The Asbury Triptych Series

Black Country

Borrowed Light Productions

Just as the moon borrows its light from the sun, what we accomplish for good is a reflection of the Creator.

Black Country

Book One of *The Asbury Triptych Series*

Published by Borrowed Light Productions

Palm Beach Gardens, Florida

ISBN 978-0-9862367-0-9 (Paperback)

Cover illustration by John Hurst. All rights reserved.

Cover design by Danny Lamb

Map illustrations by Danny Lamb and Tyler Fegley

Edited by Sherry Parmelee

Visit *The Asbury Triptych Series* website at

www.francisasburytriptych.com or www.francisasburytriptych.co.uk

Book font is Baskerville Handcut, modeled after the eighteenth-century font created by John Baskerville in Birmingham, England, during the time Francis Asbury resided there.

Acknowledgments

To attempt the writing of *The Asbury Triptych Series* requires research, much research!

During my nearly two decades of research on Francis Asbury and his biblical cavalry, I experienced the transformation of contemporary research. My task began in the late 1990s with many books obtained through inter-library loans. In time, through various connections, my efforts soon accessed antique book shops and antique book dealers. As the Internet became more of a staple for research, I was soon able to locate books and book dealers online. (I actually met one such dealer at a gas station to finalize our transaction!) At the turn of the century, the process of accessing antiquated periodicals and books from the period took a giant leap forward with Google's project to digitize books on the Internet.

In light of these developments, I would like to thank the many individuals who helped in the process. I am initially indebted to the Interlibrary Loan department of the Palm Beach County, Florida, Public Library System. I would like to thank its director, Libby Nemota, for her tireless efforts to accommodate me with obscure books and articles—by my best estimate, more than one thousand requests over an eighteen-year period. In tandem with the Interlibrary Loan department are my friends at my local branch of the Palm Beach County Library System, the Palm Beach Gardens location. There, Jim Hauser and several women named Susan (I think at one point there were at least three with that name) helped with this cumbersome task. Others assisted at the library, but Jim Hauser is easily the one who took the most interest in what I was trying to accomplish. Thank you, Jim, for your efforts; however, thanks mostly for your friendship and patience with my not-too-quiet conversations with you at the reference desk in the library. (On another occasion, I even had the privilege to teach Jim plumbing repair techniques. He is a great student.)

Several historical archivists have also aided in the research: Charles Baker and David Hallam in England, Glinda Hooper and John Wesley Weir in Ireland, and Robert Simpson and Dale Patterson at the General Commission on Archives and History for The United Methodist Church. To each of these I am indebted, as well.

For the artistic impact of *Black Country*, I am grateful for several people, beginning with the amazing talents of the cover artist from England, John Hurst. His beautiful watercolor illustration of a Black Country mother, working an iron-melting furnace with her small child dangerously close to the fire, continues to capture me every time I see it. It also amazes me that he came up with this simply through a few emails of my comments about the story. A testament to the integrity of the man is that when he shipped the painting from England, he simply sent an email stating that if I was pleased with the painting to pay him. And if I wasn't, to mail the painting back! Wow! Thank you, John, for following the Lord's leading in creating this captivating work of art.

For the implementation of John Hurst's creation, I am indebted to a young graphic artist by the name of Danny Lamb. Danny's experience coupled with his creative spirit resulted in an outstanding set of book covers. I remember sending Danny an email after opening his initial concept design for the covers. I wrote back, "Danny, I am a blessed man." The excitement and joy from seeing his work continues to resonate each time I look at the book. Danny, your work continues to bless me. Danny also favored this project by drawing some of the maps in *Black Country*. Danny, I appreciate your artistry.

Another young artist who helped with the maps in *Black Country* is Tyler Fegley. Tyler is a creative soul, an easy-going, amazingly talented artist who also has helped to take *Black Country* to a level far beyond what I could imagine. All this, and he thinks my jokes are funny! Tyler, I thank you for your talented efforts.

Another individual who helped with the graphic work is my friend Mike Kessler. Mike helped to design the series logo which resides atop the book series website and along the spine of the book. Mike is a patient man with an eye for detail. He too has endured some of my jesting. Mike, thank you for your friendship. (And your artistry, ha!)

For the book series website, my thank-you goes to another good friend. Rick Maggio, you still amaze me with your knowledge of web design and e-commerce. If you the reader haven't figured it out yet, you will soon. E-commerce is a science in itself. Thank you, Rick, for putting it into layman's terms so I can understand. I am a little worried, though; Rick didn't charge me for his amazing efforts. He continues to share that someday he will need a favor. Strange also that when I asked what kind of favor, he forwarded a YouTube video of a scene from the movie *The Godfather* . . . you know, where all the street thugs are paying homage to Don Corleone on the day of his daughter's wedding . . .

Now for the last artist who had to endure nearly eight months of working with me: my editor, Sherry Parmelee. Where do I begin? Perhaps in Scotland: Ya' know, t'is book would fall shor'dt of its achievement wit'out ya' effor'dts, Sherry. Ya' wheets, Sherry, it's all about ya' wheets! Poor Sherry, you deserve a medal! I already miss our weekly emails and adventures into my limited writing abilities. I "shutter" to think what this project would have been without you! Ha! You are an extremely patient and talented woman. Thank you, Sherry.

In closing, I would be careless if I left out my lovely wife and two daughters.

It was my wife who, after I wrote several versions of screenplays about Asbury and Hosier, urged me to abandon the screenplays (which received some attention, but had failed to attract interested parties) and write this story as a novel. After nearly a decade, I listened to her. Yes, I attended Promise Keepers . . .

I would also be negligent if I left out our two incredibly loving daughters Julia and Teresa. Through the years they have patiently listened to—better yet, endured—more than anyone not interested in Methodist history would care to know about Methodist history. My daughters no longer refer to Francis Asbury and Harry Hosier by their actual names. They are serious when they ask, "How are Francis Razzle Berry and Harry Pantyhose doing these days?"

My daughters have even allowed me to take up some of their highly valued vacation time visiting museums and sites linked to Asbury and Hosier. Another of my favorite comments of theirs comes from my younger daughter, Teresa. Picture this: several anxious hours in a car with my wife, my two daughters, and my mother-in-law, attempting to locate a hard-to-find monument, the stressful journey eventually prompting my wife to comment, "It's a good thing my dad didn't come—he would not be happy with all this wandering about." The granite pillar eventually turns up in the middle of a Pennsylvania cornfield. Upon discovery of the one-hundred-year-old marker, my observant and somewhat sarcastic Teresa proclaims, "Dad, it's covered in bird poop!" I love my girls. Oh well, as I always tell myself with two girls who actually admit that history is their favorite class in school: these experiences build character.

Both Sides: A Note from the Author

Spring is a time of renewal. Even in tropical climes, new growth, different from that of the fair-weathered winter season, appears. During one of these flourishing periods many years ago, I had the privilege of experiencing confirmation in the Catholic Church. The bishop who led the mass and its ceremony associated his message with the then popular movie *The Godfather*. His message was simple, and entertainingly delivered. The bishop left my fellow candidates and me with one clear message: "Don't go to heaven alone; take somebody with you." Forty years removed from this life-changing event, the message continues to resonate.

Fifteen years after my Catholic confirmation, again in the transformational season of spring, I began another spiritual renewal. This change climaxed in the fall of that same year as I experienced what Jesus called the "New Birth," the spiritual renewal He taught to the Jewish Pharisee, Nicodemus. Although the New Birth had a deeper spiritual effect on my life, each of these watershed events, my Catholic confirmation and my New Birth experience, has molded who I am today.

Since the New Birth experience, I have chosen to worship the God of the Bible in a Protestant setting, for a time in the traditional setting of a Methodist church and for a time in a couple of non-traditional, non-denominational church settings. All of these Protestant experiences, as well as my early Catholic experiences, have opened my eyes to the loving Creator. For me, a large portion of my drawing to the God of the Bible hinged on His church, the people of God, and the manner in which they loved one another.

Many years ago, Mark Twain penned the words, "The two most important days in your life are the day you are born and the day you find out why." The book you hold in your hand, *Black Country*, is a result of the New Birth and discovery experiences in my life. I don't think Mr. Twain was referring to the New Birth as Jesus taught; I'm confident he meant the day that an individual receives the privilege of life. In spite of this variation, *Black Country* is a direct result of both the New Birth and my discovery of what God was calling me to do.

In *Black Country*, as well as in the books which follow in *The Asbury Triptych Series*, I have written a story based on the true life of an amazing man, Francis Asbury. In this retelling, I have determined to write without prejudice to either Catholic or Protestant Christianity. In light of what I am attempting, it is all there, good and bad. Nevertheless, it is my deepest desire for the reader that when you experience the ugliness of Catholicism or the ugliness of Protestantism, you realize that the recounting of these atrocities is not meant to condemn a church made up of imperfect people in need of a Savior. The purpose I seek is quite the opposite: the celebration of the amazing love of our Savior. A Savior whose grace-filled, loving arms are spread wide, offering a merciful embrace for all of humanity, imperfect church included. If you don't know it, this grace and mercy did not arrive cheaply; its cost was the shed blood of Jesus on a wooden cross nearly two thousand years ago. It is my hope that in the reading of *Black Country*, you will understand more clearly the depth of this amazing love.

In debt to such an example of self-sacrifice, I would like to close with the words of the Bible, from the fourth chapter of the book of Hebrews. "Therefore, since we have a great high priest who has ascended into heaven, Jesus the Son of God, let us hold firmly to the faith we profess. For we do not have a high priest who is unable to empathize with our weaknesses, but we have one who has been tempted in every way, just as we are—yet he did not sin. Let us then approach God's throne of grace with confidence, so that we may receive mercy and find grace to help us in our time of need."[1]

---

[1] Hebrews chapter 4, verses 14–16 (NIV)

Historical Pitch: An Almost Spoiler

The following comment is for readers who are not big fans of history:

Try it, you'll like it!

Cliché, I know, but true. Consider this movie poster log line:

> On the verge of the American Revolutionary War between the Colonies and the British Empire, a young, inexperienced pastor from England sets out to forge a church in America. The unorthodox minister who preaches in taverns and at hangings attempts to succeed with a traveling ministry made up of an African sidekick who can't read, uneducated frontiersmen clothed in buckskin, several ex-thieves, gamblers, slaves, and prisoners—all barely twenty years of age and living out of saddlebags.

Does this grab your attention?

What prompts this introduction is the comment of a friend I asked to read my pre-edited version of *Black Country*. She admitted, "I'm not a fan of history." What followed her comment was an honest discussion on how to draw someone like herself to read a historical novel. Because of that discussion, this opening or "almost spoiler," as I call it, exists for those who are not accustomed to reading historical stories. **If you love history, I invite you to skip these few pages until after you have completed the book.** For those who will decide to read this preface, I invite you to complete it, not just skim through it, before beginning the novel.

Here goes.

The Asbury Triptych Series is a three-book novel about the George Washington of American Christianity. A bold assertion, I know. However, I am confident that time spent with this British young man will prove this opinion correct. It is the clear and timely goal of the three-book series to establish this personal view. The year 2016 marks the bicentennial of his departing this world for the next. Although the main character of this story never commanded forces as Washington did, nor did he become the official leader of a nation, this unconventional preacher from England who became more widely known than the first president and more widely known than any other Christian leader of the period did lead a troop of men who conquered the spiritual attention of the American populace.

The opening book of the series, *Black Country,* does something never done since the death of this individual—it seeks to give a snapshot of the culture and people he interacted with during his first years as a preacher in England. Many authors have written of his amazing forty-five-year ministry in America. But none have ventured more than a couple of pages about his time as a young preacher in his home country. The events I've written are creative non-fiction, working within the framework that history knows his whereabouts, but without additional research of these locations, the exact details are missing. I have done that research, aiming for the best possible scenario while keeping in mind that I am also writing a novel. At the very least, I have captured a true glimpse of the times. At its best, I have written a story that is in line with the main character's experience. It is also my hope that in reading this novel you will acquire the fact that *Black Country* is the author's kind gesture to the great nation which birthed Asbury, the nation I fell in love with through my research.

Equally important, *Black Country* displays a unique period of European history. Through dramatic scenes, the book delivers a reflection of the rich inheritance that forms the Bible-influenced foundation of the United States of America. You as the reader should walk away from this opening book not only with an understanding of the wisdom which inspired the greatest and most successful nation in the five-thousand-year history of mankind, but also seeing firsthand why the influences of the Bible and some of Christianity's key leaders from Europe were the surest agents of success for America.

There is one other advantage to reading this historical novel. The same events which drove the Puritans from their homeland a century before Asbury's time, the acts of an English king towards the Bible-based individuals in his dominion— these intolerable acts which removed all influence of the Puritans from the universities, the government, and the culture—parallel the same events in America for the last fifty years. Sadly, contemporary America stands at the threshold of repeating what England experienced 350 years ago: the complete removal of the Bible and its wisdom from the universities, government, and culture. **Reading *Black Country* is not only about reading history, it is also about reading the history you are living.**

Hopefully I've inspired you enough to read on. Let's begin with the book in your hand.

The story of the main character, Francis Asbury, is the perfect example of a fish-out-of-water tale. Born into a lower-middle-class family in the heart of England in 1745, this tall, thin, sinewy fellow with shoulder-length hair possesses little more than a primary school education and no formal training except his apprenticeship as a blacksmith, forging nails. His time is a time of little authentic religion; cockfights, gambling, the illicit lifestyle of the theatre are the norm. Despite these personal and societal limitations, he manages to become a preacher for a religious movement that eventually cures the rampant illiteracy and destructive addiction to gin of the British citizens of the 1700s.

The lack of religion during this period is the result of nearly two hundred years of church and government becoming one—the clergy and the politicians, most of them in pursuit of personal gain, have forgotten the bold efforts of those who gave their lives to attain religious freedom. This is odd when you consider the high cost that brought authentic Christianity to England—the martyrdom of several hundred people, most of whom were burned at the stake for their unwavering commitment to the faith. What was their biggest crime in the eyes of the governing body? These brave souls printed the Bible in English, going against the state-sanctioned form of Christianity. "Dissenters" was the label placed upon them.

By the time of Francis Asbury, the church and state have lapsed into an inseparable entity, forcing on the populace a cold and lifeless religion. Asbury's involvement with the movement led by the brothers John and Charles Wesley is eventually his ticket out of poverty and England's exit from a comatose Christianity. The efforts of the Wesleyan followers—known by the derisive term "Methodists"—begin to heal the ills of a society that had forgotten the Creator.

As a child, Asbury resides in a town where no one expects its children to escape the drudgery of the ironworking industry. Growing up in Birmingham, England, at the beginning of the country's industrial revolution means an almost life sentence of working the furnace, melting metal into steel. Added to this difficulty is Asbury's unique approach to life. Slightly unconventional because he has a sense of humor and a love of play, and slightly disobedient to his superiors as a young preacher (he has a weakness for departing his assigned routes and exploring parts of England he has never seen), the reprimands of his superiors only further his desire to wander. The young British pastor with barely enough preaching experience surprisingly decides to depart for the American colonies in 1771, only a handful of years after his acceptance to Wesley's traveling ministry.

His timing couldn't be worse. At this time, the British citizens in the colonies as well as the British clergy in America—both groups unflinchingly loyal to the English king—are leaving America and heading back to England. Why are these loyal Brits leaving the American colonies? The rumors of the pending war with the mother country, England, are forcing this burdensome adjustment. Heading in the completely opposite direction of those fleeing the unrest to come, Asbury lands in Philadelphia just a few short years before the start of the American Revolutionary War.

For the next thirteen years, Asbury travels the thirteen colonies on horseback, preaching the Word and organizing what remains of the religious movement he has inherited. He hasn't inherited much; the leaders of his group were English and have returned to England. Although the war drives many to appeal to God, the collateral damage of the conflict keeps most from attending church. Add to this Asbury's homesickness and the fact that for eight years the war inhibits his ability to communicate with his loving parents, who ache for news of his safety. For the duration of the war, his mail and any acknowledgment of his security fail to reach his parents in England.

Despite this hindrance, he sets out with whatever he is privileged to gain. In time, he develops a small team of preachers, unconventional like himself and with a passion for traveling about like himself. These are rough men, new to the faith, barely able to speak in public on spiritual ideals. His biblical cavalry of ex-gamblers, ex-slaves, ex-thieves, ex-prisoners, rugged mountain men, and any unlikely individual with a desire to preach—one even wears an eye patch and a sword at his side—set out to deliver sacred words. In taverns, barns, open fields, prisons, and at hangings, these men preach. Where does this desire to preach come from? For these unlikely fellows, this motley crew, the deep-seated yearning to share the Good News of the Bible with the people of the frontier is the natural result of a repentant heart—a heart transformed by the hearing of the words of the sacred book.

Despite the numerous hardships—the unforgiving weather and terrain which take the lives of many of these men well before their thirtieth birthday, the confused citizens who believe that Asbury and his men are British spies, and the misguided leadership in England which believes that Asbury is incompetent and in need of replacement—Francis Asbury perseveres. Some of his preachers experience imprisonment; others, like Asbury himself, encounter assassination attempts. Nearly the entire lot suffers physical beatings and verbal abuses. One attractive young minister endures a tar-and-feather attack, the cruel act bringing irreversible scars to his once-handsome face.

By war's end in 1784, Asbury is the unquestioned leader of the American version of this religious movement. His Christmas Eve ordination by John Wesley's Welsh agent of missions, Dr. Thomas Coke, establishes the official beginning of the Methodist Church in America under the guidance of Francis Asbury.

What I have described above is the essence of *The Asbury Triptych Series*, three books dedicated to Asbury's preaching in England and his first thirteen years in America. **This is only the beginning of Asbury's American ministry.** From this point onward, Asbury spends another thirty-two years in America, at the helm, administering what will become by the time of his death one of the largest churches in America. Without ever owning a home or land in America, Asbury sets out to deliver the Good News to the burgeoning young nation. His efforts bring civilization to the growing cities as well as the rugged frontier. Without fanfare, Asbury, through his personal hands-on approach, meets nearly an entire nation of people. His travels afford him the privilege of viewing each community that exists in America at this significant period of the new nation. Asbury's travels give him a clear view of the "melting pot" and the true sense of community. European, African, and aborigine come to know this man. Unbeknownst to him, his stays with families begin to establish his popularity, a popularity that easily rivals George Washington's. The citizens of the infant nation may know of George Washington, but with Asbury, these same citizens not only know of him, they personally know him, having invited him to dinner and shelter for a night during his six thousand miles on horseback each year of his ministry in America.

Undoubtedly, Francis Asbury is America's British founding father.

In northwest Washington DC, the large granite equestrian statue at the intersection of 16th and Mount Pleasant Streets, with Asbury securely atop the muscled creature chiseled with its stately head bending down to shoo away a nasty horsefly, clearly establishes his place in American history. Adding to this fact are stained-glass works of Francis in churches across America, as well as the naming of Asbury Park in New Jersey, Asbury University in Kentucky, and numerous elementary, middle, and high schools throughout the country. Quite an accomplishment for a boy never expected to amount to more than a man working hot iron in the West Midlands of England.

In closing, Pick up the book and read it. Allow the retelling of the life of this amazing young man to help you ignore the obstacles in your own life, the obstacles that are keeping you from accomplishing great things. Enjoy.

This book is dedicated to three uncles who left this earth too soon. To my Uncle Sal and my uncles-by-marriage, Uncle Lew and Uncle Howard, thank you for teaching me the joys of wandering about outdoors.

Long my imprisoned spirit lay
Fast bound in sin and nature's night;
Thine eye diffused a quickening ray,
I woke, the dungeon flamed with light;
My chains fell off, my heart was free;
I rose, went forth, and followed Thee.

Charles Wesley[2]

Chained at the hands and feet, two elderly men stand motionless before the Catholic Bishop. In the darkness of the sixteenth-century underground courtroom, the damp early-morning air reflects the room's feeble offering of candlelight. This tribunal of the Oxford Divinity School will on this day determine the fate of the two restrained prisoners, Nicholas Ridley and Hugh Latimer. Their lives depend solely on the judge that sits behind the ancient wooden table before them.

With them, many guards mill about making small talk. The Bishop at the head of these proceedings is a Caiaphas reproduction who cares little for the future of men. His concern is the same as the first-century High Priest,[3]

"Would it not benefit that one man dies than for an entire nation to perish?"

The Bishop's dark eyes emit a coldness that rises from the deep, hidden fissures of an unfeeling heart. His corpulent face remains expressionless. He begins,

"Nicholas Ridley, do you believe the Pope heir of Peter, heir to authority of the Church?"

The Bishop's question causes the elderly Ridley to shift. It is a strained effort to relieve the pain from the biting restraints of the chain that binds his hands behind his back. More cutting is the implication that a human can be heir of the Christian church. He pauses and manages a step forward. Ridley's reply is measured and gentle,

"The church was not built on any man, but on the truth that Peter confessed, Christ the Son of God."

"Wretched protestors!"

---

[2] Charles Wesley hymn "And Can It Be That I Should Gain," 1738.

[3] Caiaphas, the Roman-appointed Jewish High Priest who organized the plot to kill Jesus.

The sputtering saliva sprays from the Bishop's mouth.

"Do you choose to honor the Pope?"

The Bishop's forcefulness silences all in the room. The fifteen guards who stand at the perimeter of the room sharpen their focus on the proceedings and the two grey-haired men under the scrutiny of this Bishop of Mary—not Mary the mother of Jesus, but the infamous Mary, Queen Mary the first, aka Bloody Mary.

Ridley hesitates, but realizes the Bishop will not wait long. He gives reply to the Bishop's interrogating question about whether he chooses to honor the Pope,

"When he seeks the honor and glory of God."

Ridley's kindly nature brings a sneer from the Bishop, the kind you see on a pickpocket after successfully stealing money from an unknowing victim. He looks to the guards that stand on both sides of the pair in question.

"Remove him at once."

The two guards sharply grab Ridley by the arms and force him out of the room. Immediately two other guards abandon their perimeter watch and stand beside the shaking Latimer.

In the previous fifteen months, the manipulative desires of the English Queen Mary have materialized as she displays an unyielding commitment to return England to the Roman Church. Mary is a major obstacle to the protestors and their move away from the Papacy. Her conviction that the Bible should be printed only in Latin causes her to eliminate anyone who chooses to print the Bible in English.

The trial of Latimer and Ridley is another episode of Mary's devilish passion not only to destroy the movement of the protestors but also, more importantly, to eliminate any associations with her Protestant-sympathetic father, King Henry VIII. His divorce from her mother years ago temporarily removed Mary's royal status and her chance to gain the throne. At that time, the King also chose to abandon the Catholic Church when the Pope denied his request for an annulment. Mary has never let go of the public's label of her: the Illegitimate One.

The death of her father brought her closer to the throne, behind her sickly half-brother, Edward. Upon the mysterious death of Edward, a power struggle began between Mary's cousin, Lady Jane Grey—the Protestant public's favorite—and the one with the hidden agenda of eliminating the protestors, Mary. By May of 1553, Mary won out, had Lady Jane deported, and eagerly received the throne. Her nickname, Bloody Mary, was placed upon her by the commoners of England when she subsequently had Lady Jane executed to prevent any future rivalry. The execution was not the last killing Mary would oversee.

The Bishop interlocks the fingers of his hands in front of him, rotates the palms down and out; he cracks his knuckles. The annoying sound pierces the dense air. He peers at the remaining aged man. He thinks to himself, *he is a detestable man.*

"Hugh Latimer, step forward."

Latimer struggles to respond to the Bishop's demand; the leg irons cut into the thin skin of his ankles. Dried bloodstains cover the tops of his bare feet as they protrude from his torn leggings. He shuffles toward the Bishop until one of the guards strikes the back of his left shoulder with a fist.

"Enough!"

The Bishop completes the task of picking his nose through a finely stitched silk cloth. He sets the expensive handkerchief on the tabletop.

"Hugh Latimer, do you choose to honor the Pope, heir of Peter, authority of the Church?"

Latimer struggles with this question. As with many of the protesting commoners of the 1550s, their goal is not a separation from the church, but a cleansing of the wrongs that have spread throughout the clergy; they are Puritans seeking to purify the church. Latimer has personally witnessed the growing faith among the citizens as they secretly go against the Roman Church, printing Bibles in the local languages. He finds it strange that the Catholic Church would not welcome such gains.

It also pains Latimer that the Catholic Church of the sixteenth century is no longer the grand entity that transformed a corrupt Roman Empire a millennium before. Nor does the church inspire loving missionaries like St. Patrick, who sacrificed everything to save people from the ignorance of paganism. Latimer and thousands like him grieve for the Catholic Church, which at this time has lapsed into an organization standing in sharp contrast to the teachings of its founder, Jesus Christ.

Nevertheless, Latimer offers his reply to the Bishop's question of his loyalty to the Pope.

"I honor those who honor the Christ."

The Bishop slams his hand on the tabletop.

"Off with them!"

Immediately the two guards at Latimer's sides latch onto his arms and shoulders. He yelps in pain as they drag him out of the room, the tips of his toes carving two bloodied parallel lines in the dirt floor.

Outdoors, the sun beats strongly onto the center of the Divinity School grounds. A crowd of two hundred English protestors yells and screams at the Catholic guards who deliver Latimer and Ridley. They spit at the Bishop as he struts into the courtyard. Several of the guards who accompany the Bishop launch toward the guilty parties. The goal of the Bishop's henchmen is the same as the Bishop's: to make an example of those who choose to dishonor the Pope.

Fists and shoves seem to fly from everywhere as the guards squint into the glaring sun. The scene is chaotic. One protector of the Bishop goes down from a blow to the head. The protestor proclaims,

"Jesus, save your loyal servants!"

The guards strike back. A protestor is smashed in the chest with a club. He frantically tries to gain his breath. An additional blow to the head brings a collapse and violent convulsion. The repeated flagellations of a chain pummel another protestor into submission. Blood sprays cover the maddened guard. The Bishop's escorts gain control, but they remain on their guard; the defiance could resurface in an instant.

The protestors are not accepting this sentence quietly. The cries of the crowd drown the Bishop's words,

"Tie the guilty."

Immediately, several guards haul Latimer and Ridley to a small dirt-covered area; at the center is a wooden post. The heavy timber stands under ten feet tall. The woodpile which stands nearly three feet tall consists of short pieces of tree limbs that circle at the base of the pole. The guards shove the accused pair to the top of the woodpile, slamming them against the pole and tying them back to back. From out of the crowd comes a voice,

"Nicholas, I have powder!"

Another man in the crowd yells out,

"Ridley, your brother!"

A fight breaks out as one of the Bishop's henchmen confronts the young protestor who tries to get the attention of Nicholas Ridley. Once again, the brother attempts to give aid.

"Nicholas, I have powder!"

Ridley is well aware that placing gunpowder in the pockets of the trousers speeds the flames along. The hushed throng struggles to balance their attention between Ridley, his brother, and the approaching guard.

As the guard makes his way toward Ridley's brother, Ridley refuses the offer. Several women raise their hands to cover their faces; they begin to weep.

Ridley's brother blurts out as the guard grabs him,

"The wood is wet!"

Ridley and Latimer acknowledge the discovery. Wet wood burns more slowly.

The guards knock out the brother with a punch, and the men of the crowd resume their fight with the guards. The Bishop's men once again swing their clubs and chains at the protestors. Again they succeed in quelling the opposition. As a result, Ridley's brother lies unconscious and trampled on the ground, his head and arms bent in an unnatural way.

Several guards light the woodpile. The wet kindling begins its slow and torturous burn. The crowd pushes in, but the guards once again shove back. The citizens deplore the hopelessness of the situation. Many reply in despair,

"Damn you, Bishop!"

Some fall to their knees screaming in prayer,

"God save them!"

Others raise fists and scream. Their inability to help eventually forces many of the protestors to cower in sobbing lament. As they do, the popping sounds of the blaze rise above the saddened expressions of the crowd.

At the stake, Ridley begins to panic. Latimer realizes that Ridley is struggling; he yells,

"Ridley, play the man!"[4]

His stark words break the crowd's doleful mood, as does his additional comment,

"We shall this day light such a candle in England, as I trust never shall be put out."

Latimer's words encourage the protestors. They once again rush the woodpile, but the guards strike back, hard. Several of the men collapse from the blows of the Bishop's henchmen. Despite their repeated efforts, the fire's crackling wave grows as the wood begins to dry out. A growing wind, cold and steady, pushes the flames to accelerate and climb even further.

The blaze grows high on Latimer's side of the post. The people gasp. Latimer lets out a cry of anguish. The Bishop and his mad men scoff as Latimer grapples with the burning effects. His squirms soon turn into a confusing disorder; he goes in and out of consciousness, screaming as he comes to. The protestors cannot bear to let this continue, but they can do nothing.

Latimer fades once more, for the last time.

The crowd once again returns to their lament as they watch Ridley struggle with the effects of the fire. He suddenly breaks into conversation with God.

"Heavenly Father - -

I give unto Thee - -

Most hearty thanks - -

---

[4] Ridley, man up!

That Thou hast called me . . ."

Ridley lets out a scream of pain. The flames are now climbing higher, to his chest area, but his struggle fails to silence the petition of this brave man. He yells in pain once more, and then,

"A professor - -

Yes, you have called me a professor of Thee. I beseech Thee have mercy on this realm of England and deliver it from all her enemies."

With this last wish, the fire engulfs Ridley also. His frenzied cries resonate through the Oxford courtyard . . .

Under the six-year reign of Queen Mary, three hundred deaths of English Protestant leaders followed the execution of Latimer and Ridley. This set off a panic throughout the country of England. Many of the Protestant faith feared for their lives and fled the country. It wasn't until the death of Queen Mary that the Protestants returned, vowing to make great changes.

Upon the death of Mary, another daughter of King Henry VIII became queen. This daughter of Henry's second wife, Queen Anne, was a brilliant woman and, like her mother, a Protestant. Young Queen Elizabeth, the first, quickly repealed Mary's pro-Catholic legislation in England. This swayed the church in England to the Protestant side. Elizabeth successfully reigned over England for the next forty-five years, and so did Protestantism—but it too exhibited its prejudice, this time toward the Catholics.

Following the death of Queen Elizabeth in 1603, the Catholic James VI of Scotland became King of England. If his Catholic views weren't enough, the long-term rivalry between England and Scotland for dominance of the island caused the English citizenry to largely mistrust this Scottish king. Opposed to the abandonment of the Catholic Church by King Henry VIII, yet seeking political acceptance by the English Protestants, King James struggled in the middle of this Anglicized battle. An unexpected Catholic-led effort to kill him caused the King to rethink the approach to religion in England; he decided to merge the two churches. The combination of the Catholic and Protestant churches was solidified into the newly empowered Anglican Church.

The assassination attempt on King James also led him to further separate from the Roman Church. A recent English version of the Bible, the Geneva Bible, also pushed the King to publish his own version of the Scriptures. Despite the new Bible's Protestant-friendly aspect of being printed in English, the King James Bible of 1611 was a Catholic-influenced translation. Naturally, the new "combined" or Anglican translation eliminated the scathing commentaries against the corruption of the Catholic clergy.

Over the next 150 years, the King James Bible was the source material that set the English Parliament above the monarchy. This change was largely the result of the careless acts of monarchs who tried to force their style of Christianity on the people. There were laws and persecutions against Catholics when Protestant kings were in power and similar atrocities against Protestants when Catholic kings were in power. This abuse of power caused several key individuals to rise up and lead political and military actions against the abusive kings. This transition became the beginning of political parties in Parliament. The English Civil War was also a result of this struggle.

It became clear that the influence of the writings of the Bible, specifically passages that taught that having a king would lead to a loss of freedom, were changing the political landscape in England. An enlightened populace began to sow the seeds found in the writings of Moses: individual liberty and representative government. From this time forward, England would respect the monarchy as long as it honored the "Anglican" approach to religion and submitted itself to the power of the Parliament.

By 1750, nearly two hundred years later, this Parliament-led, Anglican approach to the church in England caused the church's leadership to become indistinguishable from the leadership in Parliament. The cries of the sixteenth-century political philosopher and Protestant pastor Reverend Richard Hooker, two centuries before, went out: there must be a separation of church and commonwealth.

***

In 1755, Birmingham, England, is the engine that drives the infant Industrial Revolution. The appearance of her inhabitants is rough. Their ragged and grime-covered clothing is a clear indication of the strenuous work of the laborers in the world's largest manufacturing center of metal objects. The West Midlands town is comprised of hardworking men and women who labor in the ironworking industry. The work days are long and the compensation is low. In Birmingham, a resident is fortunate to enjoy one meal each day. Their hovel-like dwellings rarely have more than one room for living space.

It is the wish of many in this town that their children will rise to much more than beating the hammer on the anvil. For most, that goal proves nearly impossible. The numerous smokestacks of the shops blacken the midday sky, not only contributing to the region's label of the Black Country, but also casting a thick-anchored shadow of doubt that any child will escape most dreaded Birmingham.

A middle-aged man stands on the perimeter of an outdoor event, wearing the traditional white collar of the Anglican priesthood. His black clerical robe flows in the brisk late-summer winds. He is a stocky man, not too tall, his quiet disposition a reflection of his wise and creative heart. He is also an artist, the poet of a fast-growing national movement.

The event the preacher has chosen to partake of is a cockfight.

Outdoors, the gathering of roughly a hundred people forms an informal circle, a "cockpit." It is as if the entire group is yelling for the sake of yelling.

"Kill the bloody cock!   "No, bloody yow[5]!"

The coarse British accents bellow at each other, at the competing fowls, and even at God as they stare at the vacant middle-space at the center of the cluster.

In the center are two bloodied cockerels battling for their lives. The jeering of the crowd appears to spur the fighters on. The panic of the conflict forces the cocks' tiny pounding hearts to squirt rivulets of blood from the wounds previously inflicted by the opponent.

At this point in the battle, both birds stumble from exhaustion. They rise and flounder about like the drunken crowd that yearns for the scrap to continue. The fight slows as one bird begins to falter again. Almost miraculously, the palpitating heart brings new life to the challenger. Despite the new life, his revival is temporary. In time, the contest is complete as the weaker fowl expires and the stronger bird deliriously struts about.

Several young boys attending the event run up and spit on the dead bird.

The owner of the victor steps on the neck of the losing fowl; he picks up the winning bird and twists its head, bringing instant death. He raises the bleeding champion overhead to a cheering crowd. Blood runs down his thick, hairy wrist and onto his shirt sleeve. In the crowd, money changes hands immediately and the raucous group readies for the next competition.

For the citizens of Birmingham, and specifically for this group, forgotten are the hard-fought efforts of Latimer and Ridley two centuries before.

The people of the Black Country enjoy their drinking as much as they enjoy gambling and cockfights. Crude flasks full of the latest concoction from the British West Indies—that sugary drink called rum—travel among the gloved hands with fingertips missing. Several at the event sit on the outskirts of the crowd, too inebriated to stand. A scraggy-looking woman blurts out,

"Give us Wesley."

The cry of the short, overweight woman standing near the black-robed preacher is barely audible; she tightens her lips, exaggerating her chubby cheeks and her impatient frustration.

---

[5] West Midland accent for the word "you."

The woman is dressed in a sticky linen shift, called a smock by the residents of the West Midlands. The see-through garment reveals numerous clammy stomach rolls. Black soot from the furnaces that melt Birmingham's iron mostly covers the outfit. The remainder of this Black Country ensemble is soaked in an ever-increasing supply of sweat. She tries again, this time as loud as she can,

"Give us Wesley!"

Her fist-raised plea catches the attention of a tall, thin man dressed all in black. Under a wool cap, the deep trenches of his weathered face reveal a slight smile. Towering over everyone else in the crowd, he comments to several standing close by,

"You heard the lady."

Several drunken men anxiously and mockingly search for a lady.

"In thish crowd?"

The slurred slight has several laughing, including the man in black and the constantly perspiring woman.

As the banter proceeds, the preacher slowly makes his way through the crowd. The disheveled appearance of the unruly group does not dismay his enthusiasm or affection for the crowd. He approaches the center of the gathering; one drunken man pats him on the back.

"Gives ush Weshley."

Spit flies from the heavy-tongued admirer. The preacher kindly acknowledges the intoxicated man and continues. The preacher who has bravely stepped into the cockpit is Charles Wesley, the younger brother of John Wesley.

Once having the opportunity of adoption of their child by a wealthy family in Ireland, Charles's father and mother were grateful when he refused the generous offer that would have brought ease and success. In fact, the person taken in his place became an Earl, the grandfather to the Duke of Wellington. Despite this opportunity declined, this son of a musician and pastor is an educated man, an Oxford graduate and an ordained minister.

In Birmingham, as well as in the majority of England's working-class settlements fueling the beginnings of the industrial revolution, the brothers John and Charles Wesley are striving to lead a revival of the Christian faith. Their efforts to reform the clergy of the Anglican Church make them household names; however, most of the credit goes to John. Charles is the forgotten Wesley. Charles respects the hard work of his brother, but there are times when the lack of recognition stresses him. This stress drives his art.

For twelve years, Charles's passion to write averages roughly three hymns each week. In fact, although many consider his brother John the architect and intellectual leader of the Wesleyan movement, it is the music and poetry of Charles that teaches, inspires, and wins the hardworking masses of England.

The Church of England does not favor the success of the brothers. Unfortunately for the state-sanctioned church, the enthusiasm of the movement isn't taking place within the well-funded walls of that establishment or under the supervision of its clergy. Instead, John and Charles are winning the people by offering their liberating message of hope against traditional norms, outdoors, to the hardworking people of the countryside—those who would not dare to frequent a church, the "undesirables," as expressed by the Anglican leadership.

To worsen the antagonism, the authentic lifestyle and religion of the brothers easily exposes the irreligious acts of the Anglican leaders, many of whom are inextricably linked to political corruption. To the Wesleys, God is more concerned with the salvation of the individual and less concerned with the continuation of a corrupt religious entity. The Wesleys respect the sacredness and orderliness of a church community, but they realize that it is the responsibility of the individual to get right with God. John and Charles are adamant that no association with a religious group, regardless of its political and social connections, enables one to achieve salvation.

The Anglican leadership, beneficiaries of the sacrificial contributions of numerous men of the past like Latimer and Ridley, are guilty of the same prejudice evidenced by their Catholic and Protestant predecessors two hundred years before. In the minds of the state-church leaders, the Wesleys and their followers are illegitimate Christians, even if John Wesley has made it clear that the movement subjects itself to the Church of England. In addition to the official refusal of the brothers' efforts, those who disapprove of the Wesleys place another label on their efforts: they brand the trend "sedition." Unfortunately, for John and Charles, like Latimer and Ridley two hundred years before, history is repeating itself.

Despite the heated efforts from the corrupt leadership of the Anglican Church, the Wesleyan movement continues to spread like fire amidst dry timber—mostly as it exposes the hypocrisy of the state-affiliated religious institution's concern with material wealth, societal status, and access to the King of England.

At the cockfight, Charles has made his way to the edge of the gathering's center. He steps over the bloodied remains of a dead rooster and enters the informal, shifting circle. The wet, blood-stained soil causes Charles to surmise, *many battles preceded the one I viewed*. The crowd begins to yell,

"Praise be for the brothers Wesley!"

Charles welcomes their approval, alert and aware that their loyalties can divert quickly.

Charles considers the group that stands, and sometimes sways, completely around him. He decides to open with the words that brought him expulsion from the refined church in the English town of Islington.

"Outcasts of men, to you I call . . ."

These are the words that England's affluent congregations like Islington find offensive. They would never see themselves as outcasts. However, to the inhabitants of Birmingham, these words are a beautiful and thoughtful welcome. Charles continues,

"Harlots - -
And publicans - -
And thieves."

The group's verbal approvals grow in volume. Several men congratulate each other on their promotion from outcasts to harlots, publicans, and thieves. Once again, Charles speaks.

"He spreads His arms to embrace you all;
Sinners alone His grace receives;
No need of Him the righteous have;
He came, the lost, to seek and save."

The smiles of many in the crowd soften the hardened feel of the rabble. The tall, thin man in black rubs his left elbow with his right hand. He nervously places his right hand inside his trousers pocket and replies,

"Calling us to the prostitutes of Islington, are we?"

The crowd bursts into cheers at the comment. Charles's gentle face sneaks a smile toward his rough-looking advocate. The citizens of Birmingham nod their approval at Charles's authentic gesture toward the man. They are well aware of Charles's religious work among the prostitutes and prisoners of the English town of Islington, the work that led the refined parishioners there to complain about Charles and ban him from preaching inside the church building.

Charles quips,

"At Islington in the vestry,[6] the churchwardens demanded my license. I wrote down my name;[7] preached with increase of power on the woman taken in adultery. None went out.[8] I gave the cup.[9]"

The man in black nods his approval as cheers rise once again from the coarse crowd.

---

[6] Room attached to the church. Charles was banned from preaching inside the church itself.

[7] I gave them a copy.

[8] People remained to hear the entire sermon.

[9] I even distributed communion.

Ideal Flat

Ah! Whither should I go,
Burdened and sick and faint?
To whom should I my trouble show,
And pour out my complaint?
My Savior bids me come;
Ah! Why do I delay?
He calls the weary sinner home,
And yet from Him I stay.

Charles Wesley[10]

This brisk morning, the grey West Midland sky seems solid as it awaits Birmingham's foundries' daily offering of black smoke. The region's familiar layers of moisture thicken the air. Heat rises from chimney tops as furnaces stoke to capacity. Steam gambols above the endless smokestacks of the family-run factories that continue for more than four miles in all directions. Within minutes, the clear, dancing atmosphere above the stacks turns dismally dark, dimming the muted silver lid. The entire town grunts and groans as the metalworking industry awakes for another round.

Birmingham and its sister cities of Walsall, Wednesbury, Darlaston, and Newton Village are the primary towns of manufacturing in the region. Small rivers and narrow dirt roads adjacent to one of the world's richest deposits of coal connect each hamlet. On any given day, massive trains of forty or more pack horses drag wood-wheeled pallets of coal from the pits at Wednesbury and Walsall. Their destination is the furnaces of these small villages and Birmingham.

Underground, the rich supply of coal is close to forty feet deep, running nearly the entire length of the eight-mile loop from Wednesbury to Walsall and Newton. The black mineral, close to the surface, is easily available to anyone who desires to dig. The abundant supply is another fact contributing to the region's label, the Black Country.

The new day unfailingly brings with it the appearance of the Brummies, the underfed, unschooled, and sometimes barbaric preteen boys of the Birmingham region. Mysteriously these urchins appear, as if sprouting from the ground. One by one, they converge into an unorganized group. The local fabricators despise the harmless, devious adventures of the miniature hoodlums. The talented

---

[10] Charles Wesley hymn "Ah! Whither Should I Go?," 1741.

pilferers remain a nuisance. One of the boys, noticeably taller than the others, yells out,

"I'll give you a palin!"[11]

This is the twelve-year-old leader of the group; he lands a closed-fist punch on the left cheek of the lad in front of him. The assaulted ten-year-old boy falls to the ground, holding his cheek and crying in pain. Several others scurry in to pound and kick the unfortunate and defenseless youth.

The ringleader of the ravenous group is the tallest and the oldest. He has appointed himself supreme leader of these tiny rabble-rousers as they pass the day pursuing dishonest gain. He continues to escape the notice of the local Anglican school, mostly because his family is no threat. For strategic reasons, the Church of England seeks the children of the more religious families, specifically the Wesleyan ones.

One ten-year-old boy stands on the perimeter of this unruly group, silently watching the fracas. He's an extraordinary boy with a trademark joy, a sweetness bursting forth in the ease of his frequent smiles and laughs—a result of the encouraging brilliance and welcoming hugs of two loving parents, so lacking in the life of the unhappy thug.

This is Francis Asbury.

The leader of the miniature mobsters turns toward the happy lad.

"Asbury, you retreating as before?"

The leader points a dirt-encrusted fingernail at the lad outside the hungry pack. Francis gives no reply to the chief who will not wait long for an answer. The leader barks another warning.

"Just as well, I'll be givin' you a palin soon."

Francis nervously fumbles with his coat seam, sure that his nemesis is an unhappy fellow.

Francis Asbury, tall for his age—actually an inch taller than the pugnacious leader—observes more than most. Recently he surprised the group when he stood up to the brute. Since then, the threats from the chief have been mostly verbal and at a safe distance. Francis's joyful demeanor puzzles the quarrelsome troublemaker. Moreover, Francis fails to realize that the punk is actually afraid of him. Nevertheless, his reluctance to participate in the ringleader's schemes stems mostly from his confidence that the group's daily activities are wrong.

The leader takes charge.

"Nigel, you take a whack at it."

---

[11] I'll give you a thrashing!

The pudgy Nigel quickly darts off for the building nearby. This two-room factory is already running at full capacity. The two men inside are busily fabricating metal buttons and buckles for uniforms. Sweat drips from their brows and forearms as the pair keep a pressured pace, seemingly oblivious to the brood outside. More than a dozen preteen boys creep toward the front of their business; the chubby Nigel perceives that he is undetected as he makes his way around the back of the shop.

Francis decides to watch from a distance. Nigel focuses his effort. His target is a chicken that roams at the rear of the metal works. The bird freely wanders in and out of the structure, oblivious to the youth. Nigel's plan is to nab the fowl and run to the river Rea on the town's perimeter.

Glancing up from the heated piece of iron he is working on the anvil, the metal artisan notifies his assistant of the approaching brood.

"Friends, indeed."

At this prompting, the assistant sneers, grabs the red-hot poker from the furnace, and departs for the rear storage room. Today, the fabricator and his assistant have a plan.

In the back room, the assistant notices Nigel. He mumbles to himself,

"There's our ill-smelling winner."

The spiv's[12] stout frame stumbles as he sneaks up on the unsuspecting chicken. The bird casually hops away from Nigel's inadvertent warning. It continues to feed on seeds nestled in the sparse, low-growing grass. Worried about discovery, Nigel decides to lie low behind a trash pile. The numerous flies that hover around Nigel and the atrocious smell of the discarded items strive for his attention, but he forces his concentration on the fowl as it enters the storage space. Confident that no one has spotted him, he rises from his crouched cover and resumes his focused task.

The assistant hidden in the back room remains silent; the usual darkness swells with an uncommon reddish glow.

Returning to the front of the establishment, the infamous leader begins the deed. He approaches the proprietor.

"Good day, sir."

The business owner silently eyes the lad standing tall and confident before him. Upon no reply, the young man continues as planned.

"Might we inquire a position?"

---

[12] A petty criminal, street thug.

The boy smiles as he turns around toward his lemmings. They, too, are sure that the merchant has no inkling of their ruse. The shopkeeper replies,

"Might I suggest honest pursuits?"

The comment spins the punkish leader around.

Precisely at that moment, a sound shrieks from the back of the building. Nigel's screams of fear interrupt the knavish[13] discourse. Industry paraphernalia forms a cacophonous melody as the assistant chases Nigel with the hot poker. The ironworker comments,

"Quite the composer, your young pal. Lads, when will it sink that you are doomed to finish your days in Birmingham?"

The ringleader bows his head, confident that the fabricator knows they are up to no good. The young thug turns around in time to catch the glower of Francis. Further on, Nigel hop-skips away, smoke rising from his scorched trousers.

Francis turns and departs for home—alone.

The three-mile walk to Newton Village gives Francis plenty of time to think. These outings with the Brummies always leave him empty, at times even surfacing slight feelings of inadequacy quite foreign to Francis. These unfamiliar emotions drive him to crave the familiar happiness; he yearns for it. If not happiness, something more: a sense of fulfillment. He senses better and knows with a strange certainty that there is more to life than the daily routine of banging out an existence in Birmingham. Among such company as the Birmingham guttersnipes, the ten-year-old is not finding that which he aches for: a strong sense of purpose.

Newton Village is a small town, a suburb of Great Barr, situated between Birmingham and Wednesbury. The coal-rich hamlet is showing signs of the burgeoning metal trade as small family-run factories spring to life. Nearby, there is even a large ironworking forge, or as some call it, an "ironworking community."

Francis's home in Newton is a two-story cottage, where he lives with his mother and father. Elizabeth, who goes as Eliza, and Joseph count it a blessing to reside in one of Newton Village's nicest structures. Attached to the Asbury home is another cottage. There are also two barns and a village pub, The Malt Shovel, on the Asbury property.

The red-bricked home faces west. The black slate roof covers two oversized second-story dormers, which provide an inordinate amount of daylight to the upstairs rooms. One room is Francis's bedroom, the other the bedroom of his parents. The upstairs windows seem to serve as an early invitation for Francis to look west.

The Malt Shovel is both pub and brewery. A natural spring benefits the small domestic brewery. The pub is a natural stop for the overworked drivers delivering

---

[13] Untrustworthy.

the West Midlands coal to the surrounding areas. Walking past the pub and brewery, Francis quickly climbs the three brick-covered steps to the entrance of his home. He makes his way in, calling loudly,

"Father - -

Mother . . ."

Francis's calls fall silent.

Built early in the eighteenth century, the Asbury cottage is a sturdy structure; compared to the one-room hovels of the area, the home is rather luxurious. The inglenook fireplace of the main room is where the iron spit and kettle warm already prepared dinners. Eliza accomplishes the larger cooking needs at the adjacent brew house before bringing them back to the home.

Francis walks over and peeks into the pot as it hangs over the pit; it's empty. The hungry youth is disappointed. At the back of the room is a door to the rest of the house and the outdoors. Francis heads for the door.

Outside, he races down the steps, calling again,

"Father - -

Mother . . ."

 Once again, no one answers. He heads for the bathroom facility.

The Asburys share a toilet hut[14] with the family in the cottage next door. Unfortunately, customers of the pub also frequent it. Once each week the nightsoil man must clean it. Although the home contains no running water, a well taps into the property's natural spring.

Francis bursts out of the bathroom and heads for the two barns; he enters one. The barn is not as well-built as the cottages; several fist-sized holes dot the dilapidated wood siding, mostly caused by necessary penetrations of the past. Strangely, they remain unrepaired. Each barn structure serves a unique function: one for tool storage, the other for supplies of the pub. Francis is in the tool barn.

Again, Francis stands alone; he looks over the various gardening implements of his father's trade, each neatly stored in its proper spot. The methodical spacing and sense of order is in sharp contrast to the barn's worn structural appearance. A foot-long piece of the barn's siding draws his attention as it sways in the wind. Feeling somewhat dejected at the conditions of the barn, he exaggerates an exhale. He too has heard the rumors: the neighbors agree that the condition of Joseph's barn is dangerous. At times they wonder what keeps the structure from collapsing, surmising that the prayers of Eliza must surely hold the rickety beams together.

---

[14] Outhouse.

Francis smiles at this strange but welcomed thought of the townspeople.

"Good afternoon, Franky."

His father's greeting breaks the silence. He turns to reply,

"Good day, Father."

Joseph busies himself, gathering up a prized set of gardening shears. The implement is superbly sharpened and clean. He safely wipes the tool with a rag.

At the same time, Francis stares at a spot in the center of the barn floor. Joseph notices his son is uncommonly quiet and staring at the infamous location; he prompts him,

"Dreaded spot . . ."

Francis looks toward him, realizing that his father is remembering the incident from a few years before. That day of memory ended differently than other days.

Previously, at the end of each day, Joseph would put away his tools. This is who Joseph is. Despite the condition of the barn that is the property of the drinking establishment, Joseph is adamant about orderliness—so much so that in the past when he had attempted to fix the structure, he was sharply rebuked. On the dreaded day that sparks Francis and Joseph's memory, the exhausted Joseph decided to leave his recently sharpened implements in a wheeled barrel that he utilized for work, leaving it in the middle of the barn floor.

Joseph divulges,

"There are times I awake in fear. Others when I regret the danger I almost placed upon you."

Francis nods his head and shrugs in agreement; he welcomes the loving concern on his father's face. Again, Joseph reveals himself,

"I am forever grateful that I decided to put my tools away, before . . ."

Joseph pauses. The trusting look on his son's face prompts him to continue,

"Before you came crashing through the ceiling that evening."

On that evening, providentially, feeling guilty that he hadn't straightened up his tools, Joseph returned to the barn and put them away; he then filled the wheeled container with ashes from the barn's fireplace. Joseph continues,

"The fall from that distance would surely have killed you."

Francis continues to agree; his father lifts his eyes toward the ceiling and continues,

"The protective hand of God was on us both that day; He aided me in placing the barrel perfectly, right where you came crashing through."

Francis remains quiet. At this point Joseph is confident as he concludes,

"That shall always remain a mystery to me. But one thing that is not mystery: God has a purpose for your living, Franky, for you came very near to life's end."

As his eyes water slightly from the retelling, Joseph turns away from his son. He doesn't want Francis to see the deep emotions that remain. As he resumes his task of gathering some of the gardening implements, his thought to himself is clear: *Enough said.*

The Malt Shovel is grateful for Joseph. Because of his extraordinary abilities as a gardener, the owner offered him and Eliza the cottage and the use of the barn. The property looks magnificent. His abilities have also landed him the prestigious position of tending the gardens of the area's richest families. He now urges Francis,

> "Franky, today we shall have need only of our long shears and the short trimmer."

Francis quickly gathers the implements and places them in the wheeled barrel. His father is quick to respond,

> "We have no need of the barrel today; trimming shall be minimal."

Francis gathers the tools in his hands. Joseph once again gives a command,

> "We must tell Mother that we leave and shall return for dinner."

Francis hurries off to tell Eliza.

> "I shall take care of that, Father."

Joseph is grateful for his son's willingness to help, and even more grateful that Francis is enthusiastic about what Joseph does for a living. Joseph is truly an artist. The beautifully manicured landscapes are magnificent works of art standing in sharp contrast to the surrounding communities. His attention for detail allows him to participate, with much success, in a tradition that dates back to the first-century Roman conquerors of Britain.

Today, Joseph and Francis will complete the weekly maintenance at the elegant Hamstead Hall owned by the Wyrley Birch family.

Joseph walks with Francis along the perimeter of his customer's property; as he does, he instructs his son.

> "The goal, dear Franky . . ."

> "I know, Father, you've mentioned before; the goal is to create an outdoor space that is well ordered, with clean lines, delineating planned spaces."

Joseph smiles; Francis continues, imitating perfectly the hand gestures of his father.

> "We accomplish this through the neatly cropped high-walled hedges. Plant and trim" (he over-accentuates PLANT AND TRIM) "in a way that creates the tiny niches that house the owner's works of art."

Joseph loves when his son takes notice of the fine details and layout of a proper English garden. He reaches to trim a wayward sprig.

> "Notice the vertical line, Franky; it must be maintained."

Francis looks to the sharp line of the closely trimmed hedge approaching eight feet in height. He peeks around the corner of the plant and exclaims,

> "Fantastic!"

Francis is admiring the hidden space, which reveals a cast garden bench.

Joseph quickly moves toward the center of the property, on to the boxwoods.

Francis follows, catching up as his father inspects the sharp, trimmed edges of the lower plants forming the perimeter of a knot garden, by far the most fascinating contribution of the formal landscape. Once again, Joseph instructs his son.

> "Franky, you shall find that the knots should not exceed twelve inches in height. This shall provide clear view toward the filler plants."

The uniform boxwoods intertwine in numerous crossing designs along the garden paths and walkways. The meticulous patterns resembling the letter "x" result in consistent spaces for additional plantings. These are the location of the filler plants.

In the open areas, taller flowers and herbs like roses and fennel proliferate.

Francis reaches toward a thriving rose bush.

> "Ouch!"

Francis inspects the puncture wound on his forefinger. His father offers a warning,

> "Display care, my son; the rose is beautiful, but it can also bring pain."

Francis moves to another woven hedge and rubs his hand across the top.

> "Father, the plant gives a beautiful smell."

He quickly moves his fingers to his nose. The pleasing aroma brings a smile to Francis's face.

> "The sage plant, Franky; it is beautiful in both sight and smell."

Joseph continues to inspect the hedge made of the fragrant herb. He commends the garden's appearance,

> "All is as it should be."

Francis and Joseph take an additional moment to appreciate the blessing of the structured artistry and its fragrance.

> "Father, can Sarah experience the beauty of the sage?"

The question catches Joseph by surprise. He closes his eyes. Fighting back a distant emotion, he looks to his son.

> "I would venture to think that Sarah is enjoying much more than a neatly trimmed garden."

Francis smiles up at his father, his eyes partially closed, as the midday sun peeks through a rare opening in the West Midland sky. Joseph fluffs the hair on the top of Francis's head as they lean in for an embrace.

When Francis was three years old, his older sister Sarah, then five, suddenly took ill. Within days it became apparent that she was in grave danger. The family sought help, but to no avail; she died, leaving Elizabeth and Joseph heartbroken.

Joseph offers more,

> "She is in the midst of the Savior."

Francis nods his head in agreement.

Recovery for Joseph and Elizabeth was different for each. Joseph's work eventually helped him to accept the loss. Eliza struggled for several years. Depression set in quickly. Young Francis witnessed many a day when his mother would blankly stare out the window of their home's main room. Her heart could not deal with such a great loss. In time, her yearning for answers caused her to suffer a personal breakdown. Francis's bereaved mother was suffering, in hopeless grief.

> "Father, I am thankful that Mother is well again."

Joseph is grateful also; he replies to Francis's honesty,

> "It was several years before Mother sought remedy with God, undoubtedly a result of the itinerants in Newton."

Francis smiles in agreement with his father's statement. In spite of his young age, he remembers the long days spent waiting for Father to come home and rescue him from a home silenced by a desponding mother. Without sensing it, these days also chiseled into his tender heart a longing for God.

Francis responds,

> "Men like Pastor Jones."

> "Yes, Franky, wise servants like Pastor Jones. Without him, I suppose your mother may have never left off sobbing at the window."

Eliza was influenced by the traveling preacher James Jones, his efforts eventually causing her to pore over the Scriptures. The sacred words brought healing to her torn heart. Eliza's blank stares through the window eventually turned into time with the Creator; there she spent many hours reading the Bible.

> "This was a strange sight for you, Franky. I believe you had grown accustomed to seeing your mother weeping. Now she stood there, praising our Lord, and reading the Bible."

Francis excitedly offers,

> "I love to sing with you and Mother!"

Joseph gives a chuckle.

> "I suppose you do. I enjoy those times with you and Mother also."

After a few years, both Joseph and Eliza find comfort through their faith. Eliza's passion for the Word of God and her parental desire to teach her only child results in Francis being able to read the Bible by six years of age. Francis reads the sacred script daily. In time the precocious child is found questioning his playmates about their religious health. This quickly earns him the nickname "The Methodist Parson."[15]

Joseph and Eliza are generous people—so much so that Joseph's unrestricted approach to kindness slightly hinders the Asburys from accumulating much in the way of material gain. He is quick to aid neighbor or stranger, whenever the need arrives. The young Francis keenly observes this trait in his father.

Also not escaping Francis's notice is the benevolence of his mother. Eliza's rebirth initiates what will become an Asbury family tradition for more than half a century. Eliza and Joseph eagerly take up the cordial task of inviting the traveling preachers that come to the West Midland region to stay at their home. The extra room downstairs makes for the ideal flat, perfect for housing Wesley's tired itinerants. The room can sleep several comfortably; even the stair landing upstairs can provide accommodation for one more. Moreover, the cottage's nearness to the pub prompts a never-ending supply of prayer needs.

Although The Malt Shovel gardening provides additional income for the Asburys, they disdain the drunken patrons of the tavern. This experience, coupled with Joseph's exposure to the wealthy families for whom he labors so arduously, causes Joseph and Eliza to want more than a future in metalworking for dear Franky.

They have seen both sides of the wealthy—their ability to help others, and their seeming passion for self-destruction. Wisely, Joseph and Eliza dislike the materialism evidenced in some of these families. For the Asburys, material wealth is a means of blessing others, much in the same manner that they have been touched by those for whom Joseph labors.

When all is considered, the religious rebirth of Joseph and Eliza is the sole guide of their child's life. Before long, a local leader in the Anglican Church begins to notice young Francis's religious fervor.

[15] The Wesleyan faithful are called Methodists.

What Does a Wesleyan Child Know?

To make the symbols of atoning grace,
An office-key, a pick-lock to place.

J. Wesley Bready[16]

Two dozen adults and children are crowded, shoulder to shoulder, in the main room of the Asbury home. Several men are on their knees, others are standing, all with heads bowed. A handful of preadolescent boys and girls join Francis, leaning on each other between the jambs of the open rear door to the stairwell; they too are silent in prayer. Almost a dozen women sit quietly—some in chairs, others on wooden crates—in supplication to the Lord. In front of the fireplace, a tall, thin man stands, head bowed and silent. His dripping-wet clothes indicate he is one of Wesley's itinerant preachers. He is a man of above-average height and wide shoulders. His broad-brimmed hat hangs on the black iron spit above the ebbing fire to dry.

This is James Jones.

Preacher Jones handles the large Staffordshire circuit for the Wesleyan movement, a route covering several hundred miles. He is known for two significant events in his life: the first, a violent encounter alongside John Wesley during the Staffordshire riots of 1743 and 1744, when the uprisings against the Methodists plagued the entire Black Country; the second, his personal donation to build a Wesleyan chapel in the West Midland town of Tipton Green. He not only donated the money to build the structure, he also erected the building on his own.

Preacher Jones raises his head and hands toward heaven; with eyes closed, he begins,

"Thus says the Lord to his anointed,
"I am the LORD, and there is no other;
There is no God besides Me.
I will gird you, though you have not known Me,
That they may know from the rising of the sun to its setting
That there is none besides Me.
I am the LORD, and there is no other;
I form the light and create darkness,

---

[16] John Wesley Bready, in *This Freedom—Whence?* He writes on the corrupt "blind guides" leading the Anglican Church in the eighteenth century. They were using religion for political gain.

> I make peace and create calamity;
> I, the LORD, do all these things."[17]

The itinerant stops.

The room's inhabitants remain silent.

He lowers his hands and head.

Outdoors, the violent evening wind slams the cold November rain against the home. A dooryard tree[18] snaps under pressure; it flails across the wall at the front of the cottage, then quickly departs, destination unknown.

Leaving his companions, Francis walks to the center of the room. His steps are barely audible above the sound of the bellowing weather outside. In a voice that sometimes cracks from the beginning stages of adolescence, he offers the following:

> "Rain down, you heavens, from above,
> And let the skies pour down righteousness;
> Let the earth open, let them bring forth salvation,
> And let righteousness spring up together.
> I, the LORD, have created it."[19]

The lad turns and quietly makes his way back to his peers.

Pastor Jones smiles, as do Joseph and Eliza. They are pleased with Francis. His dissertation is appropriate, not only due to the harsh weather conditions, but also as the completion to the passage in Isaiah chapter 45 which the traveling preacher was praying. Several of the adults silently marvel at the young boy's knowledge and recall of the Scriptures. Pastor Jones closes the prayer,

> "Amen."

Behind the itinerant, the flames of the fireplace occasionally hiss as they evaporate small droplets from the driving winds that continue to push moisture through the cracks of the adjacent window's wooden shutters. He steps to the middle of the room and, without notes, he begins.

> "My young friend is correct. This evening's tempest is much like the raging storm destroying the Christian spirit of this nation. Whether leaders of Parliament or the very clergy of our own Anglican Church, they have departed from biblical wisdom. Only righteousness shall exalt a nation.
>
> "Moreover, what of the maddened citizens of the Black Country, those led astray by the Anglican clergy playing the part of the mob? I've seen a woman removed from her home, held down by five or six men, that

---

[17] From the Bible, Isaiah chapter 45, verses 5–7.

[18] A small growing tree, usually no more than six feet tall.

[19] Isaiah chapter 45, verse 8.

another might force her. She struggled to resist until they changed their purpose, beat her much, and then departed. I've witnessed the crazed populace as they entered the home of a Methodist, pulled part of it down, broke some of its goods in pieces, and carried the rest away.

"The Bible is replete with examples, times when the Lord will allow for the uncomfortable, for it is the uncomfortable that brings forth a spirit of repentance onto a nation. If we are wise, we will allow God's work, God's most holy work, to prosper in such times."

The room's inhabitants are silent. Several of the women look away from the preacher, staring at the floor as they consider the plight of the woman at the hands of the mob.

Preacher Jones continues,

"Rain down your righteousness, Father. This is my prayer for all of England, that they should welcome the hardships—the hardships that drive us to You."

All in the room nod in agreement. Preacher Jones once again raises his hands as well as his face toward heaven as he continues.

"Almighty Father, may you continue to rain on all of England, Ireland, and Wales."

The men in the room concur,

"Hear, hear."

At this the itinerant relaxes and makes his way toward the fireplace. He turns to look in the direction of Joseph Asbury and then to the entire group.

"Save for the raging storm outdoors, I release you all for the evening."

The group quickly redirects its attention. Several of the men advise that the departing guest wait for the storm to subside. At this, several women reach for the neatly wrapped items on the Asburys' kitchen table. With packages in hand, they approach James Jones. The long-lost smile of the preacher is quickly evident. The roasted beef and venison, wrapped tightly with dried bulrush reeds, are worth more than gold to the itinerant; the gifts are gratefully received. He places the food into a worn leather saddlebag resting next to the fireplace.

Buzzing on the far side of the room are the children. The boys playfully tease the girls and the girls politely resist the annoyance of the boys. Without prior notice, the boys' attention diverts as the women surrounding the itinerant return to their husbands. The boys abandon the girls and launch for the preacher. Pastor Jones has a surprise: he darts toward them. He stops short of the unsuspecting group and delivers the following:

"First, a riddle!"

The girls want to be included in the challenge; they twitter with excitement as they make their way toward the preacher. They arrive and he continues in an animated manner,

"Out of the eater came forth meat, and out of the strong came forth sweetness."

Francis looks stumped; the boys give the same look as they proceed, as usual, to follow Francis's lead. The girls, however, exchange confident smiles.

The group quickly splits in two, boys on one side of the room and girls on the other.

The girls, all dressed in delicate dresses, gather in an orderly circle and whisper to each other about the riddle. Each respectfully waits her turn to offer suggestions. It is apparent to the adults in the room that the girls are making progress toward a solution.

Unlike the tidy group of girls, the boys stand in a loose and disorganized huddle. One boy drags his forearm across his running nose while another blurts out to his companions,

"It has to do with Samson."

Immediately the rest of the boys grab the lad, each one admonishing,

"They shall hear!"

Francis leans in and gives warning,

"Quiet, you will let on."

The boys draw closer and focus.

At the edge of the room, Joseph and Eliza, along with several parents, watch the children. The excitement on the young faces is a welcome sight. Pastor Jones, unlike many of the Anglican clergy, enjoys encouraging the younger people. His weather-worn face seems to glow as he watches the children wrestle with the riddle.

Within a minute's time, Francis approaches the itinerant.

"We have solved the riddle."

Several of the girls verbalize their unhappiness with this. One places both hands on her hips and complains to her companion,

"Francis is always right."

The girls continue to fuss.

Pastor Jones is stern.

"There shall be one chance; if incorrect, the girls will be given ample time to solve the riddle."

Francis nods his head to acknowledge the warning.

One of the boys approaches and tugs on Francis's trousers. The pair come together and talk quietly. The other boys join in, forming an impromptu huddle.

One girl cannot bear it; she exclaims,

"Stalling!"

Her cry quickly rallies the other girls.

"This is not fair; they fail to have answer."

The plea of the leader of the girls causes Joseph to laugh and inquire of the itinerant,

"Pastor Jones, seems that Francis and his chums are not ready for a reply.
Might young Nancy and the girls have the first go at it?"

Francis turns from the boys' huddle to peer at his father, who lets out his signature laugh. Eliza pokes her husband.

"Do not tease, Joseph."

Joseph continues to laugh, hard and loud.

Francis slowly exits the huddle and heads toward the entrance door. Everyone in the room focuses on the boy. As if in unison, several adults tilt their heads in a quizzical nod, wondering what Francis is doing. Eliza looks back at the adults and shrugs her shoulders; she is equally mystified.

Mid-departure, Francis pauses and turns toward the boys. The leader of the girls, Nancy, rushes to Preacher Jones and boldly proclaims,

"He fails to have answer."

Because of her action, Francis abandons his pause and heads toward the boys. He walks past his companions and steps forward in front of the itinerant and next to Nancy. He stands nearly a foot taller than the ten-year-old girl, but she is up for the challenge; she makes an offer.

"Pastor Jones, the girls and I are ready, but we shall allow Francis his chance."

Francis is uncomfortable with Nancy's show of fair play. He fumbles for a reply, but has none.

Preacher Jones inquires of Francis,

"Francis, are we stalling or do the boys possess an answer to the riddle?"

Francis looks to Nancy, and then to the preacher. His pause indicates that he is somewhat hesitant.

"Yes - -

I believe we do."

Francis wears a befuddled look. His uncertainty has Nancy staring down the opposition. Other girls raise the cry again,

"Stalling!"

Francis looks to his pals, then turns back toward the itinerant.

"The riddle, I - -

Rather, we - - believe is from the book of Judges."

Francis pauses to look again to his group. The boys shrug their shoulders in uncertainty, which agitates the girls.

"They fail to have answer! The boys are stalling."

The girls are relentless. One tiny redhead in the back of their group puffs her cheeks in frustration.

Francis spins toward the itinerant and continues,

"The riddle deals with Samson's riddle to the Philistines when they were seeking his death."

Once again, Francis stops and turns toward the boys. The puffy-cheeked girl blurts out,

"We all know this, Francis. The riddle, what is the riddle?"

The young girl in the back of the group is once again unhappy with Francis's delay, as is Nancy, who now stands with arms folded tight, staring down Preacher Jones and sporting a supple crease in her brow.

Francis appears worried, especially in light of Nancy's look; he thinks to himself, *it is becoming almost scornful.*

The boys' mood reveals their nervousness; Francis silently mouths a plea toward his helpers.

At this Nancy stomps her foot on the wooden floor, her eyes still focused on the itinerant.

Once again, Joseph bellows a laugh. Francis wisely turns toward Pastor Jones, who gently prompts,

"Francis, it seems that you and your group do not have the answer."

Immediately Francis's demeanor changes as a broad smile crosses his handsome face—a scheming smile.

"We have answer."

Francis continues,

"Had it all along. The eater and the strong is the lion that Samson subdued, and the sweetness that came forth is the honey from the beehive resting inside the dead lion's carcass."

The boys burst into laughter. Francis does his best to hold a straight face, but he too gives in to a laugh.

Nancy turns and departs in frustration to her girls. She offers them the obvious,

"They knew of it all along!"

The girls are made furious by the boys feigning ignorance. Nancy vows the consequences of her displeasure.

"Francis Asbury, you shall have yours!"

His artful companions hug Francis.

During the solving of the riddle, the storm outside has managed to subside. The adults in the room decide that the evening is over; they quickly gather their children and offer their farewells to each other and to the itinerant.

Preacher Jones approaches Joseph.

"You possess an amazing child."

Joseph bellows his familiar laugh as Eliza chuckles and delivers the evening's linens to the itinerant.

"Joseph and I most heartily agree. Pastor Jones, do sleep well tonight."

The itinerant tips his head and smiles as the Asburys extinguish the room's candlelight.

"I shall."

Joseph and Eliza depart for their bedroom upstairs.

When the first ray of morning light is barely detectable, Francis bounds down the wooden stairs of the cottage and bursts outdoors through the front door.

He makes his way carefully along the soaked ground to the tool barn. Along the way, he spots the remains of the dooryard tree that snapped the evening before. The three-inch-diameter trunk cleaved roughly twenty inches above the ground. This sight gains his curiosity. He slows to look in several directions for the remainder of the tree; it is nowhere.

He continues on his way.

In the barn he finds Pastor Jones kneeling in silent prayer. He quietly takes a seat on an overturned wooden bucket used to gather water from the spring that services the brewery. Francis pulls his long legs in, raising his knees and resting his forehead on them.

The itinerant is aware that someone has entered the sacred space. He turns toward Francis.

"Come, let us talk to the Father."

Francis almost leaps from the bucket and kneels beside the preacher. Pastor Jones begins,

"Father, I thank Thee for this young man, one who displays a remarkable hold on the Holy Scriptures. May you continue to guide him in Your desired direction. Amen."

The pair rises together.

"May I have a moment of your time, Francis?"

Francis walks to the overturned bucket.

"Sit here, Pastor Jones."

One of the itinerant's knees makes a loud cracking noise as he bends to sit; the grimace on his face indicates that the joint is bothersome to him. Francis locates a block of oak wood at his father's tool bench. It is a sizable chunk, approximately eighteen inches long and ten inches wide on each side. He does his best to roll the hardened cube several times toward the preacher. Once the task is completed, he sits.

"Francis, you possess the tenacity of an itinerant. How old are you now?"
Without hesitation Francis replies,
"Shall reach my thirteenth year this summer."
The young boy beams; Pastor Jones chuckles.
"It is barely November."
Francis is amused also. The preacher continues,
"How are your studies at Sneal's Green?"
Francis doesn't answer.
The usually sanguine boy reaches for a small stick on the barn's dirt floor and draws in the damp earth. The preacher realizes that Francis is avoiding the question. He gently grabs Francis's hand; the boy looks up to the itinerant.
"You are a smart young man, Francis. Your instructor must be pleased?"
Despite the encouraging words, Francis looks away; he is uncomfortable with the question. The silence has the preacher concerned.
Francis finally responds,
"I enjoy the historical aspects of the Bible."
The traveling preacher is relieved.
"I am confident that your instructor has shown the Bible to be a most accurate historical book. But the Bible is more than a recounting; it also heals."
Francis drops the stick and raises his eyes to look at the preacher.
"As with Mother?"
Again, the preacher is pleased.
"Precisely, as with your mother. When first my travels brought me to Great Barr, dear Elizabeth was awash with grief. Still, she would occasionally appear at the outdoor engagements. In time God began to speak to my heart; 'Go to her' was the compelling message delivered. Therefore, I proceeded to follow the Lord's leading. I failed to know, but Elizabeth had already been prepared by God to be cleansed by His healing power."
The itinerant has Francis's undivided attention.
"I recall Mother sharing how you explained to her that Sarah was with Jesus."
"Yes, Francis. I shared with her of King David, when his child from the wife of Uriah died. David was clear: 'But now he is dead; why should I fast? Can I bring him back again? I shall go to him, but he shall not return

to me.[20] The wise king realized that not only was the child safe with God, but also that he needed to continue to live for the Lord, for someday this would allow him to reunite with the child, in heaven. This truth seemed to bring hope for living to dear Elizabeth. It was not long after that your mother became a regular participant at the preaching events, eventually inviting me to preach and lodge at the cottage."

The preacher's words bring a smile to Francis's face, radiating the deep-seated thankfulness anchored in his heart. Pastor Jones rubs Francis's hair.

"Come, it is time."

The pair rise and walk side by side as they exit the barn. The itinerant looks to the thick, overcast skies, a remnant from the storm of the previous evening.

"It is best I depart immediately."

Unhappy with these words, Francis kicks at the ground, then rethinks his action.

"I shall fetch your horse."

The boy departs for the rear of the property.

Later that evening, Francis is inside his home. The young man slowly raises his eyes from the printed pages of the family Bible. Natural light from the downstairs window has ceased hours earlier. In its place, a well-burnt taper flickers on the ledge of the shuttered window. His mother has a stern warning for him,

"Francis, you shall spoil your eyes."

He ignores his mother's advice. Tomorrow Francis will return to school. Eliza urges again,

"It is best you set down for the evening, Francis."

The young boy reluctantly closes his Bible. He extinguishes the taper and plods up the wooden stairs.

***

The jubilant noise of the teenage boys in the schoolyard of the Anglican Charity School travels several blocks away as they play a crude version of cricket. Around teatime, six days each week, the unrestrained sounds of the Black Country's factories fall silent. In place of industry's cacophonous wave is the tousled melody of the students.

At this time in history, cricket is the single-wicket version. This style pits one batter against one bowler, the two competitors aided by a fixed set of fielders. For adults of the late 1750s the game is one of many vehicles for gambling. For the

---

[20] 2 Samuel chapter 12, verse 23.

students at the Anglican school the competition is for much more: the results establish the pecking order of the group.

Decades before, the Church of England established the Anglican schools for primary education. The goal was to educate the less fortunate. Learning to read resulted in reading the Bible. The schools taught Latin and Greek as well. The success of the program sent many to the secondary level. In some instances the pupils learned farming, working the land that attached to the school. From the inception, the main purpose of the school has reflected the Bible's teachings of taking care of orphans, the poor, and the disadvantaged. Throughout most of England, the local congregation supplies the students' food and clothing, free of charge–but in the Black Country, relying on the struggling locals for such provision would be next to impossible.

In their panic over the unprecedented success of the Wesleyan movement, the Anglican clergy and their obsession to stop what they described as "unbridled enthusiasm" distorted the altruistic purposes of the Church of England's school system. The boys are well aware of the church's fixation on the unwelcomed revival. Even the required uniforms are a constant reminder of the clergy's aim for control. The school boys are dressed in brown cloth and cap, the stiff white collar a prompt to keep their behavior in check. Nevertheless, the restricting clothing fails to keep the boys from enjoying their daily opportunity to break from the classroom.

Francis Asbury stands face to face with his best friend, Thomas Ault. They became friends two years prior, when Thomas's family moved to Great Barr.

Before Thomas's birth, the preaching of George Whitefield converted his father, Robert. Shortly thereafter, the preaching of John Wesley converted his mother. Because of their conversions and involvement with the Wesleyan movement, the family endured many atrocities in the 1740s and 1750s. It was the Staffordshire riots of the 1740s that mostly affected the Ault family.

Two years ago, the Ault family once again faced opposition when the magistrate of the nearby town of Aldridge forced them to leave; their crime: participation in the Wesleyan movement. The local Bishop ordered their home ransacked by selected citizens friendly to the Anglican cause. The anti-Wesleyan mob threw the Aults' household items into the street for others to steal. The horde of rioters then burned the home to the ground.

Those who persecute the Ault family are not limited to individuals of the community. Even Thomas's grandmother rejected her own daughter for her new religion. Through it all, the Ault family grew stronger, counting it a blessing to suffer persecutions for the sake of the Savior and realizing that better awaited them in heaven.

At the schoolyard, Francis and Thomas do not participate in the boys' game of cricket. They carry themselves as the obvious leaders of the classroom—in their opinion, they no longer need to prove themselves on the field. Both are handsome and tall, each wearing shoulder-length hair beneath his school cap. Francis's confident posture and appealing straight nose seem to convey his steadfast passion for justice. This craving is another attribute in line with his burgeoning focus on detail, the focus that his father enjoys encouraging in his son. Thomas's gentle mannerisms communicate that he is a compassionate listener and trusted friend.

Thomas inquires of Francis,

    "What of your parents?"

With his arms folded tight, Francis does not reply to Thomas's question. He's almost holding his breath as he stares at Thomas. He finally exhales, relaxes, and lowers his arms. He turns from his friend, who patiently waits for a response.

    "Father will hear nothing of the sort . . .

    Wishes that I remain."

Thomas is disappointed with the information. He pushes for more,

    "And your mother?"

Francis places both his hands in his pockets and slowly steps away from Thomas. He looks to the ground, struggling to respond, almost as if not wanting to reply; however, he does.

    "Mother has attempted to release me also, but Father's proclamation
    continues: 'the needs of a proper education.' "

The ringing of the school bell sends the cricket-playing boys rushing by the pair. Francis ignores them. He stands with hands in pockets, staring at the ground. Thomas gently urges,

    "We had best return to class."

The players shuffle into the stuffy space designated for learning. Dust swirls dance in the sunlight beaming through the sole window at the back of the room. The middle-aged instructor, Arthur Taylor, stands silently next to the window as he always does, watching as the boisterous youths take their seats. He dreads this moment. In Taylor's opinion, if the church is picking up the expenses, the boys should not play games while attending school.

The portly instructor is dressed in early eighteenth-century coattails and waistcoat, the monochromatic colors of the outfit in keeping with his inflexible personality. He has yet to embrace the contemporary styles of the middle eighteenth century. The times have brought Instructor Taylor's biggest fear: change. By 1750, men's waistcoats and tails—in fact, the entire ensemble—are no longer one basic color. The riches of the infant industrial revolution invite new freedoms, as the world offers its favorable views to the prospering country of England.

For the last century, France has been the leading influencer of Europe. The elaborate styles of the French have dominated the arts, fashion, and industry. Its influence has spread to Spain, Portugal, Germany, Holland, and with some hesitancy, England. The French language has also become the language of Europe, displacing Latin except in learning and law—but these developments are limited in scope. The French people are a people still under the papacy; the Roman Church inadvertently continues to keep its citizenry in the dark by refusing to allow the Bible to be printed in the local language. As a result, only those who read and understand Latin gain the wisdom found in the Scriptures.

Conversely, England's citizenry, under the influences of the Protestant and Anglican Churches which call for the Bible printed in English, benefit greatly. Passages in the Old and New Testament admonish able-bodied persons to work, sell, profit, and share from their abundance—the success of which relies on the incorporation of these biblical concepts into the country's laws, businesses, and organizations. Because of this focus on biblical production and entrepreneurship, the island nation prospers. The greater burden of this recent development is shouldered on the backs of the working class.

These edifying ideals bring to life a focus on one particular concept, that of capitalism or the free market. Capitalism is the fuel that energizes the nation, inspiring its inhabitants to produce—not for one's own consumption, but with others in mind. Even the nation's women are inspired to this concept with a passage from the book of Proverbs. In chapter 31 of the Old Testament book, the wise woman considers a field and buys it. From her profits she plants a vineyard. She then gathers the harvest of the vineyard, selling the fruit for additional profit. From these profits, she takes care of the needs of her family and the nearby poor. The practice is in its infant beginnings. It does experience resistance from the monarchy; however, the work ethic is proving itself valid, even traveling outside England to the colonies in North America. Though initially the best benefits are bestowed upon a select few in England, the financial success of free industry brings with it the ability to participate in acquiring luxurious items such as fine clothing.

The new fashions of England are deliberately less audacious than the French designs, but they are a welcome change. In light of such changes, many talk of providing sporty blue uniforms for the students. However, the staunch Instructor Taylor will have nothing to do with it.

The students complete the task of returning to their desks as Instructor Taylor removes a lit candle from its wall-mounted holder at the back of the room. Francis and Thomas arrive as Taylor proceeds to light two similar candles on opposite sides of the classroom. The two boys quietly walk in and take their assigned seats. Taylor frowns at their tardiness. He completes his chore and returns the candle to the holder at the rear of the room.

Taylor slowly draws the gloomy drape over the lone window in the classroom. He mumbles through a contorted expression as the room begins to flicker in candlelight,

"All is as it should be."

The boys fidget as the instructor makes his way to the front of the classroom.

Motionless, Francis sits tall at his desk.

Instructor Taylor arrives at the front of the room. In his right hand is the infamous fescue, the device designed to be an aid in teaching—but in the hand of Taylor, the stiff, slender pointer is less an instrument of instruction and more a tool of discipline. In the past he has used it to attack hands, foreheads, cheeks, and forearms of the students in his charge.

His familiar technique is to snap the pointer portion of the tool onto the extremity of choice. The resulting small red welt usually disappears by the time the students finish the day. During other efforts of regulation, the foot-long weapon launches at a student who has unfortunately fallen asleep during class.

Taylor begins a familiar rhythm as he taps the fescue in the palm of his left hand. The slow and steady pace borders on being hypnotic. Without notice, the overbearing man stops the tapping and turns toward Francis.

"Master Asbury, your lesson, please."

Francis looks to Thomas sitting at his right side. He pauses, then slowly rises to his feet. Apprehensively clearing his throat, he begins,

"All of Creation was spoken into existence . . ."

As Francis continues with the creation account, Instructor Taylor walks to the rear of the room.

With all the students facing forward, Instructor Taylor is out of view. As the recital continues, the imperious man silently mocks Francis. In an odd fashion, the instructor distorts his face and waves his arms about. The students are ignorant of the silent gibes, or at least Taylor thinks they are.

Francis completes his recital and waits for the instructor's response. Taylor delivers it with a sneer that communicates contempt.

"Well done, Master Asbury. You may be seated."

***

At the Asbury home, Eliza stirs the small iron kettle that hangs on the iron spit above the fireplace. In one corner of the room, a handmade wooden table with three chairs is neatly set with three plates and a vase of dried cut flowers. From the rear of the room, Joseph walks in with an armload of firewood.

"This evening, winter shall settle in."

Eliza acknowledges Joseph's comment about the seasonal weather, which will bring a chill. She replies,

"I've prepared a warm stew."

Joseph is grateful for her love demonstrated on a daily basis, a warm and hearty meal.

Beyond the rear door of the main room, Eliza and Joseph can hear young Francis making his way slowly down the wooden staircase. His steps are slow and labored: one step, pause, then another, pause, then another . . .

Joseph looks to Eliza. They both are thinking the same thing: *This is unusual.*

The door opens and Francis walks, head down, into the room. His despondent appearance saddens Eliza. She says nothing, and looks to her husband. Joseph ignores the situation and sits for dinner. Eliza and Francis sit also.

The wooden table constructed by Joseph is made of oak, stained to a dark finish. It is a sturdy piece of furniture. Its finish matches the oak chairs, also made by Joseph. The highlight of the table and chairs is the natural rush seat panels, once again meticulously constructed by Francis's father.

The seat panels are from bulrush that grows in a local bog at Sutton Park. The plants selected are usually hand-cut to eight feet in length, laid out to dry in the tool barn, and eventually woven to the seat rails. The drying process takes about one week. Once completed, the gathered material requires a little more than a year to gain its beautiful golden finish.

The Sutton Park property is the former royal hunting grounds of King Henry VIII, deeded to the people of the Birmingham area in 1528. The 2,400 acres of wetlands, heaths,[21] marshes, and ancient woodlands are freely accessible to the public. The Park contains an ancient Roman road, 1.5 miles long and cambered in typical Roman fashion, allowing the surface water to drain from the center. On rare occasion, the Birmingham youths will find coins from the reigns of Constantine and Diocletian.

On this evening, Francis is content to say little; he enjoys the hot meal his mother has prepared. Now and then, Eliza peeks at Joseph.

Joseph remains silent, choosing to ignore the subdued demeanor of Francis.

---

[21] A heath is a large open area, usually with sandy soil and scrubby vegetation, especially heather.

Finally, it is too much for Eliza to bear.

"Francis continues to struggle with his instructor . . ."

Eliza wants to continue, but she politely waits for Joseph's reply. Joseph pauses from his dinner, looks to Francis—then to Eliza—and then returns to eating.

Eliza deliberately drops her spoon to the table alongside her bowl, the noise catching the attention of both men. In silence, she stares at her husband. The next words do not come from Eliza.

"The instructor is cruel!"

Francis's words are quick and loud. He doesn't mean to, but he startles his mother. Again his words fly out,

"Mother, he dislikes us!"

With Francis looking at Eliza, it is hard to tell if he is speaking about the instructor or his father.

Joseph gets up from the table and leaves the room through the front door. Eliza bows her head in disappointment.

Outdoors, Joseph busies himself, winterizing the herb and vegetable garden. On his knees, he spreads dried straw over the fertile ground. He is alone for a few minutes, and then Francis approaches his father, slowly.

He kneels beside Joseph.

"Father . . . may a child be struck?"

Joseph continues with the task.

Francis cautiously peers at his dad. From the corner of his eye he notices his mother, standing inside the home at the main room's window. With a torn heart, she watches the two most important men in her life.

Joseph replies as he focuses on his task,

"Mother and I have struck you."

Joseph will not look at Francis. His gentle reply is not what Francis expected. His father is a man who is not afraid to speak openly, with decisiveness—but mostly with a commanding tone, seldom with gentleness. Francis thinks about his words.

He begins to help his father with the garden cover.

"But Father, you strike when deserved."

Joseph pauses, then finally looks to Francis. Francis welcomes his father's response. He considers this the proper time to ask the question that is burdening his heart.

"Father, must I attend?"

Silence.

Joseph turns away.

Francis is unhappy with his father's response.

In the background, Eliza continues to stare through the window. She loves her husband but cannot understand why he doesn't see the danger their son is facing. She is torn. She wrestles with the thoughts of submitting to Joseph's decision to leave Francis in school and her intuition that their child, their only remaining child, is daily experiencing harm.

Francis gathers his feelings; he rises and slowly makes his way indoors.

Later that evening, in front of the fireplace, Joseph and Eliza sit quietly. Each chooses not to speak to the other, joined only by the cracks and pops of the fire. Young Franky has long gone to bed upstairs.

Eliza turns to Joseph. In a gentle tone, she reminds him,

> "Our son has expressed this before."

Joseph fumbles with the drinking cup in his hands, steam rising from the hot tea. He continues to stare into the fire, almost aloof to his wife's hint. With great care and gentleness Eliza leans in toward her husband; she whispers,

> "Joseph, you are a good man, but you are a good man who chooses to do nothing . . ."

The next day finds the students of Sneal's Green racing out the schoolhouse door. Once again they set up for the daily game of cricket. Trailing the group are Francis and Thomas. With a quickened pace, Francis begins to kick stones that lay on the ground. Thomas does his best to keep up with his focused friend. Francis blurts out,

> "Father must consider it a cross to bear."

The tone of Francis's statement reveals his frustration with his father's failure to remove him from the Anglican school.

> "As if he wishes for the vulgar acts to continue."

Thomas aches for his friend.

Trailing his companion, Thomas reaches for Francis in an attempt to turn him around, but unexpectedly his friend comes to a complete halt. Thomas ceases his attempt to grab Francis and quickly offers,

> "Francis, your father is as all our fathers, desiring solely our escape from this most dreadful Birmingham."

In frustration, Francis places both hands on his hips. He stares toward the cricket players, saying nothing. Thomas gently adds to his observation,

> "This battle is larger than Francis."

Francis grimaces at Thomas's gentle warning. He resumes his stone dance, centering his anger as he savagely kicks rocks, one by one.

After several kicks Francis ceases the battle with the ground and aggressively spins toward Thomas, locking eyes, almost violent.

> "Do you suppose that I fail to realize this, Thomas? The only difference that exists between you and me is that my ***home—my home*** has yet to be burned to the ground."

Francis completes his statement with a pointed finger shaking inches from Thomas's face, silencing him with his abruptness and his emphasis on the word "home."

Thomas fully understands what Francis is implying. Although the Asbury home still stands, the vulgar acts of the instructor on Francis, the savage snaps of the fescue and the mocking sneers, have in effect destroyed Francis. Francis is adamant.

> "I vow the outrageous behavior shall not continue!"

Thomas stands in silence, worried for his dear friend.

Almost on cue, the crazed din of hammers returns as Birmingham's artisans once again practice their craft. The noise regains its place of importance dominating the town's atmosphere. Amidst the clamor, Francis sharply grabs Thomas's right arm.

> "It shall cease this day, I vow so."

He pushes away Thomas's arm, pauses, then turns to depart for the classroom. It is difficult, but Thomas manages a reply.

> "Then I shall stand with you, but Francis . . ."

Francis stops his departure mid-turn. Thomas stretches to lightly grab Francis by the right arm.

> "I realize it is said often and on occasion, by those we possess little or no respect for, but please - -
> Please, be mindful of your vows. They can lead one to much strife."

Francis gives no reply. He pulls his arm free, turns, and walks away.

Inside the fusty classroom, Francis focuses on the past. He focuses on the humiliating feelings, the apprehension of attending school, the embarrassment in front of his peers; in his mind, the numerous strikes from the fescue and the confrontational remarks about his family's association with the Wesleyan movement play on.

This shall end today. He again bolsters his thoughts. *Regardless, I will take a stand.*

Thomas admires his friend's courage as he takes his seat next to Francis.

Francis's thoughts are elsewhere—so much so that when he hears his name, he is uncertain as to why it was called . . . but he is most certain as to who it is that has called him.

Instructor Taylor taps his fescue, waiting for Asbury's reply.

The students, as well as Francis, are silent. They begin to worry when Francis is not so quick to reply to the question.

He knew it would come to this; however, he didn't think it would arrive so soon. Uneasy, Francis turns to Thomas. Thomas smiles a look of encouragement, but inside, Thomas doubts that this situation will end well. He's confident that Francis possesses the strength to stand up for himself. He's seen him do it when bullied by the local street boys. Because of this courage, the Brummies no longer attempt to extort items from Francis. However, Taylor is a larger threat than the Birmingham guttersnipes are—a danger that extends beyond the schoolyard to his family.

Francis slowly rises to his feet. His hands at his sides begin to shake. In order to hide the trembling, he locks them behind his back. He clears his throat.

"The Creator . . ."

Francis's voice cracks, and he pauses. The students stare at Instructor Taylor, all fixed in silence.

Francis clears his throat again. The belligerent instructor cuts him off.

"Enough!"

Taylor's slapping of a student's desktop underscores his angered command. The students freeze with fear.

Taylor begins pacing at the front of the room, causing several boys to squirm. They try their best to contain their nervous shifts, but it is difficult.

Francis releases his hands from behind his back, but he cannot control the shaking. He fumbles for a comfortable position. Finally, his hands rest at his side, trembling, as he remains standing.

Patrolling at the front, Instructor Taylor once again begins the tapping of the fescue in the palm of his left hand. His thoughts race as he decides how to handle such insubordination.

His scornful look is enough to melt Birmingham iron. So are his words:

"What does a Wesleyan child know of the Creator?"

No one dares a response to Taylor's rhetorical question. He glares anger at his subjects. The students instinctively wince and look away.

Francis decides to sit; in doing so, he accidentally bumps the leg of his desk. The leg's base creaks across the floor.

The noise infuriates Taylor. He turns toward Francis, his stout and hairy arm pointing the fescue.

"What of ya'?"

The instructor poses the question, expecting no reply. He's gripping the handle of the teaching implement so hard that his big-skinned knuckles are turning white.

> "And the rest of ya, your Wesleyan doctrine—huh, you do possess a doctrine?"

As the students recoil in fear, Taylor makes his way to the desk of Francis.

He hovers over the nervous lad. Francis's entire body begins to shake. He stares at the fescue, which now has returned to its methodical and steady rhythm on Taylor's left palm. Taylor's words seem to threaten the existence of the lit tapers.

> "Asbury, stand and deliver."

Francis's labored swallow seems to echo through the classroom. Warily he stands, aiming for minimal distraction. His measured pace is noticed by all, including Taylor, who continues to harass.

> "Master Asbury, daylight is fleeting."

It's a difficult task, but Francis succeeds in rising quietly to his feet.

Instructor Taylor stands uncomfortably close. Francis looks into the face of his instructor. The redness of his inflated cheeks is less than a foot away. As calmly as he can, Francis delivers,

> "The Good Lord rested on the seventh . . ."

With his left hand, Taylor smacks Francis, mid-sentence, across the face.

> "That was not the question posed!"

Guilt feelings flood Francis: *Yes, I was not paying attention.*

Sound reflection soon surfaces: *But I have done nothing deserving of this.*

The demeaning act stuns the emotions of the students. Thomas is pained; he wishes to respond, but fails.

Many students lower their heads. They do not wish to see Instructor Taylor humiliate their pal once again. Francis stands silent, staring down Taylor, eye to eye.

Francis whirls his head to look toward Thomas.

Thomas looks away.

Francis quickly returns his focus to Taylor. On cue, Taylor responds,

> "Does a man have the right to go against the King's Church, the established Church of England?"

Taylors's low monotone voice indicates that the statement is for Francis alone.

Francis wants to reply, but instead he experiences an obscure, random thought: *Perhaps the Bishop has noticed Mother's prayer meetings.*

Immediately following this thought, Instructor Taylor slices his fescue across the top of Francis's shaking forearm. The students gasp as Francis winces. Francis will not take his eyes off Taylor.

With an open hand, Taylor smacks Francis across the face once again. Francis cannot stop the trembling that is welling up from deep inside; his eyes remain fixed on his instructor.

Several students try to hide the fact that they are wiping away tears. It goes unnoticed by Taylor. The adrenaline rush of dominating this situation captivates him.

Francis has no options at this point; he is frustrated and panic-stricken. His measured exhale through his nostrils humors Taylor; he continues to goad.

"Appears we are not all Anglicans."

Cradling his forearm, which bleeds profusely, Francis turns to leave. Taylor slaps the desktop.

"Sit down, Master Asbury!"

Francis doesn't look back. He proceeds to the door at the rear of the classroom. The action rivets the students toward Francis's response. Even Thomas is surprised that Francis is standing up to Instructor Taylor.

In a rage, Taylor hurls the fescue at the exiting Asbury. The students cower in fear as the implement of discipline misses Francis and bounces off the wall, hitting another student. Taylor is not done; he launches one last verbal attack.

"Master Asbury, you are destined for failure."

The Pretenders

There is a far kingdom
A ways from here,
Beyond the storm and the sea.
There will be no need of darkness
And none for tears
When that far kingdom I see.

The Gray Havens[22]

In the crowded prison cell, Charles Wesley attempts to comfort the ten-year-old boy. The timid lad stole a chicken. This day, he will hang for his crime. The boy is wedged among twenty-five men and two women who will discover that their earthly lives, too, will abruptly run short.

The eyes of the thin lad dart around the room. His attention is split between the loving preacher and the nefarious prisoners that surround him. Under his disheveled brown hair, his innocent, sweet smile barely sneaks out of a young face that has already experienced too much of life's hardships. Charles offers comfort,

"The Lord shall not abandon."

The cacophonous noise of multiple conversations makes it difficult for Charles to hear himself or the child. Worse than the rolling din are the horrid smells emanating from bodies that have not been bathed in months. The child's odorous breath has Charles fighting the urge to hold back as he leans in to the child. Charles asks the boy,

"Are you afraid to die?"

I would venture this too deep a question for one so young. Charles wrestles with the thought.

The boy fumbles with a rip in his leggings. He fails to raise his eyes to the preacher. Charles reacts to the stark smell of the boy's clothes as it wafts the embedded odors of the grotesque prison. Smears of blood mixed with mud and human excrement cover the outfit; the child's fingernails are caked with the putrid soil from the prison's dirt floor. Despite the challenge, Charles remains patient.

The boy gives no reply.

---

[22] From the song "Far Kingdom" by The Gray Havens, lyrics by David Radford. Used with permission.

From the corner of his eye, Charles notices a small rat as it weaves through the degenerates, sometimes scudded along by a well-placed kick from one of the prisoners. The bold rodent makes its way to the perimeter of the room, then scurries back into a hole between the mortised stones on the edge of the cell. Its podgy frame temporarily blocks the room's only source of light as it creeps through the small opening at ground level. Charles turns to the lad and offers,

"You must be reconciled to God."

These words appear out of place. He debates to himself, *can a child so young stand accountable for sin?*

Charles has seen this situation before. The boy is one of the forgotten children of England's mid-eighteenth century. The demoralizing impact of the slave trade with its poisonous effects has created an entire industry and generation of orphaned lads. This boy is as many, a victim of enterprising men who kidnap children for the much-needed labor on the slave ships that set sail daily from England's ports. Even at the highest levels of government and society, the detestable practice of child abduction is ignored, considered necessary for the welfare of the nation's economy. This practice, among several others, brings an epidemic rise in crime on the island nation's streets. The savagery of the slave industry, like a toxin that works its way back to the clean source, has come full circle.

Depending on viewpoint, it is fortunate that the lad was able to escape the hands of his captors before they bound him and placed him on an outgoing slave ship. The majority of these young boys and girls never make it back to the homeland, finding themselves sold into years of plantation labor, without pay and with no hope of leaving the West Indies. Most die a premature death from the rigors of their indentured servitude. Equally unfortunate for this boy, the cruel streets drove the starving lad to steal.

As Charles wrestles with his thoughts about young children and the accountability of sin, the Sheriff arrives. He is a big man whose demeanor is cold and cruel. In his hand is a driving whip. He quickly raises the implement, creating the loud and distinctive snap that catches everyone's attention. Immediately the group falls silent. He bellows a command,

"All must load - -

Now."

His words are sharp and to the point. His penetrating gaze scans the destitute group, catching Charles's eye. Without hesitation he snarls,

"The boy shall load into the cart - -

Now."

Charles struggles with the unexpected interruption. He replies to the Sheriff,

"But the boy has not received the sacrament."

The Sheriff is unmoved by his plea.

"He loads now."

Charles realizes that the boy must depart. It is his wish to give the boy communion, but he decides to heed the barbarous officer.

Outdoors, the twenty-seven other prisoners are loaded onto the large wooden cart. The driving team consists of two powerful horses. The black Friesians are typical for their breed: large, rather stocky, and with the familiar feathers.[23] They each stand close to seventeen hands high. The Sheriff's drivers are two rough-looking men in their mid-twenties. Each carries a whip to control both their cargo and the unruly crowd that will turn up for the hanging show.

Charles lifts the boy, the last to be loaded onto the cart. The lad is overwhelmed, his cherubic face fixed in a lifeless stare as he nervously fumbles with his tattered clothing. The cart jerks forward and the prisoners are on their way to the gallows.

On board, a raucous argument breaks out among the captives. Several of the men push and shove. One lands a closed fist to his opponent's face. Another draws back to strike a male prisoner, but accidentally jabs a woman in the temple with the point of his elbow. She screams in pain, pushing and shoving as she climbs over other prisoners in her effort to retreat as quickly as she can from the impromptu brawl; she knows that the men who engage in this fight are in competition.

Decades before, men heading to the gallows prided themselves in doing so confidently. It became a rite of passage for the men about to die to dress themselves in their finest clothes and display no fear. The watching public would commend the behavior of the prisoners, expressing that they died as gentlemen. The accolade that the men are fighting over today hearkens to this old custom. In the latter portion of the 1750s, the ritual has transformed into the prisoners fighting for a coveted prize: a pair of white gloves supplied by the Sheriff. The prisoner who gains the white gloves dies as a gentleman. The winner of the distorted competition celebrates when he struts onto the gallows, gloating over his achievement.

As the fight continues, the boy tries to take it all in, but the situation is beyond his level of comprehension. He snaps out of his panicked stupor when one of the drivers cracks the whip to end the fight. The men immediately cease their battle. The boy begins to cry in fear.

---

[23] Long, silky hair on the lower legs, deliberately left untrimmed.

Charles follows alongside the moving cart. His aim is to comfort and pray for the young boy—a task which will become much more difficult as the cart approaches town. Charles temporarily diverts his attention away from the boy and looks forward, beyond the cart. He notices the edge of town and the mob that eagerly awaits the arrival of the prisoners.

The Sheriff also notices the large crowd. He complains,

"Shall take at least three quarters of an hour to reach the gallows."

The prisoners yell their approval as they notice the masses that have gathered for the day's events.

At town's edge, the atmosphere is carnival-like; nearly all of the more than one thousand townspeople are intoxicated. As if attending a local fair, individuals are selling food, clothing, and other items. A favorite purchase among the more boisterous attendees is sot's comfort,[24] the juniper-berry-flavored grain spirit that is slowly destroying a generation. Despite the epidemic of extreme drunkenness created by the drink, the situation incites moral outrage among the majority of the sober citizens. Their cry is for legislative measures to curb the unbridled destruction of the virtue of the nation. There is little chance of those cries being heard today.

At the event, dogs freely wander about, barking at the fights that break out among the raucous crowd. Sticks, clubs, cloaks, and kerchiefs wave in the air as the drunken viewers roar and sing. On occasion, the thud of a club will send a dog whimpering on its way.

All this attention renews the sense of competition among the prisoners. In the cart, the battle for the white gloves resumes. This time several more have decided to compete for the distinguished position. The men quickly wind up in a struggle. One of the cart drivers turns around sharply and cracks the whip above the conflict.

Outside the cart, the drunken townspeople fight. They curse at the driver.

An additional whip snap slows the clash, but the brawling quickly resumes as several men realize the crowd is viewing them. Arms and fists fly as the prisoners begin landing punches on backs, backs of heads, and backs of necks. The driver once again turns around; this time three quick snaps of the whip draw blood from several of the combatants. The rumble comes to a halt, still unsettled.

Charles battles his way through the crowd, his efforts to stay alongside the cart becoming extremely difficult. Wiping away his tears, the young boy stands and looks for Charles. The rubbing of his tears leaves dirt smudges across his face. He spots the itinerant, now roughly ten yards behind the moving cart.

---

[24] Gin.

Charles blurts out,

> "Look to the Son of Man lifted up. That whosoever believeth on him might not perish, but have eternal life."

The burgeoning crowd causes the cart to separate from Charles.

Nearing the gallows, the crowd becomes even more uncivilized. The sense of confusion grows as the inebriated men on the ground land horrific blows. Skulls and bones are cracked by the violent strikes. No one of any right sense would dare enter into this tumult. Slivers of swinging sticks that have collided in mid-air injure innocent bystanders. Blood from clubs that have hit their mark splashes through the air as the intensity of the group increases.

Ahead of the cart, several women scream in horror as they scurry about in search of something. A club that missed its original mark strikes one woman. Another is knocked out by a deliberate strike. Yet another of the crazed women screams uncontrollably, still attempting a search. It seems she has lost her small child in the fracas. The cart of prisoners continues forward, forcing her out of the way.

Finally arriving at the gallows, the mob swamps the cart.

The Sheriff and his drivers crack the whip on several as they push in. The crowd quickly backs away. Spurred by contemptuous anger, one of the drivers launches from the cart and lashes at the people. In fear, they try to scatter, but they are too many to move to safety. The attacker is able to catch one unfortunate individual, a small boy who screams as he holds his right eye. The crack of the whip plucked the sphere from its socket. Blood pours down his cheek.

As the crowd disperses, the clearing reveals several trampled men and children lying motionless on the ground. The crazed woman kneels above one small child.

Today is not an ordinary day; according to the locals, it is a "good show," with twice the normal number of prisoners being hanged. At the front of the wooden platform created for the event are several "resurrection women." To the crowd, the women are extra entertainment as they feign mourning for the deceased. Several are good at it. Although the inebriated attendees believe none of the cries, the women do their best to display sadness for those about to die. In truth, the women work for local surgeons attempting to obtain bodies for dissection.

In the distance, Charles struggles through the crowd. A brawler set to destroy anything in his path nearly knocks him down. Charles dodges the frenzied fighter and pushes toward the front of the gallows.

The Sheriff directs the prisoners as he disembarks,

> "Men to the left, women the right."

The women are hanged on the entrance side of the gallows, then removed, semi-strangled, and burned in public. This is a new procedure—as some call it, "an improvement from past actions," when the women were removed from the ropes semi-conscious and pressed to death under iron weights.

The crowd cheers the prisoners as they stand in front of the gallows. The appearance of the young boy seems out of place. The mob mentally blocks out the inappropriateness of the situation.

Up to this point the gathered throng was beyond control, but this act of the prisoners standing still and facing the crowd seems to calm them. One in the audience yells out,

"Crown the petitioner!"

All in attendance yell as they eagerly await the awarding of the white gloves.

Charles weaves his way forward to the boy and kneels in front of him. At this, a woman in the crowd tosses a head of rotten lettuce at Charles. It strikes him in the back. A boy around ten years of age sneaks behind the woman who tossed the salad and picks the pocket of her drunken husband. The inebriated man catches the lad in the act and a fight breaks out. Charles doesn't flinch, but continues to kneel in prayer.

Sensing danger, the frightened boy steps to Charles. He bows his head and places it on Charles's shoulder. The rotten fruit and vegetables begin to fly, consistently hitting Charles and the boy with pinpoint accuracy. The lad begins to weep. Charles reaches out and hugs him, partly to protect, partly to share in his weeping. The boy grabs on tight.

The vegetable hurling ceases as one prisoner in the lineup steps forward and raises his hands above his head. This action brings the roaring cheers of the crowd. Like a guest of honor, he peruses the gathering. He looks to his right and to his left; none of his fellow prisoners wishes to contest his proclamation. His action has silenced the others who were vying for this prized position.

The Sheriff comes forth and hands the white gloves to the victor. The mob is elated as the prisoner dons the coveted apparel. Upon completion, the Sheriff gives the command that all have been waiting for.

"Hanging spectacle begins!"

At this announcement, the prisoners begin to climb the steps of the gallows.

Lagging behind, the young boy will not let go of Charles.

It is a trying moment for the loving preacher. In tears, Charles kisses the lad on the forehead, then rises to his feet. Taking the small hand in his, he leads the underage felon to the steps. At the platform base, the boy latches onto Charles. The Sheriff is not happy with this; he makes his demand,

"The boy climbs, now!"

The Sheriff's warning brings a rippling wave of silence to the crowd. The boy will not release Charles, and Charles will not deliver the boy. The crowd begins to chant,

"Wesley, Wesley, Wesley . . ."

The crowd knows this acclamation will incite the Sheriff's wrath toward the preacher. Charles begins to worry. He decides he is willing to brave a scourging by the Sheriff and continues to hug the boy.

Again, the Sheriff levies his command.

"The boy climbs now."

Charles ignores the Sheriff.

The Sheriff grabs a whip from his driver and makes his way to the pair. The crowd's cry grows louder,

"Wesley, Wesley, Wesley!"

One man in the crowd attempts to incite the Sheriff.

"Hang the preacher, too!"

The crowd roars its approval.

Charles bows his head toward the lad and whispers,

"Look to the Son of Man lifted up. He shall not fail you."

With all the courage that a tear-filled ten-year-old can muster, he acknowledges the statement of the kind itinerant, but he still refuses to leave the preacher. The clamor of the crowd rises with each step of the Sheriff as he comes within striking distance of Charles.

Charles's attention totters, first on the boy, then on the Sheriff. With each of Charles's looks to the Sheriff, the crowd howls in excitement. The Sheriff grasps the handle of the driving whip.

He snaps the whip in front of his determined steps. The crack causes several nearby to wince. Their eyes instinctively blink. The sheriff coils the whip for another round.

Charles begs of the lad,

"It is time, my son."

The boy releases Charles; he turns and slowly walks up the steps to his departure. Charles struggles with his emotions: *This is surely misguided.*

The crowd hoots and hollers, decrying the unwanted result; they wished for the Sheriff to whip the preacher.

The crowd quickly resumes its cheers as a rope is placed around each convict's neck. The loudest approval is for the white-gloved leader of the misfits.

As if to further the trauma for the young boy, his noose, which hangs three feet lower than the rest, is on the furthermost end of the gallows. His frail little body begins to tremble uncontrollably as his benumbing fears grow with each bound neck he passes. At his location, the Sheriff's helper places the rope around the tiny neck.

All standing and roped. Charles turns and makes his departure. The Sheriff barks out the command and the stark sound of the wooden floor collapsing coincides with multiple unison grunts.

As each of the convicts dangles from a rope, the reaction of the crowd is universal—not only for each attendee here today, but also for each city and township in which these hanging shows occur. Each person in attendance stands in stunned silence, trying to comprehend the unnatural sight of human bodies jerking and then rocking from a rope, their feet twitching a yard away from life.

Amidst the silenced crowd, Charles brings his leaving to a halt and turns toward the Sheriff. His words carry throughout the gathering.

>"We sacrifice the lives of men, not for the reformation, but for the diversion of the populace . . ."

Charles sets out from the crowd, dejected that he could not save the young boy. But he has a journey ahead. He will collect his horse and depart.

Still shaken by the day's events, Charles sets off on the road to London; he has been summoned there by the Archbishop of Canterbury, the Most Reverend Thomas Herring. Charles is not alone; the energetic man who delivered the Anglican summons joins him. The pair, both on horseback, plans to be in London by nightfall.

The man who rides with Charles is in his mid-forties and dressed in an Anglican robe; he twitches as if ready to burst with excitement. Despite the slightly pudgy man's jovial disposition, he is aware of Charles's despair over the recent experience with the hanging show. He decides it is best to remain quiet as they travel along one of England's ancient dirt roads.

Like Charles, he has a fondness for the creative process—he is an artist, having participated in the theatre from an early age. However, unlike the Wesley brothers who grew up with a father in the ministry, the Anglican preacher who travels this day with Charles grew up in an environment that is highly unconventional for a future minister: his childhood experience included manual labor, while aiding in running the family hostelry, the Bell Inn in Gloucester.

At this establishment—the grandest of its kind in town, boasting two main halls, one of which was an auditorium used to stage plays—he cleaned floors and guest rooms. These chores gave him the opportunity to interact with the community's outstanding citizens of trade and commerce, while subjecting him to the entire experience of real life. Despite the occasional local clergyman that would frequent the inn, the young lad quickly found himself encountering life with members of society's seamy side: gamblers and ladies of the night, thieves and questionable members of Parliament.

It was from such undesirables that he picked up the skill of using one's hands mischievously—for picking pockets. In this setting he also perfected his ability to scheme by watching the corrupt bobby and politician. Unfortunately, it was also in this environment that he acquired the knack for breach and betrayal, as he daily viewed the making and breaking of promises by those wheeling and dealing with the constable and MPs.[25]

Although some of this exposure was valuable to the boy—for he quickly gained the ability to connect with various types of people, even picking up tips for narrative and storytelling—the experience was also a tempting peek into the seductive side of life, which would prove an irresistible allurement in the young boy's nearing of adolescence.

The fact that his father passed away when he was two years old brought further strain to his unconventional family life. Subsequent to this, his mother's remarriage failed miserably. Much of this dysfunction undoubtedly contributed to his struggles in grammar school. Despite his personal battles, it was at this time that his above-average ability for oral delivery and recitation began to emerge.

His outstanding proficiency in memorizing lines of dialogue allowed him to participate in many school plays. This fulfilling experience soon led him to passionately pursue the craft of acting, in which he quickly excelled. Despite the success, his studies of gesture, voice, and emotion brought the impressionable teenager into close contact with the sinful eighteenth-century theatre, tempting him with its lustful desires and pursuits, furthering him into a lifestyle of debauchery.

After several physical arguments with his mother, he sought to leave the family home and live with his brother. His mother, now abandoned by her second husband and finding it hard to maintain peace in her home, had no problem giving the rebellious teenager permission to leave.

It wasn't long before he realized that this newfound freedom was not as glamorous as he had believed it to be. He quickly concluded that he needed to straighten out his life.

Nearing the age of eighteen, he began to reconsider his sinful lifestyle—so much so that he yearned to enter secondary education. His mother and his grammar school principal were surprised when he mentioned that he would like to attend Oxford. Since his mother could not afford to pay for such prestigious schooling, his only hope for attending the distinguished place of learning would be to gain a scholarship as a servitor, working as a house servant to the wealthier Oxford students. It would be a difficult task, but by the encouragement of his

---

[25] Ministers of Parliament.

principal, he was able to obtain the grant and enter the school, though at the bottom of the Oxford social structure.

The school rules forbade a servitor to interact with the wealthy students. Entering the fine learning establishment at the age of seventeen in the year 1732, the restraining of his outgoing personality in his commitment to the rules soon left him lonely and detached. Providence eventually smiled upon the young man when fellow student Charles Wesley reached out and invited him to participate in the Holy Club.

The Holy Club was a group of Oxford students, led by John Wesley, who sought to make their faith an active part of their daily lives. In contrast to the sinfulness of the early eighteenth-century student life at Oxford, the Holy Club actively pursued a life of prayer, Bible study, and moral accountability to God and each other. Their methodical approach to holiness earned them the derisive label of "Methodists." The Holy Club quickly became an important part of the young man's life.

This preacher, gifted artist, Oxford graduate, and friend of Charles Wesley is George Whitefield.

Upon his graduation from Oxford in 1736, George became an overnight sensation. Having been ordained a preaching deacon of the Church of England, within a year's time he found himself preaching to congregations beyond full capacity of the Anglican church buildings. This was a unique experience for England; never before had a minister of the Gospel drawn such large crowds. The scheduling of additional services to handle the overflow was not enough. Out of necessity, George soon began to take the pulpit outdoors, into the streets.

What was drawing the masses to hear him? There was nothing spectacular about his appearance. He was slightly overweight. Due to a childhood battle with measles, one of his eyes was permanently crossed. In addition to these uninspiring characteristics, he was not a tall man, nor one that would evoke leadership.

His nickname of "Dr. Squintum," ridiculing his physical deformity, was given to him by one critic who wrote and performed a mocking theatrical production burlesquing the cross-eyed preacher. George earned the additional nickname of "Dr. Preachfield" by another artist who wrote a scathing play distorting his childhood exposure to the seamier side of life, suggesting that the women he ministered to were actually his sexual companions and employees.

Undoubtedly, what drew people to hear him were the unique characteristics attributed solely to George Whitefield. First, he was an unconventional Anglican preacher; contrary to the church's clergy of the day, he preached and prayed extemporaneously. He felt that this approach, without notes, opened his work to the leading of the Holy Spirit. However, this method opened the door to much criticism from his fellow Anglican clergy and leadership.

Second, and most notably, his admirable theatre influences surfaced during his preaching. His audiences, which soon began to number into the tens of thousands, were drawn to sermons richly adorned with theatrical realism, bringing to life the characters of the Bible. One of London's famous actors, David Garrick, had grown fond of George's presentations, which often incorporated dancing, crying, and screaming. He confessed, "I would give a hundred guineas if I could say 'Oh' like Mr. Whitefield." Garrick continued, "He could make one weep by the way in which he pronounced 'Mesopotamia.'"

Several writers of the day, enamored with George's incredible gift for oratory, proclaimed that he preached like a lion. Estimates indicated that he preached to more than two million people during the summer of 1739. Many of the day felt that his audacious field preaching was shaking the core of stagnant religion in England.

Nevertheless, George was not the type to remain in one place for too long. At the height of his fame in England, the twenty-two-year-old George approached the brothers Wesley. He wanted them to continue what God was doing through his preaching, urging them to take the Gospel to the citizens of England via the open field. At first John and Charles were against the idea, but they soon agreed to accommodate George's request. This agreement helped George fulfill his desire to depart England and launch on his first preaching tour in America.

His August 1739 arrival in Philadelphia coincided with local papers that boasted, "No one alive has preached to as many people as George Whitefield—perhaps no one throughout all of history."

George's arrival in the colonies seemed to be ordained of God.

At this time in history, several regional revivals had broken out. Throughout New Jersey and Pennsylvania, men like William Tennent and Theodore Frelinghuysen preached to the masses coming to faith. On the western front of New Jersey, Pennsylvania, and Connecticut, David Brainerd was experiencing conversions among many of the Native American tribes of the Delaware Nation. In Massachusetts, Jonathan Edwards, acknowledged by many as America's greatest philosophical theologian, was barely keeping up with the revival in his Puritan church.

However promising these developments were, each of these new-birth experiences was isolated from the others. In hindsight, it seemed that God had a plan for the American colonies, and the young George Whitefield was going to play heavily in its design. That which was about to occur in Philadelphia would transpire throughout the thirteen colonies.

Immediately upon George's arrival, the citizens of Pennsylvania thronged to hear him. In Philadelphia, standing on the courthouse steps, he preached to more than 78,000 people. Among this crowd was George's soon-to-be best friend, Benjamin Franklin. The booming power of George's voice impressed Franklin. The Americans quickly gave George the nickname "The Marvel of the Age."

Despite his great oratory skills, it was more than George's gifted voice that was gathering the people; more importantly, it was the "common to the faith" approach of George's message—a departure from the isolationist Puritan- and Quaker-influenced religion, and more resembling the first-century believing community. This unique Christian message began to unite the numerous denominations in Philadelphia.

This pattern of uniting those traditionally at odds with each other held true for all of his travels throughout the thirteen colonies, bringing together the entire awakened commonwealth under the Gospel of Christ. In the summer of 1739, and during each of George's five trips to America since, God has blessed his efforts in the colonies as the divisive, denominational spirit of Europe ebbed away, bringing together the American populace into one common experience of faith.

George caught up with Charles after returning from a preaching tour of Scotland. Like America, Scotland too is enamored with George's abilities and is also crying out for the brothers, John and Charles. This longing for the Wesleys and Whitefield in Scotland is in sharp contrast to the trio's reception at home in England.

Like John and Charles, George has had the uniquely British experience of physical expulsion from an Anglican pulpit or two. His message is consistent with the Wesleyan revival, emphasizing salvation by faith alone—although his version of the faith is slightly more Calvinistic[26] than the Wesley brothers would like. This emphasis on faith alone is the irritant that incites some of the Anglican clergy in England against the movement, causing them to label it "fanatical." There is an additional fear: the clergy leadership that looks down on the trio is actually more concerned with the Wesleyan revival waking the populace to the corruption of the Anglican clergy, which is benefiting financially from their close relationship with the MPs in Parliament.

---

[26] Following the teachings of John Calvin. The faith of the Wesley brothers was more Arminian than Calvinistic. The "sticking point" with Calvinism is the idea that some are predestined by God for eternal life and others are not. The Wesleys had difficulty accepting this concept.

The expulsions of John, Charles, and George are not officially from the Primate,[27] but the upcoming meeting with the Archbishop seems to indicate to Charles and George that their days of preaching from a Church of England pulpit are coming to an end.

Despite the grieving silence of his riding companion, George can only remain quiet for so long; he looks to the sky, then to his dear friend. He's careful to be considerate.

Lifting a hand to his tilted ear in his trademark theatrical delivery, he offers the following:

"Hark! Methinks I hear the saints chanting their everlasting hallelujahs, and spending an eternal day in echoing forth triumphant songs of joy."

He lowers his hand as he slowly peers above the treetops that line the ancient dirt road. With gentle nods of his chin he acknowledges,

"Yes, yes, heaven's inhabitants are at this moment rejoicing in the presence of the Savior."

He tilts his head toward Charles.

"And do you not long, my brother, to join this heavenly choir?"

Charles stares at the neck of his horse, unable to release his saddened thoughts about the child who departed for heaven this day. *How can one celebrate the . . . ?* He catches himself mid-thought and slowly raises his eyes to meet those of the smiling George.

It is difficult, but Charles welcomes the warmth of his fellow preacher, the preacher with the unconventional face. He reaches deep and gives a hopeful reply.

"The lad is among those who rejoice."

"Yes, Charles. I've heard you express it on many occasions: "Look to the Son of Man lifted up." Shall we do the same?"

George begins. His bold and melodic voice echoes through the hardwoods.

"And can it be, that I should gain . . ."

He looks to Charles, and Charles joins in:

"An interest in the Savior's blood!
Died He for me? Who caused His pain!
For me? Who Him to death pursued?
Amazing love! How can it be
that Thou, my God, shouldst die for me?
Amazing love! How can it be

---

[27] Head of the Anglican Church.

that Thou, my God, shouldst die for me?"[28]

It is late afternoon as the pair slowly approaches the outskirts of the busy city of London. In view are the dirty and overpopulated streets, appearing as a maze in need of deciphering. They realize that they must take special care to navigate the crowded cobblestone corridors filled with people, carts, and horses wet with the dampness of the ashen sky, all trampling through the slippery, flooding waste material. There are also numerous horses tied to trees, they too standing in the raw sewage. As with most eighteenth-century European cities, the waste matter overflows from the wastewater system built along the edge of the streets. However ingenious the system, it doesn't prevent the discharge from constantly spilling onto the roadway.

George and Charles make their way through the clamor of England's largest city. The horde of people is loud as they busy themselves with making a living. On one side of the road, shabby street vendors in tattered clothing pawn their goods to the numerous shopkeepers along the crowded way. Across the street, a butcher in his blood-stained apron almost knocks down a salesman as he tosses a shovel full of refuse from his day's messy work.

It takes nearly an hour, but finally George and Charles finally depart the city, heading east toward the River Thames. They are thankful to leave the crowded and noisy borough. They plan to cross the river over the newly completed Westminster Bridge.

More than twenty years ago, the 1736 act of Parliament authorized the building of the bridge adjacent to the great Westminster Abbey. The bridge would replace the horse ferry that existed a few miles to the south, south of the Archbishop's palace at Lambeth.

Realizing that the new bridge would greatly affect the income of the Archbishop who drew revenues from the horse ferry, Parliament built into the act compensation for the reduced revenues. As expected, with the completion of the bridge, most people abandoned the use of the ferry and took to crossing the river north of the Archbishop's residence, at Westminster Bridge. As also expected, the Archbishop's financial condition greatly improved because of his political connections.

As night begins to fall, the pair eases their horses onto the stone structure. The bridge consists of more than 3,000 tons of Portland stone, the same limestone material used in the construction of St. Paul's Cathedral. The impressive thirty-foot-wide span is more than 1,200 feet in length, 300 feet longer than the London Bridge. The bridge took eleven years and nine months to build. Charles makes the comment,

---

[28] Charles Wesley hymn "And Can It Be That I Should Gain," 1739.

"We have preceded the watchmen."

The realization brings apprehension to both men.

At each of the piers that support the bridge's thirteen arches, a small, covered alcove, meant to provide dry cover during rain, brings the unsettling concern for George and Charles. In recent months, robbers and cutthroats finding perfect cover in the dark recesses of the alcoves have accosted several travelers. These acts of violence have inspired the appointment of twelve evening watchmen as the obvious solution to the problem. As grand as the idea is, the guards have yet to establish a routine starting time.

Charles looks to the sky and welcomes the rising full moon as it sheds its light onto the darkening landscape. The ever sanguine George seems to be reading his mind.

"The sun will not harm us by day, nor the moon by night."

Despite George's recital of the verse from Psalm 121, Charles is not as confident. The pair continues, cautiously.

The crossing is uneventful; the recent hoodlum terrors are non-existent tonight.

Approaching the end of the span at the south bank of the Thames, the pair can barely see the outline of Lambeth Palace. Originally called Lambeth Manor, this is the London residence of the Archbishop. It has been the home of each Archbishop since the fourteenth century. The location is ideal, with its close proximity to Westminster and the Royal Court—an unending reminder that the Church of England is inextricably attached to Parliament. In the distance, the pair spots the imposing entrance.

Morton's Tower—named after Cardinal John Morton, who commissioned its building in the late fifteenth century—is the main entrance into Lambeth Palace. The impressive red-bricked structure consists of three buildings, their exteriors representing some of the first brickwork accomplished in London. The corners of each of the three structures are finished with Tudor-style cast-stone quoins, the alternating square and rectangle architectural details neatly stacked above each other from the ground to the roof line. The middle building, which contains two arched double wooden gates, one larger and one smaller, serves as the main entrance. Each gate boasts a cast-stone surround. The larger of the two gates resides beneath an oversized second-story room that originally housed Cardinal Morton, and now serves as a flat for the gatekeepers. On either side of the center structure are two huge five-story battlement towers.

George and Charles dismount. Surprised to find the gates open and unattended, they grab their horses' reins and make their way through the larger of the wooden gates.

As they walk through the entrance of the massive structure, they each take notice of the open doorway to the first-level room of the south tower. They stop and peek inside. The darkness of the evening makes it difficult, but they can barely see, on the far-side wall, two iron rings fastened to the wall about head-high. George offers a comment,

"Strange article for an ecclesiastical."

The comment elicits a slight chuckle from Charles. In the sixteenth century, the Archbishop utilized the space as a prison cell. The room no longer serves that purpose. The pair shuffles from the room's entrance and continues into the courtyard.

From several outbuildings, several gatekeepers in a hurried frenzy quickly join the pair; strangely, they race past George and Charles, heading straight for the tower entrance. The itinerants decide to stop and watch the development.

At the entrance, twenty gatekeepers, some carrying lighted lanterns, each in full-coated dress, line both sides of the entrance, standing shoulder to shoulder with hands at their sides. They quickly become one unit, like a guard of honor.

Within moments, a large procession enters the Morton Tower gates.

A coach, drawn by four horses, slowly makes its way through the gates. Preceding the carriage are twelve footmen, four rows walking three abreast. The entourage stops and two additional footmen from the rear of the coach race to the nearest side of the carriage. From within the vehicle, the Archbishop steps down to the cobblestoned courtyard. George whispers to Charles,

"The great potentate and his servants."

His comment once again brings a slight chuckle from Charles.

George will not let up, intimating again,

"For this, he receives annually eleven thousand pounds."

Charles chokes on George's comment, but is able to reply, though not as soft-spoken,

"While the local clergyman must fight for his ten?"

Several guards peer in the direction of the pair. Charles twitches uncomfortably, knowing that he has spoken out of turn. The footmen's attention soon returns to the Archbishop.

Disturbed by George's revelation, Charles quickly makes a calculation: *The Archbishop receives an annual salary . . .*

"One thousand times the amount of an Anglican priest!"

Charles catches himself as he utters the last words aloud. George once again comments, this time at a level the footmen can hear,

"Crass and self-seeking; this dominating society leads the populace into frigid rationalism."

Charles shakes his head in disappointment.

Making their way into the office of the Archbishop, George and Charles await the arrival of the Most Reverend Thomas Herring. Even in the flickering candlelight, the opulent beauty of their immediate surroundings takes the pair by surprise. High-arched ceilings, each delineated with hewn wooden beams, tower above a room large enough to serve as a formal ballroom. The smooth hand-troweled plaster walls fade into the immense arches above, flowing from the wood-paneled wainscoting that rises roughly eight feet above the impeccably polished oak flooring. Strategically placed around the perimeter of the room are Venetian-style pane-glass windows, each window centered and rising into arched dormers more than thirty feet above the room's hardwood floor. Each window is designed to cast the daytime sunlight onto the numerous granite busts of past Archbishops decorating each of the room's four walls.

In front of the ever-frugal itinerants, a sixteenth-century hand-carved wooden desk sits prominently in the middle of the vast workspace. To their left they notice two beautiful ebony-stained arched double doors.

Slowly, the doors begin to open.

Two of the uniformed footmen that were part of the Archbishop's entourage enter the room. One of the attendants, obviously focused on a required task, trots past his partner; arriving at the desk, he slowly slides back the oversized wooden chair. Within moments, the second attendant joins his associate, each standing on either side of the pulled-back chair.

The Archbishop arrives, escorted by a third attendant, and makes his way to the desk. Once there, he pauses to view George and Charles.

Out of respect, the pair rises from their seats. The three footmen gently escort the Most Reverend Thomas Herring into his chair. George and Charles remain standing as Archbishop Herring dismisses his attendants and addresses the pair.

"The church wardens of Islington have informed me that you have resorted to creative approaches in reaching their citizens."

This comment is for Charles. Charles knows it, but fails to reply. George responds instead,

"He has accepted my advice."

Charles peers at George; he did not expect him to toy with Herring's derisive comment.

The Archbishop picks up a piece of parchment that lies on the desk. He crumples the paper and strategically places it in front of George.

At Islington, when the refined members of the church urged the church wardens to ban Charles from speaking—they were unhappy with Charles inviting some of the town's prostitutes into the service—the members never planned on the actual outcome. They envisioned Charles attempting to scale the pulpit of the dignified church as the wardens swiftly snatched the preacher, sending him outdoors. They had ensured that the pulpit guardians would place themselves at the foot of the pulpit stairs, waiting for Charles to arrive.

Instead, when the moment of reckoning arrived, Charles perceived their intentions; he simply walked to the front of the sanctuary, feigning that he was heading for the pulpit. The wardens stiffened, determined to stand their ground. Once Charles gained the attention of the congregation, he turned and departed, quietly walking outdoors.

Inspired by George's boldness in reply to the Archbishop, Charles responds,

> "The whole congregation followed me outside, where I climbed onto a tombstone and preached."

Without hesitation, George adds to Charles's reply,

> "How was Charles to realize they desired a day in the field?"

The Archbishop is not happy with George's remark; he ignores the comment and moves to another point of contention. With a pompous attitude, he notes,

> "Vicar Saunders has informed me that you are planning a tabernacle."

George nervously fumbles with the arm of his finely crafted chair; he fails to know how to properly respond. He is indeed breaking ground on a chapel, within walking distance from the illustrious St. Martin-in-the-Fields, an Anglican church.

Throughout most of its history, St. Martin's Church in London has had a distinguished record of practical Christianity, in large part exemplifying the experience of the church's namesake, the fourth-century Roman citizen who lived out his Christianity during his service as a Roman soldier. The soldier's notoriety began on a bitterly cold winter's night in Amiens, France. As the eighteen-year-old soldier entered through the city gate, he found an almost completely naked beggar leaning against the stone wall of the city. In a gesture of kindness, he removed his sword and his cloak. He split the covering into two pieces, wrapping one of them around the beggar. Later that evening, Martin dreamed that Jesus appeared to him, dressed as the beggar wearing his cloak; upon the sharing of this dream with the church the next morning, the church baptized the young soldier. After completing his mandatory time in the Roman army, Martin spent the rest of his life until his death at age eighty traveling house to house and speaking to people about Jesus. The St. Martin's church building is the resulting monument dedicated to this Christian service of Martin.

Despite its distinguished history, the clergy of St. Martin's has temporarily strayed from its Christian focus. The current leader of the church, the stately vicar Erasmus Saunders, has made it his goal to stop the evangelistic movement of George Whitefield. The vicar has no sympathies with the thriving movement that he too has labeled "fanatical." He has hindered George from preaching at St. Martin's, aiming to shut down the London ministry of the vibrant preacher.

Nevertheless, outside the traditional setting of a church building, George has had great success in London. His plan for the "Tabernacle" on London's Tottenham Court Road is George's reply to the attempts to stifle his efforts in London. It is also an obvious move since the masses coming to hear Whitefield and the Wesleys will require the protection of a warm building during the harsh winters.

The considerable public support for George and the brothers Wesley ensures that the tabernacle will rise. Tottenham Court Road Chapel will be a large building, seventy feet by seventy feet, with a double-bricked exterior. In line with George's love for the arts, the tabernacle will sit in the middle of London's theatre district, a prominent location for Christian outreach to the debased artistic community.

The Archbishop is not pleased with George's silence. He comments,

"Failure to reply indicates your acknowledgement."

George continues to abstain from responding to the Archbishop; his opinion, if expressed verbally, would be highly disrespectful.

Archbishop Herring adds to his discovery,

"I am informed that the structure shall contain a vault beneath the chapel."

At this comment, Herring gives a wry, almost devious, smile. However, his gesture fails to stifle the confident George for long. He clears his throat and replies,

"Yes, the tabernacle shall possess a vault, for my ***predetermined*** day of departure."

The Archbishop laughs aloud at George's emphasis of the word "predetermined." His facial expression turns sour as his mood transforms into that of an accuser. He responds,

"You tend to a non-conformist, a dissenter. Your message is that of the seducer and a bringer of the Pretender."

George once again has no reply that is appropriate for this accusation. He and the brothers Wesley have heard the complaint before.

The Archbishop turns to Charles.

"You, Mr. Wesley, are bordering on excommunication. Have I not forbidden you the use of Pier's pulpit?"

Charles sits in silence. He is being admonished for refusing past orders by the Archbishop to cease preaching at the church of Charles's dear friend, Henry Piers, in Bexley.

Charles quickly surmises, *Henry will have to make a decision.* He realizes that Henry may sway in favor toward the Archbishop. He worries for his friend who desires the security of the establishment.

Charles offers a reply,

> "Our supreme purpose is to make men aware of the Creator."

> "I shall not have this fanaticism strike at the heart of the King's Church!"

The pair lean back in their seats in reaction to the Archbishop's angered tone and the unexpected   slamming of the desktop with his fist. He continues,

> "By what call do you preach the Gospel? A dispensation of the Gospel is committed to me, by the Apostle Paul."

There is a long, extended, and uncomfortable silence.

Charles looks to George. It is as if they can read each other's minds. They find it hard to comprehend being attacked for their religious activities. Charles replies,

> "Your Grace has taught me, in your book on Church Government, that a man unjustly excommunicated is not thereby cut off from communion with Christ."

The Archbishop is not happy with the indication. His reply is strong and direct.

> "Of that I am the judge."

He is judge. This is blasphemy! Charles's thought is not unique. Many of the local ministers have long realized that the leadership of the Anglican Church, the "High Church," acts as though they can say and do as they please. Their corruption has also tarnished the non-believing public's opinion of the English clergy.

Charles attempts to sway Herring.

> "Do you not perceive George's success as a spiritual sign, and sufficient proof of his call?"

The Archbishop rises to his feet; he stares at his desktop as he fumbles with various parchments upon it. He slowly raises his eyes to view the pair, then responds,

> "I forbid both of you to enter Pier's church in Bexley."

At this, Herring turns to depart; his footmen rush to his side and escort him out of the room.

Pappous

Christianity is essentially a social religion;
To turn it into a solitary religion,
Is indeed to destroy it.

John Wesley

Joseph Asbury sits at the kitchen table.

Through the main room's window, he watches as several men with smutty faces hobble across the front garden. He quickly gathers that the coal drivers have spent more time than they should at The Malt Shovel. One of the men stumbles over his own feet; in order to gain his footing, he accelerates past the boozy group.

One of his chums lets out a loud belch as he tries to grasp the situation.

"B'runnin' home, is we, Edmond?"

Edmond, in his battle to stay upright, doesn't hear a thing.

Joseph scowls through the window as he watches the stumbler continue to stagger.

"Wretched pub."

The inebriated man trips over a covered annual bed. The fodder cushions his face-first fall to the raised ground.

Eliza enters the room and comments,

"Husband, you really must gain higher pursuits."

Eliza's comment brings a slight smile to Joseph's face. He is thankful that she can help him through his frustrations. Although the pub is a source of income for the Asburys, it can be an annoyance with men coming and going at all hours of the night. However disturbing the establishment may be on this early evening, Joseph's dissatisfaction is much deeper than the occasional drunk limping across his well-protected prized planting areas.

Joseph bows his head over the table.

From across the room Eliza hears him slowly release a heavy breath as his elbows brace on the tabletop; his stumpy hands grasp the sides of his head.

Eliza sighs, too; she also struggles with the recent event of Francis walking out of school. She knows the pain that Joseph is dealing with. For some time he had suspected that something wasn't right at Sneal's Green. Eliza reaches out,

"Joseph dear, West Midlands shall not seal our son's fate."

Joseph slowly raises his head from its protected position. But not for long; he resumes his former position, once again slumping over the table.

A knock at the door breaks the quiet moment. Eliza respectfully waits for her husband, but when he doesn't move, she softly walks to the door and opens it to find a familiar face.

She invites the young visitor,

"Please come in, Thomas."

Thomas clears his throat as he timidly enters the Asbury home. His reddened eyes are immediately drawn to his pal Francis, sitting on a chair next to the inglenook fireplace.

He darts for Francis. The impact of his hug on Francis's neck almost knocks his chum out of the chair and into the fire. Francis's elbow bangs the iron spit that rests over the day's embers.

"Is this your attempt to heal, Thomas?"

Thomas steps back, realizing he needs to go more gently with his friend.

Joseph raises his head. He's happy to hear his son speak.

For Joseph, this unsettling episode has brought the dreaded feelings of putting his son in danger. *The boy had warned of this before.* This thought continues to repeat itself, each time deepening his sorrow for young Franky—and his anger toward the school instructor.

Thomas offers a belated greeting.

"Good evening, Mrs. Asbury."

All in the room are surprised to see the young girl who has silently followed Thomas into the home.

She must have floated in, Joseph thinks to himself.

The girl is Francis's fierce competitor from the riddle on prayer night, Nancy Brookes.

The drunken chorus on the Asbury front lawn breaks the unexpected moment:

"Away to the Sons of Anacreon we'll fly,

And there, with good fellows, we'll learn to entwine

The Myrtle of Benus with Vacchus's vine."

Joseph doesn't hold back.

"Bladdered buffoons!"[29]

He shakes his head.

The intoxicated choir abandons its attempt at Greek mythology and erupts into laughter. One in the group comments,

"Benus with Vacchus's vine . . . shall it rather be Venus with Bacchus's vine?"

They all agree, wheezing and guffawing at their inebriated condition and the silly consonant change.

---

[29] Drunken fools!

Inside the Asbury home, the delicate girl walks confidently toward Thomas and Francis.

Francis rises to his feet. As he does, he reveals his left forearm, which is the beneficiary of his mother's thorough bandaging. Despite her loving efforts, the wound's dressing is far from flattering.

As they stand facing each other, Francis is more than a foot taller than Nancy. She looks to Thomas, Joseph, and Eliza, and then proceeds to gently remove a white ribbon from her hair. As the ribbon unfolds, her cascading ringlets frame her affable smile. The ribbon is made of silk, beautifully hand-embroidered with the finest of stitching on its borders. In the middle of the woven band an embossed cross, also in white, highlights the beauty of the accessory.

With the hair ribbon in hand, she reaches forward and carefully lifts Francis's left hand.

Eliza takes a deep breath as she watches from the side of the room.

The compassionate Nancy continues, gently wrapping the ribbon around the forearm bandage.

A tear begins to trickle from Eliza's eye.

Her task completed, Nancy slowly lowers Francis's hand. Her touch is delicate, barely detected.

For the first time, Francis notices a unique quality about his childhood companion: her face. To Francis, her let-down hair displays something new. In this moment, he finds that he has never paused long enough to consider the face of the blossoming young lady standing before him. A strange emotion overtakes him, a slight attraction. He catches himself gazing at her.

Uncomfortable with the discovery, he hastily quips,

"Thomas aims to help me heal."

The boys laugh together, awkward and loud.

Francis nervously looks to see if Thomas noticed his admiration of Nancy. To his relief, Thomas apparently missed it. Nevertheless, Francis is once again compelled to look at Nancy's face. Slightly embarrassed, she smiles and looks to Eliza. Nancy senses Francis's attraction, expressed in his unexpected smile—a smile noticeably wider than on most occasions.

Wiping the tear from her face, Eliza holds out her arms to embrace Nancy. Nancy is delighted to return the hug; with several quick steps she reaches Eliza and the pair hold each other tightly, Nancy's face beaming with her budding smile. Eliza fights back the emotions and invites the young girl,

"Come with me; I shall give you choice of my ribbons."

Nancy accepts Eliza's generous offer.

Next morning, Father readies to leave for the day's work. Mother has been up for hours already, and the studious Francis sits at the window, reading his Bible. Eliza shares with the men,

"I have invited a gentleman for prayer this evening."

Focused on their tasks, they fail to notice Eliza's comment. She offers more,

"Invited the Aults."

Eliza is unsure if the Aults can join them for dinner. She mentions it to gain Francis's attention, which it clearly does. She continues,

"I shall see Thomas today."

Francis immediately closes his Bible and races through the rear door of the room. The accelerating stomps that signal his ascent of the wooden stairs are heard by Joseph. He smiles as he thinks to himself, *the boy has long forgotten the wound.*

However, the short duration of his smile and his return to a somber expression reveals to Eliza, *it will be a while until his father's wounds find remedy.*

Surprisingly, Joseph comments,

"I shall check with Mr. Birch this day."

Eliza pauses to think before she replies to Joseph's announcement. She is not happy about the comment, especially with its indication. What she fears most in life has a better than average chance of materializing.

This worry has kept her up most of the night. In fact, this is the reason she awoke this morning well before her customary five o'clock. Joseph is going to approach one of his employers, Mr. John Wyrley Birch, to place Francis into an apprenticeship.

She says nothing as she returns to cleaning up the morning meal.

The Birch family has agreed to hire Francis to work around the estate. The position will have Francis doing odd jobs on the massive property. Knowing the large staff, it is doubtful that Francis will be doing anything important. In Joseph's mind, *this is sufficient;* he's glad Francis will be safe, *and I will get to see him several days each week.*

This venture will actually be a return to the neighborhood of birth for Francis. For Eliza, the town of her childbearing awakens painful memories, bringing focus on the loss of her dear Sarah.

Adding to her affliction, the employment requires that Francis live on site. Eliza is uncomfortable with the arrangement. In her mind, *the boy is only thirteen;* she fears that the wealthy family will make the wrong impression on Francis. More importantly, she is struggling with the fact that she will be living in a home without children.

For Joseph, the fears of the empty nest are not a concern; he favors this job opportunity, especially if he can avoid committing Franky to a life in the wretched ironworking industry. Regardless of the result, one thing is clear: Francis's school days have ended. From this point forward, Francis will be learning from the academy of real life.

Along both sides of the meandering River Tame, within the ancient parish of Handsworth, resides the stately Hamstead Hall. The timber-framed two-story mansion, finely constructed and filled in with brick, sits to the southwest of the numerous trees that line the gentle bend in the waterway.

The Creator's artistry along this portion of the river abounds with vegetation, bushing out and standing erect. The prominent stalks of reedmace, with its dark-brown sausage-like pods fixed atop bending spires, wait on God's timing to launch their species-saving seeds. The plant, which at times is incorrectly labeled as bulrush, launches it seeds through an elaborate bunching of pappi, tucked together neatly within the tubular housings. The airborne liberators burst from the seed pod as lighter-than-air, downy parachutes carrying the cargo which ensures the plant's continuance. A blast of wind, and the pappous escorts set out on their predestined venture.

Embracing the visual beauty of the estate that straddles both sides of the river, six bedrooms and six reception rooms overlook the substantial property consisting of numerous large gardens and orchards, obviously the handiwork of Joseph Asbury. The owner of this prestigious property is Mr. John Wyrley Birch.

Mr. Birch is a big man, over six feet tall. He is the town's Sheriff, the magistrate of the working-class towns of the Black Country. He is virtually a one-man enforcement brigade. Single-handedly, he weathered the Birmingham food riots of '56 and '57. He has won the loyalty of the Methodists by bravely standing against numerous malicious mobs set on the destruction of the lives and homes of the Wesleyan worshipers. The townspeople respect this man of high standards, a man willing to put the rioters in their place, a man who also enjoys the benefits and comforts afforded by great wealth.

The elegant Hamstead Hall has been in the Wyrley Birch family for more than four hundred years. The original thirteenth-century structure was remodeled in 1690, then rebuilt in 1735. The current estate boasts four additional cottages for shepherds and keepers.

It is in one of these cottages that Francis Asbury will reside.

There will be plenty of work for Francis and his coworkers. The bountiful complex consists of rich, fertile soil, the best in the Tame River Valley. The numerous fields of crops and heads of livestock that inhabit the lush hills not only enhance the beauty of this majestic homestead, but also secure a never-ending list of chores and assignments for the laborers.

In addition to the impeccably kept grounds and abundantly producing orchards, the estate includes an extensive library of more than two thousand volumes and a cellar boasting nearly five thousand bottles of choice wines.

Supplying the much-needed water and feed for family and flock, much of the estate's help find themselves busy with the Hamstead Mill, the two-wheeled water-powered mill located on the river running through the prestigious property. It consists of four large millstones that finely grind the corn harvested in the fields. The mill also acts as a pump, delivering the water from the river to the house. Other than loading sacks of grain and corn, it is highly unlikely that Francis will have much to do with the mill. It is a complex facility, meant for an older, more experienced hand.

Later that day, Eliza rushes in with the cast-iron kettle containing the evening's dinner. Her forearms hardly look strong enough to convey the heavy load. Her wrists strain to carry the meal as steam rises from the brimming pot. She arches upward and hangs the container over the spit, noting aloud,

"If only that spit was an inch or two lower."

She removes a well-worn dishrag from her apron and wipes her sweaty brow. Given the need of preparing meals at The Malt Shovel and then carrying them home, she has a right to complain, but she doesn't. She soon is rushing to the low cupboard to gather the evening's dinner plates.

The heavy shoes bounding up the wooden stairs notify Eliza that Francis is home. Simultaneously, Joseph steps through the main room's front door.

"Mr. Asbury, your timing is impeccable."

Joseph bows to Eliza's greeting.

"Dear wife, I trust your day was productive as your husband's?"

Eliza slumps her shoulders, her slight frown revealing her disappointment. She inquires anyway,

"Shall the Birches put on Franky?"

Joseph hesitates to answer, gauging her potential reaction. He acknowledges her emotions by asking,

"Eliza, have you made peace with the circumstance?"

Eliza fumbles with the dinner plates, not rushing to reply.

Joseph stands silent. He respects the wisdom of his wife, so he patiently waits for her answer.

"Husband, I have."

The knock at the door causes Eliza to jump. Joseph lowers one shoulder and turns back toward the front door.

"Wife, I shall answer."

Eliza adjusts her outfit as she takes one last look at the set table. She is satisfied with the presentation. She readies herself as she turns toward the door; Joseph checks one more time.

"Wife, if you are ready?"

"Husband, I am."

Joseph opens the door.

The man who stands at the door is nothing out of the ordinary: of moderate height, with a thick midsection and heavy black eyebrows. His somewhat attractive face fashions a large smile. He sets down the large handled case he carries and removes his hat.

"Joseph Asbury?"

Joseph nods affirmation.

"Please come in, Mr. Taylor."

David Taylor is a traveling shoemaker and salesman. He is the past chamber master for the noble family of the Countess of Huntingdon, who, upon David's conversion to Christianity, encouraged him to begin preaching. Taking advantage of her friendship with John Wesley, Lady Huntingdon arranged for David to become a traveling preacher for the Wesleyan movement. His efforts have led to the formation of societies, which are slowly adapting to Baptist principles. These General Baptists[30] have become vigorous workers for the kingdom of God and enjoy their friendship with the Wesleyans. David is now an itinerant Baptist preacher, and largely responsible for the successful Barton-in-the-Beans Baptist Church. From there, he and several others are reaching out into the surrounding communities of Warwickshire, Derbyshire, and Nottinghamshire.

David owes much to the daughter of the Earl of Ferrers, Selina, Countess of Huntingdon. Selina was married to Theophilus Hastings, Earl of Huntingdon. Two of her sisters-in-law, Lady Margaret Hastings and Lady Elizabeth Hastings, became fond of the Oxford Methodists. Due to a bout with severe illness, and becoming bored with aristocratic life, the Countess gained a saving faith through the influence of Lady Margaret and Lady Elizabeth. She too became a fan of the leaders of the Oxford Holy Club, George Whitefield and the brothers Wesley.

---

[30] These believers did not condemn those who baptized their infants, but emphasized that adult baptism by immersion was necessary for proof to the community of true conversion. This view, in addition to the belief that baptism is essential to community but not a requirement for salvation, they held in common with the Wesleyans.

At one point in her faith walk, the Countess's husband sent for an Anglican Bishop to restore her to a "saner mind." The learned Bishop tried to woo her from the Methodist leaders, but failed miserably. At one point in the unpersuasive arguments, the Bishop expressed his regret about ordaining George Whitefield. In typical Lady Huntingdon style, she gave the Anglican leader the following reply: "Mark my words, my Lord: when you are upon your dying bed, that will be one of the ordinations upon which you will reflect with pleasure."

Thirteen years ago, in 1746, Lady Huntingdon became a widow. From this point forward, the spreading of the Gospel message became her life's passion.

Moving in the most aristocratic circles, Lady Huntingdon was not ashamed of her lowly Wesleyan friends. She invited John Wesley to her residence at Downington Park, where, in the midst of the pomp and circumstance, he preached to her stylish acquaintances. His message was well received. On another occasion, she sent for Whitefield. He too met with much success among the Countess's well-to-do friends.

The efforts to preach to the women bedecked with elegant plumes on their heads led many of high society to become devout Christians, but there was the occasional skeptic. One fair lady, the Countess of Suffolk, burst into a violent rage as she castigated Lady Huntingdon to her face, proclaiming insult by the "cross-eyed preacher's" (Whitefield's) words. Upon completion of her diatribe, she departed, never to associate with Selina again.

This event failed to destroy the evangelistic determination of the noble lady, instead inspiring her to greater heights for the kingdom of God. She consistently demonstrated her courageous zeal by her generous donations to the cause. She reduced her personal expenditures, even going so far as downsizing her residence in order to support traveling preachers. These same funds built chapels for the poor. She discharged her personal servants, one of whom was David Taylor. She sold the luxurious carriage and ancestral jewels to aid in the acquisition of theatres and halls in England, Ireland, and Wales, which were quickly converted and opened as places of public worship. She also had given generously toward the founding of Princeton College in the colony of New Jersey. Her donations to the cause of Christ were fast approaching half a million pounds.

Initially, Lady Huntingdon raised a small controversy with John Wesley. Her practice of encouraging a lay ministry with new converts did not sit well with the founder of the Holy Club. But as she did with David Taylor, she was quick to gauge the authenticity of a man's faith, and felt no hesitation in sending and supporting David and others like him to preach to the populace. This practice, as well as the traveling system she was establishing, served as another confirmation from God for John Wesley to send forth his preachers. Although this practice of sending out men new to the faith put her at slight odds with the Wesleys, the disagreement eventually faded in light of the great work that some of these men were accomplishing.

Her passion for the island nation inspired Lady Huntingdon to devise a plan for the evangelization of the entire kingdom. Methodically, she divided the nation into six districts. In her mind, each district would require regular visits by what she termed "canvassers," traveling preachers who would spread the Gospel throughout the entire country.

The canvassers quickly became household names, not only for their connection to members of the nobility, but also because of their successful labors. Men like Henry Venn, John Fletcher, William Romaine, Augustus Toplady, and Martin Madan, as well as Whitefield and the brothers Wesley, have become the most popular dissenting ministers[31] in all of England.

Nor have her efforts been aided solely by the labors of men. Many of her noblewomen friends have accompanied her on numerous tours throughout England and Wales, these outings in support of her many canvassers. Despite the success, she and her ladies have chosen to take a more private approach to the outreach, counseling the new converts behind the scenes. In addition to teaching the new believers, these titled women share their personal conversion experiences and offer administrative advice to the traveling preachers in their efforts to conquer new territories. Lady Huntingdon and her workers are especially eager to reach the villages of the West Midlands.

This evening, resupplying the Asburys' shoes and praying with the family are David Taylor's reasons for visiting the Asbury family. Eliza is excited to welcome the Countess's protégé to her home.

"Mr. Taylor, it is a pleasure to see you once again. Please do take a seat." Eliza invites the traveler to sit at the kitchen table.

"Joseph, please summon Francis."

Joseph exits through the rear door; his steady footsteps are heard traveling up the wooden stairs.

"Eliza, I am grateful for the opportunity to refresh the family's footwear."

"I treasure the thought of a bespoke[32] shoe, Mr. Taylor. But first we shall enjoy the evening's dinner and a time of prayer."

Joseph and Francis arrive. As they take their seats at the table with Mr. Taylor, Eliza refreshes Francis's memory.

"Francis, Mr. Taylor is the pious man I spoke of this morning."

---

[31] Evangelical Christians opposed to the stoic rationalism of the Church of England.
[32] Custom-made.

The young boy bows his head in respect at his mother's comment.

Eliza readies the evening meal. Her joyful mood is evident as she lovingly prepares each plate. She completes her task and Joseph rises to escort her to her seat; she smiles at her husband as he slides her chair closer to the table.

The group prays, and they quickly dive into their meals. Joseph inquires,

"What of your travels, Mr. Taylor?"

Joseph's question moves the itinerant to put down his eating utensil, the polite gesture in keeping with his gentle spirit.

"The home circuit has grown; many of the members travel more than twenty miles each week. We have need of establishing additional centers for the worship community, perhaps as many as five, including the one at Barton. There is talk of Melbourne, Kegworth, Loughborough, and Kirby, as well as Barton."

The Asburys are impressed. Mr. Taylor continues,

"The work at Barton is truly a group effort. The two have become a band of seven preachers. The Barton preachers travel up to forty miles each week, spreading the Gospel. Christ blesses the work."

Joseph looks to his son. Francis is listening intently to Mr. Taylor's words.

Eliza offers a comment,

"With Christ as the focus, the work shall always prosper."

Joseph adds,

"Not the focus of a man, but the focus of the firm foundation."

Mr. Taylor nods in agreement and looks to Francis.

"The foundation is the key . . ."

Rising from the table, Mr. Taylor looks to Joseph and Eliza.

"If you will allow me?"

"We would be honored."

Joseph's reply sends Mr. Taylor to the home's entrance. He retrieves his large traveling case as Francis grabs a few quick bites of his dinner.

Mr. Taylor opens the case to reveal several styles of footwear. Also inside the box are tools of the shoemaker's trade: a wood-handled awl and a metal shoe-sizing stick. He removes the awl. With the pointy metal device, he scratches his right ear.

With mouth full, Francis chuckles. Mr. Taylor smiles at Francis's ability to catch the jest. He offers,

"Handy tool."

Next, Mr. Taylor gently places the sizing stick onto the floor. The brass instrument is precisely marked for determining a patron's shoe size. He motions to Francis.

"The foundation of anything worthwhile is most important. Take, for instance, the many styles of shoes that I craft."

Francis sets down his fork and listens as Mr. Taylor removes the shoes from the case. One by one, he lays them side by side on the wood floor.

"If you are keen to notice, I have laid out the footwear in order of the prominence of their foundation. I speak of the heels. Note the heels of each. On this end is the jack boot. A sturdy leather boot, mostly worn by men. The heel of the jack boot is solid wood, made of beech. In the rare case that it is for a woman, the heel would be made of alder—a softer wood, but also a sturdy material. On the extreme opposite end of the lineup is the boot pump."

He gently lifts the boot pump, his stumpy, hairy fingers in sharp contrast to the delicate appearance of the fabric accessory. He turns the shoe to reveal the bottom.

"The boot pump is created with one thin layer for the sole. The material is cowhide. It fails to be as durable as wood. Do you know the sole purpose of the boot pump?"

Francis tilts his head. The look of uncertainty on his face signals Mr. Taylor to continue.

"The boot pump is a small covering for the foot. Worn inside a pair of boots, like the jack boot. It serves to save the wearer from embarrassment. When the individual is assisted in removing his boots, he fails to appear barefoot."

Francis laughs aloud. So does Mr. Taylor. He is pleased that the jest hit the mark with Francis. He resumes,

"In between these extremes, the jack boot and the boot pump, are various levels of heels, each foundation exhibiting a stronger or weaker property. On this end, close to the boot pump, is the pump; its materials are thin and light. The pump is suitable for running and dancing, or any other lively exercise. Note the heel, or in this case, the sole. It is quite thin, made of white sheep leather. This foundation will work for a season, but in time it will prove unsuccessful. Next to the pump is the ordinary shoe, its sole of a slightly heavier material, leather or wood. However, the leather sole is not as heavy as the wooden heel of the jack boot. The heel of the ordinary shoe is much sturdier than the sole of the pump, but again, not as strong as the heel of the jack boot."

All through the presentation, Francis nods in agreement. With each nod, the itinerant knows that he has laid the groundwork for the true focus of this lesson.

"It is the same in life, Francis. Our lives can take on many foundations; some will last for a season, others for a season and a half. Nevertheless, the truest foundation that will last for a lifetime of seasons and beyond is the foundation of Jesus the Christ. In it we find true prosperity."

Francis responds,

"Prosperity, as with the families that Father labors for?"

Mr. Taylor seeks clarification.

"Do you suggest the wealthy families of the West Midlands?

Francis nods his head to confirm. The itinerant continues,

"There are times when God will prosper a family with an abundance of wealth, but the prosperity I speak of has little to do with material gain. The prosperity I reference is the blessing of God's peace and wholeness. This prosperity links inescapably with righteousness. In the book of Psalms, the great King David expressed this significant truth when he penned the words of Psalm seventy-two:

" 'Give the king Your judgments, O God,
And Your righteousness to the king's Son.
He will judge Your people with righteousness,
And Your poor with justice.
The mountains will bring peace to the people,
And the little hills, by righteousness.
He will bring justice to the poor of the people;
He will save the children of the needy,
And will break in pieces the oppressor.'[33]

"David composed this most significant Psalm to his son Solomon, who would be king. David was a loving and caring father, much like your own."

Francis smiles as he peeks toward his father.

Joseph appreciates his son's gesture of love. For the first time since the injurious incident, Joseph experiences a slight feeling of self-forgiveness. His pursed lips tighten as his eyes water slightly from the edifying comment of the itinerant and the acknowledgement of his son.

Mr. Taylor continues,

"David is asking the Almighty to imbue his son the King with a spirit of wisdom—a wisdom that derives from a focus on justice—in order that when he reigns, he will reign not as the worldly tyrants do, but as a wise king. King David adds that peace is the result of wisdom that has

---

[33] Psalm 72, verses 1–4.

righteousness for its foundation: 'The mountains will bring peace to the people and the little hills, by righteousness.' "

Mr. Taylor walks over to Francis and bends down onto one knee. He is face to face with the boy.

"Young Franky, take full notice of the physical attributes that King David speaks of. The mountains and the hills can at times be barren places. Nevertheless, the King's writing informs us that when justice reigns, a justice that is focused in righteousness, even the places most barren shall be enriched with God's and the King's blessing."

Francis's eyes lock onto the eyes of the traveling preacher. Mr. Taylor adds one more thought,

"Christ is the full representation of righteousness. With Christ as the firm foundation of your life, you too can reign as a righteous king. But more importantly, in righteousness you are fulfilling the royal law, the law of the Most High King."

"What is the royal law?"

Francis's question has intrigued his parents. They are pleased that their son is following this most important lesson. Mr. Taylor replies,

"The royal law, the law of the Most High King, is to love God and to love thy neighbor as thyself."

***

Yawning as he walks outdoors, the thick morning air layers itself onto Francis's protected arms and shoulders. He has yet to grow accustomed to waking before four a.m.; however, it has become a regular habit since his meeting with the Baptist itinerant, David Taylor. The preacher's words brought to Francis a conviction that there was something more to religion than he was acquainted with. Since then he has endeavored to establish a regular time of early morning prayer before his Bible reading and the beginning of his work day at the Birch estate.

Francis makes his way to the horse barn to gather the team. They will haul yesterday's load of corn from the receiving area to the mill. Several young boys in their early teens join him along the way. Each of these lads is apprenticed to the Wyrley Birch family. A few, like the quiet Charles and the fiery Gage, have had their rough times, being from Wesleyan families that survived the punishing mobs. Others, like the stocky and stubborn Ordmond, are here for disciplinary reasons, acquired by the magistrate with the hope of bettering their futures. All have one thing in common: they follow the leadership of Francis. Francis's early-morning voice cracks as he gives the command,

"Secure them with these."

Francis hands two sets of leather reins to one of the young boys, who eagerly sets off for the task of preparing the horses. Francis clears his voice and speaks again.

"Remainder to follow."

Francis leads the half-dozen boys out of the barn. In total darkness, they make their way toward the river.

Like an advancing night-feeder, Francis leads the group as he weaves his way through the numerous hardwood trees that in daytime enhance the beauty of this fine property. As they draw nearer to the Tame, the gentle sound of the waterwheels, slowly churning away, grows louder.

It is not long before the boys arrive.

The gradual lightening of the pre-dawn sky reveals the twin wheels that sit in the river. Approaching ten feet in diameter, the wheels are vertically mounted and made of wood, constructed out of the local white oak. With precise consistency, the mechanism runs day and night, not unlike the river of which it is a part. The system, built in the traditional undershot fashion, allows the flowing water to strike the thirty wooden paddles at the bottom of the wheel's circular arc.

The Birch family grist mill is a wonderful creation. The technology dates back to the Byzantine general Belisarius during his siege of Rome in the early sixth century. The Birch's system captures the energy created by the flowing water of the river. This power is transmitted via a series of shafts, axles, and cogs to two sets of two large millstones, each weighing close to a ton and rotating a fraction of an inch apart from one another in flawless harmony.

Early on in his training of Francis, Magistrate Birch observed the boy's keen interest in the mechanical workings of the mill; he was also impressed with Francis's ability to grasp the inner workings of the facility. In fact, Francis was so intuitive about the mechanism that he had on occasion offered to Mr. Birch the possibility of other uses for the mill. For these observations, Mr. Birch rewarded Francis with a leadership position in the mill. There is an additional reason that Mr. Birch has allowed Francis to take this leadership role: he is impressed with Francis's commitment to reading and teaching the Bible to the other hired hands.

On this day, Francis will train the new boys who have joined the property's work force, instructing them in the mill's traditional function of grinding corn.

Except for the horizontal shaft that connects to the moving waterwheels, all is still as the boys enter the wooden structure.

"Fetch me the light."

Francis's request sends one of the lads into an adjacent alcove; he quickly returns with a lit taper. Francis enters the main room of the mill and lights several candles that hang on the walls. One of the boys voices his opinion of the facility.

"Outstanding!"

The lad's comment sums up the group's opinion as the flickering candles display the intricate machinery within the three-story building. The main shaft from outdoors leads to a pair of cogs, which leads to two vertical shafts, also with cogs. High above, from the third-floor level, two wooden chutes drop to the second floor. At the second floor, two sets of double millstones reside, looking like two sleeping giants waiting to awake for an adventurous journey.

The snorting of the team of horses outside announces that the corn has arrived. Francis moves to the doorway and gives direction.

"We shall load."

Francis leads the group outdoors.

The first rays of the rising sun now illuminate the entire grounds. In a matter of seconds, Francis has scaled the wooden cart loaded with sacks of corn kernels. Like a commanding field general, he quickly has the boys climbing up and passing the heavy bags into a wheeled cart.

"Load to the grain hoist; it shall lift the bagged corn to the third-level loading window."

The boys are quick to listen, at least, all but one. Francis redirects his efforts.

"Continue, as I engage the lift."

Francis climbs down from the cart and grabs the arm of the somewhat unconcerned individual, the sluggish Ordmond.

"Follow."

Like a balky mule, the burly lad reluctantly lumbers behind the nimble Francis.

Inside, Francis directs Ordmond to stand by the lift cog. The boy slowly makes his way to the long iron rod and stands beside it, staring blankly at the workings of the machinery. Francis does his best to explain.

"Once I engage the lift cog, we shall proceed upstairs to receive the grain."

The young boy nods as if he has grasped the entire workings of the mechanism, though the knowledge is far from him.

Francis grabs the long iron rod that attaches to an iron shaft, next to the wooden lift cog. He slowly lowers the rod; simultaneously, the wooden cog lowers to engage an iron cog attached to the rotating horizontal shaft. Upon contact, the vertical-lift shaft spins, and the loading cart outside begins to raise the loaded sacks of corn. Francis's eyes are beaming.

"We climb!"

Francis motions the boy to the stairs and bolts up them, well ahead of Ordmond.

The pair waits at the third level, watching as the load of corn sacks slowly rises. Within minutes, they receive the first of several loads that the boys will load downstairs.

The routine is the same for each load. Francis locks the loading cart into place, then disengages the lift. He and the lad quickly load the sacks into two hoppers. Once the chutes are loaded, Francis sends the loading cart down.

After several loads of corn, Francis and Ordmond head down the steps to disengage the lift cog. The loading operation is complete.

Francis turns to locate Ordmond, but he is still traversing the stairs. *He shall not last long.* Francis keeps his thoughts to himself.

With a leader's confidence, Francis yells for the other boys to enter the structure. They arrive, playfully bumping into each other, but eager to learn. Francis begins,

> "The corn is loaded into the hoppers above; once I engage the pit wheel,[34] the wallowers will begin to do their work. The two wallowers are the vertical iron cog-like wheels that transfer the energy from the horizontal shaft that connects to the waterwheels. It accomplishes the task by intersecting with the horizontal wooden cogs on the vertical shaft. The reason each cog is not made of iron is to help reduce the noise level - - And threat of fire."

With the mention of fire, the boys stand still. Several of them peer around the large wooden structure. They hadn't noticed before, but there are few exits from the building.

Francis is aware of their fearful looks.

> "There is only one exit and entrance to the building—a dangerous prospect in the event of a fire."

The boys stand up straight as Francis continues,

> "Once engaged by the pit wheel, the wallowers power the two large vertical shafts that go to the second-story millstones. Today, the stones will break down the corn into a powdery substance that the Birches use for baking. The flour millstones of the Birch mill are the best available: Cullen stones imported from Cologne, Germany."

Francis points to the millstones above. He enhances the presentation, demonstrating the movement with his hands.

> "For each pair of stones, the setup is the same. The running stone[35] is balanced, lying a fraction of an inch above the lower stone; close to the thickness of brown paper lies between them. There are carved furrows in

---

[34] Cog-like gear.

[35] Upper stone.

each stone, each furrow laid out to direct the ground corn to a perimeter collecting bin. From there it is directed through a spout below the stones, through another chute, and to the lower level for bagging."

"The entire process is quite simple. The corn flows through the hoppers to the grinding stones via a chute called the slipper. The slipper places the corn onto the bed stone[36] at the center. The metal rod that rises from the running stone controls the rate of corn flow. It serves to vibrate the slipper and the hopper above, ensuring a constant trickle of material. The rod's constant chattering is aptly named - -

The damsel."

Simultaneously, the boys laugh.

Francis smiles, too—the same sly smile that fooled the girls during the Bible riddle. He resumes,

"Once the corn is flowing at the proper rate, the upper stone rotates via the power of the vertical shaft connected to the horizontal shaft below. The ground corn eventually works its way to the perimeter of the bed stone, moved along by the carved furrows in both stones, grinding the corn as it travels over the bands of ridges in the lower stone.

"On the lower floor, the lead miller will sample the final product by rolling it between his forefingers and thumb. This 'rule of thumb' test determines if adjustments to the gap between the two stones are necessary. The closer the gap, the finer the grind. I can adjust the gap distance by a corkscrew located on the main shafts of the millstones."

Francis looks to the silent group. He turns and departs, making one quick pass of the machinery.

The boys watch as he returns to them. With face aglow, Francis announces,

"We shall begin."

Francis grabs the iron rod that connects to the pit wheel; he releases a catch lock and slowly lowers the mechanism. The entire machinery comes to life as the wooden cogs make contact with the wallowers. Amazed, the boys watch as the cogs power the shafts and the shafts power the millstones above.

The millstones quickly accelerate to life. Francis instructs,

"The rotation of the waterwheels outdoors is roughly ten rotations per minute; through the numerous cogs, the millstones will rotate to almost one hundred and twenty rotations per minute."

Francis once again has the boys' attention.

---

[36] Lower stone.

Francis heads toward the stairs; he must shout above the accelerating noise of the metal rod.

"I'm confident you can hear the damsel chattering away . . ."

The boys laugh.

With his arm, he motions to the group to follow. They quickly follow Francis to the second story, the noisy millstone level.

Barely audible above the din of the machinery, Francis offers more instruction.

"I will place one to monitor this station. The greatest danger of fire exists when the millstones run out of corn. The bare stones rubbing together will produce numerous sparks that can ignite the Hurst frame.[37] The one placed here shall guarantee that the stones never fail to have material. If this occurs, you must disengage the millstones with this emergency release."

Francis hesitates, and then sneezes. The grinding operation makes for much dust.

"The greatest danger to life exists in the machinery. You must take every precaution to maintain your distance from the rotating cogs and shafts. Your very clothing can be the vehicle that escorts you to a sudden death or dismemberment. I urge you, watch for the cogs."

Having assigned one eager lad and returning to the lowest level of the building, Francis instructs several of the boys in the bagging process. The grinding stones have already produced enough material to load into sacks. As he instructs, a deep voice surfaces from behind the group.

"Master Asbury, how fares our fine grist mill?"

The familiar voice of John Wyrley Birch spins Francis around.

"Good morning, sir."

"Francis, may I have a moment of your time?"

Francis abandons his teaching and quickly departs with the big man.

Outdoors, both men squint as they adjust their eyes to the bright morning light. Francis is thankful to escape the noise of the mill. Mr. Birch continues,

"The wife and I would like to reward you for the fine work you are doing at Hampstead Hall. We wish for you to join us for this evening's production at the theatre."

Francis is surprised, yet happy to be included in the family's outing. He shrugs his shoulders.

"I shall be honored."

"Very well, this evening it shall be."

---

[37] Wooden structure that supports the cogs and shafts.

Mr. Birch exits. Francis is thankful for the opportunity; he considers it a small gift from his boss.

Later that day, Francis is in his Hampstead Hall sleeping quarters. He is agitated, pacing the floor of his one-room cottage. *I spoke before thinking.* He darts for the handmade wooden dresser, erratically fumbling through the one drawer that contains all his clothing. *I should never have accepted the Birch's invitation to the theatre.*

In Francis's mind, he fails to possess the proper clothing for attending a formal theatrical production. A knock at the door causes Francis to abandon his search.

"Do come in."

The front door slowly opens. Standing at the doorway, with arms full, is a preteen boy. He announces to Francis,

"Master Birch mentioned you may have need of these."

The lad walks in and places the assemblage of formal wardrobe onto the bed.

Francis is stunned. He stares at the collection of handsome materials sent over by one of Mr. Birch's sons. As the young boy turns to depart, Francis rushes for words.

"Please inform the Birches that I am most grateful."

The young boy bows and heads off for the main house.

Francis quickly focuses on the mound of clothing. As he works his way through the pile, he remarks to himself, *I have never seen such finery.*

He holds up a tan-colored silk waistcoat. The beautiful sleeveless garment is crafted in the short style—the front buttons arranged from the neck to above the mid-stomach, as opposed to the long style with buttons continuing to the waistline. He is confident that this will suit him well.

Francis continues to search through the clothing and comes upon a fine jacket. *The material escapes me.* It is a most striking deep blue. *This shall work well with the tan waistcoat.*

He sets the jacket aside with the waistcoat. Next, he discovers a fine pair of white stockings, as well as two pair of breeches, one in brown, the other in the captivating dark blue. Yet another jacket, also made of the mysterious material, lies at the bottom of the pile. This additional jacket, in red, *is of the finest details.* Francis automatically inclines to the embroidery: *a tiny white vine, with almost undetectable small yellow flowers*, makes up the perimeter of the fine garment's edges.

Perhaps the article is too ornate - -

Perhaps not.

The door to the cottage bursts open as the fiery young boy, Gage, rushes in. He is quick to comment,

"Taking to the theatre, are we?"

Francis spins to reply to the lad's question.

"The Birches have invited me to Birmingham."

Before Francis completes his sentence, Gage is rifling through the pile of clothes. He soon solves the mystery.

"Cotton, Francis! You've a jacket—no, two—of the fine material."

Francis moves toward the jackets.

"The material is cotton?"

"Yes, have seen of it in Birmingham."

Francis rubs the fabric of the blue jacket, marveling at its feel. Gage continues,

"Expensive material, grown in the American colonies."

Francis considers Gage's words. *The colonies must be a fabulous place*. Gage rattles on,

"How will you reconcile these decorations with Wesley's 'give all you can'?"

Gage's comment hits Francis hard. The Wesleys consistently teach that one should gain all they can in order to give all they can. His feelings of guilt heighten with the rising flush in his face. He is sure Gage can see it. He also wrestles with the knowledge that this self-sacrificing view is precisely the ideal of his parents. The uncomfortable emotions linger as he considers his mother and father and their example of generosity—an example which leaves little room for finery.

Francis diverts his attention as he subconsciously attempts to accommodate his desire for the fine clothes *that the Birches have given* . . . In time, he has done just that.

Upon arrival at the Moor Street Theatre, Francis is surprised to find both wealthy and not-so-wealthy mingling together. Those who do not possess the wealth of the Birches are attending in their normal attire, some even in work clothes. At first Francis has no opinion of the matter, but eventually he relishes the fact that he, *unlike many of the locals, is dressed in a fine suit for the occasion*.

He also peruses the footwear of the attendees. His smile is almost boastful as he considers the handsome pair of shoes the Birches have lent him, crafted from elegant red Moroccan calfskin.

Again, Francis basks in the luxury of his ensemble.

The Moor Street Theatre of Birmingham began in 1740, situated north of Birmingham's commerce center, the bull ring. The theatre, which was the first of its kind in the West Midlands, is located in a back lot, between Moor and Park Street. The theatre has outlasted two subsequent small playhouses.

Prior to the building of the theatre, productions occurred in street booths and converted barns. Although the King does not sanction Moor Street Theatre, its successful performances continue to draw profitable crowds. Recently, the theatre has drawn competition from the completion of the magnificent King Street

Theatre. Actually an extension of London's Theatre Royal Drury Lane, the King Street Theatre is beautifully crafted for indoor viewing. The locals as well as the wealthy families like the Birches continue to support the Moor Street Theatre with its cozy outdoor feel, boasting a pit, a balcony, and two galleries.

Francis and the Birches take their seats in one of the galleries. They are among the last to arrive. All in attendance wait for the traditional opening as Mr. John Ward steps from behind the upstage curtain. He walks downstage to the front of the audience.

John Ward is the founder of the Moor Street Theatre's resident group of actors, the Warwickshire Company of Comedians. The talented company's growing popularity is due mostly to the leadership of Mr. Ward. Their repertoire includes not only the works of Shakespeare, but also those of several well-known English playwrights such as William Congreve, Nicholas Rowe, John Vanbrugh, and John Dryden. Many who have caught the performances are quick to realize that this collection of actors is as talented as the more famous individuals performing in the London theatre. In fact, the burgeoning popularity of the Moor Street Theatre has traveled well beyond the Birmingham area. However encouraging this may be, it is this adulation—and its accompanying profits—which has caused the opening of the competing King Street Theatre.

The audience falls silent as Mr. Ward walks to the edge of the stage and prepares to speak. The quiet gives Francis one more opportunity to appreciate the evening's opportunity and the fine outfit he is enjoying more and more the longer he wears it. He strokes the fine cotton sleeve of his jacket.

Mr. Ward begins,

> "It brings great happiness to realize our fair audience has refused to subscribe to the drawling, face-making puppies that inhabit the theatre at King Street."

Mr. Ward pauses as the gathering politely applauds. He continues,

> "As shared in times past, I am committed to work the dogs a penny'orth[38] for daring to cross my circuit."

The crowd once again approves.

At the completion of the light applause, Mr. Ward turns stage left, heading for the oversized chair on the perimeter of the stage.

Taking his place as the play's narrator, he begins:

> "Afraid of spirits, ghosts, witches, and fairies, the Widow Bumper and her over-productive body approaches the Marvel of the Age, Dr. Preachfield.

---

[38] Penny's worth.

With fifteen children, two since the death of her husband and another on the way, the good Widow Bumper longs for a compassionate ear - -

Arm, leg, even a torso . . ."

Insinuating sexual suspicion, a male actor, comfortably cross-dressed as the Widow, enters stage right.

Simultaneously, the character of Dr. Preachfield walks on stage from the center of the upstage curtains.

Downstage, the pair rushes to embrace. The Widow immediately begins to rub her upper torso onto the chest of Dr. Preachfield.

"I assured my uncle, 'Oh, you are a very good man, quite full of the spirit.' "[39]

---

[39] Paraphrased from the 1746 production, *A Will or No Will* by Charles Macklin.

All need to be saved.
All can be saved.
All can know they are saved.
All can be saved to the uttermost.
The Methodist Theological Tradition[40]

With her hand closed in a fist and raised above her head, Elizabeth vents her frustration.

"Trifling, Joseph - -

This is trifling with transgression."

Standing face to face with his wife, Joseph is well aware of her insinuation. Despite her angry stare, he will not respond. To do so would only incite harsher comments.

Joseph looks down at his feet and slowly turns away. Continuing in silence, he moves to the kitchen table and takes a seat.

"Husband, have I not warned?"

Joseph places his right elbow onto the tabletop. He raises the strong fingers of his right hand to support the lower-right portion of his cheek. He takes a measured breath and appears ready to deliver words.

He says nothing.

Huffing in frustration, Eliza puffs out her cheeks as she moves to the main room's window. She looks out into the dark evening where the partial moon wrestles with numerous clouds. Once again, she exaggerates an exhale; it ends with the setting of her hands on her hips. The movement gathers her dress at the waistline.

She laughs mockingly as she considers, *again, we traverse this path.*

In a moment of distraction, Joseph's eyes are drawn to the curvature of her hips. The flickering light from the fireplace shadows her profile onto the adjacent wall. Several times his eyes move back and forth from her hips to the wall. The argument is now eclipsed by his attraction. The view surfaces his fondness for her gentle curves, which have grown softer with age. But he realizes this is not the right time to pursue such pleasures, and wisely moves on.

---

[40] As noted by David J. A. Hallam in his book *Eliza Asbury: Her Cottage and Her Son,* quoted from *Groundwork of Theology* by John Stacey.

Complaining aloud to herself, Eliza continues,

> "The theatre! The Lord delivers this house from the pit of despair and you wish to deliver our son to the theatre?"

She turns sharply toward her husband and forcibly demands,

> "What of this theatre, Joseph? This play has our dear Whitefield running a brothel. Shall Francis perceive our faith as cover for immoral activities?"

Eliza waits for his reply. Hearing none, she lets fly again.

> "Your attempts at finery shall ruin our son!"

In his reserved manner—a manner that at times frustrates Eliza—Joseph clears his throat to speak, then pauses.

After nearly a minute of silence, Eliza grunts in frustration.

Joseph finally counters,

> "Most theatre is admirable - -
> Portions going so far as to inspire reverence."

Eliza rushes at Joseph. Within inches of his face, she stops and stares.

He has seen the look many times in the past. She retreats slightly and points at Joseph.

> "Husband, you are well aware that I speak not of the theatre, but of a deeper issue."

Once again, Joseph turns from Eliza's stare. Gently, she reaches out with her hand and turns her husband's face in her direction.

> "Husband, remove the finery from our son . . ."

***

Outdoors, Francis continues to trudge through the dusky forest of the surrounding neighborhood. Not far from home, he has been gone for more than an hour. He is happy to be out, uncomfortable with overhearing his parents while they argue.

Aided at times by the nearly full moon peeking through the thickening cloud cover, he ventures along the dense hardwoods of the Bromwich Forest. To the southwest of the Asbury cottage, the Sandwell Valley flows as a sloping woodland. For the past quarter hour, Francis has been able to walk along the eastern bank of the River Tame. The banks are exhibiting the first signs of spring grass, the dense sedge that will blanket both sides of the river by the end of summer. He is happy that the season is changing. Spring always seems to bring a sense of hope to Francis, but tonight he wrestles with the thought that his mother is extremely upset about the play he viewed at the Moor Street Theatre. *It is likely that my attendance will sacrifice my employment with the Birches.*

In the distance he spots the sensational flames that leap from two large brick smokestacks, adding an unnatural glow to the valley sky. The dancing light rebounds from the thick atmosphere, creating darkened silhouettes on the surrounding hill country. He stops to take in the view. While he watches the night sky's display, the lapping sounds of four large waterwheels divert his attention downriver. The sight increases his curiosity.

Francis has heard about the forge located on the Old Mill Farm. His father has spoken of the many items created there, noting that the forge is one of the larger operations in the West Midlands. Captivated by the concept, Francis crosses an ancient wooden footbridge and ventures onto the forge's adjacent property.

Francis slowly makes his way onto the farm. It is a large property, with at least two dozen acres leading into the grounds of the foundry. Within a few yards, he is clear of the hardwoods. In the vast open space slightly lit by the struggling moon and dancing flames, he notices many large objects in the field. It takes a few minutes of walking, but he is able to determine that *these oversized items are cows—Alderney cows,*[41] *sleeping upright.*

He resumes his trek, making his way closer to the forge.

This farm serves to supply food to the estates of the Earl of Dartmouth, including the great Sandwell Hall. It produces vegetables, fruits, and herbs, with the full working farm raising livestock. The horses, poultry, pigs, and sheep, as well as the cows, freely wander the entire property.

Francis is careful where he steps.

At the forge, he quietly makes his way to a partially shuttered window at the front of the operation. He maneuvers the shutter to peek inside and is fascinated with what he finds.

The first item to catch his attention is a mechanized contraption that connects to the waterwheels outdoors. He recognizes the various cogs and wheels attached to the long beam that travels between the wheels and the object inside the structure. They are similar to the mechanisms of the Birch mill. What he doesn't recognize is the apparatus that rests in mid-air, roughly four yards above the ground and on the end of another sizeable oak beam.

He surmises, *the huge head is made of cast iron.*

"It must weigh more than seventy stone[42] . . . perhaps as much as a grinding stone from the mill."

---

[41] A breed similar to the Jersey cow, known for its high-quality milk.
[42] About one thousand pounds.

Francis is alarmed as he catches himself saying these words aloud. He looks to see if anyone has noticed. *There is one gentleman. A tall, thin man at an adjacent window; he seems unaware.*

He is. The slender worker turns and busies himself with a task. Within moments, he turns and heads for the area where the monstrous hammer-like machine resides. He appears to supervise as four young boys arrive. The lads, close to Francis's age, carry a large object. They proceed to load the black, fibrous rock, roughly one yard each in length and breadth, onto the iron table below the oversized mallet. Francis notices, *the rock resembles a burnt stone.*

"Center the bloom!"[43]

One of the young boys yells to his companions. Frantically they calculate the location of the item on the flat iron table. They look to the stony object, then to the hammer above. The boys complete their task and are quickly on their way to another part of the building.

The angular man from the window now raises an iron lever that connects to the beam from the waterwheels. He immediately backs away as the large hammer begins to drop.

The resulting strike upon the object sandwiched between the massive hammer and the iron table is deafening. Francis instinctively covers his ears with his hands as he backs away from the window. *This is unbearable!* The hammer raises and drops again, then again. The pounding works its way to a constant pace. Despite the ear-splitting clanging of the mechanism beating the iron-ore bloom, Francis draws back to the window. *This is most fascinating . . .*

***

Back home, a knock at the Asbury door officially puts a temporary end to the argument between Joseph and Eliza. He rises from the table and walks to his wife.

"I shall remove the finery from Francis - -

And from Joseph."

The pair give each other a quick embrace. Joseph releases to answer the door. Outside stand a man and a woman. With them are a small boy, carried in the woman's arms, and four additional children, three boys and a girl, standing behind the couple.

"The Foxall clan, I presume; please do come in."

Joseph's invitation moves the family inside.

---

[43] Iron ore burnt in a smelting furnace. The material is beaten to remove its impurities.

Mr. and Mrs. Thomas and Mary Foxall have recently moved to West Bromwich from Monmouth, Wales. Thomas is from a large family involved in ironworking. His move to this locale is motivated by the burgeoning iron industry in the West Midlands.

Mary and Eliza have become good friends through their times together in worship at the All Saints Church in West Bromwich. Eliza steps forward to greet Mary and the children.

"I have attempted this only once before; I shall make an honest effort."

Eliza is going to recite their names to the best of her memory.

"You must be John and you are twelve years of age, two years younger than my Francis?"

The scruffy-looking boy affirms that she is correct. His mother notices that on the back of John's breeches are several patches of dirt marks. She quickly sets the youngest son down to stand on the floor. He wobbles slightly, but quickly gains his balance. She reaches for John, brushing clean the offending backside.

Elizabeth continues the attempt.

"Following John is young Mary, ten; Joseph, eight; Benjamin, seven; and Henry, almost five."

"Eliza, I am impressed!"

Mrs. Foxall congratulates Eliza as she successfully completes her task. Eliza invites the family in.

"Please do take a seat."

Around the main room of the Asbury cottage, Joseph has placed several additional wooden chairs that he recently constructed.

"My dear husband has once again blessed me with additional seating. In times past, you would have been placed on blocks of oak."

The children laugh at Eliza's jest. She once again offers her hospitality.

"To whom shall I bring a warm glass of tea?"

Joseph and Thomas Foxall make small talk as the ladies prepare and distribute the evening drink.

The sound of the door at the rear of the house signals that Francis has returned home. Eliza immediately abandons her chore and hurries to the rear doorway to the stairwell. She leans in and whispers to Francis,

"Francis, we are about to begin."

"Yes, Mother."

Francis and Eliza enter the room. He is surprised to see the entire Foxall family.

"My deepest apology, Mother; I did not realize . . ."

Francis was under the assumption that tonight's meeting was for the adults.

"It is quite all right, Son. I would like to introduce you to Mr. and Mrs. Thomas Foxall. Their son John is close to your age."

Francis spots the boy. He is thin and short. Francis cannot help but think, *John is short for his age.*

There is a break in the conversation between Joseph and Mr. Foxall. Joseph offers to Francis,

"Mr. Foxall is the superintendent at the Old Mill Forge in the Sandwell Valley."

The comment stops Francis in his tracks. He nervously looks about the room. Joseph notices his uneasiness.

"Are you all right, Son?"

Francis mumbles his reply,

"Quite - -

Yes, quite all right."

For a moment, Francis is unsure how to react. His conscience is bothering him. He doesn't want to incur a scolding for wandering so far from home in the dark, but he is fascinated with what he saw. On his return home from his little adventure, he had ventured a thought of working at the forge.

"I am aware - -

Well aware of the forge; amazing operation."

With mouth frozen and head tilted, Joseph anxiously waits to see where Francis is going with this.

Mr. Foxall is quick to reply,

"You should pay visit."

I already have. Francis keeps this thought to himself. Mr. Foxall continues,

"I shall make you an offer. A growing young boy of your size would do well to spend time in the trades. The hard work will aid you in becoming a man."

In excitement, Francis stands silent. He wants to burst out, *yes!*

He looks to his mother; she is doing her best to be polite. Then to his father, whose blank stare has transformed into a look of honest inquiry.

Joseph pauses to look at Eliza. She drops her head and turns from Joseph.

He determines to inquire anyway.

"I have tended to avoid the trades. Not on account that I do not believe hard work good for a man—sometimes dangerous, but good. Eliza and I have rather wished for our son to gain a decent education. However, that has proved unsuccessful. Nevertheless, at times we have sensed God securing Francis for other tasks."

Mr. Foxall listens patiently. He realizes that the Asburys' opinion is the same as most of the public's—that men who begin in the trades seldom leave. He also can sense the concern and worry of Joseph and Eliza for the safety of their son. The forge is a hazardous workplace.

Before he can share his thoughts, Joseph comments,

"Franky and I would be honored to view the facility."

Francis instinctively leaps to his feet. Each in the room quizzically looks to the youth, who stands silent, looking quite ready to launch through the ceiling.

Joseph leans forward toward Mr. Foxall.

"I suspect there is more to tell."

The two laugh and shake hands. Each is pleased with the development, but not as pleased as Francis.

The following morning, Joseph and Francis make their way out of the barn. Joseph playfully ruffles Francis's hair. Francis smiles; he's happy to spend the day with Father, and even happier at the prospect of working at the forge.

From their home, Joseph and Francis head southwest toward the River Tame. At the waterway they turn south, proceeding along the eastern bank. Along the river, Francis takes the lead. His father is surprised that the boy seems familiar with this part of the valley.

Along the way, they encounter the dense forest-like hardwoods native to the Bromwich Heath. The pair comes to what seems like a fork in the path. Francis instinctively takes the left-hand fork.

"Franky, should we not maintain along the river?"

"The trail will divert us around the marsh."

Whoops.

Joseph stops walking. With his right hand, he scratches the back of his head.

"Seems like Franky has been this way before . . ."

His son hears Joseph's murmur, but he doesn't answer. He continues down the path, keeping the "whoops" thought to himself.

Francis's lack of reply and continuation of the trek leave Joseph no option. Shaking his head, he ventures the thought, *I'm confident the boy has been this way before.*

Joseph laughs, softly at first. His humor soon transforms into his signature laugh, hard and loud. Francis can't hold back a smile. He beams as he continues to lead his father through the forest.

The sound of the waterwheels grows stronger as the pair nears the operation. At close quarters, the entire foundry resembles a callathump[44] with the churning on the river and the clanging inside the structure. Francis cannot help but think, *it seems as if the entire mill is operating at full.*

---

[44] A loud, boisterous parade.

"Father, the mill boasts of four waterwheels."

Joseph spots the huge apparatus and nods in agreement.

"You have been this way before."

The pair ventures indoors. Inside the structure, the noise is close to unbearable, as is the heat. Immediately Joseph and Francis begin the industry's standard ritual of wiping the sweat from their brows. One of the line workers shouts,

"Fetch Foxall!"

The demand sends a lad of about ten years of age running off into the distance.

Francis observes that the line worker is tall and stocky, around seventeen years of age, and covered in black soot from the forge's furnace. In his right hand is an iron hammer. Francis notices the hammer and the large hand that grips the tool. The young man's forearms amaze Francis. *The one on the right is larger than the one on the left.* Francis finds this odd.

The big fellow eyes Francis, not happy that he is almost as tall as he is. With a mocking attitude, he questions Francis,

"Plannin' to join the trades, are we?"

The comment makes Francis uneasy. In uncharacteristic fashion, his eyes look away from the inquirer.

In his commanding voice, Joseph warns the young man,

"We have business with your supervisor."

With a nervous twitch the youth turns and shouts again,

"I told you to fetch Foxall!"

Several young lads about Francis's age scramble for the far end of the building.

From a distance, Joseph and Francis spot Mr. Foxall. The unmistakable bounce in his step signifies his happiness at seeing the pair.

Mr. Foxall is not a tall man, but of average height. He is dressed in the typical outfit of the ironworker of the day: sturdy leather trousers to below the knee, with a sleeveless waistcoat revealing the stocky shoulders and arms beneath his shirt. His legs at the thigh are uncharacteristically thick, evidence of many years spent working the treadle hammer.[45] Foxall calls out as he approaches,

"Been looking forward to this!"

Upon arrival, Mr. Foxall immediately hugs Francis. Both his comment and his smile convey his joy at this occasion.

"Joseph, shall you view the facility?"

"It would be a pleasure."

---

[45] This is a smaller version of the water-driven hammer that Francis spotted through the forge window. The treadle hammer is manually operated by pushing a flat iron pedal with one's legs. The typical forging processes require that the pedal be pushed by alternating legs for an entire day's work.

Mr. Foxall turns and heads for the furnace at the far side of the operation.

"Follow me."

The pair doesn't miss a step; they are right behind him.

"Francis, the Old Mill Forge is an entire industrial community—an ironworking manor, as some are apt to call it. We not only receive iron ore to process into steel, we also produce articles for trade throughout Europe and the American colonies."

And to America? Francis looks to his father. Joseph too is impressed.

Mr. Foxall continues,

"On site we both manufacture and live. It is a self-contained community with the required furnaces to handle the forging and casting houses, as well as facilities for the workers' housing, the iron-master's house, the school, and a store for personal items. One last element of this community: there is also a church."

Mr. Foxall pauses on the word "church." He stops and turns toward Francis, staring into the young man's eyes as though trying to read the mind of the growing lad.

"Are you ready to join this community?"

Francis looks to his father again. Without hesitation, Joseph nods his approval. That is the confirmation that Francis requires.

"I am."

Once again, Mr. Foxall is turned around and moving. He arrives at the first of three furnaces.

"Old Mill originally began as a bloomery forge, this furnace evidence of the foundry's small beginnings. Since then it has grown into the blast furnace and finery forge that you see around us today. On the far end of the property is a slitting mill, where we process iron for the numerous nail manufacturers of the Black Country. In time you will understand the difference.

"In short, the bloomer forge processes raw material, iron ore, into wrought- iron blooms. The blooms are beat for strengthening with the water-powered trip-hammer. This is a most common practice for beginning operations. The advantage of a bloomery forge is the low initial cost. Two men can easily produce enough wrought iron to make a living.

"Conversely, the blast furnace is a more expensive process. The blast furnace turns iron ore into pig iron, a liquid form of steel. This requires substantial amounts of fuel to burn the raw material. The much-sought-after fluid is generally poured into prepared molds for the manufacturing of various items.

"Lastly, the finery forge turns out the products of the day. These products will change from time to time, subject to the whims of the buyer. The Black Country is called 'the toy manufacturer of the world' for its ability to handle this ever-changing demand."

He moves on to the next furnace, much larger than the previous, and constructed into the side of the hill. The furnace stands roughly fifteen yards tall. At the middle, it is about five yards in diameter. At the floor level are two large arched openings where two workmen are collecting the melted iron.

Mr. Foxall continues,

"As demonstrated here, the blast furnace is built into the hillside. Iron ore, charcoal, and limestone are the key elements fed into the fire from the top. At the side of the furnace are two water-driven bellows. They are made of leather and are roughly seven yards in length. Each leather bellows operates alternately of the other, blowing air through an iron pipe into the fire mixture. The result is a stronger fire producing molten iron, which will collect on the sand- covered floor at the bottom of the furnace or casting house. The men are gathering it as we speak. As you can see, the puddles of liquid iron resemble a sow and her piglets . . ."

"Pig iron!"

Mr. Foxall laughs at Francis's interruption.

"Yes, Francis, the proper term is pig iron. The pig iron is brittle, too brittle for the blacksmith. It will require further firing and treatment to become useful for his purposes. Eventually, the softer iron will be turned into wrought iron by the additional workings. Nevertheless, pig iron is useful for castings."

Mr. Foxall points to an additional furnace.

"Turning iron into steel requires continuous firing. That is the function of this third furnace."

He indicates the furnace on the adjacent wall.

"The round brick oven has an iron grate at the bottom where coal is loaded. The coal piles up around a clay coffin that will hold the bars of wrought iron produced in the bloomery and blast furnaces. Each bar is one yard in length. Once the fire starts, it will be tended constantly. The process depends on the quality of the coal. Good coal will allow for a shorter burn time—roughly three days and nights. The lesser the quality of the coal, the longer the period of burn, at times reaching more than five or six days and nights of non-stop burning. Reaching the critical minute of the operation, the steel is cut into narrower bars about half an inch in width. These bars over here, cut into short two-inch pieces, are gadds. They are samples for the potential buyers of the steel. The secret to the process is the treating of the iron with a chemical agent at the critical minute, when the iron has turned to steel. The men daub the product with tallow once the red-hot surface cools. This process allows the iron to be utilized by both black and white smiths."

Francis interrupts,

"A whitesmith?"

Mr. Foxall continues,

"I believe you to be familiar with the work of the whitesmith. He manufactures many of the items hanging in Joseph's barn—the scythes, reaping-hooks, axes, hatchets, and pruning shears."

"Gardening implements."

Both Francis's reply and his animated eyes indicate that he fully understands. Mr. Foxall is impressed.

"Correct. The products of the whitesmiths require temper with a different heat and chemical additive to prepare them for a bright edge. The items of the blacksmiths are much different, requiring another process. The final products of the blacksmiths consist of objects like plows and carts for farming, shoes and spurs for horses, bolts and hinges for doors, buckles and buttons for clothing, nails and spikes for construction. There are many more items, as deemed necessary by the purchasing public. When they demand something anew, we proceed to produce it."

"What of the slitting mill?"

"Francis, you impress me. The slitting mill is our busiest operation. There we take sheets of iron and heat them in order to flatten them. The thinned material eventually feeds through a slitting machine where four cast-iron discs, connected to water-driven rollers and covered in hardened steel, slice the sheet into strips. These strips are then cut to length and shipped to the nailers."

Mr. Foxall walks toward a steel anvil. On top of the ironworking device is a small iron sledgehammer with a wooden handle. Mr. Foxall picks up the hammer. With a slow turn he reaches and places the tool into Francis's hands.

"This shall become your constant companion."

Francis looks at the hammer, then around the facility. He didn't notice before, but each individual working at the forge is carrying the implement.

"Guard it as your very own."

I will . . . Before long, Francis is putting his constant companion to work.

Coming down hard with a stroke of the hammer onto the horn of the anvil, Francis blinks as the wrought-iron piece in his gloved hand breaks in two.

"Again?"

He slams the remaining section to the ground.

He looks around the forge. Several young boys the same age as Francis watch him as he fumes. Francis sneers and the boys quickly get back to their tasks.

Francis is making nails, a simple process and a beginner's task. This is Foxall's tried-and-true apprenticeship program. You learn to make nails so when you work in the slitting mill you will know the importance of manufacturing proper sheets for the forge's end customers. Francis isn't comfortable with the mundane chore; he expected more—working a large furnace or constructing a more adventuresome item like the scabbard of a sword.

In the eighteenth century, nail-making is the backbone of the ironworking industry. Once mastered, the process can easily have a preteen boy or girl pumping out four nails per minute or two hundred and fifty per hour. At this point, Francis is struggling to make one per minute or sixty per hour. The so-called simple process is turning out to be more difficult than he expected.

He once again accidentally breaks another heated rod of iron. As he slams it to the dirt floor of the forge, a voice emerges from behind his work area.

"Ya' can have fr'deedom fr'dom sin."

The unfamiliar voice with the Scottish accent causes Francis to abruptly turn around. Standing before him is a tall, thick man dressed in the traditional outfit of a Wesleyan itinerant. The somewhat handsome man with a broad nose repeats,

"Ya' can have fr'deedom fr'dom sin."

This time Francis understands what he is referring to: Francis's slight burst of anger toward the wrought-iron piece that broke in his hand. He nods his head in agreement.

"My actions do warrant correction."

The preacher politely extends his hand.

"Alexander Mather."

Francis completes the polite gesture.

"Francis Asbury."

The Wesleyan itinerant who was born in Brechin, Scotland, travels the Staffordshire circuit. Incorporated into the large circuit are the nearby towns of Darlaston, Wednesbury, Wolverhampton, and Birmingham. These, Mather attends. The twenty-seven-year-old preacher with the slightly sloping eyelids has a unique religious history.

Mather grew up in a God-fearing family. From childhood, his parents did their best to keep him from evil company, but his father was a strict disciplinarian. Before his conversion and entrance into the ministry, Mather was a baker—first with his father, then with others in London. His conversion prompted him to convince his boss and the other bakers of London to refuse to bake on Sundays. The effort met with much success; only two of the numerous bakers refused the request. Over time, his boss became wealthy; Pastor Mather and many others were convinced that it was the decision to honor the Sabbath that contributed to his success.

The itinerant is a hard worker. As a baker he once spent a three-year period working nearly twenty hours each day; the grueling schedule and a perceived call to preach eventually prompted him to enter the ministry.

"Ya' must learn to bear'rd wit' disappointments."

Francis tilts his head. Alexander repeats himself,

"Ya' must learn to bear'rd wit' disappointments."

"Bear with disappointments?"

"Pr'decisely what Ah' said, bear'rd wit' disappointments."

Francis smiles at the preacher's forcefulness and thick accent. He replies,

"What you have said is wise. I have heard of it often, from my father."

"Ya' faither is truly a wise man."

Once again the thick accent throws Francis; it takes a few seconds, but he eventually nods in agreement. The itinerant continues,

"My faither was a rigid and severe man. So much so that when Ah' was a child of twelve years, Ah' made a foolish decision and ran off wit' the Scottish rebels. Financed by the French King, we were to fight the English. Ah' planned to engage for a year certain. In that short period of time Ah' saw many mighty ones fall on Culloden Heath and Inverness. On every side they fell, yet Ah' myself was mercifully preserved. When Ah' came near to my senses and returned to the house of my faither, he refused me. At the time Ah' failed to realize, but my faither too was a wise man. He realized that the English King would hunt for rebels like myself, a Jacobite rebel. In love for family and me, he refused me shelter. Divine providence looked down upon me.

"In time, Ah' was labored to a baker in London, a man who feared God. The man providentially led me to the Foundry Kirk[46] started by the brothers Wesley in London."

---

[46] (Church) The Foundry Church in London was originally an abandoned building, once a foundry casting guns for the King. John and Charles Wesley purchased the building, turning it into the cradle of Methodism.

Francis has patiently followed the preacher's story. He agrees that they both had the privilege of growing up with a wise father, but his thoughts have wandered several times during the retelling of Alexander Mather's childhood story—so much so that he worries that the preacher may require a detailed response. He sharpens his focus.

Francis is fixated on the itinerant's original greeting, *you can have freedom from sin.* Alexander senses Francis's distraction.

"Ah' feel Ah've lost ya' in story?"

Francis dips his right cheek toward his shoulder, his nervous twitch indicating more. He admits,

> " 'Freedom from sin'—your comment moves my heart. It also proves challenging."

"Foxall tells me that ya' regularly read the Bible and ya' struggle wit' the concept of fr'deedom fr'dom sin? It's as plain as the breeks[47] on ya' legs. The fr'deedom ya' so earnestly seek cannot be found in doin'; it is only found in the Savior. Jesus has already provided the fr'deedom; ya' must yearn for'd it, embrace it . . ."

Francis nods his head in agreement, silently vowing to understand. Pastor Mather smiles as he departs.

"Ya' day is nearin' its end. Enjoy ya' evenin'."

"I shall."

That evening, Francis thinks about the words of Pastor Mather: "You can have freedom from sin; it cannot be found in doing, it is only found in the Savior." He falls asleep thinking of this.

The sun has yet to rise on this Sabbath morning. The thick air wafts from the mouths of each worker as they plod toward the chapel of the Old Mill Forge. It is a simple building, an outcropping of the burgeoning ironworking manor. Francis is among the slowly waking group.

Inside, the bulky itinerant Alexander Mather, his broad and lively smile indicating that he has been up for a couple of hours before this five a.m. service, welcomes the men. To each man who enters, the preacher gives a welcoming embrace. The men are grateful for the enthusiastic greeting, but if the truth were known, they would much rather start their only day off sleeping in bed.

Each man sits; Pastor Mather takes his place, standing behind a worn wooden table at the front of the room. He slowly looks to the men before him. The plain and undistinguished clothing of the men reflects the paucity of the structure. It is a simple chapel with wood blocks for seats and articles of industry lying about.

---

[47] Trousers.

Bare walls and a dusty window complete the structure, which has the main purpose of bringing together the working men of the forge to worship God.

Each man holds his Bible in hand. Pastor Mather begins,

> "One day, goin' hastily along the street, a loaded cart stood in my path. It was nearly filled up. In spite of this, Ah' went on, thinkin' Ah' could get by—but just as Ah' was goin' by, the cart moved. It caught my basket of baked items. Immediately, the cart crushed me against the wall and dragged me. The draggin' seemed to go on very long, so long that Ah' feared for my life."

Pastor Mather pauses. The sleepy men have been prompted to life by the opening of the story. Their eyes are wide and focused on the itinerant dressed in black. He continues,

> "Ah' eventually arrived at a shop window. Providentially, it gave way. Through the window, Ah' tumbled into the cobbler's shop and was released of the devilish hold of the cart. Everyone who saw it supposed Ah' should be crushed to death, or at least that my arms and legs would be broken. However, Ah' received no hurt at all, besides a lit'l bruise on the back of my hand. This rescue from certain death was the second time in my life that the guid[48] Lord made an attempt to gain my undivided attention."

The men remain silent.

> "Is the guid Lord aimin' for ya' attention? My message this glorious mornin' is simple: ya' must be reconciled to God. Ya' life will end in certain death unless ya' gain victory over sin. Sin is crouchin', nay, has already snatched life fr'dom ya'. Before ya' very birth, sin reigned in ya'. Ya' can have fr'deedom fr'dom sin. That fr'deedom is only found in the Savior, Jesus the Christ . . ."

Pastor Mather raises his hands for prayer. In unison, the men rise to their feet. The short and simple prayer sends the men on their way.

Francis is the last to exit from the simple chapel. Outdoors, Pastor Mather approaches to greet the young man, with papers in his hand. He presents them to Francis.

> "Fr'dancis, Ah' would like ya' to spend time wit' the writings of a dear friend. Please enjoy this sermon of George Whitefield, 'Walkin' wit' God.' Ya' will greatly prosper fr'dom his efforts."

Francis bows his head as he receives the documents.

> "Thank you. I am most grateful. I vow to read them."

---

[48] Scottish accent for the word "good."

Francis departs. His thoughts are fixated on the words that keep ringing in his head: *You can have freedom from sin.* He is drawn to their implication that he is a prisoner.

Francis departs the Old Mill Forge for home, welcoming the walk through the Bromwich Heath. He also welcomes the thought of a warm meal cooked by his mother.

Later that day at the Asbury home, Francis and two of his friends await his mother's dinner. Outside in Joseph's barn, they are engaged in discussing an excerpt from Whitefield's sermon that Pastor Mather gave Francis earlier in the day. Francis reads the portion in question.

> *Perhaps it may seem a hard saying to some, but our own experience daily proves what the Scriptures in many places assert: that the carnal mind, the mind of the unconverted natural man, nay, the mind of the regenerate, so far as any part of him remains unrenewed, is enmity—not only an enemy, but enmity itself—against God, so that it is not subject to the law of God, neither indeed can it be. Indeed, one may well wonder that any creature, especially that lovely creature man, made after his Maker's own image, should ever have any enmity, much less a prevailing enmity, against that very God in whom he lives, and moves, and hath his being. But alas! So it is. Our first parents contracted it when they fell from God by eating the forbidden fruit, and the bitter and malignant contagion of it hath descended to, and quite overspread, their whole posterity.*

"Whitefield is correct, all of humanity is prisoner."

With much enthusiasm, Francis expresses his opinion to Thomas Ault and Thomas's friend, William Emery. The two seem slightly amused at Francis's urgency.

The trio faces each other, each seated on a block of hardwood in Joseph's tool barn. Thomas's long legs stretch casually in front of him. His chin rests comfortably on his hand, supported by his elbow resting on his thigh. Francis is bent forward, almost pensive, with his knees tucked under his chest. Whitefield's sermon rests in his hands, inches from his face. William, who is several inches shorter than both Thomas and Francis, sits cross-legged, watching Francis concentrate on the paper.

For a moment, the steady and gentle winds of late May work their way through the numerous holes in the barn's dilapidated wood siding, caressing the silence at the end of Francis's proclamation that "all of humanity is prisoner." Francis lowers the sermon papers.

> "It is most true, Thomas. You are prisoner. I am prisoner. William is prisoner. I sense this deeply. I fail to comprehend my escape."

Thomas quietly reflects on his friend's comment and confession. He leans back against the wall and casually crosses his legs at the ankle.

"Francis, it seems you are focused in the wrong direction. My father also has communicated often that 'we are sinful creatures.' However stark this truth may be, I fail to believe that we are to maintain this 'prison,' as you call it. Perhaps we should seek the advice of the clergy . . ."

Thomas's unexpected pause leaves everyone waiting for his next words. With a wry smile, the kind more often found on the face of Francis when he's up to something mischievous, Thomas offers,

"Or your mother?"

Francis understands what Thomas is indicating—that Francis on more than one occasion has had to deal with Elizabeth's controlling tendencies. He quickly responds,

"Let us consult with clergy."

Francis silently justifies his decision. *Mother would not mind our Sabbath visit cut short.*

After dinner, Thomas, William, and Francis make haste for St. Margaret's, the Anglican parish church in Great Barr. The trio decides to attend the last service of the day. The timing of the service has allowed Francis to finish his Sabbath visit with his parents, but as the daylight proceeds west, the boys make their way to St. Margaret's.

St. Margaret's Church takes its name from Margaret of Antioch, martyred for her faith by the emperor Diocletian during his persecution of the Christians in the fourth century. Erected in the thirteenth century, the church is a handsome brick structure with a magnificent seven-story spire at the entrance.

The boys quietly make their way into the sanctuary, quick to notice the beauty of the structure. Inside, several stained-glass windows escort natural light into the cast-stone, columned place of worship. The boys are impressed with the wooden beams that support the high-arched wooden ceiling. The opulence of the space is beyond anything they could have imagined.

The large room, which appears to hold about two hundred people, has only a handful of occupants. The boys take a seat in the hand-carved pew in the back. Within moments, the Anglican priest enters at the front of the room and ascends the pulpit.

The boys gradually focus in on the words of the priest as he begins to read his sermon.

" . . . an history so full of important and interesting events as that which this day recalls annually to our thoughts, cannot but afford them very different subjects for their most serious and useful employment— for today we revisit the patron saint of childbirth, St. Margaret of Antioch. During the degenerate leadership of the emperor Diocletian, she was to fall. The daughter of a pagan priest, she was converted to Christianity and subsequently driven from her home by her father."

The boys continue to listen attentively.

"As providence would have it, she became a shepherdess. As a shepherdess, she eventually came under the notice of a magistrate of Rome. The lustful advances of the man, Olybrius, were promptly denied by the woman who had vowed her virginity. Threatened with death unless she renounced her vow of virginity and her Christian faith, Margaret's stance brought forth the wrath of the Roman Empire. She was imprisoned. In prison, she had an encounter with Satan himself, disguised in the form of a dragon. According to all accounts, the great deceiver swallowed dear Margaret. Providentially, the cross which she carried in her hand so irritated the throat of the dragon that he purged her from his stomach. Upon the appointed day of her execution, she was burned at the stake, but the flames failed to bring pain or death. The magistrate immediately had her bound hand and foot and thrown into a boiling vat of water. In prayer, her restraints were miraculously cut and she stood to her feet unharmed. In desperation, Olybrius ordered her decapitation. This act was carried out and brought forth the prefect's desired effect."

Thomas and Francis look to each other. They have each sensed the other's opinion. Francis is the first to respond,

"This is mere myth and legend."

Francis's complaint causes the pair to rise together. The half-dozen people attending the service do not notice their standing. Francis and Thomas turn to depart; William quickly follows them out of the building. Francis mutters on the way out,

"Blind priests! I should have honored your request, Thomas."

Thomas tilts his head as he considers Francis's last comment. *What request?* Disgusted by the waste of time, Francis says with a grimace,

"We shall talk to mother . . ."

Thomas tries his best to keep up with Francis's hurried pace. Although he wants to, he decides not to gloat that he was right in the first place. Francis once again resolves,

"I shall settle this matter this evening."

Francis's stern comment brings a slight chuckle from Thomas. Partway home, William Emery informs his companions,

"I shall leave you, Francis and Thomas, as I've an early start in the morning."

Francis and Thomas wish him well as William departs. The remaining pair heads in the opposite direction, away from Francis's eventual destination of the Old Mill Forge, back to the Asbury home in Newton Village. Along the way, Francis belabors a thought to himself: *Shall be a late return this evening.*

Inside the Asbury home, Eliza's widened smile will not diminish as she proclaims,

> "The desire of the Savior, my son, reveals the true nature of your heart—a heart although stained with sin, still fit and ready for triumph. You truly are set aside for God's work, a dissenter on the path to righteousness; and you as well, Thomas."

Francis is not paying attention to the praises of his mother. He fumbles with the iron spit of the fireplace.

> "You boys should attend the Old Church at West Bromwich. You may catch the last service of the day."

Francis comments to Thomas,

> "We will have to travel in darkness . . ."

Francis heads for the front door. He is out the door before Thomas can rise from his seat. Thomas rises and gives a cordial reply,

> "Good evening, Mrs. Asbury."

Thomas races to catch up.

Francis and Thomas begin their mile-and-a-half trek to the west toward the Bromwich Heath. Their destination is the West Bromwich church—All Saints Church, or "the Old Church," as Eliza called it. If the pair hurries, they can make the eight o'clock evening service, the last on the Sabbath.

The thick forest quickly grows damp after sunset. The boys soon reach the River Tame and proceed north along the east side of the waterway. Their destination is the Jone Bridge, north of the intersection of Wigmoor Brook and the Tame.

Along the way, they surprise several animals. The reduced light makes it difficult to determine what is actually scurrying away from the pair. Another few steps, and again—swoosh into the underbrush, the sudden flurry fairly scaring the boys each time. Francis informs his friend,

> "Father often warned to travel this path by daylight."

Francis's comment does not bring comfort to Thomas. Thomas notes,

> "These harvest mice are bold."

Francis ponders Thomas's comment, but does not reply. The pair continues.

Swoosh - -

> "Ow!"

> "Are you all right, Thomas?"

"Passed right over my boot. Moggy's[49] paradise!"

"The spring weather has excited these forest rodents. Stay close, Thomas; I doubt they will approach the both of us."

Thomas leaps right behind Francis, and the pair continues cautiously.

"Ah!"

Thomas spins around.

"Brushed the calf of my boot."

Francis stops short and Thomas slams into him.

"Do watch where you are treading! Now, Thomas, we are talking about the smallest rodent in the forest. The harvest mouse is smaller than the palm of my hand. They fail to jump high enough to reach your calf."

"This one was quite successful . . ."

Francis shakes his head and continues. In less than ten seconds, Thomas once again complains,

"Ow."

Francis stops short again.

"What was it now, Thomas—the middle of your thigh?"

"My shoulder blade."

Francis cannot hold back.

"Your shoulder - -

Ha!"

Francis begins to step away, but suddenly halts.

"Ow!"

He lets out a scream.

"Thomas, that grazed my scalp!"

He rubs the side of his head. Thomas notes,

"Seems these mice are both bold and agile."

"Hilarious, Thomas. These fail to be normal field mice."

"As I have been saying, Francis."

Francis mockingly shakes his head at Thomas's comment. A few steps forward, and one of the animals hits Francis in the stomach.

Thomas and Francis both jump in fright. The animal bounces off Francis's midsection. He frantically swings his forearm forward, knocking the creature up into the air. It lands on Thomas.

"Hoy!"

Thomas bats the rodent toward Francis.

---

[49] A cat's.

It hits Francis in the chest and falls to the ground, lifeless. The entire exchange has lasted a mere five seconds. The young men stand there, breathless, each too petrified to move.

"Pick it up, Francis."

"You pick it up."

"No, you pick it up; you fail to believe that this tiny rodent can do much damage."

Francis looks to his feet. He can barely make out the tiny silhouette of the mouse as it lies motionless on the forest floor. He doesn't want to, but he slowly bends down to grab it.

He pauses before coming into contact with it. Thomas senses his fear and goads Francis,

"Well, go ahead, my brave friend; pick up the mighty mouse."

Francis places his right hand, and then his left, gently around the seemingly lifeless vermin. *The soft downy fur still is warm with life.* Francis comments,

"It's not dead, Thomas."

Francis rises to his feet, the mouse securely cupped in the palms of his hands.

"Well, look at it. You must look at it, Francis."

Francis sighs. He slowly pulls back his thumb. Surprised by his discovery, he conveys his findings.

"The brownish fur looks spotted."

"Spotted?"

Francis's comment perplexes Thomas. Francis slowly pulls back two of the fingers of his right hand.

"Thomas, you must look at the mouse also."

Thomas takes a deep breath.

"Well, all right."

Francis slowly raises the rodent toward Thomas. He closes his fingers around the creature before it is visible to Thomas.

"You must open your hand for me to view it, Francis."

Francis chuckles.

"Are you prepared, Thomas, prepared to meet the mighty mouse?"

"I am."

Francis slowly peels back his fingers, creating a nest for the object in his hands.

"A bird?"

"Yes, Thomas. We have been doing battle with birds."

"Look at the markings! It is most beautiful."

The pair ponders the bird in Francis's hands. The majority of its tiny body is light brown in color. The chest area underneath is a frosty white with dark-brown speckles. Thomas ventures a question.

"Should we set it down?"

Francis hesitates, then replies,

"Perhaps we should bring it with us. It may get eaten by the bold and agile harvest mouse."

Thomas laughs as Francis gently prepares the bird to travel in his hands. The pair continues north along the Tame.

The bird in hand is actually the song thrush, a bird native to the West Bromwich region. The beautiful creature is attracted to the gold-yellow flowering scrub plant for which the area is named, the broom plant. The hardy shrub thrives in the few open and sunny areas around the Bromwich Heath. It is also the plant used by weavers to make brooms.

The tiny birds have an extensive repertoire of songs and musical phrases. In fact, the song thrush possesses the largest musical vocabulary of all the thrushes. The bird will on a regular basis whistle unique little tunes, repeating them for long periods. The local residents of West Bromwich consider it a blessing to hear such beautiful music. The bird is a favorite of many throughout the English countryside.

The song thrush also plays a role in the lives of those who do not like the residents of West Bromwich. Those wishing to have such a beautiful plant with its vibrant yellow blooms cascading along their village's open areas look upon the settlement, originally called Brom Wich (meaning a village where broom grows), with jealousy. The begrudging outsiders call the inhabitants of West Bromwich "throstles"—not because of the pleasant sounds of the song thrushes that inhabit the region; they are sarcastically alluding to the disagreeable braying of the hundreds of freely wandering donkeys that are also attracted to the thriving broom plant.

At the Jone Bridge, Thomas, Francis, and the bird cross the Tame. The old wooden bridge, barely wide enough for a horse and cart, is reassuringly sturdy. The pair quickly crosses the river and begins heading slightly west.

The boys are able to make better time now. Although much of the forested land continues, some of the hardwoods have been cleared and converted into fruit tree orchards. This is due to the efforts of the Lord of the Manor House, a landed property sold off into lots by the royal knight and philosopher, Sir Samuel Clarke. One of his purchasers is Josiah Turton. Francis and Thomas are actually traveling through the property of Mr. Turton.

The orchard planted by Mr. Turton is unique to this area of England. Upon the advice of the caretaker of the old Manor House—or the West Bromwich Hall, as it is known—Mr. Turton has decided to plant White Muscadine grapevines, Newington and Red Roman nectarine trees, Newington peach trees, Gorls Bury and Orange Burgamott pear trees, Mapell plum trees, Turkey apricot trees, and Bleeding Heart and Black Heart cherry trees.

Along the way, Francis pauses.

"Thomas, these trees must be of the fruiting variety. Note the precise planting arrangement."

It is difficult in the greying evening light, but the moon that continues to grow toward full allows Thomas to make out the uniform rows of plantings and small fruits beginning to grow. Francis continues the horticultural lesson.

"Each tree appears to have many twins. A few more months and we shall need to return for a harvest."

Thomas's wide grin affirms his agreement with Francis's observation.

The boys begin to make a turn to the south. They soon pick up what appears to be a dirt path. This is actually an ancient road, one of the remaining artifacts of the Roman Empire. The wider-than-normal dirt road, with its characteristic camber, heads directly in the direction of the church. The boys continue up a slight grade that increases for a few hundred yards. As they proceed, they can see in the distance the lights of the Old Church, which sits upon the highest point of the surrounding land.

"Father has shared that the ancient missionaries traveled this road, bringing the Gospel to Britain, perhaps as early as the seventh century."

"I have heard of it often as well, Francis."

The boys make their way to the front of the Old Church. It is a simple structure, a three-story straight-run design of approximately eighty feet in length and forty feet in width, completely made of brick. The entrance is through the side of a bell tower standing nearly forty feet high.

"Thomas."

Francis motions for Thomas to look up at the bell tower. Thomas responds,

"Beautiful glasswork."

Francis acknowledges his observation. The boys don't realize it, but the glass- and brickwork of the building dates back to the fourteenth century.

They enter the church and find themselves standing at the nave.[50] Realizing that the service is well underway, the boys take a seat near the rear of the room.

---

[50] The central approach to the high altar.

Immediately the entire congregation of thirty people stand to their feet. In unison, they begin to sing,

> "Rejoice, the Lord is King!
> Your Lord and King adore;
> Mortals, give thanks and sing,
> And triumph evermore.
> Lift up your heart,
> Lift up your voice; rejoice;
> Again I say, rejoice."[51]

At the far end of the nave, a tall, thin man dressed as a Wesleyan itinerant raises his hands as he sings. This is Henry Venn. Several men around him also raise their hands and voices to heaven. Francis comments to Thomas,

"This is most remarkable. Such a sweet sound."

Francis enjoys the moment. He too stands as the congregation begins the second verse,

> "Jesus the Savior reigns,
> The God of truth and love;
> When He had purged our stains,
> He took his seat above.
> Lift up your heart,
> Lift up your voice; rejoice;
> Again I say, rejoice."

The voices of the gathering grow louder and more jubilant as the hymn progresses. The boys' experience is completely different from anything they have encountered in a church before. Although they slightly lag the congregation as they try to grasp the lyrics of the song, they find themselves standing and singing as loudly and joyfully as their fellow worshipers.

The hymn ends and all remain standing. Henry Venn walks toward the altar at the front of the sanctuary and ascends the pulpit.

"Glory to God; mercy to me, a sinner."

"Oh no . . ."

Francis frantically looks about the seats that he and Thomas occupied moments before.

"Francis, you act as if you have lost something."

"I have . . . the bird."

As soon as Francis completes his sentence, nature's music begins.

> "Puk, puk, puk. Chip, chip, qui'd-qui'd qui'd, qui'd-qui'd-qui'd.
> Puk, puk, puk. Chip, chip, qui'd-qui'd qui'd, qui'd-qui'd-qui'd."

---

[51] Charles Wesley hymn "Rejoice, the Lord is King," 1746.

"Thomas, where is the bird?"

Thomas has no idea. In a panic, the boys search the area around their feet. They simultaneously bend down, bumping heads.

"Ow!"   "Ow!"

"Thomas, you must . . ."

"Puk, puk, puk. Chip, chip, qui'd-qui'd, qui'd, qui'd-qui'd-qui'd.

Puk, puk, puk. Chip, chip, qui'd-qui'd, qui'd, qui'd-qui'd-qui'd."

In the raised pulpit, Pastor Venn lifts his hands toward heaven.

At this, the bird appears from the row of seats in front of Thomas and Francis. The creature promptly flies to the pulpit and perches within inches of Pastor Venn, on the beautiful oak-wood rail that surrounds the top of the hand-crafted speaker's stand.

"Puk, puk, puk. Chip, chip, qui'd-qui'd qui'd, qui'd-qui'd-qui'd.

Puk, puk, puk. Chip, chip, qui'd-qui'd qui'd, qui'd-qui'd-qui'd.

Puk, puk, puk. Chip, chip, qui'd-qui'd qui'd, qui'd-qui'd-qui'd.

Puk, puk, puk. Chip, chip, qui'd-qui'd qui'd, qui'd-qui'd-qui'd."

Thomas looks to Francis.

"Francis, shall we leave?"

Francis has no reply. He looks to the people around the church. No one is saying a word.

Pastor Venn begins,

"As the songbird sings of Your splendor, Almighty Father, we are reminded that if we fail to praise You, even the rocks and the birds shall cry out."

"Puk, puk, puk. Chip, chip, qui'd-qui'd qui'd, qui'd-qui'd-qui'd.

Puk, puk, puk. Chip, chip, qui'd-qui'd qui'd, qui'd-qui'd-qui'd.

Puk, puk, puk. Chip, chip, qui'd-qui'd qui'd, qui'd-qui'd-qui'd.

Puk, puk, puk. Chip, chip, qui'd-qui'd qui'd, qui'd-qui'd-qui'd."

With this last chorus complete, the bird flies to the north side of the church. Several of the worshipers smile as the feathered creature wings above them. A young girl of seven waves her arm in an attempt to catch the passer-by. The bird decides to land on the window ledge beside a young man—a rather handsome young man.

The slender individual is Richard Whatcoat. He gently rises from his seat, his mannerisms smooth and quiet—so smooth and quiet that the bird instantly hops onto his extended pointer finger.

Confident that the winged visitor is content, Richard slowly turns and makes his way toward Francis and Thomas. Along the way, the bird cranes its neck to take several genial looks at his escort, almost as if to say, "How are you doing today, Richard?"

Francis and Thomas watch the proceedings, each struggling with the embarrassment of causing a disturbance. Francis nervously taps the edge of his seat, occasionally venturing a glance at the others in attendance. Uncomfortable, he lowers his eyes toward the back side of the pew in front of him. Thomas, he notes, is also diligently staring at nothing.

Richard approaches the pair.

"Your beautiful companion is searching for you."

Richard, nine years older and six inches taller than Francis, extends his long, thin arm and offers the bird to Francis. The uncertain Francis places both hands forward to receive the creature. The bird doesn't hesitate; it hops into Francis's cupped hands. He quickly secures the bird there for the rest of the church service.

The All Saints congregation is happy that Francis has regained the bird. They return their attention to the pulpit, where Pastor Venn has patiently watched the proceedings. He once again raises his hands.

"Almighty Father . . ."

Upon the completion of Pastor Venn's prayer, the congregation surrounds Francis and Thomas. The atmosphere of the occupants inside the church has become one of genuine fellowship. Each individual has not only approached and welcomed the young boys, but has also warmly invited the boys to return.

The men of the congregation are quick to discover and admire that Francis is working at the Old Mill Forge. One gentleman, Mr. Jonathan Turton, a direct descendent of Josiah Turton, invites the boys back to his home for a late-night snack. Francis responds,

"We appreciate the offer, but we must be going; I've to awake by four in the morning."

Francis's declining of the offer doesn't deter Mr. Turton.

"Thomas, are you employed?"

Thomas is quick to answer,

"Not at the moment, sir. I must complete my studies before Father will allow me to apprentice."

"I would like to make you an offer. I will need help in a couple of months, help with harvesting my many fruit trees. Do you think you can spare a couple of weeks to lend a hand?"

Thomas looks to Francis; Francis has that wide grin again. It doesn't escape the notice of Mr. Turton.

"Plenty of fruit to take home to the family . . ."

The generous offer has Thomas thinking, and Francis can almost read his friend's mind. Thomas inquires,

"Plenty to share with family and friends?"

Thomas's question amuses Mr. Turton.

"I suppose the bird won't eat too much."

The boys are silent. Mr. Turton furthers the deal,

"Yes, plenty for your friends, those that fly and those that walk . . ."

Thomas is relieved. At this, Richard Whatcoat approaches the two young men.

"Francis and Thomas, I shall be heading your direction this evening. May I travel with you?"

The stately young man waits for the boys' reply. Francis thinks to himself, *Thomas and I sought answers from the pastor, but the bird episode has dwindled my courage to ask.* He responds,

"It would be an honor."

In the thickening night air, Francis and Thomas make their way with their new friend, Richard Whatcoat. Richard is a polite young man, free of envy and pride. Words of encouragement are a regular part of his conversation. Francis and Thomas are easily drawn to Richard.

"As sober a life as I have led, I continue to struggle with the fact that my heart is hostile toward God."

Richard's comment comes as a surprise to the pair; it also directs the conversation in a deeper direction. Francis offers his feelings,

"I too struggle with God; the Scriptures are plain enough, but I sense the imprisonment of my soul. I deeply sense it."

"Francis, you and I are saying the same thing. For a time, I was confident that my good work toward God and others was the direct path. Through the efforts of men like Venn, I realized that the Scriptures call my good works 'filthy rags.' Pastor Venn portrays it well: 'My heart has enmity with God.' At times I forget the damage my sin nature has caused, my eternal separation from my loving Creator."

Francis quickly responds,

"And separation from our fellow man. How can our hearts which long for God be antagonistic toward God? I sense the truth of this also. Thomas and I talk of it regularly. Our lives are well ordered, but still we are imprisoned. It is the sole reason that we ventured to the Old Church this evening."

Richard walks along, quietly pondering the honest confession that Francis has offered. Francis and Thomas wait for his reply.

"Puk, puk, puk."

The bird in Francis's hand trills a few sounds as it squirms. Richard smiles as he offers,

"Your beautiful companion calls."

Francis nods his head in agreement. With a gentle movement, he opens the palms of his hands. Immediately the bird is airborne, gone into the night air. Disappointed, Francis comments,

"With no effort, he is free."

The trio look to each other as they consider Francis's comment about the bird.

***

The early-morning fog obscures the familiar landmarks of the Old Mill Farm. It is the Sabbath once again. The men of the forge slowly make their way to the rugged chapel. Inside, Alexander Mather gives his good-morning embrace to each man as he enters the makeshift church. With each hug, he adds his greeting,

"Guid mornin'."

The men numbly raise their hands as if to say, "Likewise." The preacher's thick Scottish accent is nearly incomprehensible to them.

Mather makes his way to the front of the room. The cold, damp air causes each man to huddle close as he prepares for the itinerant's message. With Bibles in hand, the men in desperate need of sleep bow their heads in preparation for prayer.

"Almighty Faither, we enjoin our hearts to Ya's. May the words of my mouth br'ding the ultimate healin' of the Savior."

The men settle in for the message.

"Ah' ask one thing of ya' men gathered on this damp mornin': to believe now, to come to Christ now, wit'out any other qualification than a sense of ya' own sinfulness and helplessness.

"Do ya' desire to end the enmity that ya' heart possesses against God? The solution to ya' predicament is simple: to believe. Place ya' faith in the One who died for all the wrong in ya' life, the One who longs to embrace ya' wit' a far greater hug than ya' received this mornin'."

At this last statement, a slight smile is evident on the faces of the men.

"Again Ah' ask of ya', believe now, and do not put it off. Come to the Savior; He has given ya' the qualifications necessary to overcome ya' sinfulness . . ."

Enmity with God. These words of Pastor Mather' seem to dance in Francis's mind. *These were the same words used by Richard Whatcoat one week ago.* Francis's thoughts bring unexpected comfort to him. *I feel near to you, God. So near.*

With the service complete and his Bible tucked under his right arm, Francis races back to his cabin. Pastor Mather and the others watch Francis as he runs across the Old Mill property. Pastor Mather gives a slight smile, pleased with the development, *even if Fr'dancis failed to bid farewell.*

Inside his cabin, Francis shuffles through some papers piled on his bed.

"Found it!"

He places several sheets between the pages of his Bible. He's off again.

He rushes from the cabin and heads for the heath and, ultimately, the Asbury home.

At the Asbury cottage, Francis quickly makes his way up the brick steps to the front door. He bursts into the main room of the house.

"Mother?"

"Father?"

No reply. Finding the home empty, he heads through the back door. He rushes down the steps outdoors, aiming for Joseph's barn.

In the barn, Francis pulls up an oak-wood block, placing it near the exterior wall of the structure. He sits down, pulls his legs up close, and lodges his head between his raised knees. In silence, he begins to pray,

> *Almighty Father, today I have received such blessing, blessing more than I can fathom. Today a sinner was brought near to You. So near to You that I am forever changed. I thank You for this overwhelming privilege.*

The opening of the barn's entry door causes Francis to cease his prayer. He raises his eyes and spots a familiar face.

"Thomas offered that you would be here."

The young man is William Emery, the friend of Thomas Ault.

"Will you pray with me, William?"

"Of course, Francis."

William reaches for an oak block. With one quick move, his short, stocky hands pull it over in front of Francis. He kneels before the block, bending forward and placing his elbows onto the wood. The two young men are silent as they bow their heads.

Francis begins,

> "My beloved Creator, my emotions are awakened from their slumber. For a time, You have pursued me, patiently waiting for me to turn toward and not away from You. This very day, You have not only awakened my emotions, You have brought to life something much deeper, as if my entire being is satisfied in You."

For roughly two minutes, the pair remains silent. The only sounds are the occasional shifting of position, as William's knees grow tired of remaining in the bent position. In time, William realizes that Francis is also moving. He raises his eyes to view Francis wiping away tears.

The pair instinctively rises from prayer together.

"Francis, what has transpired? You seem ablaze with excitement."

"Much more than mere excitement; today I was brought to Jesus Christ, who graciously justifies my guilty soul through faith in His precious blood."

William's face brings forth a beautiful smile, a very full smile. His clean white teeth gleam as his eyes express an uncontrollable abandon.

"Francis, I am thrilled to hear. Thomas is correct; you truly are set apart."

Must Jesus bear the cross alone,
And all the world go free?
No, there's a cross for everyone,
And there's a cross for me.

Thomas Shepherd[52]

Dividing the gentle nation of Ireland almost completely east and west is the majestic River Shannon, the river that draws its name from the Celtic goddess, Siona. There are two well-known versions of the legend. One tells of a brave woman who broke custom by catching and eating one of the large salmon that consistently return to the waterway from the open sea each autumn. Another story tells of an audacious female who dove deep into the well of knowledge at the source of the Shannon, again an act that went against the norm. The common element of the stories is the bold rebel breaking with tradition and eventually heading westward. In one account, she is forever searching at sea; in the other, dead from drowning.

From its origin in the northern county of Cavan to its terminus at Limerick, the beauty and stillness of the two-hundred-mile-long river embodies the welcoming nature of the island nation located to England's northwest. This longest river in Ireland emerges from a small pool on the slopes of the beautiful mountain known as Cuilcagh. Along its meandering path southward, the waterway interacts with three large lakes, one of them the third largest in Ireland: Lough Derg, the final body of water along the river's course. The remaining two lakes are Lough Ree and Lough Allen. Each of these bodies of water supports an abundant array of plants and wildlife.

It is around the peaceful lakes of the River Shannon that the rare blue-eyed grass grows in abundance. Its dense iris-like clumps, driven to freely wave in all directions by the summer lakeshore winds, provide a captivating sight in the early mornings of July and August. During these months, after sunrise, the tiny star-like purple-blue and white flowers begin to open. From a distance, the tiny yellow centers of the cerulean blooms appear as a gathering of shy little eyes, peeking in all directions. The reeds stand tall and erect in the watery meadows that make up the slough of the river, magnificent sentinels proclaiming that autumn isn't far away. The proclamation of the reeds fills the sudden silence that arrives in mid-

---

[52] Thomas Shepherd hymn "Must Jesus Bear the Cross Alone?," 1693.

July, a rush of quiet signaling the end of the mating season for the spring and summer resident birds.

It is these gentle glances of the small perennial flowers which the blue-eyed rider on horseback enjoyed a handful of months ago, as he traveled from the town of Terryhoogan in eastern Ireland to his homeland in the northwestern portion of the country, the town of Drumsna in the picturesque county of Leitrim. The rider is Robert Strawbridge.

Robert slows his horse to a stop and dismounts. As he stands alongside his chestnut-colored escort, he fumbles with the saddlebag attached behind the cantle[53] of the saddle. He gently removes a mysterious gift, wrapped in brown shop-paper. Unfurling the plain cover, he smiles; *a perfect offering.* His thought broadens the smile on his attractive face. He carefully wraps the present once again and returns it to its safe chamber.

In the year 1732, Robert was born in the town of Gortconnellan, Drumsna. The town's name means "the ridge over the swimming place." It is here that the southeastern flowing River Shannon makes an almost ninety-degree turn, proceeding northeast. As if having a mind of its own, the flowing body of water unexpectedly turns again, this time heading north. It eventually turns back to the east, then finally regains its original course toward the south. The resulting curve of the backtracking waterway creates a natural loop blessed with some of the country's most fertile and wooded lands. From these abundant furrows, the gentle sloping of the land up from the winding river culminates in the stunning majesty of the Leitrim mountains. Adding to this visual crescendo are the numerous islands of the waterway, a resounding example of divine artistry.

Robert grew up on a farm with a privileged view of the river, the land a gift from his direct ancestor almost 150 years ago. Robert is from a line of the planted Englishmen placed in Ireland by the English King James. To the Catholic in Ireland, this displacement of Irish settlers by the Anglican King amounted to a military and religious conquest. Others astutely point out that the infiltration by the English leadership was an effort to modernize an archaic, even brutal, society. Regardless of one's opinion of good or bad, the transplanting of the English settlers not only ended centuries of killings by feudal clans, it also brought development of several new cities along the river. The town of Drumsna became one of these new urban areas.

---

[53] The rear part of a saddle.

Robert grew up in an Anglican household, the second son born to his parents. As a gesture to their disgruntled Irish neighbors, Robert's father named him after his maternal grandfather, in keeping with the long-held Irish tradition of naming the oldest son after the paternal grandfather and the next son after the maternal grandfather. From an affluent family, Robert has gained the benefits of an education; he is intelligent and eloquent in speech. He is also a strong man, a carpenter by trade, his sturdy frame topping out at just under six feet tall. His shy but brilliant eyes highlight his shoulder-length hair and handsome face. His gentle smile has warmed the hearts of many, including the one who has given him reason to return to his homeland from the distant town on Ireland's western side.

It was in July that Robert began the more than seventy-mile trek on horseback to see his father. Robert had been away for some time. This summer of 1758 capped off a two-year spiritual journey for the young tradesman from Drumsna; in 1756 he had experienced a Christian conversion. Fitting with Robert's personality, his experience was not a common one, taking place under the guidance of an unlikely mentor, Laurence Coughlan.

Unlike Robert, Coughlan was more in keeping with the traditional Irishmen of the eighteenth century, a real Hibernian. Born in Drumsna to a Roman Catholic family, Coughlan had not experienced the benefits of privilege that Robert had; he was a man of little education. Despite his limited beginnings, he found himself transformed by the words of the Bible, taught by the preaching of Wesley's itinerants in the year 1753. His new birth inspired him to vigorously study the Word, eventually leading him to preach to the inhabitants of Drumsna. Within two years, Wesley had recruited him to join the itinerant ministry. A year after that, he was on his way to preach to the fishermen of Newfoundland.

Early in his ministry, one of Coughlan's first hometown converts was Robert's younger brother, Leonard. Coughlan's evangelistic efforts toward the sixteen-year-old touched the heart of his older brother. In keeping with Robert's "all in" approach to life, he abandoned his trade and started to preach.

His independent spirit soon became evident. His Anglican experience, much like Coughlan's Catholic experience, gave Robert the opinion that he wanted no part of institutionalized religion. Within months of setting out to preach, Robert's zeal for reaching the lost souls of Leitrim County caused him to regularly distribute communion and baptize new converts. It didn't matter to Robert that John Wesley strictly forbade the Wesleyan itinerants from distributing the sacraments. Even if it meant going against the norm, Robert was determined to bring the entire Christian experience to each person he met.

This distribution of the sacraments by those who were not ordained did not originate with the individualistic Robert. A few years before, many of the new converts in Ireland who wished to preach had themselves licensed under the Toleration Act of 1689. Awarded with this provision, men like Thomas Walsh, along with the brothers Charles and Edward Perronet, set out on their own, boldly distributing the Lord's Supper and offering baptism to the faithful.

Despite the unconventional individuals who preceded Robert, the Anglican and Wesleyan faithful in Drumsna considered Robert's individualistic approach too zealous. Within a few months of his initial efforts, they asked him to leave. Unshaken by the resistance, he collected his horse and went on a preaching tour of the neighboring counties of Sligo and Kilmore, ending up in the county of Armagh and the town of Terryhoogan.

In Terryhoogan, Robert was the frequent guest of a wealthy farming family, the Balances. In addition to their agricultural pursuits, the three Balance brothers owned more than one-third of the local rental properties. In fact, it was the Balance family, committed to their Wesleyan faith, who invited Robert to come to Terryhoogan from the nearby town of Tandragee. They admired his preaching as well as his carpentry talents, especially his ability to construct thatched roofs.

Before his encounter with the Balances, Robert's arrival in Tandragee forced him to take a part-time job as a carpenter, erecting buildings. The Balance family, highly active in the local Methodist society at Terryhoogan—the "mother church" of the Wesleyan movement in eastern Ireland—had heard about the vibrant preacher from the west. As soon as they could, they traveled to the neighboring town of Tandragee to hear Robert preach. Pleased with what they heard, they invited the struggling preacher to their hometown, where Robert found an enthusiastic audience for his ministry. In addition to agreeing to make Terryhoogan a regular preaching stop, he accepted an offer to work on a special building project: the erection of an addition attached to the residence of John Balance. Considering the payment the family was offering, his decision to settle in Terryhoogan was an easy one.

Situated in a beautiful sloping meadow, the Balance home is typical of the local architecture. A stone foundation supports an earthen floor and eighteen-inch-thick mud and stone walls. Resting on the walls that provide coolness in the summer and secure heat in the winter, oak beams support a wood framework that is the foundation of the thatched roof made of rye and wheat stalks.

Eighteenth-century thatched roofs have changed little since they first came into prominence during the Middle Ages. Like the ancient craft, the process remains slow and laborious. As Robert has expressed to many a passerby, "It can take five thousand or more handfuls of straw to complete the average thatched roof."

Each handful of stalking material is first hand-cut from local sources. Next, the harvested straw is prepared for drying, laid flat, and tied into bundles. After drying, the bundles require trimming to the desired length, usually around three feet. After this preparatory process, the bundles are ready for installation onto the wood framework that will support the roofing material.

The key to a waterproof roof is in the slope of the roof's framework. The steeper the pitch, the more quickly the rain and snow will run off the roof, ensuring no infiltration. The average slope for proper waterproofing is between forty-five and sixty degrees. Bundle installation is from left to right and from the bottom roof edge up to the peak or ridgeline. The bundle rows overlap from one- to two-thirds of the bundle length. Over the decades, installation of multiple layers stacked more than three feet deep leads to the attractive, thick appearance of the roofs.

The need to hire someone like Robert came as a surprise to the Balance brothers. Unexpectedly, the first carpenter they hired remained only long enough to build the foundation and walls of the tiny addition. One morning he failed to appear for work. After several days of the hired man's absence, they realized he had left town. They struggled with the abandonment; *had they done something to offend the gentleman?* It wasn't until the recommendation of a friend to go see the fiery preacher in Tandragee that they experienced any relief from their loss.

In Tandragee, the three brothers—William, George, and John—first found Robert not in a pulpit, but on a roof, surrounded by bundles of thatch. After polite introductions, light conversation, and discovering that the preacher was running low on funds, they had to force themselves not to ask the obvious question. They seemed to silently agree that they would first hear him preach.

In the hearing, they were not disappointed. His eloquent manner of speech and occasional bursts of passion for the subject, added to his charismatic appearance and divine inspiration, were unmistakably an irresistible and winning combination. The Balance brothers were convinced that not only could he help them complete their little building project, he could also easily become a regular itinerant for the healthy Wesleyan society in Terryhoogan. After the sermon, they asked the inevitable question. Robert did not hesitate; he would follow them to Terryhoogan.

The project the Balance brothers had in mind was a prophet's chamber, modeled on the idea found in the Bible in the second book of Kings. The story is told of the Shunammite woman and her husband who regularly entertained the prophet Elisha as he ministered throughout the countryside. The woman said to her husband, "Look now, I know that this is a holy man of God, who passes by us regularly. Please, let us make a small upper room on the wall; and let us put a bed for him there, and a table and a chair and a lampstand; so it will be, whenever he comes to us, he can turn in there. "[54]

Although the Balance addition differed slightly from the chamber in the Bible story, being built on the ground level in lieu of upstairs, the nine-foot-long, seven-foot-wide, six-foot-high room would be enough to hold a small bed, a lamp, a table, and a chair.

His initial stay in Terryhoogan found Robert preaching three nights each week. During six days each week, he worked on the Balance addition. Robert was thankful he had found kindred spirits in the Balance family, and even more thankful for the building project. It was a simple task to a man of Robert's talents; before long he was well on his way to completing the roof. To Robert, *things could not be better.* He was free to preach to a highly receptive audience and he was also gainfully employed. However, he was mistaken; things were about to be better.

Within a few days of his arrival in Terryhoogan, Robert met a young lady by the name of Elizabeth Piper. She was an outgoing young woman, and somewhat high-spirited; she was attractive in form and considerate by nature. Most important to Robert, she and her family were devoted Wesleyans.

Their chance meeting was unavoidable. From the Balance residence, where Robert toiled daily on the thatched roof, a cobblestone walkway led to the house next door, where Elizabeth resided with her family. After several visits and deliveries of food and refreshments to Robert, he fell in love with the girl next door. Knowing her daily schedule, he would plan his work to finish a row precisely at the expected time of her arrival. Without fail, the plan was successful. As she would be gracefully making her way along the stone path, Robert would begin his last batch of stalks. As he made his way down the ladder, he would fight his nervous feelings by doing his best to think of a cheerful greeting.

It would have saved Robert much anxiety if he had only realized that the feelings of attraction were mutual. For Elizabeth, the godly preacher with the admirable carpentry skills was hard to overlook, especially in light of those shy eyes that gleamed so appealingly when he allowed them to. When he also began sharing that charming smile, it wasn't long before she, too, was "all in."

Robert's meeting with his father this summer was to ask his permission to marry. The elder Strawbridge had hesitated at first. He knew well that his son didn't take commitments lightly. He had watched as Robert grew in the faith, the faith that led him so far away. His strongest advice to his son was found in the Bible: "When a man has taken a new wife, he shall not go out to war or be charged with any business; he shall be free at home one year, and bring happiness to his

---

[54] 2 Kings chapter 4, verses 9–10.

wife whom he has taken."[55] His father was adamant that Robert take time off from preaching to be with his bride.

Now, as Robert rides along, the advice of his father replays in his mind. He finds great joy as he daydreams of his plans with Elizabeth. He is confident that he can put aside the time to spend several months enjoying the fruits of their relationship. Shall they make a temporary home in the prophet's chamber, or shall they pursue settling down elsewhere? Should the two of them do as many young couples and sell all their personal items and sail west for America? This is 1758, and the excessive government taxation is stifling many young people's ability to gain the necessary foundation that would ensure even a minimal lifestyle. These apprehensive young men and women are choosing to risk all as they pack up and leave their beautiful homeland.

Robert thinks to himself, *the resulting tasks from the move would easily provide for one year away from the ministry—an entire year planning, embarking, and setting up home in a new land.*

Although these thoughts are at times deeper than he wants to consider, they are truly a comfort—for the gentle time of summer has passed; it is November and the days are short. He has long left the beauty and comfort of a summer along the River Shannon. His journey takes him into the heart of the island nation, and into the heart of eastern Ireland. The riding is hard as he traverses the rocky, irregular mountains and terrains of the counties Cavan and Monaghan. The numerous inland lakes decorated with their striking well-wooded landscapes somewhat lighten the arduous ordeal. In Robert's mind, these evidences of divine Creation help to shorten the journey.

He once again stops his horse. Spinning around in the saddle, again he reaches to check on his saddlebag. He eyes the brown shop-paper. Convinced that the item in the leather bag is safe, he spurs his horse forward.

As Robert and horse approach the town of Tandragee, the landscape begins to level out. Looking to the east, he can see the endless farmlands that will lead him to his Elizabeth. Horse and rider pause. In the distance, a small herd of red deer make their way toward a brook. Robert marvels at the creatures as each animal cautiously tightens its stance, turning to the right, then to the left. Convinced of their safety, the entire group steps to the water and lowers their heads to take a much-needed drink.

---

[55] Deuteronomy chapter 24, verse 5.

Robert raises his eyes to the mid-morning sky; again, it is grey. He surmises that the sun has been up for only two hours, barely rising by eight o'clock. He knows he shouldn't rest for too long, for he longs to see his dear Elizabeth. The autumn season limits his daylight, for the skies will darken by four o'clock this afternoon. Adding to the gloomy season, the sun has failed to show itself for the last two days. This time of year, it is counted a blessing if the clouds clear for more than an hour or two each day. The weather, which strives to compete with the glowing thoughts that eddy in Robert's head, is a constant drizzle, with temperatures hovering not far above freezing. Adding to this, the chilling and constant winds of ten to twelve knots from the North Atlantic Ocean as it curls north of the island nation have buffeted the horse and rider for the past four days.

Nevertheless, Robert is undaunted by the challenging season. Within moments, he is urging his mount on toward Terryhoogan.

Robert indulges in the joy he is experiencing. He is happy to marry one whom he feels is the perfect complement for him, *God's chosen helpmate for me.* He gently reaches into his saddlebag, careful to maneuver around the item in shop-paper. Pushing it aside, he removes a one-page document neatly wrapped in white ribbon. His thick hands untie the ribbon, which he tucks firmly between his thigh and the saddle. He opens the rolled parchment, careful to make sure it is right-side up. The words on the page are handwritten in a beautiful style. Robert reads:

𝕴 **publish the banns of marriage between Robert Strawbridge of Drumsna, County Leitrim, and Elizabeth Piper of Terryhoogan, County Armagh. This is the first time of asking, if any of you know cause or just impediment why these two persons should not be joined together in Holy Matrimony, ye are to declare it.**

He raises his head from the wedding declaration his father prepared for him; an identical version awaits reading in the Strawbridge's hometown church in Drumsna. In the distance, he sees that he is coming upon familiar surroundings. As he finally enters the grounds of the Balance family farm, his horse whinnies as if realizing he is nearly home. Robert too breathes a deepened sigh as he catches sight of Elizabeth moving toward him. He hurries to wrap the paper as he brings the horse to a stop and dismounts.

Robert reaches into the saddlebag and gently replaces the holy document, once again careful not to damage the worn leather bag's other contents. The task completed, he turns and heads toward home. He quickens his pace on foot, and after two dozen strides, he is at the cobblestone walkway that joins the home of John Balance and the home of the Piper family. He has also reached Elizabeth.

The two embrace.

Robert enjoys the softness of her body. Even through several layers of dress and coverings that protect his dear Elizabeth from the cold, he can sense the tenderness of her frame. Their hug, as they each catch their breath, turns into a kiss. The gentle endearment pushes the cold away.

Robert pulls his lips from hers and looks into her glistening eyes.

"Eliz, I have missed you so."

With an uncontrollable smile, she gives a slight giggle.

Robert says with a laugh,

"The tip of your nose, how it rises slightly when you chuckle—I have missed that the most."

They both laugh, then kiss again.

The next three weeks seem like an eternity for the young couple. Each Sunday, the local priest reads the banns of marriage in the Terryhoogan parish of the Anglican Church of Ireland. With each reading, Robert and Eliz sit anxiously waiting for the awkward but welcomed silence that follows the reading. Each time, the result is the same: no objections to the marriage of Robert Strawbridge and Elizabeth Piper. They smile as they each grasp the other's hand more tightly, reading each other's thoughts: *We belong together.*

Robert and Elizabeth depart from this Sunday's service, welcoming the walk along the dirt road that leads to the Balance farm. These strolls together have become a joy to them both. Along this path they have shared their hopes and dreams, their likes and dislikes. Unlike previous times on this path, however, today carries special significance. Elizabeth raises the obvious question.

"However long until word arrives?"

Robert shrugs his shoulders.

"Cannot say; one week, perhaps two, and word shall arrive from Drumsna."

On three consecutive Sundays, the reading of the banns also occurs in Drumsna, as required by the 1753 Act of Lord Hardwicke. According to the ruling, marriages are legal only if the reading of the banns of marriage takes place on three consecutive Sundays in the churches of the bride and groom. These readings allow an opportunity for the congregations to give reasons that the intended bride and groom should not marry. If no oppositions occur, the couple may marry. Failure to comply with the act would result in the marriage being void in the eyes of the Anglican Church. Despite their eagerness to marry, Robert and Elizabeth must wait for word to arrive from the west. They plan to marry on Christmas day, only weeks away.

Marrying on Christmas day is a common custom. An eighteenth-century Anglican wedding is mostly a religious and legal event, with little in the way of ceremony. The bride and groom typically arrive at the local parish, worship in song, pray, say their vows, take communion, and go on their way. Only immediate family participates in the service. The couple hopes for clear weather and a sharing with those present of their love for each other and for God.

This Sunday is also significant in the fact that following the final reading of the banns, Robert and Elizabeth will dine with the Balance family. The mid-afternoon meal is an attempt by John Balance to calm the nerves of the anxious couple.

Standing next to each other on the front stoop of the Balance home, Elizabeth leans on Robert's arm. The pair has arrived on time, precisely at two o'clock. With his free arm, Robert raises his hand to knock on the door.

The lifting of the wood latch and the creaking of the oak door precede the words of the kind and generous John Balance.

"Robert, Eliz, before long you shall have answer."

Robert nods his head in sheepish agreement. Elizabeth is thankful that John has noticed their strain. John continues,

"Please do enter before the weather cools dinner."

The young couple chuckle as they thankfully enter the home.

The fireplace residing in the exact center of the main room easily warms the Balance residence. The home is evidence of a landed family.[56] The ceiling is high; visible are the hewn support beams—the structure that secures the thatched roof—and the large masonry stones that line the fireplace flue to the ceiling. The oversized fireplace, which also serves for cooking, provides ample heat for the main room's occupants.

Mrs. Balance invites the pair to sit. They each take a seat on the handmade oak chairs facing the fireplace hearth. John steps forward. Realizing the strain that Robert and Eliz are under, he decides to open with a story. With the crackling of the wood fire in the background and Mrs. Balance seating herself behind him, he stands in front of the anxious pair and begins,

> "When first it arrived it held such beauty and splendor, its artistry spreading in all directions as the foam of a freshly landed wave of the Atlantic. As for many, it would be some time before its value would emerge. The centerpiece of winter and the relief of a late summer harvest, the little tuber would come to the aid of the oat . . ."

John hangs on the letter "t."

---

[56] An English family that was given Irish lands.

"For some, a luxury bringing income, for others, necessity, for their lands had been taken; in either case, a bountiful fare. This earthly manna, considered inferior to crops of earlier days, is highly nutritious and gives robust reason for the survival of the past frigid peril."[57]

Rising from her chair, Mrs. Balance quietly makes her way behind her husband to tend to the boiling cauldron. The large three-legged iron pot stands atop the wood fire. Removing a cloth from her apron pocket, she wraps the material around the iron ladle that rests on the stone hearth adjacent to the fire. The hearth, expertly crafted, surrounds the oversized see-through fireplace in the shape of a circle. She lifts the utensil, places it into the bubbling stew, and stirs.

In the pot are additional evidences of a well-to-do family: farm-raised meat and wild game diced with carrots, turnips, leeks, and potatoes. The aroma rises on the gentle steam, filling the entire room. Mrs. Balance leans over the pot, drawing in both the pleasing smell and the embracing warmth.

John continues,

"Robert and Eliz, have you considered . . ."

With deliberate over-emphasis, he lifts his right arm straight out from his side. With his fingers stretched wide he moves his hand, arm fully extended, making an exaggerated arc. Midway through the flamboyant pattern, he closes a fist. The act terminates when he withdraws the closed hand, placing it into his coat pocket.

The young couple waits for what may be next, but nothing is forthcoming. John stands silent with his left hand hanging at his side and his right hand in his right side coat pocket.

Robert leans forward in his chair. Uncomfortable with the awkward pause of the storyteller, he struggles with placing his hands in a relaxed position. First, he tries to rest his hands on top of his thighs; this fails. Next, he moves his right hand under his thigh. This too becomes unsatisfactory. He decides to cross his arms in front of his chest. At this, he looks to Eliz. She appears relaxed, but has nothing to add. Her calm elevates Robert's frustration; he stands abruptly. With hands extended out from his sides and palms up, he bursts out,

"What of this, John? Are we to solve a riddle?"

Robert's outburst shocks Elizabeth, as well as Mrs. Balance, but John merely chuckles.

"My dear friend, as I mentioned when first you arrived, before long you shall have answer."

---

[57] The "little ice age" of 1650–1720, when temperatures were much lower than normal.

Robert forces his hands onto his hips. He shakes his head in disbelief and sits back in his chair, sliding back and releasing a huge breath that puffs wide the thin lips of his mouth and inflates his cheeks. Eliz lets out a slight laugh. She recalls that those were the precise words offered by John when Robert and she arrived, *before long you shall have answer.* She ponders, *was he foreshadowing this riddle from our arrival?*

Smiling at the young girl, and at his wife who has returned to her chair, John removes his right hand from the coat pocket. In it, he holds a potato.

Robert shakes his head again, this time finishing with shoulders slumped and eyes looking at the floor. He is obviously not approving. Eliz bursts into laughter.

Robert raises his eyes to catch Eliz laughing, which brings some comfort. He relaxes his countenance as he places both hands on his hips and raises his right leg to cross over his knee. John carries on undaunted.

> "Robert, are you aware of the efficiency of the potato? Harvest rarely takes more than two months. The lesser sorts can lease an acre or two, plant, gather, and sell in time to pay me my rent. I needn't remind you that the vegetable has aided in making me a wealthy man. Why, it has also helped to thicken my stews . . ."

Robert nods his head, this time in agreement, but his reply is tinged with sarcasm.

> "Yes, John, I acknowledge the blessed attributes of the sacred item you hold in your hand."

John smiles widely at Robert's brusque comment. He has come to realize that Robert is a man with a determined and sometimes fiery personality. He decides to continue the banter.

> "This is manna, for certain—a manna that appears below the ground, an earthly manna."

Robert stands, interrupting John's bold proclamation of the attributes of the potato.

> "I agree that the potato is an earthly manna, but shall it expedite that which I long for - -
> Permission from the west to marry?"

This time John cannot hold his reaction; he begins with a wide smile and then bursts into laughter, as does Eliz once again. Robert would rather continue experiencing satisfaction by furthering the point, but he finally gives in and smiles.

The three weeks that follow the dinner with the Balances are especially long for Robert and Eliz. Robert attempts to busy himself with final preparations of the prophet's chamber. His frustrations surface at times, especially when he runs short of reeds for the thatched roof. The slight outburst subsides when a resident of Terryhoogan comes to the rescue with a supply of dried rye reeds. The kind man easily recognizes Robert's nervousness about the impending marriage. The older gentleman even goes so far as to check back a time or two to ensure that Robert has no additional construction needs.

As for Elizabeth, she eagerly chooses to involve herself with the local Wesleyan society, attending to the sick and aged. This is her manner of bringing comfort to herself; she is bold in both proclaiming and living the teachings of Jesus.

Word finally arrives, just in time for the Christmas wedding. Robert's father, mother, and younger brother, Leonard, make the cross-country trek, arriving on the day that Robert completes the addition. The young couple is naturally overjoyed at their arrival. Over a plate of bread lovingly baked by Elizabeth in a turned-down cauldron, the extended family of five rejoices at the favorable results of the reading of the banns in Drumsna. They also rejoice in the fact that tomorrow is Christmas, the day of the wedding.

Christmas morning arrives after an anxious night. Robert awakes tired from several bouts with sleeplessness. Eliz too is weary; fitful sleep was her ordeal as well. Robert and his brother, father, and mother walk toward the Piper home. Unnoticed by the preoccupied Robert, it is a rare day—the sun has peeked through the grey December sky. As Robert's mother hums a Charles Wesley hymn, his father gains Robert's attention.

"The good Lord is smiling upon you, Robert."

Robert raises his eyes toward his father, who is looking skyward. Robert decides to take in the unusual occurrence. For the first time in several days he exhibits his handsome smile, the sun's reflection in his light-blue eyes adding to his attractive beam. He replies,

"He is indeed."

The family reaches the cobblestone path to the Piper residence. Suddenly, Robert diverts his course.

"Wait here."

He runs into the newly completed prophet's chamber. His mother and father, unsure of his detour, stand quietly waiting for him to emerge from the little building.

Robert is not gone for long. He returns and proceeds past the family without saying a word. The elder couple shrug their lack of understanding to each other and continue to follow their son. His mother offers,

"Something demands his attention."

"A little something for tonight. Traveled with me from Drumsna."

Robert's sharing brings a smile to his mother.

Within moments, all are standing at the front door of the Piper residence. Robert the junior is nervous. He didn't expect to be; this day has played in his mind on many occasions. He expected to stand tall and confident, but now he feels inadequate for the day's sacred task.

Inside, the members of the Piper household are hurrying to prepare for the day's cherished event. The knock on the front door of the home inspires her mother and father to give Elizabeth one last hug. Elizabeth is grateful. Her mother brushes away a slight tear on her daughter's cheek as they release to answer the door.

The door opens and both families stand silent, looking to each other. Robert is the first to react; he extends his hand to reach for Elizabeth. She instinctively holds out her hand and curtsies. Robert gently kisses her hand, then raises his head and offers the opening words of the day,

"My love, my heart trembles for you."

"As does my own."

Mr. Piper places his left arm around his wife's shoulders and pulls his teary-eyed partner close. The elder Strawbridges react in much the same manner. Mr. Piper offers an invitation,

"Shall we not come in?"

All enter the Piper residence. In the main room, several chairs sit in a semi-circle around a small oak table. The table is in front of a lit fireplace, and on top of the table is a worn Bible. The Bible is a treasured artifact from the time of Queen Elizabeth I, when she sought to convert the Irish Catholic faithful into the reformed church. Its faded covers contain the first Irish translation of the Scriptures, created by Bishop William Bedell of the Church of Ireland almost seventy-five years before.

The work is unique in that Bedell completed his translation before the 1641 Cromwell invasion; this delayed its publication. Bedell's death in 1642, and the confusion of the outbreak, delayed the final printing for more than thirty years. Robert Boyle, Earl of Cork and famed scientist who discovered Boyle's Law, completed the task of publishing this version of the Bible. Boyle was a religious man; the emphasis of his scientific work focused on the relationship between the power of the Creator and His creation. This man of science was adamantly against all dissertations that detracted from an appreciation of God's power in Creation. He regularly gave lectures for proving the Christian religion against what he termed "notorious infidels." He completed the printing of the Bedell Bible in 1685.

Mr. Piper stands at the table and nervously fumbles with the carved wood cover of the Bible. Ceasing his fidgeting, he raises his head and begins,

"Please do sit. I have prepared a fire."

Each takes a seat. Mr. Piper continues,

"On this glorious morning, my heart is warmed not by the fire burning in the pit, but from a fire that gently kindles through the impending bond that will be forged today. Mrs. Piper and I count it a privilege to give our daughter . . ."

Mr. Piper's voice falters. He once again looks to the table and fiddles with the Bible. In his pause, he tightens his lips to fight back his deep emotion. It is a difficult task, but he is soon able to continue.

". . . our loving daughter, the child we have raised, the young girl who bounced from chair to chair inside our home, the woman who is the apple of our eye and who today will partake in the sacred ceremony of Holy Matrimony. I ask that we all stand and sing a hymn."

All rise from their seats. Standing next to each other, Robert and Eliz each grasp the other's hand. Mr. Piper begins,

"Author of the peace unknown,
Lover of my friend and me,
Who of twain hast made us one,
One preserve us still in Thee . . ."

Robert and Elizabeth look to each other. Their uncontrollable smiles convey their deepest feelings for each other. They raise their eyes to heaven as they join with their parents in the Charles Wesley hymn.

"All our heightened blessings bless,
Crown our hopes with full success.

"Center of our hearts Thou art,
End of our enlarged desires;
Stamp Thine image on our heart,
Fill us now with holy fires.
Cemented by love Divine,
Seal our souls forever Thine.

"All our works in Thee be wrought,
Leveled at one common aim,
Every word and every thought,
Pure in the refining flame.
Lead us through the paths of peace,
On to perfect holiness.

"Let us both together rise,

> To Thy glorious life restored,
> Here regain our Paradise,
> Here prepare to meet our Lord,
> Here enjoy the earnest given,
> Travel hand in hand to heaven."[58]

Robert and Elizabeth both draw comfort from the singing. Viewing their immediate families joining together to praise God is a unifying experience for them. The couple once again turn to each other and smile. Robert mouths his words to Eliz: *I love you.*

Mr. Strawbridge raises the question of the day.

"Shall we make our way to the Divine Service?"

All agree it is time. Mr. Strawbridge interrupts,

"Before we depart, I propose we give thanks to the Lord for this blessed day."

All bow their heads to pray. The elder Robert walks to the table. Standing next to Mr. Piper, he lifts the aged Bible and opens to the book of Psalms, carefully paging through the historic printing. Arriving at the intended text, he begins to read.

"Blessed is every one that feareth the Lord; that walketh in his ways.

"For thou shalt eat the labour of thine hands: happy shalt thou be, and it shall be well with thee.

"Thy wife shall be as a fruitful vine by the sides of thine house: thy children like olive plants round about thy table.

"Behold, that thus shall the man be blessed that feareth the Lord. The Lord shall bless thee out of Zion: and thou shalt see the good of Jerusalem all the days of thy life. Yea, thou shalt see thy children's children, and peace upon Israel.[59]

"Glory be to the Father, and to the Son, and to the Holy Ghost, as it was in the beginning, is now, and ever shall be, world without end. Amen."

The parish church that services Terryhoogan is in Tandragee and is part of the Ballymore Parish. The stone building dates to the mid-seventeenth century, although the church's congregation goes as far back as the fourteenth century. Inside the building, Robert and Elizabeth stand before the church warden. He is a rather tall man, with a bald pate. Elizabeth's nervousness abates slightly as she considers, *the man's thinning grey hair is too long at the ears.* This thought soon fades as she focuses on the day's most important event. The church warden escorts the families down the church's main aisle, past the handful of local residents who

---

[58] Charles Wesley's "Hymns for Christian Friends: 16," 1749.

[59] Psalm 128, King James Version.

have decided to view the wedding. He instructs the wedding party to stop, facing toward the Lord's table. All stand still and await his words.

Alongside the couple are Mr. and Mrs. Strawbridge, their son Leonard, and Mr. and Mrs. Piper. The groom and his family stand on the right, the bride and her family on the left. Walking from an adjacent room, the Anglican priest approaches the couple. He pauses in front of them, stopping at a small table with a Bible lying on its top. He raises his hands and begins,

> "Dearly beloved, we are gathered together here in the sight of God, and in the face of this congregation, to join together this man and this woman in holy matrimony; which is an honorable estate, instituted of God in the time of man's innocence, signifying unto us the mystical union that is betwixt Christ and His Church; which holy estate Christ adorned and beautified with His presence, and the first miracle that He wrought, in Cana of Galilee; and is commended of Saint Paul to be honorable among all men: and therefore is not by any to be enterprized, nor taken in hand, unadvisedly, lightly, or wantonly, to satisfy men's carnal lusts and appetites, like brute beasts that have no understanding; but reverently, discreetly, advisedly, soberly, and in the fear of God; duly considering the causes for which matrimony was ordained."

Staring straight ahead, Robert finds solace in the biblical significance of this ceremony. The slight pounding of his heart is lessened by the thought that from long ago, men and women have come together in this holy union; *very long ago, since Adam and Eve.* His thought is interrupted as the priest continues,

> "Considering the causes for which matrimony was ordained, first, it was ordained for the procreation of children, to be brought up in the fear and nurture of the Lord, and to the praise of His holy Name. Secondly, it was ordained for a remedy against sin, and to avoid fornication; that such persons as have not the gift of continence[60] might marry, and keep themselves undefiled members of Christ's body. Thirdly, it was ordained for the mutual society, help, and comfort, that the one ought to have of the other, both in prosperity and adversity. Into which holy estate these two persons present come now to be joined. Therefore if any man can shew[61] any just cause why they may not lawfully be joined together, let him now speak, or else hereafter forever hold his peace."

An older gentleman in a pew near the back of the church clears his throat.

---

[60] Self-restraint and abstinence.

[61] Show.

Robert's emotions change instantly. He spins toward the individual and catches the senior citizen closing his eyes and dropping his chin on his chest. The clearing of his throat was the catching of the saliva that collected while dozing off. Robert is relieved. His father turns toward his son.

"The Lord is shining upon you this day, Robert."

His father's comment is clearly meant to lighten the moment for his nervous and sometimes over-reactive son. Robert nods his head in agreement, but he fails to smile. The priest focuses on Robert and Elizabeth.

> "I require and charge you both, as ye will answer at the dreadful day of judgment, when the secrets of all hearts shall be disclosed, that if either of you know any impediment, why ye may not be lawfully joined together in matrimony, ye do now confess it. For be ye well assured that so many as are coupled together otherwise than God's Word doth allow, are not joined together by God; neither is their matrimony lawful."

Both Robert and Elizabeth shake their heads in the negative. The priest now looks toward Robert.

> "Wilt thou have this woman to thy wedded wife, to live together after God's ordinance in the holy estate of matrimony? Wilt thou love her, comfort her, honor and keep her, in sickness and in health; and forsaking all others, keep thee only unto her, so long as ye both shall live?"

Robert leans forward; with a shaky voice he replies,

> "I shall."

The priest nods his head in agreement and looks to Elizabeth.

> "Wilt thou have this man to thy wedded husband, to live together after God's ordinance in the holy estate of matrimony? Wilt thou obey him, and serve him, love, honor and keep him, in sickness and in health; and forsaking all others, keep thee only unto him, so long as ye both shall live?"

Without hesitation, and with a volume slightly louder than expected, she responds,

> "I shall."

The priest smiles at her enthusiasm.

> "Who giveth this ready woman to be married to this man?"
> "I do."

Upon his reply, Mr. Piper reaches across to take Robert's right hand and place Elizabeth's right hand into it. He gently backs away to return to the side of his wife.

The priest clears his throat and proceeds.

> "Robert, face Elizabeth; grasp hands and repeat after me: I, Robert, take thee, Elizabeth, to be my wedded wife."

"I, Robert, take thee, Elizabeth, to be my wedded wife."

"To have and to hold . . ."

"To have and to hold . . ."

The vows continue, as Robert promises from this day forward to remain faithful to Elizabeth for better, for worse, for richer, for poorer, in sickness and in health; to love and to cherish, "till death us do part."

"According to God's ordinance . . ."

"According to God's ordinance . . ."

"And thereto I plight thee my troth."[62]

"And thereto I plight thee my troth."

Upon completion, the priest has Elizabeth recite the vows. Facing Robert, she completes the Solemnization of Matrimony requirement of the Book of Common Prayer. Her lovely smile transforms her tremulous words into a beautiful offering of her heart.

The priest turns to Robert.

"Robert, please take the ring from atop the Bible. Place it upon the fourth finger of her left hand and repeat after me."

Robert reaches to the Bible. His sturdy hands, marked from years of hard work, gently lift the symbol of his vow from the holy book. As he turns toward his bride, he places the ring into his upturned palm. The gold piece seems to soften the muscular hand. Temporarily departing from the immediate task, he glances at Elizabeth's eyes; they are moist with happiness. He looks to her hands; they are smooth as a June rose petal. He lovingly takes her hand and gives in to his urge to caress the top of it with his thumb; *so soft*. She smiles.

"Place the ring and repeat after me."

The priest's command breaks Robert's focus. He completes the requested task, sliding the ring onto her finger and looking to the priest, who proceeds with the next words.

"With this ring I thee wed . . ."

"With this ring I thee wed . . ."

"With my body I thee worship . . ."

"With my body I thee worship . . ."

"And with all my worldly goods I thee endow . . ."

"And with all my worldly goods I thee endow . . ."

"In the name of the Father and of the Son and of the Holy Ghost."

"In the name of the Father and of the Son and of the Holy Ghost."

"Amen."

---

[62] A lifelong pledge of faithfulness to one's promise.

"Amen."

"Robert and Elizabeth, please kneel before the Lord's table."

The young couple does so. The priest continues,

"Let us pray. O Eternal God, creator and preserver of all mankind, giver of all spiritual grace, the author of everlasting life; send Thy blessing upon these Thy servants, this man and this woman, whom we bless in Thy name; that as Isaac and Rebecca lived faithfully together, so these persons may surely perform and keep the vow and covenant betwixt them made, whereof this ring given and received is a token and pledge; and may ever remain in perfect love and peace together, and live according to Thy laws; through Jesus Christ our Lord. Amen."

The priest reaches down and joins together the right hands of Robert and Elizabeth, then raises them in the air.

"Those whom God hath joined together, let no man put asunder."

The priest clears his throat to speak at a raised volume; the words resound through the ancient church building.

"For as much as Robert and Elizabeth have consented together in holy wedlock, and have witnessed the same before God and this company, and thereto have given and pledged their troth either to other, and have declared the same, by giving and receiving of a ring, and by joining of hands; I pronounce that they be man and wife together, in the name of the Father and of the Son and of the Holy Ghost. Amen."

The priest isn't finished.

"O merciful Lord, and heavenly Father, by whose gracious gift mankind is increased; we beseech Thee, assist with Thy blessing these two persons, that they may both be fruitful in procreation of children, and also live together so long in godly love and honesty, that they may see their children Christianly and virtuously brought up, to Thy praise and honor; through Jesus Christ our Lord. Amen."

Separating from their parents, the young couple's walk from the church to the Piper's residence has never happened so quickly. However, their destination is not the Piper's residence; this night, their wedding night, they will proceed all the way to the prophet's chamber. With rapid steps the pair make their way to the entrance of the little space. For a moment, each pauses to consider the wooden door that invites them to enter their united future. Slightly out of breath, the couple's measured panting eventually causes them to look to each other. Robert gently grasps Elizabeth with his right hand. His heart has never pounded so fast. With his left hand, he pushes open the door.

Entering the small room, Robert turns toward his bride and lifts her in a passionate embrace. Without hesitation, the two embark upon a gentle kiss.

Robert interrupts their kiss and lowers Elizabeth back to her feet. With his right hand, he motions her toward the object he has painstakingly protected since his departure from the west coast of Ireland a month ago. Grasping her hand, he escorts Elizabeth to the head of the bed. On the tiny table adjacent is a dried clump of the iris-like blue-eyed grass, with its purple-blue petals all gently dried, resting upon the oak stand. He lifts the plants and offers them to her.

Her smile conveys that she is thankful for the gift. However, mindful that this is her wedding night, she sets the arrangement back onto the table, arches her neck, and embraces Robert for a kiss.

Robert once again interrupts the kiss as he pulls away to share,

"Clearly we heard the priest's proclamations of the honorable accounts for marriage. I look forward to these blessed times."

"As do I, Robert."

He is happy for her welcoming response. He bravely offers,

"Perhaps some of them shall arise in America?"

Without hesitation she answers,

"Perhaps some of them shall. Kiss me, my husband."

***

The three physicians are the best John Wesley could find. The wearied doctors who struggle to keep up with Wesley's busied schedule marvel at his stamina; they can barely match the pace of the untiring man. Each of the trio is of the same opinion: *He is a man impassioned with a mission to reach the entire world.* Wesley once again recognizes their frustrated sighs, and replies before they can complain.

"The world is my parish."

This is Wesley's seventh trip to Ireland. The group is walking along the dirt road that leads toward the county of Limerick. Traveling through the rural scenery with Wesley and the doctors is Irish itinerant Robert Swindells. He is a favorite of Wesley, the first Wesleyan preacher to proclaim the Gospel in County Limerick. The county consists of four key settlements on the various land holdings of the Lord Thomas Southwell. Court-Matrix, Killiheen, Ballingrane, and Pallas are the principal villages of the transplanted German citizens of the Palatine region.

From the thirteenth to seventeenth centuries, the ancient Palatine region of the Rhine of Germany was a beautiful state, well-timbered, with bountiful vineyards and fertile plains growing corn. The self-governed land evidenced its abundant prosperity by its striking castles. It was a region largely successful due to its Protestant influences, which printed the Bible in the local language. These were the Lutheran towns of Heidelberg, Mannheim, Worms, and Speyer. This all came to an abrupt end in 1709 when the King of France, King Louis XIV, became attracted to the region's wealth and took it for himself. The Catholic King's actions were also a continuance of the centuries-long European religious persecutions that went back and forth between Protestants and Catholics.

All at once, the King leveled the cities of the Palatine, forcing the citizens of this beautiful land to escape to the forest, where their attackers hunted them down like wild animals. Once captured, the German citizens were stripped naked by the King's men and left to die in the harsh winter. Other Palatine citizens received scarcely better when their oppressors kidnapped them and dragged them to France. Even the graves of the deceased were violated for the silver and gold contained within. In a matter of months, the entire Palatine world had been burnt to the ground.

Despite the atrocities, roughly ten thousand of the Palatines escaped to Rotterdam, Holland. Upon hearing of their trials, Queen Anne of England sent for them; they shipped immediately to Great Britain. Upon the arrival of the ships, the entire group set up camp in the streets of Camberwell and the Blackheath commons of south London. Discovering that nearly three thousand of the immigrants were Catholic, the Protestant Queen promptly sent them back to Germany to die. The remaining seven thousand struggled to live outdoors in not much more than lean-tos, surviving by their own industrious creativity as well as the kindness and compassion of the British citizens.

Months into their survival on the streets of London, an American mayor of Albany, New York, Peter Schuyler, viewed the suffering Germans. Walking the London streets with Mayor Schuyler were four Mohawk Indian chiefs he had brought from America—he had originally set out with five, but one of the Mohawk leaders had succumbed to illness and died at sea. The four extroverted chiefs easily attracted much attention from the German visitors and the citizens of London. The attention they so enjoyed inspired them to regularly walk the busy streets. One of the chiefs explained that the German immigrants reminded him of the gentle Dutch settlers in America. He liked the Dutch, so much so that he offered property to any of the German exiles who would come to America and settle on his land along the Schoharie Creek west of Schenectady, New York. Nearly three thousand of the Palatines came forward and accepted the offer.

Of the remaining four thousand, some eventually felt welcomed enough to make a home in England. Others moved on, finding acceptance in County Kerry, Ireland. The remaining thousand landed on the estate of Lord Southwell, in County Limerick, Ireland, the destiny of Wesley and his doctors.

Lord Thomas Southwell—the second Baron Southwell, his family having settled in County Limerick in the early seventeenth century—was a generous man. He invited the remaining German families stranded in London to settle on his 4,800-acre estate in Rathkeale, in the four key hamlets. The properties were dotted along the picturesque and winding River Deel. He quickly offered land at half its value and timber to build houses.

Lord Southwell's plan was simple: the displaced Palatines would lease the land at five shillings per acre for three lives.[63] Each family received eight acres and a credit account of forty shillings per year for seven years, to procure needed items of stock and farming tools.

The diligent and frugal Germans quickly set up successful farms of hemp and flax. Not all of the German settlers were farmers by trade; their initial farming efforts were merely an attempt at survival. In time, those who were more inclined to other industries abandoned their farms and set up vineyards or became men of the trades: carpenters, masons, shoemakers, butchers, weavers, schoolmasters, and herdsman.

The county of Limerick has prospered by the efforts of the energetic and hardworking Palatines. Approaching the flourishing hills, one is quick to notice that somewhere along the way, limestone walls neatly crafted by talented masons, and accented with vibrant hedge materials and stately hardwood trees, have upstaged the traditional thorny hedges that mark the edges of farms. Despite the vast improvements to the value of Lord Southwell's holdings, the fifty-year lease period is nearing its end, and this expiration will no doubt raise the rents to nearly triple their current amounts. This fear has spread among the German citizens, prompting the rumor that many will be leaving for America.

John Wesley, Robert Swindells, and the three physicians approach a tiny home with white, limed walls reflecting the few hours of sun left in Limerick. Standing at the front door is an elderly woman, who frantically waves her hand.

"Mr. Wesley, please do hurry; Thomas hasn't much longer to live."

Wesley takes off in a short-legged stride; he is surprisingly fast for a little man. The physicians and Swindells follow several yards behind.

Entering the home, John bows his head to several women who appear to be weeping. With handkerchiefs covering their mouths, they point him to the single door at the rear of the main room.

---

[63] Fifty years. The German settlers' leases are due to expire in 1759.

John enters through the bedroom door; the stench of sickness immediately invades his nostrils. He instinctively covers his mouth. Realizing that he may have offended his dear friend, he removes his hand, walks to the bedside, and places his hand on the forehead of Thomas Walsh. The young man is barely alive; the only signs of life are the breath vapors that rise amidst the thick damp air. John instinctively rubs his hands together for warmth.

The three physicians enter the room and waste no time in working on Thomas. One pulls back the heavy wool bedcovering to reveal a thin man whose chest rises and falls under much exertion. John's fearful thought lingers: *He has lost so much weight.* The emaciated twenty-eight-year-old opens his eyes and turns toward the arm that has once again placed its hand upon his forehead. He forces a gaunt smile to John, the effort evoking a horrid cough. One physician moves to press on Thomas's chest cavity, causing the rawboned man to let out a groan of pain. The doctor is quick to pronounce,

"Pulmonary consumption."[64]

Ignoring the doctor's proclamation, Thomas's weak voice strains at a question for John.

"How did you part with Mrs. Wesley the last time?"

The question shocks John; it prompts the realization that his itinerants know of his troubles with his wife, Mary. He gently responds,

"Very affectionately."

"Why, what a woman is this? She informed that your parting words were, 'I hope to see your wicked face no more.'"

Silence.

His wife's slander cues a restrained mental response: *She is resolved to blacken me at all events.* Wesley purses his lips and rubs the clammy forehead of his dying itinerant. He offers,

"There are more pressing matters, Thomas."

Thomas's diagnosis of pulmonary consumption is devastating; this is the greatest killer of people in eighteenth-century Europe. A small tear trickles down John's face. He allows the tear to wander as he gently strokes the hair of his traveling preacher. His thought is singularly focused: *Tragic.*

Thomas Walsh is one of Wesley's best itinerants in Ireland. By his own words, John has proclaimed, "No man has gained more sinners for the kingdom," easily marking Thomas as the best of Wesley's preachers not only in Ireland, but also throughout all of England, Ireland, and Wales. His is a loving approach to Christian community, uniting individuals on the foundation of the Scriptures and the teachings of Jesus.

---

[64] Tuberculosis.

The tiny island of Ireland seldom receives credit for its valuable contribution to pure religion. Some of Christianity's brightest lights hail from the gentle nation. Thomas Walsh is certainly one of the church's best representations of a life prepared and transformed in Ireland, sent out for the promotion of the teachings of the Bible. Born in 1730, in a small farming town outside of Limerick, his father Edmund and mother Helina were faithful Roman Catholics, teaching him the Lord's Prayer, Ave Maria, and the 133rd Psalm. The writings of the Psalmist, which pointed out the blessings of brotherly unity, became seared into his memory. *"Behold, how good and how pleasant it is for brethren to dwell together in unity!"* [65]

His childhood education involved teaching by one of his brothers who had studied for the priesthood, but left the Catholic seminary upon discovery of teachings that seemed to misalign with the life of Jesus and the Scriptures. Torn between the leanings of his older brother and his parents, who continued to urge loyalty to the Catholic Church, his young heart began to search out God. It wasn't long before young Thomas abandoned any church teachings that did not line up with the Bible. With the eighteenth-century Catholic Church sadly having departed from many of the teachings of the Bible, Thomas was quickly drawn to the influence of his Protestant brother. Despite this pulling away from the church of his parents, he clearly held a special place for all people regardless of their faith—Protestant or Catholic, and even those who professed a lack of faith. It was this pure desire to reach individuals for the kingdom of God in lieu of the kingdoms of earth that propelled Thomas to Christian stature. His words were powerful: "It may be asked, then, why did I leave this communion, since I thought so favorably of them? I answer, because I was abundantly convinced, that as a Church they have erred from the right way and adulterated the truths of God by the traditions of men; which the Scriptures, and even celebrated writers themselves, abundantly testify."

At the age of nineteen, wanting to teach, he left for the town of Newmarket. Being a man of high moral character and above-average teaching abilities, he quickly gained many students. Despite his teaching success, his heart struggled. One evening on his way home from the school, he came across the Parade, the public meeting place in the county of Limerick. To his amazement, there was a Protestant preacher expositing to a largely Catholic crowd. He paused to listen to the man's words that rang throughout the gathering place under the thirteenth-century King John's Castle, overlooking the River Shannon. "Come unto me, all ye that labor, and are heavy laden, and I will give you rest." This simple yet

---

[65] Psalm 133, verse 1.

profound approach of preaching the words of Jesus to the people of the street suddenly anchored Thomas's unsettled soul. In an instant, he realized that he should be doing the same.

Thomas's initial efforts were not without opposition. After one preaching occasion, he encountered a young woman whose heart was transformed for the Lord during his sermon; she informed him that she had attended today's exhortation with the intention of stabbing him with the knife she had purchased for the occasion days before. This would not be the only time that individuals would seek his harm. Despite the threats, he remained at the task.

The street preacher who inspired young Thomas to become a traveling itinerant is the preacher who now stands beside Thomas's deathbed, Robert Swindells. Thomas closes his eyes and moans as the doctors poke and prod his failing body. John continues to stroke the young man's head. Robert leans over from the opposite side of John and gently kisses Thomas's forehead. One physician breaks the blessed moment.

"The disease is in its last stages."

John doesn't move; he continues to look toward Thomas's thin and wearied face. The doctor continues,

"Consequently, beyond the reach of any human help."

"Then we shall continue to pray."

The sounding of a horn outside interrupts John's measured reply. A cow's horn, in lieu of a bell, summons the worshipers in Ballingrane. John lovingly looks to his friend, hoping that the horn will remind Thomas of his times with God. Thomas clears his throat to speak. Once again, he strains to open his eyes as he turns toward John. His words are barely audible.

"By reminding sober men to read the Holy Scriptures, we will not suffer them to be deceived."

Tears spring to John's eyes. He forces his lips tight in an effort not to weep openly. Thomas once again lets out a ghastly cough, then closes his eyes and returns to lying flat against his straw pillow. The physician gives his best medical advice.

"We shall not bother Thomas further."

All turn to depart the room. John pauses as his thoughts wander. For some strange reason he yearns for another young preacher, *half as bold as dear Thomas.* He surmises that the Lord is prompting him that one as successful as Thomas awaits his discovery. He bends down and kisses Thomas on the cheek. Wiping away his own tears, he too leaves Thomas's presence for the last time.

The days that follow find John refocusing his efforts, certain that he heard from God correctly that "one as successful as Thomas awaits his discovery." John enthusiastically attends the Limerick Wesleyan conference beginning four days after his visit with Thomas. Opening the gathering of Ireland's Wesleyan itinerants, Wesley offers his deepest feelings about the young preacher. Standing at the front of the room, he begins,

> "I knew a young man who was so thoroughly acquainted with the Bible that if he was questioned concerning any Hebrew word in the Old, or any Greek word in the New Testament, he would tell, after a little pause, not only how often the one or the other occurred in the Bible, but also what it meant in every place. His name was Thomas Walsh. Such a master of biblical knowledge I never saw before - -
> And never expect to see again."

The room is quiet. Present are Wesley's top preachers in Ireland: Joseph Whitford, John Haughton, Jacob Rowell, Joseph Cownley, Robert Swindells, Samuel Larwood, James Morris, Thomas Kead, and John Fisher; the only one missing is Thomas Walsh.

In addition, present at this conference are fourteen young men who wish to become part of the movement. John Wesley, heavy in heart for the impending loss of his young preacher, looks to the new candidates who stand before him. *Can such a man be among them?* He abandons his thought and begins the conference.

> "Who are now proposed as traveling preachers?"

> "Brothers William Thompson, William Harwood, John Furz, Philip Embury, and several others."

The deep voice of the portly, good-looking Robert Swindells resonates in the small room with the low ceiling. Wesley continues,

> "Have the applicants step forward."

The fourteen men make their way to the front. Slightly nervous, they proceed to Wesley's side. One by one, each kneels quietly before their leader. Wesley, in an unguarded moment, inquires,

> "Are you prepared to join the swaddlers?"

All in the room hold back a laugh. The candidates appear stoic, too anxious to consider a light moment. John's reference to the word "swaddler" marks a derogatory label given to the Methodists by an unruly crowd in Dublin almost ten years before. On Christmas day in 1749, John Cennick was preaching to a near rabble in Swift's Alley. He drew from the words, "Ye shall find the babe wrapped in swaddling clothes." An individual obviously ignorant of the Christmas story called Cennick a "swaddler." The mob was too accommodating to let the label die out. From that point on, the Irish Methodists received the label "swaddlers." During the Cork riots that followed, the attacking crowds boldly announced, "Five pounds for a swaddler's head!"

The solemn gathering waits for the conference to proceed, each man saddened by the deteriorating condition of Thomas Walsh. Wanting them to abandon their heavy hearts, John forces a slight smile and attempts a prayer.

But he remains silent. Silently weeping, the words fail to materialize. John doesn't fight the desire; he realizes that the uncontrollable emotion is God's Spirit. He allows it to continue. At its completion, he closes.

"Amen."

The conference selection proceeds as planned. Each man's name is placed before the itinerants, and they vote on every one. The questions of the candidates are straightforward: *Have you faith in Christ? Are you going on to perfection? Do you expect to be perfected in love, in this life? Are you groaning after it? Are you resolved to devote yourself wholly to God and his work? Do you know the Methodist doctrine? Have you read the Sermons? The notes on the New Testament? Do you know the Rules of the Society? Of the Bands? Do you keep them? Do you take no snuff, tobacco, drams?*[66] *Do you constantly attend the church and sacrament? Have you considered the Twelve Rules of a Helper? Will you keep them for conscience' sake? Will you preach every morning and evening, endeavoring not to speak too loud or too long and not lolling with your elbows? Will you diligently and earnestly instruct the children, and visit from house to house?*

Selected for admittance on trial during the conference are William Harwood, William Thompson, John Furz, and three others. Philip Embury and the rest go unchosen; they remain on Wesley's reserve list.

Upon completion of the conference's closing prayer, the itinerants, old and new, exit outdoors and busily make their way to their assigned circuits. Left behind are Robert Swindells and John Wesley. Wesley bids Robert farewell. The two embrace, reading each other's pained emotion over the losing of their friend and co-laborer, Thomas Walsh. Without saying a word, Wesley releases, turns, and departs.

Swindells, noticing that one candidate has remained, makes his way toward the back of the room. Sitting alone and dejected is Philip Embury. Robert notices the young man staring at nothing; he remembers that Philip went unchosen as a traveling itinerant. He approaches and offers consolation.

"Aye, tomorrow's winds shall bring better happenings."

Philip shrugs his narrow shoulders and continues to stare at the dirt floor. Robert again attempts to invoke conversation.

"Brother Philip, shall you return to Ballingrane?"

---

[66] A dram is a shot of liquor.

Barely audible, looking at his feet dangling from the chair and kicking the soil beneath them, Philip replies,

"I shall."

"I hear that your local preaching is received well; it would do Ballingrane well if you were to continue preaching on Sundays."

Robert pulls up a chair, sits, and places his thick hand on the back of the unhappy lay preacher.

"Several share that your carpentry business is doing well."

"It does well."

Robert smiles, he is happy that there is still life in the young man. He invites Philip to consider,

"Have you not family in Court-Matrix? I hear that your talented hands have constructed a beautiful church building there."

"The building is sound, a reflection of the simple and clean mandates of Wesley."

Philip pauses, then continues,

"But the Lord's call on my life seems more than mere sticks and mortar . . ."

Robert is silent. He nods his head as encouragement for Philip. After careful thought and consideration, he offers,

"If you sense the Lord's call, then Providence shall reveal if there be grand work for you."

Philip is relieved that Robert somewhat understands his struggle. He expected to depart the conference as one of Wesley's circuit-riding preachers traveling all over the country of Ireland. He settles himself and offers,

"I shall not dismiss the Lord's call on my life, but for now that call shall lead me home, in Ballingrane, where I shall preach each Sabbath. Perhaps it is through my carpentry and farming that the Lord will open the door to my heart."

"Perhaps that is precisely where He shall reveal His plan."

Robert rises and departs, leaving Philip alone with his thoughts. Philip is somewhat dejected; *my very conversion was by the hand of John Wesley himself.* This thought only serves to frustrate him more. He gets up from his chair, kicks the dirt with the heel of his boot, and departs for home. Heading out the door, he complains,

"My carpentry and farming shall fail to meet the rising rents . . ."

O Lord, I know not what I am,
But to You I flee for refuge.

William Wilberforce

"Now is the time for us to go."

John Wesley's advice to his friend, Mr. Francis Ward, and his three other companions fails to move them. The three men and Mrs. Ward all seem to reply in unison,

"It shall be fine, John. The mob will not return this evening. They have all dispersed to their families."

The mob they speak of is the group of protestors that surrounded Mr. Ward's house earlier that afternoon. With heated anger, the unruly group sought out the "preacher" staying with the Ward family. John and the men standing before him earnestly asked that God would disperse the aggressors. Shortly after the prayer, one by one the men bent on violence left the scene. After half an hour, not one man remained outside the Ward home.

To avoid offending his hosts, John takes a seat. He feels otherwise, however: *They will return.*

Just before five o'clock, Mr. Ward darts to the room's exterior window. John looks to his companions. Mr. Ward rushes to close the wooden shutters and turns back, staring at John in open-mouthed silence. Within minutes, the mob is once again surrounding the Ward residence, this time in far greater numbers.

"Bring out the Minister!"   "We shall have the Minister!"

The cries of the unruly gathering are repeated again and again.

Inside, John stands to his feet; with unflinching determination, he makes his way to the front door. Mr. Ward stands to block John from exiting.

"They will kill you, John."

Mr. Ward's companions join in,

"Back away from the door, John."

The advice of his companions fails to alter his intent. Like a consistent and gentle wind, John raises his arm and moves Mr. Ward aside as he opens the front door of the home. The crowd's volume rises to a crescendo. John's words are barely audible,

"May I have a private moment with you?"

The man to whom John is speaking is undoubtedly the leader of the group. He stands nearly a foot above the crowd, making him almost fifteen inches taller than Wesley. His long, thin grey hair appears dirty as it hangs below the black hat on his head. In his right hand is a wooden club roughly twenty inches in length and three inches in diameter. John is inviting the man inside.

The man, dressed in the tattered dark clothes typical of a drover,[67] looks to his fellow rabble-rousers. He raises his open hand and the crowd falls silent. With full confidence that he can handle Wesley and the three men standing behind the preacher, he enters the building alone.

John calmly turns his back on the man as he escorts him to the center of the main room. Mrs. Ward shuffles over and closes the front door. The stinging body odor of the mob's leader fills the room.

John turns and faces his guest.

> "If tonight is the night that I am to meet my loving Creator, I am prepared."

John's comment surprises the drover; with his left hand, the one not holding the club, he nervously fumbles with a hole in his trousers near the upper left thigh. Wesley again makes a comment,

> "None is like the God who rides upon the heavens to thy help."

This comment relaxes the mob leader. His shoulders settle as he gazes at the others, his face appearing as one who has been disarmed of pretenses. John inquires,

> "May you go and bring one or two of the angriest of your companions?"

The drover nods his head and turns. He makes his way across the room and exits, closing the thick oak-wood door behind him. Once again, the crowd raises its volume.

Within moments he reenters the home, this time with two men from the mob. These two are complete opposites, one as tall as the drover, the other a short, stocky man with extremely large forearms. The stubby fingers of his bloated hands powerfully grip a wooden club. He slams the club into the wall as he enters the room. His tall companion immediately forces open the wooden shutters at the window, causing the crowd outside to scream at the home's inhabitants.

Over the din, Wesley offers again,

> "If tonight is the night that I am to meet my loving Creator, I am prepared."

The two men and the drover all stand in silence. The protesters outside manage to curb their violent accusations; they desire to hear what is said inside.

---

[67] One who drives the carts full of coal.

In his gentle manner, Wesley continues,

"None is like the God who rides upon the heavens to thy help."

Once again, the assailants are reduced to lambs. John makes a request of the men.

"I bid you, make way that I may go out among the people."

The three men quickly make their way to the door. As they open it, the grumbling noise of the mob fills the room. The crowd's enthusiasm quickly escalates, and again they are shouting.

"Death to the preacher!"   "Death to the enthusiast!"

Escorted by the three changed bullies, John makes his way to the center of the mob. Soon he is making a request of Mr. Ward,

"Fetch me a chair."

From the house, Mr. Ward hands a chair outdoors. The seat quickly moves over the heads of the more than five hundred who have gathered to persecute the Methodist preacher. It reaches Wesley within moments.

Climbing atop the wooden chair, Wesley begins,

"What do any of you want with me?"

Immediately a reply from the crowd confronts Wesley.

"We want you to go with us to the Justice!"

"That I will, with all my heart - -

However, I ask, will the Lord absent Himself forever? Moreover, will He be no more entreated? Is His mercy gone forever? And is His promise come utterly to an end for evermore?"

No one in the crowd has an answer. The wave of silence ripples to the edge of the mob.

"Presumption is one grand snare of the devil, in which many of the children of men are taken. They so presume upon the mercy of God as to utterly forget His justice. Although He has expressly declared, 'Without holiness no man shall see the Lord,' still they flatter themselves that in the end, God will be better than His word. They imagine they may live and die in their sins, and nevertheless escape the damnation of hell."

A woman in the crowd cries out,

"The gentleman is an honest man!"

At this, several men sigh and turn away. They are the first to initiate the departures. Many in the crowd begin to disperse. Several women lead the proclamation against those who persist in harming Wesley.

"He is a just man . . ."

John remains silent as members of the crowd take leave. Despite the predominant change in attitude, roughly two hundred set on violence remain. After several noble attempts by the women to disperse the mob, he offers,

"Shall we go to the Justice tonight, or in the morning?"

"Tonight . . ."   "Tonight . . ."   "Tonight . . ."

The crowd is unanimous.

The distance to Bentley Hall from Wednesbury is two miles. Halfway along the route, the darkening skies of the approaching evening burst open with a heavy rain. As he walks, Wesley thinks to himself, *this will surely disperse the mob.*

However, the mob continues to follow. Nearing Bentley Hall, several of the group run on ahead to summon Justice Lane. His son answers the knock on the front door of the Lane residence. Once he perceives the nature of the mob's visit, the young man races upstairs to his father's bedroom. The Justice is already in bed.

"What have I to do with Mr. Wesley? Go and carry him back again."

The Justice's reply launches his son downstairs. The pounding on the door is resonating throughout the entire house before he can return. The young man opens the door; more than two hundred people greet him. One at the front confronts the young man.

"Why aren't you displeased that they sing psalms all day; aye, and make folks rise at five in the morning?"

The question takes the young man by surprise; standing silent, he has no answer for the intruder's unexpected complaints. The complainer continues,

"What would you advise us to do?"

"I advise you to go home and be quiet."

The reply disappoints the unruly group. They voice another plan,

"Justice Persehouse will see us."

The mob quickly seizes Wesley and retreats for the town of Walsall.

Walsall lies southeast of Bentley Hall. Located at the midpoint between Bentley Hall and Great Barr, the town is successful in the production of items necessary for the proper operations of horses. This has developed into a thriving leather- and rope-making industry. Along with the miners and mechanics associated with the ironworking industry, Walsall's hardworking inhabitants number roughly 1,500 families. A town of determined ruffians with access to plenty of rope is far from advantageous to the diminutive itinerant.

Along the way, a messenger arrives.

"Mr. Persehouse is in bed. I urge you to turn around."

Once again, the mob is unhappy. One in the group gives his advice,

"Let us return home."

The recommendation disappoints many in the crowd. The people begin to depart.

Now only fifty surround the Methodist preacher, with the majority of their sentiments turning in his favor. The club-wielding drover tosses his weapon to the ground. He places his arm on the shoulder of the itinerant and turns him back toward Wednesbury.

Even the weather begins to cooperate as the rains begin to abate. An occasional opening in the clouds reveals several stars of the northern sky. Wesley considers the development a promise from God that all is as it should be. He relaxes slightly, but remains alert.

After half a mile, a mob of three hundred meets the group. The drover, now one of Wesley's protectors, gives the news:

"The Walsall mob!"

The drover's warning puts Wesley's escorts on alert. One of the women in the group hands her club to the drover and departs. Immediately, the Walsall mob charges the Wednesbury mob. Many on both sides assault each other. The friendly group runs off, leaving Wesley in the hands of the Walsall attackers. Only the drover and a handful of men remain to defend the preacher. John attempts to reconcile with the group.

"Gentlemen, please . . ."

Wesley's attempt to gain their attention is in vain. The rabble rage on all sides, each bent on reaching the Methodist preacher. With anger, the group attacks the drover and his men; they vanish from view as they are pushed to the outskirts of the mob.

Wesley is alone among the unruly crowd.

Three men grab Wesley by the shoulders and begin to drag him along. A thrown rock strikes the preacher in the mouth. He instinctively cups his mouth with his right hand as blood pours from between his fingers. With his left hand he reaches into his coat pocket for a handkerchief. The mob pushes him along as he wipes away the blood.

Within a few minutes, they arrive back at Walsall. Seeing a door to a large house standing open, Wesley attempts to go in. From behind the opening the owner proclaims,

"Oh no, you don't!"

"Ow!"

A man in the group drags Wesley by the hair, pulling him back into the middle of the mob. They once again shove him down the main street. Wesley continues his attempt to reason with the group.

"Shall we not . . . ?"

"What have I . . . ?"

Wesley's efforts are of no use. Suddenly, without warning, the assailants get into an argument amongst themselves. Two men want to hang Wesley; several others want to throw him in jail. *This could release me,* Wesley thinks to himself. At the other end of town, he spots a door to a home standing half open. Wesley begins to sidle toward the open door. Unaware of his intention, the arguing mob fails to notice as he slips from their midst and makes for the door.

The disagreement quickly subsides when one man punches another in the eye. Gingerly holding his head, the injured man staggers from the scene.

Wesley is relieved when he reaches the door. Again, the homeowner gives warning,

"They would pull my house down to the ground."

The man who suddenly appears in the doorway will not allow Wesley to enter. John pleads his cause,

"Are you willing to hear me speak?"

Wesley awaits an answer. There is none. He pleads with the man again.

Silence.

At this point, Wesley can hear the howling complaints behind him. The Walsall mob catches up to the Methodist preacher. They are not happy that he has evaded the crowd.

"Knock his brains out . . ."   "Down with him . . ." "Kill him at once . . ."

The angry cries of the crowd continue as they push in on Wesley. He thinks to himself as they nearly smother him, *if I falter, I shall be crushed to death.* To protect himself from falling, he raises his hand to the shoulder of a man standing next to him.

Another man in the crowd swings a wooden club; it bounces off the raised hand of Wesley. Despite the intense pain, he will not lower his hand. From out of the crowd, the drover appears. This time he has brought help: forty men from the Wednesbury group. He and his companions muscle their way into the mob to surround Wesley. Pushing and shoving away any who are not their own, they accomplish their goal. The drover puts the unruly group on notice.

"Nay, we will hear him first."

It is a difficult task, but with this request, the mob falls silent. Realizing that God has provided a window of opportunity, Wesley begins,

"What evil have I done? Which of you all have I wronged in word or deed?"

He pauses.

"Those who speak disparagingly of the inhabitants of Walsall warn that they are a light people, suddenly moved to affrays and insurrections."

The mob considers the last comment. Several of the Walsall group dislike the label. As blood continues to ooze from the cut on his lip, Wesley finally has a chance to look at his hand that received the blow; it is missing skin. He attempts to speak, but nothing comes out. The mob senses something is wrong. A man in the crowd remarks,

"Even God seeks to silence him."

The crowd pushes into Wesley. The drover and his bodyguards push back, clubbing several men. By now, the Walsall women are scurrying away. Wesley's protectors once again quell the violence. In silence, Wesley makes his request to God: *Protect me, Father.*

The mob begins to cry out again,

"Take him away!"

Wesley's emotions totter; he senses God's provision, but is well aware that he is staring into the scowl of madness. Several in the crowd push in again. Their leader orders several men to grab the drover. The task is difficult, but they make the attempt, seeking to separate him from Wesley. His strong arms, especially the one with the club, warn otherwise. He bashes one of the oppressors on the cheek bone. The man's arms go stiff as he falls unconscious to the ground. The group tramples him. The other attackers grow frightened enough to retreat.

Wesley's voice returns,

"Forgive them, Father, for they know not what they do."

Immediately, the leader of the unruly mob, the one set on taking the drover away, turns toward Wesley.

"I will spend my life for you. Follow me, and not one soul here shall touch a hair of your head."

At these surprising words, three of his Walsall accomplices join him to confirm his stand. They move in close to Wesley. The drover and his men are leery of this sudden change, as is Wesley. The new arrival continues his verbal efforts to help Wesley.

From the side of the mob, a burly voice booms through the crowd.

"For shame. For shame! Let him go."

The big man, his outfit covered in blood, is the town butcher of Walsall. He continues,

"It is a shame that you do this."

With both arms, the burly man pulls four men from the crowd. With little effort, he tosses two of them to the ground; the others run off as fast as they can. The mob parts in the middle as Wesley, the drover, and their four newest escorts make their way through the crowd. The butcher joins the deliverers midway as the group heads for the bridge out of town.

On the near side of the bridge, the Walsall mob is once again spurred on by their anger. The escorts do not hesitate; they plunge Wesley forward, ramming through the enraged group. Wesley's men pound several with their wooden clubs. The frightful effort is successful as they break through.

The mob doesn't give up. They pursue, aiming to catch up. The butcher snatches a club from one in the crowd and begins to fight off the unruly mass. The drover from Wednesbury joins the butcher; they both deliver several direct hits to the heads and chests of many of the attackers. As men fall to the ground in pain, women from the earlier Wednesbury mob on its return trip home turn and join in the defense of the preacher. This delay provides enough time for several of the women to escort Wesley out of town.

Wesley and his deliverers begin to race through the surrounding meadows. After a few steps, Wesley stumbles to the ground. The attacking group notices and attempts to dart around the butcher and the drover. In the mud, Wesley's thoughts are urgent: *Get up, must not remain on the ground.* One of his female escorts yanks him up by the arm. They quickly are on their way once again, leaving the mob behind.

Wesley makes it safely to Wednesbury.

Such was the atmosphere in Wednesbury in October of 1743.

Wesley's 1743 visit took place at the midpoint of a two-year period of violence toward the Methodist faithful in Wednesbury. At the time, brave men affiliated with the movement—men like James Jones, the preacher God used to reach Eliza Asbury—suffered many atrocities. Over time, it became evident that the parish church vicar of Wednesbury, Edward Eggington, was spurring on the hostilities toward the Methodists. Well into the next year, several homes of prominent Wesleyans were broken into, their houses ransacked and personal belongings thrown into the streets and stolen. Riots began. Children watched in disbelief as mobs forced their parents from their homes, their mothers raped and their fathers beaten in the streets. Neighbors refused safe haven to children who ran from the advancing mob. The destruction of homes and personal property was repeated often. Even the chief constable of Wednesbury, a Wesleyan convert, suffered attacks and beatings.

Public announcements proclaiming that the Methodists must come to town and sign a paper of recantation were posted throughout the Black Country. Even the press, on the payroll of the High Church, distorted the accounts. The following article was printed because of the riots in Wednesbury against the Methodists:

> *By a private letter from Staffordshire, we had advice of an insurrection of the people, called Methodists, who upon some pretended insults from the Church party, have assembled themselves in a riotous manner; and having committed several outrages, they proceeded at last to burn the house of one of their adversaries.*[68]

---

[68] From *The London Evening Post*, February 18, 1744.

The violence against the Methodists quickly spread beyond Wednesbury, until the entire Black Country was embroiled in hostilities toward the followers of Wesley. It soon became easy to spot the homes of the Wesleyan faithful; they were the homes that possessed the marks of violence and destruction.

In the winter of 1744, many of the Walsall residents once again participated in a miraculous rescue of those plundered in Wednesbury and other local areas. As an angry mob was leaving Wednesbury with their Wesleyan spoils, they made the mistake of traveling through Walsall. The residents of Walsall, notified of the approaching group, raised a body of men and confronted the unruly crowd. The residents were successful in regaining many of the stolen items, placing them at the town hall and posting a notice throughout the surrounding areas that any who had suffered the violent acts of property might come and retrieve their personal items.

Wesley thinks back on those days seventeen years ago. *Lord, Your delivery from Wednesbury's fury I know, having lost only one flap of my waistcoat and a little skin from one of my hands. I never saw such a chain of providences before, so many convincing proofs that the hand of God is on every person and thing, overruling all as it seemeth to Him good.*

He turns to the young assistant helping him with his clerical robe.

"Then they roared amain,[69] but I walked straight through them, and none offered the least rudeness."

He smiles as he considers and shares of one event during the period.

"The oppressors continued their harassment, venturing to fool the masses in the form of entertainment. *Trick upon Trick,*[70] the most dreadful of plays, intended to speak against the Methodists, was performed at Moot Hall in Newcastle, with the Edinburgh Company of Comedians at their best to perform the farce. However crafty they may be, they mock God's work at their own peril. The performance begins, and fifteen hundred are rudely surprised as the support beams holding the first few rows collapse. Several hundred well-paying patrons are thrown together, screaming in panic—not unlike the panic that awaits, come the Day of the Lord. All settles and the second act proceeds smoothly, at least until the support holding the cheaper seats makes a horrendous cracking noise. Many flee the pending doom; those left in their noisy seats are delivered to their new location several inches lower in elevation than they started. The Almighty has an alarming sense of humor. Again, the worried flee, as well as the actors. After many efforts, the players are coaxed to return to the stage. This continued effort is met by the Almighty's third and final

---

[69] With full force.

[70] A play burlesquing John Wesley and the Methodists, opening in 1743.

act as the gallery seats come crashing to the ground. The three hundred remaining patrons are certain that these latest victims are crushed to pieces. Not a single person is killed or hurt; such is the mercy of God! As the remaining patrons wander about, Mr. Este, the actor to play the Methodist in this abominable production, approaches the panic-filled audience and begs to continue. The remaining patrons agree. As the people begin to take their seats, the stage on which Mr. Este stands drops more than six inches! This last scene sends Mr. Este running in the utmost confusion and the remaining patrons as fast as they can, out the nearest theatre door."

The assistant chuckles at the sharing of the story.

These are glorious days. John Wesley is thankful as he walks between the nearly ten thousand people present for today's visit to Wednesbury. The Black Country town, once known for its bull-baiting, cockfighting, and antagonism toward the Wesleyan movement, is overflowing with joyous followers of Wesley. He makes his way up the steps to the house on Meeting Street.

Standing at one end of the meeting room, John gazes at the two dozen individuals crammed into the small structure. His eyes move to the window and the throng of people outside.

"I shall deliver outdoors."

Upon this announcement, everyone in the house exits.

Since 1760, the house on Meeting Street is where the local Wesleyan society gathers for its meetings. It is the center of Wednesbury Methodism. Despite the movement's overwhelming popularity, it never intended to compete with the local parish church.

On days like today, the Monway Field next to the meeting house is no longer the historic field known for its white clay used in making quality tobacco pipes; today it is the center of the Black Country and its long-awaited embrace of the unhindered religion espoused by the brothers John and Charles Wesley. Dressed like a Quaker and surrounded by his brother Charles and two other itinerants, John climbs the wooden structure, a loading stand used to convey corn into the carts of the drovers.

Upon the makeshift pulpit, Wesley begins,

"I count all things but lost, for the Excellency of the knowledge of Christ Jesus my Lord."

The crowd settles in. The town's visitors more than triple the population of Wednesbury. John finds delight in the young men in the front of the crowd. He thinks to himself, *the six of them seem to hang on each of my words.* He offers a silent prayer on their behalf. *May the words of my mouth and the meditations of my heart rise pleasing to You, Lord.*

These young men before John Wesley are Francis Asbury and Richard Whatcoat, in company with Francis's pals: the two Thomases, Thomas Ault and Thomas Russell, and the two Jameses, James Mayo and James Bayley. Francis and his friends from the Old Mill Forge wait eagerly in silence for John's next words. Beyond the young boys, Eliza and Joseph Asbury stand with the Foxall family.

Wesley continues,

" *'You must be born again.'* John chapter three, verse seven.

"If any doctrines within the whole compass of Christianity may be properly termed fundamental, they are doubtless these two: the doctrine of justification, and that of the new birth; the former relating to that great work which God does for us, in forgiving our sins; the latter, to the great work which God does *in us,* in renewing our fallen nature. In order of *time,* neither of these is before the other; in the moment we are justified by the grace of God, through the redemption that is in Jesus, we are also born of the Spirit; but in order of *thinking,* as it is termed, justification precedes the new birth.

"We first conceive His wrath to be turned away, and then His Spirit to work in our hearts.

"How great importance then must it be of, to every child of man, thoroughly to understand these fundamental doctrines!"

John's brother Charles approaches the stand. He is dressed in the black gown of the Anglican clergy. John invites his brother to join him.

The preacher's stand is a series of four steps to the wooden platform. Charles hesitates as he places his foot on the first step. The rickety platform sways slightly to the right as Charles rises to the second and third steps; instinctively he places his right hand on the rough-sawn oak handrail. He stops to look at his brother. John nods his head twice; *the platform is safe.* Once at the top, the brothers stand shoulder to shoulder.

Charles raises his hands and the gathering of people readies to sing. Charles gives the downbeat. As he swings his hands lower, he begins to sing. John and the entire crowd join in,

"Come, sinners, to the Gospel feast;
Let every soul be Jesus's guest.
Ye need not one be left behind,
For God hath . . ."

John raises his hands to stop the singing. He is adamant; his hands signal to stop the singing, *now.* The unexpected interruption brings a rippling silence. Eventually all is quiet.

John clears his throat. He looks to his left.

"You are bleating like cows in that corner."[71]

The guilty parties look away in embarrassment.

John slowly looks to his right.

"And there is a man on my right who has been singing a false note."

Francis and Richard look at each other, struggling not to laugh. The guilty man on the right raises his hand to speak.

"Dear Wesley, I vow to make amends."

The entire crowd remains silent. Many look away as John gazes in their direction. He continues,

"Is not our singing a vital part of our faith?"

He looks to the gathering on the left, the bleating cow section. Some of them bow their heads; others nod their heads in agreement. John continues,

"I urge you, sing lustily and with a good courage. Beware of singing as if you were half dead, or half asleep, or as a cow bleating for its mate. But lift up your voice with strength. Sing modestly; do not bawl so as to be heard above or distinct from the rest of the congregation, that you may not destroy the harmony . . ."

He looks to the man on his right. The guilty party raises his right hand and nods his head in the affirmative.

John has more,

"Strive to unite your voices together, so as to make one melodious sound. Sing in time. Whatever time is sung, be sure to keep with it. Do not run before nor stay behind it, but attend close to the leading voices, and move therewith as exactly as you can; and take care not to sing too slow. This drawling way naturally steals on all who are lazy, and it is high time to drive it out from us, and sing all our tunes as quick as we did at first.

"Above all, sing spiritually. Have an eye to God in every word you sing. Aim at pleasing Him more than yourself, or any other creature. In order to do this, attend strictly to the sense of what you sing, and see that your heart is not carried away with the sound, but offered to God continually; so shall your singing be such as the Lord will approve here, and reward you when He cometh in the clouds of heaven."

Wesley looks over the enormous crowd. They silently agree with his comments.

"Well then, shall we?"

---

[71] Elk cows will bleat for their males during certain parts of the rutting season. Elk roamed most of the United Kingdom up to the end of the eighteenth century.

Charles raises his hands and begins again. The entire crowd is together on the downbeat.

> "Come, sinners, to the Gospel feast;
> Let every soul be Jesus's guest.
> Ye need not one be left behind,
> For God hath . . . bid all humankind."

All are focused and singing. John nods his head; he is well pleased.

> "Sent by my Lord, on you I call;
> The invitation is to all.
> Come, all the world! Come, sinner, thou!
> All things in Christ are ready now . . ."

The day's event marks a milestone for Wednesbury; no longer shall its residents persecute the Methodist movement. From this point forward, towns like Wednesbury and Walsall proudly join the revival of the church.

Two hours have passed since the people departed the grand event; the setting sun peeks through the horizon of a spring sky. Francis and Richard sit on the trailer platform that earlier in the day supported the brothers Wesley. A gentle breeze carries the organic, earthy smells of the Monway Field. Francis nudges Richard as he comments,

> "Were not we alive when Mr. Wesley spoke?"

Francis's raised, open hands animate his words.

> "And his brother's voice—a Christian artist!"

> "Yes, Francis, the brothers are the outworking of a holy and loving God - An artist God."

Richard's comment has the two looking skyward. The rare sight of a West Midland sky with the arrays of red and orange splashing on the horizon, highlighting the wispy sprays of the last clouds of the day, is too beautiful to resist.

> "Francis, did it slip by that Wesley confirmed what we hear from Mather and his companions?"

Francis nods excitedly.

> "As if they and Mr. Whitefield - -

> "All of them penning the same sermons: 'The spirit of God removes our enmity with God—through faith we are saved.' They paint a masterpiece that offers freedom as easy - -

> "As easy as the song thrush's release from my hand."

Richard is impressed with Francis's observations. He turns his head toward his companion.

> "And a true freedom, untarnished by the nature of man."

Francis bows his head to look at his feet, hanging over the edge of the platform.

> "Thank you, Richard; this thought warms my soul."

"You are quite welcome, Francis. Tomorrow as always?"

"I shall meet you in Wednesbury, eight o'clock sharp."

The Wesleys' visit to Wednesbury inspires the young men. Each makes it a point to grow in his faith. Francis and Richard, along with half a dozen other young men, establish the habit of taking in four sermons on the Sabbath. For the first few months the routine is the same: an eight o'clock morning service at Wednesbury, two services in West Bromwich during the day, and a final service at five p.m. back in Wednesbury. Thomas Ault, James Mayo, James Bayley, and Thomas Russell, the same boys who attended the Wesley sermon at Monway Field, faithfully join Francis and Richard. Occasionally, Thomas Ault's friend, William Emery, joins the group. Eliza and Joseph are happy that Francis and his friends earnestly seek the Lord—though at times, Joseph suspects that the boys are more interested in attending the meetings for other reasons.

Francis and his pals enter the doorway of the Old Church, also known as All Saints Church, in West Bromwich. The usual gathering of thirty is present. In addition, several locals from Wednesbury and Walsall push the attendance to near fifty.

The boys, all sixteen years of age, make their way into the nave, led by Francis's tall, slender frame. Following his elongated stride, step for step, are the usual four pals, the two Thomases and the two Jameses. Francis glances toward the south side of the nave. It is evident he has spotted someone important to him. He chooses to sit on the opposite side of the room. His companions file in behind, doing likewise.

On the south side of the building is one of the reasons the young men are so eager to attend worship services on the Sabbath. On the opposite side of the room in which Francis and his pals sit are some of West Midland's most attractive young ladies. Once again, the seven beautiful young women who sit quietly awaiting the Sabbath service, among them Nancy Brookes, are a refreshing sight for the All Saints members. Nancy and her companions are dressed in delicate white dresses with matching linen capes, their outfits topped off by small gypsy hats with lace wings. Appearing as beautiful white blossoms in a monotonous display of Black Country grey, the girls have the boys' undivided attention.

Standing next to the girls is Richard Whatcoat, who offers a cordial greeting.

"Good morning, ladies."

The girls are flattered that the twenty-five-year-old Richard would notice girls only slightly into their teens. They are easily drawn to his steady demeanor and slender face. He tips a slight bow to them.

As if on cue, Francis reacts to Richard Whatcoat, who has strategically placed himself in the open bench area behind the girls. He waves to his friend. Richard returns the obvious gesture, then turns to ask the girls,

"Do you fine ladies mind if I am joined by my dear friend?"

Francis, followed closely by the other boys, is up and moving before the girls can respond to Richard's question. The boys jostle for position as Francis edges his way to sit right behind Nancy. She glances at him briefly, long enough to let him know that she has noticed. She then turns to her friends, slightly raising her chin and giving the look that a female lion gives to the other lionesses in her den: *He's mine.*

The boys are quick to offer a hello; the girls give slight acknowledgement, but return to looking forward. Within moments, the girls are smiling to each other with excitement. Each of the boys and girls carries a King James Version of the Bible. Francis's Bible has a beautiful white ribbon dangling from the pages. He plays with the end of the ribbon that hangs out of the Bible. The ribbon is the one Nancy tied around Francis's bandaged forearm when his school instructor viciously cut it almost four years ago.

The West Bromwich group of Methodists is actually a satellite gathering of the much larger Wednesbury group. The West Bromwich faithful continue to worship at the parish church, All Saints. Fortunately for the Bromwich and Wednesbury worshipers, the vicar of All Saints, Edward Stillingfleet, has gained the confidence of the local family of nobility, the Legge family.

Edward is an Anglican priest who is sympathetic to the Methodist cause. The current Earl of Dartmouth, William Legge, grandson of the first Earl of Dartmouth, secured him for the All Saints church. Brother Dartmouth, as he insists on being called, is a devoted Methodist and member of the Wednesbury Methodist society. William and Edward are both friends of Selina, the Countess of Huntingdon. Through her, Vicar Stillingfleet has been able to secure the most notable itinerants of the Wesleyan movement. Today, one of the Countess's close friends and advisors, Pastor Henry Venn, returns to the Old Church.

The boys and the girls settle themselves as the stately Venn ascends the pulpit. The thirty-seven-year-old man has a religious pedigree of clergy ancestors tracing back, uninterrupted, more than two hundred years, to the times of the Reformation. When Henry was fifteen, his father, an Anglican priest, passed away. At seventeen, he gained entrance into St. John's College, Cambridge. He eventually obtained a Rustat Scholarship[72] for Jesus College, also part of Cambridge University.

---

[72] Started by Tobias Rustat, servant to King Charles II in the seventeenth century, for the children of deceased Anglican priests.

During his university years, Venn not only exemplified his religious fervor, he also displayed above-average ability at the game of cricket. He was easily one of the best players at the school. Nearing completion of his education and awaiting ordination, he played for Surrey in a public match of cricket. The game results were in his favor. At its finish, he threw his bat to the ground, proclaiming, "Whoever wants a bat which has done me good service may take that, as I have no further occasion for it." When his friends inquired of his reason for such action, he replied, "Because I am to be ordained this Sunday, and I will never have it said of me, 'Well struck, Parson!' " Despite the pleadings of his friends, tutors, and instructors, he remained faithful to his vow.

Venn is currently the vicar of Huddersfield Parish Church. He accepted the position two years ago, leaving his role as chaplain to the Countess. Despite his success with Lady Huntingdon in spreading the Gospel via her biblical cavalry throughout England, Ireland, and Wales, he felt called to the parish position. He is one of a handful of Methodist preachers at this time who are ordained in the Anglican Church; the Wesley brothers, Stillingfleet, William Grimshaw, and a few others are fortunate enough to gain that honor.[73] Despite the High Church's fear of the evangelical movement, Pastor Venn's pedigree allows for some forbearance when it comes to his involvement with the brothers Wesley, George Whitefield, and the Countess. The Church of England is also happy that Venn's work in Huddersfield, like Stillingfleet's in West Bromwich, is fully submitting to the Anglican structure by meeting in the parish church.

Traveling with him today is twenty-seven-year-old Thomas Hawes, the new chaplain to the Countess and her aristocratic friends. Thomas is a bright young man, his wisdom easily displayed when he, along with the Countess, helped Henry Venn to abandon his distorted view of works salvation.[74]

Thomas seats himself in the front row of the church and listens quietly as Venn begins.

> "We can make no atonement to a violated law. We have no inward holiness of our own; the Lord Jesus Christ is the Lord of our Righteousness."

With these opening words, Pastor Venn has everyone's undivided attention, especially that of Francis and Richard.

---

[73] George Whitefield, although ordained, is considered too Calvinistic to be Methodist, yet is still looked on with suspicion as one who is dangerous to the cold and lifeless formalism of the Anglican Church.

[74] The view that good works will get one into heaven.

Venn continues,

> "Cling not to such beggarly elements, such filthy rags - -

> "Mere cobwebs of pharisaical pride. However, look to Him who hath wrought out a perfect righteousness for His people. Do you find it a hard task to come naked and miserable to Christ? I beg you, come. Come divested of every recommendation but that of abject wretchedness and misery, and receive from the outstretched hand of our divine Immanuel the riches, the super-abounding riches of redeeming grace.

> "Were I a wise man, these words would have originated with me. However, they didn't. Providence shared these words with me at a critical time in my life when I went back to my former mistaken ways of religiosity. These were not the words of a man, but of a woman—my dear friend Selina, the Countess of Huntingdon. As well as for myself, they are also the words for many a weary soul that tires of doing good. For good shall fail as an admittance into the kingdom; doing good is merely an indication that you have already secured entrance into the kingdom through Christ and Christ alone, and equally as important, He has secured your heart. There must be no conditions. He must be the only Mediator between God and sinful men, 'no miserable performances,' as the dear Countess so wisely wrote. She and others like our dear Thomas called me to abandon my reliance on works and to preach Christ crucified as the only foundation of the sinner's hope, to preach Him as the Author and Finisher, as well as the sole object of faith.

> "Faith—this is the gift of God."

Francis stares at the cover of his Bible. The vicar's words are releasing an invitation in his soul; he finds himself silently asking God, *Doing good will fail; why does this thought bring peace to my soul?* This appealing proposal lingers long, causing Francis to miss much of Venn's remaining message.

At the completion of the service, Francis and his pals wait for the adults to vacate the chapel. The two Jameses and the two Thomases make small talk with the girls. Well, at least one of the Jameses, James Bayley, is conversant. James Mayo is shy to begin with; in the presence of the girls, he is completely silent.

Among the girls is Nancy. Quietly looking forward, she patiently waits for Francis to join in and offer conversation, but he does not. Francis has turned toward Richard, still seated behind him.

"The gift of God—faith is the gift of God, Richard."

Richard looks to his companion, then is distracted by the man approaching from behind Francis. Richard silently nods to his pal in agreement as the oncoming gentleman offers a question.

"Young man, may I have a word?"

Francis turns to his right. Standing before him is Vicar Venn.

Francis hesitates. He thinks to himself, *what - - do you call me? Why would such a man of God call me?*

"Yes, Vicar."

Francis fumbles to make his way out of the pew; Nancy watches as the young man to whom she would gladly give her heart makes his way to the front of the church.

At the front, Francis stands facing the venerable man who gently holds the Bible in front of him with both hands. Francis nervously fumbles with his own Bible and then the hem of his coat sleeve. Venn begins,

> "I have a word for you, young man—a sacred word, from Paul's letter to the Ephesians. That which you seek is found in the second chapter of this most amazing epistle: 'For by grace are ye saved through faith; and that not of yourselves: it is the gift of God, not of works, lest any man should boast.' "

Francis is silent. Venn, observant man that he is, leans in and whispers to Francis,

> "You insult the giver when you attempt to pay for the gift."

Francis says nothing as he looks into the loving eyes of the Vicar. Deep inside he senses a peace that transcends all understanding; he knows *the Word of God has made a deep impression on my heart.*

Francis makes his way back to his friends. Nancy is the first to notice.

"Francis, your face."

Francis tilts his head in ignorance. He ventures to ask,

"What of my face?"

"It has a countenance of joy."

Embarrassed, he turns to Richard.

" 'Tis true, Francis, you do give off a joyous glow . . ."

***

The Wednesday night meeting is several hours away. Francis wipes his brow with his left forearm as he considers this thought. From his right hand hangs his iron mallet. He lays the tool onto the anvil in front of him, desperately in need of a break. He has been beating on the anvil for more than twenty minutes straight. Thirsty, he turns and walks toward the exit of the forge.

Walking past several young men beating out pieces on their anvils, Francis notices his pal, James Mayo. James is creating the main shaft for a monkey wrench. The piece will eventually join other parts that will comprise the entire assembly for the much-needed tool utilized by the more experienced ironworkers at the forge. James focuses on the hypnotic rhythm resulting from his blows. His hammer beats the red-hot iron once every three seconds. Each stroke is gentle enough not to snap the iron and finishes with a subtle bounce after the main stroke.

Francis stops to watch. As he stands there looking at James, he considers his unusual friend. James doesn't have to work at the forge; he is from a wealthy family. The Mayo family has been in West Bromwich for more than one hundred years. In 1716, when Sir Samuel Clark purchased a portion of the ancient feudal estate of the lords of Bromwich, several of the town's wealthy men purchased additional out-parcels of the old manor estates. James Mayo's ancestor, John Mayo, was one of these men. Considering this fact, as well as his own family's limited means, Francis finds James's hard work admirable.

James hasn't noticed that Francis is there. Francis attempts to gain James's attention by singing in time with the strokes of the hammer,

> "O for a thousand tongues to sing
> My Great Redeemer's praise,
> The glories of my God and King
> The triumphs of His grace."

Without missing a beat, James surprises Francis by joining in on the Charles Wesley hymn.

> "My gracious Master and my God,
> Assist me to proclaim,
> To spread through all the earth abroad
> The honors of Thy name."

Several of the young men around Francis and James take notice; they adjust their blows, mimicking the rhythm of James. They too begin to sing,

> "Jesus, the name that charms our fears,
> That bids our sorrows cease;
> 'Tis music in the sinner's ears,
> 'Tis life and health and peace."

The entire forge has caught on. Several men hop from the blast furnace, grabbing their hammers and a piece of wrought iron. They too play the beat as they make their way toward the singing group. Others abandon their anvils and do the same.

At the impromptu gathering, every man from the forge is now singing in time,

> "He breaks the power of canceled sin,
> He sets the prisoner free,
> His blood can make the foulest clean,
> His blood availed for me.
> He speaks, and listening to His voice,
> New life the dead receive,
> The mournful, broken hearts rejoice,
> The humble poor believe."

As the men complete this last line, Mr. Foxall arrives. Immediately the men cease their singing. However, James, Francis, and a couple of boys around them do not notice Foxall's arrival; they continue.

The men of the group try to give notice. James and Francis, along with the few, fail to understand. They continue.

Each eventually stops as he catches a glimpse of Foxall, even Francis and James.

An uncomfortable silence falls as each looks to the other, uncertain of their boss's reaction. They know he is a man of God, but he is also a man who reports to others; he has a schedule to keep. Mr. Foxall walks into the group. The gathering parts, allowing their supervisor to head straight for Francis and James.

At James's anvil, Mr. Foxall lifts James's mallet from his hand.

The men grow uncomfortable, some nervously fumbling with their hammers, others rubbing the backs of their necks, not sure what Foxall is going to say.

Foxall methodically looks to the entire group, going eye to eye with each man. They are a motley bunch, with faces, arms, and clothes covered in the black soot that floats around the forge. He says nothing. The musky smell of body odor, fire, and industry wafts through the spontaneous gathering. In his baritone voice, Foxall offers the following:

> "There are so few words that never grow old - -
> Jesus!"

Foxall's proclamation concludes with the hammer raised in the air. With sweaty, chiseled forearms pumping their own hammers in the air, the entire group repeats the word,

> "Jesus!"
> "Jesus!"
> "Jesus!"

After the third iteration, the men, including Foxall, stop and smile at each other. He then poses a question.

> "Would you men protest a break?"

The reply is unanimous,

"No!"

Outside, Francis immediately dashes for the oak-wood water bucket resting atop an oversized tree stump. Along the way, he anxiously surveys the surrounding area. *A most welcome break;* his thought edges him even faster as he races for the tree. As he expected, he is first in line, well ahead of several others his age.

From several sources around the building the young men appear, all thirsting for water, all aiming for the tree stump. Francis gratefully wipes his brow as he gently lifts the iron ladle from the bucket. It slightly overflows with water. He watches as the water flows down the sides of the container. The scoop rises to reach his lips.

He drinks slowly. *Pleasant,* is the thought that surfaces in his mind. The voice from behind him almost startles Francis.

"Shall Thomas and James attend your meeting this evening?"

Francis does not recognize the voice. With the ladle still raised to his mouth, he turns around. His eyes open wide as he brings his agreeable quenching to a sudden halt. Unexpectedly, he loses his grip; the ladle begins to fall to the ground. He fumbles to catch it, and the dipper's remaining water splashes onto the man standing before Francis.

The man doesn't flinch.

"I would gather that you require more need of refreshment than I?"

Francis quickly bends to pick up the dipper. Midway, he returns upright and attempts to wipe the water from the handsome quilted waistcoat of the visitor. Black sooty smudges appear on the beautiful hand-crafted garment.

"Oh, my deepest apologies."

Francis wipes his hands on the front of his leggings. He looks to his hands; they remain dirty.

By now, Francis has gained an audience. The hardworking young men and boys try not to laugh as Francis attempts to make amends. A young boy around twelve years old scurries in to retrieve the fallen ladle. Staring at the nobleman who stands before him, Francis is unaware that he has lost the coveted spoon.

The well-connected man standing before the teenage ironworker is William Legge the Second, Earl of Dartmouth, the noble of residence at Sandwell Hall. The Old Mill Farm that surrounds the forge supplies beef, fruits, and vegetables for the Earl and his family.

As he regards his sullied outfit, the handsome thirty-year-old British statesman puckers his right cheek in disappointment. Raising his head, he comments,

"Many years ago it became evident that touching iron will leave a sooty trail."

He smiles at Francis and continues,

"Not to worry—I shall address this unfortunate circumstance later. Again I ask you, shall Thomas and James attend your meeting this evening?"

Nervous and ashamed that he soiled the Earl's expensive garment, Francis replies,

"I would expect both shall attend."

The nobleman standing in front of Francis makes a request.

"I wish that you should convey these to them both."

The Earl has in his hands a handsome leather binder filled with parchments. The notebook is more than an inch thick and is secured with a wide leather strap. He offers the book to Francis.

Francis is hesitant to reach for the booklet. He moves toward the lad drinking at the water bucket and snatches the ladle from the young boy. The lad flinches, then quickly turns to retaliate. He reconsiders when he finds himself staring into Francis's midsection.

Francis dips some water from the bucket; he pours it onto his left hand, switches hands with the ladle, then pours water on his right hand. He hands the spoon back to the young boy and proceeds to clean his own hands. After rubbing them together, he wipes them on his trousers—no more trail of black soot. He looks to his hands once more, and is satisfied that they are clean enough.

He reaches to receive the notebook. When it arrives in his hands, he ponders its contents; *there are many pages inside*. Francis attempts to look at the documents. He pauses and speaks to the Earl,

"Touching iron will leave a sooty trail."

Brother Dartmouth smiles at Francis's proclamation. He laughs aloud as Francis once again wipes his right hand, this time on the back of his trousers. Francis slowly returns his gaze to the Earl and asks,

"May I?"

"Of course."

Francis gently removes the leather strap that binds the notebook. He lifts open the front panel and finds a cover sheet labeled "Apostle of Wiltshire." He is quick to look to the Earl, but soon returns to the papers that are captivating his attention; he thumbs to the next page.

The Earl's attractive face is once again lit by a smile. Francis's enthusiastic reception of the documents slightly amuses him, especially as Francis's eyes dance around the page. Within a few moments, Francis raises his head toward the nobleman.

"John Cennick?"

"Yes, John Cennick, the sermons of John Cennick—a wonderful man of God. I am convinced his writings shall be of great value to your class meetings. Please pass them along to Thomas Ault and James Mayo."

"I shall."

The meeting the Earl mentions is a Wesleyan class meeting, one of two important gatherings that are the life-sustaining core of the Wesleyan movement. The other meeting is the band meeting. Both ideas are the ingenious invention of John Wesley.

Geographical location determines one's participation in the class meetings. Membership requirements are simple; first, there must be a personal desire for salvation, evidenced within the local community. Second, once the individual is converted, they must have a desire for holiness. The meetings are generally limited to fewer than two dozen men, women, or children, separated by gender and age unless the group is too small to segregate. When applicable, this separation of the sexes uniquely allows women to participate regularly in positions of leadership. There is a probation period, usually around one hundred days, to determine whether the individual is serious about his or her faith commitment. The atmosphere of the gathering is one of fellowship, with a time of prayer and singing as well as open discussion among all who participate. The conversations deal with matters of faith and personal struggles.

Due to the public nature of the class meeting, the more delicate and personal issues are discussed and handled in a general sense. The depth of these discussions varies according to the size of the group and the openness of the individuals involved. The leader of a class meeting is one who exhibits a depth of Christian understanding and compassion. These caring men and women serve as role models of Christian love and fellowship. They are also the lay leaders, and in some cases, the future preachers of the Wesleyan community.

The class meeting is actually the result of a serendipitous discovery by Wesley. In an effort to raise monies for a facility used by early Methodists in Bristol, Wesley appointed a leader to manage a small group of worshipers. The leader was to collect a weekly donation toward the purchase of the structure. Over a period of several months, it became clear that not all the members could contribute on a regular basis—in fact, the frank discussions resulting from the shortfall of funds revealed that many of the members were enduring hardships previously unnoticed by the preachers and members of the Bristol Wesleyan society. As the leader of the group relayed the various excuses to Wesley, John realized that this was actually the device he had been searching for: a method that would recreate the first-century church's sense of community. He immediately set out to establish this regular meeting arrangement wherever his influence spread.

The band meeting is slightly different, being a voluntary gathering of followers of the Wesleyan movement who meet weekly, men on Wednesday nights and women on Thursday evenings. This group is much smaller, usually fewer than six, and is more intense in nature. In addition to the evidence of conversion and a desire for holiness, the main requirement of band meeting participation is a hunger for a deeper spiritual commitment. The participants are there of their own accord, separated by gender, confessing to and praying for one another. The commitment requires the pledge to honor one another's human dignity as each attempts to mature in the faith. These members are constrained to secrecy regarding the personal confessions. Each is his brother's or sister's keeper. The discussions are deep and sometimes uncomfortable as they address the most intimate problems of life. Each member is set on encouraging the other to "fight the good fight" when dealing with the sinful issues that arise. As with the class meetings, the band meetings end with prayer and singing.

Despite the High Church's suspicion of these Wesleyan societies, they are springing up all over England. Whether the informal class meeting or the intimate band meeting, both small groups are serving to enhance the evangelical spirit within the Anglican Church.

The small groups are not only changing the Anglican Church from the inside out, they are also changing the cultural atmosphere of England. The study of the Bible and other books in these gatherings is raising the intelligence level of the common people. The self-led gatherings of miners, laborers, mechanics, and merchants are also fostering ideals of participative self-government. With the barriers of class, wealth, and gender removed, a spirit of self-help and mutual service become the pillars on which the movement stands—and succeeds. Many make it a goal to learn how to read, first by memorizing Charles's hymns and then by learning to decipher the written letters of these hymns. In the spirit of Christian fellowship, these same individuals, having taught themselves, go on to teach their own children and the children of the surrounding communities.

The occasional visit from Wesley's studious traveling preachers also lifts the intelligence levels of the local citizenry. Wesley's demand that his preachers read at least five hours a day from books on a list established by John himself—books he calls "the most useful books"—has created an intellectual cavalry out of mostly uneducated men. These increased levels of understanding among the populace are so evident that when the English politicians address the peasantry, they now must attempt to appeal to strict ethical and religious principles. This is a change from the politicians' dealings with the peasants in the past, and is also in sharp contrast to the political leaders' current dealings with other groups like the middle and upper classes. Wesley's goal is to move people to act on their own behalf, fostering independence among the underprivileged while urging those with abundance to social responsibility. Where there once was ignorance and vice, there is now godliness and order.

From deep within the forge the cowbell rings, sounding the return to work. Francis instinctively turns to leave. After a half step he turns back toward the nobleman.

> "Oh, my deepest apologies; I must return . . ."
>
> "Enjoy the sermons, Francis. I am happy that you shall consider their wisdom."

For the rest of the work day, the book of Cennick's sermons remains within Francis's view. On more than one occasion he is tempted to open it, but reconsiders in light of his soot-covered hands.

That evening after work, Francis hurries home with his new treasure. He wastes no time in preparing himself for the night's class meeting. He longs to spend a few hours with the book, but he must get ready for the evening's gathering. A quick bite to eat and he is on his way.

The dark meeting room is on the second floor of the two-story brick building on Paradise Street. The structure is on the heath, directly across the street from the beautiful Dagger Hall, a building built entirely of oak. Dagger Hall is owned by the Turton family, owners of the fruit-tree orchard Francis and Thomas Ault traveled through on their first visit to Old Church in West Bromwich.

The meeting room is incomplete, recently abandoned for a second time by a frustrated preacher, James Wheatley. Wheatley is the originator of the space; unfortunately, he did not finish the room because of personal troubles.

Wheatley was once one of Wesley's preachers. In 1751, John expelled him for his teachings that clearly violated Scripture. The upset Wheatley headed out of town for Norwich, where he developed a following. In time, he returned to West Bromwich, determined to rival Wesley and continue spreading his distorted views of the Bible.

Wheatley's views were not new; the first-century church dealt with individuals who took the freedom of salvation by faith alone and distorted it into license. The Apostle Paul dealt with such abuse in his letter to the Romans.[75] Dealing with Wheatley and his gathering of followers, Wesley was swift in his discipline of the talented and outspoken Welsh cobbler-turned-preacher. Wheatley called his followers "my dear lambs." Upon his expulsion by Wesley, the irony of this label

---

[75] Romans chapter 6. This distortion was known as "antinomianism" in Wesley's day, coming from the Greek term meaning lawless. It is the exact opposite of legalism and originated in the Gnosticism movement during the times of the early church.

did not escape John and other Wesleyan preachers who braved verbal and physical harm from the so-called "Wheatley lambs."

In the building on Paradise Street, the wealthy and generous Jonathan Turton climbs the steps to the second floor. The stairwell is dark, its fusty smell occasionally highlighted by an errant cobweb. In the hand of the angular man is a lit taper, which flickers as he slowly enters the upstairs room. He pauses to catch his breath, then methodically makes his way toward the glass window on the other side of the room. A hint of moonlight enters the musty space. He counts to himself, *four, five, and six.* He stops long enough to take a deep breath—not winded, merely cautious. He lowers the candle to look at the floor. His discovery brings a smile. He gently raises his right leg and takes one large step toward the right, then continues to the window.

At the window, he places the candle into a wall-mounted holder. The room appears to oscillate in the candlelight as it catches a slight draft from the adjacent window. At the front of the stuffy room measuring thirty feet square is a three-legged pulpit; it is nothing more than three narrow wood spindles holding a flat oak-wood top, the entire assembly barely big enough to hold a Bible. During the daylight hours, the only window in the space—a rather dirty window, if one takes an honest look—dimly lights the pulpit as well as the room. The horizontal hanging wood planks lining the walls of the room are incomplete and bare. Some are marked with small scrapes and notches carved out by a knife. The majority of these boards are rough-sawn; leaning on them usually results in a slight tear in one's clothing. Other parts of the wall where planks are missing reveal the substructure of the second-level exterior wall. The wooden floor is equally challenged. A series of planks is worn from foot traffic, the whitewash finish almost completely rubbed off. Most of the boards are structurally sound, but a few show visible stress from past leaks through the room's window and roof. Many who visit the upstairs room know to avoid these spots for fear of the boards giving way, sending them crashing to the floor below. This is the reason for Mr. Turton so carefully counting his steps; he doesn't want to tread on one of the weakened areas.

Mr. Turton makes his way to the pulpit and places his worn Bible onto the wood top. He struggles with the fact that he has not made it a point to improve the forsaken space. His thoughts quickly shift as he ponders the wood pillar that stands at the exact center of the room. Rubbing his left elbow with his right hand in his characteristic manner, he analyzes the situation: *Ten on the right, four men and six boys; and seven on the left, three women and four girls.* Confident that the room has enough space for the slowly growing group, he kneels to pray.

"Almighty Father, I come to Thee as a sinner, one in desperate need of Your merciful grace. I lay aside all pretenses that I am worthy of such love. May You bring courage to this room this evening—courage to all who attend, and courage to a young man who will stand before family and peers and bring a word from your Word . . ."

Tonight's meeting is a class meeting of those Methodists who live close to West Bromwich. The Asbury family falls into this category. Tonight's meeting is also a special meeting, for the young man for whom Mr. Turton was praying will pray and read Scripture, and will also speak about the Scripture he has chosen to read.

Mr. and Mrs. James Bayley are the first to arrive, along with their son James. He is a thin young man, about two inches shorter than the five-foot-nine Francis. His passion for hard work has earned him a position on Dartmouth's Sandwell estate. The younger James is an outgoing, talkative young man; this has given him opportunity to become a good friend of Francis.

Facing toward the makeshift pulpit, father and son seat themselves on the left side of the room. Mother proceeds to the right. The process repeats itself for the Ault family as well. Thomas Ault, along with his brother Jabez, coax their father to sit on the front row. It is not a difficult decision when they consider that there are only two rows. On their own, James Mayo and Thomas Russell arrive. Both boys are stocky and slightly shorter than Francis. They are the quiet and almost methodical pair from the Asbury group of pals. Their unmistakable slow gait makes it appear as if they are brothers. Almost scaring them out of their quiet demeanor as he springs to his feet, Thomas Ault quickly greets them.

"A rather exciting evening!"

James Mayo and Thomas Russell smile in agreement. Thomas embraces them both.

Three women are next to arrive: Ann Firm, Sarah Mullin, and Ann Cutler. The middle-aged ladies are slightly winded from the climb upstairs. They pause to catch their breath. Noticing their struggle, Mrs. Ault rises from her seat to escort the women to the right side of the room.

Thomas Ault walks to the center post in the room, then turns and motions for James Mayo to follow. As Thomas Russell takes a seat, James walks slowly toward his friend. Thomas poses a question,

"Would you venture a guess that he shall not show?"

James sharpens his focus to quickly peer at Thomas. His reply is almost sharp.

"I've never known him to back away from a commitment."

Thomas silently nods as he considers James's reply.

"Nor have I."

At the acknowledgment James relaxes, enough for Thomas to grab his right arm and try to pull him toward the distressed portion of the floor. James has been here before; he pushes Thomas away.

"Thomas, you devil!"

James turns and heads for his seat, shaking his head and laughing quietly at his friend's attempt at a practical joke.

The young men are soon delightfully distracted as Nancy Brookes arrives along with three of her friends. Thomas Ault is quick to respond,

"And a rather blessed evening."

Thomas's statement is deliberately audible to his friends and the four lovelies who have entered the room. The girls make their way to the right side of the room, the hems of their dresses floating an inch above the floor. Alone at the post and now bowing politely, Thomas Ault attempts to greet the young ladies.

"Why, hello . . ."

They ignore the kind gesture and proceed to their seats. James Bayley offers Thomas a word,

"A far cry from our dear Francis . . ."

His sarcastic slight of Thomas has the three young men laughing. Holding back his laughter as he struggles for decorum, Thomas rises from his frozen bow. From his seat next to James, Thomas Russell takes the mature route.

"Should not we pursue more profitable ventures? I suggest we sit and pray for our dear friend."

Thomas heads for his seat next to his companions.

As the three boys bow to silently pray, Mr. Turton nervously paces at the front of the room. *Attendance could be much larger than expected.* With sixteen people already present, his original estimate of seventeen is not far away. *Room cannot contain much more than nineteen.* He tries not to recall that it could actually contain close to fifty people if the floor repairs were completed. He crosses his arms; raising his right hand to his face, be begins tapping his teeth on the bent knuckle of his pointer finger.

The men in the room, Mr. Ault and Mr. Bayley, notice Jonathan's unsettled gesture. They instinctively get up and slide their chairs to the right side of the room. Their deed accomplished, they proceed for the back of the room. Looking around, the verbal James Bayley speaks up.

"He has arrived."

James rises from his seat. He bounces with excitement as he walks to the young man who has entered the room.

"Grand evening, Francis."

Francis welcomes the hug from his friend, but doesn't reply. Keeping his eyes on the floor, he tightens his lips together and nods. James wisely withholds comment and returns to his chair. The two Thomases are aware of Francis's reaction. They look to each other, each thinking the same thing: *He is quite nervous.*

Soon after Francis's arrival, his parents enter the room. Joseph escorts Eliza to her chair with the ladies. With the task politely completed, he turns and heads for the rear of the room, standing next to Mr. Ault and Mr. Bayley.

The three gentlemen say nothing. Joseph takes in a measured breath. The men make eye contact with Joseph, nodding their confidence that Francis will do well tonight.

Following the Asburys, three additional young ladies enter the room. Realizing that Francis is already heading for the front, they hurry to their friend Nancy Brookes. Their arrival fails to go unnoticed by Francis's pals.

Francis faces the group as he stands next to the front row, purposely avoiding eye contact with his pals. He nervously stares at the rickety pulpit. *This is near to impossible.* Self-condemning thoughts begin. He fumbles with the ribbon that hangs from his Bible. From its position, it appears to mark a passage somewhere in the New Testament. *I am a poor, ignorant, foolish, and unfaithful creature.* His thoughts continue to buffet his trembling soul. *If only my vitals would settle.*

In the midst of his emotional battle, he raises his eyes to find nearly two dozen familiar faces staring at him. His focus darts from the people, to the pulpit, to the window, and back to the attendees. He decides to look at his shoes. He ventures to end by staring at the floor space in front of him. But no; on to the ceiling, where he spots the flimsy waves of a spider's web attached to the top of the wood pillar. He quickly returns his gaze to the floor space at his feet.

He ventures to look out again, and this time meets with success—the unsettling encounter unexpectedly coming to a halt as he catches a most inviting sight: beauty itself, fashioned with delicate, softened edges. It doesn't come naturally, but as he gains the confidence to linger, the effort becomes a gentle and pleasing experience—one in which he finds himself, as in times past, drawn to gaze in an almost audacious fashion. This exquisite creature not only gives pleasure to the eyes, but also seems to satisfy his deepest sense of purpose. It comes as a surprise, but in the face of his dearest Nancy, he is finding inspiration to face the unknown.

Fearing discovery, he moves his focus to the window, then back to Nancy. To the window and then back again. With each glance in her direction, he senses an easing of his internal struggle. She is fully aware of his glances, edging her gaze slowly in his direction, careful not to startle his awareness of her. With the slightest smile, she lifts her eyes—eyes that can't help but reflect the sparkle of the flittering candle, eyes that are slowly turning toward her expectant companion . . .

"Francis . . ."

Shaken by the deep voice, Francis ends his fanciful flight.

Instantly, the nervous feelings return. He nods to Mr. Turton as he points toward the likely-to-collapse pulpit. Francis makes his way to the crude podium. The spindle legs slightly twist and creak as he sets his Bible onto the oak top. He begins,

"Sh- Sh- Shall we pray?"

The room is eerily silent as the people bow their heads and wait for Francis's offering to the Lord. A long and uncomfortable silence follows. Small noises become apparent: the wind gently blowing through a crack in the window frame, a stray dog barking in the distance, the squeaking of the pulpit as Francis pushes his weight onto the wooden top.

Dry with fear, his throat will not bring the words.

The stomach discomfort has now progressed into a slight trembling of his hands. As he struggles with the quickening pulse that runs through his arms and chest, he moves to open his Bible. *Perhaps I shall read a Psalm for prayer.* He accidentally knocks the sacred book onto the floor.

Several women gasp as the Scriptures thud onto the wooden plank floor. Nevertheless, everyone continues to sit with head bowed, imagining what has transpired. Francis bends and picks up his Bible.

Again, there is a protracted silence.

Francis raises his head and searches for Nancy. It's not that there are a multitude of people in the room; it is Francis's slight panic that has caused him to lose sight of her. *Her face, I fail to see her face.* It finally dawns on him, *her head is bowed like the rest.*

Unexpectedly, Francis finds himself amused. He silently laughs to himself, *Almighty Father, what shall I gain from earthly pursuits?* He pauses to reconsider his thoughts. *Please help me to speak.*

The completion of his quiet prayer brings a lessening of the inner trembling. He is able to take a slow and deliberate breath. He begins again.

"I shall read from the Gospel of John."

At this, the attendees raise their heads. In the background, the sound of feet ascending the steps changes the mood. Several people look to the top of the stairs, waiting to see who has arrived.

Francis welcomes the distraction. He looks to his hands; they continue to shake slightly.

At the entrance to the room is a young man, neatly dressed. It is William Emery. Francis smiles, then motions for him to take a seat.

"Please be seated."

Francis is surprised that the words have come out so easily. He continues with his planned reading of the Scriptures.

"The Gospel of John, chapter . . ."

Another set of footsteps on the stairs interrupts Francis. All in the room once again wait for the new arrival.

The heavy steps indicate that the newcomer is a man. Within a few moments, a tall, stocky man enters the room, his familiar face bringing further comfort to Francis. The itinerant preacher removes his hat and bows his head toward Francis.

"Master'd Asbur'dy, my deepest apologies."

"Quite all right, Pastor Mather."

With the attendance at twenty-four, the room is beyond normal capacity—or, more accurately, normal capacity before proper repairs. Pastor Mather takes his place along the rear wall next to Joseph. Francis smiles at his father. Joseph returns the smile, and Francis begins.

"The Gospel of John, chapter fourteen.

" 'Let not your heart be troubled; you believe in God, believe also in Me. In My Father's house are many mansions; if it were not so, I would have told you. I go to prepare a place for you. And if I go and prepare a place for you, I will come again and receive you to Myself; that where I am, there you may be also. And where I go you know, and the way you know.'

"Thomas said to Him, 'Lord, we do not know where You are going, and how can we know the way?'

"Jesus said to him, 'I am the way, the truth, and the life. No one comes to the Father except through Me. If you had known Me, you would have known My Father also; and from now on you know Him and have seen Him.'

"Philip said to Him, 'Lord, show us the Father, and it is sufficient for us.'

"Jesus said to him, 'Have I been with you so long, and yet you have not known Me, Philip? He who has seen Me has seen the Father; so how can you say, 'Show us the Father?' Do you not believe that I am in the Father, and the Father in Me? The words that I speak to you I do not speak on My own authority; but the Father who dwells in Me does the works. Believe Me that I am in the Father and the Father in Me, or else believe Me for the sake of the works themselves.

" 'Most assuredly, I say to you, he who believes in Me, the works that I do he will do also; and greater works than these he will do, because I go to My Father. And whatever you ask in My name, that I will do, that the Father may be glorified in the Son. If you ask anything in My name, I will do it.'

"The Gospel of John."

The room's attendees remain as quiet as they were during the reading. Francis scans the room. With each face, he finds himself in a comfortable setting. This peace is unexpected, undoubtedly the blessing of God. If it were up to him, he would linger in this moment, with the peace of God settling into his soul. But he wisely begins.

"Jesus's words, 'I am the way, the truth, and the life, no one comes to the Father except through Me'—these most vital words of the Savior clearly reveal that He possesses no competitors. This is His adventurous claim, that by no other means may humanity come to the Father. The courageous statement is full of risk, for if it shall be proven otherwise or if Jesus shall be revealed a fraud, His claim to exclusivity is clearly ineffectual.

"Shall we consider the transforming power of Jesus? Throughout our lives we have encountered individuals whose hearts have changed toward the Savior. Were not these turnings authenticated by the actions of these we encounter? Have you heard of any other god that can change a man's direction? I have not. Have you heard of any other religion that boasts of such transforming power? I have not. Only Jesus can change a heart, He is truly the way, the truth, and the life.

"The pen of Charles Wesley conveys it best,

'Jesus the name, high over all,
In hell or earth or sky;
Angels and mortals prostrate fall,
And devils fear and fly.
Jesus! The name to sinners dear,
The name to sinners given;
It scatters all their guilty fear,
It turns their hell to heaven.' "

Francis raises his hands to pray. He looks to his hands; *they fail to shake*.

Francis's heart is overjoyed; he is experiencing a perfect peace. His breaths are sure and deep. *Oh, for this moment to never end.*

By now, he realizes that he should pray. Expecting the attendees to consider him strange for gazing at his raised hands for such a long period, he looks to the congregation. To his surprise, he finds that all their heads are bowed. He decides to linger for an additional moment, his heart pounding with excitement. He begins his prayer and quickly concludes,

". . . and Father, in the name of our appointed Savior, we thank you. Amen."

Pastor Mather is the first to react. He leaps from the back wall, his hastened steps drawing the attention of all in the room. With his hat in his left hand and Bible in his right, he approaches the young sermon-giver with open arms.

With one large grasp, the big man's embrace smothers Francis.

At the back wall, Mr. Ault and Mr. Bayley grip each of Joseph's hands in a hearty two-fisted handshake.

"The Lord has blessed you, Joseph."

His pursed lips revealing that he is fighting back deep emotions, Joseph acknowledges Ault's encouragement.

At the front of the room, Francis glances toward his mother; she sits in her chair, in tears. Mrs. Ault and the other women offer smiling comfort. The sight of his mother's emotion moves Francis also; still in the embrace of Alexander Mather, he has to struggle to raise his right hand to wipe away a gentle tear that has journeyed down his cheek.

All in the room are now standing. Near to Eliza is Nancy, surrounded by the other young girls. Her eyes lock onto Francis's, her most pleasing smile giving forth an unquenchable inner joy. Each of her companions gently clings to her arms as they share in her happiness.

Mather mentions to Francis,

"Fr'dancis, later on, Ah' would like to encourage ya'; may Ah' have a private moment?"

Francis is quick to respond to the itinerant's question.

"Yes, Pastor Mather."

As the group begins to disperse for the evening, Francis's friends come forward, each offering their pal a firm handshake and embrace. Especially moved by the evening's results, Thomas Ault's hug lasts longer than the others. Each display of love and friendship confirms for the watching itinerant what is deep in his heart. In front of his companions, Mather urges Francis,

"Fr'dancis, this special group of ya's should form a band."

The boys fall silent. Francis too stops to ponder this suggestion. Almost immediately, the boys begin mumbling amongst themselves. Pastor Mather tries to understand what they are quietly discussing. He presses Thomas Ault,

"Master'd Ault, ya' question my idea?"

Thomas is hesitant to reply; he looks to Francis, then to the other young men. Francis lightly shoves Thomas.

"Go ahead, Thomas, ask."

Thomas doesn't say a word.

The strange silence causes Mather to question Francis,

"What is it, Fr'dancis?"

   With his trademark smile, the smile that displays that Francis is up to something, he replies,
   "My pals fail to understand that which you ask - -
   They fail to comprehend your Scottish accent."
   Raising the hand that holds the Bible, Pastor Mather breaks into a hearty laugh. He brings his arm down hard onto Francis's shoulders. Francis almost buckles from the impact. The boys, including Francis, smile at the preacher. Mather is quick to respond,
   "Ya' boys are somet'in' else.
   "Fr'dancis, organize ya' band . . ."

Two Are Better Far Than One

Woe to him, whose spirits droop,
To him, who falls alone!
He has none to lift him up,
And help his weakness on;
Happier we each other keep,
We each other's burden bear;
Never need our footsteps slip,
Upheld by mutual prayer.

Charles Wesley[76]

Francis's closed-mouth, reticent smile instantly appears upon hearing the words of his dear friend, Thomas Ault. Thomas voices them again,

"Fantastic, Francis, purely fantastic—it is that which you are born to."

Thomas's enthusiastic delivery adds to his heartfelt statement. Nevertheless, Francis's smile fades; he remains lost in a fixed stare. Even the stoic James Mayo offers encouragement.

"Could not have declared it better myself - -

Thomas is dead right; you are born to preach."

Francis's riveted look remains. With his unmistakable short-legged stride, James Mayo makes his way, unnoticed, closer to Francis. Standing in front of his friend, he waves his chunky right hand in front of Francis's eyes. The serious look of the young man who seldom has a down moment does not waver; he remains frozen in concentration. Disappointed, James huffs aloud, then turns and walks away.

Resting his chin in his right hand supported by the elbow leaning on his thigh, Francis finally replies.

"You fail to know that which I experienced."

The words bring his friends in closer.

Thomas Ault, James Mayo, James Bayley, Thomas's brother Jabez, and Thomas Russell have all gathered for their first-ever band meeting. Following the advice of Pastor Mather, the young men have decided to meet once a week in an effort to deepen their faith in God. On this Sunday afternoon in Wednesbury, they have unanimously appointed Francis their leader. James Mayo prods,

"Go on, Francis . . ."

---

[76] Charles Wesley hymn "Two are Better Far Than One," written to his wife, Sally, 1749.

James's encouragement elicits more from Francis.

"I was sharing - -

That which I experienced was most unsettling."

He pauses. Uncharacteristically, he leans his supporting hand away and lowers his head. It is as if he is waiting for something.

Francis's cessation of speech leads to an uncomfortable silence. In the background, the lazy vocal expressions of garden birds, their stomachs full from a morning of foraging, announce the arrival of midday.

The awkward quiet causes the older boys to attempt to identify with Francis's comment. They nervously fold and unfold their arms and give quick eye contact to each other; James Bayley rubs his scratchy beard stubble with the palm of his hand. Each wishes that Francis would say something, anything. Finally, the less mature Jabez blurts out,

"We all are unsettled when speaking in public."

Francis slowly lifts his head to give Jabez a bleak stare, causing the youngster to look away with embarrassment. *You have no idea.* With a sigh, Francis finally gives in.

"This was far more than a nervous outing, Jabez. That which I experienced was truly planted deep in my soul."

Leaning back in his chair, with both hands nervously tapping on his thighs, he offers more.

"At first I enjoyed the pleasant array of God's holy comfort, His unmistakable Advocate, inhabiting my countenance. Welcomed as it was, I proceeded as Thomas proclaimed, with great success. Nevertheless, later that evening, alone in my room . . . that is when the turmoil began - -

When the buffeting began. The painful murmurings of an ancient time surfaced from within me. Every fiber of my muscles began to twitch uncontrollably."

Francis's companions are mystified; this is not what they expected to hear from their spiritual leader. Each decides to sit, while the confession moves Francis to stand. With head down, he begins to pace from one side of the room to the other. On close inspection, it is clear that his hands are trembling slightly. In a shaken fashion, his tall and sinewy frame still pacing, Francis explains,

"As I lay upon my bed that evening, longing for the precious peace of the Almighty, my soul struck hard against me, as if the pounding originated from the core of my back, transmitting to the backs of my thighs, then the fronts. My chest ached in fear. It was well into the night that I wrestled with these rumblings, nay, feelings—if they were feelings. Rolling to the right and then to the left was my ordeal, a vigilant watch. One thing was certain: sleep came at high cost that fateful night.

"My cry was that of King David: 'Cast me not away from Thy presence, and take not Thy Holy Spirit from me.' "

The boys continue to sit in silence. For once, the young men who usually have to work at focusing for more than a few seconds are locked into each word that comes from their troubled friend. Francis continues to pace, but at least he has raised his head a little.

"It soon became clear that this struggle was more than the trembling of a sinful body; this battle was a resolute contention with a memory."

Francis brings his methodical pacing to a halt. He raises his hands to his face; in the palms of his calloused hands, he weeps. From deep within his soul, the quiet crying emerges. His companions look to each other in silence. This is their truest friend, their leader, and a kindred spirit to each of them.

Turning to stand with his back to the group, facing the window, Francis lifts his head from his hands. He proceeds to peel back another layer.

"A memory - -
Memory of one whose severity filled me with such horrible dread."

Francis's words bring a slight feeling of embarrassment to the group; almost in unison, the confession causes each to remove their focus from Francis. Slightly uncomfortable, they each look to the wooden floor of the meeting room. It is difficult, but each eventually refocuses on Francis, who now has turned toward his companions. Wrapped in a deep look of concern, he nervously scrapes his top teeth across his bottom lip.

In an effort to be considerate, James quietly rises from his chair. At least it is an attempt; his awkward movement causes his wooden chair to loudly scrape the floor. All but Francis turn their heads toward James and look with apparent disdain on his rude slip. This doesn't bother James; he brings forth the inevitable question, the question each of Francis's companions is longing to ask.

"Of whom might this memory be?"

The question causes Francis to focus his gaze toward the window. With his left hand resting on the sill, he pauses as he raises his right hand, balled into a loose fist; then lowers his head, gently touching his lips to the tawny skin of his thumb and forefinger. Several seconds elapse before he raises his face to speak. As if talking through the window, Francis continues,

"Memory I imagined concluded long ago.

"A few years back, I found myself frightened beyond understanding, trembling and alone, lying in bed—failing to settle, forever trembling. Back then I was aware of its source; however, time has made clear that which I continue to deal with . . ."

Francis pauses again. This time he walks from the window and takes a seat among his friends. Taking a slow, deliberate breath, he looks to each of them as he struggles with a powerful emotion, almost too embarrassed to reveal the source of his difficulty. Nevertheless, he knows he needs to air his deepest fear. Pressing onward, he continues,

> "That which causes me to tremble - -
> Which causes me to tremble are the striking words of my old instructor, Arthur Taylor: 'Master Asbury, you are destined for failure.' "

Francis looks to each of his friends, whose eyes remain fixed upon the strained face of their companion. This brings comfort to Francis. Satisfied that his friends are trying to identify with his pain, he continues,

> "That hideous man filled me with such horrible dread that for me, anything was preferable to going to school. The daily beatings escorted the nightly trembling into my life. Taylor was a great churl—Thomas, you are aware of this. He caused me much suffering, and that suffering seems to have returned."

The young men say nothing. They look to Francis, then to each other. All look to Thomas Ault as he steps toward Francis.

> "Our instructor was indeed a great churl."

Thomas's acknowledgement causes Francis to nod. The sigh in Thomas Ault's voice reveals his pain on Francis's behalf. He places his arms on the shoulders of his dearest friend.

> "Has not the good Lord made way for you to move beyond that odious fellow?"

Francis nods his head. The others also rise and move in close. The look on Francis's face, the slight smile that peeks from the left side of his lips, conveys his thankfulness for their encouragement.

> "He has, but I continue to struggle."
> "Wherein lies your struggle, Francis?"
> "The recent event has brought the revelation that my struggle of outright fear may have transformed into a cry for purpose. I refuse to become Taylor's obnoxious proclamation - -
> I refuse to become a failure."

The young men seem to relax as they ponder this statement. James Mayo walks to the window. Jabez and his brother look to each other. Thomas gently encourages Francis to continue.

> "Go on."

Once again, Francis pauses to gauge the acceptance of his pals. With some reluctance, he offers the root of his difficulty.

"I have given this struggle much thought. The conflict has resulted in a revealing question. At what point do my yearnings to accomplish become sinful pride?"

The friends return to their pensive looks. None has answer; they're not spiritually mature enough to come close to an acceptable reply. Realizing that this is beyond his ability to comprehend, James Mayo turns from the window, uncomfortable with the silence of the room's inhabitants. In an effort to lighten the present mood, he decides to change the subject.

"What of Sutton?"

James's question regards the town of Sutton Coldfield. A young man of Francis's age, who resides in that beautiful country town on the outskirts of Birmingham, has invited Francis to his home. The teenager, Edward Hand, met Francis at a Sunday service in West Bromwich. After the service, Edward approached Francis and requested that he lead a meeting in prayer and Bible reading at his home in Sutton. The appeal was a surprise to Francis, for in the request he was also encouraged to exhort on God's Word "if he felt so led."

Amidst the group's silence, Francis shares his desire.

"I shall move onward to that which I am called to."

Francis's reply brings some relief to the group. However, Francis once again lowers his head and stares at the floor. James continues the thought,

"Shall it benefit for us to accompany you?"

Francis is silent. He once again scrapes at his bottom lip with his teeth. Slowly he raises his head and looks to James Mayo.

"I would count it a favor . . ."

Francis and his pals waste no time as they depart from their first-ever band meeting. Francis's willingness to preach in Sutton gives the group new life. At the edge of town, they begin their trek through the forest of ancient oak trees that lies east of Great Barr.

They proceed slightly north of due east from Great Barr. For Francis, this is familiar territory; he is instantly flooded with pleasant memories of his childhood. With his father, Francis enjoyed the sights and sounds of the heaths, marshes, wetlands, and forest that lie due west of Sutton Coldfield. In the past, the father and son's destination was most often the bog at Sutton Park. From these wetlands, his father would harvest the bulrush reeds for making the beautiful handcrafted seat covers of the oak-wood chairs that are part of the Asburys' furnishings. Along the way now, Francis cannot help but smile as he remembers the many hours spent examining the plant life. Even at the tender age of five, he realized that the plant creation was important to his father.

Francis pauses. The young men stop also. Following Francis's lead, all fix their sights skyward, above the treetops. They lean backwards, stretching to take in the view. High above the leafy elms a large bird, a kingfisher, makes its way westward. In its claws is a large fish. Francis offers his opinion of the encounter,

"I would venture either trout or carp . . ."

The boys nod their heads in agreement with Francis's observation; their wide smiles convey that they are of one mind as they eagerly welcome Francis's changed mood. Each, too, is pleased to embrace the sun-warmed view skyward.

Sutton lies slightly less than four miles from Great Barr and slightly more than four miles north of Birmingham. The population of almost 1,300 enjoys plenty of fresh water from the many natural springs that lie on the town's outskirts to the west. This is also the large, heavily-wooded area of Sutton Park. The park consists of almost a fifth of the more than 13,000 acres that make up the parish of Sutton Coldfield. The sixteenth-century deed of King Henry VIII continues to allow the residents the right of pasture, fishing, and hunting in the park. Several large man-made lakes boast of the area's most productive fisheries for food. In addition to the lakes are the dense forests of large oak trees. Several other hardwoods exist in abundance: elm, larch, pine, beech, spruce, and sweet chestnut.

The seven man-made lakes or pools date back to the twelfth and thirteenth centuries. Originally built in the twelfth century as a fish pond, Wyndley Pool is the oldest of the retention areas. From it, the local population continues to eat well. Another pool constructed in the fifteenth century, also for the sole purpose of fish production, is Keeper's Pool. As with the Wyndley Pool, Keeper's Pool boasts a large population of perch and bream. The traditional recipe for the small fish originates from the fifteenth century and consists of baking the fish in flour, seasoned with spices such as pepper, saffron, and cinnamon. The largest of the pools is Powell's Pool. Formed thirty-one years ago in 1730, it contains slightly more than forty-eight acres of water area. The lush Canadian pond weed and blanket weed that grow near the shorelines provide a natural cover for predator fish like carp and pike, some of which can grow to a weight of thirty pounds.

Two of the pools were created to provide water to mills: Blackroot Pool, constructed four years ago to supply water for a leather mill, and Longmoor Pool, celebrating its twentieth year of continued use by a mill that produces buttons. The construction of the pools is ingenious; simply by damming small streams with quarry stones, water from a local river is redirected to a predetermined location. The altered water supply for Sutton's pools comes mainly from several small tributaries of the Plants Brook. The productive river currently supports eleven mills: the leather mill on Blackroot Pool, two corn mills, a button mill on Longmoor, a cloth mill, a saw mill, and several metalworking mills.

Asbury and company are happy to notice the first body of water. They pause to take in the magnificent view of the largest of the pools in Sutton Park, Powell's Pool. The dense hardwood trees that surround the body of water act as a protective rampart. The towering timbers sway as the tiny shimmering leaves catch the strong winds aloft. As the boys walk beneath the lake's perimeter sentries, a small but well-traveled dirt path emerges amidst the fertile, shade-covered soil.

The boys eagerly quicken their pace. Francis hops over a fallen limb; the youngest of the group, Jabez, leaps over the same rotted branch and moves slightly ahead of him. The two Thomases will not be left in the rear; they eagerly pick up the pace, racing each other to the lead. The two Jameses decide that an alternate route will gain them advantage and launch into the dense undergrowth that parallels the ancient trail. Their slow trot immediately turns into a series of vaulted hurdles as they race toward the shoreline.

Within a few minutes the entire group is standing at the water's edge, pausing to catch their breath. None utters a word; the beauty of the lake has their undivided attention. They do their best to capture all that the scene affords.

On the right, a grey heron with its unmistakable black head plumes wades along the striking bog-bean plants at the water's edge. The orchid-like white flowers with the purple-tipped buds buzz with bees mesmerized with the act of pollination. Behind the beautiful blooms, the long-legged bird slowly moves along the shoreline. Mid-step, he darts his powerful orange bill into the shallows. Up he lifts, and in his bill wiggles a small bream fish. It struggles for a short period, until the wise bird raises his bill and swallows the fish whole. At the completion of the bird's afternoon snack, Francis raises his right arm parallel with the ground.

"Give listen . . ."

Francis's advice has the boys taking in the unique sounds. In the distance, the grey heron splashes the water in an attempt at another fish. Nearer, the commotion of flying insects vibrates with a swirling sound; mingled with the resident orchestra are the almost lyrical notes of the yellowhammer perched in the hardwood trees. The brilliant yellow and golden head and chest feathers are as vivid as its whistle which seems to say, "a little bit of bread and no cheese."

Again Francis instructs his chums,

"Look . . ."

He points to a spot nearby on the left; it is a male reed bunting. The tiny bird hangs onto a swaying reed. If the little creature has noticed the pool's newest visitors, he fails to show it. The boys continue to watch in silence as the sparrow-sized bird with the black head displays its summer finery, the duller color of the broad neck collar continuing to highlight the darker head. [77]

Hearing the numerous retellings of Francis's adventure with a little bird, the impetuous Jabez reaches for the unsuspecting bunting; it quickly launches to flight for safety.

Looking behind them, the boys catch the glimmering light of the sun as it begins its late afternoon descent. The angelic beams struggle to rain through the thick-leaved branches of the hardwoods. The trunks and branches of the trees are blackened to silhouettes as each ray of light darkens their color from behind. The more successful streams reach all the way down to the forest floor, illuminating the blankets of white-flowering wood anemone that thickly cover the areas at the base of the trees. Francis gives a final directive,

"We must make way; shall be evening soon."

Francis's comment sends the boys further eastward.

As they enter the grasslands of the park, they catch the gentle scent of the yellow-flowering gorse. The bright blooms of this bushy, dense evergreen relative of the broom plant gives off the slightest hint of coconut when brushed. The boys enjoy the fragrance; it brings a simple pleasure to the hot walk through the park's driest portion of land. As with the broom plant, the gorse is a hardy shrub, one of the few that will thrive after a fire. The seeds that burst from their pods in April and May can remain dormant under the soil for several decades and are usually the first to sprout after a scorching. The flowers of the plant are more than aesthetically pleasing; these striking yellow blooms with the tropical scent are also used to color and flavor teas, beer, and wine.

The home of Edward Hand is located in the Hill Hook section of Sutton Coldfield. The twenty or so randomly placed cottages of the community are located on the northwest limit of Sutton. This makeshift village is mostly populated by poor widows and the elderly, who are dependent on help from the local parish. These residents must sign a twenty-one-year rental lease with the Warden and Society of the King's Town of Sutton Coldfield, also referred to as The Corporation. The remaining younger citizens, like Edward and his family, are also required to sign a lease for the "government" housing. These are families of hardworking artisans, among them weavers, carpenters, masons, tailors, cordwainers,[78] and bricklayers. Their work is carried out at their homes and, like

---

[77] In the winter, the head of the male reed bunting will turn a streaked brownish-red color. The collar is still existent, but in a duller buff color.

[78] Shoemakers.

Edward Hand, some are followers of the brothers Wesley. As for Edward, he is thankful that he can eke out a living making shoes.

Inside the wooden structure—Cottage thirteen to The Corporation—the home of Edward Hand is small but adequate. Twelve people are crammed into the main room of the home. Like the Asbury home, it too has a fireplace. At the rear of the room is a door, opposite the entry door, which leads to the outside toilet room.

Edward and James Mayo have the same build—in fact, the two appear as short, stout brothers. Edward lumbers to the front of the room to begin the introductions. With a slight feeling of nervousness, he begins,

"Everyone, it pleases me so to introduce my new friend, Francis Asbury."

Each in the room nods a greeting. Edward continues,

"He is joined by his companions, Thomas Ault and Thomas Russell, James Mayo and James Bayley, and young Jabez, who, bearing their similar resemblance, I presume to be the brother of Thomas Ault. That would make two Thomases - -

And two Jameses - -

And a Jabez - -

I believe."

Edward's guests chuckle at his verbal efforts to summarize his observation. A knock at the door quiets the gathering.

"I was unaware of additional guests this evening."

With these words Edward tilts his head slightly, puffing out his lower lip to signify his surprise. He makes his way to the front door. His short legs and steps draw attention to his slight sway to the right and to the left.

As Edward opens the door, the gathering is surprised—the young men in the room are quite pleasantly surprised—to see Nancy Brookes and four of her friends, dressed in their beautiful white dresses. Edward politely offers,

"May I be of assistance?"

Nancy curtsies to Edward.

"We long to hear Francis Asbury this evening."

"Well, do come in; he happens to be standing right over there."

With jubilant faces, the girls shuffle in, conscious that every young man in the room is eyeing them. They immediately head for Francis and his companions. Also aware that every male in the room is watching, Francis is quick to voice his invitation.

"Welcome, Nancy."

She once again curtsies, this time toward Francis. Without hesitation, he sweetens the welcome.

"My heart is warmed that you would attend."

He bows to Nancy. As he rises, she softens his formal greeting.

"My heart has a fondness for your preaching."

Francis blushes slightly. Thomas Ault nudges Francis aside as he steps forward for a greeting.

"Fair Nancy, it would truly be an honor for me to escort you to your seat."

Standing almost a foot taller than Nancy, Thomas extends his left elbow. She gently smiles at Francis as she places her right hand around Thomas's long, thin arm, resting it on his forearm. Thomas beams at Francis, then turns and escorts the girls to their chairs, the boys trailing closely behind. Francis smiles at Thomas's audacity. He follows the group toward the front of the room.

The room becomes silent as Francis walks to the makeshift pulpit. This time his podium will be a small, square wooden table with four stout legs. The piece looks strong enough to stand on—not that Francis would do such a thing; he would bump his head on the low ceiling. The oak wood of this piece is stained a dark walnut, almost black.

As with the meeting room in West Bromwich, the space is simple: a single window, rough-sawn wooden walls and floor. The inglenook fireplace, which lies dormant for the summer, resembles the one at the Asbury cottage. Other than the flies that buzz in and out of the pane-less window, the room is silent as its occupants eagerly await Francis's exhortation. He raises his hands as he looks to the gathering.

"Shall we pray?"

As heads bow, Francis looks to Nancy. She bows in prayer like the others. Francis admires the shape of her delicate forehead, her fair skin accentuated by her hair—fastened up, as usual, beneath the clean white gypsy hat with lace wings, but enough peeks out to catch Francis's attention. His heart quickens when he looks at her. He is surprised that she knew about the meeting tonight, surprised and pleased she chose to attend. In the midst of this digression, Francis begins to feel his slight nervousness abate. He realizes that this is the Lord's advocate, the Holy Spirit, once again bringing an indescribable peace. *Thank you, Father.*

"Almighty Father, we lay aside our assumptions and pretensions. Cause us to see You with clear vision on this most splendid summer's night. Amen."

The attendees raise their heads as Francis opens his Bible to speak.

I would like to walk about. Francis decides to abandon the oak table. With his Bible in hand, he turns to his right. With three short steps he is in front of the window; he leans his back against the sill. This relocation is beneficial, as he is comforted by a slight breeze that cools the back of his neck.

He begins,

> "The Gospel of John has been my focus for this evening's gathering. In fact, tonight's discussion, like my earlier message, will once again have its origins in chapter fourteen of the book of John—specifically, Jesus's statement in verse six: 'I am the way, the truth, and the life. No man comes to the Father except through Me.' "

> "On a previous occasion, I offered that Jesus makes a bold claim: that only He can bring humanity to the Father. This adventurous proclamation is full of risk. On the outset, His statement may appear narrow, for it immediately excludes all other paths or religions. Some may go so far as to infer that the words are callous and cold. In contrast, it is my goal to persuade that this statement is far from narrow, callous, or cold. I aim to win your opinion that the statement is all-inclusive, a loving declaration bringing the deepest sense of hope. For by it, humanity has a clear word from its Creator; no longer does humankind wander about without communication from above. The Almighty has cared enough to make Himself known, and He does so without reservation. Despite the cries of exclusivity, the act on its own, the Almighty choosing to reveal Himself, removes all sense of restriction. For the statement that follows in verse twenty-three opens the door to all of humanity, 'If anyone loves Me . . .' "

Francis lifts himself from the window sill and walks to the far side of the room. Standing in front of his new friend, Edward, he leans down. Almost face to face, he poses a question that all in the room can hear.

> "The Christmas story—what does it offer? Is it not 'Peace on earth, goodwill toward some?' "

Everyone in the room, Edward included, looks puzzled by Francis's question; the quote doesn't sound correct. Francis keeps his vigilant stare on Edward as he continues,

> "The passage in Luke assures us that God's goodwill is not toward a few, does it not? The Scripture assures us that His goodwill is for all: 'Peace on earth, goodwill toward men.' "

Francis gently places his right hand on Edward's left shoulder and brings forth a question.

> "Edward, do you love the Savior?"

Edward nods his head, *yes.*

Francis rises from his direct conversation with Edward. The entire room is silent as he turns; even the continuous buzzing of the flies has ceased. All eyes are focused on Francis as he gently walks to a position front and center of the room. The only noise is the muffled click of his wood-heeled boots touching the timbered floor.

He turns toward the congregation.

"Who here tonight shall say as Edward, that he or she loves the Savior?

"I urge you, allow this claim to resonate as the deepest longing of your heart: 'If anyone loves Me . . .' "

A knock at the door breaks the silence. One of Edward's guests rises from his chair to answer it.

"Good evening, might I enter the prayer meeting?"

"Richard!"

Francis's acknowledgment of Richard Whatcoat prompts Edward's friend to welcome the traveler.

"I trust I have not missed any of this evening's thoughtful considerations?"

Thomas Ault and company laugh as they find humor in Richard's encouraging but formal words. Francis cuts short the amusement.

"Always generous, Richard; please do come in. You are just in time for prayer. Would you like to open?"

Somewhat hesitant of Francis's offer, Richard, the oldest individual in the room, removes his hat and steps forward to the front. Standing next to Francis, he first gives a kindly bow to his friend. Then he opens,

"Father, as a wise bird once revealed to me, You have made it remarkably easy for mankind to know you. May our time this evening fail to be hindered by our shortcomings; we seek to acknowledge you as Creator God . . ."

Outdoors after the prayer meeting, Francis and his friends, including Richard, make small talk with Nancy and the girls. The group moves in and out of various light and energetic conversations. The girls enjoy the attention; the boys are nervous, but persistent in the chase. As the evening progresses, each girl slowly pairs off with a boy. In time, Richard finds himself standing with Francis and Nancy. He politely excuses himself for the evening.

"Francis, I must not delay. Your words this evening were a tonic to my soul."

"Thank you, Richard."

Francis and Nancy find themselves isolated as the others have all wandered away. The smile on each of their faces is evident. A slight nervousness causes Francis to search for words. *Her dress, compliment her dress . . .*

"My heart is warmed by your preaching, Francis."

Francis nods his thanks, glad that Nancy had something to say.

"My soul is drawn to the Savior on account of your words."

"Is it truly so, Nancy?"

"Why, yes, Francis. The Savior seems to bless your efforts."

"How so?"

"The stirrings of the people, the stirrings of my friends - -
The stirrings of my heart."

Nancy's brilliant eyes sparkle as Francis lingers on her last comment. The flickering street lamp shadows her silhouette as she stands with hands clasped behind her back, nervously scratching the ground with the toe of her right shoe.

In complete silence, Francis has no reply. Nancy continues,

"I long for you to prosper in your endeavor."

The quiet that follows is uncomfortable for both.

After a few moments, Nancy reaches out her right hand to gently grasp his left. The smoothness of her palm glides easily across the calloused hand that grows more muscular every day from the work at the forge. She finds comfort in holding his hand, a big hand that shifts to gently blanket hers. In silence the two look at each other. Francis is the first to glance away, but he quickly returns his eyes where he wants them, on her eyes.

"Your words stir my heart; I too long for the success of my endeavor."

"Your success shall come to pass, Francis; one would have to be negligent to miss this."

Francis dips his eyes toward the ground. Nancy is unsure of his implication. *Is he sad, or is he shy?*

He reaches forward with his right hand. Nancy senses a slight trembling in his left hand that she continues to hold. She is expecting more as he takes hold of her left hand.

"Dearest Nancy, you have been a comfort for some time . . ."

Francis hesitates, nervously scraping his bottom lip with his teeth. Uncomfortable, he shifts the pressure of each hand's grip. Back and forth, he alternates between his right and left hands. He senses that his palms are growing warmer. Nancy wants to say something, but she is patient, longing to hear Francis express his deepest feelings.

"Dearest Nancy, my Nancy, it would honor me if you would continue to encourage my preaching."

"I shall, Francis, I shall . . ."

On several occasions during the week that follows, this evening's events will come to mind for Francis; he is especially drawn to reliving his conversation with Nancy. Her words about the stirrings of her heart bring a euphoria he has not experienced before. It is difficult at times, but he has to force himself to refocus on the tasks of the forge, all the while hoping for another opportunity to preach, and to meet with the girl who has brought to life such strong feelings.

The summer heat causes the temperature inside the forge to rise to almost unbearable conditions. In his wisdom, Mr. Foxall has enacted a policy that allows the men to break for water each hour. Water break is one of James Mayo's favorite occasions, as it affords him the opportunity to prod Francis about his true feelings for Nancy.

"Francis, the men shall call for water soon. Shall we make our way?"

Francis doesn't reply as he focuses on his anvil. It is clear that James's comment didn't register.

"Say again, James . . . ?"

"I said, the men shall call for the bucket soon; shall we make our way at this time?"

Again, the suggestion fails to prompt any recognition.

"Enough with you, then . . ."

In haste, James departs for his coveted water break. Francis remains focused on his task. He mumbles to himself as he arranges several iron pieces on the table next to his anvil. Abruptly, he looks up from his work.

"James? What are you asking of me? - -
Where has he wandered?"

James is nowhere in sight. Francis quickly abandons his attempt to locate his pal. He lowers his head and concentrates once again.

"I shall scarf in order to weld . . ."

Francis begins the process of preparing the ends of his pieces to weld together. He is no longer an apprentice; his progress has earned him the opportunity to move beyond the chores of a beginner. The mundane task of forging nails is long behind him. Having passed his journeyman testing, he is no longer at the master's beck and call, sent here and there to run errands, or to build monkey wrench tools for more accomplished blacksmiths. The additional and more welcomed benefit of graduation is that Francis no longer has to sleep on the dirt floor near his anvil—required to build discipline into the blacksmith hopefuls—or to work the bellows and treadle hammer until his arms and legs ache from the strain.

He is not so sure he is ready to scarf. Over the past year he has built his confidence, fine-tuning his hammer technique while pounding out thousands of nails and more than a hundred horseshoe blanks. He enjoys watching the masters and has even picked up a few helpful hints when the older men have felt generous. Regardless of his feelings, he strongly desires to proceed with the project.

Scarfing is a technique whereby each strike of the hammer onto the heated iron piece creates a flattened shape. This new shape is eventually manipulated and wrapped around a second piece of iron, much like a scarf placed around the neck. It is a difficult process, most often left to master smiths. The delicate technique easily frustrates those who have not mastered complete control of their hammering skills. Nevertheless, Francis is determined to build this special item.

He thinks of the master smiths in the adjacent room, pounding out the endless custom items. *I can do this.*

Francis proceeds, patiently heating up the first piece of iron. It is roughly one inch in diameter and one yard in length. He lays the tip of the iron rod into the fire. In a short time the piece is the desired orange color; he removes it from the heat and begins the process. With the heated piece resting on the anvil, Francis slowly applies several well-placed blows with the hammer. Lighter-than-air sparks leap from the metal as he continues the process. He is careful not to push the heated iron too fast; this is a slow and deliberate procedure. As he works, he is thankful that none of the miniature comets leaping from the anvil touches his face; he already has several locations that will never grow facial hair. He pounds the rod until the end flattens from the repeated light blows.

Completing this initial phase of the task, he lays the scarfed rod aside. *That fails to be as difficult as expected.* He now lifts a second rod and places it into the fire. In a matter of minutes, the iron piece is ready. He lays it on the anvil, then picks up the first rod and reheats it for about thirty seconds. Now both rods, the tips brilliant orange, are softened and hot.

He proceeds to mold the flattened edge of the first piece around the softened end of the second piece. With each measured stroke of the hammer, Francis takes great care to surround the second piece of iron. It requires a few minutes, but the two pieces soon weld together. This effort results in a new piece in the shape of an elongated upside-down "V," much like a tripod missing the third leg. Francis raises the new object as James returns from his water break. He inquires of Francis,

>"Francis, the men missed you on break. What are you working on?"
>"Oh, just a little thing."
>"What sort of 'little thing'? You are attempting to scarf?"
>"I call it a gift thing."
>"The scarfing, has it been accomplished correctly?"

James looks at the contraption that his friend is creating. He scratches his head.

>"Francis, this resembles nothing that I am aware of. When did you obtain the ability to scarf?"
>"Oh, it shall. Where is your faith, James?"

James shakes his head; he has nothing to say. He is not sure what the object may become.

Suddenly his face beams with a smile. Francis catches the changed demeanor but ignores his friend and returns to the project. The usually calm James blurts out,

> "Dear Francis, I believe I have had an epiphany!"

A rare occurrence! Francis's thought causes him to chuckle to himself. James continues,

> "That which you are painstakingly focused upon, this object that would cause you to miss a much-needed break, is quite possibly a gift for Nancy, is it not?"

Francis halts what he is doing and looks to James. The two stand silent, staring at each other. One face beams; the other is focused and adamant. The stone-faced Francis responds,

> "James, you appear as if you have discovered a distant planet."

James continues to glow, an odd thing for the stoic lad. Maintaining his calm and collected look, Francis continues,

> "I shall not divulge whom the gift is for; it is intended as a complete surprise."

> "I shall maintain it is a gift for your fair Nancy."

Francis shakes his head. He turns and resumes his work on the parts.

James returns to his position at his anvil, only a few feet away from Francis. For the remainder of the day, completely out of character, James continues to inquire about the gift. Francis does his best to be polite, but he refuses to reveal the recipient of the gift. For hours he continues, calculating, then pounding, then more precise calculating, more intense pounding. At times he comes across as if he is ignoring his dear friend. He isn't ignoring James; he is merely focused deeply on the task—though if truth be told, the constant chatter of one who seldom speaks more than a few sentences each day does fatigue him just a little.

From deep within the forge, the boys' supervisor approaches.

> "Asbury, here are the remaining rods for the final batch."

The heavy-set man drops roughly fifteen iron rods on an adjacent table, the clanging of the delivery barely heard above the din of the forge. Francis yells back,

> "Shall begin them on the morrow."

> "Not my decision when you begin; Foxall only expects completions. Better plan on completing by sundown tomorrow."

> "The batch shall be finished by tomorrow eve."

Francis returns to the work at hand. James cannot hold it in any longer.

> "Enough, Francis; you must divulge the purpose of your generous undertaking. It must be important enough to risk your responsibilities at the forge."

Mid-swing of a downstroke with his hammer, Francis halts in order not to crush James's hand. James is holding his hammer on top of Francis's anvil.

> "James, you must attend to your work; several of your projects lack completion due to your continuous distraction."

> "As long as you fail to reveal the recipient of your gift, I shall remain."

Several nearby workers slow their pace as they vacillate between listening to the banter of James and Francis and working on their projects. Once again, Francis aims to dismiss his pal.

> "James, return to your work. I shall not let on."

The man on the left of the arguing pair, Trevor, shakes his head as he butts in,

> "James, your pal is in love; let him be."

James turns and looks to Trevor. Trevor is an imposing figure, taller than the boys, with stout arms and a nasty scar that begins at the front of his neckline and terminates at the back of his neck, a remnant of the Wednesbury riots that killed many Wesleyan followers.

James reluctantly lifts his hammer from Francis's anvil. He returns to his own work space, lifting up an iron rod and placing it into the fire. Once more, he begins to inquire,

> "As your friend . . ."

Trevor and several men let out a laugh. Francis too begins to lighten his mood. With that almost devious look, he smiles at James; his words are clearly heard by James and the men.

> "Let - -
> Me - -
> Be."

Francis's slow delivery in response to James's perky requests is met with the sound of James's grumbling; his complaints continue to entertain the ironworkers. Trevor delivers the decisive blow:

> "He is in love, James—something I am confident you may never become aware of . . ."

The men laugh again; so does Francis. James shakes his head and frowns. He is soon preoccupied with his work responsibilities, recalling that tomorrow is Saturday and the project that Foxall expects of him and Francis is due that evening.

Francis considers the Foxall project. *I shall complete on time.* He is more interested in the day that follows; *I look forward to being at home.*

That Sunday at the Asbury Cottage, Eliza is overjoyed to see Francis. He is also happy to be in the presence of his parents. Their Sunday afternoons have become a regular occurrence. As usual, Eliza has lovingly prepared one of Francis's favorite meals, a thick, beefy stew. Homemade bread and the staple of summer, fresh vegetables from Joseph's garden, highlight the dinner. Eliza notes,

"Father has planted quite the garden this summer."

Eliza's comment, intended for Francis as he stands looking at the inglenook fireplace, goes unanswered.

"Say again, Mother . . . ?"

"I was sharing how Father's garden this summer is better than in years past."

"I am sure."

Francis continues to analyze the fireplace. He takes in a deep breath of the meaty stew as its pleasant aroma rises above the fire.

"Now, Francis, I hope you do not intend to sneak a tasting."

"I shall wait for the table, Mother."

The arrival of the dinner plates signals to Francis and Joseph to ready themselves for the meal. They both head for the rear door and The Malt Shovel's spring to wash.

Outside, the cool air of the approaching evening is beginning to settle in, with a linen-like mist rolling in from the west. The two men stand above the water bucket, shirts removed, washing their face and hands.

"Franky, your hard work is turning you into a man."

"Indeed?"

"Look at you. Your arms and shoulders bear the marks of strenuous work."

Francis looks at his arms. He hadn't noticed it before, but when he turns his elbows inward to see his shoulders, his triceps bulge out. His arms are no longer sinewy; they are gaining muscle definition.

"Your right forearm is slightly larger than your left."

This fact had also escaped Francis's notice. He slowly admires this new discovery.

"Look at your hands, Franky; they appear stronger than your dear old dad's."

Francis smiles at his father.

" 'Dear old dad.' I shall not grow weary of such a label."

Joseph laughs, hard and loud. He breaks from his joyous outburst long enough to wisely advise Francis,

"Mother waits."

At the table, Francis and his parents pause to give thanks for the day. Upon completion of the prayer, Joseph and Francis immediately begin the feast. The table is generously set with a meal that will serve far more than three people. This is Elizabeth's deepest joy, preparing a meal for her son. Despite her palpable pleasure, she does not begin her meal, but remains still, holding her fork in her hand. She clears her throat in the way that only a mother can.

> "One meal each week fails to satisfy my motherly desires. It is my wish you would attend more often, Franky."

> "Our son is quite busy, Eliza. His responsibilities at the forge demand that he gain the proper rest."

There is a long pause as Joseph and Eliza look to their son for response. His reply is delayed as he unashamedly enjoys the meal. After an oversized spoonful, he senses that the conversation has stopped; he raises his head, slurping a hasty gulp of stew.

> "Rest escapes me."

Eliza sets down her fork, a look of concern on her face.

> "Rest escapes you?"

Francis realizes that his answer should justify the strain he has bought upon his mother. He decides to be completely honest.

> "Thomas and I meet the others in band one night each week; we also attend the Wednesbury class meeting an additional night. The Lord has recently bestowed opportunity as I have been preaching an evening in Sutton, at the home of a recent and dear friend, Edward Hand . . ."

Francis's rattling ends as quickly as it started. He slurps another mouthful of dinner as Joseph defends his son.

> "Eliza, it seems little time is left for Franky to visit."

She picks up her fork and returns to eating, plunging it into her food with short, sharp strokes, pouting the pout that pushes her upper lip toward her delicate nose. With mouth full, Francis raises his head to see that he should offer more. He swallows the warm, meaty stew and continues,

> "The Sutton gatherings are growing; Edward speaks of an additional night of prayer. As I rise at four o'clock, finishing late the night before makes for a difficult schedule to keep."

Eliza abruptly halts her eating.

> "Few hours' sleep, Franky? I worry for your health."

> "Eliza, our son shall weather this season; it is the Lord's will. I am confident of this."

Francis's smile broadens as he listens to his parents bicker over their beloved son. *I do miss these tiny battles . . .*

As the Sabbath day of rest ends, Francis wrestles with his thoughts. Sitting in front of the fireplace as his parents spend the last hours of daylight selecting vegetables from the garden for next week's meals, he thinks of his responsibilities at work as well as his growing ministry in band and prayer meetings. He ponders the next prayer meeting in Sutton. *How will it all fit into a schedule?* Then, *Will Nancy attend?*

Returning to the forge, Francis is grateful that tomorrow evening is another meeting in Sutton. He stops long enough to catch the moon peeking in and out of the fast-moving clouds. He looks forward to a good night's rest and work tomorrow.

The next day at work goes more quickly than usual; the schedule is busy, with barely enough time for the mandatory water breaks. At day's end, Francis is both surprised and grateful that another evening in Sutton is upon him. He hurries to his quarters to wash, change clothes, and pick up his Bible. After a quick bite to eat at the forge's kitchen, he is on his way.

This night in Sutton finds Francis standing in front of a room packed with thirty people. The room is obviously overcrowded. The sound of Edward Hand as he attempts to silence the gathering is barely audible. Francis decides to give aid. Standing, he clears his throat and announces,

"Our dear friend Edward wishes to speak."

"I say, our dear friend Edward wishes . . ."

The room full of young men and women, not one over twenty years of age or under the age of sixteen, quickly becomes quiet. Francis motions to Edward.

With a bashful smile, Edward acknowledges Francis's help. For Edward, speaking in front of so many people is unpredictable—at times, he is as peaceful and fluid as the River Thames, and on other occasions, the words and thoughts are difficult and labored. The thirty young adults quietly wait for Edward to begin. This gathering is unique, a revival of sorts, among the young people of Sutton and the surrounding areas. Several of the attendees have traveled from as far away as Walsall and Wednesbury.

Edward begins to speak; the words are easy tonight.

"Brothers and sisters, due to the unexpected success of our prayer meetings, we must heed the fact that if we fail to be respectful of the room's limitations, we shall be forced to look for other accommodations."

The young crowd begins to mumble. Considering this rude, Francis takes over.

"What my dear friend Edward is implying is for all to bow for prayer."

Edward smiles his agreement with Francis's statement, more than happy to exit the front of the room and hastily take his place at the back.

The group lowers their heads to pray.

"Heavenly Father, our most sure provider, we acknowledge that it is You who freely bestows this time of refreshing upon the household of our dear friend Edward. Have mercy upon us for failing to recognize this sooner than we have. Guide us . . ."

A loud pounding at the front door causes Francis to cease his prayer. The young men and women immediately raise their heads, each looking to the entrance. Several make their way to the open window for a look. The pounding, they have noticed, was far from friendly.

The pounding occurs once again. One of Edward's friends is the first to recognize the individual at the door.

"Hastings!"

The mention of the town's magistrate causes Edward Hand to look toward the floor, his face flushed with fear and disappointment. He immediately heads to the window and closes the wooden shutters. The entire group looks to Francis. He hesitates to answer, but makes his way to the front door and asks of Edward,

"What of Hastings?"

Edward fails to reply. The two Thomases and Jameses push their way through the crowd; they plan to answer the door with Francis. Francis is thankful to see his pals behind him. He pushes away the thought, *I'm not comfortable with this.* James Mayo urges,

"Go ahead, Francis; we stand with you."

James Mayo's deep-toned voice gives Francis the confidence he needs. He slowly reaches for the door latch. His hand resting on the wooden handle, he hesitates. *Lord, I entrust this gathering into Your loving arms.*

By now, the girls have all gathered around Nancy at the far end of the room, several large young men standing in front of and behind them. These children of the Wesleyans remember well the persecutions from the past—and for several, the persecutions of their parents. A few of the young men also guard the rear door of the house. One of them reassures the girls,

"Not a stone shall harm you."

The girls are thankful for the protector's comment, but they still fidget with fear. For a third time, the magistrate pounds the front door. The girls huddle closer than before; one whimpers with tears. Francis lifts the wooden latch and opens the door. The eerie creaking of the oak-wood hinges precedes Francis's greeting.

"Good evening."

The magistrate, a stocky man roughly four inches shorter than Francis, is not impressed. The dictatorial judge raises his right hand in a fist. From the balled flesh, he slowly extends his pointer finger, palm up, raising the tip of his finger within inches of Francis's face. In a dark voice, he warns Francis,

"Convey to Mr. Hand that his gatherings must cease."

Francis is silent with fear. His thoughts race between self-preservation—he has an urge to run—and protective leadership—he wishes that no harm come to the group. Almost simultaneously, his thoughts move to Nancy. Now his courage is bolstered; *I shall protect her with my life.* He finds himself wishing to slam the door in the face of the town's leader, but he wisely stifles the impulse.

"Yes, we shall bring this evening's meeting to close."

"You shall bring every evening's meeting to a close; Mr. Hand may no longer entertain such a disobedient group."

Disobedient group? Francis's thought brings a strange feeling to the surface. He is sure that his face reveals the flush of emotion driving his anger. *We harm no one; we only seek to honor our Lord and Savior.*

James Mayo steps alongside Francis.

"Francis, I shall help in dispersing our friends."

I didn't plan to disperse anyone. Francis wisely keeps that thought silent.

James reaches for Francis's hand holding the door. This action is enough to send the town's leader away. With more exertion than he expected, James releases Francis's tightened grip from the handle and shuts the door. Francis peers at his friend; in a low and adamant tone, he presses James,

"What are you doing, James?"

James's reply is equally stern.

"We shall disperse this gathering before harm replaces prayer as the evening's theme."

Francis looks to the floor. He raises his left hand and simultaneously strokes both sides of his chin with his thumb and forefinger.

"I believe you are correct, James."

Francis steps to the front of the room. It is an easy task to gain the undivided attention of the group; in silence, they wait for Francis's direction. Outside, the light wind brushes against the home. The low, shallow whistle created by the less-than-airtight jambs of the front door and window add to their sense of alarm.

The thud that hits the roof causes the twelve young women to scream. The men instinctively jump and look up.

"Francis . . . ?"

Nancy's uneasy request causes Francis to step toward her. He reaches her as the second thud hits the side of the brick home, the impact ending with a strange spreading sound. The odd noise repeats again, this time on the opposite exterior wall—and then again, on the slate roof. James is quick to guess,

"They torch the home!"

James Mayo is the first to burst through the front door; two hundred men and women, set on violence, greet him. The mob rushes for the front of the home, moving James back inside. His face conveys the fear that has gripped him. He pushes the words out,

"Francis, we cannot exit!"

Several of the attackers force the window shutters open, slamming one of them against Edward's back. In pain, he spins to close them. Francis drags Nancy toward the exit, the rest of the group following close behind.

"Edward!"

The group lurches back as they notice the flames that have attached themselves to the wooden window shutter. Edward opens the shutters as James Mayo and Thomas Ault remove their jackets and beat the flames out. Realizing that the opened window will invite further threat, Francis gives warning,

"Watch yourself!"

Within inches of Edward, James, and Thomas, a flaming torch-branch enters the room through the window and lands on the interior floor. Nancy's cry fills Francis with anger toward the perpetrators. This time some of the young men immediately remove their coats to beat out the fire, as smoke begins to fill the room.

Grabbing Nancy by the hand, Francis rushes for the front door. He turns and urges,

"All shall exit together."

"Francis, it is certain violence with a mob out there!"

"It is certain death in here, James."

Francis is adamant. The other young men each grab the hand of a young lady, several of whom are now in tears. Simultaneously, hard objects begin hitting the outside of the front door. The pounding is continuous, each thud followed by several more in rapid succession. James knows what it is; he offers his grave observation.

"They are stoning the residence."

"Then we shall brave a stoning!"

Francis's harsh tone reveals that he has had enough. Having moved to the rear of the room, Thomas Ault quickly advises Francis,

"Listen, the rear door! No pounding on the rear door."

His observation has several moving to the rear, but Francis counters,

> "Stop; we shall exit the front of the residence."

Thomas considers this ill advice. He confronts his friend,

> "Are you mad, Francis?"

Francis loses control of the group as the mob once again forces open the window shutters, launching another torch-branch into the room. Each individual lunges for the perimeter of the room. Several quick-thinkers extinguish the flames. Francis repeats his command,

> "Everyone, move to the front door; we must exit now."

Not all heed Francis's directive. Some gather behind Francis, ready to exit outdoors. Others still favor the rear door. He once again gives his order,

> "Follow close; I shall aim for the park. The cover of darkness shall allow us to break away."

This time the other James, James Bayley, speaks up.

> "This is madness, Francis; we shall be heading straight into a tempest!"

> "I am fully aware, James. This is our surest option."

> "Surest option? Why not exit the rear of the house?"

Everyone in the room is staring at Francis. He hesitates, then states,

> "For I know that which lies to the east."

James and the group look to each other in puzzlement. Several voice the inevitable question: *Why not exit the rear of the home?* The room's returning silence is rivaled by Francis's long and deep breaths that forcibly make their way through his nostrils. Enraged by the event but confident that they have not thought this all the way through, he offers his reply.

> "You question the harm of the rear door? You fail to realize that which resides on the other side of the rear door - -
> The rest of the town's inhabitants."

James does not reply. Francis has now gained control of the entire group. He once again proclaims his demand,

> "Ready yourselves."

James lowers his eyes to the ground as the truth sets in: *There really isn't a better option.*

Francis grabs the door handle. It vibrates from the impact of the stoning. Despite the continuous pounding, he opens the door and rushes out. As stones hurl through the door, the group begins to exit the home. Outside, the gathering of young people runs in single file. They head straight for the mob.

The stoning strikes several of them instantly. Francis, too, is badly bruised from the outset, taking injury to the top of his head. Blood begins to run down his forehead and into his eyes. He ignores the pain as he brushes away the warm fluid with his left forearm; holding tight to the hand of Nancy with his right, he races forward.

The decision to head straight at the violent gathering slightly disarms the harmful group; they expected the youths to run toward town, where the majority of the mob awaits. Their surprise causes a slight interruption of the pelting. The cease-fire is a welcome surprise to Francis and his group. One by one, the young men and women aim for the mob.

The fearful event has heightened the young people's senses. Their nostrils begin to sear with the burning smell of wood, which they are confident is from the house. As Francis and his group continue through the raging crowd, the stone-throwing begins again. Two burly men hurl fist-sized rocks with all their might, their stubble-bearded faces cocked in malicious glares. One by one, two boys supply them with endless ammunition; they are barely the age of ten.

With heads bowed, the young people continue to advance. They haven't the opportunity to feel; they must act. Two of the young men stumble after a hard strike. Another friend of Edward's begins to stagger, his injury to the chin bringing immense pain. If any of them goes down, they will surely be stoned to death. The young man with the chin affliction grabs his face, regains his footing, and continues his charge. The others do as well.

Without notice, several women in the mob perceive the young people's action as hostile; they turn and run away from the advancing prayer group. This only serves to enrage the hostile men; they continue to seek harm.

Right through the middle of the maddened residents the young people travel. Several men swing and kick at the teenagers. One kick to the shins almost downs one young man; with all the strength he can muster, he stays upright. The same with a well-placed punch to the ear; cupping the side of his head, the elder teen continues. Although the hostile group is allowing them to pass, the stoning and thrashings do not let up.

Eventually Francis and company find themselves clear of the assault. They head for Sutton Park. Their strides are growing weaker, but their panicked emotions will not allow this fact to register. Francis pushes the group further on.

Several yards into the park, the young people begin to realize that they have made a safe escape; they slow their pace, eventually ceasing to run. They gather roughly two hundred yards into the park.

The evening wind has increased, making a haunting sound as it swooshes through the tree tops. Intermittent clouds allow the waning moon to occasionally light the surrounding woodlands. This is not a welcome sight for the group. Several of the young ladies begin to weep uncontrollably. The young men, on guard for potential townspeople who may have ventured to follow, do their best to comfort their frightened companions. Edward Hand realizes that the front of his waistcoat is covered in blood. It is his blood; the inside of his forearm bleeds profusely. His close friend Stepney uses his necktie to form a tourniquet. One young girl suffering from a head gash, the back of her beautiful white dress smeared with blood, faints in the arms of her protector. James Bayley and Thomas Ault do their best to catch their breath; bent over with hands on their knees, they arch their heads upward and turn toward the home of Edward Hand. Strangely, it is not engulfed in flames.

Francis and Nancy turn and look to each other. Their hands are tightly gripped, so much so that Nancy's barely has any feeling in it. The slowing of adrenaline has caused them to experience a sense of reality as they too struggle to catch their breath. Nancy's entire body begins to shake, and without warning, she begins to weep. She pulls her hand away from Francis's and embraces him.

***

The Old Mill Forge is operating at a hurried pace. Men and boys race about as the preparations proceed as planned for a large delivery that Mr. Foxall has slated for completion today. Francis and James are at their anvils, putting the finishing touches on their items. In front of the pair stands a young boy, who politely inquires,

"Francis, shall I combine your rods with James's?"

The boy standing before them is eight years younger than Francis; next month he will celebrate his ninth birthday. Young Henry Foxall has inherited the sturdy good looks of his Welsh lineage. The wide-eyed boy stands with hands on hips, his tilted head of thick, wavy hair highlighted by his thin-lipped smile. Again, the lad offers his services.

"I can move them for ya, Francis . . ."

Henry is fond of Francis. Since his eighth birthday, Henry's father has allowed him to visit the mill each Friday. He loves his father and he loves the forge, but Francis is the one he enjoys being with the most. Francis doesn't mind the young boy's attention; lately, the two are inseparable. Francis responds to his little friend,

"James and I shall require your services at the dinner break."

Henry nods his head with three short bursts. Immediately he runs off, eventually heading outside. Francis smiles.

"He shall return well before dinner break . . ."

James chuckles at Francis's comment.

"I do say, Master Henry seems as though he shall follow you to the ends of the earth."

"I do say, if we fail to complete our order, his father shall launch us toward that very end."

Francis returns to the anvil. The three years of working the hammer have not only strengthened his body, they have also enhanced his talent for administration. He rarely misses a deadline. He and James have become a dependable team; their work habits are methodical, largely due to Francis's leadership. This allows them to finish most projects slightly ahead of schedule. This week's assignment is no different; Francis spends a few minutes putting the final blows to his last piece of iron, while James still works on finishing his own. As if to let James know that he once again has finished his portion of the project ahead of schedule and ahead of James, Francis proclaims,

"Complete."

To further the verbal poking, Francis declares,

"James, I shall take a water break and return to work on the mysterious gift."

James shakes his head. Several of the men working nearby pause, in hopes of catching James's reply. There is none; he will not pursue the opportunity that Francis is dangling in front of him.

Returning to the anvil from his water break, Francis pauses to look at James. James will not acknowledge Francis. This only brings that notable wry smile to Francis's face.

He turns and retrieves the gift project from under his work bench. He removes each item from the box and holds it up for examination—pausing in an exaggerated manner with each item in order to tease James—and lays the object onto the tabletop. The project is complete; all that is required is to prepare the gift for transport. Francis drags a wooden crate from the side of his work area. The box measures eight inches wide by thirty-six inches long by twenty inches high. Francis places the box on top of his anvil.

Piece by piece, Francis places the gift into the box as he verbalizes his intentions.

"I shall make presentation tomorrow - -

At my home."

James is saying nothing. Francis continues in his effort to shake out a response.

"A beautiful dinner is planned . . ."

James will not bite. Francis tries the direct approach.

"Haven't you the slightest inquiry?"

James continues to work at his anvil. It is difficult, but he decides to keep quiet.

The men around James see it differently.

"I'll place a guinea he gives in."

"Make it two he shan't."

The men vent their amusement as they watch James working the anvil, wrestling between focusing on his work and glancing in Francis's direction. The wiser of the betting coworkers comments,

"Shan't be long now, our James will give in . . ."

Francis lovingly places each piece into the box. He has constructed a wooden lid for the crate out of oak. He places the top and secures it with two nails. As the second nail rests flush with the wood, James speaks.

"Oh, all right, Francis; when shall you present it to Nancy?"

The winner of the bet cannot help but voice his joy.

"Ah ha, that shall be one guinea for me!"

The men settle their bet as James puts down his hammer and walks to Francis. Face to face, he inquires of his friend,

"Francis, you must let on. Am I not your closest friend?"

"A friend, yes. Closest?"

Francis leaves James hanging for an answer, then offers him a slight concession.

"Please do come by; Mother shall put out a plate for you as well."

James is ashamed that he gave in. He also cannot reconcile the fact that Francis will not divulge the secret. He grunts as he turns to head back to his anvil. Along the way, he sneers at the betting men. They laugh at the frustrated young man, and one of them wisely offers,

"On the morrow, he shall be there . . ."

The man is correct; tomorrow I shall be at the Asbury cottage. Not happy with his friend, James continues the thought to himself. *I shall follow Francis home from Old Church . . .*

***

The gentle summer breeze flowing through the main-room window of the Asbury cottage does little to cool Eliza as she hurries to set out Sunday's afternoon meal. She pauses briefly, raising her right hand to her forehead to wipe away the thin layer of sweat that causes her hair to stick to her temples. This is but a slight inconvenience; even the extra portions of Francis's favorite beef stew that she has lovingly prepared serve to remind her that her son is at home once again.

Upstairs, Francis and Joseph put on clean clothes. The two meet in Joseph's bedroom and take turns peering into a palm-sized piece of mirror framed in walnut. Adding to the challenge of seeing oneself in the little mirror, Francis's adolescent excitement causes him to fidget around the room. Sensing his son's enthusiasm, Joseph exclaims,

"She shall be pleasantly surprised!"

Francis considers his father's comment. *She shall.* His eagerness has him asking his father for advice.

"Shall I present before or after dinner?"

"Either shall evoke the fondest emotions of the fairer sex."

This reply causes Francis to beam. He unexpectedly bolts out of the room and down the stairs.

Today is not only the Sabbath, but also a special day for Francis: he has invited his close friend to meet his parents. Joseph and Eliza have heard much good about Edward Hand, but they have yet to meet the young man. They look forward to welcoming this contemporary of Francis into their home.

Entering the outskirts of Newton Village, James Mayo is surprised to discover that he has arrived at the same moment as Nancy. He had planned to follow Francis home from the morning's worship in West Bromwich, but a family matter delayed him. Nevertheless, he picks up the pace of his walk; within moments, he is alongside the young lady. He politely gains her attention.

"Good afternoon, Nancy."

"Hello, James."

"On your way to the Asburys'?"

"Why, yes, I am. How did you know, James?"

"Oh, just a thought."

The pair continues to the front garden of the Asbury cottage. James offers his hand to escort Nancy up the three brick steps. She gratefully accepts. At the door, James releases her hand and knocks.

Inside, Eliza stands still. She calls out,

"Franky!"

She rushes over to the kitchen table to make a final adjustment, eyeing each plate that is set for today's gathering. There are four places set.

Francis and Joseph arrive together. Francis is quick to offer,

"Mother, I shall answer."

Before opening the door, Francis pauses. He looks over at the cast-iron pot that steams with the day's meal, hanging above an ebbing wood fire. *Perfect.* He opens the door.

"Nancy - -

And James. Do come in."

The pair enters and Joseph approaches, offering a kindly welcome.

"You do not fail to grow prettier every day."

"Thank you, Mr. Asbury."

Nancy laughs at James's reply to Joseph's comment. James notices the kitchen table, neatly set with four plates. *Only one additional plate.* He begins to see that this is a special gathering for Nancy.

In the background, Eliza inquires of her son,

"Franky, you failed to . . . ?"

Francis interrupts his mother.

"Mother, you remember James Mayo from the forge."

"Yes, I do. Hello, Nancy."

Nancy curtsies to Eliza. Eliza returns a smile, then turns and heads for the room at the rear of the house, quickly returning with two additional plates for dinner.

Another knock sends Joseph toward the front door, where he stops and turns.

"Eliza, are we prepared?"

"Yes, Husband, we are."

Joseph opens the door.

"Mr. Asbury?"

"Yes, you must be Edward Hand."

"Yes, sir, I am."

"Please do come in."

Francis hurries toward the door.

"Mother and Father, this is my friend from Sutton, Edward Hand."

Joseph and Eliza politely acknowledge Edward. Elizabeth invites all to dine.

"Everyone, please do take a seat. Dinner is prepared."

After prayer, the group enjoys the dinner. Edward is quick to surmise that Joseph is more talented than most gardeners. He offers a compliment,

"Mr. Asbury, this is by far the best produce I have ever partaken of."

"My husband's vegetable and herb gardens are well known."

During the meal, Edward and James focus on their food. Each is grateful for the robust offering. While all enjoy dinner, Francis and Nancy take turns catching a glimpse of each other. Francis is happy that she is here. Nancy worries that she has food on her lips; after every forkful she nervously raises her napkin to wipe her mouth.

Having finished his meal well before the group, Joseph offers a question to Edward.

"Francis tells us that your prayer gatherings have grown beyond capacity?"

Edward pauses to look at Francis; he is unsure how to answer Joseph. *It seems as though they fail to know of the recent developments.* The hesitant look on Francis's face proves to Edward that they remain uninformed. Realizing that he needs to be completely honest with his parents, Francis takes over.

"My deepest apologies, Edward; I have failed to share with my parents."

Eliza is quick to inquire,

"Failed to share?"

Eliza levels her gaze at Francis. He responds directly,

"Mother, Father, the prayer gathering this week past was less than successful."

Joseph attempts to offer encouragement.

"Perhaps there were other commitments?"

"No, Father, the event was amply attended. The problem arose with the local magistrate."

"Reverend James Hastings?"

Edward is surprised that Mr. Asbury knows of preacher and magistrate Hastings. He responds,

"Yes, Mr. Asbury, the warden of Sutton ordered our gatherings to cease. He came prepared with some of the townspeople."

Hiding his shock, Joseph gently asks,

"How many townspeople?"

Francis hesitates. He looks to Edward, his father, and finally his mother, then answers truthfully,

"My estimates place it at more than two hundred, with triple that awaiting us in town."

Eliza's gasp is the only sound heard above the summer breeze working through the jambs of the front door. She slowly pushes her plate away. Tapping the tabletop with the tips of the curled fingers of her right hand, she pushes away from the table and exits outdoors.

"Father . . ."

"She will make peace with this, Franky. Edward, how shall your family proceed? The warden represents the connected Church."

Edward's face reveals a despair not unlike that of losing a limb. He responds to Joseph,

"We fail to possess the influence to gain a hearing."

"Edward and Francis, it had failed notice before, but I now detect marks of persecution on each of you. Have you failed to divulge the entire truth?"

Francis looks down at the tabletop. Edward leans back in his chair, his eyes on the ceiling. Nancy decides to bring all that has happened to light.

"Mr. Asbury, my companions and I . . ."

Unable to complete her sentence, Nancy breaks into tears. James places his right arm around her shoulder as she weeps uncontrollably.

The front door opens and Eliza comes in. She makes her way toward Nancy.

"Come, dear."

Nancy rises from the table. Her embrace of Eliza brings a slight watering to Francis's eyes as the two most important women in his life depart for the rear room.

"Mr. Asbury?"

"Yes, James."

"Could not Wesley's itinerants give counsel in this matter?"

"I believe so. Perhaps this is an issue for Mather. However, you are dealing with a connected public servant. 'Public servant' . . ."

Joseph mocks the label. The three young men agree with Joseph.

Francis desires to move on. He asks,

"Father, if it is well with you, when Mother and Nancy return, I would like to present my gift."

"It would be a most welcome change. I will fetch your mother and Nancy."

Joseph exits the room. In the silence that follows, James approaches Francis about the gift.

"Francis, is Nancy aware?"

"James, you must let life proceed its course."

Not aware of the private dealings about the gift, Edward offers thanks to Francis.

"I appreciate your father's advice, and I shall present it to the family. I pray that Pastor Mather will provide a workable solution."

Joseph escorts the girls into the main room. Edward, James, and Francis have moved the kitchen chairs in front of the inglenook fireplace. Nancy smiles at Francis; he had hinted that there was something special occurring today. Everyone except Francis takes a seat. Standing at the firebox, Francis begins,

"Mother, for some time my heart has been warmed toward a certain experience. It has inspired me to do well. On this day, I would like to make my affections known, for they are rooted in the deepest appreciation and love."

James nervously places one hand at a time underneath his thighs. He can hardly contain himself. He is impressed with Francis's mature approach to such a delicate subject. Francis continues,

"On this beautiful summer Sabbath, I would like to present a gift."

Francis turns toward a wooden box covered with one of Eliza's quilts. Elizabeth tilts her head as she exclaims,

> "In all my busyness, I failed to notice . . ."

Francis smiles at his mother's surprise.

> "Mother, I would like to present this gift in appreciation of your many years of love demonstrated toward Father and me."

She tries to fight it, but Eliza's eyes well up.

> "Franky, I am moved to tears."

As Nancy smiles, Eliza wipes her eyes with the handkerchief she removes from her apron pocket. Francis places his hands on his mother's shoulders and lovingly advises her,

> "Please do remove the quilt."
>
> "Yes, Son."

At this point, James sits with the look of one who has just found out he has been pickpocketed. Edward beams for his pal. Joseph repositions his feet and hips to sit slightly higher in his chair, thinking, *This is my loving son.*

Eliza rises and removes the quilt. She stands back a step, crossing her arms and placing one hand under her chin, the hand with the rolled handkerchief in it. She gathers herself enough to ask,

> "What have we here?"
>
> "I have placed two nails on the sides of the top; Father, shall you lend me a hand?"

Joseph rises; in his hand is a small iron pry bar. He proudly exclaims,

> "First chance to use this gift that Francis crafted for me."

Joseph shows off the tool Francis presented to him this morning.

The creaking of the nails pried from the oak-wood box causes Nancy and Eliza to squint. Nancy's beautiful face smiles widely for Francis. James is still, locked in a lifeless stare at the side of the wooden crate. Joseph gently lays aside the top of the box. No longer flushed with tears, Elizabeth nudges her husband. She draws a laugh from the group when she offers,

> "I must take a look."

Eliza places her arms on her husband's hips and peers from behind him into the box. The numerous iron pieces are beautifully presented in the sturdy oak box; nevertheless, Elizabeth is unsure what the gift actually is. As is everyone, except for Francis and Joseph. Elizabeth excitedly blurts out,

> "Franky, you must share what is in the box."
>
> "I shall. Allow me to erect it."

Eliza and Joseph back away as Francis approaches. He removes the three large pieces from the box and sets them on the floor. He next moves to the inglenook fireplace and removes the iron skillet that hangs from the rusted spit.

> "Edward, lend a hand . . ."

Edward springs to his feet. Francis directs his friend as he hands him the cast-iron pot.

> "Place it on the table. James, recover from your stupor and hold the left side, while I erect the right."

James immediately rises to give aid. Francis hands him one of the tripod pieces. He assumes that this is the left portion of the gift; he is still trying to figure out how he could have interpreted such a large item to be a gift for the delicate Nancy. Francis then removes another tripod from the box and places it on the right side of the fireplace. Next, he takes apart the existing iron spit and legs that Eliza uses for warming the daily meals. In its place, he erects the newer and sturdier version.

At once, Elizabeth understands what the gift is. She impulsively responds,

> "Franky, my heart is touched."

Wiping a tear, Eliza comes up behind Francis as he stands back to admire the work. She places her arms around his wide shoulders.

> "You are such a thoughtful son . . ."

> "Mother, it is crafted a couple of inches shorter in an attempt to ease your daily burden."

Thankful for Francis's consideration, Eliza hugs her son.

That evening, Francis and James experience an amusing walk back to the Old Mill Forge. James easily admits that he has gained a new level of understanding about his friend; *he loves his parents*. He also sheepishly verbalizes what each now know:

> "One should never assume anything."

The young men's laughter continues as they enjoy the new crispness of the evening temperatures that signify the approaching end of summer. Francis inquires of James,

> "Shall you attend the meeting with Pastor Mather and Edward Hand tomorrow evening? We decided on meeting at the forge church."

> "I shall attempt to be there for our friend . . ."

The next evening finds Francis in the worship room of Old Forge, meeting with Edward Hand, Mr. and Mrs. Hand, and Pastor Alexander Mather. James has decided not to attend, desiring an early evening of rest. Candles dimly light the room. At the front are five wooden chairs placed in a semi-circle around a small wooden crate on the floor, not more than eighteen inches high. On top of the box is an open Bible.

All sit in the chairs with heads bowed in silent prayer. Pastor Mather closes the prayer and poses a question.

"Edward, shall you or your parents seek a seat in Parliament?"

Mr. and Mrs. Hand chuckle at the itinerant's question. Edward and Francis are mystified; *what is so funny?* The Scottish itinerant leans in toward Francis. With his thick accent he asks,

"Master'd Asbur'dy, ya' plannin' on enterin' the Parliament anytime soon?"

Francis squints his left eye nearly shut. He cautiously responds,

"No, sir."

"Well, guid."

Mr. Hand quickly lets them in on the private joke.

"You see, Francis, and Edward as well, you cannot seek the aid of the Toleration Act enacted by Parliament nearly seventy years ago if you have plans to enter Parliament."

The boys both nod their heads to signify that they think it all makes sense. *Subsequent to the explanation it still fails to be funny—a mystery, but not funny.* Francis keeps that thought quiet.

But recalling to mind their English history, the boys soon understand Pastor Mather's joke. Their enlightened response urges Mather to continue,

"Young Edward, as Ah' can tell, ya' surest option to maintain ya' prayer meetin's is the Toleration Act."

The Toleration Act Pastor Mather refers to is a law on the books of Parliament from 1689. It allows dissenting Protestants[79] the right to freely worship in the manner of their choice—provided they are not seeking political office. This ruling is the result of more than three decades of religious persecution by King Charles II, and more than seven decades of Puritan persecution by the English monarchy.

Subsequent to the coronation of Charles II in the mid-1600s, a twofold approach to eliminating the dissenting Christians began. First was the random imprisonment of thousands of leaders of the Puritan movement; second was the enactment of legislative action aimed to silence the evangelical purists for good.

The first of the stifling acts meant to remove access from the evangelical faithful was the Corporation Act of 1661, which served to eliminate all political influence of the Puritans. The act was clear: If anyone planned to serve as a Member of Parliament, he must swear a solemn oath that he would not take up arms "on any pretext whatever" against the King. It was the second portion of the act that dealt a blow to the Puritans. This odious provision stated that aspiring

---

[79] Christians who do not agree with the state-sanctioned Anglican Church of England.

members of the legislative body must receive the sacraments according to the rites of the Church of England. Due to the Puritan refusal of participation in the Anglican Church, this immediately removed the Puritan influence from the governing body.

Following this assault on religious freedom was a three-part legislative action aiming to undermine the ideals, education, and culture of the Puritans. The 1662 Act of Uniformity forced every clergyman and schoolmaster to "declare his unfeigned assent and consent to the use of all things in the said book contained and prescribed, in these words and in no other." That book was a prayer book that was clearly anti-Puritan. Upon the enactment of this law, two thousand Puritan ministers—20 percent of the entire English Anglican clergy—who could not of their own conscience submit to such a ruling were eliminated from their positions. These vicars were the heart and soul of the healthy portion of the Anglican Church leadership. Almost instantly, those who would lead the church toward a heretical despondency were running the Church of England.

The reaction of the expelled Puritan clergy to the Act of Uniformity was to set up shop in secret, meeting in private homes, conducting worship services according to the dictates of their own consciences. As word of this development surfaced, Parliament retaliated with the Conventicle Act of 1664. This nefarious law "punished with fine, imprisonment, and transportation on a third offence, all persons who met in greater numbers than five." The meetings implied by the ruling were gatherings of dissenting worshipers, namely, the Puritans. The act of transportation meant that after the third offense, the guilty parties would become subjects of the state, resulting in the state selling them into permanent slavery on the West Indian plantations.

Providentially, and thought by many as a direct response to the anti-religious acts, in 1665 the Great Plague arrived. In London alone, more than 100,000 citizens died from the disease. This horrifying predicament sent the Parliament fleeing to Oxford and the remaining clergy (the not-so-religious clergy) scurrying away as well. Immediately, the expelled Puritan clergy stepped in to minister to the sick and dying. They buried the dead and consoled the bereaved. These bold men of God went forth, armed with the truth written in the Bible and the passion that the Spiritual Law superseded the State Law—a concept that would later show up in the writings of John Locke about Christianity and governments, as he proclaimed that no civil law should ever violate the laws of Scripture. Ironically, the Puritan clergy returned to the churches they had been forced to leave, proceeding to conduct services as if nothing had ever happened.

Despite its fear of the deadly pestilence, Parliament was not finished with the Puritans. In 1665, in a strike at the Puritan clergy who had returned to their old churches, it enacted the Five Mile Act. The ruling prohibited any dissenting (Puritan) clergymen or schoolmasters from returning within five miles of any town, borough, or parish in which they had previously taught or preached.

These acts of Parliament completely removed all Puritan influence from the government, church, and culture for the next twenty-five years. Not until the Toleration Act of 1689 was enacted by a new King and Queen, William and Mary, did conditions improve. However, this gesture—clearly a politically motivated act, intended by a Protestant King and Queen to gain a slight advantage over Parliament by winning the favor of the Protestant dissenters—fell far short of the efforts needed to revive the Puritan culture. For by now, more than four thousand of its clergy and teachers had been made prisoners by the powerful anti-Puritan Parliament. For nearly three decades, this determined effort by the governing body had successfully purged the Puritan influence from university, social, and political circles.

For the Puritans, these events served to solidify one of their community's deeply held convictions: that there should be a clear distinction or separation between church and state. Their experience mirrored that of the Pilgrims almost a century before, demonstrating once again that when the state's influence oozes into the church's sphere of operation, the net result is devastating to religion.

Clearing his throat, Pastor Mather once more repeats his advice to Edward Hand.

> "Apply to Parliament for protection under the Toleration Act. It should provide the necessary elements to allow ya' prayer meetin's to continue."

O might each obtain a share
Of the pure enjoyments there;
Now, in rapturous surprise,
Drink the wine of Paradise;
Own, amidst the rich repast,
Thou hast given the best at last;
Wine that cheers the Host above,
The best wine of perfect love.

Charles Wesley[80]

Autumn has arrived in the West Midlands. The winds of the advancing season have once again increased as the temperatures drop. The ground cover in its blunt colors of brown and grey fails to silence the vibrant orange and red expressions of the fall leaves singing, almost shouting, from the limbs above. Neither can the falling mercury calm infatuated hearts.

Hand in hand, Francis and Nancy walk the soggy, leaf-covered dirt road to the Asbury home. They have spent most of the day together. It started early with Sabbath worship at Old Church in West Bromwich. Among the gathering was the usual crowd: Francis's close friends, the local adults, and the young people—many young people. Several of these young ones are those who were beginning to enjoy the exhortations of Francis at the home of Edward Hand, the same individuals who braved the stoning at the last meeting in Sutton.

Francis gently squeezes the soft and delicate hand; he lingers on his thought, *such tender skin.*

Francis and Nancy have grown accustomed to attending worship together on Sunday. Their deep faith is an added element of attraction for both. It was in the initial phases of their faith walk together—specifically, the persecutions in Sutton at the hand of the town magistrate, Reverend Hastings—which brought them closer emotionally. During several visits together on the first days that followed that dreadful night, the pair could not deny their feelings for each other.

The Sutton persecutions stayed with the young people for some time. At first, the event cancelled completely the prayer gatherings started by Edward and Francis. Not until nearly a month later did the young people feel safe enough to voice their desire to gather again. Some did gather, though not many, in a private

---

[80] Last stanza from the hymn Charles Wesley wrote and had sung at his wedding to Sarah (Sally) Gwynne on April 8, 1749.

home—but it wasn't the same. The fellowship of the initial gatherings was missing, as was the unofficial leader of the teenagers, Francis.

The smaller group, as well as the remainder who did not gather again, clearly seek to honor the Lord in spite of the fact that one thing has become apparent among them: they miss the energy of people their age gathering to praise the Creator. Regardless of their interests, the more vocal ones have made their opinion known. The public knowledge of this longing is the driving force of Francis's task for the evening.

Francis's steady footsteps slow a bit as he poses a question to Nancy.

"Do you believe she shall resist?"

Sensing the concern in Francis's tone, Nancy ponders the suggestion as the pair ease their pace.

"I believe it would bring her joy. At the very minimum it would bring you home more than once each week."

Francis nods his head in agreement. He characteristically scrapes the top of his bottom lip with his teeth. Nancy smiles; she finds the slight downward curl of the right side of his lower lip endearing.

Before reaching the steps to the Asbury cottage, Francis releases Nancy's hand. She doesn't mind. She has come to realize that Francis is uncomfortable showing such signs of affection for her in front of his mother. He leaps the three steps in a single bound, grips the wooden handle, and opens the front door to his parents' home. He turns toward Nancy with a vaunting nod, then bows as she walks in.

"Fair Nancy, please **do** enter the Asbury cottage . . ."

Nancy giggles at his greeting, complete with its deepened and formalized voice, its emphasis on the word "do," and the silly hand gesture waving her in. She responds,

"You should have pursued the theatre."

"A delicate subject in front of Mother."

The two laugh at the private joke about his mother and the theatre. Inside, Eliza hears the front door open; she races down the stairs. Halfway, she verbalizes her discovery:

"My Francis is here!"

Skipping the last step, she leaps toward her son to enfold him in a strong embrace. She pauses for a moment to turn to Nancy.

"Hello, Nancy."

Francis responds to his mother with a nod of his head. Nancy is more polite.

"Good day, Elizabeth."

"Today's dinner shall not be as usual."

With this unexpected declaration, Eliza releases Francis and nervously runs her hands over her hips to straighten her dress. Without warning, she bolts through the rear door of the main room. Francis shakes his head. His thought worries him: *She is nervous; how can she know what I'm about to ask?* He turns toward Nancy and remarks,

"This shall prove challenging."

Nancy smiles at his concern. She gently reminds,

"Have faith."

Francis makes his way to the fireplace. Hanging above the low fire is his mother's iron kettle, steam issuing from under its lid. He grabs the dishrag hanging on a nail next to the iron spit he lovingly constructed for his mother. He tilts his head back and forth as he admires his handiwork. Placing the rag onto the kettle lid's handle, he slightly lifts the heavy cover with both hands. *How does Mother manage this?* He is grateful that she does.

In the kettle, a hot soup is warming nicely. The aroma of herbs rises to please Francis; *the welcoming scents of sage and thyme.* He searches for the spoon that his mother uses to stir the soup and finds it lying on the hearth. He maneuvers the lid to his left hand and reaches down for the spoon. Lifting the utensil, he prepares to place it into the kettle for a taste. With his left hand, he raises the heavy lid higher. Looking at the soup, he notices something different: the mixture isn't the usual golden liquid he has grown to love; instead, the soup seems to be almost red in color. Although the mixture smells marvelous, its appearance is new to Francis. He prepares to taste it anyway.

"Francis, remove your intentions."

The stern voice of Elizabeth brings Francis to a halt. He turns to find her standing at the rear door to the room. Raising a steady hand with finger pointed, she once again gives warning.

"You shall wait for dinner."

Francis reluctantly returns the spoon and lid to their designated places. With hands nervously finding rest at his sides, he glances at Nancy; she holds back a laugh. He decides it is best to say something, anything, to change the subject.

"Where is Father?"

"He is outdoors, planting the beans for next summer's harvest. I suggest you remove temptation and lend aid to him outdoors."

Francis lowers his eyes and moves to the rear door. He pauses long enough to give another quick look to Nancy. She smiles. Francis is lost in *that incredible smile;* he moves on, heading outdoors in search of Joseph.

Fall plantings . . . he must be at the south side of the barns. The thought has Francis making his way around the buildings. *There he is.* Joseph prepares the ground where the bean plants will reside for an early summer harvest next year. Without looking at his son, Joseph suggests the obvious.

> "Mother has forced you from the kitchen?"
> "One could say I brought it upon myself."

Joseph laughs and motions to his son.

> "Pull up a block and lend hand."

Francis moves to the pile of a half-dozen chunks of moss-covered, unsplit oak left over from the stock his father cut for winter. He grabs one and plops it down right next to his father.

> "Breathing room, provide some breathing room, Francis. Move halfway
> down the wall; you can begin there."

Joseph's stern advice causes Francis to rise, lift his block, and move roughly two yards away. His father follows behind. Attached to his waist belt is a woven bag. He reaches his hand into the pouch, pulling out a small handful of its precious contents.

> "Mazagan beans—not as productive as the larger beans, but an early
> producer - -
> And much stronger against the winter cold."

Nodding his head to acknowledge the lifelong wisdom coming from his father, Francis receives the valuable items. With his hand full of seeds, it finally dawns on him: *How shall I dig the soil?* As only a father can do, Joseph is already on the spot with a small spade for his son.

> "You'll require this."

He hands the uniquely designed digging tool to Francis. Joseph turns to return to his portion of the plantings; he continues down the wall, giving his son clear directions.

> "First row, two fingers from the wall, seeds a handbreadth apart."
> "I am aware, Father."
> "I am aware you are aware. The row plantings are to be a handbreadth
> apart also. This bunching will protect the seedlings from frost before
> transplanting."

Francis methodically places the seeds in their rows, careful to set each seed firmly and cover it with the rich, loamy topsoil. Before long, he is once again in a safe and familiar setting: gardening with his father. He proceeds unabashedly.

> "Father, my band aims to meet Wednesday evenings."

Knowing that his son rarely has only one thing to say, Joseph waits for additional communication. It's not long before Francis continues,

> "We seek to gather in a home - -
> Our home."
>
> "I see no problem with the five or six of you meeting here, Francis. Have you discussed your plans with Mother?"

Expecting an immediate response from Francis, the lengthy pause causes Joseph to slowly look up toward his son; the stop in conversation also indicates to him that Francis is yet to mention his full intentions. Joseph wisely expects that something else is coming; he waits as he returns to his planting chore.

His expectations are correct. Francis continues,

> "Well, Father, the band meeting may take on more of a class meeting appearance . . ."
>
> "Oh?"

Joseph once again halts his planting, scratches his brow with his forearm, and looks to his son. Sensing that his father has paused, Francis looks to Joseph. Returning to his planting, he goes a step further.

> "Father, I wish to move Edward Hand's gatherings to our home."
>
> "Were not more than thirty present for the gatherings in Sutton? That is quite larger than a band or class meeting."
>
> "Well, yes, Father. You see, we've nowhere else to meet. Sutton is closed off and the class meetings in Wednesbury and West Bromwich are . . ."

Francis stops mid-sentence, pausing in his planting also. He stares at the ground for a moment. By now, Joseph is fixated on watching the actions of his son. He is familiar with the body language that always gives the full account of the story. Joseph inquires,

> "The meetings in Wednesbury and West Bromwich are . . . ?"
>
> "Well, Father, they are boring."
>
> "Boring?"
>
> "Well, not boring; I didn't mean to imply boredom. The meetings are a blessing. However, they just are - -
> Far from young."

Joseph is quiet. This is not what he expected. *Boring? How can they appear boring?* As Joseph ponders his son's comment, Francis cannot help but bring forth his deepest feelings.

>"The meetings in Sutton were rather exciting; young people from several towns joined me— joined us and our little gathering."

>"Thirty people are far from a little gathering. Have you considered the consequences of your efforts? What if the thirty turns into forty? What then, Francis?"

Francis purses his lips. He hadn't considered the gathering growing; *that would be a fantastic experience.* He keeps that thought silent.

>"Francis, I will have to talk with Mother. I will clean up; dinner is nearly ready. Remain outdoors for a time; it shall be safer."

Joseph's cocked smile causes Francis to hold back a laugh.

>"Father, thank you for talking to Mother."

Joseph grunts as he rises, his popping knees once again reminding him of his age. *My legs have lost their youthfulness.* He rubs the top of Francis's head as he limps his way toward the rear door of the home. Francis remains sitting, silently pondering *what shall Mother say?*

Francis resumes the planting. He gently places in the ground the few seeds left in his hand. He unexpectedly hears the rear door of the home open as he covers the last seed. He turns to find his father walking at a hurried pace, straight for Francis.

Joseph announces,

>"Mother would like to speak with you."

With one fluid movement, Francis bounces to his feet. Facing in Joseph's direction, he petitions his father,

>"What did she say? Is there concern?"

>"She requires your presence."

The look of distress on Francis's face causes Joseph to add,

>"Come along, Franky."

Francis reluctantly takes his first step; with head slightly bowed and eyes fixed on the ground ahead of him, he proceeds slowly to the rear door.

Upon entering the home, he can hear his mother and Nancy talking in the main room. He quietly cracks open the rear door to peek at his mother; *she appears calm.* He takes a deep breath and enters the room. Eliza turns and greets her son.

>"Francis, Father and I would love to host your friends."

Francis is genuinely surprised and greatly relieved. He wants to hug Nancy, but he wisely decides to wait until later. He walks to his mother and hugs her as Joseph enters the room.

>"Franky, Mother expects you this Wednesday eve."

Francis pulls away from Elizabeth's embrace.

"This Wednesday! I shall have to—we shall have to spread word immediately."

"Proceed as you wish, my son; shall mean more of Mother's soup for me."

Nancy chuckles at Joseph's quip. Strangely, Joseph's comment reminds Francis of his earlier question. With a short, sharp turn of his head toward his mother, he ventures to ask,

"Mother, what kind of soup have you prepared? It appears peculiar."

"Your father obtained a few tomatoes. Many of the women have been raving about the qualities of the fruit. I decided it was time for the Asburys to try them."

Francis thinks to himself, *the tomato.*

"The fruit fails to be poisonous?"

"Now really, Franky, would Mother try to poison us? She may disfavor a few of my habits; nevertheless, she would never . . . well, there was the time with the theatre . . ."

"Enough, Joseph; we have put that behind us."

Wednesday evening would come quickly for the hardworking Francis. He found himself racing from the forge in the dark on Monday and Tuesday evenings after work, so that he and Nancy might seek out many of the young people who had gathered at the Sutton meetings. They painstakingly spread word of the upcoming meeting to their friends in West Bromwich, Wednesbury, and Sutton.

On the scheduled Wednesday the meeting went well, the initial gathering succeeding as if the previous meeting had been held the week before. The young people found it natural to come together as a group. The only negative during the event was Elizabeth expressing her disappointment at running out of food for the nearly two dozen who had gathered. Equally successful were the following three gatherings during the remainder of the month. With each meeting, the number of attendees grew—so much so that the last meeting forced many of the young people to stand outdoors. This development was the inciting incident forcing yet another decision, the subject for this evening's gathering.

The young women, eighteen in all, gather in the tiny main room of the Asbury cottage. The atmosphere is one of expectation. At the center is Nancy. She stands with both hands snugly placed inside the pockets of the petticoat beneath her dress. The recent fashion development has intrigued several of the young ladies. One of the girls instructs,

"The access slit resides just below the button on each side of the dress. Through this fashionable opening, Nancy is able to reach the pockets

below. And if Nancy were feeling a bit daring, she could attach the hidden
cord sewn at the bottom of the dress to one of the sweet little buttons,
exposing a bit of her petticoat."

The girls flutter at the thought.

Over the last month, Nancy's unflinching support of Francis—as well as the not-
so-private budding relationship between them—has caused her to become the
obvious leader of the fairer sex for the evening gatherings. The young ladies
excitedly talk and share about numerous unrelated things; at times their
conversations border on prating, at least until the exchanges include references
to Francis and Nancy as a couple. On multiple occasions, Nancy quietly mouths a
reminder to the others that Francis's mother knows little of their companionship.

Outdoors, twenty young men assist Joseph. The resourceful gardener has
grown accustomed to these Wednesday evenings and the numerous extra strong
hands available, especially since it is the busy fall season.

Joseph shouts an order to the young men.

"Quickly, before Francis arrives, give attention to the spinach."

With this command, the nearly two dozen young men make their way to the
northeast corner of the large vegetable garden, where the numerous rows of
spinach reside. Joseph continues,

"The spinach must be clean of weeds. Look for chickweed and the
running weeds. These must be eradicated to ensure successful completion
of the harvest at month's end."

Immediately, the group descends on the designated portion of the garden.
With battalion-like precision they begin to remove the unwanted intruders.
Handful by handful, every undesirable weed lands upon a makeshift pile of
discards. Satisfied with the results, Joseph turns and leaves, almost trotting as he
disappears into his tool barn.

Inside the structure, he moves at a hurried pace. Knowing that many hands
accelerate the work, he surmises that he has only five to seven minutes before the
young men will have the spinach beds clear of chickweed—clear of all weeds.
Grabbing several small shears and cutting tools, he races back outdoors.

As Joseph approaches the young men, James Bayley offers a question.

"Doing some cutting, are we?"

Mid-stride and without missing a step, Joseph responds,

"Hurry; before Francis arrives we must shear my herbs: sage, savory,
thyme - -
Oh, and the hyssop; I almost forgot the hyssop. I would also like to cut the
mint, tarragon, and sorrel, as well."

James smiles; by his mental calculations, he determines that the remaining work Joseph intends will require about fifteen minutes. He finds it amusing that the enterprising gardener has figured out the exact amount of time he has before his son arrives from the forge. He responds to Joseph,

"How shall we cut?"

"Cut close to the surface of the ground or near the heads, depending on the plant. You shall know which will reproduce; these shall be cut near the head."

James receives the cutting implements and distributes the tools to several of his friends. In front of Jabez Ault, he pauses to ask,

"Are we old enough to handle sharp objects?"

Jabez feels somewhat disrespected.

"Almost fourteen!"

He shrugs off the comment and snatches a set of small shears from James. All who have received a cutting implement follow close behind James as he leads them to the bed full of aromatic plants.

Inside the Asbury cottage, Nancy and several of her friends help Elizabeth with the last-minute preparations. During the first two meetings of the month, Elizabeth did her best to provide a small snack, sacrificing much of her jarred fruit. The peaches and nectarines were tasty to all. However, the generous offering meant that she and Joseph would go without the precious luxury during the upcoming winter. Although it pained Elizabeth, after several requests, Nancy and the girls convinced her to offer only a brewed tea. This arrangement proved advantageous last week, especially when the number of attendees approached forty.

Joseph and his troops enter the home as the girls are setting the tea onto the kitchen table, the heavy oak piece now sitting in a corner of the main room. Elizabeth arrives with an armload of cups she has borrowed from The Malt Shovel tavern next door; she places them on the table. All additional furniture resides outdoors, making room for everyone to stand indoors and sit outdoors.

The arrival of the men enlivens the girls. Observing them, Elizabeth almost leaps toward Joseph, delighted that these young people are growing closer to God in her home—and satisfied that the spiritual growth is happening under her watchful eye. With a little extra effort, everyone fits into the Asburys' main room.

As if on cue, James Bayley turns around and opens the front door of the home; in walks Francis, along with his forge companion, James Mayo. Immediately the shoulder-to-shoulder gathering turns toward tonight's teacher. He is greeted by many speaking at once.

"Francis, we are eager to hear you this evening."

Francis smiles and bows his head in gratitude. James Bayley and the quiet James Mayo nudge their way through the group and lead Francis to the center of the room. The always-talkative James Bayley turns toward Francis, the first to offer what both are thinking.

"The home shall split! We must make arrangements for a new location."

Francis remains silent. He ventures a look around the crowded room. He moves his head several times from left to right, his gaze eventually coming to rest on his close friends, James and James. He quietly offers,

"Perhaps it is the Lord's desire for this evening."

The two Jameses look to each other. James Bayley seems mystified by Francis's response, but James Mayo looks as if he knows a little more. They both shrug their shoulders.

Francis raises his right hand to speak.

"Everyone, it is my wish . . ."

The crowd tries to quiet, but it is difficult. Francis gives it another attempt.

Everyone, I wish to pose a question."

Each in the room ceases to speak, focusing on Francis. He continues,

"As much as it may pain my dear mother, I seek to offer a suggestion."

Francis pushes slightly forward, inching his way toward the kitchen table, toward his mother and father. Again, he speaks.

"I seek to offer a suggestion. It has come to my attention that a space has become available in West Bromwich."

Immediately the chatter begins. The young men ask each other what Francis may be suggesting. The girls' intuition causes them to realize that Francis is hinting at moving the meetings to a new location.

Francis raises both hands to gain their attention. Once the volume is reduced to a low murmur, he continues,

"The space, once improved, could easily handle fifty people."

This excites many in the group. James Bayley responds,

"But can we afford such luxury? Not many of us are blessed with a blacksmith's salary."

Thomas Ault, Thomas Russell, and several other young men laugh at James's quip. Even the stoic James Mayo chuckles. Amidst the roomful of increasing amusement and gentle banter, Bayley raises his arms to quiet the gathering. They reduce the volume somewhat as he continues,

"It was my aim only to provoke laughter. The offer which you propose, Francis, is fantastic! The space shall be our own."

The murmuring of the group becomes a steady chatter of ideas. Standing at the kitchen table, Francis looks to James Mayo, motioning that he is going to pour himself a cup of tea. He silently mouths to James, "cup of tea?" James nods his head. As he pours, Francis is surprised that no one has yet asked the location of the available space. He hands James his cup. After pouring his own drink, Francis raises his cup to toast his pal. The two sip their tea as Francis once again ponders the lack of concern over the building's address. He smiles to himself. The omission doesn't bother him; he and his friends are young, *and at times, we fail to consider important details.*

By evening's end, Francis is able to divulge the whereabouts of the new meeting space. The space is actually a familiar one, located on the Bromwich Heath on Paradise Street across from Dagger Hall—the space where Francis first exhorted, the old James Wheatley home. Upon identifying the location, the obvious question of the evening is whether the dilapidated wooden floor of the second story space will hold up. Francis's reply is to the point:

"It shall require work."

Francis's band does their best to ease everyone's concern. James Bayley, along with Thomas Ault, vows to gather the necessary materials for a proper and safe floor. Even the usually quiet-in-public James Mayo chimes in,

"Francis, could not the Turtons be counted upon for aid?"

The Turtons are the wealthy family that owns the West Bromwich fruit tree orchard, where Francis and Thomas Ault were invited to aid in the fruit harvest a couple of years ago. The well-planted area is also the orchard that Francis and Thomas secretly traveled through under the cover of darkness, to which Francis hinted at returning to "borrow" some of the precious fruit. The Turtons own the structure directly across the street from the abandoned Wheatley home, the beautiful Dagger Hall. Francis agrees with James; approaching the family would be a great way to begin the process of raising sufficient funds to acquire the deserted room.

The next few weeks find the nearly forty young people busily seeking help from anyone who will listen to their plea. Their request is simple: "We require money for supplies to acquire and repair the neglected space." The procuring of the materials is actually easier than most had predicted. Crate suppliers to the forge have been eager to donate some of their containers as materials. In addition, their supervisor at the forge, Mr. Foxall, has contributed the necessary nails to accomplish the repairs. The young men are eager for the work to begin.

With an ample supply of materials for the repairs, Francis is appointed the task of gaining permission to begin the restoration. He asks Thomas Ault to accompany him to the town magistrate. They leave Newton Village on a Friday morning, Mr. Foxall having allowed Francis to take the time off from work. Mr. Foxall's words are clear: "Take only the time necessary to accomplish the request, then proceed back directly and return to work." Francis is thankful for the kind gesture from his supervisor.

Down the main road of West Bromwich, Francis and Thomas walk at a brisk pace. Hope and expectation grow with each stride of their long legs. The effort's deepened breaths cause the crisp autumn air to waft like miniature spirits from their mouths.

Approaching the brick building which houses the magistrate, the two cannot hold back.

> "Thomas, we can begin this very evening!"
>
> "Before this evening, Francis! Thomas Russell has taken this day off from his father's business. He agreed to transport much of the donated wood this morning."
>
> "If only Foxall would allow us a day off."
>
> "Francis, if our legs were broken, I doubt we would be afforded time away from the forge."
>
> "Yes, Foxall is quite the taskmaster."

The two revel in their slight of their supervisor. It's not that they dislike Mr. Foxall; it is actually a custom of the trades to never admit that they enjoy working for their boss. They silently smile at each other, knowing that it is a privilege to work for Foxall. They continue along.

Francis and Thomas pause in front of the magistrate's entrance door. Both are slightly out of breath. They look at each other. Francis raises his eyebrows and purses his lips. After a few seconds of silence, he nods his head and Thomas opens the door.

Inside, an assistant to the magistrate greets them. He is a short man, slightly overweight and balding. In his hands is a small sheaf of papers; he struggles as he attempts to roll them like a scroll. His efforts falling short, he resorts to folding them slightly as he inquires of the pair,

> "Are we to see the magistrate?"

Francis nods. The assistant continues,

> "Very well, proceed through the entrance."

Francis and Thomas simultaneously nod. They walk to the door and Francis opens it. Inside, the magistrate sits at a large oak-wood desk covered with numerous piles of paperwork. Francis's eyes are immediately drawn to the iron bar resting on the desk, which resembles the smelted bars at the forge. The magistrate raises his head toward the young men as they enter and quickly offers,

> "Please do take a seat. What have I for you today?"

Standing in front of the elderly magistrate is more unsettling than Francis had expected, so much so that the boys fail to take the offered seats. Success of the mission seemed certain before the meeting. Now he is slightly lost for words. The quiet and respectful Thomas is also silent. But the civil officer will not wait long.

"What have I for you today?"

Francis has no doubt that when he speaks his voice will tremble slightly. He proceeds anyway.

"We desire to improve the abandoned Wheatley building."

He is grateful the statement came out. The words were slightly unsteady, but understandable, and, thankfully, there was no uncomfortable ending that seems like something else is supposed to follow.

In contrast, the town's leader is stern in his reply to Francis's request.

"No work shall proceed until the space has been properly contracted."

Francis had not planned on this reply. He becomes more nervous. He is convinced that all in the room can hear the pile-driving heartbeats accompanying his deep breaths. His voice trembles, this time not so slightly, as he attempts clarification.

"Properly contracted? Are you implying a signed contract?"

"Young man, I do not imply a signed contract; my intentions are much more. I am implying a completed transaction."

Francis and Thomas stand silent and dejected. It is a difficult task, but they eventually have the courage to look at each other. In their silence, they seem to be saying the same thing. They fail to know how to accomplish it, but without speaking a word, they vow to arrange the purchase of the room.

Bowing to the magistrate, they turn to leave, long-faced and quiet, uncertain of how to raise the necessary funds. On the way out the door, Francis accidentally bumps an adjacent wooden table. On top of the small piece of furniture is a glass container. It falls to the floor, shattering in many pieces. The two young men halt their exit and turn toward the magistrate. In a sharp tone he responds,

"Be on your way, lads."

The return trip to town is a long and quiet trek. Reminiscent of their days at the Sneal's Green school, Francis's gaze locks onto the ground and he kicks at stones as he walks alongside Thomas. Thomas is silent; he says nothing as he blocks out the distraction of Francis's stone dance, choosing to reflect on the implications of the magistrate's words. His eyes fix skyward, the dark clouds furthering his doubts of their success.

As Thomas and Francis make their way home, Francis's friend Thomas Russell thumps on an oak stump outside the Wheatley space. Each swing of the wooden mallet ends with an increasingly louder grunt; he is impatient. He ceases the pounding. With the hammer dangling from his long, thin arm, he decides to venture into the wooden structure. His heart is set on doing the necessary carpentry repairs to the Wheatley space.

Thomas is from a long line of talented carpenters, taught well by his father and several uncles who still make a living in the trade. In past meetings at the space, he actually had envisioned himself improving the room which needed so much work. He had observed that the rough-hewn walls would require a proper sanding and caulking, and the floorboards bracing and replacement of worn areas. *I could easily accomplish these tasks—even the step, two-thirds of the way up, would be easily replaceable with the necessary support for safety.* He is confident that the work would bring him satisfaction and recognition from his friends; however, if his deepest thoughts were known, he also longs to show off his skills to one of the girls who frequent the young people's gatherings.

Climbing the wooden steps, the lanky Thomas makes a mental note: *The edges of the steps require finishing.* At the infamous step in need of support, he wisely lifts his foot to the step above. His angular frame is perfect for his trade, his long arms and legs facilitating his ability to reach into, above, and around difficult and tight spaces. His tall, thin body not only aids him in his work, but also, unbeknownst to him, has drawn the attention of one of Nancy's close friends. He maneuvers up the stairs, carefully ducking his head and batting away cobwebs as he enters the second-floor space.

Thomas and the girl who finds him attractive would make an interesting couple. They would have their common ground, for she, too, is from a hardworking family that makes a living through the skill of carpentry, assembling wheels for the horse-drawn carts that pull the pack trains of coal. She and Thomas also come from families drawn to the Wesleyan movement. Despite these compatible circumstances, the point of interest for this couple would not be what they share alike, but what they do not possess in common: she is approximately half his height.

The girl is pretty in face and witty in personality, her beautiful smile with the rounded cheeks and brilliant white teeth naturally attracting the attention of most boys. Her soft eyes with the thin brows and long lashes are magnetic to a young man. Nevertheless, the interest of the potential suitors never seems to proceed beyond the initial appeal, their lack of pursuit always ending in disappointment for her. She suspects it is due to her shortness of stature. Despite the discouraging results of the past, she continues to hope.

Entering the second-floor room, Thomas makes his way to the window and looks out, down to the grey and gritty dirt of Paradise Street. He gives a quick glance to the heath that lies directly across the street, doing battle with the oncoming winter. Back at the street, in the distance, he notices a small group of people heading in his direction. He is able to make out three of them: Francis, Thomas Ault, and Nancy. On their return trip, Nancy and two of her friends had joined Francis and Thomas Ault—unbeknownst to the young men, Nancy and her pals had followed them to the magistrate's office. It wasn't long before the girls were able to ease the boys' distress about the building acquisition, their kind words of encouragement acting as a healing embrace.

From the second-floor window, Thomas Russell squints to make out the last two individuals who lag behind the threesome. It is clear by their outfits that the two in question are both female, as they are in dresses. He is uncertain as to the identity of the tall young lady. But before long, the identity of the second girl is made clear by the fact that she is much shorter than the rest of the group. She is the girl who admires him; moreover, she is the girl he admires.

He nervously turns from the window and looks for a place to set down his hammer. He discovers a chair on the far side of the room and shuffles toward it. In his haste, he has forgotten about the room's peculiar shortcomings; during his second step, his foot lands squarely onto a dilapidated portion of the floor. The crack of the wood and the sudden drop of his frame cause his emotions to race. Instinctively, he reaches simultaneously for the pole at the center of the room and the oncoming floorboards.

"Aaaagh!"

His knee stops at floor level. His long arms had reached the post, but they were not able to keep his foot from completely penetrating the floor. His brow begins to sweat; he is in pain. He maneuvers in an attempt to free his leg; placing both hands on the floor, he tries to push himself off it. His efforts fall short. The injury brings great discomfort, but he is more worried that Francis and the girls will see him in this desperate situation.

Again he tries to lift himself from the predicament by pulling on the pole, but he can't manage it. His thoughts dart in several directions: *I can't feel my foot. Is it broken? Shall the group discover me? Is skin penetrated? Do I bleed?* He attempts to push off the floor again. He reaches down with his left arm; it is difficult, but he pushes up, aiming to free his foot. It will not release; the foot is wedged between the cracked board and an adjacent support beam. *Oh my, she shall find me incapacitated. Francis shall be amused. He shall tell the rest, or worse, my father.*

Thomas attempts to reconcile with his fears, but he fails to find comfort in the face of such a humiliating discovery. Below him, he can hear the sound of the front door opening. The gentle mumblings of the group are plainly audible; *they have arrived.*

Francis's louder voice below causes Thomas Russell to once again squirm in his attempt at freedom. He gives several jerks of his foot and feels an incredible pain shear through his calf muscle.

"Aaaagh!"

His scream brings Francis, Thomas Ault, and the girls to a halt. Thomas Ault is the first to respond.

"Thomas Russell?"

"Believe so."

Francis's reply coincides with his leap toward the stairs; within seconds, he is racing up them. Skipping every other tread, Francis is scaling the flight quickly. He, too, encounters the building's shortcomings as he fails to skip the cracked step along the way, his foot landing directly on the fragile board. At the crack of the wooden step, he instinctively slides his foot sideways, jamming it into the solid oak stringer.

"Aaaagh!"

Once again, Thomas Ault is quick to respond.

"Francis?"

Nancy and her girls cringe at the thought of Francis being hurt. As Thomas hurries to the stairs, two voices simultaneously deliver a declaration.

"Aaaagh, my leg!"   "Aaaagh, my leg!"

Thomas on the floor above and Francis on the stairs below are both in pain. The girls follow Thomas Ault up the steps. Upstairs, Thomas Russell finds it odd to hear Francis scream in pain; *something unexpected must have occurred.*

On the steps, Thomas Ault stops at Francis. As he begins to inquire, Nancy quickly interrupts him.

"Francis is hurt."

Nancy scoots around Thomas to gently place her hand on top of Francis's right shoulder. In different circumstances this would be a most pleasing and enjoyable event for him, but he is slow to respond.

"I shall be all right; however, my leg and foot feel most unwell."

He reaches for the side wall of the stairwell as he gently lifts the ailing limb. Nancy maneuvers herself under Francis's shoulder as she advises,

"Sit, Francis; you mustn't stand on the foot. Sit."

"Very well."

Francis accepts the counsel, leaning his back against the wall and sliding down to a sitting position.

Working her way around Nancy and Francis, Thomas Russell's admirer darts up the stairs and disappears toward the second-floor room.

Thomas can hear the staccato steps as they approach the second level. He drops his chin to his chest; *she is here.* The door to the upper room squeaks as it opens.

Catching sight of Thomas, the young girl quietly gasps as she covers her mouth with clasped hands. She catches herself before attempting to leap to his side.

> "Thomas, can I proceed?"

She is worried about additional shortcomings of the floorboards. In an almost grumbling reply, Thomas responds,

> "It is safe—the additional deficiencies lay closer to the exterior walls; you've no need for worry."

She slowly lifts her foot and takes the first step; she is cautious, yet anxious to reach Thomas. Step by step, she repeats the motion, releasing a breath of relief with each completed movement.

Realizing that she has successfully traversed the shaky floor, Thomas turns to greet her.

> "Dearest Mary, I pray your day has progressed more satisfactorily than mine?"

Pausing to answer, her eyes search Thomas for additional ailments. She is confident that only his foot is injured. Slightly worried, but realizing that Thomas has made a humorous comment, she reluctantly decides to make light of his predicament.

> "I've hadn't a chance to sit all day."

Thomas laughs aloud. The sudden movement brings a pain in his calf that causes him to quickly shrink back. The reaction fails to escape Mary's notice.

> "You are in pain, Thomas."

> "It is true, Mary; my leg at the calf is most painful."

> "Can you raise enough for me to place my shoulder under yours?"

> "I fail to know. Perhaps we should await Thomas."

> "Thomas shall be aiding Francis. Come, rise up and I will attempt to lift you."

> "As you wish."

Thomas has answered before thinking. He does not think she will be able to help him; however, he decides to try. Pulling up on the post, he begins the task. Mary slowly works her little frame under his shoulder—an easy task, considering her small stature. Thomas comments,

> "It is actually quite comfortable to have your support."

Mary smiles. *I wouldn't trade this opportunity for the entire town of Bromwich.* She keeps this thought to herself.

By standing almost upright, Thomas is able to wiggle his trapped foot as he leans on Mary's shoulder. He realizes that if she were to move to the pole, she could support the bulk of his weight. He advises,

"Mary, move to the pole. You can lean against it as I proceed to free my foot."

She does so.

This move allows Thomas to push even harder as he lifts his aching foot. As he does, Mary notices the blood running down his leg. She can clearly see that he has punctured his calf; it bleeds, but slowly. Keeping this news to herself, she decides to offer encouragement instead.

"A bit more, Thomas, and your leg shall be free."

Thomas finds comfort in her words. He gently lifts his leg once more; twisting his foot inward, he is able to gain a few more inches. Again he lifts, this time curving the end of his foot down and inward; it at last breaks free of its prison. Thomas immediately stands to both feet.

"Aaaagh!"

"Thomas, you needn't stand; lean against the pole while I retrieve a chair."

Thomas does as Mary instructs. She pushes away from Thomas and heads for the window on the other side of the room. Thomas is quick to caution,

"Slowly, Mary—there shall be another precarious location just to the right of the window."

"I can see it. The chair is just in front of it. I shall maintain care."

Mary is able to reach the chair; she brings it to Thomas. He is thankful as he sits.

He takes a deep breath as he looks toward Mary. His uncontrollable smile accents his eyes as they meet with hers.

"Thank you, Mary. Thank you for caring for me."

She smiles; *he must mean so much more than the current incident.*

Thomas Ault bounds into the room. He doesn't hesitate to share,

"Thomas, you and Francis both require medical attention—we shall leave immediately."

Thomas Russell nods his head, looking to Mary as he speaks.

"Mary and I shall require assistance in getting downstairs."

"I will help you both. Francis and Nancy are attempting to descend the stairs."

On the stairs, Francis leans on Nancy's shoulder. One step at a time, the two head for the first floor. Three steps into their journey, the front door to the structure opens, and two men in the midst of conversation can be heard walking inside.

"Yes, John, the Wheatley building is available."

The two men who have entered are John Turton of West Bromwich and his nephew and namesake from Staffordshire, John Turton the younger.

The younger John Turton has recently graduated with a Bachelor of Medicine from University College, Oxford. In addition to his medical training, he is a mathematical and philosophical genius who recently received recommendation into the Royal Society.[81] The recommendation alone is a distinguished honor, but there is a good chance he will also receive the fellowship. The young man, nine years older than the seventeen-year-old Francis and the same age as Francis's friend Richard Whatcoat, has a desire to practice medicine in London.

Nearing the bottom step, Nancy recognizes John Turton the elder. She calls out,

"Mr. Turton, we require your assistance."

The two Turton men dart for Francis and Nancy as they notice the pair limping onto the bottom-floor landing. John the younger is quick to direct,

"Have a seat, young man, whilst I take a look at your foot."

"You may want to proceed to Thomas, upstairs."

"In due time; you must take a seat."

Francis nods his head and points to the chair in the building's lobby. The elder John Turton offers Nancy relief from her burden.

"I shall take him from here."

"Thank you, sir."

Bracing Francis on his shoulder, he moves him toward the chair. Francis lets out a groan, then persists,

"You must attend my friend upstairs. I shall fare well, but I fail to believe so for Thomas."

"Thomas Russell?"

Nancy responds,

"Yes, upstairs."

John the elder knows Thomas Russell. Pointing toward the steps, he urges John the younger to proceed. Francis warns,

"Beware the sixth step; it gives way - -
As well as several locations upstairs."

The younger John stops. He turns to look at Francis, who repeats his warning.

"As well as several locations upstairs."

"As well as several . . ."

Echoing Francis's words, John the younger shakes his head and resumes his departure to the second level.

One step at a time, he proceeds toward the upstairs level. He successfully traverses the infamous sixth step and continues upward.

---

[81] Great Britain's learned society to promote scientific study, founded in 1660.

At the upstairs landing, John gently pushes open the door to the room. He senses the stale, dry smell of the room as he catches sight of Thomas Russell supported by little Mary and Thomas Ault. He responds to his discovery,

"I shall take over from here."

"Thank you, sir."

John points Mary aside as he works his way under Thomas's other shoulder. Amidst Thomas's occasional groans, the three men make their way toward the steps. John looks to the floor and spots the hole that caught Thomas's leg.

At the bottom floor, Francis and the elder John converse.

"I remember you and your friend. Both of you worked my fruit trees several autumns past."

"It is as you say, Thomas Ault and I . . ."

"Yes, Thomas Ault. How is your fine friend?"

"You may ask him yourself; he should be making his way down the steps with your nephew and the injured Thomas Russell."

Thomas Ault, Mary, Thomas Russell, and John the younger enter the room as Francis completes his sentence. Frustrated with his injury, Francis closes his eyes and rests his head against the wall behind him.

The four of them appear strained. Mary darts off for a chair; placing it next to Francis, she advises,

"Sit, Thomas."

He does so, groaning slightly in pain as he drops into the seat.

Going down on one knee in front of his new patient, Thomas Russell, the younger John begins his examination.

"Let us have a look."

Gently maneuvering Thomas's injured foot, he says nothing. The only sound is his occasional muttering to himself. After several inspections of the injured leg, he pauses; then, appearing confident, he looks Thomas in the eye.

"Your leg does not appear broken; lacerated, but gratefully, unbroken. A good preparation of the cut shall result in a quick recovery. I recommend a poultice of onion placed upon the puncture to purify the blood."

"Onion?"

Thomas Ault questions the medical suggestion. Mary and Nancy tilt their heads; they too question the soundness of the advice. John the younger is quick to affirm,

"The application of a slice of onion to the wound shall aid in the healing process."

Francis lifts his head from the wall he's been resting on. Opening his eyes, he looks to the young doctor and delivers a question:

"Onion? Where in the Lord's creation is the medical community applying onion to open wounds?"

"Francis."

Nancy's harsh tone matches her look of disappointment and displeasure with Francis's question, which has bordered on sarcasm. She holds the frown while staring at Francis. Noticing her reaction from the corner of his eye, Francis decides to ignore her displeasure. John the younger replies,

"The colonies, in America."

The doctor's answer sharpens Francis's attention; he clears his throat as he leans in for more. The young doctor is happy to continue.

"The native tribes have long been successful with the use of poultice for treatment of wounds. The onion, as well as several herbs and plant leaves, are commonly utilized—natural or boiled, depending on the ailment."

"The colonies sound like a fascinating place."

"They appear to be, Francis; a fascinating place and a fascinating people. Now for your foot."

Rising from his kneeling position, the young doctor slides sideways and kneels on the same right knee in front of Francis. Once again, he gently inspects an ailing limb.

"Can you turn the foot?"

Francis slowly turns the foot inward, giving a low grunt as he grimaces. He notices from the corner of his eye that his honest expressions are upsetting Nancy. *Shall attempt to hold back to avoid furthering her worry.*

With the gentleness associated with his industry, the doctor raises Francis's injured foot. He inspects the heel as well as the arch. Palpating the arch brings a sudden jerk and quickened breath from Francis. John the younger raises his eyebrows in reaction to Francis's expression of discomfort and advises,

"The swelling around the foot alarms me. The injury shall require the application of leeches to reduce swelling. I can arrange for the treatment at the home of my uncle."

The girls, as well as Francis and his friends, grimace in disgust. Thomas Ault remarks,

"Leeches! Would not proper rest allow for the accumulation to subside?"

Far from being offended, John the younger is pleased by Thomas's inquiry and quickly offers his encouragement.

"You appear to have an interest in the field of medicine. Your suggestion does hold merit. Remaining off the foot would be a more novel and, to some, proper approach. However, I would not rule out leeches; they are an interesting group of creatures."

"Francis's mother would soundly rule out leeches."

The young people simultaneously laugh aloud at Thomas's comment. The laughter doesn't last long; the girls contort their faces as they shiver at the thought of leeches draining life's fluid from Francis's foot.

Francis closes his eyes and gently places his head back against the wall. He mumbles,

"First the magistrate and now leeches . . ."

For the next two weeks, the friends of Francis and Thomas Russell take turns daily attending to the personal needs of the two young men. Nancy and her associates complete the majority of the mundane chores: bringing food and water, propping up Francis's injured foot, supplying the next onion slice for Thomas's poultice. At times, several girls, along with a couple of boy tag-a-longs, cram into the small bedrooms of the injured. In the Asbury cottage, it is a given that Elizabeth will be present whenever a female nurse arrives. Francis doesn't mind; his constant mental response is *such is Mother*.

As for the forge, Mr. Foxall isn't happy to lose Francis's labor for a fortnight. Through several of his companions, Francis assures his boss that he will return as soon as he is able, but it is a struggle for the young man. He is enjoying the attention, especially from Nancy.

On this cold and darkening day, the fourteenth day of Francis's injury, the afternoon sun is preparing for its evening trek. Outdoors, the November winds escort a stark reminder of the approaching winter and its sharpened temperatures. The knock on the Asbury front door comes as a surprise to Elizabeth as she descends the stairs from Francis's bedroom. She has delivered his dinner as usual, nearing sunset. In her hands is a pillow that Francis no longer requires for the propping of his ailing foot. She hurriedly takes the last two steps, tosses the pillow onto the chair next to the kitchen table, and heads for the front door.

Pausing before she answers, she adjusts her dress, then reaches for the door.

The chilling wind buffets against her face as it rushes into the room, causing her to squint for a moment. She focuses her eyes to see that there are two men standing on the front stoop. One man she is familiar with: Mr. Joseph Russell, father of Francis's injured friend, Thomas. From his clothing, it is evident that the other gentleman is a distinguished man of honor. She pauses to think, *the face is somewhat familiar* . . . All of a sudden, she remembers. The recognition causes her to nervously straighten her outfit. She instinctively reaches to assure that her hair is under its covering, then quickly returns both hands to her sides as she greets the visitors.

"Lord Dartmouth, Mr. Russell, pleasantly unexpected; please do come in from the cold."

> "Thank you, Mrs. Asbury."

The handsome nobleman bows his head as he enters the home. He and Mr. Russell remove their hats as they attempt to rub off the cold. Elizabeth is quick to offer,

> "Please draw near to the fireplace to warm yourself, and please, call me Elizabeth."
>
> "Thank you again, Elizabeth."

Lord Dartmouth once again bows his head, the polite gesture bringing a flush to Elizabeth's face; *such a handsome fellow*. She once again adjusts her outfit as she inquires,

> "On such a cold evening, may I offer a warm drink?"
>
> "No, thank you Mrs. Asbury—excuse me, Elizabeth. Mr. Russell and I seek a meeting with your son."
>
> "Very well, you will have to proceed to his bedroom. He has been confined for a time— well, I mean, Mr. Russell, you would obviously know of the misfortunes of Francis and your son."
>
> "Yes, Mr. Russell has informed me of the boys' unfortunate injuries. Is he well enough to meet?"
>
> "Quite well; I suspect the numerous young ladies who attend him on a regular basis have long passed their necessity - -
>
> He is quite well indeed; plenty of time and willing help for recovery."

The men both hold back a laugh. Elizabeth chuckles as she confesses her thought,

> "Like most men, I would gather."
>
> "Yes, Elizabeth."

Elizabeth turns toward the stairs and invites the men to see her son.

> "First room at the top of the stairs. The bedroom door is open."

The two men once again bow their heads toward Elizabeth as they make their way up the stairs. Elizabeth heads for the rear door of the main room, humming as she exits.

Upstairs, Francis can hear the approaching steps on the wooden stairs. The sound has interrupted his thoughts as he watches the afternoon sky make its customary departure into darkness. For a time, his view through the west-facing window has fostered several thoughts about his future. At first, there was the religious gathering of young people. His concern for their spiritual lives as well as his own occupied some of these musings. He misses his new friends, especially Edward Hand. This focus on the youthful worshipers naturally led into strategy for accomplishing the needed repairs on the Wheatley space, *if only they would allow our work to commence*. Francis is surprised where this last thought seems to be leading each time it has occurred. *The injuries of Thomas and myself are the Lord's mechanism to force us to abide by the magistrate's ruling; the Lord's ways reside much higher than ours.*

In addition to the thoughts of the Wheatley space, Francis has recently ventured a completely new idea, one that he is not ready to share with others. He would love to discuss it with Nancy, but it has been two weeks since they have been alone with each other. He is cautious to consider the idea aloud, afraid that his mother or father would highly disapprove. Nevertheless, he finds himself returning to it more often than he expected, and to the individual who had initially shared of it—the young doctor, John Turton.

The light knock on his bedroom door jamb causes Francis to sit up in his bed. He turns to find Lord Dartmouth and Joseph Russell standing at the doorway. He politely invites them in.

"Mr. Russell, Lord Dartmouth . . ."

Francis shuffles his legs to the side of the bed in an effort to stand before the Earl of Dartmouth. The Earl interrupts his attempt.

"Francis, you shall not rise. Please remain as you are."

"Yes, Lord Dartmouth."

"I prefer Brother Dartmouth, please."

"Yes, Brother Dartmouth."

Francis nods his approval and repositions himself in his bed. As he does, William, the Earl of Dartmouth, begins,

"Francis, Mr. Russell and I have been considering the group you have assembled into what appears to be a fine society of young people. It is our wish that you should continue your endeavors. It has come to my attention that a certain property would allow for this welcomed association to continue. However, before I begin to share that which I am prepared to offer, I would venture a question."

Francis sits up a little higher in his bed; the Earl has his undivided attention. William continues,

"The Wheatley space that is available—however did you discover its attainability?"

Francis is slow to respond. He looks about the room, nervously scraping his teeth across his bottom lip. Neither man speaks. Francis stops the nervous habit, raises his head, and looks to the Earl and Mr. Russell.

"My good friend from the foundry, James Mayo . . . his father happens to live next door to the Wheatley building. It was Mr. Mayo, John Mayo, who informed of the space's availability."

"Very well. I had received word that you visited the magistrate about the property; it brought concern that the estate agent of my hiring was failing to accommodate my needs."

"Lord Dartmouth, my friends and I are incapable of purchasing the property at this time; we only sought to improve it."

"Well, I admire your optimism. If you will allow me, I would like to make an offer in regard to said space. I am prepared to aid Mr. Russell and Mr. Bayley, the father of your friend James Bayley, in the outright purchase of the space. The acquisition would be on the condition that a certain young man would establish a Wesleyan class of enthusiastic young people within the confines of said space. I am also prepared to supply the necessary funds for materials needed to complete the structure for said meetings."

Francis has not moved since the beginning of the Earl's declaration. The Earl's desire to acquire and dedicate the space for the worship gatherings is causing great excitement in Francis's mind. His thoughts run wildly: *We could meet regularly. With the Earl's help, the space could be improved beyond anything we might achieve. The space would be available at all times.* He pauses to refocus. He feels his neck starting to tighten; he would like to tilt his head to relieve the natural pressure that builds up when one has been lying in one position for too long. He decides to wait; he wants to hear more from the nobleman. *But I really need to crack my neck . . .*

Brother Dartmouth continues,

"Francis, if you shall agree to lead the class meetings in the abandoned Wheatley building, I would be most happy to supply the means to accomplish the needed improvements. Shall you step forward and lead?"

Without hesitation, Francis responds,

"I shall."

Francis is surprised at the words that were blurted out without thought. The two men both laugh at Francis's enthusiasm. Mr. Russell comments to the Earl,

"I believe we have made the correct choice."

Francis leans forward and cracks his neck: *pop-pop-pop*, the sound fills the room.

The next morning, Francis is on his feet. The incredible news of the Wheatley building acquisition is the perfect medicine for healing a young man who has grown used to not working and to regular nursing visits from the opposite sex. Francis eagerly desires to share the incredible news with Nancy, but he knows he needs to get back to the Old Mill Forge. Vowing to himself to see Nancy as soon as he can, he heads straight for the foundry. He looks forward to a return to work, not only for the income, but also to share the good news with James Mayo.

Outdoors at the forge, several of his coworkers greet Francis. Standing around an almost roaring fire, they are finishing a mid-morning break. One by one, the greeting is the same: "Happy for your return. Now, no further delay; proceed to work." Each brief encounter brings a slight smile to Francis's face. He is happy to be among the men. This is a tight-knit group, each aware of the other's yearnings to provide—some for families and others, like Francis and James Mayo, for something bigger than themselves. Their banter is their embrace, an expression of their love and concern for each other. The chiding is also a silent acknowledgment of the privilege to work.

As Francis enters the doors of the forge, Mr. Foxall greets him. It is his daily habit at break time to stand beyond the door jamb and watch his most important resource, his men. Glad to see Francis's return, Mr. Foxall welcomes his youngest blacksmith.

"Mr. Asbury, your return brings me pleasure."

"Thank you, sir."

"I see that the men have given warm welcome. No doubt they long for the entertaining discussions of the adolescent relationships in which you and James Mayo regularly participate."

"I believe you to be correct, sir."

With his head slightly bowed and after a brief moment of hesitation, Francis makes his way toward his anvil. Foxall pats him on the back as he passes. The anvil appears as he left it, neat and orderly. Like his father, his work space is almost sacred. Not only does each tool and item have its proper place, each tool and item is also returned to its designated space at each day's end.

At the anvil, Francis and James once again share the day together. Francis has much to tell. After a few unimportant exchanges, Francis delivers the news he is aching to break.

"The Earl of Dartmouth has decided to purchase the Wheatley building for our gatherings. He went so far as to require my leadership of the youthful congregation."

James pauses in his work, but fails to reply to Francis's exciting news.

It is not that he is uninterested; the problem lies in the fact that he already knows about the acquisition. In fact, the news has already spread throughout the entire town. Even Edward Hand, several miles away in Sutton, has been notified of the incredible development. James struggles for his response. He doesn't want to sound like he is out of touch with the current event, but he also doesn't want to disappoint his best friend. He decides to respond,

"The Earl shall purchase a building?"

"Yes, the Wheatley building, for our gatherings. Is this not a fantastic turn of events?"

"It is, Francis, it is. What of the required repairs?"

"The Earl has agreed to give additional aid for its improvement."

James admires Francis's enthusiasm. He is also happy that he did not spoil the moment. He smiles at his friend and returns to pounding on the anvil. It isn't long before the banter begins.

"Francis, are we planning any projects for your fair Nancy?"

Francis, as well as several coworkers within hearing distance, laughs aloud at James's goading.

The sale of the Wheatley building occurred ten days after Francis's return to work. By then, the young people were more than ready to begin repairs. From the very evening of the completed transaction, the random pounding and clapping of hammers, nails, and boards became a constant sound emanating from the second-floor window of the abandoned building. On occasion, a girl's laugh or shriek would launch from the wall opening overlooking the Bromwich Heath, as one of the young men would tease. After a full day's work through the weekdays and Saturday, Francis and his pals, along with many of the young women, worked well past midnight as they slowly turned the dilapidated space into a safe and functional room.

For Francis and James Mayo it was a tough schedule: up at four a.m. for work at the forge, then working at the new space until midnight. The Earl provided supplies. Even Mr. Foxall, along with several suppliers, donated nails and wood materials from the forge and the Sandwell estate. Thomas Russell and his faithful assistant Mary capably led the entire project. The work was hard for all, but the fellowship was pure and encouraging. After three weeks of hard work, the core group of individuals rejoiced in prayer and song as the space was ready for completion.

The Methodist meeting room on Paradise Street across from the Bromwich Heath quickly becomes a gathering place of young people set on growing in their faith. Every Wednesday night the faithful arrive, some earlier than others, each waiting for Francis and James Mayo to appear. Francis and James always arrive last and together. They are rarely apart, spending almost every waking moment in each other's company. Considering that they bunk in the same room on the Sandwell estate, it is only for a few hours during Francis's Sunday visits with his parents that they fail to spend time with one another.

Due to the enthusiasm of the gatherers, the Wednesday evening prayer gathering soon expands to an additional evening. Francis doesn't mind the extra night; he has by now progressed in his ability to speak and pray in public. Prior to this, in spite of the regular opportunities to speak, public discourse was always an adventure for Francis. At times he would begin slowly, his voice trembling slightly. At other times he would speak without reservation from his opening words. The slow, trembling beginnings did not bother him; he had grown accustomed to this. He knew that it would only take a few moments for God's Spirit to inhabit his efforts; when this occurred, his voice would calm and his thoughts would flow freely.

Francis is thankful for the opportunity to lead. His speaking, praying, and preaching talents are blossoming into a West Midlands movement. He marvels that more young people attend the gatherings each week. As word spreads of the successful prayer gathering in West Bromwich, Francis is surprised to see the Wesleyan itinerants starting to pay regular visits on these Wednesday and Thursday evenings.

This evening is no different, as more than fifty young people gather in the meeting room. Standing at the back wall for the entire evening are two of Wesley's itinerants, along with Francis's friend Richard Whatcoat. Nearing the evening's end, the tall, stocky itinerant dressed in black pushes his squared shoulders off the wall and approaches Francis at the front of the room. The itinerant is familiar to all who have come together on this cold winter's night, as he has labored for several years in the West Midlands. In his right hand is his Bible and in his left is his black broad-brimmed hat. Standing in front of Francis, he announces,

"Fr'dancis Asbur'dy, Wesley has need of ya' efforts."

Francis smiles at the thick Scottish accent of Alexander Mather. He also begins to think about the itinerant's comment. *Wesley has need of my efforts* . . . He wants to reply, but hesitates. He doesn't want to seem to assume more than the remark deserves. As he glances away from the corpulent face of Mather, the itinerant is quick to press,

"Young man, have ya' considered my comment?"

Francis slowly returns his eyes to the preacher; *perhaps this is more than it appears.* When he remains quiet, Mather pursues the subject.

"Several of us on the circuit would like to offer'd ya' the opportunity to lend hand. On occasions, our load is too much to bear. We desire a competent aid in our r'dounds. Would ya' be willin' to assist in the immediate area? We believe ya' could accomplish the needed tasks one or two nights each week. Simple tasks—prayin' wit' the sick, readin' the Bible to the elderly. This would be welcomed aid in our efforts to br'ding the Gospel to the West Midlands."

Mather's offer brings a ripple of silence to the entire room. Each individual turns his or her gaze toward Francis.

Francis senses the attention that everyone is paying to him. He instinctively looks to those present. To his right are his closest friends, the two Thomases and

James Bayley. At his left side is James Mayo. Directly in front of Francis and behind Mather is Richard Whatcoat. Each smiles in anticipation of Francis's reply.

Searching the room, Francis looks for Nancy. His heart begins to pound strongly. For a moment, he wonders whether this reaction is because of the chance to help the Wesley brothers, or if it is the nervous feeling he sometimes has when seeing Nancy. The emotion doesn't end his search; he finds her as he looks across the shoulder of Thomas Ault. She stands quietly, gently smiling with closed lips.

Inside, Nancy is happy for Francis. She always knew that such an offer would occur. She thinks to herself, *I was the first to see his abilities*. She gently blinks her eyes twice as she catches Francis's glance. He cannot help but release a broad smile in return.

Francis once again looks to Pastor Mather and replies to the suggestion,

> "If you and the others will give aid, I would consider it an honor to help the Wesleys."

> "We would also like to offer'd ya' the leadership role at West Bromwich."

Francis is surprised. Mather makes note,

> "Ya' shouldn't be surprised; ya' practically are leadin' the entire West Bromwich class here each evenin'. Look r'dound; have ya' not considered it peculiar that not only the young attend? We will have to train ya'; however, we are confident ya' will succeed in ya' efforts. We are also confident that ya' class of mostly young people will soon be attractin' more older, borin' people."

Francis glances away, worried by the itinerant's last comment, "more older, boring people." *He must have talked with Father.* He looks once more to Pastor Mather. Mather's smile and his steady look into Francis's eyes convey a sense of belonging that Francis has never experienced. *Me, part of Wesley's team! Men like Alexander Mather. This is too wonderful to express with words.* The stocky Scottish itinerant reaches forward and embraces Francis. The young man senses a new beginning for his life.

Within days, Francis finds himself engaged in the life of a class leader. Mather, Whatcoat, and others began to train him for this new role, a vital role in the healthy life of the Wesleyan movement. As class leader, Francis will be in constant contact with the members of his class. His goal as class leader is a clear one: to observe and record the faith of the members. New for Francis will be that whenever he senses anyone failing to live within the guidelines of their professed biblical faith, he will be responsible to help or confront them, urging them onward toward the goal. Since he already has a full-time job at the forge, Francis will have to attempt this task in the evenings after work.

Francis's responsibility is not as detailed as in his band meetings with his friends; the monitoring of the faith of the class members will be accomplished mostly through personal confessions in the weekly meetings. The more public setting means that the accountability factor will be of a more general sense. Since Francis's group of young people is too large for one class, he will have to meet a minimum of two nights each week, splitting the group in half. He quickly realizes that he will be investing four nights every week: two for the class meetings and two for the prayer and exhortation evenings. He doesn't mind the extra nights; *it seems right for me to do so.*

His first class meeting goes well, or well enough to most. Personally, he has a hard time splitting the group that gathered beforehand. The young people don't mind; the split is simple: men and boys on one night, women and girls on the next. This arrangement also matches what the Wesley brothers expect of full-fledged Wesleyan society meetings. The initial class meeting begins like the many that follow: Francis stands and offers an opening prayer, followed by the singing of a hymn, and he then gives a personal account of the condition of his faith and the struggles and temptations that have occurred in his life the week before. From there he turns to the first individual on his left and inquires, "Well, brother, how do you find the state of your soul this evening?" The process repeats itself until everyone in the room is questioned by Francis.

Francis is a natural for this role. He enjoys the interaction with others and relishes the unspoken assurance of common ground between him and the class members. On a lighter note, since his appointment by Mather, on numerous occasions his mother has reminded him of times in his childhood where he would question the vitality of the faith of his close friends. Elizabeth's strong opinion is that this role is natural for Francis; it is Joseph's opinion also.

The class meetings are demanding. Francis seldom is ready to head home before midnight. He soon finds himself in the strenuous routine of waking at four a.m. for prayer, working at the forge until five p.m., praying until six, hurrying to eat dinner, and then racing off to the class or prayer meetings that always seem to last well into the night. Four nights each week, he repeats the process. Despite the demanding schedule, the formality of the class meetings seems to spark more interest in the prayer and exhortation gatherings for both Francis and his friends.

Each week the demanding schedule tires the young man, but however strenuous the routine is, Francis always set his sights on the end of the week. On Saturday evenings, Francis takes a break from his ministry and his work, to spend time with Nancy.

On this particular Saturday, Foxall, pleased with the crew's hard work, has allowed Francis and the men to leave work early. About an hour before nightfall, the young couple walk hand in hand as they proceed along the River Tame as it pours from a lake adjacent to the forge. They set out toward the dried-out stump of an oak tree that lies on the outskirts of the Sandwell estate. Along the way, Nancy is too excited to keep quiet; when she is confident no one else can hear, she inquires of Francis,

"Do you find pleasure in your efforts, Francis?"

"I do."

"Please do tell more."

"More? What more do you require?"

"Francis, there is more; your face tells all."

Francis fails to respond. Nancy continues,

"There is much more; you are scraping your teeth on your lip."

"Huh?"

"Your lip—you seem to scrape it when you are unsettled. I've seen it before; it is actually rather winsome. Do tell me more."

Francis self-consciously stops the scraping. He pauses mid-step, bringing Nancy to a halt also. As the November winds weave through the oversized limbs of the hardwoods behind the young couple, Francis opens up.

"I am troubled - -

Deeply troubled. At times I feel unworthy."

Francis nervously releases his grip of Nancy's hand. The aimless waving of his arms reveals the reality of his struggle. Both hands eventually find rest in his pockets. Nancy urges,

"Go on . . ."

"Who am I to ask - -

Of one's soul condition with God?"

Francis hesitates. The long silence compels Nancy to gently prod,

"Please continue."

"Humbled, I am humbled to sit and listen to the struggles of others, especially when the expression of their struggles - -

Could easily be coming from my lips."

Not surprised by his sharp tone, Nancy reaches out her hand for his. Francis pulls it out of his pocket and curls his fingers around hers. Growing calmer, he invites her to listen.

"Come, Nancy; do sit."

Francis lifts her arm, aiding her to sit atop the oak tree stump.

"Pastor Mather warned of these feelings. He was adamant; no man can sit in judgment of another."

"Do you feel led to judge, Francis?"

"No, but I do feel led to discern. Nevertheless, my discernment brings guilt. Their struggles are my struggles, Nance; should I not be above these temptations as a leader?"

Nancy hesitates. She is ready to respond, but doesn't want to hurt Francis's feelings. She knows him well: *He is a natural leader, and natural leaders can grow to focus too much on themselves.* She places her other hand on top of the hand holding hers. Gently and slowly, she advises,

"Above temptation? No. Within temptation? Yes."

She gently squeezes his hand and continues,

"I too have heard Mather. And others like him. Their words apply to you. Francis, you are truly becoming a leader when you realize and accept your shortcomings."

Francis grudgingly grunts an acknowledgement. He looks into Nancy's eyes and responds,

"Thank you, Nancy."

He raises his arm and kisses Nancy's hand. As he lifts his eyes, Nancy responds,

" 'Tis a most beautiful Saturday."

It isn't; the winds howl, the temperatures sting, the sky is dark with ashen soot, and the clouds thicken. However, do these two notice? Despite the worsening weather, Francis agrees with Nancy, *'tis a most beautiful Saturday.*

Saturdays may be for Nancy, but Sundays are for Mother. Each first day of the week, Elizabeth expects her son to enjoy the elaborate dinner she plans for his pleasure. Despite the obvious effort that goes into producing the lovingly prepared meal that sits atop the Asbury table, this Sabbath finds Elizabeth quiet and somewhat detached. She has once again arranged dinner for the two most important men in her life, but something is different. She removes her cooking apron and takes a seat at the table with Francis and Joseph. Her words are quick and to the point.

"Francis, offer thanks to the Almighty."

"Yes, Mother. Almighty Father, we acknowledge Your provision in today's meal; may it nourish our bodies to proper physical and spiritual health. Amen."

The men do not hesitate to begin. Elizabeth fumbles with her table napkin. Several times, as the men slurp and plunge into the meaty stew, she runs the course fabric between her thumb and forefinger. Her exaggerated exhales go unnoticed by Joseph and Francis. Francis finally pauses in his eating. With spoon in hand, he offers a question.

"Father, have you taken winter inventory?"

Each winter, Joseph assesses the status of his tools. With a doctor's precision, he carefully inspects each cutting implement for defects. He is mostly concerned with the condition of the cutting edge. In the past, he would have had to pay not a small sum of money for the sharpening of the defective items. That is no longer the case; in recent years, he has had the privilege of asking his son to take care of the annual chore. He responds to Francis's inquiry,

> "I have. I shall review my needs with you before your departure this eve."
> "Very well, Father—"

Elizabeth interrupts,

> "Joseph, you speak of cutting implements; have you failed to remember our earlier discussion, or do you choose to ignore it?"

Francis halts his eating. With spoon resting mid-stroke of its return journey to the bowl, he tilts his head in a quizzical nod and glances at Elizabeth. He cautiously inquires,

> "Mother, it seems as though things are somehow amiss?"

Failing to look at Francis, Elizabeth stares at Joseph, her stern face broadcasting her disappointment with her husband. Joseph nervously taps his spoon on the tabletop. His downturned eyes remain focused on the oak-wood tabletop. He gently sets down the spoon and fumbles with the edge of his neatly wrapped cloth napkin, which until now has remained untouched alongside his dinner plate.

Elizabeth blurts out,

> "Well, have you not spoken to our son?"

Joseph again twists the edges of his napkin, pressing it between his thumb and the tabletop. He slowly offers,

> "Well, haven't had any opportunities to . . ."
> "Joseph dear, we agreed to speak to Francis; specifically, you agreed to speak to Francis. Is it not the proper time to do so?"

Joseph clears his throat. It is four or five seconds before he raises his tabletop gaze to look toward Francis. At first, he fails to make eye contact with his son—instead, his eyes bounce from Francis's handsome chin, to the picture on the wall behind him, and then back to Francis's face—never the eyes, only some pronounced area of his son's attractive countenance. Elizabeth once again must intervene.

> "Joseph, our son."

Again, he clears his throat, the deep tone emitted from his masculine frame echoing off the kitchen wall. He begins,

> "Francis, it has come to our attention, more correctly, Mother's attention . . ."
> "And your attention as well, Joseph."

"Yes, Elizabeth, my attention as well—that you have taken fancy to a young girl."

"What your father is precariously offering is that several of the townspeople have noticed you and Nancy Brookes spending much time together."

"It is true, Mother. Nancy and I do spend time together at class meeting as well as prayer meeting. She is my contemporary."

"Your father and I are worried that Nancy has become much more than a contemporary to you, Francis. We are alarmed by the reports that your evenings together on Saturdays are more than a casual occasion."

Francis is silent. He stares at his father. *She cannot be serious, Father. I am seventeen years of age, old enough to marry if I choose to.* Out of respect for his mother, Francis keeps this thought to himself.

Francis decides to respond with a half-truth.

"I am quite busy throughout the week. Nancy and I have barely enough time to establish a relationship."

Elizabeth huffs as she rolls her eyes toward the ceiling. She retorts,

"I should have concluded that the two of you would . . ."

She stops her sharp reply mid-sentence. Joseph spreads his arms and places both of his burly hands palms-down on the edge of the table. The table moves slightly at his strong grip on the oak wood. He leans forward and offers,

"Elizabeth, Francis is a young man of marrying age . . ."

"Marriage?"

Joseph backs his head away slightly in retreat. Nevertheless, he continues,

"I do not mean to imply that he and Nancy will be marrying. However, several young men his age throughout history have become husbands. Besides, I find Nancy to be a proper candidate for our son if he did desire to marry."

Elizabeth is silent. Joseph finally makes eye contact with Francis and continues,

"Francis, I commend you for your choice. As a young man, you have made great strides recently. I admire your attempts to aid Wesley's movement; I also admire your commitment to the forge. I believe that if you were to require the aid of a good woman, I could not fault you. It is precisely the recipe that has aided me in becoming the man I am today."

The silence in the room is uncomfortable, yet satisfying.

The eyes of Joseph and Francis remain steadfast and at peace with each other. Joseph offers a smile to his son; Francis lowers his eyes, and then returns the smile. Simultaneously they turn to Elizabeth, who is wiping her eyes that are joyfully wet. Her uncontrollable smile glows with respect for her husband and love for their son.

> *In ancient times the office of a priest and that of a preacher*
> *Were known to be entirely distinct . . .*
> *From Adam to Noah, it is allowed by all that the first-born in every family*
> *Was of course the priest in that family,*
> *By virtue of primogeniture.*[82] *But this gave him no right*
> *To be a preacher, or a prophet . . .*
> *For in this respect God always asserted*
> *His right to send by whom He would send.*
>
> *John Wesley*

Quietly walking along the exterior wall of Joseph's tool barn, Elizabeth spies the first pods of Joseph's bean plants as they push through the soil, nearly a month early. The overcrowded planting has allowed the vines to survive the harsh temperatures of the winter months, their safety enhanced by their location on the more temperate south side of the structure. She gently bends to talk to the numerous white buds and the tiny emerging bean pods.

> "March in the Midlands, a rather hazardous journey for fellows like yourself . . ."

From around the barn, Elizabeth can hear someone approaching. Their steps are fast and pounding. Her biggest fear, a drunken patron from The Malt Shovel? She turns her head sharply and begins to rise.

> "Mother, Mother, where are you?"

Careening around the corner toward Elizabeth, Francis nearly knocks her over; the heel of her palm braced on the hard soil saves her from falling completely to the ground. With an alarmed huff she pushes herself to her feet and snaps toward her son,

> "Francis, to what do I owe such a startling visit?"
>
> "Developments, amazing developments!"
>
> "In mid-week?"

Francis pauses to catch his breath. He bends over, one hand on his knees, the other wiping the sweat from his forehead. He rises from his crouched position to aid his breathing, arching backward for a deeper breath. Elizabeth wonders,

> "Franky, have you run all the way from Sandwell?"
>
> "Pastor Mather . . ."

---

[82] The right of succession belonging to the firstborn child.

His reply causes him to lose his breath; he places his hands on his hips to breathe deeply. Elizabeth coaxes,

"Yes, Pastor Mather . . . ?"

"Pastor Mather has asked of me . . . asked of me - -

To preach. Locally."

"Preach? A local preacher? Francis, this is indeed an amazing development."

"Most assuredly. I am to start as soon as I can arrange - -

My schedule. Thomas Ault has agreed to help with our band, and Pastor Mather has given his permission. I shall continue to conduct the West Bromwich meetings; in addition, I shall preach at least three to four times each week - -

In time, three services on Sundays."

Elizabeth tilts her head toward the ground. She mutters, loud enough for Francis to hear,

"Three on Sundays, and when shall a mother spend time with her son?"

Francis hadn't thought about this. His shoulders drop in frustration. *Happiest day of my life, and she frets about time with her son.* As he considers his thought, it leads him in a better direction: *I am sorry, Mother.* With his right hand, Francis reaches to lift his mother's downcast chin. She shuns the effort and heads for the rear door of the home.

Undaunted, Francis scoots forward, ahead of her.

"Mother, I hadn't considered; I do beg your forgiveness. Perhaps I . . ."

Elizabeth slows her departure as Francis ponders the situation. She turns toward him, expecting a solution, but there is none at this time. She replies,

"Humph."

She is not pleased with Francis.

Hours later, as dinner ends inside the Asbury cottage, Joseph and Francis excitedly discuss the day's development. For a time, it is almost as if Elizabeth is absent from the table.

"Franky, your two years as leader of Bromwich have prepared you well."

"I know, Father, but it troubles me also."

"Troubles you?"

Francis fumbles with the edge of the table. He finally looks to his mother, then back to Joseph.

"Father, the position requires that I continue to work . . ."

"Yes, the local preacher is an unpaid position; I realize that, Franky."

"What I am trying to say, or consider, is how to spend time with you and Mother. I am required to hold at least three services on the Sabbath."

Joseph lifts his strong hand and rubs the front of his chin. His thick thumb and forefinger stroke the sides of his chin; he is deep in thought. Francis yearns for a solution; he decides to voice his thought.

"It pains me to trouble you, Mother."

Joseph responds,

"Franky, you will have to give it time. Sleep on it. The solution will come."

"Sleep on it." Later that same evening, Joseph's words ring in Francis's mind, leading him to focus on another thought: *if only I could.* Pastor Mather's invitation keeps him from sleeping. For the last hour, he has on several occasions rolled from his back, to his stomach, again to his back, and again to his stomach. Several times he has found himself stopping mid-turn to rest on his left side. The identical pause occurs on turns toward the right side. All efforts end with little success. *This restlessness is somewhat maddening.* He rises from his bunk and wraps himself in his blanket, then slips on his shoes and walks outdoors.

The cold, crisp air greets him at the door. Looking to the night sky does little to lighten his burden; the sky is black with cloud cover, not even a small clearing *tiny enough to permit at least one beam of light from the moon to wander in.* He wraps his arms tightly around himself; the air has brought a slight chill. He returns to his room.

Quietly making his way under the covers, Francis settles into his bed. In the bunk next to him, James Mayo snores his quieter snore. Francis is thankful that the chorus hasn't turned into the traditional full ensemble. *James, you are a fierce snorer.* Lying on his back, Francis's thoughts soon wander to the past two years; *they transpired so quickly.* He fights an audible laugh as he thinks of the time that Thomas Ault and James Bayley argued over who was to help out on the evenings that Francis led the girls. James won out when he raced Thomas the half mile from Newton to the Jone Bridge. Thomas's losing of the footrace didn't silence his argument, so James furthered the humiliation by shoving Thomas off the bridge, sending him splashing into the Wigmoor Brook. James's triumphant observation ended the competition: "Seems you are far too wet to hold a service."

Francis's thoughts ramble on; he considers the times of great spiritual significance. *Many of my friends have deepened their faith commitments, even young Jabez.*[83] He wipes away a slight tear as he remembers the elder couple who regularly brought food to the young worshipers. *Oh, how I miss Hannah's fresh-fruit offerings. Her always-patient husband, Edward, who would wait until each individual had departed, always aiming to offer a word of encouragement, persevering through my neophyte ramblings about the demanding schedule and a faith not too accomplished in the sacred text.*

---

[83] Jabez Ault, younger brother to Thomas.

Lord, may I too aspire to be as diligent an encourager as Edward and Hannah are.

His thoughts wander to a more pressing concern: *what to do with Mother. I do love her so, but I am a man of nearly twenty years. Able to wander about as I please . . . I will have very little time, perhaps no time at all, to spend in Newton. I desire a solution that suffices the needs of all.* The thoughts of his mother and father soon lull Francis to sleep. In the morning, he will begin a new facet of his life, a phase that will demand much more of his time and energy—much more than even he expects.

***

The man on horseback sits high in the saddle. He is clearly tall and thin, and he is clearly one of Wesley's itinerants. An escort joins him, and they slowly make their way toward the Methodist meeting room on Paradise Street. Several of the townspeople move in to greet him as they pass.

"Good morning, Pastor Glasbrook."   "Good day, James."

James Glasbrook is the preacher riding into town. In front of the old Wheatley building, he reins in his Arabian mount. The small-muzzled horse exhales through his large nostrils and stops obediently. The itinerant swings his right leg over the horse's prominent tail carriage as he dismounts.

As he busies himself with removing the leather saddlebag draped behind the saddle, many of the young boys of the town race toward the traveling preacher.

"Pass'r Glasbrook, Franky awaits!"

The tiny, frail boy who appears to be ten years of age proudly places both of his hands on his hips. He cannot help it; his broad smile fails to hide his excitement, for he is bringing news of Glasbrook's newest helper, who waits inside the West Bromwich meeting room of the Wesleyan faithful. Several more boys about the same age arrive in time to catch the dip of the preacher's hat as he launches the saddlebag over his shoulder. His formality honors the youngsters, who are overjoyed to see a "real itinerant preacher."

Glasbrook's riding companion waits outdoors with the horses, where the young boys continue to admire the muscular animals.

Inside the dark lobby, Glasbrook makes his way toward the stairs and begins to ascend. Without fear, he places his right foot onto the infamous sixth step, chuckling at the memory of the stories Mather has shared.

"We do have a past, don't we?"

Entering the second-floor space, Glasbrook finds Francis sitting in a chair with his back against the window wall. Francis leverages himself off the adjacent window sill with his right hand and rises to greet his mentor.

"Good morning, Pastor."

"Good morning, Francis. I have been privileged to meet several of your faithful flock. They gave such a rich welcome to me below."

"A flock, yes, but faithful—that will require slightly more effort."

The itinerant smiles at Francis's quick wit. He doesn't hesitate to reply,

" 'Slightly more effort' . . . perhaps a running theme for the day. Please, have a seat. I am anxious to get started."

The angular pastor walks to the other side of the room and retrieves a chair for himself. Placing the seat directly in front of Francis, he shrugs his saddlebag off his right shoulder and onto the floor, kicking up a slight dust cloud and the musty smell of kiln-dried floorboards. Glasbrook sits.

Reaching into the leather bag, Glasbrook removes several documents. Each handwritten document appears neatly produced. He quickly shuffles through them, satisfied that all is in order. He clears his throat and suggests,

"Before we proceed with the guidelines for a helper, I would like to open with prayer."

Francis nods his head in agreement, and the two bow their heads as Glasbrook prays,

"Heavenly Father, You view us as we truly are: poor, naked, miserable, and helpless sinners; yet despite our lowly estate, You offer a loving and merciful hand to lift us from the miry pit. We humbly submit our efforts to You on this glorious morning. Amen."

They lift their heads and Glasbrook begins.

"Francis, as I am aware that you are currently apprenticed at Sandwell Forge, I have chosen to amend some of the requirements of a helper. It is important that you grasp the intention of these rules. In time, if you are fortunate to progress, you will have ample opportunity to embrace the letter of these imperative guidelines, as well as the spirit conveyed therein.

"What we do hinges solely on prayer. Do you comprehend the importance of this?"

"Yes, I do."

"Very well. You must daily devote to prayer at least one hour when you rise and an additional hour before you retire for the night. Many of your fellow helpers rise at four a.m. for this discipline. They also manage to lay aside the events of the day at five o'clock in the evening for a time of supplication. In the past, Wesley made it a point that only prayer was to occur during this period. The conference has recently amended this discipline: prayer as well as meditation and Scripture reading may take place during these hours."

The itinerant leans forward a bit; he clears his throat as he shifts the documents to his right hand. With a serious expression, he makes his point:

"Be ever mindful, your efforts shall surely fail without prayer. Is this clear?"

Francis humbly nods in agreement.

"Very well, Francis. I shall continue."

"Excuse me, sir."

Francis's interruption catches Glasbrook by surprise. He nods his head as he raises his hand, gesturing for Francis to continue.

"Conference—what did you mean when you commented that 'the conference has recently amended' . . . ?"

"The conference, Wesley's annual conferences - -

The meeting of his itinerant preachers. Do you . . . ?"

Francis's puzzled look prompts Glasbrook to elaborate.

"Since 1744, the Wesleyan preachers have come together on a regular basis to discuss the movement and its requirements—items such as doctrine, prayer, and fasting, as well as the imperative proclamation of John Wesley himself that the movement shall remain within and submit to the Anglican Church rules. It is at the conferences, also, that the itinerant preachers receive their assigned circuits. Does this help?"

"Yes."

"Then I shall continue. As helper, it is your duty, in the absence of a minister or traveling preacher, to feed and guide the flock. There may be times when you are called upon to exhort; times when you shall meet the entire society, as well as the bands; times when you will meet the sick. You may even have to step in and bring discipline when a band leader fails to confront the disorderly. Do you foresee any obstacles to meeting these requirements?"

"No, I do not."

"Good. There are several rules that aid the helper. First, be diligent. Never be unemployed a moment. Never be triflingly employed. Never while away time; neither spend any more time at any place than is strictly necessary.

"Second, be serious. Let your motto be, 'Holiness to the Lord.' Avoid all lightness, jesting, and foolish talking.

"Third, converse sparingly and cautiously with women; particularly, with young women in private."

In the chair, Francis nervously rocks his thighs as he places his hands under them. Within seconds, he removes his hands from their secure position and fumbles to place them in a comfortable spot. Glasbrook is quick to notice.

"Converse sparingly and cautiously; you do understand the importance of this?"

"Yes, Pastor Glasbrook, I do."

The pastor clears his throat again. He leans forward in his chair; he's within inches of Francis's face. With a commanding confidence he conveys in a quiet tone,

"I understand you are fond of a local girl. Is this true?"

Once again, Francis anxiously looks for a proper place for his hands; he settles with them on his knees. His strong hands grip each other tightly as he responds,

"Yes, I am fond of a certain young lady."

"Then this next rule is especially important - -

Take no step toward marriage without acquainting us with your design."

Francis raises his right hand and scratches the back of his neck. With a questioning tilt of his head, he takes a deep breath. Sensing Francis's uncomfortable plight, Glasbrook offers,

"Marriage doesn't remove your privilege to preach, but it will terminate your chances to travel."

At this point Francis becomes distracted; he has noticed a strange marking above Pastor Glasbrook's right wrist. He hadn't noticed it earlier, but it appeared when the pastor reached back to return to the seat-back of the chair. In a way, it is a familiar marking—a scar, but much worse than the one on Francis's own forearm.

Catching Francis staring at the mark, the itinerant observes,

"You have taken notice of the permanent marking of my arm . . . ?"

Glasbrook brings forward his left hand and begins to roll back the white shirt cuff and dark coat sleeve covering his right arm. The action slowly reveals a nasty scar that goes well up to his elbow.

Francis's face is flushed with shock. Noticing the young man's reaction, the pastor offers insight.

"Several years ago I had the privilege of traveling with Wesley. The beautiful island nation of Ireland was verging upon an awakening. Amidst this movement, many were turned against us.

"One glorious day in June, William Ley, Wesley, and I arrived in Carrick-Upon-Shannon. Our plan was to preach to the good people of this scenic town. Many there took notice of our arrival. In thirty minutes, or perhaps just under one hour, a local esquire, the justice of the peace, approached us. In his hand he held a drum, and behind him was an unruly mob set to disrupt the gathering. He paused to turn and speak his vile words toward the group that neared one hundred persons. By then, Wesley was already in the garden behind the house, preaching his sermon; I stood on the rear balcony overlooking John and his faithful. Inside the home, William Ley remained at the front door, resting in a chair.

"I hadn't noticed the approaching group until I was alarmed by the commotion of the esquire beating William with the stick he intended for the drum. I immediately bolted shut the door to the rear yard, the sole access to Wesley out back, and stood my guard. The approaching justice of the peace divested himself of his drum, accepted a walking cane from a nearby resident, and proceeded straight for me. I braced myself, fearing not only the wooden walking implement that could easily become a weapon, but also the several dozen who followed the man into the home. As several of the group carried William outside, the man of law bent on violence approached.

" 'Where is Wesley?'

"My reply was simple enough:

" 'He is not inside, and you are not going through this door to the outside.'

" 'Where is he?'

"His second request was much more forceful. Pushing at me, he demanded that I step away from the door. I would not. Subsequently, he turned and parted the crowd behind him, thus making his way out the front door.

"Within moments the brawling leader was out back, at the garden wall.

"Intent on stopping Wesley, the crazed man scaled the garden wall. It was a difficult task for the portly fellow, clawing his large frame upward; however, he succeeded. Once over the wall, he launched for John, bumping him with his chest as he proclaimed,

" 'You shall not preach here today.'

"The obnoxious visitor added a few unsavory curses and proclamations, but I needn't elaborate.

"In a manner that only John Wesley could accomplish, he recovered his balance, straightened his coat and hat, and then gently responded to the madman,

" 'Sir, I do not intend it, for I have already preached here today.'

"This infuriated the man. He began to beat the ground with his cane. At this, Wesley calmly walked away and entered the house from the rear door where I stood.

"When the lone attacker came to the realization that Wesley had left, he must have quickly darted for the rear door.

"Unobserved, he entered through the door. Catching sight of him, I leapt to stand in his path as he aimed for Wesley; he immediately began to beat me with his stick. With my right arm, I braced myself against the wall. He proceeded to lower the club, beating my arm until the flesh was blue and torn. I would not release the wall, fearing that if I did so, I would retaliate. After a dozen blows and my blood that flowed, he realized I would not release. One final blow snapped the stick in half. With half his weapon lost, he turned from me and with the defeated club swiped Wesley's hat off his head. He spent the next minutes valiantly beating and stomping the hat of that dear man, at least until a gentleman rescued the maligned item from his wrath."

By now, Francis is sitting in silence, his jaw stiff from remaining slightly open and without movement for nearly the entire length of the story. He gains his composure, closes his lips, and looks to the floor. *"Fearing I would retaliate."* Glasbrook's brave words resonate in his mind. *I don't think I could have just stood there.*

The pastor gives enough time for Francis to meditate on the event. He then suggests,

"Let's move on, shall we?"

The lad raises his eyes to his mentor; however, he is without reply. Glasbrook resumes his reading.

"Believe evil of no one; unless you see it done, take heed how you credit it. Put the best construction on everything. You know the judge is always supposed to be on the prisoner's side.

"Speak evil of no one, else your word, especially, would eat as doth a canker. Keep your thoughts within your own breast, till you come to the person concerned.

"Tell everyone what you think wrong in him, and that plainly, and as soon as may be; else it will fester in your heart. Make all haste to cast the fire out of your bosom.

"Do not affect the gentleman;[84] you have no more to do with this character than with that of a dancing-master. A preacher of the Gospel is the servant of all.

"Be ashamed of nothing but sin: not of fetching wood, or drawing water; not of cleaning your own shoes, or your neighbor's.

---

[84] Don't present yourself as a man of high stature, a man of society.

"Be punctual. Do everything at the time.

"You have nothing to do but to save souls. Therefore, spend and be spent in this work. And go always, not only to those that want you, but to those that want you most.

"Act in all things, not according to your own will, but as a son in the Gospel. As such, it is your part to employ your time in the manner which we direct; partly, in preaching, and visiting the flock from house to house; partly, in reading, meditation, and prayer. Above all, if you labor with us in our Lord's vineyard, it is needful that you should do that part of the work which we advise, at those times and places which we judge most for His glory."

Francis's meeting with Pastor Glasbrook lasts nearly an hour. At meeting's end, the pastor bids him farewell and departs for his waiting horse.

From the second-floor window of the meeting room, Francis watches nearly a dozen preteen boys below as they surround Wesley's itinerant. Paying adoring reverence to the traveling preacher, they are delighted as he leaps astride his mount, tips his hat to the group, and launches his horse toward the edge of town.

From the window ledge, Francis ponders the morning's events. *How long before my call to a society in need? Oh, that it is soon!* Pastor Glasbrook's admonitions ring in his mind: *Prayer, it all hinges on prayer; speak evil of no one; be diligent; called upon to exhort.* This last counsel, "you may be called upon to exhort," excites Francis. He envisions himself standing in front of a few dozen people in some distant corner of Staffordshire.[85] He can see himself sharing from the Scriptures; his mind darts to certain Bible passages. He changes course quickly as he envisions himself aiding an old man, offering comfort in his waning days; offering instruction to a young group of boys . . . *"Converse sparingly and cautiously with women; particularly, with young women in private."* This thought brings his jubilant daydream to a halt as several occurrences come to mind.

On several occasions during his two years as the leader of the West Bromwich class, he found himself in private with a young girl from the gathering. Although he clearly did nothing deemed inappropriate, he admits that his thoughts—or more accurately, his attractions—to a few of the opposite sex surfaced in his mind during counseling. He vows to pay close attention to this potentially destructive temptation.

The two weeks following the meeting with Pastor Glasbrook find Francis occupied with his tasks at the forge. Each morning he leaps from his bed with excitement; after a few moments to awake, he jumps right into his time of prayer. Four a.m. is nothing new for Francis; his regular routine before his call to the

---

[85] The county in which Francis resides.

local preacher position found him awake at this time. This aids him greatly, allowing him to start work earlier than most, and helping him to finish his tasks ahead of time. This rising well before daylight becomes an unavoidable requirement when the demanding schedule of his weeknight commitments to the West Bromwich society begins.

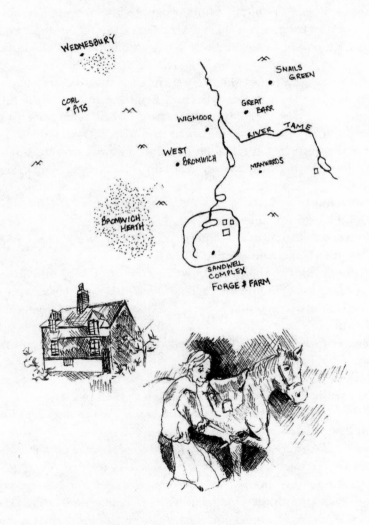

It is slightly after five a.m. On this morning, Francis walks through the cool mist that rises from the hardened ground. Every other step finds him tapping an anonymous stone forward with his right foot. This is different from the stone dance that he has exhibited in the past, as when he grew frustrated with the cruel school instructor. This is a happy tapping, a gesture of expectation. *Shall Pastor Glasbrook call this day?* The thought gives energy to Francis's steps. He pulls back his foot and belts the innocent stone several yards.

As he makes his way along the familiar path to his work area, he spots several other workers who have begun their day earlier. After a few steps, he is in their presence; with a nod of his head, he gestures a quiet hello. The men return the same.

Looking up, he spots James Mayo. He surmises that he has been at the anvil for almost an hour. Like Francis, James has long been accustomed to the early risings, although now that Francis spends the first hour of the day in prayer, James must venture alone in the dark mornings. The complacent James doesn't mind; he understands that Francis has taken on new and important responsibilities. He is actually excited for his dear friend. Looking up from his work, he offers a greeting.

"Good morn', Francis."

"Good morning, James."

"Prayer was productive, I expect?"

"Yes, James, most productive - -"

"More productive than you think."

James pulls out from beside his anvil a folded envelope. He extends it toward Francis, who is slow to respond.

"For me?"

"Yes, Francis, for you. Pastor Glasbrook dropped it by this morning, must have been half past four. Told him you were sleeping in."

"James!"

"Not really. He was thrilled to hear you were in prayer."

Francis snatches the document from James and pushes open the folds of the parchment. In sturdy handwriting he reads:

Wolverhampton, Methodist Society. Attend Mrs. Hanson. She is affected with illness.

Francis basks in the thought of correspondence from Glasbrook, but the jubilant feelings soon subside. *Affected with illness. What shall I say to one who is sick?* Surprised by Francis's changing facial expressions, James doesn't know what to think.

"Francis, you seem askew . . ."

Francis continues to stare blankly. The thick morning air exhales from his mouth, which remains slightly open. James nudges his friend.

> "Francis, everything all right?"

> "Excuse me, James. All right enough."

He is still staring into the morning vapors. James responds,

> "Seems far from accurate . . ."

James's uncertain shrug of his shoulders catches Francis's peripheral vision. He turns toward his friend.

> "I beg your pardon, James; I am lost in thought. Glasbrook has asked that
> I attend a woman in Wolverhampton, a Mrs. Hanson. What shall I say to
> a sick woman?"

> "Aha. Well, he did mention that he would return to talk with you around
> noon."

> "Return . . . why didn't you mention?"

> "Francis, you have left little room for conversation."

Raising his eyebrows and tilting his head, Francis puckers his left cheek and lip, indicating irony.

> "James, you have a way with the obvious."

> "Ha!"

For Francis, the lunch break cannot arrive quickly enough. As the morning drags on, he has difficulty completing his tasks for the forge. Several times during the morning, the usually stoic James has to spark conversation. It isn't that James is experiencing a rare inclination to converse; he is rather worried by the nervous dabbling of his friend. From the anvil to the door, then back to the anvil, then again to the door . . . Francis cannot seem to focus on his work. The back and forth finally stops at noon, when the forge's midday bell rings.

Francis darts outdoors, James following right behind. Struggling to keep up, James blurts out,

> "I would think that he could easily find you."

Francis ignores the advice and continues to race for the grounds.

Arriving at the oak stump with the water bucket, Francis pauses to gaze around. He nervously taps the fingers of his right hand on the rim of the drinking container.

> "Why hasn't he arrived? He did say noon, didn't he? What day do I visit?
> What shall I say? Wolverhampton, eight miles' walk. Shall take two hours
> to walk. Shall not arrive until eight, perhaps nine this evening. It was this
> evening? James, did he mention this evening?"

James stands silent, his head bowed, staring at an unusual sapling at the base of the stump. Slowly raising his head to look at Francis, he laughs.

"There shall be difficulty living with you in these conditions. I am hungry. Care to join me?"

"No, he shall arrive shortly."

"Very well."

In the distance, at the perimeter of the forge property, the horse carrying Pastor Glasbrook finally arrives. Francis anxiously taps his fingers again; it is a struggle, but he is able to remain at the water supply. He wants to race toward the itinerant, but he wisely chooses to wait. The majestic Arabian stops within two yards of Francis. The settling brings a relieved exhale from both the horse and Francis.

"Good afternoon, Francis. Have you received my memorandum?"

Before Francis can respond, he notices another horse and rider entering the property. The distraction has James also turning to view the newcomer. He quickly informs Francis,

"Almost forgot, Lord Dartmouth has also requested that you visit Mrs. Hanson. He too would like to talk with you before you attend her this evening."

"Lord Dartmouth? James! Oh, very well."

The nobleman brings his horse to a stop next to the itinerant.

"Young Pastor Asbury, how are your parents?"

"Most kind of you; they are well."

"Someday, it is my wish to gain the talents of your dear Joseph. Seems that the Goughs and the Birches will not allow him another opportunity."

"Both estates do keep Father busy."

"Very well, then. I understand you have agreed to attend my dear friend. She is nearing her end of days."

Francis nervously rubs his hands together. *She is to die soon?* The thought makes him even more nervous; he scratches the back of his head with his left hand. Brother Dartmouth continues,

"Have you secured arrangements for travel?"

"I shall depart at six, upon completion of my evening prayer."

"Very good, Francis. I will attempt to send word that you shall arrive before seven."

Once again, Francis raises his left hand to scratch the back of his head. He forces a question.

"Seven? I would expect closer to nine. Wolverhampton is at least eight miles' walk."

"Walk? Dear boy, you shan't walk. Mrs. Hanson is in no condition to receive you at nine."

The nobleman turns to Glasbrook. He pauses to think, and then asks,

"Might a horse be obtained for Francis to borrow this eve?"

"It may."

"Never mind; I shall have one brought 'round this eve. Francis, I expect you to head straight home once completing the visit. Valuable horse. Is that understood?"

"Yes, Lord Dartmouth."

"Brother Dartmouth. Please, Francis. Call me Brother Dartmouth."

"Yes, Lord, Brother, Dartmouth."

"Close enough. I shall talk with Foxall; they shall bed down my animal for the night."

Francis is surprised—actually, excited—that he will have use of a horse. The excitement evaporates quickly. Nervously running his top teeth over his bottom lip, he looks to the itinerant and poses the question,

"What shall I say to a sick woman?"

Glasbrook and the nobleman give a slight chuckle. Pastor Glasbrook responds,

"It is the business of a visitor of the sick to see every sick person within his district thrice a week. Are you prepared to take on such responsibility?"

Francis nods his affirmation. The itinerant continues,

"Very well, then. You are to inquire into the state of their souls, and to advise them as occasion may require. Talk of their disorders; seek to procure advice for their medical condition. Relieve them of any burdens that bring strife. These are the key responsibilities."

Lord Dartmouth adds,

"Knowing our dear Mrs. Hanson, she would be eternally grateful if you were to pray, listen, and stoke a fire for her tea."

"Yes, Francis, stoke a fire for her tea. Can you handle such heavy responsibilities?"

Francis's jubilation returns. *I tend to over-think these things.* He turns to the itinerant to answer,

"Yes, Pastor Glasbrook, I can handle 'the stoke.' "

"Very well. You have an assignment, you have a horse, and you have opportunity to comfort a dear saint on her final journey toward Home. Do well."

"I shall."

The rest of the day is a blur to Francis, working the anvil, contemplating what he will say to the elderly woman. The five o'clock bell sends him running out of the forge. At his anvil, James Mayo laughs aloud as his hurried friend almost falls when his foot catches a stray piece of iron lying in his exit path. A couple of the men nearby also find Francis's frantic departure amusing.

Halfway back to his cottage at the forge, Francis stops.

He stands motionless, staring at the sun as it sets to the west of Forge Mill Lake. He's seen this before—a captivating event, the sky glistening with various shades of blue and white. He shifts his focus to the various ducks resting upon the flat water and the thousands of northern lapwings scattered along the lake's shoreline. In spite of the inspiring scene, the torn expression on his face clearly indicates that he is confused. *Evening prayer?* Since his meeting to become a local preacher, the five o'clock bell has sent him to prayer. *Shall I pray before I depart?* The words of itinerant Glasbrook emerge: "Be ever mindful, it surely will fail without prayer."

All right, then. Francis turns and heads for the barn where the borrowed horse resides.

The stable boy from Lord Dartmouth stands alongside the forge's barn, the structure housing several of the horses which are part of the Sandwell estate. From the looks of it, the young boy who stands holding the reins has spent several hours grooming the beautiful animal. The horse of noble ownership is a black Connemara pony.

The sturdy, short-legged horse with the defined pony head notices Francis as he approaches. He bobs his head twice. Francis pulls his head backward, surprised by the horse's welcoming reception. The attendant offers,

"You must be Francis. Churchfield is most ready."

"The horse's name is Churchfield?"

"Yes, after the estate my lord recently built. The Connemara is smart, well-tempered. Will serve you well."

"Yes, I understand."

Francis wrestles with his thoughts and emotions for the evening.

First, he is excited; this is his first assignment as a local preacher. Second, he is hesitant; he will be bringing comfort to one who is about to pass into eternity. Third, he is unsure; he has never ridden a horse before. Fourth, *I am only slightly familiar with the required journey to Wolverhampton . . . and I shall be returning home in complete darkness.* Fifth, *I must spend time in prayer. Can anything else bring challenge to this day?*

The stable boy urges Francis to mount.

"Place your foot here."

Francis temporarily puts aside the worries and follows the direction. The young man continues to offer instruction about the animal.

> "Although he is short at the knees, he is quite strong. The breed hails from the mountainous west of Ireland. Good stock, gentle personality. He shall serve you well."

Good stock, Irish mountains, short at the knee . . . the random thoughts frustrate Francis. He fumbles with the horse's reins and nervously offers,

> "I'd best move on."

> "To move forward you gently tap him at the ribs. He shall continue until you pull on the reins. Pull left or right for turning. The horse is all you need. A gentle soul. I shall remain on site until your return."

If I return. This thought of Francis is strong. The stable boy gives one last piece of advice.

> "Keep him from the shore grass—easily distracted, could make for a wet ride."

Oh dear. A horse drawn to the reeds growing along the riverbank. In addition, this animal occasionally forgets he's eating on the precarious sloping side of a riverbank and falls in. Francis shakes his head as he lightly puts his heels to the horse, and the pair is on their way.

Moving away from the lake at Sandwell Forge and onto the level ground along the River Tame, Francis reminisces about his time along the waterway. He has spent many a day walking along its fertile banks, some of these walks blessed with the company of Nancy. The lake boasts of many waterfowl. This time of year, spring and early summer, brings the first set of wildflowers and the screeching cries of the lake's most vocal residents, the northern lapwing.

The beautiful birds show up by the thousands, resting and courting on the banks and grasslands that surround the lake. Francis and Nancy find it inspiring. The birds have a most unusual mating ritual. Several of the male birds will simultaneously take flight, their goal the completion of their highly acrobatic, erratic, and unusual flight designed to attract willing females. The black-and-white bird with the tinted green back climbs straight up in the air; it soon ceases to ascend, hammer-heading toward the earth in a sudden downward descent. The shrill cry of the bird as it awkwardly and uncontrollably spirals toward the ground, its oversized wings flopping loudly in the wind, can easily frighten the unfamiliar viewer.

Watching this ritual, Francis once again considers the unusual custom: *tottering birds.* He continues northwest along the riverbank; he will parallel the Tame for some time. At the wilderness town of Willenhall, he will have to depart from the waterway and head west toward Wolverhampton.

Francis spots the moon. It is up early, having risen midway through the afternoon. The sight of the celestial body in its nearly-full waxing gibbous phase brings a slight comfort to Francis's worry of his return trip in darkness. *I suppose you shall light my way home.* Francis's relaxed feeling prompts him, *I suppose this is as welcome a time as any* . . . As Churchfield slowly strides along the river, Francis begins to pray.

Surprisingly, praying on horseback comes easily to Francis. He finds that the methodical pace of the animal aids him in reciting several of the key Scriptures that have come to mind, almost like praying to music. *For I know that the Lord is great, and our Lord is above all gods. Whatever the Lord pleases He does, in heaven and in earth, in the seas and in all deep places. He causes the vapors to ascend from the ends of the earth* . . .[86]

Francis and Churchfield continue at a steady pace. Overhead, a large flock of lapwings moves in unison eastward. Suddenly, the entire flock turns north, then south, and finally southeast, heading toward Forge Mill Lake. This is typical; these several hundred birds will eventually join the large flock already in residence at the lake.

The River Tame at this point is shallow and fast-moving. The setting sun is slowly reducing the crispness of the waterway's features, but Francis can still see that the banks are gently sloped in most areas, while other areas show signs of erosion. In the worn portions of the waterway, the bank is a straight drop of about seven or eight feet in height. Francis is mindful to keep Churchfield clear of the tempting grass at these locations.

As they approach the Ford Brook, the sun has completely set; darkness eagerly aims for its advantage. Francis is anxious; *I desire light. The path is treacherous.* His fear subsides as his eyes adjust to the beams from the moon as they filter through passing clouds. As the sky clears a little, the moon illuminates the path, creating spreading shadows through the branches of the occasional hardwood tree.

He crosses the brook and continues northwest toward Willenhall. He catches a familiar scent as the odor of cattle and their byproduct waft through the thick night air. He twitches his nose and smiles at the experience.

Willenhall is an ancient hamlet dating back to the eighth century. It is a satellite village of Wolverhampton; in fact, the residents of the parish must proceed to Wolverhampton for weddings and funerals. Before the discovery of coal, the Willenhall farms were engaged in an abundant production of wheat. When coal arrived on the scene, the population of three hundred soon refocused their efforts on harvesting the black fuel for the ironworking industry.

---

[86] Psalm 135, verses 5–7.

In addition to the local coal mines being carved daily out of the ground, lock-making is a main industry of Willenhall in the eighteenth century. The process is an arduous task, requiring endless hours by young apprentices. The locks are cheap—a penny each for a Willenhall lock—so cheap, that it is well known that if a Willenhall locksmith drops a lock, he will not bother to pick it up; he could manufacture another one in less time.

Francis slowly makes his way past a small backyard workshop. The rasping sound of several files going at once pierces the darkness. Francis thinks to himself, *it is well past six o'clock.* He finds it odd that the four youngsters, and what appears to be their mother and father, are still bent over the vice, filing away at keys. *When shall their day come to a close?* The thought brings thankfulness that he works for a generous individual like Mr. Foxall.

He departs the Tame and heads slightly north of west. *Should be roughly three more miles.* At this point in the journey, the generally flat land begins to undulate. From conversations with his father, Francis knows that there is an ancient road, the London Road, which travels directly to Wolverhampton. In the opposite direction, the road goes all the way to London from Wolverhampton. *Shall make the road and pick up the pace.*

Within a few minutes, Francis does precisely that. The words of his father come to mind: "The dirt road has its advantages: a direct route to Wolver, few obstacles, and only an occasional pot-sized hole." Francis is relieved to find the ancient route.

Before his departure, Pastor Glasbrook had also given Francis advice about Wolverhampton. He mentioned that the Wesleyan society there is new, having been formed seven years prior, in 1758. The society is largely the result of the open-air preaching of George Whitefield in 1753 and John Wesley's efforts in 1757, when he formed a society in nearby Bilbrook.

There were also ominous warnings from Pastor Glasbrook. He spoke of the 1761 incident which nearly killed Alexander Mather. It was a struggle seasoned with a few bruises and cuts, but he managed to flee. In response to his successful escape, the town burned an effigy of the Scottish preacher. Glasbrook continued, "Two years ago, the locals attacked and leveled to the ground the Wolverhampton Methodist meeting house on Rotten Row."[87] Four individuals, including the local attorney, Mr. Hayes, were responsible for the uprising. By the influence and subtle threats of a lawsuit from Lord Dartmouth (Brother Dartmouth), the guilty Mr. Hayes had rebuilt the structure at his own expense.

---

[87] Now known as Broad Street.

Traveling due west, Francis approaches Rotten Row, the street where the home of Mrs. Hanson is located. The home is on the far end, opposite Francis's entrance. There are several simple brick houses lining both sides of the street. In the lighted darkness, he can see each sturdy home topped with a thatched roof. In the distance, the moonlight reveals a large structure—a very large structure—roughly a thousand yards from the end of Mrs. Hanson's road. The building's silhouette becomes much clearer as Francis makes his way down the street.

The oversized monument with the large spire is St. Peter's Church. The sound of several men in deep discussion interrupts Francis's gaze at the distant edifice. He hadn't noticed them earlier, but the group of seven men is about fifteen yards ahead of him, standing on the left side of the street. The conversation grows clearer as he approaches.

These are men of commerce; nearing the men, this thought is unmistakable to Francis. Graziers[88] and farmers boldly attempt to convince the resident butchers to raise their wholesale purchase prices. Francis is amused by the animated gestures of one gentleman; *he would make for a convincing preacher.*

Passing the men in their deep negotiations, Francis approaches the brick house of Mrs. Hanson and directs his four-legged escort toward the front door. Dismounting, he pauses to give a silent request: *Father, settle the rumblings within me. Help me to be of service to Your elder servant. Place within me the words.* Francis secures Churchfield and heads for the front door.

The young woman who answers the door is happy to see Francis. He estimates that she is nearly the same age as he is, slightly shorter and quite attractive. She invites him in.

> "Brother Dartmouth had sent word of your coming. The mistress of the house awaits."

Francis follows. The home is rather simple, much like many of the homes in Great Barr. Nearing the doorway at the bedroom, the young woman advises Francis,

> "I shall escort you to her."

She gently takes Francis by the hand and draws him into the bedroom. The gentle touch matches her kindly personality.

Mrs. Hanson lies quiet, not moving. Francis is uneasy; he scrapes his top teeth over his bottom lip. The young woman gently calls,

> "Mrs. Hanson? The young preacher is here."

Slowly, Mrs. Hanson's eyes begin to open. She smiles toward the young woman and turns her head toward Francis. His attractive escort whispers as she lets go of his hand,

---

[88] A person who grazes cattle for market.

"I shall leave you to be with her."

"Very well."

The young woman gently touches the back of his arm and departs. Francis notices a chair not far from the bed. He begins to pull it over, then stops.

"May I?"

Pointing toward the wooden seat, he waits for Mrs. Hanson to answer. She looks at the young preacher and responds,

"Please do."

"Thank you. Mrs. Hanson, I am Francis Asbury. It is my pleasure to meet with you."

Francis pulls forward the seat and sits. Mrs. Hanson gives a slight chuckle.

"A young man like you, pleasure to meet with an old woman as myself? I should think your time would be much better spent chasing my helper. How old are you, Master Asbury?"

The question strikes him as odd. However, he responds,

"This summer I shall turn twenty."

"I thought so. Would you read to me the sixteenth chapter of John? Its words would bring great comfort to me at this time."

Francis leans forward in his seat and opens the Bible in his hands to the book of John. Mrs. Hanson turns her eyes away from Francis, toward the moonlight that eases through the sole window in her bedroom. He begins,

" 'These things I have spoken to you, that you should not be made to stumble. They will put you out of the synagogues; yes, the time is coming that whoever kills you will think that he offers God service . . .' "

Francis pauses; *this is a most odd request.* He looks to Mrs. Hanson. His pause causes her to purse her lips; she is not happy. She turns toward him; it is evident she wants him to continue.

" 'And these things they will do to you because they have not known the Father nor Me. But these things I have told you, that when the time comes, you may remember that I told you of them.' "

"Enough."

Her gentle yet raspy request causes Francis to stop. The silence is awkward. Francis sits back in his chair and looks about the room. *Is she expecting me to expound on these odd verses?* Returning her eyes to the window, the old woman begins to speak.

"Francis, the sixteenth chapter of John is Jesus's farewell to His disciples, is it not?"

"It is."

"Very well; I shall be departing this life soon, to an embrace in eternity by our Heavenly Father."

"Yes, Mrs. Hanson."

"Yes, Mrs. Hanson?"

Her forehead creases with Francis's response. In a stern voice, she continues,

"Much more than, 'yes, Mrs. Hanson.' These words that Jesus shared with his disciples, I share them with you."

Francis ponders her statement, *I share them with you.* He leans forward.

"Are these words of yours intended for me?"

The elderly woman turns her eyes toward Francis. With a most serious look on her face, she advises the young man,

"God has called you to preach the Gospel. His call will require you to leave the familiar. For some reason, the unfamiliar will bring strife, perhaps pain. I urge you to follow that call, even if it were to lead you headfirst into a storm."

Francis raises his right hand and grasps his chin. He is silent. Once again, Mrs. Hanson turns her head toward the window, but she has not finished speaking.

"You know I was in attendance when Whitefield preached here some years ago. His voice thundered through the air, deafening many into new life. His words brought me to new life. However, not all embraced the life-giving truths of his proclamations. The terrible time upon Mather . . . the burning of his likeness. Horrible events. The burning of the meeting house."

Francis finds it odd that she is going on about persecution. He glances at a small wooden stand at the head of the bed, to his left, and notices a copy of *The Gentleman's Magazine*. The London-based newspaper is the preferred periodical of the British wealthy. He surmises that *Lord Dartmouth must have given her a copy.*

As Mrs. Hanson continues to speak at length about difficult times, Francis finds himself perusing an article that has caught his attention:

Extracts from a Journal
written by Mr. John Bartram of his Travels into Carolina

John Bartram, appointed botanist to His Majesty George III, writes the article, in which he details his dealings with the Catawba Indians in the colony of Carolina. Francis considers what he is reading: *the Catawba Indians for many years maintained a bloody and revengeful war with the five united Indian nations of New York . . . the Catawbas always pursued them so closely that they generally obtained a sufficient revenge; they sometimes chased them as far as the Susquehanna River, bringing back many scalps as a token of their victory . . .*

Francis stops reading. He hears Mrs. Hanson's next words clearly; she has shared them once already.

> "Follow the call, even if it were to lead you into a storm."

Confident that she has completed what she set out to do, Mrs. Hanson calls for her attendant, then turns toward Francis and dismisses him.

He rises as the young woman enters the room. *I ventured to bring a word to this dear old saint; instead, she brought a word to me.* Francis continues to ponder this thought as he exits the home.

Outside, he asks of the young woman,

> "A visitor of the sick should attend three times each week; do you desire that I visit again?"

> "I am confident that my mistress would enjoy your visits, however long they shall last. Please do."

> "I shall return in two nights."

The ride back to the forge is a unique experience for Francis. At times he is clearly on the verge of being lost, especially when the moon ducks behind clouds for minutes at a time. On one occasion, he estimates that the total time of darkness is nearing fifteen minutes. The challenge of riding through a forest with no natural light brings an eerie feeling to the local preacher. Adding to this is the unexpected interaction with Mrs. Hanson. Thoughts of the Bartram article sharpen his anxiety into outright fear. However, to his surprise, it is in these moments of distressed emotion that Francis can sense Churchfield taking charge. In complete darkness, the horse walks confidently in the direction of home. The animal knows precisely where to go. On several occasions, Francis has cause to marvel at this development.

A couple of hours later, nearing the Sandwell Forge, he once again reflects upon the prophetic words of the elderly lady: "Follow the call." He wants to leave off the storm portion, but it sneaks through. His thoughts also move to America; *will the storm I shall face be found in the far-off land of the American colonies, the land of the Catawbas and the Indian nations of New York?* Strangely, his mind recalls the medicinal advice of John Turton the younger: *"the natives in the colonies . . . the poultice of onions . . . and herbs applied to the cut."* This last thought lingers until he considers Mrs. Hanson's beautiful attendant. He toys with the thought of seeing the girl again; *strange, I failed to obtain her name.* His thoughts quickly return to the work day ahead and to Nancy.

These thoughts linger in Francis's mind for the next several days, especially when news of Mrs. Hanson's passing arrives the day after his visit with her.

The next Sabbath finds Francis in a familiar setting, the home of his parents. Once again, Elizabeth prepares an outstanding meal, and the three of them are delighted to be together. Francis opens the conversation.

"Father, Mother, it is well that we gather."

"Yes, Son, it is. Mother, would you agree?"

"As much as it pains me when you depart, it is a most welcome emotion on your return. However, I fear this privilege is quickly drawing to a close."

Francis looks to his father and nods his head. They both realize that Mother is anxious over his work as a local preacher, for the day is approaching when Francis will not be able to accommodate his Sunday visits with his parents. Francis tries to encourage his mother.

"Yes, Mother; however, I shall find a solution to this dilemma."

Elizabeth says nothing, quietly returning to her dinner. Spoonful after spoonful, she continues in silence. The men allow her time to contemplate.

After a few minutes, Elizabeth wipes her face with her napkin, rises from her chair, and departs from the room. Joseph and Francis sit silently watching as she walks through the rear door to the back room. Joseph leans in to inquire of his son,

"Have you any suggestions, Franky?"

"I do not. I fail to see a solution."

Francis taps his spoon on the table. The nervous act causes Joseph to respond, again leaning in and speaking quietly.

"Franky, although you are a man nearing two decades in age, without the commitment of the itinerancy or marriage, your mother continues to view you as a child."

"Father, I am committed to my work - -

And my preaching."

"You might consider talking to her about it."

"I have tried, Father."

"Try again; she is a mother, and shall be all her days."

"I shall."

Francis's next assignment arrives the following week. On a pleasant Saturday afternoon, he is to venture to the nearby town of Bilbrook, where Glasbrook has instructed him to meet with the "new members." To Francis, the assignment seems a simple one.

Bilbrook lies an additional three and a half miles to the northwest of Wolverhampton, a total of eleven miles from the forge. Lord Dartmouth once again lends Churchfield to Francis. As before, the horse bobs his head twice, this time adding a slight nicker, when Francis arrives to collect him.

The trek in daytime is much more enjoyable. The budding plants of spring and the dense green sedge along the riverbank reveal signs of promise. Churchfield is clearly thankful for the early growth of the springtime grass. Francis is thankful to be a local preacher; the position sits well with him. Occasionally he daydreams of being a traveling itinerant, but these thoughts seldom gain much ground. Upon entering the town on horseback, Francis heads toward the Bilbrook meeting house.

With a large smile and a slight spring in his step, his Bible in hand, Francis embraces the pleasant May afternoon. Inside the home, the leader of the "new members group" greets him. He is a tall, thin man nearing forty years of age.

"Francis Asbury, the ride from Sandwell must have brought on a thirst. Would you care for tea?"

"Would be most welcome."

"Please, have a seat. I shall summon the members; they anxiously await."

The tea is the perfect refreshment for Francis. He gulps it down and wishes for more.

A strange noise begins to emerge from the adjacent room into which the class leader has disappeared. It rises at first as a gentle mumbling; before long, the mumble raises to a roar. The door bangs open and two dozen boys and girls, five to ten years of age, burst into the room. One particular girl appears younger than the others. The atmosphere quickly changes to one of complete excitement and confusion. Several of the older boys launch for Francis and nearly knock him out of his seat. Pushing and patting them aside, he struggles to his feet. Several girls shriek and laugh as another boy pulls their hair. Once Francis is standing, a boy about seven years of age leaps into his arms. The impact knocks Francis off balance and back into the chair.

Entering the room, the class leader shouts above the din,

"I shall return near the end of the meeting."

It's difficult, but Francis is able to get the words out:

"How long shall class meet?"

"Shall see you in an hour."

An hour? The thought stumps Francis. *How shall I keep such a brood calm, better yet, busy, for upwards of an hour?* Francis sets down the boy. *How do I quiet this group?* The thought drives him to blurt out,

"We shall head outdoors."

With a battalion-like response, the entire group launches itself, the boys and girls squeezing through the front door of the meeting house as one unit. Despite a few bruises, the youngsters make it through and anxiously await Francis's arrival outside.

Shaking his head, he makes his way for the door. He pauses at the doorway to view the group. Three boys are now pulling the hair of the girls. The girls are screaming and laughing. One lad decides to run through some standing water; his breeches soon drip with the silty liquid. *These children border on anarchy.* Francis ventures out.

Standing in front of the active gathering, Francis has the boys and girls separate into two groups. This brings a slight reduction in volume. He announces,

"We shall have a riddle."

The youngsters jump and scream with excitement. Francis raises his arms and the girls grow quiet, but the boys' disorderly behavior continues. Francis looks about; *the girls seem to be controlling themselves. I must help the boys to emulate this.* Smiling to himself, he continues,

"All right, quiet down. Quiet, please."

It is difficult, but the boys finally settle down. All is silent. Francis begins,

"Consider the riddle: the Hebrew woman Deborah, the judge of Israel— was she priest or prophet?"

No one in the group responds. A boy chews on his thumbnail; another lad scrapes at the dirt with his heel. One girl begins to raise her hand, then quickly retrieves it.

Very well. Francis is thankful that the group stands silently contemplating the identity of Deborah. After a moment, Francis reveals the facts.

"Deborah was a prophet, or more correctly, a prophetess. In the times of the ancient Hebrews, the prophets and prophetesses brought important words from God. Because of the words which God spoke through her, she proclaimed the wisdom that allowed the Israelites to succeed in battle. Deborah spoke for God. To be a prophet or prophetess of God is not a right to be seized, but a gift to be exercised with profound responsibility."

One boy raises his hand to speak.

"Pastor Asbury, may we play ball?"

Humbled by the insignificant question, Francis drops his head and looks to the ground. *Ball? What of the lesson?* He counters,

"Only if you have grasped the lesson from the Bible. Was Deborah a priest or a prophet?"

In unison the boys and girls respond,

"A prophet!"

One girl, who comes across as the leader of several other girls, stands rather upright. She straightens her skirt and responds,

"More precisely, a prophetess."

Francis smiles.

"Very well. We may play a game now. Have you a ball?"

One of the boys darts for the side of the meeting house and returns with the inflated bladder of a pig. He yells to his friends,

"Choose sides!"

Immediately, two boys charge the lad. In response, he places the ball on the ground and kicks it to one of his friends on the other side of the gathering. The girls scatter; they want no part of the activity. No one has chosen sides, but it doesn't matter; the boys begin the game.

Francis takes a seat on the ground. The girls slowly make their way toward him, and one by one, each takes a seat alongside the local preacher. All watch the boys as they kick the ball in several directions. Francis comments,

"This game seems to lack boundaries."

The girls giggle. One of them stands and approaches Francis. She can barely reach to look eye to eye with him as he sits. She urges Francis,

"You should play. A fun game for boys."

Francis smiles at the bold youngster.

"How old are you?"

The girl holds up four fingers. Another girl blurts out,

"She is three years of age."

Francis responds to the three-year-old,

"Very well, I shall take your sage advice."

Running onto the field, Francis is nearly double their size. One young lad kicks the ball right at him. Francis grabs the ball with his hands, places it on the ground, and gives it a strong kick. The ball launches high and long. One boy exclaims,

"Roit bosta!"[89]

For nearly the rest of the afternoon, Francis and the boys continue their play. At times, Francis must take great care to avoid a collision with the youngsters, fearing accidental injury to the lads.

From behind the girls who sit alongside the makeshift field, an elderly man makes his way toward the group. He inquires of the girls,

> "Young ladies, shall you wear out your clothing before its time? Please rise from the ground and preserve the dresses which your parents have painstakingly provided."

In unison, the girls rise to their feet. Somewhat embarrassed, they look to the ground. The elder man continues,

"Who is the young man playing with the boys?"

---

[89] West Midlands slang for "The best!"

None of the girls answer. They nervously move about; some place their hands behind their backs, others kick the dirt. One girl finally clasps her arms in front of her and responds,

"That is Pastor Asbury. Francis Asbury."

"Pastor!"

The old man's reply startles the girls. They sense that he is unhappy with the revelation. The old man marches toward the field, approaching Francis with short, quick steps. The boys, as well as Francis, are unaware of the newest player on the field; they continue the game. The elder man shouts,

"Pastor Asbury!"

Francis stops short. He turns to see the white-haired man, slightly bent over at the shoulders. He responds,

"Yes, I am he."

"Pastor Asbury, are we uncomfortable with taking sport?"

Francis smiles and returns an invitation.

"Come, join the sport! The children freely accept all."

"Does not Wesley admonish to use time wisely?"

At this, the pig-skin flies by, nearly hitting the elder man in the head. He flails his arms, his timing slightly off with the arrival of the accelerating projectile. He scowls at the approaching young boy who focuses on retrieving the ball. In passing, the lad offers an apology.

"Failed to warn."

The older man huffs and extends his arms with hands palms-upward, complaining to Francis,

"Such fribble, from a man of God?"

The old man turns and departs, obviously frustrated with Francis.

By day's end, Francis is exhausted. *I fail to ever run as long as this.* His thought does little to help him catch his breath. Sitting on an old tree stump and surrounded by the children, Francis notices the approaching class leader, who upon arrival immediately expresses his gratitude to Francis.

"Thank you, Francis. Never expected to be three hours."

"It is well. The afternoon seemed to progress quickly."

The boys immediately begin to whine. They know what is next; their newest pal shall leave. They surround Francis, each pulling on part of his garments, and offer farewell. Francis does his best to reach down and thank each boy for the time together. Several girls nudge in and offer Francis the same. The class leader responds,

"The children take well to you. We must arrange for a return visit."

At this revelation, the boys and girls cheer excitedly, and Francis thinks to himself, *please, do not rush this decision.* Francis walks on, gathers Churchfield, and sets off on his return journey.

Over the summer, Elizabeth's biggest worry materializes: Francis spends almost every Sunday in June, July, and August preaching in Wolverhampton, Walsall, and Bilbrook. Several times there is a slight relief when he speaks at a late service in West Bromwich, for this location allows his mother to hear her son preach. The summer schedule sharpens Francis's preaching abilities, and the West Bromwich faithful grow to enjoy his improvement.

In order to please his mother, Francis finally arrives at a solution. The first weekend in September finds him once again at the dinner table with his parents.

Francis opens the conversation.

> "Mother, it is time that I shared with you. The summer months have demanded much of my time."

He looks toward his mother; she is fighting back tears. Francis gently continues,

> "It has pained me also. After many hours of debate with myself and discussion with James, I shall make an offer. If it pleases you both, I shall make the necessary arrangements."

Elizabeth tilts her head with interest, her softening facial expression exemplifying the hopefulness that has arisen from Francis's words. Raising a handkerchief, she wipes away tears. Joseph encourages,

> "Continue, Franky. Mother and I long to hear."

> "Very well. If it is well with you both, I would like to move back into my room upstairs. It would . . ."

> "Oh, Son!"

Elizabeth's interruption ends with her tears of joy. Joseph jumps in,

> "Franky, this is a grand idea. Is it practical? Have you discussed this with Foxall?"

> "Does not matter; it is settled."

Francis lets out a slight laugh at his mother's words, then answers his father's question.

> "I have."

Francis looks to his mother; again, she wipes away the tears. He too sheds a slight sign of emotion. Wiping away the liquid from beneath his eye, Francis continues,

> "Mother, I have made the arrangements, expectant of your positive reply."

His mother and father laugh aloud. Through a slightly cracking voice, she responds,

"Is it that evident?"

Moving back home allows Francis to enjoy a daily meal with his parents. Even on the Sabbaths that require him to preach at five a.m. in West Bromwich, eight a.m. in Walsall, and five p.m. in Wednesbury, Francis manages to squeeze in a midday meal with his family. Although the necessity of traveling on foot to each of these destinations is bringing Francis near to exhaustion, he is happy that the simple act of eating a meal together pleases his mother and father.

After a few months, Mr. Foxall finally becomes comfortable with the new arrangement; he understands and admires Francis's determination to ease the worry of his mother. He is also impressed with Francis's tenacity to persevere as a local preacher. The schedule is demanding: four nights each week and a full day on the Sabbath, all in addition to a full week at the forge. Mr. Foxall is not only impressed, he is also slowly realizing that he needs to reach out and help Francis in a special way. Thus the meeting with Alexander Mather about to take place on this crisp autumn morning.

At the entrance to the forge, Foxall and Mather stand face to face—or almost, as Mather is nearly six inches taller than the ironworker. The voice of the stocky Scottish itinerant is confident and can be heard by several passersby as they enter the forge for their day's work.

"In time, Thomas, in time. Ya' would do well to postpone ya' intentions."

"Why, Alex?"

"It is a fine gesture; however, Ah' advise against it. Allow for this to mature."

Thomas is not happy with Pastor Mather's resistance. Squeezing his forehead with his thick right hand, he offers one final consideration,

"Allow me the first sight of a favorable time."

"Ah' shall, Thomas, Ah' shall."

In an attempt to silence Foxall, Pastor Mather clears his throat and moves his eyes toward his left. Thomas understands; approaching from the left is Francis. The pair acknowledges the situation; nodding their heads, they shake hands and depart.

Mather tips his hat to Francis.

"Guid mornin', Fr'dancis."

With a voice that cracks from early-morning dryness, Francis responds,

"Good morning, Pastor Mather."

"It is indeed. May Ah' have a bih'[90] of ya' time?"

---

[90] Bit.

Francis rubs his eyes as he nods his head yes. Noticing this, Mather asks,

"Up early in prayer?"

Francis once again agrees. The itinerant continues,

"Would like ya' to make a rather lengthy journey this Saturday. Ah' have confirmed the use of Brother Dartmouth's horse. Ah' hear ya' have grown quite fond of him. Ya' will need to head to Ashbourne in Derbyshire, to a Mrs. Dobinson. Their class shall meet wit' ya' as ya' br'ding a word. Are ya' comfortable wit' such a long journey?"

"I shall be. Father will counsel me on the proper path to Ashbourne."

"Hoots![91] Venturin' out on ya' own sits well wit' ya'. Ah' was looking forward to travelin' wit' ya', but if ya' . . ."

Mather stops short of completing his sentence, thrilled to see that he has caught Francis off guard. Francis fumbles,

"Together, well - -

My deepest apology, sir. Did not mean to imply . . ."

"Quite all right. Ya' are expected to preach three services on Sabbath also, in Ashbourne."

Francis stands silent. He has barely recovered from incorrectly assuming that he would take this two-day journey on his own. *Must be a large group at Ashbourne.* His first thought comes out verbally,

"If we were to travel all night, seems it leaves little enough time for return. What of Monday's work at the forge? What of Saturday's, as well?"

"Ya' guid boss has agreed to allow time for a return the day followin', and a day off on Saturday."

Francis once again stands silent. He cannot believe the development. *This is strangely new. The past few months, Foxall has accepted the preaching and teaching that pulls me from the property. Must admit, it has been very fulfilling, almost purposeful. I enjoy the forge, but traveling about . . . my soul seems prepared for this.*

The journey from the Asbury cottage in Newton Village to Ashbourne will start by proceeding east to the town of Sutton Coldfield, the hamlet of Francis's friend, Edward Hand. Francis and Alexander will then proceed due north to Lichfield to join an ancient Roman road, Rykneld Street, known as Ickneild Way before the thirteenth century. Joining the Rykneld, their northeast travel will parallel the River Trent as the cambered road undulates through grazing fields and hardwood forests. Eventually, they will cross over the Trent. Continuing on the primal road, they will once again cross a body of water, the River Dove. Once across the Dove, they will turn to the west and follow the winding waterway as it

---

[91] Well then!

eventually turns to the north, ascending into the hilly surroundings of Ashbourne. The fifty-mile journey will take twelve hours on horseback. Leaving before dawn, the pair plans to meet with the class on Saturday evening and cap off the night by attending a love feast. The weekend will culminate with Francis preaching three services on Sunday.

The cool predawn air of the West Midlands autumn streams from the nostrils of the two horses that stand prepared to take Francis and Alexander to Ashbourne. Churchfield is skittish, mostly due to the crisp weather. Even in the darkness of the early morning, he can sense Francis's approach. As is his custom, the horse nickers, this time much louder than on previous occasions. He nods his head twice as Francis extends his hand to rub the animal's nose. Churchfield draws his head nearer to accept the affectionate gesture. Francis responds to the dear creature's greeting,

> "My stocky friend, you do amaze. We've an arduous journey ahead; have we prepared?"

Churchfield bobbles his head left to right. Francis cannot help but laugh aloud.

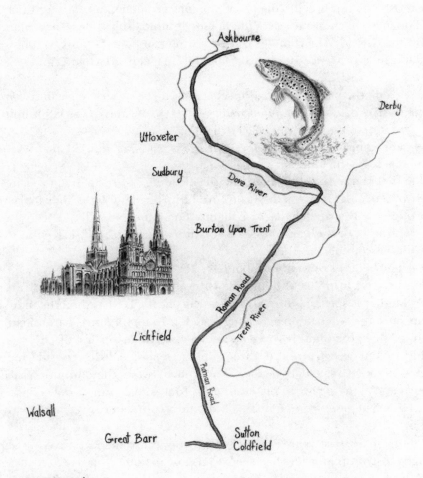

Ashbourne

Derby

Uttoxeter

Sudbury

Dove River

Burton Upan Trent

Roman Road

Trent River

Lichfield

Roman Road

Walsall

Great Barr

Sutton Coldfield

West Bromwich

Mather's horse, Algernon—Alger for short—stands nearly seventeen hands high. The palomino-colored Andalusian is a mighty-looking horse. The favorite choice for war horses, this powerful animal is both intelligent and beautiful. The breed, which originates in Spain, is widely spread over the European continent. Characteristic of the breed, Alger's cream-colored mane and tail are thick and long. The massive chest increases the horse's intimidating appearance. Standing next to Churchfield, Algernon dwarfs the loving Connemara pony. But however formidable its appearance may be, the Andalusian is at heart a loving and sensitive creature.

At 5:15 a.m. the pair set off on horseback. Francis is quick to surmise, *through Sutton in the dark . . . should be an interesting effort.* He decides to voice this opinion.

"Sutton in the dark can be a challenge."

"For some wit' less experience. Alger has made the journey many a time."

Francis accepts the itinerant's experience.

As the first rays of sunlight creep into the morning sky, the pair approaches the park of royal decree. In a less-than-comfortable offering of light, they make their way through the thick patch of gorse plants. The familiar smell of coconut wafts about, causing both men and horses to breathe deeply of the refreshing scent. Pastor Mather comments,

"The benefits of ramblin' about."

Francis sneaks a smile. Although he is hesitant to share it with his traveling partner, Mather is speaking directly to Francis's heart. He has thought about this trip ever since the Scottish preacher suggested it. In fact, Francis barely achieved four hours' sleep the night before—up at one a.m., up again at half past two. He was able to fall asleep around three, only after repeatedly considering the journey's distance, calculating the approximate time they would arrive in Ashbourne. Waking again at his customary four a.m., Francis dove right into prayer. His excitement made it difficult to hold a coherent conversation with the Creator.

For most of the past year, Francis has grown accustomed to traveling about. Although most of his journeys have kept him close to home, this trip to Ashbourne will be the farthest he has ever had to travel. Considering these implications, Francis is excited.

Mather's observation brings Francis's early-morning daydreaming to a halt.

"We shall proceed north, past Edward Hand's. The Rykneld lies a short distance beyond."

Mather turns his horse to the left, and Francis and Churchfield follow.

The morning's rays grow stronger; no longer do the shadows remain mysterious. Once again, Francis silently rejoices at the beams of light permeating the numerous branches of the hardwoods that provide cover for the travelers. A crisp wind gambols above the treetops, promising a sharp welcome when the pair wanders from beyond their protective canopy.

Remnants of the Rykneld mark the path from this point forward. For the next seven miles, the men will have a clear path to follow to Lichfield. As the road emerges from the protective forest of Sutton Park, the chilling wind begins to have its way with the men. Both riders simultaneously pull up on their coat collars to keep their necks warm.

Without notifying Francis, Mather decides to pick up the pace. Alger takes off at a slow trot. Francis quickly spurs Churchfield to follow. Turning around to speak to Francis, Mather offers insight.

"Creatures require a bih' of a run."

Francis and Churchfield soon pull alongside Alex and Alger.

Within a mile or two of Lichfield, Mather slows his horse. Francis pulls back on the reins, and Churchfield's trot slackens. Eventually the Irish pony comes to a stop next to Alger. The pair stands at an intersection. Francis remarks,

"The middle of nowhere and, strangely, there lies an intersection?"

"Havers!"[92]

Francis is slightly alarmed by Mather's reaction. He looks away from the itinerant, to his right, staring down the long, straight road that intersects with the Rykneld.

Mather interrupts his thoughts.

"Watling Street."

Francis looks back toward Mather. He remains silent as he looks to the preacher, uncomfortable with responding without knowledge. Mather offers more,

"Far from nowhere. The lasting impressions of Rome. Just as the Rykneld, Watling is also an old Roman road, to London fr'dom here."

Francis nods that he understands. He looks to the Rykneld; it begins to head in a northeasterly direction, Watling to the northwest and southeast. Uncomfortable with Mather's impromptu lesson, and unclear on what appears opposite than indicated, he hesitantly raises a question.

"Shall we remain on the Rykneld?"

Mather smiles, the kind of smile that finds humor in Francis's inexperience with England's countryside.

"Yes, Fr'dancis, the Rykneld is the proper route. We shall arrive Lichfield, then proceed across the Trent. We shall cross water twice. The River Trent first, then the Dove."

---

[92] Nonsense!

"Very well, along the Rykneld we shall proceed."

Francis prompts Churchfield forward. Mather smiles again.

Within two miles of Lichfield, Alexander and Francis find themselves in a beautiful cherry orchard. The trees have already fruited, the branches mostly bare. The distinctive round canopy shapes created by the farmer's faithful pruning ensure a prosperous fruiting season next year.

The trees form an unusual arena of sound. Several families of adult green woodpeckers perform their familiar chirps, urging their fledglings to take flight. Many of the little ones hide within the cavities of several hardwood trees that surround the orchard. They continue to arch their necks for dinner, unaware that the start of autumn signals the last of these free meals. The secluded hideaways carved out by their persistent parents earlier in the year are no longer big enough to fit the grown youngsters. The cacophonous sound borders on the comedic. The distinctive loud, laughing-like cry of the green bird with the red stripe on its head and the black mustache is repeated often. Adding to the airborne orchestra are the striking colors of the male of the species, with his more distinct green feathers and the red marking within the middle of his black mustache.

Francis offers,

"Father always loved the sound of these chubby birds, boldly laughing at us as they fed upon the ants of the ground."

"By far the largest of the species."

Francis nods; Mather's comment about the green woodpecker being the largest of the woodpecker species in England is indeed correct.

A mile further on, Francis notices a large three-tiered structure on the horizon. Gradually, as the animals draw them northward, the image captures his imagination. His father has spoken of the magnificent church buildings that exist throughout England, but Francis has never seen one for himself. He sits a little taller in the saddle.

The building that draws the morning's sun-rays is the Lichfield Cathedral. The structure dates to the year 669 AD, when it was built as a tribute to the one thousand Christian martyrs who met with sudden death at the hand of the fourth-century Roman emperor, Diocletian. The revised architecture of the building that greets Francis took its shape in the early portion of the eleventh century.

Some have attributed the name Lichfield to the killings of the followers of Christ, the Saxon word *lych* meaning a dead body. However, the name is also associated with the alternate Saxon meaning of the word, a marsh or morass. Two low-lying bogs surround the town of Lichfield; the town's residents call them moggs. The two sloughs connect two lakes that lie adjacent to the cathedral, Minister Pool and Stow Pool.

Lichfield Cathedral before the Reformation of the sixteenth century was a magnificent display of architectural wonder. Towering displays of stained glass and ascending buttresses of the red sandstone color delivered the welcoming eye to the three spires reaching toward heaven. Lichfield Cathedral is the only medieval English cathedral constructed with three spires. The distinct coloration of the building, the magnificent architecture, and the immense size of the structure are designed to focus hearts on the awesomeness of the Creator.

Beautiful destruction. Francis's thought reflects the truth that the beauty of the Lichfield Cathedral has long departed. The destruction of the Reformation period is evident. The violent demolition of the numerous statues and rooms dedicated to less-than-Christian purposes by the Catholic builders are a clear reminder of the stirrings of that disturbing time.

As Francis and Alex draw nearer to the building, the damage and decay from nearly 150 years before speaks to the revolution that occurred within Christianity. Francis notices a pile of broken statues, standing nearly ten feet high and covered with dead weeds and grasses that have taken root in the pile. He instinctively raises his right hand and covers his mouth. Mather verbalizes what Francis is thinking.

"Terrible time. A time of both destruction and accomplishment."

The comment causes Francis to question,

"Accomplishment? Seems anything offered to God should be delivered from destruction."

"Unity requires truth, Fr'dancis. Much of the destruction came about because of a departure fr'dom truth. Wit'out it, there can be nothin' that stands together."

The pair pulls closer to the dilapidated cathedral. Francis notices several large holes in parts of the ceilings. There are also many panes of glass broken or missing from the structure. Sensing Francis's disappointment, Mather offers encouragement.

"Fr'dancis, truth is supreme."

"I understand the need of truth; what fails me, Pastor Mather, is the perception of mankind. If an item or a group requires repair, then as well as possible, repair it. Why destroy it?"

"Fr'dancis, ya' have summarized precisely the initial focus of Luther's reformation. He sought to repair, not to replace. The sinfulness of mankind, through key leaders and their abilities to deceive through a willin' press, brought about the separation. I do not agree wit' the needless destruction of the cathedrals; however, when leaders deceive a people, and their practices contradict Holy Writ, serious actions are required."

"Pastor Mather, destruction of idols and statues I understand, but how does it come about that the roofs of a magnificent building—a building offered to the glory of God—should suffer harm from the cannonball?"

"Fr'dancis, ya' are a student of history. The cathedral's pagan items suffered under the reforms; however, the destruction of the buildin' came about fr'dom another source. The give and take of the English Civil War brought harm to the structure. Fr'dancis, do not get it wrong: wit'out truth, mankind shall never experience unity."

Francis understands. He takes in the rest of the building's destruction, more broken windows and a pile of broken pieces of stone. Pushing Churchfield closer to the rubble, he is drawn to one shard that stands out from the rest. On the random scrabble, a glimmer of gold, clearly part of a larger array of an artistic offering, stands out like an eternal light amidst the dusty-grey scrap pile. The gold piece standing out from the dreary background causes him to ponder Mather's last statement, *without truth, mankind can never experience unity.*

Pointing to the northeast, Mather advises,

"We must aim for this direction."

The pair continues for the area where they will pick up the Roman road once again. Mather continues the discussion.

"In regards to truth, Ah' pose a question. Deborah, was she priest or prophet?"

Francis is somewhat surprised by the inquiry. He can sense his face flushing a bit; *perhaps he knows of my playing ball with the children in Bilbrook.* He decides to respond anyway.

"A prophet."

"Would ya' say the honor was bestowed upon her by birth or by callin'?"

"Most assuredly by calling."

"Why so, Fr'dancis?"

"My studies of the Bible reveal no special lineage, only that she was entrusted with important information from God for communication to the ancient Hebrews."

"Very well, Fr'dancis. A prophet is called of God, not by birth, but by special callin'—a gift of God to an exceptional few to be exercised wit' a profound sense of responsibility."

"A calling to an exceptional few, a profound sense of responsibility; I understand."

"Very well."

He must know of my playing ball.

About a mile from the northern edge of Lichfield, they pick up the road and continue for roughly two miles, where they look to their right and see the northern portion of the River Tame as it slowly approaches its intersection with the Trent.

At the Trent, the men and horses make their way across the ancient stone bridge of the Roman road, still in service. On the western bank of the Trent, they proceed to follow the river as it makes its way toward the northeast. The ground begins to undulate; no longer does the morning fog lift from the drenched soil. The morning's rays give a slight warming to the journey.

The road slowly begins to move closer to the River Trent. Although it will never come closer than a half-mile, the pair continues to see that the river is near. At Burton, the men shall be placed within a mile or two of the Dove river crossing.

Burton is an ancient town along the Roman road, not much different from the other towns of the Staffordshire district. Its significance is its proximity to the River Trent.

The midday sun continues to emerge from the thinning cloud cover, the resulting warmth bringing a slight loosening of the coats. To the west, the ancient hamlet of Horninglow rises above crested woodlands. The ancient settlement is thought to be a worship mound for Vikings in the tenth century. The town's name is derived from the Old English meaning "the people dwelling at the horn-shaped tumulus."[93]

The pair continues over a gentle rolling hill, eventually heading downhill toward the River Dove. At the river, Mather pulls back on the reins and stops. He looks to Francis.

"We shall cross at Monk's Bridge and then rest for a time."

The ancient bridge dates back to the early part of the thirteenth century. Originally called Eggington Bridge, by the end of the same century it was given the name Monk's Bridge by the Crown-appointed chaplain in charge of raising funds for its maintenance. The four-arched bridge, built entirely of stone hewn from a local quarry, is nestled between two embankments that make up the sloping perimeters of the River Dove.

The pair step onto the old bridge and make their way across the river. On the north side of the Dove, Mather and Francis dismount from their horses. As the men instinctively stretch their limbs, Francis, realizing that his legs are somewhat stiff, secures Churchfield and takes a short walk. After some time, he is able to shake off the uncomfortable feeling.

---

[93] A tumulus is an artificial mound, especially over a grave.

Walking along the Dove, Francis notices several large fish hovering above the river bottom. He inquires of Alex,

"There is an abundance of fish. Do you know the species?"

"River trout."

Francis has never seen river trout. Curious, he bends to take a closer look. Several of the fish dart upriver.

Leaning back, he finds himself next to a small clump of plants with tiny blue flowers. The leaves are somewhat hairy, much like a nettle plant. With his right hand, he reaches to pick the attractive tiers of green leaves surrounding the single flower. To his surprise, the entire plant, including the roots, pops from the ground. As he inspects the root system, Mather explains,

"Alkanet plant. The monks centuries ago used to import them to dye their holy cloths red."

Francis responds,

"I see."

He snaps the green leaves and blue flowers from the roots, then rises and heads for Churchfield, where he places the above-ground portion of the plant in his saddlebag. He takes a few seconds to analyze the root system. He hesitates, and then places that in the saddlebag as well. Spinning about, he notices Mather walking away from the riverbank. *Perhaps he is in need of relieving himself.* Francis returns to the waterway to sit. As it is nearing the noon hour, the young man has begun to feel hungry.

After a few minutes, he notices Mather returning from the clump of ash trees whose leaves are turning a distinctive golden color. In the itinerant's hand is a long stick. Francis ponders the pole that is nearly fifteen feet in length; *why should he have need of a stick, and a rather long stick at that?*

Proceeding to his horse, Mather leans the stick on Alger and reaches into his saddlebag. Rummaging inside the leather storage compartment, he eventually emerges from his quest, places an item in his coat pocket, and returns to digging through the leather bag. Once again, he retrieves an item. Francis realizes that Alex is keeping the unidentified item in his hand, but it is small and hard to recognize from this distance. With the pole in his other hand, Mather walks to the riverbank about ten yards away, kneels on the low-growing grass, and begins to work on the end of the pole.

Francis decides to move in for a closer look.

The pole is unusual. While nearly two inches in diameter at the base, the top of the pole is only a quarter-inch thick. Mather places the thin end of the pole onto the flat top of a cut tree stump. Nearing fifteen inches in diameter, the cut ash tree is waist-high, perfect for a work table. Alex places the items in his hand—there is more than one, Francis notes—onto the makeshift tabletop. Francis notices a thin piece of wire nearly seven inches long and a spool of line. At this point, Mather peers up at Francis and explains,

"Braided horse hair."

With a quizzical nod, Francis acknowledges the information. Mather returns to the task. Taking the piece of wire, he bends it almost in half, forming a small loop at the end of the wire. He places the nearly three-inch-long u-shaped wire around the top of the pole, leaving roughly half an inch past the end of the pole. Next, he takes the spool of braided horsehair rope and cuts a seven-inch piece.

With the utmost care, the itinerant wraps the two ends of the wire hoop that reside on either side of the thin end of the ash pole. Mather is careful to create a weaver's loop with the braided horsehair line at the opposite end of the metal hoop, about an inch down the pole. When finished wrapping the horsehair line around the wire hoop and securing it to the pole, he threads the end of the braided rope through the weaver's loop and pulls it tightly through and underneath the wrappings he just finished. The result is that the braided horsehair rope is securely holding the wire hoop onto the end of the pole.

Next, Alex pulls out nearly fifteen feet of the braided horsehair, cuts it, and ties it to the metal loop on the end of the ash pole. Reaching into his coat pocket, he retrieves two small items. One is a dark-brown color and furry; the other is frillier and bright brown in color. Francis is confused; *what can this be?* He decides to ask.

"What have we?"

" 'Tis hand-tied flies."

"Flies?"

"Yes, Fr'dancis, flies. The darker one is made of violet-colored wool and the grey feather of a mallard."

"Duck?"

"Yes, Fr'dancis, a duck. Aware that ya' will eventually ask, the other fly is made of strands of tan-colored wool and the hair of a spaniel."

Alex ties the dark-brown fly to the horsehair line, then secures the entire rig to the wire loop on the end of the pole. He informs Francis,

"Now we shall procure a trout."

Francis is impressed; he has never fished before. He inquires,

"How shall we procure a trout?"

"Watch and learn. Perhaps ya' can ready some wood for a fire?"

Francis moves quickly; he doesn't want to miss the fishing. The task is easy, as many hardwood limbs are within a few steps. He piles the wood on top of some dried-out clumps of grass. *He did not say start, just prepare for a fire.*

Satisfied that he has completed the itinerant's request, he bolts for the riverbank. Standing a few yards away from Alex, Francis watches as the traveling preacher gently swings the long pole back and forth, behind him and then out over the water. Each time the hand-tied fly lands undetected on top of the water. But not quite undetected, for within a few minutes a loud splash removes the fly from view. This commotion causes Alex to grasp the pole more tightly with both hands and cry aloud,

" 'Tis lunch on the way!"

In the water, a trout, attached to the end of the braided horsehair line, is secured and struggling, its frantic splashing breaking the silence of the river forest. Within a minute, Alex is able to swing the fish onto the riverbank. Francis instinctively lurches for the fish; landing on his knees, he aims to grab the trout as it flops about. Mather laughs aloud as the fish successfully escapes Francis's attempts to control the catch. He advises,

"Back away, Fr'dancis; will drag him up the bank."

In less than twenty minutes, Mather is able to land five trout. After the second fish Francis wisely starts the fire, and the men enjoy fresh trout for lunch.

After the meal, Alex tucks away his new fishing pole, storing it about ten yards into the forest. He returns and informs Francis,

"Shall have need of it on our return. We must be movin' on."

With full stomachs, the pair mount their horses and continue on their way.

The River Dove is a beautiful waterway, beginning in the hills of Buxton, east of Axe Edge. Five major rivers begin in this same region: the Dove, the Manifold, the Wye, the Goyt, and the Dane. The River Dove travels forty-five miles nearly due south, its western bank in Staffordshire and its eastern bank in Derbyshire for almost its entire length. The Dove finishes its course at the River Trent, northeast of Burton, not too far from Monk's Bridge.

For the next six hours Francis and Alex travel the Derbyshire side of the river, working their way in a west-to-northwest direction. Along the way, they encounter a river full of life; trout and ducks capture Francis's attention as the river slowly makes its way uphill through lush forests of ash trees. The autumn temperatures evoke their dance, painting an elaborate display of red and golden hues. The pair journeys half the river's length—the more sedate portion of the waterway—and pulls away from its shores at the hilly outskirts of Ashbourne. From this point northward to its source, the Dove climbs amidst mountainous valleys. Francis aches to continue along the resplendent river—not only because of the natural beauty, but also, more accurately, because of the sense of adventure it prompts. He also somewhat wishes to avoid the formalities that lie ahead. He vows to himself, *shall return someday.*

At seven o'clock that evening, Alex and Francis arrive at the Methodist meeting house in Ashbourne. The members of the class meeting have already gathered, the men and women milling about as several different conversations occur together. Francis is slightly nervous at the sight of thirty new faces. He fumbles through the pages of his Bible. He has been in this situation before; *the Lord shall provide*. The thought brushes away the anxious feelings.

Pastor Mather leads off the class meeting by introducing himself and Francis. He also instructs the gathering that Francis is in charge. Stepping back from the front of the room, Alex nods his head to Francis. Francis begins.

He opens with his own faith struggles. Then, careful not to come across as inconsiderate, he inquires of each individual, one by one, about their faith and their relationships with family and friends. The simple yet profound statements of several of the key men of the town challenge him to self-reflection. At the end of the group time, he asks all to stand and sing a hymn.

During the hymn, a knock at the door causes several young teenage girls to dart for the entrance. As if they were expecting someone, they throw open the door.

The hymn prematurely ends, leaving Francis a little uncomfortable that the group didn't complete the song. Sensing the awkward silence, he inquires,

"Have we guests?"

One of the young girls excitedly exclaims,

"Oh, yes! Little Bethel has arrived."

Stumped, Francis looks to Alex. The stocky itinerant gives a wry smile, the kind that conveys "a bih' of surprise awaits." Francis remains quiet as a group makes its way into the room.

The first to enter is a woman in her mid-thirties. One of the young girls extends a welcoming hand and greets her by name.

"Mrs. Crosby."

The young girls bow as Sarah Crosby enters the room.

Behind Sarah, two women enter together: the older one, in her early forties, is Sarah Ryan; the younger woman, clearly closer to Francis's age, is the wealthy Mary Bosanquet. Francis is quick to notice that the twenty-six-year-old woman is wearing a simple yet expensive dress. He admires the look; it reminds him of the outfits of the women of the Birch family in Hamstead. The young girls who answered the door extend a similar greeting to these two women. One of the girls gently strokes the fine garment that covers Miss Bosanquet; Mary smiles, and her young admirer blushes.

Next to arrive are three young women in their mid-twenties and a nine-year-old girl. The young women are Mrs. Dobinson from Derby and Mary Clark and Ann Tripp from Leytonstone, London. The young girl is the niece of Sarah Ryan; her name is Sally Lawrence. A courteous welcome is given to them as well.

As the new arrivals make their way around the room, Francis finds them most pleasing to view. The young women and the wealthy Mary Bosanquet are slightly older than Francis, which he finds intriguing, especially in light of the admirable reception they received from nearly everyone in the room, including Pastor Mather. *Moreover, what of this "Little Bethel"?*

Pastor Mather seeks to gain the gathering's attention.

"Very well, the love feast may proceed. There shall be chance enough to return to the hymns a bih' later on."

Immediately, the men of the group depart for outdoors, while the local women exit into an adjacent room.

Francis thinks to himself, *this intermission shall provide opportunity for introductions.* With Bible in hand, he scuttles in the direction of Pastor Mather. The itinerant watches as Francis stops short of bumping into him. He decides to wait for the noticeably restless young man to speak. Francis stands in front of Alex; he cannot stand still. He shifts his weight from one leg to the other; he fumbles with the corner of the cover of his Bible. Mather thinks to himself, *oh, he is just itchin' to meet the young ladies.* He teases,

"Seems we are all a-flutter . . ."

Francis drops his head; his face turns red with embarrassment as he realizes his intentions are obvious. Mather gives in.

"Follow me, Fr'dancis; Ah' would like to introduce ya' to these fine women."

While Alex and Francis cross to the other side of the room, the men and women who departed earlier return in a flurry of activity. Several wooden tables are muscled into place around the perimeter of the room. Women dash about carrying cloth-covered bowls. As the women pass by, the round wooden bowls send forth the sweet smell of freshly baked buns. The chairs and bowls are lovingly set at the tables.

Mather once again taunts the young man,

"This endeavor outranks food?"

Francis is not amused; he nods in the direction of the woman who first entered the room. Mather acknowledges that he will introduce her.

Standing in front of Sarah Crosby, Mather gives greeting.

"My dear Sarah, how do ya' do today?"

"Very well, thank you, Pastor Mather."

"Ah' would like to introduce ya' to my young companion, Mr. Fr'dancis Asbur'dy of Newton Village, Staffordshire."

Sarah Crosby gives a slight bow. Francis acknowledges the kind gesture as Mather completes the introduction.

"Fr'dancis Asbur'dy, Ah' have the honor of introducing ya' to Mrs. Sarah Crosby, recently of Derby, and most notably, London, where she not only heard the great George Whitefield preach on several occasions, but also . . ."

"Pastor Mather, we needn't go into all that. I am content to be one entirely unworthy of notice."

"Very well. Fr'dancis and Ah' shall take this up on our return trip."

Sarah turns toward Francis and inquires,

"Shall we have the honor of hearing you preach the Sabbath? I have heard much in your favor."

With his unoccupied right hand, Francis rubs the opposite forearm as it cradles his Bible. He is slightly uncomfortable with the comment. He responds,

"I am humbled to have come thus far. While at times the Lord has allowed for some success, most oft' 'tis a humbling experience."

"Fr'dancis is too modest; he has been runnin' the West Bromwich class for some time. The Lord is callin' him to the itinerancy."

Once again, Francis displays his nervousness over Mather's comment; it is hard for him to meet Sarah's gaze. Approaching from her left are the other girls who accompanied her to tonight's meeting. Each greets Alex and Francis with a polite curtsey; the men return a nod of respectful reception. Sarah introduces Francis to the group.

"Ladies, I have the honor of introducing Mr. Francis Asbury of Newton Village, Staffordshire. He has traveled a long distance to bless us with his preaching on the morrow."

Starting with the first on the left and working her way around the group, Sarah completes the introductions. With each, Francis bows his head to welcome their acquaintance.

"Francis, I introduce each of these my companions, all of whom are humble servants in the Lord. Miss Ann Tripp, Miss Mary Clark, Mrs. Dobinson, Miss Mary Bosanquet, Mrs. Sarah Ryan, and once again, myself, your humble servant, Sarah Crosby. We pledge our humble support of the Lord's work in your life."

"It is a most welcome thought; I thank you all. Are we missing a young lady? I remember a young girl arriving also."

"Yes, Francis, young Sally Lawrence is the niece of Sarah Ryan. The nine-year-old came to Sarah after the unexpected passing of her mother. She shall remain at The Cedars until she is old enough to marry."

"The Cedars? I am unaware."

Mary Bosanquet, the wealthy young lady whom Francis finds somewhat attractive, responds to Francis's inquiry.

"The Cedars is the home that I was fortunate to purchase in London. Sarah Ryan, Ann Tripp, Mary Clark, and I reside there. And if the Lord shall look upon us with favor, perhaps Mrs. Crosby."

Tilting her head, Sarah Crosby gives a slightly mischievous smile. She quips,

"The Cedars may have me, or more correctly, hear me."

The girls laugh, as does Pastor Mather. Uncomprehending of the humor, Francis gives a slight smile, not wanting to appear without knowledge.

Mather is quick to jump in.

"The girls do far more than reside at The Cedars. Mrs. Sarah Ryan and the ladies have set up shop, attendin' to the destitute of London. From there in Leytonstone, their house takes care of London's orphans, young and old. Many are wit'out family or friend; some arrive full of vermin, half-naked and afflicted wit' distemper. Mrs. Crosby, ya' would greatly profit their efforts."

"Thank you, Pastor Mather."

Francis has no reply. As he looks to Sarah Ryan, the twenty-year-old Francis sees an older woman. Her hair in its bun is mostly white in color; the creases of her forty-one-year-old face reveal a life of struggle. Francis leans toward her and replies,

"I am humbled by your pure religion."

Mather offers more about the elder of the group.

"If ya' are humbled by her pure religion, ya' will most certainly find her years at Bristol enlightenin'. She is the former housekeeper at Wesley's New Room in Bristol. Far fr'dom her to share it wit' you, she regularly corresponds wit' John Wesley, advisin' him of the spiritual heath of the society at the seaport town."

"Quite enough, Pastor Mather."

Alex wisely honors Sarah's hand-on-his-wrist request.

When John Wesley came to the seaport town of Bristol in 1739, it was at the invitation of George Whitefield. Whitefield was seeking a favor from the Wesley brothers; he wanted them to pick up his work of preaching outdoors to the large gatherings that were continuously showing up for his sermons. On April 2, 1739, the first time that Wesley preached outdoors, he clearly saw the favorable results of such a venture. Within a month, Wesley turned the generous gifts of the new followers of Christ toward the purchase of a plot of land and supplies for "our New Room in the Horsefair." The structure became the place where Wesley taught the Scriptures to the local Wesleyan society. Eventually enlarged in 1748, the New Room, the first Methodist building in the world, soon became the headquarters for helping the poor of Bristol.

It was from this room, in the years 1757 to 1761, that Sarah Ryan led both a successful outreach to the destitute of Bristol and, more importantly, the spiritual mentoring of those who gathered there. Her work was not without controversy, the contention stemming from a jealous outburst from the wife of John Wesley when she accused Sarah Ryan of being "a whore with three living husbands." The verbal attack took place at the 1758 Bristol conference, when Mrs. Wesley spotted Sarah at the head of the table, participating in a meal with the preachers from the conference.

In all fairness to Mrs. Wesley, Sarah Ryan was slowly becoming one of John's most trusted advisors, corresponding with him through letters on a regular basis. In fact, Wesley was writing to Mrs. Ryan often, more often than he wrote to anyone else. Added to this was the fact that Sarah had years ago married a shameless bigamist who left her. She married again, this time to a sailor who callously beat her. He too deserted her, in favor of the sea. Eventually she married a third time, when the cruel sailor was reportedly lost at sea.

Despite the challenging circumstances, Wesley's choice was a wise one. Sarah truly was a blessing to all, and the perfect individual to reach the poor and forgotten of Bristol, having come from a poor family herself. Drawn to Christ by the preaching of George Whitefield, the younger Sarah, Sarah Crosby, had invited her to attend Wesley's services at The Foundry in London. Over time, the evident workings of God's Spirit in Sarah Ryan's life caught Wesley's attention. Against several who voiced a negative opinion about her past, Wesley saw her potential and put the thirty-three-year-old in a position of leadership as the housekeeper of the New Room at Bristol in 1757.

The other Sarah, Sarah Crosby, is five years younger than Sarah Ryan. She too experienced Whitefield and Wesley at a young age and, like Sarah Ryan, her first husband deserted her. She is a dynamic young lady, one of the three who formed an earlier outreach to the poor in London, that time at Moorfields. Little Bethel, as it was called by Wesley and other members of The Foundry, was led by Sarah Ryan and Sarah Crosby as it sought to meet the needs of the less fortunate in Moorfields. Now, the other girls would like nothing more than to have Mrs. Crosby join them in their similar work at The Cedars.

Returning to that topic, Pastor Mather offers,

"It would be a return to the past."

"Indeed, most nostalgic."

Mrs. Ryan's comment encourages the memory of the early outreach in Moorfields, where the wealthy and young Mary Bosanquet teamed up with Sarah Ryan and Sarah Crosby.

Pastor Mather clears his throat and remarks,

"It appears our love feast is ready to begin. Shall we?"

The entire group moves to the center of the room.

Francis has been to love feasts before. The ceremony, meant to replicate the agape meals enjoyed by the early Christians of the first century, seeks to deepen the spiritual walk of the community. The group sitting to enjoy a simple meal in fellowship together reflects that earlier experience. The gathering will also share a cup of drink—literally, as all in the group will drink from the same cup. In addition to the meal, several will come forth and preach on their conversion experiences. Prayers and hymns are also part of the enriching event.

Pastor Mather steps to the center of the room.

"Shall we bow in prayer?"

Everyone in the room bows their heads in silence. Mather continues,

"Almighty Faither, bless our lit'l gatherin' as we listen for Ya' leadin'. We humbly ask this in the name of ya' mighty Son, Jesus. Amen."

All in the room respond likewise: "Amen."

In early Christianity, the believing community came together on occasion to observe a community-wide meal known as the agape. The Wesleyan society in Ashbourne seeks to repeat such an event this evening. The Greek word *agape* means love; it implies ultimate, sacrificial love. Since the fifth century, the practice has largely fallen away. Nearly thirty-six years ago, in 1727, the Moravian Christians in Herrnhut, Germany, revisited the tradition. This reinstated ceremony made its way to the Moravian settlement in America, in the colony of Georgia. John Wesley, while in Savannah, Georgia, with his brother Charles, experienced the Moravian love feast ten years later, in 1737. After a night of prayer, the agape meal in Savannah commenced. Thanksgiving and prayer began and ended the solemn occasion. The evening impressed Wesley; he clearly saw the benefits of coming together in community. He also was delighted that the gathering touched on a key aspect of primitive Christianity, a favorite subject with him. After his May 24, 1738 conversion in London, Wesley set out to make the love feast a regular feature of the Anglican revival movement. The ceremony eventually became a standard practice with George Whitefield and the Calvinistic Methodists, as well as with the Moravian societies in England.

Surrounded by the evening's attendees, Mather raises his hands and begins a hymn.

> "Come and let us sweetly join,
> Christ to praise in hymns divine;
> Give we all, with one accord,
> Glory to our common Lord.
> Hands and hearts and voices raise . . ."

By now, all in the room are singing as Mather continues to lead.

> "Sing as in the ancient days;
> Antedate the joys above,
> Celebrate the Feast of Love."[94]

Stepping forward from the group, an elderly man begins to recite,

> "Happy the souls that first believed; to Jesus and each other they cleaved, joined by the unction from above in mystic fellowship of love. Meek, simple followers of the Lamb, they lived and spake and thought the same, brake the commemorative bread, and drank the Spirit of their Head. On God they cast their every care, wrestling with God in mighty prayer. They claimed the grace through Jesus given; by prayer, they shut and opened the doors of heaven."[95]

Another man steps forward and instructs the women,

> "Please distribute the bread."

Several of the women head for the tables and uncover the wooden bowls. Lifting the containers, they proceed to give each person a bun baked especially for the occasion. Francis breathes deeply of the pleasing aroma as he receives his.

The second man raises his hands and all in the room become silent. He sings grace,

> "Be present at our table, Lord - -
> Be here and everywhere adored - -
> Thy creatures bless, and grant that we - -
> May feast in Paradise with Thee."[96]

At the completion of the song, everyone is seated at the tables to enjoy their bread together.

---

[94] Charles Wesley's "The Love-Feast," 1740.
[95] Quoted from Charles Wesley's poem "Primitive Christianity," 1743.
[96] John Cennick's grace hymn "Before Meat," 1741.

Francis and Alex take their seats with Sarah Ryan and Sarah Crosby's group. Francis sits between Sarah Crosby and Mrs. Dobinson, who proves to be a married woman of twenty-eight years of age. Mrs. Dobinson has strategically placed herself between Francis and Mary. She offers Francis information about Sarah Crosby,

> "Francis, you are sitting next to God's very messenger to my life."

Francis looks to Sarah Crosby, who smiles at the young man. He hadn't noticed before: *She has very attractive blue eyes.* Her face is somewhat chubby at the cheeks, her nose rather thick—not someone whom Francis would find attractive, but pretty in her own unique way. *Besides,* he thinks, *she is sixteen years my elder.*

Mrs. Dobinson is close with Sarah Crosby, who had mentored the troubled young woman as she struggled in her early years of marriage. With a smile toward Francis, she continues her story.

> "My life before London was one of which I lived without God, till after I had entered into the married state, which is now near ten years ago. Before this time, the Divine Spirit frequently strove with me. I used to frequently think, when in company, that everyone seemed happy but myself; yet, I did not properly know what I wanted to satisfy my craving desires, and to give repose to my restless heart. About the year 1758, I went to hear the Reverend Mr. Romaine preach; his subject was the Good Samaritan. I admired his discourse and frequently attended his ministrations. I often wept much under his preaching, and felt a strong desire to be religious.
>
> "One Sunday, being at our parish church, and understanding that the sacrament was to be administered, it was strongly impressed upon my mind to curse it. I thought, I will not do this for the world; but the temptation sank into my heart, so that it suggested that I had done it, and that I must now be inevitably lost. The horror of mind which I felt upon this occasion was inexpressible."

The women at the table give Mrs. Dobinson their undivided attention as she continues.

> "Before this time, I had never heard Mr. Wesley preach, nor had I desired to hear him. But I was now glad to go anywhere, that I might obtain relief for my distressed mind, and accordingly went to The Foundry that evening. All that week my anguish of soul continued both night and day, and I felt no hope of deliverance. I endeavored to pray as well as I could, but it was often in the greatest terror, for I supposed that the Lord had entirely left me to the power of the enemy.
>
> "Around this time, my dear husband asked if he should desire Mr. Wesley to visit me, but I was unwilling. He then observed that he knew one who

was acquainted with Mrs. Crosby. I answered that I should be glad to see her. She soon after favored us with a visit, and took me with her to the class meetings.

"I now began to become acquainted with the people of God; I endeavored to use every means of grace and to lay aside everything that I knew to be sinful. However, my burden was not yet removed. I saw myself a wretched sinner, a hell-deserving creature, and was made deeply sensible that nothing but an interest in Christ, and a sense of the pardoning love of God, could heal my broken heart.

"With the help of Sarah, and over some time, I came to that interest in Christ; I experienced true peace and freedom."

Francis responds,

"Thank you, Mrs. Dobinson."

At this, all at the table commence the eating of their simple meal.

On the other side of the room, an elderly gentleman stands with a large wooden pitcher and a drinking vessel with wooden handles on opposite sides. The man raises the cup and gives thanks to God.

At the completion of his short prayer, he brings the cup to the table where Francis resides and hands it to Pastor Mather, who takes a sip and passes it to his left. One by one, each at the table takes a drink. At the completion, the gentleman retrieves the vessel and repeats the process for each of the remaining tables. All in the room will share the drink, which is actually tea.

Mrs. Dobinson rises from the table and excuses herself. Francis instinctively reflects on Mary Bosanquet, as she now sits beside him. He ponders possible subjects to broach with her, questions to ask of her. Without knowing exactly what he will say, he turns toward her—and she turns toward Francis at precisely the same time. The slight embarrassment causes Francis to look toward the other side of the table. Within a few seconds, he returns his gaze to Mary, who patiently waits.

Francis is silent. Mary begins,

"What of your parents, Francis? Do they reside in Staffordshire?"

"And I with them, in Newton Village. I am recently removed from a forge community in Sandwell Valley."

"The trades? How do you manage?"

"I am privileged—a most understanding employer. One who would preach, if called to do so."

"Of your parents, are they favorable towards the Savior?"

"They are. And yours?"

"Most opposed. My dear mother has sometimes expressed a belief that it would be better for the family if I were removed from it, lest my brothers, who are younger than I, should be infected by my sentiments and example."

Francis looks at the table; he is uncomfortable with the idea of a parent making such an outrageous statement toward a child, *especially a child of favorable religion.* Mary can see that this revelation has brought discomfort to Francis. She reaches her hand onto the table and places it upon his. His emotions quickly change. She continues,

"One day my father said to me, 'There is a particular promise which I require of you: that you will never, on any occasion, either now or hereafter, attempt to make your brothers what you call a Christian.' "

At this, Sarah Ryan chimes in,

"Francis, her reply will ease your worries for this dear servant."

Francis turns toward Mary and asks the obvious.

"Whatever did you convey?"

"I answered, 'I think, sir, I dare not consent to that.' "

Pastor Mather laughs aloud. The women at the table also enjoy the light moment.

Mary continues,

"Upon my reply, Father aimed to put me out of our house. Nineteen years of age and my parents wanted me out."

Twenty years of age and my parents want me in. Francis will not reveal this thought to anyone at this table. He doesn't have to, as the loquacious Mary goes on to note,

"Wealthy families also struggle at love."

Born into a wealthy London family, exposed to Methodism by a family servant and convinced at the age of seven that she should become one of them, Miss Bosanquet spent much of her preteen and early teenage years in the Wesleyan society in London. She was naturally drawn to the inspired words of Sarah Crosby. Eventually, she found herself under the tutelage of Sarah Ryan.

Mary continues,

"The more I conversed with Mrs. Ryan, the more I discovered of the glory of God breaking forth from within, and felt a strong attraction to consider her as the friend of my soul. I told her the past sins, follies, and mercies of my life, and received a similar account from her."

As her wealthy parents spent time in Scarborough, Mary, at the age of eighteen, became one of the believers in Moorfields.

"Within four years, my parents asked me to leave the home. Eight o'clock that evening, I arrived at my lodgings at Mrs. Gold's in Hoxton Square. When bolting my door, I began to look on my present situation. I am, said

I, but young. Cast out of my father's house. I know the heart of a stranger, but alas! How much more of it may I yet have to prove? I cried unto the Lord, and found a sweet calm overspreading my spirit. I could, in a measure, act faith on these words: 'When thy father and thy mother forsake thee, the Lord shall take thee up.' "

Struggling with her painful experiences, Francis hesitates to ask more. He doesn't have to, as Mary continues,

"This was my cross; for every time I went to see my dear parents, what I felt when towards nightfall I rose up to go away, cannot well be imagined. Not that I wished to abide there, but there was something in bidding farewell to those under whose roof I had always lived that used to affect me much—though I saw the wise and gracious hand of God in all, and that He had by this means set me free for His own service."

At the completion of the meal and drink, Pastor Mather steps to the center of the room. Inviting anyone interested in coming forth, he gestures with his right hand. A young man of about thirty comes forward. At his table, a young woman with two young toddlers holds back tears. A woman sitting next to her draws her near, her arm around her shoulders; with a handkerchief, she gently wipes a tear from the young woman's cheek.

Pastor Mather returns to his seat as the young man begins. Standing at the center of the room, he shares,

"Tha' Almighty knows well tha' depths of my heart. It has been quite tha' struggle to move beyond my troubles. For many a year I have wrestled with tha' gin. My dear Leah knows tha' full of it. Drink nearly sought to bring me to expire. I humbly announce that I no longer am its captive; I have obtained tha' liberty that can only be found through tha' Savior."

With head bowed, he makes his way back to his wife. At the table, several men welcome the young man with an embrace.

Sitting next to Francis, Sarah Crosby rises from the table. Francis finds this odd, and even more so as she begins to make her way to the center of the room. Francis has been to several love feasts, but never before has a woman spoken, only men. Inside and outside the church community, many frown upon the act of a women preaching or teaching in church. The majority of the opposition is within the leadership of the Anglican Church, but many who are opposed are also in the Wesleyan communities. This is ironic, considering that John Wesley's own mother conducted services for several hundred of the Epworth faithful when her husband, John's father, was away on out-of-town preaching trips. More serious are the unbelieving communities that find it an excuse for violence against the religious movement.

Sarah stands quietly at the center of the room. To Francis, an awkward silence follows, made more uncomfortable by the fact that she stands with eyes closed, hands hanging at her sides. She finally begins,

> "I have no pursuits, nor wishes, but to please Him, and no fears but to offend Him. I would live to do His will or I would die to see Him. He knows I love Him, with a measure of the same love wherewith He has and does love me."

She opens her eyes. Looking about the room, she continues,

> "As one entirely unworthy of your notice, I shall proceed."

Francis squirms in his seat; *this is most unsettling.*

> "Jesus showed me that as He had answered for my actual transgressions in His own body on the tree, so had He answered for my original sin and for every deviation from His perfect law. He then gave my heart a power to believe Him thus my whole Savior, which I never could do before–and now I felt a peace come into my soul superior to all I had ever known, and which I could not tell how to explain, till it came as though someone had spoken: 'It is the peace that ruled the heart of Christ, in the days of His flesh.'
>
> "I stand here this evening, as in many evenings past, with this same peace in my heart. I have wrestled with the call that He has placed on my life; the call to speak is not one which I receive lightly. 'Unless they are under an extraordinary impulse of the Spirit, let your women be silent in the churches.' Are these not Wesley's words? Has he not clearly defined the difference between a priest and a prophet? Wesley walks a difficult road; he aims to be an Anglican, and he seeks to acknowledge the work of God. Do the words of the Creator coming from my lips not constitute an extraordinary impulse of the Spirit? What of Wesley's clear distinction between 'an authority to preach' and 'an authority to administer the sacraments?' The early church is consistent with these practices. Did not evangelists and deacons preach? Yes, and some of them under extraordinary inspiration. Then both their sons and their daughters prophesied, although in ordinary cases a woman was not permitted to speak in church. Was not this a singular woman and not the whole of them? Wesley has correctly translated so."

Francis continues to be uneasy with this, but he is alone. The individuals in this gathering know well the preaching of Sarah Crosby. Mather reaches to pat Francis's hand, which is nervously bouncing on the tabletop. *In time he will understand.* Mather keeps this thought to himself.

Sarah goes on to relate her early successes.

"Just four years ago, Mrs. Dobinson and I set out with her husband to nearby Derby, just thirteen miles from here, with our goal clearly defined: 'to introduce His servants into this place.' Our initial attempts at setting up a class were immediately successful. Before long, more than two hundred were coming to hear of Christ. This is not the work of Sarah Crosby; this is the work of God through His servant Sarah Crosby. The result of which is the erection of the chapel on St. Michael's Lane.

"Since the time of my conversion in London some twenty years ago, I have often desired to be instrumental in turning the fallen toward God."

I too possess this desire. Francis considers his thought.

"In London, with the responsibilities of a class leader, a vision was given to me while in prayer. Jesus many years ago uttered the words that have secured my heart: 'Feed my sheep.' I answered, 'Lord, I will do as Thou hast done. I will carry the lambs in my bosom, and gently lead those that are with young.'

"I urge you, has not God the right to send by whom He would send?"

The return trip home is full of questions for Francis. Despite the success of his preaching the Sabbath in Ashbourne, he is uncertain about the experience of seeing a woman preacher. Pastor Mather urges Francis to study the Scriptures, to seek out the fact that there were men and women deacons, as well as men and women prophets.

"What of Huldah, the prophetess to Josiah's revival?"[97]

Francis knows of the scriptural references; he also trusts the words of Mather. He is certain about one thing. *One prophet I stand sure of–Deborah.* The words of the young girl in his youth meeting in Bilbrook come to mind: "More precisely, a prophetess."

---

[97] Found in 2 Chronicles chapter 34.

What may we reasonably believe to be God's design
in raising up the preachers called Methodists?
To reform the nation, and, in particular, the Church;
to spread scriptural holiness over the land.
1763 London Conference[98]

Francis dreads the completion of his morning prayer session. Stalling his rising up and leaving for work, he reaches for the blanket from his bed and places it around his shoulders. He sits on the end of his bed, staring at the horizontal wall boards of the cramped bedroom, an eight- by nine-foot room with two beds. The ceiling is low, seven feet above the wood floor. It's not that he is feeling lazy. He isn't tired; his visit to the West Bromwich class the night before ended early, before ten o'clock. He reaches up and stretches, the blanket slumping to the bed as his long arms almost touch the ceiling. He mumbles,

"Would rather skip this day's proceedings."

He falls back onto the bed.

It should be a normal Thursday in the month of January—up at four, prayer until five, off to work, quit at five, and back for prayer until six. What distresses Francis is not the work day ahead, but what stands outside his cottage door. Coupled with that is the fact that he is not in his bedroom at the Asbury cottage. Francis didn't make it home last night; he is in his old cottage, in the room he shared with James Mayo at the forge.

Last night, all was well with Francis. He led the class meeting at the Bromwich meeting room, as he's been doing for a couple of years now. The meeting was attended by several of his close friends. Nancy and her friends were present. At evening's end, the entire gathering left for home immediately after the meeting. At least, all but one. Francis found himself alone with Nancy, a most welcomed set of circumstances. The two sat talking in the meeting room by themselves for nearly half an hour. At the completion of their intimate visit, the two of them readied for departure. Walking outdoors, they discovered what had strangely escaped their notice: the entire Black Country had turned white.

January snowfall in the West Midlands is not a rare occurrence. Despite the consistent yearly averages that account for the region receiving the most snow throughout England, the packed crystals rarely pile more than a few inches deep. The snow that sits on the ground at the Sandwell Forge this morning is nearly thirty-six inches deep.

---

[98] Large Minutes, B, Question and Answer 4.

Still stalling, Francis lowers himself and reaches for the blanket once more. Lying there feeling his eyes beginning to close, he wisely drops the handmade quilt, huffs a complaint, and raises himself to his feet. Francis dreads having to trudge through the heavily packed snow. He did it last night, escorting Nancy the half-mile home through the beginning stages of the storm. Although at the time the snow depth was only a few inches, the driving wind embittered the conditions. The precipitous powder now piles up to his waistline. Francis is certain *my walk to the forge will be cold and strenuous.*

Francis grabs the bed covering that continues to coax him to stay indoors; he wraps it around his shoulders and head as he steps to the door. Placing his hand on the door pull, he creaks the wooden slab open no more than an inch. The charging wind relentlessly fills the entire room with its offensive sting. Lighter-than-air particles quickly collect on the surface of the wooden floor. Francis fully opens the door, lowers his head, and proceeds to trek outdoors.

The snowdrift has a path, cut through it by James when he left for work more than an hour earlier. Unfortunately, the snowfall has not let up, and the previous path is made nearly invisible by the fresher material filling in the majority of James's hard work. Francis raises his legs in an exaggerated fashion. The going is slow, one step, then another step, the wind-blown snow removing any sense of location. Francis trudges on in the direction of his workplace.

At the forge, a fire blazes at the building's entrance. Occasionally raising his muffled focus, Francis can see the fire in the distance. No one stands outside. It is an uncommonly huge blaze, necessary to compete with the weather. He surmises that his coworkers are inside, *protected from the harsh conditions.* He suspends his search and continues in the direction of the struggling beacon.

My elbows ache. The chilling temperatures are doing their best to wear Francis down. He continues the hurdling strides, each lift of his leg bringing a slicing distress to his knee joints. The wind grits against the one portion of his body exposed to the elements, the bridge of his nose.

Nearing the fire, Francis can barely make out a voice from inside the building. Although wind in this condition can play tricks with one's senses, he's confident this was spoken language. The sound repeats itself. Francis tilts his head, but the thick blanket refuses a clear interpretation. He would be risking harm if he exposed his ear for clarification. He leans into the wind and listens. The voice once again attempts to reach him. In an uncommon moment, the wind slows, finally allowing clarification.

"In the horse stalls!"

In the horse stalls—clearly the voice of Trevor. The large man's instruction causes Francis to raise his head. Beyond the fire, in the entrance of the forge, he can see Trevor pointing in the direction of the large wooden structure. Francis once again tucks his chin as he turns toward the livestock barn.

The building which houses the Sandwell estate's primary animals is a large wooden structure. Its three stories remind Francis of the Birch family mill in Handsworth, on the stately Hamstead Hall property. The Sandwell barn is where Francis collects Churchfield for the lengthier rounds of his local preacher duties. He continues his steady stride toward the building, edging past the roaring fire.

Pausing within the heated circle, Francis instinctively reaches his gloved hands toward the fire, rubbing them together briskly. The warmth is hard to experience; the temperature and wind discourage the satisfying glow. He places his hands in his coat pockets, tucks his arms against his chest, and proceeds onward.

Nearing the stalls, Francis experiences his usual morning hunger pangs. Normally he addresses this irritation with a snack his mother has placed in his coat pocket. That pleasure is not a possibility this morning. Unlike his normal morning desire for food, today's effort brings a discomfort that travels beyond his stomach. The annoyance this time ventures to his entire musculature; even his bicep muscles gripe with strain. The weakened feeling leaves him with a familiar craving: *Oh, for Mother's bread.*

At the entrance to the barn, one side of the oversized double wooden doors opens partially to greet Francis. A gloved hand reaches from behind the oaken slab and gently pushes the door open enough to allow Francis to enter. He vaults inside.

The warmth of the protected environment releases the strain on his body; he instinctively stretches his fingers inside his coat pockets, conscious that they no longer remain in a fisted position. The relief causes him to straighten from his bent position. He rises to see several people gathered in front of him.

Standing around the wood-burning stove are Mr. Foxall, Alexander Mather, Thomas Ault, Richard Whatcoat, and James Mayo. *This is most unusual.* Francis's thought brings the revelation that each in the group is smiling at him. *This also is most unusual; James never smiles before noon.* Francis responds to his discovery,

"Have I been uniformed of special occurrences?"

Mather chuckles. He quips,

"Seems ya've marched through it as of now."

The men in the group laugh aloud as they continue to rub their gloved hands over the iron heater. Francis nudges in. He looks to Thomas and Richard and inquires,

"Are we planning on joining the trades?"

"No, Francis; however, we are here to discuss a change in employment."

Thomas's reply has Francis thinking to himself, *whatever could this be?* Foxall approaches. He invites Francis,

"Follow me, Francis; I've something to show you."

Francis doesn't want to leave the warmth of the iron stove, but he obliges. Walking side by side, Mr. Foxall puts his stocky arm around the shoulders of the young preacher. Francis enjoys the warm reception. The pair walks past several bays containing feed for the horses, then a bay with a half-dozen chickens roaming and pecking at the hay-covered ground. Finally, the two stop in front of a horse stall. In it is Churchfield. Francis hadn't noticed, but Mather and the rest have followed them to the wooden cubicle housing Francis's four-legged friend. The horse nickers as Francis approaches. The men smile as Francis thinks to himself, *how does Churchfield know I am present? Amazing creature.*

From behind, Mather places his thick hand on Francis's left shoulder. Francis and Foxall turn to face the Scottish preacher. Thomas, James, and Richard form a semi-circle around the trio. Mather begins,

"Fr'dancis, ya' have been relieved of ya' duties wit' the West Bromwich society."

An uneasy feeling comes over Francis, an emotion of failure. He thinks back to past failures. Mather continues,

"We have chosen to replace ya'."

Once again, the announcement silences Francis; he bows his head. Mather goes on,

"We needn't look far for ya' replacement. We have chosen Thomas Ault to lead the class at Bromwich. In addition, Ah' apologize as the one who must bear'rd the news, but Mr. Foxall no longer has need of ya' services at the forge."

This proclamation brings a wearied exhale from Francis. The men in the group stand silent. Other than the sound of the chickens gently clucking in their search for seed, the room is quiet. Francis's thoughts, like the wind that blows outside, are frozen. He doesn't know what to think; his brain seems to have lost all function. With his right hand he rubs his left elbow, the move ending in folded arms. He blankly looks at Churchfield as the horse happily munches on his fodder. *Oh, to be of the animal creation.*

Mather breaks the silence.

"Fr'dancis, accordin' to these recent events, seems ya' might be available for other assignments. Might Ah' suggest abandonin' the trades and joinin' the itinerancy on trial?"

Francis's head rises quicker than a flame engulfing dry kindling. He is silent, but Mather still has a few words.

"Fr'dancis, ya' had to anticipate this was to come?"

"His projects have been lacking as of late."

James's slight has all the men laughing, including the somewhat amazed Francis. Richard comments,

"Francis, your eyes appear as if they've made discovery."

"Aye, as if you've discovered a distant planet."

Once again James has the group laughing, but more so he and Francis; it remains a private joke between the two.

Foxall once again places his hand on Francis's shoulder and offers,

"Francis, in reality, you have not been let go at the forge; neither is it final that you are relieved of your responsibilities with the Bromwich society. It is your decision. This opportunity, joining the traveling itinerants, is your choice."

The room remains silent. In the background, the driving wind outdoors has abated, replaced by the sound of Churchfield chewing on his morning snack. Francis considers the offer. *Would combine all that is best in my life, the societies, traveling about.* His thought wanders to the River Dove, *traveling about.* He responds,

"I shall accept."

In their jubilation the group embraces Francis, each coming forward, one by one, to offer a loving hug. As Foxall completes his solid clasp, an apprehension grips Francis. *I cannot afford a horse.* He voices his concern.

"Shall be a strain to gain a worthy animal."

"Already provided."

At the end of his reply, Foxall points in the direction of Churchfield. Francis is bewildered; *the creature is mine?* The puzzled tilt of his head prompts Pastor Mather to add,

"The animal has been yours for some time. Dartmouth gave it to you, but I felt otherwise. Had to force Foxall to keep it from your knowledge."

"Alex worried you would receive the gift and become comfortable."

Francis places his hands onto Thomas's shoulders. Looking him straight in the eye, Francis advises,

"Do care for the good people of Bromwich; they remain precious to this undercharge."[99]

---

[99] One less than skillful.

As with the transition from class leader to local preacher, the move from local preacher to full-time traveling preacher-on-trial brings deeper guidelines and responsibilities. Once Francis has time to share with his parents that he has a new career, Pastor Mather and James Glasbrook set up a meeting with him in the upstairs room of the converted Wheatley building.

The unusual snowfall has subsided; its more common accumulation of two inches cloaks the frozen soil. Three horses stand outside the Methodist meeting house in Bromwich. Tied to a mature oak tree, the animals huddle in an attempt to bring warmth. Inside the upper room, Pastor Mather, Pastor Glasbrook, and Francis sit in a loose semi-circle, heads bowed in prayer. The trio remains silent in contemplation.

After several minutes of silence, each raises his head in completion of his private supplications. Pastor Glasbrook offers,

> "Francis, Wesley sends word from Kingswood; he desires that I attend Bedford. Alex and myself agree, this is the Lord's open door to trial you here at home, in Staffordshire."

Francis is thankful for a position. He is happy that his assignment is within reach of his home, not so much for the luxury of living in his parents' cottage, but more in line with the fact that he will have the privilege of sharing his new experiences with his friends, and of course, with Nancy. Mather begins,

> "Although today's effort is far fr'dom triflin', James and Ah' inquire as to ya' casual opinion of this development."

Francis leans forward in his chair. He lowers his gaze toward the floor and pauses. Raising his eyes toward the itinerants, he begins,

> "The appointment on trial is rather humbling—satisfying, but bringing a slight apprehension. Nevertheless, 'tis also answered prayer. I felt torn for a time, partly in the trades, partly in ministry. The work as a local proved to be most satisfying; I enjoyed visiting the sick, and exhorting."

> "Mrs. Hanson?"

> "Yes. Dear lady. I am most confident Wolverhampton misses this light in Israel.[100] At the risk of sounding prophetic, it appeared eternal—the fate of my soul combined with a deep sense of calling, a calling that failed to subside. Not that I desired it. Ask William, Edward, or Richard;[101] on many occasions our dialogue hinged upon this concealed longing."

> "It was far fr'dom concealed, Fr'dancis. Quite obvious to many."

> "Fair enough; my gratitude for your kind words."

---

[100] A godly person.
[101] William Emery, Edward Hand, Richard Whatcoat.

Glasbrook turns the conversation in the direction of today's meeting.

"Well then, let us begin. Wesley requires much of the itinerant."

Francis settles back in his seat, prepared to absorb all he can. Glasbrook continues,

"No longer is it your business to preach so many times, or to take care of this or that society."

The comment comes as a surprise to Francis. *No longer to preach?* Noticing the slight dip in Francis's eyes as he attempts to grasp the deeper meaning of the comment, Glasbrook clarifies,

"You are to preach, Francis, but to save as many souls as you can—to bring as many sinners as you possibly can to repentance, and with all your power, to build them up in that holiness without which they cannot see the Lord."

Francis understands. Mather adds,

"Ya' must remember, Fr'dancis, a Methodist preacher is to mind every point, great and small, in the Methodist Discipline. Ya' shall require all ya' wheets about ya'."

Francis finds Alex's comment amusing, especially his thick accent on the word "wits." He smiles, and Glasbrook quips,

"Ya' wheets, Franky, ya' wheets."

Pastor Glasbrook's attempt at a Scottish accent isn't that bad. All three enjoy the light moment. Glasbrook continues,

"Wesley is adamant; his preachers will read."

"The list is extensive, Fr'dancis. Wesley has accumulated quite the library."

"Alex is correct; Wesley has stocked the shelves in London, Bristol, and Newcastle. He aims to educate the masses through his traveling preachers. The somewhat challenging list includes several divinity books, the Bible, Wesley's tracts, the works of Boehm and Francke.[102] There are also practical books on natural philosophy, astronomy, history, poetry, and Latin prose."

At this point, Francis appears slightly overwhelmed. He loves to read, but other than Wesley, the writers mentioned are unknown to him. Other than history, the subjects mentioned are foreign to this simple nailer from the West Midlands. Glasbrook can detect Francis's concern as the young preacher scrapes his top teeth on his bottom lip again. Glasbrook continues,

---

[102] William Boehm, German chaplain to the British Court, early eighteenth century. August Hermann Francke, one of the German Lutheran leaders at Halle. Boehm informed Wesley of Francke's writings.

"There are books on Latin verse; Greek prose, including the Greek New Testament; Greek verse, including Homer's Iliad; and the Hebrew Bible."

Francis is silent. He once again lowers his gaze, staring at the wooden floor of the meeting room. His shoulders droop slightly. Glasbrook emphasizes,

"Wesley requires five hours of reading each day."

Francis raises a thought, which he decides to voice.

"How then shall I visit the sick and each household if I am to spend the day reading? Shall it not benefit to read only one book, the Bible?"

"Fr'dancis, ya' must be more than the Apostle Paul. For even he required Timothy to 'br'ding the books, and the parchments.' Are ya' more than Paul?"

The door to the upper room opens; walking in is a young man, two years older than Francis. Mather waves his hand in a manner that invites Francis to hold the last thought on reading. Walking toward the group, the new arrival pulls up a chair.

The thinly built twenty-two-year-old man is shorter than Francis, with dark hair and eyebrows highlighting a round face. His thin nose is straight; however, Francis notices that it points slightly to the right side of the man's face. He is neatly dressed; Francis recognizes the fine workings and the cotton material of the coat. He surmises that the new arrival may come from a better, more polite[103] family.

Mather gives the introductions.

"Fr'dancis Asbur'dy, Ah' introduce to ya' Mr. William Orpe. William, Fr'dancis has recently been assigned to replace James on trial."

"My pleasure to meet you, Mr. Asbury."

"As well."

Glasbrook comments,

"I see that the weather has failed to keep you."

"It has."

"Very good. Francis, William is the son of a farmer from Ellastone."

This piques Francis's interest; he sits up in his chair. Glasbrook continues,

"Ellastone is not far from Ashbourne, situated along the Dove."

"Fr'dancis and Ah' rode very near there on our trips to Ashbourne."

"I remember it well."

Glasbrook turns toward Orpe to ask,

"How is Wesley?"

"He fares well. Our studies continue."

"William is a Hebrew linguist, one of the best in England."

---

[103] Polite company in this day was the well-to-do aristocracy.

Francis is impressed. Nodding his head, he considers, *quite young and already accomplished in Hebrew*. Remembering that the Hebrew Bible was one of Wesley's required readings, Francis ventures a thought: *Perhaps I shall read Hebrew . . . someday*. Glasbrook goes on,

> "William shall be assigned assistant to the Staffordshire circuit. The current assistant, Thomas Hanson, is being reassigned to Norwich."

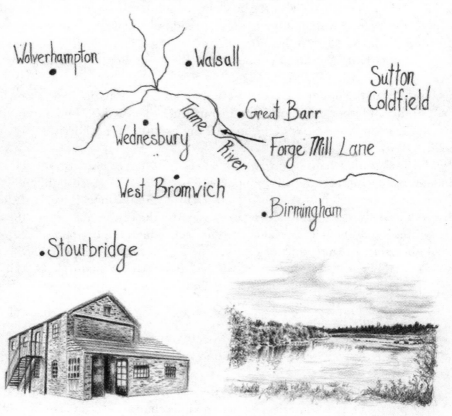

Pastors Mather and Glasbrook rise from their chairs. They secure their clothing for the harsh conditions outdoors as they gather their leather saddlebags and hats. Each looks to the other, nods, and tips his hat to the young men.

> "Francis, we shall obtain reading materials for your travels. I leave you with Wesley's sage advice. When a young itinerant mentioned that he had no taste for reading, Wesley's reply became conference record: 'Contract a taste for it by use, or return to your trade.' William, Staffordshire resides in your hands."

Upon Pastor Glasbrook's announcement, the two seasoned itinerants depart from the room. Francis is slightly uneasy; William Orpe looks barely old enough to be his boss. *The Lord is sovereign in His dealings,* Francis thinks, accepting the situation.

William leans forward in his chair as he opens the conversation.

"I understand we share a common loss."

Francis does not understand. He raises his shoulders, unsure of the comment's origin. William continues,

"Slightly more than a decade, and the emotions still bring pain. My dearest Anne."

Francis leans forward also; he's still slightly confused, but he senses a common ground. William divulges,

"I was nearly eleven when Anne passed. Only a few weeks, and she was gone. Anne was my sister. The beautiful river you became fond of on your trip to Ashbourne was beloved by my sister and me. It was never the same, subsequent to her departure."

Francis sits quietly reflecting the loss. Memories flood his mind: the main room window of the Asbury cottage, his mother sitting in tears, staring out of the window. He thought that such memories were lost to eternity. He was wrong. From a hidden place in his heart, shut away long ago, these emotions once again appear. He shares with William,

"I was very young, three years of age. I fail to remember Sarah; however, I remember Mother, weeping at our main room's window. For days . . . months . . . she would sit and weep."

The two sit in silence; neither has to say a word. Francis's previous reservations concerning William's age are no longer an issue. *To lose is to gain;* Francis's thought urges this confidence.

In this unguarded moment, William leans back in his chair and inquires of Francis,

"Do you worry about the preaching responsibilities?"

Francis finds this an odd transition. *Have been preaching for almost five years; not a difficult task.* He comments,

"I gather these duties appear as natural with one as accomplished as yourself."

William stands. Stroking the sleeves of his handsome cotton coat, he walks to the perimeter wall and ventures a look out the second-story window. He taps his hand on the window sill, begins, and then interrupts himself. He turns toward Francis.

"As natural as owning a fine colonial-made cotton coat."

He strokes the well-made garment. Francis scrapes his teeth again; the comment strikes him as not making sense. Francis once again is unsure as to who this William Orpe really is.

For the next five months, Francis and William handle the large Staffordshire circuit. They are clearly shorthanded, as the circuit encompasses not only the Black Country towns of Birmingham, Wolverhampton, Willenhall, Walsall, Wednesbury, Darlaston, and Bilbrook, but also an extended portion to the south in Worcestershire and Gloucestershire—an immensely large circuit spanning nearly 120 miles in a straight line. The pair does their best, Francis primarily in the Black Country, William handling Worcester and Gloucester.

In April of 1766, William and Francis receive word of an additional preacher assigned to Staffordshire. The plan is to meet him in Bilbrook on the first day of May. Francis is gladdened by this news; although he is happy with his new career, the task is somewhat limiting. In his mind, he hasn't ventured out. He is still living with his parents, still preaching in places that have heard him preach for the last five years. He is expecting more travel. He looks forward to the meeting in Bilbrook; *perhaps I shall be reassigned to the low country.*

On Thursday morning, May 1, 1766, Francis sets off for the familiar village. Upon his arrival, several of the youngsters of Bilbrook race off to spread the word: Pastor Asbury has arrived.

Settling Churchfield with an ample supply of grass reeds, Francis heads for the little building that serves as the Bilbrook meeting room. In the distance he can hear the children; two dozen of them now race toward him. He smiles and waves to his admirers, then darts inside the building. Laughing as he turns toward the room, he unexpectedly finds himself face to face with an older gentleman. He offers,

"My deepest apologies; trifling with the children."

"Maintains your age."

Francis smiles, surprised that the older gentleman approves of his teasing. He inquires,

"From London?"

"Yes, Wesley sent for me. The name is John Poole."

"Francis Asbury."

The front door bursts open and the children pour into the room, the invading tads surrounding both itinerants. Raising their elbows above the sweaty faces, one by one, John and Francis each rub the head of a child. The selected child squeals with exuberance; the process repeats itself often. The preachers have a good laugh.

Standing at the doorway watching the juvenile proceedings, William Orpe lets out a loud and hearty laugh. It's an effort, but Francis and John manage to turn toward their partner. Francis quips,

"Enter upon risk of injury . . ."

William smiles as he replies,

"Perhaps we shall gain the extra help for the low round."[104]

The Bilbrook class leader arrives. Standing behind William, he announces,

"Children, we must depart outdoors."

Amidst the complaints, the children begin to remove themselves from the room. Francis taps one last head; the little boy beams, his missing-tooth smile adding to the entertainment.

Quiet having arrived at last, William begins.

"John Poole, I assume. Francis and I welcome your willingness to aid in our undertaking. Wesley has summoned me to Bristol; I shall leave on the morrow. Francis, it is my intention that you remain in the Black Country; John, you shall make haste for Worcester. You may depart immediately."

Turning from William in disappointment, one thought clouds Francis: *This is far from productive.* He walks to the window at the back of the room. The departure fails to stop William as he and John make last-minute preparations for his trip south. Upon completion, William requests,

"Francis?"

William's voice is not what Francis wants to hear. He turns to face the one in charge of his ministry efforts. William informs him,

"This eve, we have been invited to the class meeting with Bilbrook. The society longs for our attendance. Tomorrow, once I have left for Bristol, you may continue in your familiar rounds."

Francis purses his lips; it is difficult, but he says nothing, only nods a less-than-hearty agreement. A sense of rejection remains with Francis for the remainder of the day and into the evening. He lies in bed this night, toying with what he calls *other options . . .*

The following day at the Bilbrook class meeting, William instructs Francis to lead, which he does. The local society is familiar with the young man from Great Barr. The tiny class of twelve adults finishes within an hour. At evening's end, several ask William to exhort. William begs to postpone this to another visit, but the people are unwilling to accept his suggestion.

---

[104] The portion of the Staffordshire itinerant circuit residing to the south, in the counties of Worcestershire and Gloucestershire.

Several attempts to depart are unsuccessful. The Hebrew scholar is clearly avoiding speaking; *this is odd.* Francis does not voice his thought. William finally relents and agrees to speak.

At the center of the small room, William stands with his back to the only window. The fidgeting of the young man's arms and hands goes unnoticed by the Bilbrook faithful; however, this nervous twitching does not escape the notice of Francis. William steps forward and begins, his voice trembling.

"The ancient Hebrew word translating for compassion is the word *hessed.* *Hessed* is compassion or another attribute, loving kindness."

Francis and the others are delighted with the teaching topic. William's voice continues to shake when he speaks, but the beginning of the subject brings promise. William continues,

"*Hessed* is an attribute of the Almighty. His unconventional love and concern for humanity."

There is a pause.

The pause after this last sentence is uncomfortable. Several men in the group look away from the speaker, unaccustomed to their preachers stumbling when speaking. William continues again,

"It is God's kindness and goodness, revealed though the covenant relationship with Israel."

William's voice gives clear indication that he is nervous. Again, an uncomfortable silence follows.

Francis is nervous for his friend. He folds his hands in front of himself and taps the heel of his boot against the wall on which he leans. Pushing his back off the wall, he decides to help William.

"The Father seeks after us."

Relieved that Francis has jumped in, William responds,

"It is as Francis describes."

Silence.

Realizing that William is not doing very well, Francis takes over. He moves to the center of the room and attempts a dialogue with William. For nearly thirty minutes, the technique works well enough to bring proper closure to the subject. Francis closes the time with a hymn and prayer. At evening's end, the class departs, leaving William and Francis with the man and wife who will provide shelter for the night. The four depart, none speaking of the evening's event.

The following morning bursts with a cool May breeze. The springtime temperatures allow for comfortable travel on horseback; *one of my favorite seasons.* Francis rejoices at the glorious sun as it rises. As William and Francis prepare their horses for departure, Churchfield nickers his usual greeting, shaking his head from left to right as Francis rubs the animal's nose. William comments,

"As jubilant as the children for your arrival. Myself, as well. Thank you, Francis, for aiding me last evening. Shall see you the Sabbath of the twenty-fifth, end of month in Wednesbury."

William climbs atop his horse and departs before Francis can respond. *He kindly acknowledged my help. He fails to be a preacher.* Francis's two thoughts remain for most of the morning.

En route for Wolverhampton, Francis has an epiphany. *Rather unreasonable to plough old furrows; the Black Country shall keep.* Francis brings Churchfield to a complete halt. He pauses, considering. After a minute of silence, the horse no doubt wondering what is happening, Francis turns the animal completely around and heads north toward the village of Stafford. Catching a dry and dusty pack-horse road, he ventures for new territory, despite the fact that there is no Wesleyan society in Stafford.

Near the ancient town, he veers slightly west to catch the River Sow. This move also clears him of the numerous marshes and wetlands that lie northwest of the village. Crossing the river, he aims northward, for a hamlet by the name of Stone.

The seven-mile trek through the dense hardwood forest takes him several hours. Nearing dusk, Francis spots the Stone parish church, St. Michael's. It is a simple structure, recently built. The large stone-tower entrance resides in the center of the front facade. The building runs straight back in a rectangular, straightforward design. The current building, constructed eight years ago, is part of the parish which began near the end of the seventh century, when the Persian King, Wulfhere, murdered his two sons for converting to Christianity. Their grieving mother commissioned the building on the site where she buried her offspring under a great pile of stones.

Thankful that he has reached the town before dark, Francis enters St. Michael's. There are a few people sitting in the wooden pews. As Francis takes in the view, the newly completed altar catches his attention. Behind the granite high altar is a three-panel sculpture. The stone triptych depicts Mother Mary holding baby Jesus in one end panel, and St. Michael in the other. The larger center panel displays the risen Jesus. *Beautiful workmanship, to the glory of God.*

In Stone, Francis seeks to furrow new ground. The handful of people in the church receive him well enough to accept his offer to exhort. As he does so, his efforts fall on mostly restricted ears; only one elderly man seems slightly interested. To Francis, *despite the lack of success, it is perhaps a beginning.* With no offer of housing for the night, Francis and Churchfield enjoy an evening's sleep under the springtime sky. In the morning Francis moves on, north again. He decides to visit a town he thinks could benefit from his preaching, the village of Newcastle-under-Lyme.

Newcastle-under-Lyme resides in the Potteries, a region that is becoming the pottery-making capital of the British Isles and Europe. The industry began here in the early seventeenth century.

Approaching the town, Francis is greeted by a large stone church building; it is the Anglican church of St. Giles, built in the late twelfth century. Beyond the towering structure that sits on a sloping hill, Francis can see a wider-than-normal street, packed with drivers moving their livestock to market. Several holding areas are roped off, many already inhabited by the animals. In addition to the pottery kilns that dot the region on the outskirts of the town, Newcastle also participates in the ironworking industry. Francis enjoys a welcoming view, passing several small family-run nail forges, much like the operations back home. The noisy shops bang and belch their industry around and above Newcastle.

Entering the grounds of St. Giles, Francis dismounts in time to catch several men and women running into the church building. He quickly ties Churchfield and proceeds indoors.

The three women and four men inside are jubilant, all talking at the same time. Francis surmises, *they must have fantastic news to share.* Six other men listen intently, trying to decipher the information.

From the side of the altar, the black-robed Anglican priest appears and hurries toward the group. Aware of his arrival, the group compose themselves, and quiet returns to the building.

The priest inquires,

"What has brought such a flurry?"

"Harold has gained employment - -

At Wedgwood's in Burslem."

The young woman who answers cannot contain her enthusiasm; she quickly takes Harold's face in both her hands and kisses him. The priest gives a disbelieving look; the rest of the group also falls silent with surprise. The newly employed young man, Harold, is reaping the benefits of a local hero.

The English potter, Josiah Wedgwood, is a native of Burslem. Like most families, Josiah's is a hardworking one, with a long tradition in the pottery industry, dating back more than one hundred years. He is a creative individual; for the last decade, the thirty-year-old one-legged potter has been experimenting with several different types of clay. The latest trial has brought forth a unique discovery, the details of which are known only to the family. Experimenting with Cornish clay and stone, Josiah has created a beautiful cream color for his earthenware. Joining this new color with his fashionable flair for shape and glaze, he has created an unmatched product, which has recently caught the attention of Queen Charlotte, the wife of King George III. In response, Josiah has not only received a handsome contract to make pottery for the King, he has also decided to name his discovery Queen's Ware, in honor of the King's wife.

Francis continues to watch as the Anglican priest inquires,

"Harold, this is most welcome. When shall you initiate?"

"Day after the Sabbath."

Harold's face beams. The priest once again inquires,

"And your parents, have they affirmed this advantage?"

"They have."

"Well then, I've one admonition for you. Recognize the wise words of the Apostle Paul: You would do well to be in the world, but not of the world."

Standing amidst the group as they receive the sage advice of the Anglican priest, one man who accompanies the grateful Harold is not happy with the biblical advice. With a barely concealed smirk, the man who appears as an uncle or older relative to Harold offers,

"Harold, you have heard it said of Wedgwood, 'Fashion is infinitely superior to merit.' I perceive this is precisely the nature of Paul's warning."

Harold nods in agreement; however, he is alone. The group, the uncle's wife included, does not appreciate that the uncle would smother the enthusiasm of this happy event. Displeased with her husband, the wife quips,

"Wedgwood also pronounced, 'Few ladies you know dare venture at anything out of the common style till authorized by their betters.' "

The priest leads the group with an amused smile; the others follow suit. The wife tips her head toward Harold, who does his best to keep silent. Turning from his wife, the uncle notices Francis standing at the entrance to the church. He asks of the young man,

"Been watching the proceedings?"

"I have."

The men wave the young stranger into the room. Francis approaches the group and introduces himself, as do the others. The priest, John Fernyhough, questions Francis,

"Great Barr, you've come a great distance from home. Away on business?"

"Of sorts."

"What sort of business?"

Francis hesitates; he has no indication of the priest's reaction toward the Wesleyan movement. If he is hostile to it, persecution could result. If he is friendly, acceptance could easily occur. A Scripture comes to Francis's mind: *Therefore whoever confesses Me before men, him I will also confess before My Father who is in heaven. But whoever denies Me before men, him I will also deny before My Father who is in heaven.*[105] Francis proceeds,

"I am an itinerant for John Wesley."

All in the room look to the priest; he has lowered his eyes to stare at the beautiful stone floor. The movement pushes Francis to worry. Raising his eyes toward Francis, the priest responds,

"Have we a word of exhortation?"

Francis eyes the group; their warm facial expressions embrace his deepest yearnings, to preach the Word. He replies,

"I do."

Although the receptive gathering is small, Francis clearly senses the Lord's leading in this wandering-about venture. Despite the insecure feeling of preaching in front of an ordained priest, he does his best. The Anglican priest, too, is clearly receptive to the idea of a Wesleyan preacher offering a word to his congregation. All receive it well. After spending the night at the home of the Anglican priest, Francis sets out again.

Continuing in his desire to wander about, Francis heads east. *Perhaps Ashbourne by nightfall.* The crispness of the morning air is fading fast as the sun rises well above the horizon. Aiming in the direction of the welcoming orb, Francis will travel through portions of the ash and lime-tree forest, the sturdy hardwoods appearing as an impenetrable arena. However, before he enters the well-shaded portion of his journey, he pauses to admire the numerous trees that surround him. Never before has he seen such beauty; the artistry escaped him upon his arrival the afternoon before. The branches of the trees are completely covered with oversized bunches of the downward-facing pale pink flowers. The paper-thin blooms with multiple petals discreetly hide the few remaining green leaves of the trees. They remind Francis of the apple trees in the Turton family orchard in West Bromwich, but he suspects they're different. Again the thought arises, *all to the glory of God.*

The undulating ground signals to Francis that he soon will gain elevation as he travels. The stoic edge of the ash forest patiently awaits his arrival. *Ashbourne by nightfall;* the thought once again brings comfort.

His twilight arrival at the meeting house in Ashbourne unexpectedly finds him greeted by a familiar face. The advancing evening fails to hinder the stunning blue eyes of Sarah Crosby, *the woman preacher.* Francis dismounts from Churchfield.

"Greetings, Mrs. Crosby."

"A most welcome hello, Mr. Asbury. Seems a far turn from Great Barr."

---

[105] Matthew chapter 10, verses 32–33.

" 'Tis that. Might I inquire of whom a warm meal for myself and fodder for Churchfield may be obtained?"

"Would be most difficult to obtain a meal by standard process in Ashbourne. A preacher like yourself shall endure several of the town's women pouring forth a free dinner."

"Then I shall endure."

Sarah directs Francis inside the meeting room. The dimly lit room reveals several families standing in two loose huddles. One teenage girl walks the perimeter of the room, lighting the wax tapers that sit in little iron holders. The fifteen people, teenage girl included, turn in unison as Sarah announces,

"Seems Great Barr has freed one of its own."

As the jubilant men and women advance, Francis perceives that he may want to brace for the impact. The loving reception escorts the wearied young man into the center of the room, where Francis is greeted by an elderly, thinly built gentleman. Extending a dry, pale-white hand, Mr. Chalkey insists,

"Francis, please take a seat; the wife shall gather a substantial meal for a tired itinerant. Harry and Edmond, conduct yourselves to the back room and fetch a table for Francis."

Do I appear tired? Francis keeps this thought to himself as Chalkey's two friends depart. The resulting void in the crowd around him is promptly filled with two young boys. One, in clothing that borders on threadbare, approaches. Scratching his head, as his miniature partner weaves through the adults to maneuver alongside his companion, the threadbare boy inquires of Francis,

"Might Charles and I fodder your horse?"

"You may."

Francis grins at his little helpers. The mature Sarah Crosby approaches; Francis finds a satisfying comfort in her company. Although he has yet to reconcile with her as a preacher, he admits to himself, *her wise words bring a soothing comfort; an older sister I never had.* She inquires,

"We are a plain people, Francis, with little in the way of luxury. Shall you desire residence for the evening?"

"I shall."

Thomas and Edmond arrive with the table, sliding the thirty-inch-square oak top within inches of Francis, his knees nearly touching the underside of the scratched wooden surface. Another man delivers two chairs, placing one next to Francis, the other across from him. He invites Sarah to take the second seat, which she does.

Sarah's blue eyes communicate a spiritual excitement; Francis is drawn toward this sister in Israel. She opens the conversation.

> "Mrs. Ryan and Miss Bosanquet have summoned me to The Cedars."
> "Shall you go?"
> "I believe so. I am prepared to leave in the morning."

Two women convey three plates full of food to the table. The pleasant smell triggers hunger pains in Francis's stomach. He instinctively pushes on his abdomen in hopes that it will not utter an embarrassing bellow. The brimming plates once again catch his attention. The generous offering consists of a plate of venison, a plate of summer vegetables, and a final plate of fruit. Francis swallows hard as his mouth salivates. Sarah politely ignores his distracted reactions. After giving thanks for the food, Francis begins to feast.

Sarah offers,

> "I long to return to London. Sarah and Mary once again inspire an admirable work."
> "What of Mary's parents? Have they had reconciliation with their daughter?"
> "Somewhat; her father assisted in the acquisition of the home. His admonition was fairly clear: 'If a mob should pull your house about your ears, I cannot hinder them.' "

Francis nearly chokes on the father's cautionary words. He wipes his lips and smiles at Sarah, who returns the favorable gesture. Reaching her hand across the table, she touches Francis's forearm. The muscular limb enjoys the gentle touch.

> "You must pay visit sometime to the Cedars. Mary, Sarah, and I would welcome your calling."
> "If the Lord wills . . ."

The remainder of the evening finds Francis engulfed by the townspeople, as each one is eager to converse. The subjects flow from the seriousness of Bible references to the lightness of prime fishing spots for trout along the River Dove. The evening ends with an invitation for Francis to stay at a couple's home.

The next morning, as Francis enjoys a hearty meal of eggs and bacon, one of the couple's children startles Francis and his generous hosts as he bolts into the home. Bent over, hands on his knees and out of breath, the messenger gasps as he conveys the reason for his arrival.

> "A letter . . . for Asbury. Francis - -
> Asbury."

The young preteen boy of the house, the couple's oldest, hands Francis the written correspondence. Francis is unsure, but the letter is indeed addressed to him. He opens it and reads,

Dear Frank,

Francis pauses, surprised by the unique salutation. Surmising an urgency in the writer's tone by this shortened version of his given name, he reads on.

> *After having so firmly engaged you to supply Hampton and Bilbrook at the end of the week, I could not but be surprised to hear you are turned dictator. Certainly, you must either think I was not able to see the places properly supplied or else that I am fickle and inconsistent, and therefore you expect to hear my new mind. I take this opportunity of informing you that I shall not be at those places, and shall expect you to see them supplied in due time. It is true another preacher is come, but he goes immediately into the low round. In the meantime, I wish you would hearken to those verses of Hesiod,*[106] *"Let him attend his charge, and careful trace the right-lined furrow; gaze no more around, but have his mind employ'd upon the work." Then I should hope to hear that your profiting would appear unto all men. You have lost enough already by gazing all around; for God's sake, do so no more. I wish that I might see you on your return from Hampton on Sunday evening. I shall be at Wednesbury, if it pleases God. I have a little concern to mention. I hope you'll call.*
>
> *I remain yours affectionately,*
> *W. Orpe*

Francis stares silently at the handwritten note. Lowering the hand holding the missive, he rubs his forehead with his free hand. The mother of the house inquires,

"Everythin' all right, Pastor Asbury?"

Francis moves toward the kitchen table. He asks,

"Have you a writing implement?"

"We have."

---

[106] A Greek farmer-poet from the eighth century BC. He lived about the same time as Homer, author of the *Iliad*.

The father moves to the shelf above the fire pit and takes down a wooden box. Placing the box on the table, he opens it and removes a quill pen and a jar of ink. He sets both items onto the table and invites Francis to sit. Francis does so carefully, not wanting to bump the table; black walnut ink is indelible.

Lifting the pen, Francis dips the quill and begins to write on the back of Orpe's letter.

> *My brother, if the same you be,*
> *I hope in time appointed you'll visit me.*

Francis stops writing. He raises his eyes and stares at the room's ceiling. Tapping his left foot on the floor, he contemplates. *Perhaps a detailing of my travel.* He resumes,

> *May 1 for Stafford*
> *And then for Stone*
> *And then for Newcastle*
> *And then for Ashbourne*
> *And then William Gibson*
> *at Birmingham*

He is recounting his past two weeks and his plans for the next few days. He pauses, then sets the pen back into the wooden box. Blowing on the letter, he waits for the ink to dry.

Setting the paper on the tabletop, he rises from his chair.

"I must be riding. Thank you for your kindness."

Francis lifts the letter, folds it in half, and tucks it into his coat pocket. He dons his hat and makes his way outdoors.

William's letter has clearly upset Francis. He abandons his trip to Birmingham, the correspondence changing his plans. The words of Pastor Glasbrook resonate in his mind: *"Above all, if you labor with us in our Lord's vineyard, it is needful that you should do that part of the work which we advise, at those times and places which we judge most for His glory."* Francis worries as he aims for home.

The tree-lined edge of Newton Village has never appeared as agreeable as on the Saturday morning he arrives. Francis hurls the negative thoughts aside in favor of *Mother's warm dinners*, the thought lifting his mood.

At his father's barn, Francis dismounts and leads Churchfield inside to eat. He ties his traveling companion to a wooden support post standing in the middle of the structure. Removing the horse's saddle and bridle, Francis turns to fetch his father's wooden wheelbarrow. He fills it with hay and places it within reach of the loyal animal. The horse eats as his owner obtains a wooden bucket to fill with water. With Churchfield's needs attended to, Francis heads into the cottage.

Elizabeth rejoices as her son steps into the main room of the home.

"My Francis!"

Francis welcomes his mother's embrace. For the first time since opening the letter from Orpe, he relaxes. His mother inquires,

"Here long?"

"Unfortunately, not long. Shall attend a meeting in Wednesbury on the morrow."

It isn't until the completion of dinner that Francis feels comfortable enough to share about the letter. His parents are divided on the subject. Elizabeth naturally takes Francis's side, believing that God is calling her son to new territory, while Joseph leans more in the direction of obedience to Pastor Glasbrook's advice. Regardless of their steady opinions, both Elizabeth and Joseph love their son, saying,

"We support your decisions, Francis."

***

Entering the familiar building on Meeting Street, Francis kindly accepts the greetings from the members of the Wednesbury Wesleyan society. One portly gentleman inquires,

"Preaching this morning?"

"Do not believe that I am."

"I see."

The disappointed man waddles off. Francis moves to a chair on the far side of the room while the twenty-five attendees mill about. Sitting uncomfortably, Francis finds himself going in and out of conversations. He is not thrilled about meeting William here among those who know him best. *I haven't a choice;* he attempts to make peace with the circumstances. Laying his head against the side wall of the room, he closes his eyes in another attempt to escape tonight's requirement. He begins to drift.

"Francis?"

The familiar, delicate voice brings a smile to Francis's face; he opens his eyes and responds,

"Nancy! I expected to call upon you after the service."

"Several made mention of your arrival last eve. I assumed you would attend Wednesbury or Hampton. I'm happy to find you first round."

"I am happy to find you also, Nancy."

"Some mention otherwise."

"Oh?"

"Some talk of Ashbourne."

Her mention of Ashbourne has a stinging tinge of disappointment. As she turns abruptly and walks away, Francis is uncertain of her intentions. He rises to follow, but happens upon the doorway as the door swings open.

In walks William Orpe, dressed in his fine cotton jacket; with him is John Poole, the other itinerant assigned to the Staffordshire low rounds. Francis stands still as the men spot him and angle in his direction. Francis considers William as he thinks to himself, *he is one attached to finery.* Reaching Francis, William opens with,

"Glad you have attended."

Francis bows his head to acknowledge the greeting. William continues,

"I believe you have received my correspondence?"

"I have."

"Francis, I constructed the missive as clear as I could. The success of our circuit demands loyalty to the assignment. Rash decisions have no place - "

Francis raises his hand to interrupt.

"The decision was far from rash, William. Hampton and Bilbrook I have attended long before you were **preaching**."

William purses his lips and draws a deep breath through his thin nostrils. The comment upsets him, especially Francis's emphasis on the word "preaching." *He thinks because he is a better speaker in public that I fail to preach.* William holds this thought to himself. He responds,

"Very well, although it is upsetting that you should avoid that which is familiar. I have need of your **preaching** elsewhere."

"What of Derbyshire?"

"Derby shall fare well on its own. Francis, you seem unaware that as an itinerant you are on trial."

"You seem unaware that the itinerancy's success is enhanced most by furrowing new ground. Are we to remain in Bilbrook and Hampton and grow comfortable?"

William's response has triggered further anger in Francis. *You are barely more than my age! Moreover, you lack as a preacher!* His face reddens. Sensing the tension in Francis's demeanor, William responds,

"Brother Asbury, I expect you to remain. Hampton and Bilbrook as well as Wednesbury, Walsall, and Bromwich require you."

A deluge of thoughts runs through Francis's mind. *Hampton and Bilbrook, these are well on their own. Ingrate! I saved you from an awful engagement, and you incite. Disrespectful!* Francis turns to remove himself from the pair. In full view of Nancy, he storms outside through the front door. Struggling with her own emotions, she holds back tears.

The next two months find Francis making his assigned rounds in the Black Country. He is not pleased, but he decides to obey. *I shall not risk my itinerancy.*

***

In the northern portion of Great Britain lies Yorkshire, the largest county in England. Because of the shire's large size, it is partitioned into four sections: north, south, east, and west. Easily one of the most picturesque settings in the entire nation, the county's majestic rural landscape bespeaks the splendor of its Creator. Within the western slice of this northern paradise shines a town known for its successful woolen trade. This heavenly hamlet, nestled in a valley surrounded by verdant hills and bordering on the north side of the River Aire, is the community of Leeds.

Leading into the town from the south, a line of black-robed and plain-clothed riders on horseback slowly makes its way across the cast-iron bridge that hangs above the River Aire. Crossing Leeds Bridge, the line of Wesleyan itinerants stretches into town, all the way up Briggate Street to Holy Trinity Church. The holy entourage is greeted by many of the town's inhabitants.

Started in 1721, the construction of the church required five years to complete. Holy Trinity is largely the result of the generous offer of Lady Elizabeth Hastings, sister-in-law to Selina, Countess of Huntingdon. Lady Elizabeth's donation amounted to slightly more than 25 percent of the total funds needed to build the stately gritstone structure. The nearby Meanwood Quarry supplied the oversized stone material for the main portion of the edifice. Five towering sections of a square wooden spire of diminishing dimensions climb 180 feet above one end of the rectangular structure. Both sides of the elongated building are wrapped with several flat pilasters, the stone columns rising up to the simple yet decorative cornice line, forty feet above the ground. A detached clearstory window resides between each of these vertical uprights.

One by one, each of the Wesleyan preachers guides his horse to the magnificent structure, dismounts, and secures a location to tie his four-legged companion. The travel-wearied itinerants immediately find themselves in unexpected conversation with several enterprising local lads. These adolescent entrepreneurs have set themselves up around the church, each standing near a tree and an oaken bucket, guarding his treasured container of water and a nearby pile of fodder for the arriving horses. These crafty young men realize the need and, more specifically, the generosity of the preachers who consistently exhibit the precept in the Bible's book of Proverbs, "A righteous man regards the life of his animal."[107] After securing a choice spot for each of their horses, the preachers enter the church building.

As with other Wesleyan conferences, the mood borders on festive as each arrival adds a new voice to the hymn in progress. Several of the townspeople excitedly become a part of the celebrative festivities, these too joining in the resounding praise to the Almighty. Although the locals will leave once the conference begins, they are welcome to join in the singing—for this is not a formal gathering at this point in the proceedings; the opening of the conference is a beautiful supplication by all in the Wesleyan community. After nearly an hour of rejoicing in song, the Leeds conference begins and the local members depart.

Standing in front of the hand-carved wooden altar, John Wesley raises his hands and offers,

> "On this Tuesday afternoon, the twelfth of August, in the year of our Lord one thousand seven hundred and sixty-six, I inquire of those present: What preachers are admitted this year?"

Rising to his feet, the saintly John Pawson straightens his coat hem and responds,

> "William Orpe, William Ellis, James Brownfield, Samuel Woodcock, James Longbottom, Joseph Pilmoor, William Barker, Thomas Simpson, Duncan Wright, John Dillon, James Rea, and Richard Bourke."

Wesley invites,

> "William Orpe, please step forward."

The small, handsomely dressed young man steps forward. Wesley continues,

> "William Orpe, have you faith in Christ?"
>
> "Yes."
>
> "Are you going on to perfection?"
>
> "Yes."
>
> "Do you expect to be perfected in love in this life; are you groaning after it?"
>
> "Yes."
>
> "Are you resolved to devote yourself wholly to God and His work?"
>
> "Yes."

The questions continue as Wesley probes about Methodist doctrines.

> "Do you know the Methodist plan, the rule of the society and bands, and do you keep them?"

---

[107] Proverbs chapter 12, verse 10.

And more,

> "Do you take no snuff, tobacco, drams? Do you constantly attend the church and sacrament?"

Wesley's line of questioning is consistent with his administrative character.

> "Have you read the Minutes? Are you willing to conform to them?
>
> "Will you preach every morning and evening, endeavoring not to speak too loud or too long and not lolling with your elbows? Will you diligently and earnestly instruct the children, and visit from house to house?"

Wesley questions not only William, but also each of the preachers admitted for this year. Finishing with the new itinerants, who are now fully established members of the traveling evangelists, Wesley moves on. He assigns some of the existing preachers to act as supervisors of one of the forty circuits in England, Ireland, Wales, and Scotland.

> "William Orpe, I shall appoint you assistant of the Staffordshire circuit."

He appoints to each circuit not only assistants, or supervising preachers in charge, but also additional preachers. James Glasbrook heads for Bedfordshire, John Poole remains with Orpe in Staffordshire, and the newly elected Joseph Pilmoor is to travel the Cornwall East circuit.

Joseph Pilmoor is a striking young man, six years older than Francis. His above-average height, stocky build, and deep voice easily invite a favorable response to his life-changing message. The twenty-seven-year-old from Fadmoor in the scenic lands of North Riding, Yorkshire, has known of the Savior since the age of sixteen, experiencing the transformation under the preaching of John Wesley. He never lived with his real father, who denied he was the partner of Pilmoor's mother, Sarah. The father sued Sarah for defamation of character, but he lost the suit. Sarah did not marry until Pilmoor turned eleven. From then until age sixteen, he worked on a farm as a laborer. At the time of his conversion, a relationship with Wesley opened the door for Pilmoor to attend Wesley's Kingswood School near Bristol. Upon completion of his studies, the young man skilled in Latin and Hebrew was drawn to the itinerant ministry, accepting the invitation to preach the eastern portion of the Cornwall circuit on trial. This year he accepts full admission to the itinerancy, gaining the assignment to the Cornwall East circuit once again.

On the north side of the sanctuary, Pilmoor talks with several young men. He is naturally drawn to the Methodist society because of his attraction to the class meetings, which abandon hierarchy of social status. The landowner worshiping next to the laborer—this is the system for Pilmoor. His family squabbles and the absence of a father drive him to yearn for recognition among the more notable of civil society.

Wesley stands down from the altar for a break in the proceedings. With a coach's enthusiasm, he darts for the illustrious gathering of Methodism's future leaders and places a hand onto the shoulder of one young man, slightly shorter than Joseph Pilmoor, who leads the conversation. The young man falls silent as Wesley inquires,

> "Dear Tommy, before long you shall cover the entire coastline of our great nation."
> "Wherever the Lord shall call, to spread the eternal blessing."
> "Indeed, Tommy."

Thomas Rankin is advancing rapidly as Wesley's martinet[108] of choice. With sergeant-like discipline, Rankin carries out Wesley's requests, dealing head-on with insubordinate class leaders and preachers. Wesley's quip touches on the fact that this year's assignment moves the businesslike young man from the scenic coastlines of the southwest coast at Cornwall to the east coast at Lincolnshire. Wesley's new appointment for Rankin is not by accident. With a surgeon's precision, Wesley brings his single-minded enforcer to a new front. Wesley eyes the other young men standing with Rankin and Pilmoor as he gives his sage advice.

> "Nothing can bring hurt, if you remain calm, mild, and gentle to all men."

Rankin smiles as he replies,

> "The way of duty is the way of safety."

Wesley thrives on these words. Rankin's military-like approach to religion is a clear reflection of his father, a blameless and devoutly religious man who early on surrounded the child with a rigorous philosophy of religious habits and practices. The death of his father when he was seventeen brought Rankin a yearning for spiritual significance. Fortunately for him, the Wesleyan society in his Scottish village of Dunbar boasted of men much like his father—ex-military men who applied their disciplined manner to their faith. Growing up in the presence of these retired soldiers, Rankin gained further affirmation of his style of faith.

Also in this promising group of young leaders is Richard Boardman. He too is the same age as Pilmoor, twenty-seven, and both are one year younger than Rankin. Boardman will spend his third year in the itinerancy in the York circuit. He is pained that he will not be traveling with his friend, Joseph Pilmoor.

Wesley departs, returning to the front of the altar and raising his hands to signal a return to the business of the conference. The men's volume slowly falls to silence as they take their seats on the ebony-stained pew benches.

---

[108] Disciplinarian

Confident that he has the full attention of the room's inhabitants, Wesley announces,

> "We shall dive into more earthly affairs. Why is field preaching often omitted?"

In the front row of the pew, John Pawson rises to respond to Wesley.

> "To please the stewards."

> "To please society."

The additional response is given by Alexander Mather. Wesley replies to both,

> "Let it be so no more."

The questions and answers continue for some time, with inquiries into several items important to the preachers: "How late may the evening preaching begin? Never, except in harvest-time, later than seven. How long should a love feast last? Never above an hour and half; everyone should be at home by nine. Are all the preachers merciful to their beasts? Perhaps not. Everyone ought: one, never to ride hard, and two, to see with his own eyes his horse rubbed, fed, and bedded."

Wesley pauses from the mundane issues. Wiping his brow with the back of his hand, he breathes deeply and proceeds.

> "An earnest matter continues to lie before us. Shall Robert Williams preach among us?"

The room is no longer silent; several itinerants rise to their feet and voice their opinions. The responses form two camps: "No, we are not satisfied as to his moral character," and "Yes, he shows great progress in his moral character." Wesley acknowledges their assessment.

Robert Williams is a plain man, from Ireland, straightforward in his religious dealings. He enjoys preaching, but unfortunately, he also enjoys voicing his opinions in an impatient and fiery manner. Wesley responds to the men who question Williams's reputation.

> "We must proceed with caution. I shall reinstate appointment of Robert Williams, placing him in the east.[109] I shall also continue to maintain, he must refrain from criticizing the clergy. It proves sinful. If the blind leaders are leading the blind, so be it. It is foolishness; never shall it do well—only harm."

Once again Wesley pauses, this time closing his eyes and tilting his head toward the ceiling. To the itinerants, it is obvious that he is in silent prayer. Wesley opens his eyes and offers,

> "My authority has been questioned."

---

[109] Northeast, Belfast and Coleraine.

The only noise in the building is the gentle summer wind that bounces the limbs of a mature forest tree off one of the clearstory windows on the south side of the building.

Wesley continues,

> "The question has been asked, 'What power is this which you exercise over all the Methodists in Great Britain and Ireland?' May I give answer to those who oppose my leadership?"

The men silently give their approval. Wesley answers,

> "Very well. Zinzendorf loved to keep all things close. I love to do all things openly. I will therefore tell you all I know of the matter, taking it from the very beginning. In 1738, two or three persons who desired to flee from the wrath to come, and then seven or eight more, came to me in London and desired me to advise and pray with them. I said, 'If you will meet on Thursday night, I will help you as well as I can.' More and more desired to meet with them, till they were increased to many hundreds. The case was afterwards the same at Bristol, Kingswood, Newcastle, and many other parts of England, Scotland, and Ireland. It may be observed, the desire was on their part, not mine. My desire was to live and die in retirement. But I did not see that I could refuse them my help, and be guiltless before God."

Wesley's mention of the year 1738 is significant in that this was the year of the creation of the band society rules. Those who are questioning Wesley's leadership also dislike that he approves and disapproves of men seemingly by personal whim. Wesley responds to these complaints as well.

> "What is that power? It is a power of admitting into and excluding from the societies under my care; of choosing and removing stewards; of receiving or not receiving helpers; of appointing them when, where, and how to help me, and of desiring any of them to meet me when I see good. And as it was merely in obedience to the Providence of God and for the good of the people that I at first accepted this power, which I never sought—nay, a hundred times labored to throw off—so it is on the same considerations, not for profit, honor, or pleasure that I use it at this day.
>
> "But several gentlemen are much offended at my having so much power. My answer to them is this: I did not seek any part of this power. It came upon me unawares. But when it was come, not daring to bury that talent, I used it to the best of my judgment."

At the completion of his words, Wesley steps down from the altar; the men rise to their feet and approach their leader. Alexander Mather is the first to voice not only his but the entire group's opinion,

> "John, ya' are our dear faither. Ya' have molded a people where there was none."

Mather's words aren't the only ones to bring encouragement. Unanimously, the itinerants spend the next hour offering their devotion to the man and the movement which God birthed through his faithful efforts.

Hours later, the cool August evening settles on the grounds of Holy Trinity Church. The itinerants have departed for their assignments. John Wesley remains, in prayer with Pastor Mather. The two appear as an odd couple; Alex is nearly six feet tall, and John in his jack boots struggles to reach sixty-two inches in height. With heads bowed, they silently supplicate to the Lord. The four-day conference represents another turning point in the Wesleyan movement. All who questioned Wesley's leadership have silenced their objections, declining to confront John's responses.

Rising from prayer, Alex places his hands onto Wesley's shoulders. He informs his mentor and leader,

> "Ah' shall inform the young man of his responsibilities. He shall remain as directed."

Departing on horseback, Mather thinks about his promise to Wesley. *Oh, Fr'dancis; ya' must learn to submit to ya' superiors. Ya' contemporary, William Orpe, is worthy of such.*

> *Ah Sun-flower! weary of time,*
> *Who countest the steps of the Sun:*
> *Seeking after that sweet golden clime*
> *Where the traveller's journey is done.*
> *Where the Youth pined away with desire,*
> *And the pale Virgin shrouded in snow:*
> *Arise from their graves and aspire*
> *Where my Sun-flower wishes to go.*
>   *William Blake*[110]

Standing along the south side of his father's tool barn, Francis stares at the ground. He raises his eyes to take in the mature bean vines clinging to the wooden structure. Contemplating his situation, he abruptly brings forward his right hand and snaps a mazagan. He plunges half of the green bean into his mouth and chomps it; the juicy sphere inside the cool, crisp pod splits on contact.

The news from the man looming in front of him is far from what he expected to hear. Francis accidently spits out a bean fiber as he blurts,

> "The conference appoints William Orpe once again? He fails as a preacher."

> "Fr'dancis, Ah' understand ya' frustrations. Submission is a difficult task . . ."

> "Difficult enough; the fellow is far from a preacher. And worse - - He displays a strong inclination for finery."

> "Fr'dancis, ya' must master'd ya' sin. Have we not pursued such journeys before?"

Silence.

Francis tosses the remainder of the pod to the ground. He rubs the knuckle at the base of his left index finger, moving his right thumb in a repeating circular motion over the bony knob. He stares at the ground once again, continuing the compulsive hand massage. Alexander Mather finds this rather odd. Francis blurts out once more,

> "I move for another circuit. You must sway Wesley."

---

[110] William Blake, *Ah! Sun-Flower*, 1793.

Alex says nothing as he stares at the young man. Francis is almost rude as he continues,

> "I seek worthwhile alternatives."
>
> "Fr'dancis, ya' propose a difficult request. Ah' shall not put ya' itinerancy at risk."
>
> "Of what risk? It shall force greater liability for one of experience to submit to one with limited - -
>
> Rather, no experience."

Why, ya' are a stubborn and naïve young man. Very well. Mather responds,

> "All right, Fr'dancis, Ah' shall talk wit' William. As for now, prepare to take the low r'dound. Gloucester by week's end. Ah' suggest ya' head for the River Severn, as several small societies yearn to emerge along its banks."

Mather departs and Francis ponders the development, grateful for the appointment. His joyful steps, stone-kicking included, last only a moment; his thoughts soon launch in another direction. *If only the next meeting should meet with likewise success.* Francis makes his way into the tool barn, where Churchfield snorts his usual greeting. *Churchy.* Francis reaches out and strokes his horse, informing him,

> "I pray the Lord's blessings also on this morning's second enterprise."

Before departing for his low-round circuit, Francis spends time with his father and mother. Joseph is grateful for the appointment, Elizabeth not so grateful. Regardless, after several suggestions from both, Francis is on his way, he and Churchfield heading down the road to West Bromwich.

The Sandwell Valley utters a melodious poem as the moss-covered path plows through the lush, sleepy white offering of wood anemone as they loop about. As if begging Francis to stay, the flowers remain longer than usual this season. Above the floor, the gnarled, knobby trunks of the numerous hardwood trees form the woody foundation of an intricate weave. Avoiding the barky branches, Francis ducks his head to escape an unpleasant tap. He is tempted to pause and collect a few of the bridal-white windflowers crowded below the arching offshoots, but he reconsiders; *these would prove faint in comparison.* He resumes his course toward the important affair at hand.

The whorled mass of vine and flower below, as well as tree and limb above, provide cover and perch for numerous diminutive but commanding offspring of the forest. Previous outings reveal that Francis is familiar with the song thrush and the harvest mouse. He marvels at the thought of catching a rare sight of the red fox or the peregrine falcon; *have not viewed one since a child.*

As if previously planned, right above Francis the familiar concentric striping of the lightning-fast bird of prey soars over the swaying tops of the highest trees, the bird's deliberate eye taking in Francis as it focuses its sharp gaze toward the ground. Francis happens to look up; *oh, yes! Magnificent creature.* His discovery lifts his emotions above the seriousness of the upcoming meeting this morning. He arches his neck to follow the falcon's course. The exciting moment ends as the bird turns toward the north and departs. Once again, the thought of the nearing encounter brings a slight nervousness to Francis. The impressive sight and exit of the falcon fails to silence his next thought, *perhaps she shall allow for forgiveness.*

Approaching All Saints Church in West Bromwich, Francis takes his usual turn toward the southwest. He continues to worry about his meeting with Nancy. The street in which she resides is only a short distance ahead. Francis looks skyward; it has turned dark. *The rain shall fall.* Francis ventures the thought in an effort to switch from his musing. The predicted precipitation begins.

The patchy drizzle is a regular September occurrence in the Midlands, brought on by a weak frontal situation. Despite the fact that the cloud cover is thick, the autumn storm lacks the more turbulent cumulus clouds of the summer. In addition to the water that falls, the outbreak of rain drops the temperature to a chilly level.

The local husbandry men, or farmers, welcome the falling precipitation. They stand at the doorways of their small thatched-roof cottages, each structure strategically placed within the neatly trimmed hedges outlining the perimeter of their hemplecks,[111] happily watching as their wind-swept crops bend in joyful absorption of the life-giving liquid.

Churchfield, having been this way before, instinctively slows in front of Nancy's home. It is a simple West Midlands home, one story high and built of brick. The house nestles in the midst of several large oak trees, representative of the oak forest that surrounds the area. Francis has developed a clear recollection of the building: three stone steps to the front door, the single window in the main room, a split in the right-side shutter. He dismounts and approaches the front door.

He knocks. Answering the door, Nancy is expressionless.

Francis removes his hat and inquires,

"Might I have a moment of your time?"

She ponders the request, looking first to Francis, then to the falling rain. With an exaggerated inhale, she purses her lips in contemplation and responds,

"Yes, Francis."

---

[111] Small pieces of ground for growing hemp or flax.

The rain ceases to fall; the resulting silence turns Francis around. He turns back toward Nancy and asks,

"Might I invite you outdoors?"

Francis is thankful that Nancy agrees. The pair heads for a familiar spot, the old stump on the perimeter of the town. Francis gently lifts Nancy's hand with his. When she doesn't resist, Francis is thankful for the small achievement. He didn't expect it; her tears and sudden departure at their last meeting convinced him that the relationship with Nancy was not intact. He escorts her to the cut tree; noticing that it is wet, he removes his coat and invites her to sit. Lifting her arm, he places her upon the outdoor seat.

The slight chill from the drop in temperature causes Francis to wrap his arms around himself as he places one foot upon the stump, alongside Nancy. Her smile invites him to continue.

"Nance, when last we met, I detected a certain struggle. May I inquire?"

Nancy shifts her gaze away from Francis and toward the ground. Audibly, she reveals nothing; visibly, it's an entirely different matter. Francis is uncomfortable; his nervous habit returns as his top teeth scrape his bottom lip. He continues,

"It is desirable that we should discuss our difficulty."

She remains silent, her eyes now shifting toward the distant horizon. Francis too looks away. Leaning his chin on the shoulder of the arm resting upon his raised knee, he looks to the dusty ground. He closes his eyes, aware that Nancy may not talk at all. He struggles with this possibility.

Lowering his leg from the stump, Francis places a hand on Nancy's shoulder and asks,

"Would you prefer that I depart?"

"No."

"Would you prefer to talk tomorrow?"

"No."

Sensing a slight improvement, Francis ventures,

"Would you prefer that I pursue the theatre?"

Nancy cannot hold back; she smiles at the silly comment. Francis is relieved; *she appears human*. Like many random thoughts that appear in Francis's mind, this thought remains with him. Nancy reaches up and takes Francis's hand as she finally speaks.

"Francis, it is difficult; nevertheless, I have conciliated with the itinerancy. At times, the concept brings much warmth—'my Francis, one of Wesley's worthies.' However, a coldness arrives with accounts of delightful and elegant potentials who weave their lives into yours in an attempt to encourage your efforts."

Francis pauses, surprised at Nancy's response. He responds,

> "I had not expected it, but I treasure your clear acknowledgment. Nancy, these potentials who convey support fail to threaten my affections for you."

Francis pauses again as he analyzes his intentions. *True, my affections for Nancy are strong.* Nancy interrupts Francis's thought.

> "Francis, I cannot compete with those wiser than myself."

The ensuing silence prompts the pair to quietly stare at each other. The awkward stillness causes Nancy to bow her head, not meeting his gaze. Releasing her hand, Francis raises his hand to her chin, lifts her face, and gently speaks.

> "Your exclusive competition is the Lord."

Nancy once again smiles; she is grateful. Francis returns the look. Reaching into his coat pocket, he exclaims,

> "I have a gift!"

> "Oh?"

> "A gift."

Francis places a small, dark-colored container into her hands. The palm-sized box increases her curiosity, resulting in an even wider smile.

> "Francis, may I?"

Francis gives two short nods indicating his answer is yes. As Nancy places her delicate hand around the elongated box wrapped in a darkish-grey skin, she remarks,

> "Unique covering."

> "The skin of the stingray fish."

> "Francis, it is beautiful."

Nancy lifts open the lid to the box. Her face conveys her surprised reaction. Francis informs her,

> "The grapes are removed to allow the aromatic liquid . . ."

Nancy interrupts,

> "Perfume! 'Tis a darling perfume bottle."

Francis is grateful she knows about the item. The crafted ceramic piece consists of a lid of three purple and blue grapes; the cap screws onto a cylindrical container surrounded by a sculpted design in the shape of three green leaves. He is also grateful that he didn't speak his opinion of the item's name, a "smelling bottle." Nancy goes on,

> "How ever did you procure such a divine article?"

> "My recent trip from Ashbourne; the Staffordshire potter assured of its restorative properties."

Nancy smiles at Francis's quip. She opens the bottle and carefully dabs a touch of the scented liquid onto her left wrist. Raising her arm to smell the pleasing aroma, she smiles that deep smile again. Francis smiles, too; he reaches forward and retrieves her arm, the beautiful fragrance attaching to his lips as he kisses her wrist.

Francis informs her,

> "I've to itinerate the low round; Gloucester by week's end."
>
> "Gloucester! A mighty journey, Francis."
>
> "I am aware; Mather warned. Father has prepared a route. I am confident it shall prove faithful."
>
> "Very well, when shall I see you?"
>
> "The hundred-mile circuit shall require two weeks before my return. I shall see you on the Sabbath at All Saints."

From Nancy's home in West Bromwich, Francis and Churchfield head southwest. They will travel a great distance from his home, twenty-five miles to Worcester from Bromwich, and an additional twenty-nine miles to Gloucester. The more than one-hundred-mile round trip for the low round circuit is a challenging effort for a seasoned preacher like Mather; the task for Francis approaches battling a small tidal wave. His inexperience as a traveler is the reason. Only a spirit of adventure, seasoned with youthful overconfidence, can launch someone like Francis fifty miles in an unfamiliar direction.

Francis's travel will once again place him on an old Roman road. The route he has decided to take functions as a pack-horse road, delivering the varied supplies, raw materials, and products of the West Midlands to the southwestern coastal towns where he is heading. The road also reciprocates, allowing for the overland transfer of imported products arriving to the Bristol port of Pill, directing the sought-after cargo to the West Midlands. The ancient path begins to the west at Wolverhampton; Francis will catch it as it heads south at the city of Stourbridge. From there he will continue in a southerly direction to Droitwich, after which the road will deliver him to the ancient Roman town on the River Severn, Worcester. From here, his travels will parallel the mighty river to Gloucester.

Departing from Bromwich, the nailing village of Stourbridge is Francis's first point of arrival. One constant for Francis on this eight-mile journey is the rolling hills that consistently grow larger on the horizon. Looking toward the lush hills on the western border toward Stourbridge, he notes the first signs that summer has departed, the amber spires of ornamental grasses blanketing the meadows as they swell in every direction.

Approaching the little town of Stourbridge, Francis begins to hear a beautiful sound. The melodic petition is enjoyable to the itinerant. He slows Churchfield and the two pause to listen to the peals of bells, *those beautiful, musical bells*, ringing across the knolls and hillocks.

"Can you hear it, Churchy?"

Churchfield grunts as he busies himself with the meadow's natural fodder.

"Come, Churchy; we shall investigate."

Prompted by the reins and poked by Francis's heels, Churchfield ends his short-term feast, raising his head and resuming the journey. The sound grows louder as they approach the village. Francis is pleased that the music has remained for nearly five minutes. The bells continue to peal.

In the distance, Francis spots the source of the symphony: a large red-bricked structure, *a church*. Attached to the building is a tower nearly one hundred feet tall. Atop the bricked, square steeple are the bells. Francis decides to stop.

Stepping down from Churchfield, Francis is approached by several young men of the town. Their sooty clothes cause Francis to assume they are apprenticed to an ironworker. He inquires,

> "Working the trades?"

One of the blades,[112] the short, stocky one, responds,

> "Naila's."

> "Nailers. Have we progressed beyond sleeping at the anvil?"

The men are surprised that Francis is aware of the tradition. The vocal one responds,

> "Yo' naila'?"

> "I have pounded my share."

> "Well den', we welcome yo' to ar' town."

The fellows share trade talk. Before long, the young men find out that Francis is an itinerant preacher, and they invite him to preach. Francis accepts. The men instruct him to wait in an adjacent open field while they gather their fellow nailers.

The young men return with Francis's congregation; they are a rough-looking group. This is familiar territory to Francis; he is excited to share from the Word with these men who are working as he did and are only a few years younger than he is. In addition to the first group of six, they have summoned an additional dozen hearers. Noticing a nearby work table, the short, stocky leader of the original group instructs two of his companions to bring it over; they immediately grab the wooden piece and deliver it, making sure it is level. The stocky leader informs Francis,

> "Yo' make-shif' pulpit."

> "Thank you."

Francis steps to the table; two men come forward, clasp their hands together, and give him a boost atop the improvised platform. Francis steadies himself atop the table and begins,

> "Shall we pray?"

---

[112] Lively young men.

All bow their heads.

>"Almighty Father, Creator of heaven and earth, all that is seen and unseen, we petition Your guidance in our affairs this day. For nothing shall remain impossible with You; where gates are closed, You open, and where gates are open, You close in a fashion that no man may open."

Francis's prayer ends and he begins a short exhortation from the Gospel of John. The men are attentive, several nodding their heads in approval. One man bows his head into the palms of his hands. Francis is confident, *the words are bestowing new life. The men* . . . The thought emerges that the entire group is men; there are no women present. Francis pauses for a moment. He finds this discovery odd. He continues,

>"For God so loved . . ."

The impact from behind is unexpected. Francis struggles for something to grab as he plummets backward, off the table that is rotating under his feet.

As he smashes to the ground, the men rush Francis.

Unbeknownst to Francis, one of the group approached the gathering from behind him and shoved the table forward. Francis decides to accept his fate; *harm shall come*.

The men lightly push and poke the fallen preacher, verbally mocking him.

>"Naila' preacha'. Yo' fail to reason, tables ar' fo' workin', not fo' standin'."

Laughing loudly, the obnoxious group turns and departs from Francis, leaving him lying alone on the ground. Francis is surprised, *certain of an awful course*. He gets up and heads for Churchfield. Gathering himself, Francis mounts the horse and leaves Stourbridge.

For the next twenty miles, Francis proceeds through randomly strewn oak forests, rolling fields, and tiny hamlets, each consisting of one or two thatched-roof houses. The numerous hills along the route will eventually result in a two-hundred-foot drop to the destination of Worcester. However, the journey is deceiving—although resulting in a net decline, there are several instances where Francis and Churchfield will once again climb to a height as much as, if not more than, previously descended. The process repeats itself several times before achieving the final descent into Worcester.

The town of Worcester has its origins within the Roman reign of Constantine, though it is uncertain which Constantine—the son of Constantine the Great, Julius Constantine, or Constantine Chlorus, the father of Constantine the Great. Regardless, the city is one of several strategically important Roman settlements located along the River Severn, the center hub for many Roman military roads—one of which Francis is traveling on from Stourbridge.

Worcester is a walled city. For ease in commerce, only one of the ancient entrance gates remains. The historic roads affiliated with the town form strategic, direct routes connecting London to Wales, the Midlands to the port town of Gloucester, and, venturing to the northeast, Worcester to Derby. Travelers from the island nation and beyond regularly visit this city of commerce with its ten thousand residents.

Arriving in the town, Francis finds a mix of open fields intermingled with rows of houses, each simple brick structure usually topped with a thatched roof. Strangely, Francis encounters several houses with a cone-shaped roof. Atop the roof, emitting smoke, a funnel-like turret bends at a slight angle. The heated air prompts him to question, *whatever for?* Francis has no idea; it is an unfamiliar architectural feature.

Continuing along, an opening in a stone wall marks where an oversized gate used to reside. In fact, the metal gates, each more than ten feet wide, lie aside the doorway which escorts Francis further into the settlement. Francis correctly surmises, *these must account for the ancient Roman walls of which Father spoke.*

From the first century until the seventeenth century, the Worcester residents raised several sets of barrier walls in order to protect themselves from invading forces. The Roman, Anglo-Saxon, and Norman empires each contributed to the building of the walls. Each new protective boundary uniquely expanded the territory of the town. Francis will pass through several sets of these as he heads in a southerly direction. For the last fifty years, the locals systematically eliminated the imposing gate and columned structures associated with the entrances; now only one gate remains. In fact, several sections of the walls, which have not been necessary since the English Civil War almost 120 years before, have become valuable as perimeter walls for new development within the town.

Off in the distance, the Worcester Cathedral stands near the edge of the Severn. Francis once again is disappointed to find a fractured church building. Portions of the grand structure damaged in the English Civil War appear to list, aching for restoration. As Francis views the afflicted areas, he remembers his conversation with Pastor Mather. Mather's words are nearly audible: "Unity requires truth." He thinks of the English Civil War and Cromwell's attacking forces. He also thinks of the Reformation. The recollection causes him to ponder Luther and his sixteenth-century attempts to repair instead of separate.

The open fields adjacent to the many row houses and buildings bustle with people milling about. *'Tis fair day?* The day of the week is Friday, so Francis doubts his thought. In addition to the hundreds of people who walk the streets, the fields are full of cattle, horses, and sheep. *Market day?*

Francis is correct; Fridays in Worcester are days set aside as market days, highly important to the farmers and graziers of the area. Several of the suppliers travel a great distance to make their living, a majority of which is earned on these designated days.

In addition to the herds of animals, several grassy fields already have horse-drawn wooden carts surrounded by a raucous crowd of people. Each cart is piled to the top with a strange kind of produce. The oversized vehicles are hitched to teams of multiple horses, some with four, and others with six. Francis ponders, *a substantially less amount of pullers than the transports of the West Midland coal packs.* Nevertheless, one thing is clear to Francis: *the industrial wagons do not hold coal.* The precious cargo that many are clamoring to bid on is a green, dried plant resembling an oversized pinecone.

Francis and Churchfield move toward one cart and its proprietor for a closer look. The owner of the wagon stands before nearly twenty people. In an informal circle, the impromptu guests enjoy the back-and-forth of several men as they bid on the mysterious produce. The banter reminds Francis of his friend James Mayo. One man yells his bid of a shilling; the other replies, "Three!" The farmer delights in the verbal battle that is slowly raising what will amount to a good year's wages. The bidders continue,

"Three shillings sixpence."

"Oh, we've money on yo' get-about day. Four shillings!"

The crowd cheers. Before Francis realizes it, the gathering swells with an additional thirty people who have decided to watch the proceedings; they surround Francis and Churchfield. Sitting atop Churchy, Francis has the perfect view—he is at eye level with the farmer who stands on a wooden block, next to his team and cargo. Francis decides to inquire of a young boy who has taken a liking to Churchfield. The lad strokes the horse's nose as Francis poses the obvious question,

"What is the produce on which the men bid?"

"Hops! The men are malters in need of the plant."

"I see."

Francis knows of malters; his parents' cottage is part of a local malter's operation. He is unaware of the plant, however, never having seen it used at The Malt Shovel. The discovery has Francis seeking to move on; unfortunately, the tightening crowd prohibits this.

Hops are the seed cones of the hops plant. The vining plant is dried and used in brewing beer. Francis draws in a breath; the plant's unique, woody-pine aroma fills the open-air space. Worcestershire, as well as Sussex, Surrey, Hampshire, Herefordshire, and Kent, possess the ideal soil for growing the hearty plant. In these counties, hops are added to the ale mix to create beer. The Malt Shovel at the Asbury Cottage in Staffordshire continues to brew true ale, which has no hops added.

The market is a lively place, too lively for Francis. The mood of the people reveals a sense of excitement and celebration. Asking to preach to this crowd, which is also partaking of the hops-enhanced ale, seems impossible to the itinerant. He decides to continue his journey, determining it best to spend the night in or near Tewkesbury. Begging pardon, he slowly works himself and Churchfield out of the gathering.

Departing Worcester through the opening in the ancient wall, the cambered pathway under Churchfield's hooves continues southward along the east side of the Severn. *There it is again.* Francis has spotted another house with the cone-shaped roof. He is unaware that the conical-topped structure is an oast house, utilized in the preparation of the hops harvest.

There are three rooms in the traditional oast house: one for an oven or kiln, another for drying the hops, and another for cooling the dehydrated plant. Once the plant dries in the drying room, strategically placed above the kiln, the hops move to the cooling room before their loading for transport. The unique shape of the roof allows for a superior draft of the fire. In addition, the cone-shaped roof tops out with an adjustable cowling; the pivoted attachment captures the ideal airflow to aid the kiln firing.

Francis returns his focus to the Severn, the longest river in England. The source of the waterway is in the Plynlimon Hills, the highest point of the Cambrian Mountains in Wales. Each year, the soggy moorlands receive almost the entire reservoir of the depressions coming off the Irish Sea and St. George's Channel, the powerful Atlantic storms dropping massive amounts of rain. The sponge-like, moss-covered plateau soaks in the precipitation to the point of saturation, forcing the excess liquid to run downhill toward England.

The route along the river is scenic. The late summer/early autumn grasses blanket each side of the river's shoreline. The purple and pinkish spiny flower heads of the teasel plants are beginning their annual fade, aiming for the attractive tan color cherished for cut-flower arrangements. The waterway is swift, meandering several S-turns and oxbow lakes through the countryside, its erosive flow creating high-walled cliffs on the faster outer edge of the channel and a gentle, shallow slope on the slower inside edge. The long-term effects of such an arrangement create a constant winding path through the flatter lands of its course.

As Francis travels in a southeasterly direction, he notices a stunning view in the distance and guesses that the distant mountain range is the Gloucester and Evesham Vales mentioned by his father. Francis has never traveled through mountains; he is fascinated by the fact that if he ventured a little to the east of his current destination, he could try this new experience. He reconsiders, remembering the words of Mather: "Ah' shall not put your itinerancy at risk." Francis decides to maintain his course, continuing his riverside trek. Periodically, though, he finds himself raising his eyes to take in the view, drawn toward the magnetic scenery in the distance.

Approaching a small hill, Francis and Churchfield climb toward the building at the top of the mound. The rocky ground gives challenge to the pair. Several times the horse stumbles; however, the strong animal presses on.

At the top, Francis is pleased to find a downhill view into the town of his destination. In the distance, the Gloucester and Evesham Vales form a spectacular backdrop to the little village of Tewkesbury. Francis turns his gaze to the southwest. All is as expected: rolling hills descending toward the town, scattered fields for grazing . . . Francis abruptly brings his search to a halt.

Turning to look back to an almost southerly position, Francis is amazed at the sight. In the distance, on the edge of the town, sits a massive stone church. Francis remembers what his father told him: "Tewkesbury is an ancient town; the Benedictine monks established an abbey there in the year 1102." Taking nineteen years to complete, the structure had several additions over the centuries. As Francis stares in the direction of the intersection of the River Severn and the River Avon, the magnificent Romanesque tower of the abbey continues to steal his attention. Yes, he needs to cross the Avon; however, the sight of the Tewkesbury Abbey in the distance causes him to pause.

Filled with excitement, he taps Churchfield and the pair heads downhill, fast. As he approaches the Avon in an easterly direction, Francis spots a four-arched bridge over the waterway, leading into the town of Tewkesbury. He continues toward the overpass.

Upon entering the rampart of the bridge, the cambered roadway gives way to a dirt-covered path. At the bridge, Francis notices a sign reading "King John's Bridge" as he guides Churchfield onto the slightly curved crossing. The pair crosses the river as the sun begins to set. Entering the town, the road dead-ends into the main street of the village, High Street. Francis turns southward. He is anxious to locate anyone who would sympathize with his work. His thoughts fluctuate; *why should I go against Mather's aim?* He once again begins to doubt his efforts.

Heading in a south-by-southwesterly direction, High Street veers, becoming Church Street and heading in the direction of the religious building. Francis's sense of excitement fails to compete with his fascination with the huge church. Approaching the immense structure, a visitor joins Francis. He is a hairy creature, short in stature, and quiet. Tipping his hat toward his fellow traveler, Francis offers,

"Heading south, are we?"

The new arrival doesn't answer; he stares at Francis, tilting his head slightly. He remains silent.

"Very well, then; Churchy and I shall converse on our own."

Francis shrugs his shoulders, his amused response going unnoticed by his new companion. At the church grounds, Francis dismounts. The town is quiet. The only other existence that Francis notices is his new friend—the quiet, non-speaking friend. Francis tries again,

"Traveling tonight?"

The bewhiskered visitor walks over to Francis and sniffs his leg.

He is a dog, a hairy dog. Francis strokes the friendly creature. Despite the chalky feel, the fur is unusual, *almost like human hair.* The wheat-colored hair hangs long at the jowls but is thick and curly on the body. A touch of grey and dark brown gives a terrier appearance. The thin black skin of the dog's lip-line complements the shiny black nose. He appears to smile as he gently draws in air to pant, the white of his lower teeth showing enough to prompt an amusing comparison.

"Slightly turned. Like James."

James Mayo's two middle teeth of the bottom row also slightly turn from each other. As Francis walks toward the entrance to the abbey, his furry friend decides to tag along.

Inside the magnificent church, Francis gazes in awe at the height of the ceiling, the impact made even more dramatic due to the immense length of the church. Francis guesses that the building is over three hundred feet in length. The abbey's floor plan is cruciform[113] in layout. Francis surmises, *the perpendicular cross-section is at least two hundred feet in length.*

Looking upward, the view is imposing. The elevated vaulted, arched ceilings reach to more than six stories in height. Each arch originates from a massive circular stone column nearly four stories tall, starting from a corbel-styled bracket in the shape of a head and launching upward from there. Nine of the six-foot-diameter cylindrical columns line each side of the thirty-three-foot wide center

---

[113] In the shape of the Latin cross.

nave. Francis stands silently alongside his four-legged companion, which sits with mouth closed as if to honor the sacred space.

A loud, surging force emanating from the far end of the abbey breaks the silence. As suddenly as the organ-like chord began, it ends. Francis and the dog have each tilted an ear. Once again, there is silence. Following the short interval, several metal tools and tubes clang together, offering an additional unexpected sound to the new visitors. Again, silence.

Francis takes a few steps in the direction of the unfamiliar tones. The dog follows. Before his third step, a gentleman emerges from the right side of the distant altar. He is dressed in the traditional clothes of a man who works with his hands for a living. The short, skinny arrival hurries toward Francis and the dog.

As he approaches the pair, the man is mumbling to himself. Several times he raises his hands, as if to convince an invisible companion of his point. In his left hand he holds a fine instrument, small and made of metal. Francis correctly guesses that the man's work is highly specialized.

Reaching Francis, the man continues, walking right by the unannounced pair. Francis turns to watch the preoccupied worker. The man stops mid-comment, then turns and faces Francis.

"Milton himself shan't rescue the meantone."[114]

Francis and the dog are unenlightened. Realizing this, the man explains,

"The organ, the gallery's organ—'twas the gift of Hampton Court."

Francis continues in ignorance. This time the reply is loud,

"Milton himself played the bloody instrument!"

"Poet John Milton?"

"Yes, at Hampton Court. In the days he was secretary to Cromwell."

With the mention of the historical Oliver Cromwell, the strange and focused man has Francis's attention. The remainder of the evening proves beneficial to Francis. As long as he continues to show interest in the technician's effort to tune the massive organ, Francis and the dog remain in his favor. By night's end, the kind man offers Francis a place to sleep. Naturally, the offer does not include Francis's companion. At evening's end, Francis and the organ tuner depart for the night's arrangements. The furry pal departs also, satisfied with his night of adventure.

In the morning, Francis is surprised to find the dog sleeping in the barn alongside Churchfield. Francis comments,

"Very well."

---

[114] Eighteenth-century method for tuning an organ.

The trio sets out for Gloucester, but before long, the dog turns back to Tewkesbury. Francis nods his goodbye, and Churchfield snorts what Francis guesses is a friendly fare-thee-well. With the dog backtracking for home, the pair moves on toward Gloucester.

Gloucester is a port town. Residing on the River Severn, this southwestern settlement established by the Roman Empire is a cathedral village. The eleventh-century King William I, also known as William the Conqueror, commissioned his chaplain—an outgoing and enterprising monk named Serlo from Mont St. Michel in Normandy—to raise funds to construct a cathedral. Over the next seventeen years the dedicated Serlo accomplished his goal, allowing the start of construction in the year 1089. For the next 550 years, the Abbey of St. Peter was the center of Christianity in the city by the river.

The dissolution of the Catholic monasteries by King Henry VIII in the year 1540 ushered out the monks of the abbey and escorted in Protestant leadership, along with a new name for the abbey: Gloucester Cathedral. King Henry's reign marked the beginning of turbulent transition for the next two hundred years. Beyond the Catholic and Protestant atrocities toward each other, the Anglican influence eventually opened the door for the new dissenters, men like George Whitefield and the brothers Wesley.

Gloucester is the birthplace of George Whitefield. His mother's Bell Inn on Southgate Street is only half a block away from his childhood school of St. Mary De Crypt. John Wesley visited the town in the summer of 1739, addressing overflowing crowds in a field belonging to George's brother. For the last twenty years, the locals have been mostly against the Methodist movement, their interest in Wesley and Whitefield merely an exercise in curiosity.

Francis and Churchfield enter the town via Westgate Street. The road that travels southeast in the direction of the Cotswold Hills will intersect with the Northgate, Southgate, and Eastgate Streets, all four streets meeting in the center of town. Francis's father directed him to search out the old Cordwainers' Hall, where he is to find a local preacher by the name of John Brown. Joseph mentioned that the small chapel was located near Northgate Street.

Continuing along Westgate, Francis spots the magnificent cathedral to his left. Drawing on Churchfield's reins, he coaxes the horse to a standstill. Francis is awestruck. This building is clearly the largest he has viewed since his time as a local preacher. *There are no words. Almost holy.*

A rumbling noise causes Francis to look behind his horse. The oncoming team of six horses pulling a cart loaded with timber inspires Francis and Churchfield to immediately move out of the way. Safely on the side of the road, they watch as the heavy lumber comes to a stop. The driver and his assistant climb down from the wooden-wheeled rig. The driver, a tall, thick man covered in dust, advises the young man,

"Yo' shall be killed getting about like that."

"My apologies."

"Yo' astray?"

"Why, yes—looking for the Methodist meeting house."

"Dat' large buildin' behind yo', not too distant, is da' Methodis' meetin' room, a cordwainers' hall. Good day, sir."

"Good day."

Francis turns toward the south and heads for the edge of the River Severn. Approaching the river, the houses improve in appearance. He is drawn to the attractive brick homes, much nicer than any he has encountered in his hometown or in any of his travels. *The Methodist here must do quite well.* The thought gives Francis a quiet confidence that this visit shall prove successful.

Nearing the homes, he takes in the sight of several men standing street-side. He approaches to inquire,

"May I ask of the Methodist meeting room?"

One responds,

"The field here at the waterside has proved most advantageous for such outings. Might we inquire as to your needs?"

"Yes, you may. I am an itinerant for Wesley. Hoping to preach this day to the Methodist faithful."

"You've arrived at a most opportune time. Please set up to preach here at the quay. We shall make arrangements for the faithful."

"Very well, thank you."

Simple enough. Francis's thought is pleasing to the itinerant. A quiet peace removes any hesitations he has had since the table incident in Stourbridge. He dismounts and secures Churchfield to an oak tree at the water's edge. Waiting for the townspeople to arrive, a strange thought enters his mind: *the small chapel resided near Northgate Street.* His father's words contradict where he is now. *Perhaps Father's advice is slightly off.*

In the distance, several dozen men and women approach Francis. He is thrilled to see not only adults, but also a dozen small children. *The children shall hear of Jesus's love.* Francis recognizes the look of the men in the group. These sturdy miners of the local coal deposits are consistently covered in clothing marred by the carbonized mineral.

Before long, Francis stands amidst eighty people. His joy causes his heart to pound strongly; *O what would one not do, what would one not suffer, to be useful to souls and to do the will of the great Master!* Excitement fills the gathering as several announce their expectation of the afternoon's events to come. Francis raises his hands and begins,

"The love of our Lord and Savior, Jesus Christ - -
To you is the word of this salvation sent."
"Before we begin, we request a baptism!"

The interruption halts Francis's greeting. He responds,

"A baptism?"
"Yes, a baptism."
"Shall da' preacha' enjoy a baptism?"

Francis doesn't know what to think; *they request that I baptize someone?*

The men of the group rush Francis. Before he can react, Francis is hoisted overhead of seven men. They carry him into the river. The water splashes as they wade into the twelve-inch-deep waterway. They escort him to the center of the river, onto a sandbar. There they push him down and roll him in the mud. Francis begins to cough, the wet soil making its way into his mouth and throat. He struggles for breath as the men continue to ensure his discomfort. A rush of water burns as it sucks through his nostrils. One man grabs Francis's leg and drags him, ensuring his jump[115] fills with the shoal's moist top layer. Squirming to free himself of the penetrating silt, Francis experiences the proclamation of one of the men,

"Dis' should fill yo' trousers wit' real substance."
"The bore!"

The announcement by another of the aggressors causes the men to flee. Francis is relieved. He lies in the mud, coughing and catching his breath. He sits upright, placing his head between his knees. He can hear the scoffing of the men in the distance, the mocking laughs of the women and children. He ignores their taunting. He is thankful that they are on the shoreline. Strangely, none are departing; they continue their verbal harassment. Francis isn't moving, content to rest in the shallow water, away from immediate harm. Despite the distant sound of the river and the obnoxious perpetrators, he lowers his head for silence. After a few seconds he is comfortable that he can stand without feeling winded, so he rises to his feet.

As he turns around, he finds himself staring into a five-foot-high wall of water.

The rushing wave levels Francis. His footing lost, he finds himself pushed and rolled under a moving slab of water. He struggles to regain his footing and his breath. Failing this, he attempts to swim for air. This effort falls short also. Buffeting and battering, the water will not allow him to surface or to breathe.

---

[115] Short coat.

Panic sets in; Francis needs to breathe.

In the racing current, he is able to draw forward his knees. Bringing them to his chest, he thrusts his feet toward the bottom. Finally connecting with a solid surface, he launches upward.

The first breath out of the water coincides with the audible gasp of a man in panic. Francis instinctively paddles his arms to stay afloat. With his head above water, he begins to feel his feet dragging the bottom. The water is growing shallower; nevertheless, it continues to rage.

Several submerged tree limbs bring Francis's floating to a sudden stop, the tangled weave of branches above the waterline causing him to protect his face and eyes with his hands. His cheek slams into a snapped portion of the timber; he is certain that the scrape has resulted in a deep gouge.

Despite the jab to his face, the blunted branch is a help; Francis is grateful to have something to hold onto. The mass of limbs braces him against the strong current. His lower back is in pain; holding on with his left hand, he maneuvers his right hand from the tree and moves his closed fist through the water to massage his lower back.

Looking toward the shoreline, he catches a glimpse of Churchfield. The horse's reins are taut, caught in a clump of downed trees on the bank. The current has the animal pushed away from the tangle, downstream. Churchfield struggles to maintain his footing. Francis surmises, *the colliers[116] must have pushed him into the oncoming wave.* Standing to his feet, Francis realizes that the water level has risen above his waistline; the white water is settling, but the current is still moving swiftly. He plants his feet firmly to keep from drifting away.

Francis struggles for a solution for reaching the shoreline. He notices that downstream there is an exposed sandbar near the slower-moving inside portion of a meander in the river.

He lets go of the limb.

Drifting fast, he lunges in the direction of the shoal, pushing with one foot and then the other. The motion resembles a one-legged rabbit, buoyantly hopping. Nearing his target, Francis exerts himself in one last leap, landing on the edge of the sloping sand. After two large, hard-fought steps, he is up on top of the miniature island.

Only three feet separate him and the shoreline. He catches his breath and looks in the direction of Churchfield, observing that the horse continues to struggle. *Hold on, Churchy.* Francis worries for the animal.

Francis takes a deep breath and leaps.

---

[116] Coal miners.

Landing face-first in the tall teasel thicket on the shoreline, Francis finally senses peace. He lies still for a moment, taking several relaxed breaths. Remembering that his work is not complete, he pushes himself to his feet and launches upriver for Churchfield.

At the horse, Francis analyzes the situation. He must slide down the three-foot embankment covered with autumn-colored ornamental grass. The waterline is clearly visible; the water is flowing at a moderate pace. He must move back into the moving water. Francis also notices that Churchfield has not recognized that Francis is there. No neighing, no shaking of his head—the usual greetings of the animal are non-existent. The horse focuses, straining to keep his footing. Francis doesn't hesitate; he slides down to the animal.

Standing with one foot on the land and the other in the water, wedged against the horse's front leg, Francis secures his stance. He works his hands up the length of the reins; grasping the ends, he finds that they are hooked around an angled branch of a large tree limb. The tangle looks deliberate, wrapped three to four times around and tied in a knot. *Their aim was to kill you, Churchy.* Pained by this discovery, Francis feels anger begin to rise.

Francis unties the leather straps, careful to maintain pressure into the flow of the stream. He is certain, *release shall ensure a solid drag.* Winding the last few inches of reins around his hand, he steps forward to the other side of the tree. The branch is thick, big enough to brace himself with. His intention is to release the hold and maneuver Churchfield up the bank.

With one quick whip, Francis removes the last wrapping of the straps and holds on.

The current moves the horse nearly one yard; Francis arches his back over the top of the branch. *The load is excessive. This shall surely fall short.* Francis's knuckles are turning white, the bloodless grip threatening to fail.

Churchfield snorts through his nostrils, the rushing water threatening to fill the horse's lungs. The animal stomps, splashing water onto Francis. Francis takes several short breaths; the strain is becoming too much for him. He is pulling with all his strength, his leg and back muscles nearing their limit. With one strong yank, he leans forward and launches backward. The tree limb snaps.

Horse and rider are launched downstream with the current.

Churchfield is able to get his footing; unfortunately, the moving water forces him to trot in the direction of the flow. The resulting break of the branch has Francis floating on his back in three feet of water, tangled in the reins. He attempts to roll over onto his stomach to gain footing. The effort forces his face underwater; he instinctively rolls onto his back again.

I must draw my legs forward to stand in the roll; Francis considers the maneuver before launching.

He launches.

Rolling onto his stomach, he draws his feet forward. They plant splendidly, allowing him to push upright. With all his strength, he launches, standing to his feet.

He slams face-first into Churchfield's rear end.

Churchfield whinnies his usual greeting.

Shaken from the impact, Francis is able to stand—barely. Somewhat disoriented, he leans onto the animal, wrapping his arms around Churchfield's rump. He notices that the horse isn't moving either. His four legs are firmly planted on the sandbar that earlier aided Francis.

Francis struggles to Churchfield's side and hangs onto the animal's thick mane. He strokes the horse's neck.

"There now, Churchy; the worst is behind us."

To their right, three feet away, the shallow slope of the bank once again affords a climb out of the river. Francis turns Churchy toward the shoreline. Holding the reins, he leaps onto dry land, then calls to the horse and pulls him over. The pair shuffle out of the waterway, safe on the hard-packed soil above the river.

The miniature tidal wave that hit Francis in the middle of the River Severn is a natural phenomenon which occurs three to five days each month, starting usually one to three days after a full and new moon. Known as a tidal bore, it is actually the incoming tide from the Atlantic as it enters the ever-narrowing channel of the river. Much like forcing water through a funnel, the rapidly decreasing width in the waterway upstream causes the incoming flow to rise above the natural downstream flow of the river. In the past, many unknowing individuals have ventured out onto a sandbar, assuming that the dry land is a constant feature of the river. As the tidal bore approached, they, like Francis, quickly discovered that it isn't.

Taking inventory, Francis inspects his four-legged companion. All is well.

Taking personal inventory, all is far from well. His face is bleeding from a shallow puncture; his lower back drives a knotty pain toward his right thigh. Scrapes and bruises scar his hand and forearms. In addition, his wet trousers and jump are loaded with river bottom. He does his best to remove the sediment.

Francis looks around the river; his enemies have departed. He wipes off his trousers again and finds mud caked on his coat also. A slight chill causes Francis to begin to shake. He grabs Churchfield's reins and heads inland.

Within a few yards of the waterway, he secures his companion and gathers wood. The biting cold prompts Francis to collect more wood than normally necessary for a comfortable blaze. Before long, he is able to raise a fire. Sitting next to the warmth, he fails to gain comfort; his body continues to tremble. Looking to Churchfield, he notices the horse leaning toward the fire. Francis jumps up and gathers the remaining timber, putting the entire collection onto the fire. Within minutes the flames leap upward, pushing both horse and rider back for safety.

As the miniature inferno warms, Francis and Churchfield draw comfort from its yellow and blue flames. Churchfield is also exhausted; he lies down on his side. Francis has never seen the horse settle in this way. He slides up against the pony's round belly and reclines, drawing warmth and rest from his companion. Reaching his hands into his pockets for warmth, he finds the compartments are torn. In fact, further inspection reveals that much of his jacket is torn and ripped from the thrashing of the Severn Bore.

Settling himself for a while, Francis has time to reflect. He is troubled. In addition to his torn jacket and his physical and emotional ailments, Francis suffers from a more menacing injury, deeper than the emotional strain brought on by the harassment of the locals. It is also more significant than the physical pains of a strained back, a bruised face, and swallowed mud. Spiritually, something has changed. Francis can sense it—as if a protective covering is missing, *as if my Advocate has abandoned me.* The thought naturally segues into a sense of loneliness and self-accusation. *Lord, I have forced my wants upon Your work.* Francis struggles with the claim, *I have brought this upon myself.*

Francis and Churchfield awake at the same time; approximately two hours have passed. Francis unwraps his arms, which have aided him in keeping warm. The glowing fire continues to emit comforting vapors. Francis pulls himself to his feet. Limping slightly, he rubs his lower back. The horse rises as well. The pair stretch around the fire, gradually working away from the inviting warmth. Francis inspects his clothing; it is partially dry, prompting him to turn his back toward the fire to allow the rising flames to continue the drying process. Francis welcomes the blaze's abundance as it soothes the pain in his lower back.

Standing at the fire pit, Francis notices Churchfield making his way to the water's edge. Something clearly has the horse's attention. Assuming his companion just needs a drink, Francis continues to warm his clothing. Occupying his thoughts with the recent developments, he pushes aside thoughts of self-doubt; *I fail as a preacher.*

Churchfield whinnies. The jubilant noise causes Francis to abandon his dejected thought. Turning in the direction of the river, he walks toward his companion. The horse is shaking his head left to right and whinnying. *Strange, that is his usual greeting for me.*

At the water's edge, a huge splash causes Francis to run toward Churchfield. The horse stands there, watching the water. The object in the river is gone. Francis is puzzled by the sound. After a few moments of an unsuccessful search, Francis grabs Churchfield's reins, mounts the horse, and departs upstream along the river.

Continuing along the river, Francis and Churchfield head northward for Tewkesbury. Although the original reception was less than successful, Francis notes to himself, *at least the villagers were not forcing me into the river; I can visit those in prison.*

For the next two months, Francis wisely spends time in the friendlier town of Tewkesbury. He avoids going home, knowing that his facial and body scars would bring grief to his mother. In Tewkesbury, his time is divided among several nailers who share living expenses in a one-room building on the corner of High Street and Quay Lane and other nailers who live on nearby Smiths Lane. During the day, Francis meets them at the central gathering place of the men and women at Nailers Square, around the corner on the west side of the buildings, facing the River Avon. In the evening, the two locales take turns allowing Francis to bunk with them. Despite not being able to do much with it, one of the women does her best to mend his jacket.

During his lengthy stay, one of Wesley's key men, John Pawson, pays a visit to Francis from Stroud, south of Gloucester. The itinerant has heard of Francis's ordeal at the river and has come to offer encouragement to the young man. Francis is thankful for the kind gesture. Although Pawson knows of the attack, Francis is hesitant to divulge his truest fear. This despair is one of the main causes of the visible strain beginning to show on the young man's face. His anxiety has him reconsidering the itinerancy. After several days, Pawson departs on an errand for Wesley. Francis almost asks to leave with Pawson, but in the end decides to remain.

Inevitably, Francis's time with the nailers leads him to attend young men and women in the Tewkesbury jail. The two-story stone structure resides west of the abbey, its entrance facing the empty lot on the River Avon. The jail is the old bell tower of the abbey, becoming the jail when King Henry VIII allowed the local citizens to purchase the building as their own chapel. The structures were purchased for the value of the lead roof and bells, slated for melting and sale.

The first of December, 1766, is a cold day in Tewkesbury. As usual, Francis rises early, making his way for Nailers Square. The usual young men arrive at first light and find Francis sitting atop the iron bench crafted by the local nailers. Francis's daily prayers have transformed the iron seat into a prayer bench. Despite their initial hesitation, the men now expect each morning to find their new friend, bent from the waist over, elbows on his knees and face in the palms of his hands, supplicating to the Lord. Francis's consistent prayer for the men is evident not only in the softened demeanor of the nailers, but also in the rejuvenated emotions of the preacher.

Francis raises his head from prayer; several men stand silently waiting for him to finish. Francis quips,

"Well, I'm not about to make you breakfast."

"Seems yo' have food to eat we know not of."

Francis smiles his trademark wide-grinned smile.

"Seems some have paid attention to the teachings."

"And some of us enjoy da' restful sleep."

The entire group finds humor in the jest. Rising from the bench, Francis remarks,

"I shall not remain. Shall venture once again toward Worcester."

Unexpectedly, the group expresses its desire that Francis remain. The young men and their wives enjoy the young preacher's company. In fact, several of the marriages which previously were unstable have improved through Francis's teaching and preaching of the Word. One of the rough-looking nailers steps forward. Face to face, placing his hands on Francis's shoulders, he shares,

"Expectin' yo' on return trip."

"Very well, I shall enjoy the company of the nailers once again."

Within ten minutes, Francis and Churchfield are on their way.

Heading north toward King John's Bridge and its passing over the Avon to the eastern bank of the Severn, the pair travels a familiar route. Along the waterway, a large splash catches Francis's attention. He attempts to draw Churchfield to a stop, but the horse continues forward. Francis once again pulls the reins.

"Churchy!"

The horse finally stops. He leans his head toward the water, drawing Francis's attention to the river. Along the bank, a large, dark water-creature hovers just below the surface. Churchfield gives his customary two nods, then his left-to-right shake of the head and familiar whinny. Francis is slightly jealous.

"Someone you fail to introduce, Churchy?"

Francis watches as the elongated grey marine animal gives a gentle bend to its tail. Intrigued, Francis leans toward the river. The friendly river inhabitant glides forward. As if walking with a pal, Churchfield moves forward on his own. Francis is fascinated with the creature; his face conveys his surprise.

"Now, Churchy."

The horse ignores Francis.

Francis doesn't mind. He enjoys watching the creature.

The creature is a grey seal. This is not an uncommon sight upriver on the Severn. After a few minutes traveling alongside their spotted companion, Francis advises Churchfield,

"We must continue, Churchy. Bid farewell to this miniature Leviathan."

With a gentle snort that implies "I would rather walk with my friend," Churchfield reluctantly raises his head and moves toward the bridge.

Once over the adjacent river and reaching the Roman road, a sense of confidence comes to Francis; *doing that which He created me for*. He is happy to be wandering about once again.

The fourteen-mile trek should take three hours, the road escorting Francis through several hills, valleys, and pastures, sloping from the riverbank. Over his left shoulder and in the distance beyond the river, the Malvern Hills rise from the misting earth, their browning masses no longer green, the winter season forcing its hand. On the outskirts of Worcester, Francis once again encounters the strange-looking oast houses. One by one they appear, each attached to a farm and pasture. The sight of the rising smoke as it dances above the peculiar turrets reminds him of the numerous nail shops of Staffordshire; *oh, to be in Staffordshire*. Along the damp ground, the mist rises midway to the height of the treetops; hovering, it mysteriously attaches itself to hill and dale.

Entering the town from the south and through the former location of the thirteenth-century St. Martin's Gate, he heads for the damaged Worcester Cathedral. The unpromising midday sky is grey and cold, the slight drizzle and wind ensuring that horse and rider are less than comfortable. Adjusting the collar of his coat for warmth, Francis brings Churchfield to a halt. In the distance, a faint but steady rhythmic sound catches Francis's attention. Tilting his ear, he ascertains that the measured tones are clearly drumming; he's confident it is the cadenced tapping of several musicians—perhaps British soldiers. He abandons his destination of the cathedral and ventures deeper into the walled city, toward the persistent sound.

Nearing the large wooden building from which the drumming emanates, Francis reins in his horse and slides from his back, pausing to observe the details of the structure. Built of oak timber set into concrete siding and painted white, the building has a high roof line nearly three feet higher than normal special-use structures, a slate roof, and no windows. Out front, Francis notices several British soldiers standing at attention outside the oversized double wooden doors to the structure. He approaches the men, aiming for one short, stocky guard.

"Would you welcome the efforts of an itinerant preacher?"

The men are silent. They glance at each other and continue to say nothing. Dressed in their proper military uniforms, the young men are an imposing sight. Each stands tall and straight. The soldier Francis decided to address looks to his companions once again, then finally responds,

"Very well. Correction shall complete shortly. Please do join us."

The soldiers turn and head in through the wooden doors. Francis follows.

The large open space inside the building is actually a riding school where the horse soldiers receive their training in combat riding. In addition, the space has one other use: the discipline of soldiers whose behavior is inconsistent with the British army.

Inside, the drummers which Francis heard from afar are lined up at the far end. They continue to play, although in a low-volume, steady drum roll. Their unique yellow-jacketed uniforms capture Francis's attention, until he notices the large wooden apparatus in front of the drum line. Hanging from what appears to be a hangman's gallows but without the raised platform is a man with his hand raised. Actually, the thumb of his right hand is connected to a rope that is taut and clearly supporting his weight. At the other end of the man, whom Francis has surmised is a soldier suffering discipline, the bare arch of the man's right foot rests on the rounded point of a wooden stake buried upside-down in the ground. The soldier, who is dressed in his military uniform minus the red coat, periodically shifts the weight of his right leg in an attempt to relieve the pressure on his foot. Unfortunately for the soldier, this weight shift results in an excessive amount of strain on the thumb. Francis inquires,

"How long has he suffered in such a manner?"

"As long as the Captain requires. Sometimes one to one and a half."

"Hours?"

"No, preacha', days."

Francis is astonished; *the man must dangle in such a manner for a day?* The soldiers notice that the revelation troubles Francis. One of the soldiers, a tall, thin man with uncommonly dark eyes, offers,

"We shall gather the men; plan to preach out back. They shall assemble in fifteen minutes."

The tall soldier departs, and the remaining two escort Francis past the drum line and the hanging man.

Outdoors, the horse soldiers gather. They are a group of twenty-two men, dressed in their military red coats and their winter boots that reach above the knee. Several have removed their black tricorne hats. They stand quietly as they watch Francis thumb through his Bible. Francis is comfortable with returning to his standard sermon from the Gospel of John, about Jesus being the way, the truth, and the life. He raises his hands for prayer and the men bow their heads.

Partway through his sermon, the drum line brings its monotonic rhythm to a halt. The silence causes Francis to stop. Within moments, the drummers make their way toward Francis and his impromptu gathering.

With their drums in hand, the specialized soldiers in their bright yellow coats with red-and-white shoulder, wrist, and edge bands are in sharp contrast to the red-and-white uniforms of the horse soldiers. On the front of the yellow drums carried by each drummer are the Roman numerals XXIX, signifying the 29th Regiment of Foot. Francis continues to stare at the unique outfits, observing the white wigs of the drummers tucked neatly under the black-and-white mitre hats.

The men are black!

Francis doesn't verbalize his surprise, but the men sense his reaction. Francis has never seen anyone with dark skin. He stares at the drummers, unable to resume his preaching. He continues to stare; it is hard to resist the sight of these sharply dressed men, their bold yellow uniforms highlighting their brown skin. One of the drummers tips his head and motions to Francis,

"Please continue."

His deep, almost melodic voice returns Francis to his intended purpose. The remainder of the sermon is a blur to Francis; thankfully, it is a familiar recital. Finishing the Bible lesson, he concludes with prayer.

At the gathering's end, the lead drummer once again approaches Francis. The tall, angular man inquires,

"Might we hear your preaching again?"

"I shall attempt preaching this evening, in town."

"Very well, my men and I shall attend."

For the remainder of the afternoon, Francis contemplates his discovery: *the King's army possesses black drummers.*

By six p.m., many of the town's residents have shown up to hear the traveling preacher. Standing in front of nearly seventy-five people, Francis peruses the gathering made up of village woolers, men and women who work sheep's wool for export. Village cobblers, butchers, and malters also join the small crowd. There are nearly twenty soldiers to the left of Francis. He looks for the drummers, but they are not present. He begins with prayer,

"Heavenly Father . . ."

The people are silent as Francis concludes his prayer and begins to speak.

"I have had many trials from Satan, but hitherto the Lord has helped me against them all. I stand a miracle of mercy! O that I may always be found faithful in doing His will!"

With the Bible in his right hand raised above his head, Francis is suddenly interrupted by a man on his left.

" 'Tis the devil's rebellion. Yo've no right to go against the King's Church. Yo' border on da' rebel."

The man protesting Francis is one of the soldiers of the 29th Regiment. He is a tall man with a rough-looking face and dark eyes. Shocked by the outburst, the thoughts in Francis's head suddenly stop. He tries to focus on the situation, but it suddenly seems surreal; his emotions are still raw from the Gloucester dunking. As his mind darts to the river baptism, a slight panic comes over him. He lowers the arm holding the raised Bible; his hands begin to shake.

The objecting soldier looks to his fellow fighters; they're not accepting Francis's preaching without a protest. One of them bursts toward Francis as he cries,

"Yo' shall suffer for going against our King!"

The announcement causes the crowd to disperse. Women hurriedly push their children away, caught between Francis and the oncoming soldiers set to do bodily harm. The soldiers grab Francis by the arms; with two pulls, he is face-down in the dirt. The soldiers kick him in the ribs. In the legs. One jumps up and lands his heels in the middle of Francis's back. Francis is defenseless; the sand cakes in his nostrils as he gasps for air.

One soldier grabs his legs and drags him backward through the dirt. The other soldiers continue the pounding with well-placed kicks from their military-issue boots. They twist his leg and turn Francis over, exposing his chest and stomach to injury. A stiff kick to the side of his face knocks him unconscious.

The screams of the women in the crowd are the last sounds he hears.

Francis awakens lying in a bed. He cannot raise himself to see where he is; the pain in his lower back is unbearable. Rolling slightly to his right, he notices a soldier in a yellow military jacket standing in the doorway. The soldier inquires,

"Pastor Asbury, may I enter?"

Francis tries to speak, but he cannot. His jaw aches with a sharp, piercing pain. He attempts to nod approval, but this too proves futile; his head aches at the temples, and he senses that portions of his face are swollen. Disregarding the lack of response, the black British soldier from the drum line of the 29th pulls up a chair and sits next to Francis.

Francis awakens again, this time realizing that he must have fallen asleep. He instinctively turns to his right as he remembers the black soldier. He is still there, quietly waiting for Francis to regain his senses.

"Pastor Asbury, you must rest. The gracious people of Nash's shall nurture you. I've arranged to move you when strength returns. For now, you shall remain."

Francis cannot physically acknowledge the statement; he closes his eyes and thanks God for the safe and thoughtful provision.

It is three days before Francis can sit up. When he does, the lady who runs the almshouse, Mrs. Percy, informs Francis,

"Many took yo' for dead."

Drawing a breath, Francis swallows. His throat is scratchy and dry. His heavy tongue aims to moisten the inside of his mouth. It is a slow process. The painful condition of his face causes him to force the words out.

"Where am I? What has transpired - -
To place me here?"

"Wasn't for the drummers of the Twenty-Ninth, you would ha' been killed."

"By whom?"

"Da' soldiers of the Twenty-Ninth. Dey' accuses you of being Wesleyan.
Is it true? Yo' one of Wesley's?"

Francis keeps silent. Despite the welcomed return of his saliva, the stinging pain of an empty stomach begins to compete with the pain in his head and back. Mrs. Percy offers,

"Here is tea. Yo' need to replenish. In answer to yo' question, yo' are in the Nash Almshouse."

Francis receives the cup and sips slowly. The bruise on his jaw draws comfort from the warm liquid as he swallows. He takes another sip, this time holding it to the right side of his mouth, the side with the injury.

Walking into the room, the drummer draws Francis's attention. He looks to the tall man. He is dressed in his vibrant uniform, the white trousers highlighted by the yellow, red, and white jacket and the black leather boots rising above the knee. His ornamental oversized jacket cuffs are rolled back to reveal his dark skin. The soldier bows his head and remarks,

"Seems our patient is flourishing."

"He is."

"You shall find Mrs. Percy's tea as perfect remedy."

Francis returns the nod and responds,

"Yes, it brings wellness."

The polite soldier once again pulls up his chair within arm's length of Francis. His gentle, deep, melodic voice informs him,

"The house of Percy is generous; however, it is limited. I shall make arrangements with the Knapps; I would guess your health allows travel tomorrow."

"I shall not burden Mrs. Percy more than necessary."

Francis sets down the teacup on a small wooden stand next to his bed and looks to his dark-skinned attendant. *He seems extremely kind.* Francis draws comfort from the man's gentle and caring manner. Shifting to the immediate task, he braces himself to lift his legs to the side of the bed, successfully placing both feet on the floor. He notices that his boots are missing and is embarrassed that his bare feet are exposed to the two people in the room with him. Strangely, he thinks back to the shoe lessen he received at his parents' home when he was nearly thirteen.

"How I now see the wisdom of boot pumps."

Mrs. Percy laughs aloud, as does the drummer. Before attempting to stand, Francis asks of the drummer,

"Might you lend hand?"

The African stands to his feet and extends his hand. Francis notices the thick-wristed appendage and its protruding thick vein that travels the broad underside of a well-developed forearm muscle. The drummer offers,

"My name is Joshua, Joshua Charlow of St. Kitts."

"My pleasure, Mr. Charlow."

At this, Francis extends his right arm forward. Joshua gently pulls the itinerant to his feet. A little lightheaded, Francis manages to balance. He also manages to notice that Joshua is nearly six inches taller than he is. Francis informs him,

"Well, Mr. Charlow, take me to my horse and I shall follow to the Knapp residence."

Joshua remains silent, staring at the floor. Francis inquires,

"My horse—what of Churchfield?"

Joshua places his right arm onto Francis's shoulder.

"We shall locate your horse—your Churchfield. As of now, we've no record of its whereabouts."

The news hits Francis hard. A feeling of sadness mixed with guilt pushes aside the little confidence he gained in the last few minutes. He sits back onto the bed, saying nothing.

The extended silence prompts Joshua to offer,

"Pastor Asbury, your horse shall show. For now, we must move you to the Knapp residence. Mr. and Mrs. John and Anna Knapp have heard of your plight. They are a loving and generous couple of your stripe: Wesleyans."

"Mrs. Percy informed earlier, but the memory escapes me; where do I reside now?"

"The Nash Almshouse—from what I have learned, set up nearly four centuries ago. For the destitute, run on its own, apart from the King. By the generous contributions of private individuals. Great idea, biblical."

"Thank you, Joshua. Joshua, one more question; how do I know you?"

"You don't."

Mrs. Percy interrupts,

"Joshua and a few of his drumma's rescued yo' from the Angli soldiers. They aimed to kill yo'."

"Why rescue a despised Wesleyan?"

"Pastor Asbury, I believe Mrs. Percy and I have heard it often from preachers like yourself: 'The Lord rescues us to rescue others.' Is this not true?"

"It is."

"Well then, there is your answer, Pastor Asbury. Besides, does not the name Joshua mean 'God rescues'?"

Francis nods his approval.

"Joshua, you must call me Francis."

Outside the Nash building, three drummers of the 29th have a horse-drawn chaise waiting to escort Francis to the Knapp residence in the adjacent hamlet of Lowesmoor. Leaving the city, they venture northwest through a tree-lined connecting road. The lofty oaks focus the travelers' attention toward the end of the neighboring street. There, a single-standing white house made of timber in the old-country style resides two hundred yards outside the walled boundary of Worcester. Joshua advises,

"Our destination. My men and I shall stay with you until nightfall. In the morning we have an assignment and then we shall visit in the afternoon."

"Assignment?"

"Yes. Military orders."

"May I inquire?"

"Very well, Pastor Asbury—rather, Francis. In the morning, my fellow drummers and I shall flog the Angli soldiers who persecuted you."

"Flog. You - -

Allowed to . . ."

"Yes, Francis. It is a requirement of the King's army that drummers flog the insubordinate soldiers. Seems Command believes we possess the arm strength to establish a clear understanding."

Francis is confused. First, it is a stretch for a young man from the West Midlands to accept that an African can participate as a British soldier. *Not that I disapprove.* Before Joshua, he had never seen a dark-skinned individual from Africa. Second, this African will be doing the flogging? From his early childhood Francis has heard of flogging, but always associated with the slave trade—he's heard the stories of the infamous slave ships and the brutal episodes of endless flogging of the Africans. The surprising circumstances prompt Francis to ask,

"How do you come about as drummer in the King's army?"

"Not long ago, I was a slave of the French. The valiant efforts of Colonel George Boscawen and his brother, Admiral Lord Boscawen, changed that. The admiral gained our freedom through the British capture of the island of Guadeloupe, eight years ago - -

"Yes, in '59. The Boscawen brothers rescued ten of us, all slaves of the French. They graciously invited us to join the drum regiment for the Twenty-Ninth Regiment of Foot. The colonel felt we would greatly enhance his troop's morale, especially with the discipline. We accepted the drum positions, which provide the pay rate of corporal."

"The colonel knew you could drum?"

"We are Africans."

His own statement amuses Joshua. His bellowing laugh echoes a time of ancient civilization, the first peoples in a region not far from the Garden of Eden. The laugh leaves Francis somewhat mystified.

In front of the Knapp residence, the chaise comes to a stop. Joshua leaps down and assists Francis to the ground. Walking him to the front door, Joshua assures Francis,

"The Knapps shall take good care of you. We Wesleyans shall rescue this nation yet."

John and Anna place Francis in a two-story structure adjacent to the home. The downstairs room is one large open space; the half-finished, musty room reminds Francis of the West Bromwich Methodist meeting room that he and his friends remodeled for worship. The helpful couple guide the itinerant upstairs to a private room complete with a dormered window, a bed, and a small table with one chair. Leaving him to rest, John Knapp offers,

"You may stay as long as you require."

Francis remains silent, nodding his acceptance.

The next day's sunrise awakens Francis; he instinctively worries that he has slept in too long. He leans to his right, hoping to get out of bed. It is not an easy task. With much pain in his face and back, he manages the effort. Placing both feet on the wooden floor, he pushes off the bed and rises to stretch. Despite the pain in his ribcage, he forces a large breath and stretches carefully.

He slowly slides his feet along to the one window in his room. Looking to the west, he notices the walled city. Beyond Worcester, he can see the River Severn. His thoughts and emotions take a dive; *oh, Churchy?* Pursing his lips, he fights back the urge to weep, certain that he will never see his horse again. He prays silently, *Lord, I have not only disappointed You, I have destroyed the offerings of a loyal animal. I shall miss his welcoming neighs. However, shall I return to Great Barr?*

A knock on his bedroom door ends the gloomy thoughts. Francis responds,

"Do come in."

It is drummer Joshua. In his left hand are Francis's boots; in his right, Francis's Bible. He offers,

"I felt you would have need of these."

Shuffling toward him, Francis responds,

"Thank you, Joshua."

"Can you walk downstairs?"

"Yes, Joshua."

"Very well, follow."

Transitioning down the steps is not easy; Francis pauses after each one. Joshua patiently walks alongside Francis, ensuring a safe journey toward the lower level. At the bottom of the stairs, Francis notices the front door to the structure is open. Standing outside the door, two yellow-jacketed drummers stand at attention with their backs toward Francis. Joshua motions for Francis to head toward his fellow musicians.

At the doorway, a familiar sound greets Francis: the neighing of Churchfield. Francis bursts through the two soldiers and finds the horse tied to a post, eating grass. The animal raises his head and shakes it several times to the right and left. He ceases as Francis reaches him and hugs the horse's neck.

"Oh, Churchy, I shan't risk our separation again."

The horse nuzzles against Francis's love offerings. The accommodating soldiers watch as the pair exchange familiar greetings. Francis raises his eyes toward Joshua.

"Moreover, I shan't risk my itinerancy either. Joshua, I shall return to Great Barr."

"Great Barr? I've word that the nailers of Tewkesbury desire your preaching."

Francis ponders the corporal's statement. *Perhaps I shall return to Tewkesbury.* Joshua interrupts Francis's musings.

"Before you visit the nailers, I've one request."

"Yes, Joshua?"

"Prayer, for my fellow soldiers and myself. The colonel has informed us that the Twenty-Ninth departs tomorrow. For the colonies. I am afraid we are heading into a storm - -

At Boston."

Francis doesn't respond. Strangely, he recalls the odd conversation with the old woman who was to die in Wolverhampton—Mrs. Hanson, and her prophecy. She urged Francis to continue to follow the call, despite a storm. Refocusing his thoughts, Francis responds,

"I shall pray."

The winter month of January finds Francis in Tewkesbury; in fact, he remains among the nailers for several months. Their kind hospitality provides a home to stay in and one meal each day. Francis is grateful for the provisions. His efforts in the riverfront village lead to the establishment of a Methodist meeting house on Tolsey Lane. Francis is proud of this small accomplishment. However, his ominous persecutions in Worcester and Gloucester almost daily darken his sense of gain in Tewkesbury.

The first of April finds Francis once again at Nailers Square. Bent over on the prayer bench, he completes his supplication. He raises his head to find a familiar face patiently waiting for him to complete. The tall man remarks,

"Fr'dancis, ya' mother and faither would do well to know of ya' well-bein'."

"Pastor Mather!"

The revelation launches Francis to embrace the Scottish preacher. The two draw comfort from each other. The crisp morning air floats from the mouths of the smiling men as they release.

"Fr'dancis, word is ya' have wrestled wit' a Leviathan."

"I have, yes, I have."

"Couple in Worcester shares of ya' barely escapin' wit' ya' life. Ya' jacket conveys the same."

" 'Tis true, sir. I've stuck it out in Tewkesbury. Nailers here receive the Word with joy."

"Heard of that as well. How do ya' fare, Fr'dancis?"

Francis's demeanor sobers; he stares toward the ground. Mather is troubled for his stubborn but brave protégé.

"As Ah' thought. The low r'dound borders on toughest gr'dound for Wesley's vision; only one is tougher. Ya' have done well enough. Do ya' believe so?"

"I have invited opposition."

"Fr'dancis, ya've much to learn. Ya' did not br'ding this upon ya'self, only deepened its undesirous effects. Ya' failed to submit to the plan of God - -

And Wesley. Do ya' understand? Opposition is expected; however, wit' disobedience, it invites anguish."

"I understand."

"Ah' advise that ya' head for London. Ah' hear that several godly young women would desire ya' preachin'. They shall provide a home for ya'. Rest awhile in the town; Whitefield and Wesley shall hold conference there shortly. Ah' am proposin' to Orpe that he recommend ya' for appointment in the upcomin' conference."

Inside, Francis rejoices. His widening smile invites Mather's response,

"Ah' thought that would lift ya'. One other item: before London, make a visit to ya' parents."

"Yes, sir, I shall."

To Francis and his parents, the two days together pass much too quickly. Each evening, several of his friends join them for dinner; oddly, Nancy does not attend. Francis's stories of the little Wesleyan society in Tewkesbury, the black drummers of the 29th Regiment of Foot, the ancient buildings of worship, and the infamous outing at Gloucester entertain his faithful comrades and escort them through a wide range of emotions. Laughter, tears, anger—each of these feelings surfaces during the retellings of his adventures.

The night before his departure, Francis spends time venturing to find Nancy. Traveling in complete darkness to her home, he waits outside. No candles light the home; the family is absent. Disappointment overwhelms Francis. Without tears, he confesses his struggle to God; *perhaps our relationship is nearing an end*. He departs, his thoughts refocusing on London and the journey ahead.

The 105-mile trek from the Asbury cottage to London takes nearly one week on horseback. Like his trip to Ashbourne, Francis's journey to London occurs with Mather. In Sutton Coldfield, they take the Ickneild portion of the Roman road to the north, stopping south of Lichfield to catch the ancient Watling Street. From here, they follow the Roman road southeast all the way to London. The ancient road takes them through the towns of Atherstone, High Cross, Towcester, Stratford, Hockliffe, Dunstable, and St. Albans. By county, his course originating in Staffordshire traverses through Warwickshire, Northamptonshire, Bedfordshire, Hertfordshire, and Middlesex.

Entering the city of London from the northwest, the Watling delivers Francis and Alex due north of their destination, Tottenham Court Road Chapel, Whitefield's chapel known as the Tabernacle. Mather informs Francis that he should pay a visit to one in need. He departs, suggesting that the itinerant head directly to Whitefield's chapel.

"Ah' shall find ya' tonight at service. Whitefield and the brothers Wesley alternate preachin' there most nights of the week."

Francis nods his agreement and departs for the chapel.

The hemp farm Francis travels through bears the marks of the previous winter; large piles of prepared hemp are scattered about the farm. Unlike the summer when the fields flow with the tall, clumpy plants, the fields are currently barren. Several huddles of men and women, mostly prisoners from the workhouses, busy themselves with the pilling of the hemp. This process is the last step required in preparing hemp for spinning into fiber for material.

Francis is also thankful that it is the season of spring. He arrives well beyond the nasty portion of the hemp-preparation process—in the winter, when the plants remain outside soaking in water to rot, they give off an unbearable stench. As elsewhere, the month of April is a pleasant time of promise in England.

As Francis rides southeast on Tottenham Court Road, Whitefield's tabernacle will sit ahead on his right side, nestled among several small independent theatres in the artist district of London. Adjacent to the place of worship is a home utilized by Whitefield and his many guests who attend, usually preachers from England, Ireland, and Wales. Francis isn't planning to stay near Whitefield's tabernacle; to his mind, it isn't an option. He will seek modest accommodations, meeting Mary Bosanquet and her companions, Sarah Ryan and Sarah Crosby, across town at The Cedars in Leytonstone.

Dismounting from Churchfield in front of the home, Francis walks to the door and knocks. The voice from inside is adamant, calling,

"Enter; we are indisposed."

Tis not an English voice. Francis is surprised; he pulls on the oak-wood handle and enters.

Inside the dark, narrow hallway, Francis takes three steps and walks into a main room, much like the main room of his childhood home. The ceiling is low, as is the light level. At the opposite end he spots two men, on their knees and peering up and inside a stone fireplace. Aware of his entrance, the kneeling man on the left tips his head toward Francis.

> "I was just informing Preacher Occum of the advantage of my contrivance. Since installing these dampers, many hundreds have been set up in imitation, to great satisfaction."

The balding man completes his discourse. His face is full of black soot; he removes a handkerchief from his coat pocket and wipes his brow. The maneuver only serves to further the smudging. Standing to his feet while continuing to clean his right hand with the cloth, he approaches Francis and offers his hand.

> "Franklin, Benjamin Franklin. Son of a humble tallow-maker, boarding at Thirty-Six Craven Street in London."
>
> "Asbury, Francis Asbury, itinerant preacher for John Wesley. Boarding nowhere in particular at this time."

The other gentleman, who has still been admiring Franklin's invention, rises, turns, and walks toward the pair. He is a tall man, over six feet in height. He too extends a hand to Francis, this hand much sturdier than the aging Franklin's.

"Occum, Preacher Samson Occum. A Mohegan from the great colony of Connecticut."

"Asbury, Francis . . ."

Francis fails to complete his introduction. He is not aware of a colony called Connecticut; he assumes it resides in America. He also fights the urge to laugh. He is amused by the contrast in the two men who stand before him: one in his sixties, barely five feet five inches tall, with bulging belly, sooty face, and white splotches of hair on either side of his bald head; the other, the preacher, standing upright and straight, athletic, and towering over his companion. Furthering the picture of contradiction between the men is the wide bib-tie and black clerical robes of the preacher and the simple, plain woolen clothing of Franklin. The man of God has jet-black hair, straight as ever Francis has seen; his face is of foreign origin, almost European but not Spanish or Italian, with perhaps a touch of Asian. Moreover, the skin color of the man catches Francis the most; it is a reddish-brown color. Noticing Francis's confusion, Franklin responds,

"American Indian."

Franklin pauses long enough, or so he perceives, for Francis to process his revelation.

"Very well, you are Francis Asbury."

Francis's lack of response corresponds with the entrance of three individuals in the midst of a discussion. Unaware of Franklin, Occum, and their young guest, the group barges into the room. The first of the new arrivals can be overheard proclaiming,

"The merchants shall never agree . . ."

The gentleman making the argument is a short, jovial man in a black clerical robe. Making eye contact with the new arrival, Francis notices *one of his eyes crosses.* The second is a tall man, also dressed in a preacher's outfit, similar to the temperate outfit of Occum. The third, a short, round man, is well dressed in an expensive cotton suit. Francis is drawn to admire this man's attire; *quite fashionable.*

Trailing the three, a fourth comes into view; this is a familiar face to Francis. The last gentleman walks around the entire group and spots Franklin's black-stained face. He looks to Francis and then back to the soot-covered sage. He returns his gaze to Francis.

"Black dust seems to follow you."

Francis cannot help the reaction; he laughs before responding,

"Lord Dartmouth."

"Young Pastor Asbury, I've word from Mather that you have been itinerating."

"As best I can."

"Well then, you are on the verge of seeing it done properly. Whitefield will yield his pulpit this evening to the eloquent and exciting Samson Occum. Have you had the pleasure of meeting him?"

"I have."

"And have you had the pleasure of meeting dear Dr. Franklin? This American shall surely rob the King of all his undesirous taxes."

The group looks to Franklin; they doubt he is without reply to Dartmouth's quip. He does not disappoint.

"Being born and bred in one of the countries, and having lived long and made many agreeable connections of friendship in the other, I wish all prosperity to both sides. Unfortunately, I have talked and written so much and so long on the subject, that my acquaintances are weary of hearing, and the public of reading, any more of it. Considering this and the fact that my father was an Englishman, born in the village of Ecton in Northamptonshire—to England, I am too much an American, and in America, I am too much the Englishman."

"As usual, well done, Dr. Franklin."

The group expresses amusement at the comments of Dr. Franklin and the reply of Lord Dartmouth.

George Whitefield is the preacher with one eye that crosses. The other men with him are Lord Dartmouth, the well-dressed merchant Dennis De Bert, and Samson Occum's traveling companion from America, a Princeton College Presbyterian minister, Nathaniel Whitaker.

Occum and Whitaker are in the middle of a two-year stay in England. Their intention is to raise money for their Indian Charity School in Lebanon, Connecticut. Eleazar Wheelock, a graduate of Yale in the year 1733, owns the institution. The noted preacher and educator is determined in his efforts to educate the young Native American children of the eastern border of America. Currently, Occum and Whitaker are well on their way to acquiring more than ten thousand pounds[117] in contributions.

Grateful that Lord Dartmouth is present, Francis doesn't mind spending the day with the august group. At times, his nervousness surfaces in his verbal replies. In his own opinion, he is much too young and much too inexperienced to participate in conversation with these leaders of Great Britain and America. He

---

[117] More than two million US dollars in twenty-first-century value.

patiently longs for the familiar territory of the evening's service. In spite of his fears, the men welcome Francis.

Because of his recent experience in an almshouse, one high-minded conversation draws Francis into the discussion. Dr. Franklin approaches Lord Dartmouth on the precarious domain of charity. Francis listens intently as Franklin proffers his opinion of the effort.

> "For my own part, I am not so well satisfied of the goodness of this thing. I am for doing well to the poor, but I differ in opinion of the means. I think the best way is not making them easy in poverty, but driving them out of it."

> "I and many others agree with you, Dr. Franklin."

> "Ah, yes. However, in my youth, I traveled much; I observed in different countries, yours included, that the more public provisions were made for the poor, the elderly, the neglected, and those in general need, the less they tended to provide for themselves, and of course became poorer. On the contrary, the less was done for them, the more they did for themselves, and became richer. This is the sure foundation of the origin of our free market system. If a man shall not work, he shall not eat."

Nathaniel Whitaker jumps in.

> "I agree, Dr. Franklin. I am sure that your observations of England will reveal that which troubles your findings."

> "Correct, Nathaniel; my travels of this great land reveal that there is no country in the world where so many provisions are established for the poor and needy, so many hospitals to receive them when they are sick or lame, founded and maintained by voluntary charities."

Francis's thankfulness for Mrs. Percy and the generous offers of the Nash Almshouse causes him to nod in agreement. Dr. Franklin continues,

> "So many almshouses for the aged of both sexes, together with a solemn general law made by the rich to subject their estates to a heavy tax for the support of the poor. Under all these obligations, are our poor modest, humble, and thankful? Do they use their best endeavors to maintain themselves and lighten our shoulders of this burden? On the contrary, I affirm there is no country in the world in which the poor are more idle, dissolute, drunken, and insolent. Make them uncomfortable with their poverty and you shall bestow a Christian blessing upon them. The day you passed that act, you took away from before their eyes the greatest of all inducements to industry, frugality, and sobriety, by giving them a dependence on somewhat else than a careful accumulation during youth and health, for support in age or sickness. In short, you offered a premium for the encouragement of idleness, and you should not now

wonder that it has had its effect in the increase of poverty. Repeal the law, and you will soon see a change in their manners. St. Monday and St. Tuesday[118] will cease to be holidays. Six days shalt thou labor, though one of the old commandments long treated as out of date, will again be looked upon as a respectable precept; industry will increase, and with it plenty among the lower people; their circumstances will mend, and more will be done for their happiness by inuring them to provide for themselves, than could be done by dividing all your estates among them."

Although the economic ramifications of Dr. Franklin's argument are above Francis's level of comprehension, one thing is clear to the young preacher who has recently enjoyed the benefits of an almshouse financed by private donations. Without expecting it, he finds himself offering the observation to Dr. Franklin.

"In my recent stay in an almshouse, I failed to notice persons of idleness."

Francis's surprise at the blurting-out causes him to fidget with his hands; he eventually rests them within his coat pockets. Dr. Franklin offers,

"Then your stay could only have occurred in a privately funded institution where the proprietors have long adopted the Christian principal that if a man shall not work, then a man shall not eat."

"Yes, I would believe it to be so."

Leaning into the conversation, Lord Dartmouth confirms,

"I am quite familiar with Nash's, and yes, the facility is as you express, Dr. Franklin. The Nash family operates their almshouse according to biblical dictates vital to the free market system."

The nobleman looks to Francis and smiles. *Seems as though he is aware of my trial;* Francis keeps this thought to himself.

Tottenham Court Road Chapel—or the Tabernacle, as the locals refer to it—is the religious structure erected by George Whitefield in response to his ejection from the chapel in Long Acre by the vicar of St. Martin–in-the-Fields. The vicar holds no favor toward the radical evangelical efforts and success of Whitefield. Built of brick eleven years ago in 1756, within four years the seventy- by seventy-foot square building is rendered too small by the Whitefield faithful. Through the donation of Selina, the Countess of Huntingdon, Whitefield arranges for the building of an octagonal extension toward the front. Soon, other private donations from the Tottenham congregation erect twelve almshouses and a chapel house adjacent to the Tabernacle. The popularity of the Tabernacle soon results in regular guests like the Prince of Wales, as well as his brothers and sisters.

---

[118] A tradition of absenteeism on Mondays and Tuesdays, usually because of a gin hangover or plain laziness.

Other notable attendees include the Scottish philosopher David Hume, the son of the Prime Minister, art historian and man of letters Horace Walpole, and actor David Garrick.

A recent occurrence at the Tabernacle exemplifies Whitefield's wisdom in placing the chapel within the London theatre district. The extremely funny actor Ned Shuter happened into a worship service. At the time he was starring in the play *The Rambler*, without a doubt, he was the London favorite when onstage sporting his craft. Strutting in with his trademark dressed and cocked hat and flat-collard frock, Shuter was surprised when Whitefield in his characteristic style turned toward the celebrated actor and invited him to "ramble toward the Savior." Shuter ill-perceived the impromptu offer and proceeded to argue with Whitefield. Whitefield was patient; he allowed for a reasoned argument. Over the next few weeks, Shuter's personal demons—he drank excessively—sent him repeatedly back to the Tabernacle. In time, Whitefield's patience resulted in Ned Shuter becoming a regular member of the Tottenham Court Road Chapel society. From this point on, the local actors know exactly where to find Ned after a drinking binge: either at Whitefield's chapel, taking in a sermon, or out in an open field, preaching to himself as loudly as he can on original sin and repentance.

The London faithful at the Tabernacle are far from a homogenous group. Worshiping regularly next to the local actor, lawyer, and merchant is the farmer, plasterer, husbandman, and cordwainer. The efforts of Whitefield and the Wesleys attract all portions of society. While characteristic of other societies in England, Ireland, and Wales, class distinctions are uniquely non-existent within the Wesleyan community.

Francis and his illustrious group enter and take their seats within the chapel. Although the Tabernacle is much less ornate than the magnificent thousand-year-old churches that Francis has viewed in his recent travels, the tall, columned ceilings remind Francis of the ancient cathedrals. The chapel is full of people. There is a double-tiered gallery on three sides of the four-walled structure; these are filled to capacity. One section to his right and directly in front of the raised wooden pulpit remains empty; it can easily hold two dozen people. Francis finds it strange; *this seating has no takers.*

At the completion of this thought, Francis's attention is drawn toward a slight stir at the rear of the chapel where the entrance fronts on Tottenham Court Road. Entering the structure is an entourage of twelve people, *twelve richly dressed people.* The congregation already present marvels at the new arrivals, as does Francis; he has never viewed anything like this. The clothing of this group rivals anything he has experienced. Several women in elaborately ornate dresses, the hoop skirts enlarged by whalebone frames, glide into the room. Their high-plumed hairdos are richly adorned with oversized and colorful feathers. Several of the women sport tall headpieces made of excessive spirals of wool and horsehair, the false curls accented with flowers causing the women to appear taller than their male escorts. The obviously significant male counterparts sport their powdered wigs, though nowhere near the height of the cocooned weaves of the ladies; a sword at the side represents a necessary accessory for a couple of these flashy blades.

Upon their arrival, George Whitefield rises and exclaims,

> "She has arrived!"

In the midst of this wealthily clad group, a well-to-do but moderately dressed woman emerges. At first, Francis is surprised to see her in the midst of the extravagant group; *she appears out of place*. Francis once again catches a word by Whitefield,

> "Our dear Selina."

Francis remains mystified. He realizes that this woman must be a friend of Whitefield as well as someone special. He patiently awaits as she makes her way to the vacant seats at the front. Lord Dartmouth leans in toward Francis and whispers,

> "The Countess of Huntingdon. One of Wesley's and Whitefield's biggest benefactors. King George is captivated by Her Ladyship, calling her noble, commanding, and engaging. She truly is an honor to her sex and nation."

Francis nods his affirmative, but he is uncomfortable with the entire scene. Dartmouth can sense it, especially when Francis begins to rub his pointer-finger knuckle with the thumb of his opposite hand. The Earl once again leans toward Francis.

> "Seems the girls of Leytonstone have an open seat. I am sure they would welcome your company."

He points in their direction, right behind Francis. Relieved, Francis rises and departs toward Mary Bosanquet, Sarah Crosby, and Sarah Ryan. They see him approaching; they too are relieved, and thankful for his willingness to join them. Mary rises and motions for Francis to sit next to her; as he does, he bows a thank-you. She curtsies and takes her seat, then gently places her hand on his hand, which rests on his thigh.

> "Welcome back, Pastor Asbury."

Francis tries to resist, but it is impossible; his face broadens into a wide smile.

At the front of the sanctuary, the black-gowned George Whitefield climbs the flight of winding steps to the pulpit. The raised platform stands on a large, octagonal wooden pedestal, the entire structure nearly ten feet above the ground. Once at the top, Whitefield begins,

"They have satirically called my tabernacle 'Whitefield's soul trap.' I pray that God may make it indeed a soul trap to many of His wandering creatures."

The gathered crowd clap their hands. Soon they fall silent, and George continues,

"They have burlesqued me on stage as running a brothel. Other unworthy productions have cast me in further dim lighting. To each of them I have one reply: I am afraid Satan is angry."

The group acknowledges his observation: "Yes, Satan is angry at his success." Whitefield raises his arms, closes his eyes, and with his melodic voice begins,

"Father Abraham, whom have you there with you? Have you Catholics?"

He pauses, then responds,

"No."

He pauses again, a long pause. After twenty seconds he continues,

"Have you Protestants? No. Have you High Churchmen? No. Have you Dissenters? No. Have you Presbyterians? No. Quakers? No. Anabaptists? No. Whom have you there? Are you alone?"

By now, many in the pews squirm with uncertainty. Whitefield continues,

"No, you are far from alone. My brethren, you have the answer to all these questions in the words of my next text: 'He who feareth God and worketh righteousness, shall be accepted of Him.'[119] God help us all to forget having names and to become Christians in deed and in truth.

"Accepted of Him, many shall enter the kingdom, many who appear far different from you or me. Today, I offer you one who shall surely walk the golden streets of eternity. I welcome the Preacher Samson Occum of the Connecticut Colony tribe of the Mohegan."

Descending the pulpit stairs, Whitefield meets the approaching Occum at the bottom step. It is well that George remains one step above Preacher Occum; the Mohegan is nearly a foot taller than Whitefield. Extending his arms, he offers the Native American a loving embrace and a holy kiss.[120] After they release, Preacher Occum ascends the steps.

In the pulpit, Occum begins,

"Eternal life and happiness is the free gift of God, through Jesus Christ, our Lord.

"The life mentioned in our text begins with the spiritual life. It is the life of the soul, a restoration of the soul from sin to holiness, from darkness

---

[119] Acts chapter 10, verse 35, paraphrased by Whitefield from the King James Version.

[120] The early church's traditional greeting of a kiss on the cheek.

Of 1767   *Alien Preacher* / *377*

to light, a translation from the kingdom and dominion of Satan to the kingdom of God's grace. In other words, it is being restored to the image of God, and delivered from the image of Satan. And this life consists in union of the soul to God, and communion with God, a real participation of the divine nature, or in the Apostle's words, it is Christ formed within us."

Raising his thick arms toward heaven, Occum continues,

"I live, says he, yet not I, but Christ who lives within me . . ."

For the next hour, the alien preacher preaches on sin and its destructive nature and its obsession with destroying the image of God in humanity. In his elevated and eloquent manner, he closes with,

"Great or small, honorable or ignoble, rich or poor, bond or free, Negroes, Indians, English, or of what nations so ever, all that die in their sins must go to hell together, for the wages of sin is death. Take warning of this doleful fight before us; oh, let us all reform our lives, and live as becomes dying creatures, in time to come. Let us be persuaded that we are accountable creatures to God, and we must be called into account in a few days. Now awake to righteousness, and be concerned for your poor and never dying souls. Fight against all sins, especially the sin that easily besets you, and behave in time to come as becomes rational creatures; and above all things, receive and believe on the Lord Jesus Christ, and you shall have eternal life. And when you come to die, your souls will be received into heaven, there to be with the Lord Jesus in eternal happiness, and with all the saints in glory, which, God of His infinite mercy grant, through Jesus Christ our Lord. Amen."

The evening is an exciting event for Francis. In their eagerness to approach the preacher from America, the congregation swarms the front of the sanctuary. Francis marvels at the gathering; standing shoulder to shoulder, the high and lofty entourage that accompanies the honorable Countess, the farmer, and the merchant all eagerly await their turn to greet Pastor Occum.

Francis and the girls rise and head for Whitefield, who stands alone to the side, a rare occurrence for the popular Oxford preacher. Turning toward the young and vibrant members, he welcomes their presence.

"Pastor Asbury, I see you've found encouraging company."

" 'Tis true."

Addressing the women, Whitefield remarks,

"I'm to leave for the colonies once again, perhaps in a few weeks. Wesley wishes that I stay for the conference in August. Perhaps I shall. I've heard tell that one Pastor Asbury has a more than successful chance of admittance on trial."

"We've heard also."

Francis blushes with slight embarrassment at the remark, still uncomfortable in the presence of the venerable Whitefield. George smiles at the young itinerant.

"Francis, you shall do well to accept."

The well-dressed Mary Bosanquet offers,

"Yes, Francis, we agree. We also agree that you shall do well to preach at The Cedars each Sabbath for the next three months."

"Oh? What if I planned to join our honorable company for the colonies?"

"We would agree that you shall do well there also."

The gentle flirting amuses Whitefield; he quips,

"Methinks, Pastor Asbury, you must possess a double portion of Elijah's blessing to turn down such an **attractive** offer."

With his characteristic dramatic delivery, Whitefield emphasizes the word "attractive." Francis enjoys the verbal nod. He also is thankful for Whitefield comparing him to Elijah's protégé, Elisha. He replies,

"Perhaps; even so, make it a double portion of the blessings that prosper you and I shall easily accept departure for the colonies."

The flirting is over. The girls bow their appreciation and respect for Francis's determination to spread the Gospel.

The three months in Leytonstone are a special time for Francis. In consideration of his clear dedication to the itinerancy, Mary Bosanquet puts aside her attempts to relate with Francis on an intimate level and invites him to aid in the girls' street ministry. The platonic arrangement works well. On several occasions, as the dirty cobblestone streets of London produce a street vendor attempting to harass the young ladies for bringing aid to the less fortunate, Francis breaks into an impromptu sermon. His experienced voice easily draws a crowd and silences the objection. Most of these gatherers are grateful for the scriptural teaching, including a few of the original oppressors.

On Tuesday, August 18, 1767, Francis departs from the girls for the annual conference in London at the Foundry Chapel.

***

With the harsh winds of the winter of 1739 imprisoning the Christian faithful indoors, and the ill favor of the Anglican priests forcing the Wesleys outdoors, the providential paradox resulted in John and Charles Wesley coordinating the acquisition and renovation of the old artillery foundry of King Charles. Sitting atop Windmill Hill, north of Finsbury Fields, the building known for casting brass guns and mortars for the Royal Ordnance had sat quiet for twenty-three years.

May 10, 1716, was a day which ended not as planned. It also ended the operation of the artillery foundry. On this infamous day at the privately owned facility, captured French cannon stored on site for three years were ready for melting and re-forming into English ordnance. The molds were readied, and nearly fifty people gathered to view the operation. Men and women of royalty along with key military personnel joined the foundry's owner, Mathew Bagley, and his family for the significant event.

Unforeseen reasons caused the operation to delay. By nightfall, the majority of the spectators had departed; of the original fifty, only four remained. At the eleven o'clock hour, the French brass was finally ready for pouring into the molds. The molten liquid began its slow ooze into the cavity buried vertically in the ground. Ignoring the warnings of a journeyman founder who had spotted moisture in the bottom of the mold hours before, Mr. Bagley ordered the process to fully deliver. As the extremely hot fluid touched the latent water, a catastrophic explosion instantly killed seventeen of the twenty-five workers in the immediate vicinity of the operation. The remaining eight laborers suffered severe burns; only two survived. Searing flames injured the four spectators. Sadly, Mr. Bagley and his son were listed among the dead. The disastrous event forced the British government to set up a new facility to take over the process of producing brass ordnance.

The Wesley brothers' 1739 acquisition of the closed foundry in Upper Moorfields, London, required nearly eight hundred British pounds for subsequent renovations. The finished structure allows for seating 1,500 people in the main room. An additional three hundred can fit in a space directly behind the sanctuary. It is a simple structure, the outside built of brick and mortar, the inside adorned with several support columns and wooden pews. Upstairs are two apartments used by the Wesley family.

On this dark summer evening, the swaying yellow lights of The Foundry's lanterns hanging on either side of the entrance doors give a hallowed glow as nearly two hundred of London's faithful, along with John Wesley and twenty of his itinerants, gather for the opening evening of the conference. Allowing the locals to attend the first day's events, Wesley patiently awaits the following three days when he can focus on business.

The idea of a conference gathering of Wesley and his itinerant helpers originated mostly by circumstances outside of his influence. When forced to organize the growing number of preachers drawn to his movement, the conference of 1744 was held, representing the first organized meeting of key leadership. Originally planning to meet his itinerants quarterly, Wesley found that the annual meeting quickly became the standard procedure. The meetings usually occurred between the more pleasant months of June and August. At this point, the cities of London, Bristol, and Leeds are the designated towns for meetings, happening in turn.

Much like Martin Luther who sought to cleanse instead of leave the Catholic Church of the sixteenth century, through the 1750s and early 1760s Wesley painstakingly offered attempts to unite with the Anglican structure. Sadly, his efforts have been ignored. In the preceding year he wrote several letters to many of the clergy, hoping to form a common basic doctrine and tolerance of differences. This year is no different for Wesley; he continues to desire solidarity with the King's Church.

The attendees fall silent as John walks toward the pulpit at the front of the room. Once there, he begins,

> "Ah, many years ago, in the year 1739, I preached in the morning to nearly five thousand standing shoulder to shoulder in the fields that surround this great building. A building once set for destruction by fire, now set afire with life-giving instruction for building. On that morn, I preached on the spirit of bondage and the spirit of adoption. Later that day, from this structure meant for building an arsenal for the British army, I spoke: 'O hasten Thou the time when nation shall not rise up against nation, neither shall they learn war anymore!' It is my desire and prayer that the Church of England shall no longer desire to war with its children, that it should lovingly seek our adoption."

Seated a few rows directly in front of Wesley's pulpit, Francis looks about the room. Attendance here at The Foundry, among the brothers Wesley, George Whitefield, and other key itinerants, overwhelms the young preacher. Of the 104 Wesleyan itinerants in existence at this time, he can pick out only a dozen or so. It is easy to spot a traveling preacher; they stand out from the locals, dressed in dusty clothing and carrying a worn leather saddlebag into the sanctuary. With several, the smell of lingering body odor floating alongside their arrival reminds Francis of his gritty travels; he instinctively raises an arm to smell himself. *Not too offensive.* Realizing, too, that attendance at a conference by an itinerant is by Wesley's invitation only, he considers himself fortunate to attend—slightly overwhelmed, but fortunate.

The rest of the evening is a time of worship in song and edification through testimony. Many of the London Wesleyan society come forth to share of God's involvement in their lives, some giving encouragement through God's miraculous provisions, others building the faithful through God's provision of peace in times of trouble.

The next morning of the conference is much quieter than the evening before. Present are John Wesley and twenty of his itinerants, Francis included. Wesley directs the attendees to the room behind the sanctuary. The space designated for London's band meetings can hold three hundred people. At the front of the room, John and several of his circuit assistants seat themselves facing the remaining itinerants. Seated alongside Wesley are Alexander Mather, James Glasbrook, and Wesley's advancing disciplinarian, Thomas Rankin. The young martinet sits upright and straight, peering sternly at the itinerants. Mather and Glasbrook casually rest. The late-arriving Richard Boardman joins the august group up front. All are clearly happy to be seated next to the honorable John Wesley.

Standing and walking to the front, Wesley begins,

"What preachers are admitted this year?"

Standing from his position at the front, James Glasbrook offers,

"Richard Bourke, Benjamin Rhodes, John Allen, Alexander McNab, Lancelot Harrison, and Thomas Dancer."

"Please rise."

Wesley has each of the newly appointed full-time itinerants stand. He raises his hands and prays silently. Lowering his hands and his gaze toward the preachers, he offers,

"To be a Methodist preacher is not the way to ease, honor, pleasure, or profit. It is a life of much labor and reproach. They often fare hard, often are in want. They are liable to be stoned, beaten, and abused in various manners."

Wesley turns his eyes toward Francis. Francis is uncomfortable; he nervously rubs the base knuckle of his pointer finger. Wesley smiles at Francis, and Francis's fear flees. He is confident that he is with those who can identify with his struggle. Wesley continues,

"Candidates who are receiving full admittance, consider these warnings before you engage in so uncomfortable a way of life."

The new preachers take their seats, and Wesley moves on.

"Who are admitted on trial this year?"

Once again, Glasbrook stands.

"Timothy Janes, Francis Asbury, Joseph Peacock, Joseph Wittam, Thomas Cherry, William Hunter, William Harry, Thomas Ryan, and William Collins."

Wesley offers sage advice to the hopefuls, each of whom displays the required talents and perseverance to join the ranks of full-time itinerants; however, another year of experience is required before that decision will be finalized.

Wesley inquires,

"What preachers desist from traveling?"

Glasbrook again rises to offer the individuals who will no longer participate as active itinerants. The names are unknown to Francis. His thoughts wander as the five or six names exit from Glasbrook's mouth. Not until the verbalized reasons for one preacher's untimely exit register with him does Francis return his attention. Glasbrook elucidates,

"For the rumor and confirmation of drinking in public and for the subsequent rumor and confirmation of singing profane songs, James Stephens shall desist from traveling."

Concluding the handling of the itinerant-specific issues, Wesley moves toward the temporal. In recent years, these items have slowly demanded much more time than the original conference focus of doctrine, discipline, and appointments. The next day's meeting shall deal solely with such issues.

In the morning, the unusually warm air slows the pace of the attendees. A random yawn accompanies the rubbing of eyes fixed forward toward Wesley. One item of note: As George Whitefield sits in the front, the tireless itinerant from Wales, Howell Harris, joins him. Harris is one of two leaders of the dynamic Methodist movement in Wales. Like the brothers Wesley, his Methodist manifestations prohibit his ordination in the King's Church.

The always observant and untiring leader surmises that his group is in need of a jolt. Instead of his customary opening with prayer, he blurts out,

"How are the preachers stationed this year?"

No thoughts randomly wander now. Each of the itinerants sits up straight, anxiously awaiting the most important decision of the conference: *on which circuit shall I travel this year?* The preachers nervously rub the backs of their sweaty necks, or their forearms which ache from holding the reins for fifty weeks each year, or their knees which are sore from prayer. Wesley loves this moment; he peers at each existing and potential itinerant. The veterans like Mather and Glasbrook are amused by the event, especially when they view the younger travelers nervously avoiding eye contact with Wesley. Wesley begins,

"London: Will Buckingham, Benjamin Colley, Peter Jaco, Nicholas Manners, and Thomas Janes."

Several of the men mentioned breathe a sigh of relief; others wishing for the London circuit frown their displeasure. Wesley continues,

"Sussex: John Easton, John Allen.

"Canterbury: Duncan Wright, Alexander McNab.

"Colchester: Thomas Hanson."

Many in the group silently rejoice; Colchester is a rough coastal circuit.

"Norwich: William Minethorp, Benjamin Rhodes.

"Bedfordshire: James Glasbrook, Francis Asbury."

Francis immediately spins to look toward Glasbrook. He is thankful to team with his friend and mentor; he and Alexander Mather are Francis's two favorites, like welcomed uncles. His thoughts focus; *Bedfordshire, shall place me nearly eighty miles from home.*

The Bedfordshire circuit is forty-five miles from London. It is a large, rural-based circuit consisting of more than a thousand square miles, an expanse including numerous small societies within Northamptonshire, Huntingdonshire, Buckinghamshire, Hertfordshire, and Cambridgeshire.

The reading of the assignments continues in the same manner, completing the twenty-five circuits in England and the additional sixteen circuits in Scotland, Ireland, and Wales. The placing of the itinerants commands their undivided attention. Francis makes a mental note of William Orpe's assignment to the Wiltshire circuit.

Wesley then goes on to offer his comments on reading. Several of the new itinerants have raised concerns about the inordinate amount of time required by their leader.

"I urge you, read the most useful books, and that regularly and constantly. Steadily spend all the morning in this employ, or at least five hours in twenty-four. 'But I read only the Bible,' some are to say. Then you ought to teach others to read only the Bible, and, by parity of reason, to hear only the Bible. But if so, you need preach no more."

The young preachers hang on Wesley's last admonition, "you need preach no more." Francis and the others sit higher in their seats. Wesley continues,

"Just so proclaimed one who is an infidel; I shall not raise his name.[121] And what is the fruit? Why, now he neither reads the Bible nor anything else. This is rank enthusiasm. If you need no book but the Bible, you are above St. Paul. He wanted others too. 'Bring the books', says he, 'but especially the parchments,'[122] those written on parchment. 'But I have no

---

[121] One of Wesley's itinerants whom he expelled.

[122] From 2 Timothy chapter 4, verse 13.

taste for reading.' Contract a taste for it by use, or return to your trade. 'But different men have different tastes.' Therefore, some may read less than others; but none should read less than this. 'But I have no books.' I will give each of you, as fast as you will read them, books to the value of five pounds. And I desire the assistants will take care that all the large societies provide the Christian library for the use of the preachers."

Moving on again, Wesley aims for the temporal items.

"Shall we repeat or enforce the rules relating to ruffles, lace, snuff, and tobacco?"

As expected, the discussion among the seasoned assistant itinerants is in line with Wesley; the major concern is the dress of the preachers and the attire of the society members. "Avoid whichever tends to conform to the world's desires for fashion." "The ruffles on men's shirts do not belong on the Wesleyan faithful, especially the preachers." Francis considers his flirtation in the past with finery; he recalls his stay with the Wyrley Birch family. *I do enjoy a masterly crafted coat.* He moves on in hopes of realigning his opinion.

Wesley summarizes the issue best:

"This is no time to give encouragement to superfluity of apparel. Therefore give no band-tickets to any in England or Ireland till they have left them off."

On the issue of snuff, the clear objection is the taking of the substance during sermons. The preachers do not partake. Wesley, in his recent book titled *Primitive Physick: or an Easy and Natural Method of Curing Most Diseases* allows for the use of snuff when attempting to cure head lice, the product being rubbed vigorously into the scalp.

Drams are a different subject. Drams are spirituous liquors. England in the eighteenth century plunges to the depths of debasement with its rampant addiction to dram drinking. Wesley refers to drams as "liquid fire." Well beyond the religious community, the overall public opinion is that there should be a healthy alternative to hard drink. Ales and beers are the natural choice of many, including Wesley. Wesley's thinking on drams is straightforward:

"How shall we cure them of drinking drams? Let no preacher drink any, on any pretense. Strongly dissuade our people from it. Answer their presences, particularly of curing the colic and helping digestion."

A final issue forces Wesley to pause before divulging. The problem is isolated to the coastal towns; however, a few villages along the larger rivers also take part in the illegal operation. Wesley declares,

"How may we put a stop to smuggling? Speak tenderly and frequently of it in every society near the coasts. Carefully dispense my document, *Word*

> *to a Smuggler.* Expel all who will not leave it off. Silence every local preacher that defends it."

Wesley's recent pamphlet, *A Word to a Smuggler,* delivers a strong argument against the illegal importation of goods without paying the required duty. His view is simple: the prohibitive act harms the British King and his citizens; it is worse than a highwayman or a pickpocket, as it is robbing those you know—the King and your fellow citizens. The biblical admonitions that "thou shalt not steal" and that one must "render unto Caesar the things which are Caesar's" clearly delineate Wesley's opinion. He finishes with the exhortation,

> "If you fear God . . . keep yourselves pure."

The final day of the conference is like the opening day—a time of worship in song and edification. Unlike opening day, this time the singing and testifying are limited to the intimate group of preachers. The singing is worshipful and the sharing at times borders on the comical.

At one point, it is Wesley's turn to step forward with a testimony or encouragement for his eager troops. After peering around the room with a wry smile, John has a word for a young itinerant.

> "Pastor Asbury, some thoughts on fair Bedford."

The itinerant from Great Barr is uncomfortable with the singling-out. He darts his gaze around the room, avoiding eye contact with anyone. He places his arms across his chest, his shoulders raising slightly as he draws his arms tighter; he then settles in to receive Wesley's words.

> "On a cold November evening, I ventured into Bedford. The fifteen miles of road from St. Albans to Sundon were covered in snow. Save for a worn beaten path by a wagon that had gone before us, the deepening snow would have inhibited us completely. The road from Sundon to Bedford was in much the same condition. With much difficulty and in the dark of night, we arrived in Bedford. Our host structure was a clear reflection of the dedication of the Bedford faithful, the large congregation, without fail, worshiping in a structure built over a hog-sty. At times, the rising stench from the swine below endeavored to silence my sermon. I persevered in the knowledge of the Bedford faithful—surely they love the Gospel, who come to hear it in such a place."

Francis considers the words of Wesley.

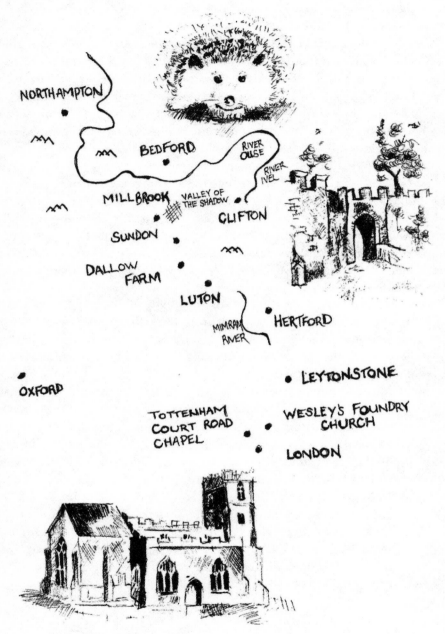

NORTHAMPTON

BEDFORD

RIVER OUSE

RIVER IVEL

MILLBROOK

VALLEY OF THE SHADOW

CLIFTON

SUNDON

DALLOW FARM

LUTON

MIMRAM RIVER

HERTFORD

OXFORD

LEYTONSTONE

TOTTENHAM COURT ROAD CHAPEL

WESLEY'S FOUNDRY CHURCH

LONDON

The acorns of one century are the oak trees of another, and
The forests of the dim centuries are the coal mines of to-day.
Centuries refuse to be self-contained, and history cannot be packed
In parcels.H. J. Penny[123]

As he joins Francis for this end-of-August departure from London, the seasoned preacher born and raised in Bedford breathes deeply of the crisp morning air. Along the undulating pathways hidden below the forest of leafy silver birch and beech trees, James Glasbrook advises Francis,
        "Hertford by day's end."
The small town in Hertfordshire is twenty miles outside London. Heading due north from the Foundry Church, Francis and James traverse the woodlands that supply building materials and fuel for London and the surrounding areas. Amidst the towering conifers, hemlock, and cypress, the radiating beauties of summer hang on for one more week. The refreshing colors of the delicate dog rose seem to court one another as they weave their spiny limbs among the hardwoods, gaining a more advantageous position as they aim for the first level of branches several feet above the forest floor. The soft white and pink flowers tease flirtatiously as the gentle breeze inspires them to wave. The attractive quality of their dark, blue-green leaves enhances their beckoning. In addition to the climbing dog rose vines, the tiny lavender and purple blooms of the blanketing wood speedwell wrestle the wood anemone for domination of the gentle slopes and meandering paths.
        Pastors Glasbrook and Asbury will both itinerate the sprawling Bedfordshire circuit and its several promising locations. Unlike the large and lively London society with its magnificent chapels, these rural spots support small, intimate classes of the countryside faithful.
        Entering Hertford from the south, James and Francis direct their horses to the open field which serves as the town's marketplace. The men dismount, securing their four-legged companions next to the wooden stocks and pillory[124] used for punishing those who break the law. James points to the pillory.
        "This time last year, our dear Benjamin spent an evening so occupied."

---

[123] H. J. Penny, *Alexander Mather: Scotsman, Baker, Methodist Preacher.*
[124] Both the stocks and the pillory were used to punish and publicly humiliate lawbreakers. The pillory was a post-mounted wooden frame with holes for securing the head and hands.

Shocked by the account, Francis asks,

"Benjamin Colley?"

"Yes. The mayor was troubled by the disorder which erupted."

"From preaching?"

"Benjamin is young and enthusiastic; the more suspect locals thought it opportunity to broaden their nefarious efforts. The mayor and his men were far outnumbered. Without question, 'twas his sole option. Other than sore shoulders and neck, our dear Benjamin fared well."

Francis's shock abates; nevertheless, he cannot fathom spending a night in the pillory for preaching. *Far worse than a near-drowning? Perhaps not.* The self-revelation helps him to deal with the hurt from his experience outside Gloucester.

Interrupting his thoughts, a tall, thin man wearing a leather carpenter's apron approaches the pair. In his right hand is a wooden mallet. The imposing figure's words precede his arrival.

"Pastors, I failed to believe Wesley would give so easily."

"Abraham Andrews. How are we?"

"Fine, doin' fine. Who've we here, Pastor Glasbrook?"

"It is with pleasure I introduce one of our newest and finest, Francis Asbury of Great Barr."

"Great Barr? All dat' seems to surface in Great Barr are naila's."

"Spent my share of evenings bedded down alongside my anvil."

"Ha ha! Wesley's men are a solid lot."

Slapping Francis firmly on the back and abruptly halting his laugh, Abraham advises,

"You've need to follow."

"Very well."

James's reply sends the trio in the direction of the southwestern portion of town. Francis tries to reach the spot on his back that still stings from the carpenter's strong slap. He can't; the striding carpenter and joiner forces Francis to push himself in order to keep pace.

As the men make their way, Hertford Castle, the tiny town's major landmark to the west, comes into view. The castle positioned alongside the River Lea is currently in disrepair. The flint walls[125] standing more than twelve feet in height mark the perimeter of the castle's grounds. All that remains in original condition are the six-foot-thick walls with navigable walkways atop. This portion of the structure is thought to be the first line of defense against an attack.

At this time, the castle is nearly eight hundred years old.

---

[125] Large stone walls covered with broken shards of flint rock set in mortar.

In 1309, the monarchy, the Pope, and the Pope's Bishops imprisoned the Knights Templar in the dungeon of Hertford Castle. They feared the order's growing wealth and power. The once-welcomed group, established to regain the Holy Land of Jerusalem from the conquering Islamic army, at the time was held suspect. Around the same time, the French wife of King Edward II, Queen Isabella—also known as "the She-Wolf of France"—arrived with her violent temper. Taking a lover, she successfully organized propaganda against her husband, displacing him and placing her fourteen-year-old son on the throne. The youth of the junior Edward resulted in Isabella and her lover, Roger Mortimer, ruling for the next three years. Young Edward's mother eventually arranged the murder of his father. Realizing the betrayal of Isabella and Mortimer, Edward III took control, imprisoning his mother and hanging her lover. Upon her release from prison, Isabella spent her final years at Hertford Castle.

Hertford Castle during the sixteenth century boasted of King Henry VIII and his many wives. Three of his more famous children—Mary, daughter of Catherine of Aragon; Elizabeth, daughter of Anne Boleyn; and Edward, son of Jane Seymour—each spent considerable time at the fortified residence. During Mary's reign as an adult, she utilized Hertford's dungeon prison to hold her Protestant martyrs. Mary's death began the reign of her half-sister, Elizabeth. During her reign spanning four decades, the Protestant Queen spent much time at the castle. During three decades of the deadly plague, members of Parliament and the courts found safety in the castle.

Walking past the castle's perimeter walls, the trio stops in front of 25 Castle Lane. Catching their breath, James and Francis view the property. Abraham offers,

"Well, it is finished."

The itinerants are unsure of his pronouncement. James inquires,

"Finished? Is it the home you speak of?"

"Far from just a home, it is da' Met'odist home - -
And a school."

"School?"

"Aye, Pastor Asbury, a school. Follow."

The three men make their way into the one-story wooden structure. Inside the main room, nearly two dozen young girls sit quietly on several rows of wooden benches. James inquires,

"You are teaching girls?"

"And boys. Each attends t'ree days each week. I've a teacher for da' boys and one for girls. Arrangement works quite well. Each attends every ot'er day."

"And does Wesley know of this?"

"Not yet. Plan on sendin' word shortly. Da' space works for da' class and band meetings as well."

"I assume the members aided you in this endeavor."

"Well, James, t'was my plan; however, few have come forward. Da' Lord blesses my business. I shan't have need of assistance, only Wesley's blessing."

"Mr. Andrews . . ."

"Francis, I don't ans'er to Mr. Andrews."

"Very well, Abraham. Whatever inspired you? To build."

"Your fellow itinerant, and quite easily. When I viewed Mr. Colley's calm demeanor in da' face of da' mayor and da' belligerent people of da' town, I knew dat' he possessed da' true religion. His confident and considerate actions drew me to bring him breakfast next morn. By day's end, despite the aches and pains brought on by da' pillory, he was in great spirits. Enough to encourage me to do all I can for da' cause."

"Well then, Abraham, Francis and I shall make known to Wesley your little school and meeting house—your successful school and meeting house."

Abraham is grateful. He gives a slight bow and offers a request,

"Pastor Asbury, would yo' bless da' girls with a lesson from da' Bible?"

"It would be my pleasure."

After Francis preaches to the children, Abraham invites the men to stay the evening. They gratefully accept. Before departing for the living quarters, their host moves to the bookshelf on the back wall of the school room. He removes a book and proceeds toward Francis.

"A gift. In gratitude. Thank yo' for teachin' da' girls."

Francis tilts his head in thanks, touched by the generous offering of the rough-edged carpenter.

The book's cover with its swirling colors of robin's-egg blue bubbled within a gold–and-tan frame not only highlights the brown leather edge binding, it also invites the young itinerant to open to its pages. Before he does, he notes the gold-leaf details of the binder: three brilliant sunbursts from the bottom up, each separated by horizontal scrolls, these in gold leaf also. Near the top are an additional trio of horizontal golden scrolls, each bordering a colored square; one in hunter green bears the author's name, Bunyan, in gold-leaf lettering. The other square, in brick red, bears the words *Pilgrim's Progress*, also in gold-leaf lettering.

Francis opens the book. The title before his inspired eyes is a familiar one to the itinerant.

The Pilgrim's Progress
From
This World to That Which Is to Come

Francis raises his eyes toward the carpenter and gives him a gentle smile.

"Thank you, Abraham; a most welcome invitation of my youth. It shall join me in my travels."

That evening, the men sit around the lit fireplace in Abraham's home. The simple home boasts of numerous carvings he has made, several in a lovely wood with a reddish tone. Francis remarks on a wooden stand that seems to glow in the firelight.

"The mysterious material is quite attractive."

"Mahogany."

"Wherever does such beauty reside?"

"West Indies - -

By way of Bristol and London."

Francis is impressed; he rises to admire the wooden stand. James too rises. The itinerants instinctively rub the smooth finish as James asks,

"This stand, shall it grace the schoolroom?"

"In time, in time. It is my desire to construct a pulpit someday. Perhaps a pulpit for Wesley himself."

"Impressive, Abraham."

Without hesitation, the carpenter is almost forward in his request.

"James, shall travels keep yo' from our little school for long?"

"Northampton and Bedford sometime this year or early next. We shall service Hertford, Luton, and surrounding areas first, for a short season. Some stops in between either way. We shall aim for three to four weeks out."

"Look forward to a return. Perhaps enrollment shall increase by then."

After a restful night, the men are on their way. The fifteen-mile journey to Luton will follow the River Mimram for the first nine miles. The Mimram is a unique waterway, with a rare groundwater system known as a chalk stream. Due to the natural aquifer that exists in the rock formations beneath the riverbed, the accumulated rainwater filters through the porous rock, which is a form of limestone. The passage through the chalk filter not only adds nutrients, it also purifies the water.

The crystal-clear river is a healthy environment for unique fish and plant life. The added nutrients serve to amplify the natural food chain: the insects are more prevalent, the plants are healthier, and the fish are more abundant.

Spotting several large brown trout hovering twenty inches below the surface of the Mimram, James alerts his traveling companion.

"Francis, look."

"Beautiful. The water is clear."

"Francis, look through the water—the trout."

"I see. You know, Mather has quite a talent for catching."

"I know. On our return through the circuit we shall obtain the swimming delicacy."

The horses eagerly escort the itinerants toward the northwest, grateful for the ample supply of water and grass on this leg of the journey. Francis pulls out his Bunyan book and begins to read.

Before long, the undulation of the cresting hills begins to glow with the area's highly valued wheat crop. The golden flush of the arcing grass is both evidence of the generous summer rains and an announcement of the approaching fall season. The tempting view is too much to resist; Francis puts down the book and reins in Churchfield for a look. The horse nickers as he lowers his head for a tasty treat. The view captures Francis's attention; *oh, for Father to view such magnificence.* The beauty of the wind-coaxed wheat easily surpasses the vertically stiff and leafy hemp fields of his previous travels in Staffordshire and around London.

The remaining six miles will take the pair through the cresting hills that benefit the Luton straw-hat industry. The local farmers grow the ideal wheat, rich in golden color and tensile strength, for the manufacturers engaged in the plaiting process. In addition to hats, the plant works its way into thatched roofs, bed mattresses, and table placemats. The plaiting process is ingenious, the braiding of seven strands of dried wheat creating a pliable material. The corded strength combined with the irresistible coloring ensures numerous markets for the finished product in and around Luton.

Francis returns to his reading. The quiet ride is enhanced by the cooling temperatures of September. Nearing the town, Francis glances up from his focused efforts and spots numerous houses with children sitting on the roof edge. He inquires of James,

"What of the children?"

"Plaiters. Young girls and boys spend nearly twelve hours each day weaving the straw into solid plaits for manufacturing. Over one, under two, pull it tight, and that shall do . . ."

"Over one . . ."

"Francis, it is quite simple. Over one, under two, pull it tight, and that shall do."

"Over one, under two . . ."

"Oh, Francis."

"Of what am I to be over and under?"

"Weaving straw. It is simple; seven strands are braided as you have attempted to recite, the outside on the right weaved over the one next to it and then under the next two strands. Repeat the process from the other side, over the one next to it and under the next two. In time, your work shall resemble a flat braid. The children do well with it. They place themselves on the roof knowing that once their braid touches the ground, their work for the day is complete."

"I see."

"Enough of plaiting. Where is Pilgrim in his journey?"

"The First Stage. Mention of his dream in the den."

"Oh, you've only begun the book."

"Considering the lessons in straw, I have progressed nicely."

James turns toward Francis and laughs aloud. After a few seconds, James shakes his head and flashes a wide smile with a silent laugh. Francis perceives the facial expression as odd. He prompts James,

"Yes?"

"Oh, the den. I'm reminded that the den which Bunyan speaks of resides in Bedford."

"Bedfordshire's Bedford?"

"Yes, Francis. In fact, the den was not a den at all . . ."

"Mother has informed me—a jail, I realize."

"Yes, Francis, a jail."

Glasbrook returns his attention forward, sending Francis deep into the book.

On the west side of Luton resides a small farmhouse on an open plot of land. The acreage slopes upward, providing an advantageous view back down to the town. Francis and James continue. Despite Francis's reading, James shares,

"I spent many days on the property as a child. Interesting home."

Without lifting his eyes from the book, Francis responds,

"Interesting in which way?"

"You shall see."

James's secrecy draws Francis's undivided attention; he raises his eyes from Bunyan's tale. The surrounding farm of several hundred acres boasts of wheat and cattle. James is thankful to reach the beginning of the residence quarters. The pair stops at the hedgerow on the front side of the house.

The Dallow Farm house is a large wooden building, its two and a half stories providing nearly three thousand square feet of living space. The thatched roof and wood batten siding give the home with three fireplaces an informal country-style appearance. Francis's gaze is drawn to the three tall brick chimneys. Their clay color is unique to this region. He also sees an adjacent building of equal height, this one clearly a barn. James watches Francis's eyes as they peer at the upper roof area of each building. He offers,

"The space above the second floor is not so easily accessible."

Francis quizzically tilts his head. With a smirk, he replies,

"The mystery continues."

James chuckles.

"Come, let us proceed."

Inside the home, the owner welcomes James and Francis. The Hale family has owned the Dallow Farm since 1640. Mr. Hale is a short man, his thinning hair softened by its striking white color. The elder farmer is a member of one of Luton's important families.

"James, it is my pleasure to receive you once again. I see you've a young associate."

"Mr. Hale, one of Wesley's newest: Francis Asbury of Great Barr."

"Pastor Asbury, James is a long-time friend of our family. On several occasions when he was a young boy, I happened upon him among our wheat fields. Has he shared of the barn?"

Francis turns toward James. It is clear he doesn't understand. Realizing this, Mr. Hale suggests,

"James, perhaps we should escort Francis to the barn."

"Francis fails to realize the significance of the barn, or that he has recently spent much time with the barn's primary resident."

"Well then, we must inform this young itinerant of a little history."

Francis delights at the mention of history, one of his favorite subjects. However, he continues to doubt the efforts of James; *what is he up to?* Mr. Hale's comment also furthers Francis's uncertainty. *More mystery,* Francis thinks to himself. Regardless of the lack of information, Francis happily follows them through the exit door.

Outdoors, the three men arrive at the adjacent two-story building. It appears to be an agricultural barn, sturdily built of wood, with several farm implements leaning against the wooden siding. The trio ventures inside.

Francis views a wooden ladder on the far end of the dirt-floor space. Next to the ladder are two small windows. The space is nearly filled with a wooden plow, a few wooden yokes, some wooden wheels, and several saddles neatly hanging on two walls. Looking at the ladder, James urges Francis,

"The ladder interests you, Francis?"

"Why the ladder? I've spotted no apparent use for the item."

James and Mr. Hale chuckle. Mr. Hale advises,

"Look closely. Rather, look up closely."

Francis does so. Peering at the wooden plank ceiling, all appears as it should: well-spaced eight-inch-wide boards, running north to south from one end of the building to the other. Francis is puzzled; he looks to James.

James is silent. Smiling, but silent. He turns toward Mr. Hale. Mr. Hale urges again,

"Look closely, Francis, at the ceiling. Note that which is hidden in plain view."

Francis looks. His frustration, evidenced by the exaggerated exhale through his nostrils, amuses James and Mr. Hale. The pair finally gives in.

"Francis, between the windows on the far end. Count over three boards."

"Yes, Francis, follow James's advice. Once you've counted the three planks, space off the end wall nearly two full strides. Tell us that which comes into view."

"Ah, I am two strides off the wall. I do not see it."

"Aha, works as well as it did some seventy-five years ago. Come, Francis; James and I shall reveal the secret."

Walking directly underneath the mentioned spot, Mr. Hale takes hold of a long pole adjacent to the ladder leaning on the far wall. From the end of the pole protrudes a small iron hook. Reaching toward the ceiling with the pole, Mr. Hale places the iron hook into an iron eyelet stained to match the wooden planking, affording it complete concealment from view below. Pulling on the metal ring, a trapdoor in the ceiling lowers to reveal a hidden space in the half-story above the two-story barn. The six planks which make up the access are cut at different lengths on both ends, appearing to match the rest of the ceiling's random cut-length pattern. Francis smiles at the two men and inquires,

"Shall we proceed above?"

Francis's eyes are wide with the promise of a risky undertaking. James responds,

"We shall."

Mr. Hale fetches the ladder. Francis hadn't noticed before, but the two ends of the ladder have similar iron hooks, like the pole. Mr. Hale places the hooks of the ladder into the opening above. The apparatus is just long enough to hook into two eyelets strategically placed on the top side of the access door. Once the ladder is secure, Mr. Hale invites,

"Shall we?"

It is a somewhat shaky undertaking, but the men climb to the space above.

In the room above the barn, Mr. Hale informs Francis,

"This space is sacred. The meeting place for a body of believers—believers running from the King who despised them. The leader of this group of Pilgrims was imprisoned for preaching without a license. This well-spoken and determined leader of the religious dissenters preached in this space on numerous occasions. Francis, do you know of whom I speak?"

"I cannot say so."

"Very well, Francis; the individual Mr. Hale has been alluding to is the writer of the book you have been reading on our journey from Hertford. John Bunyan himself was the itinerant preacher who on numerous occasions held church in this space above the rafters."

Francis is silent. The significance of the room captivates his thoughts. He envisions Bunyan standing here, in the loft covered with hay, preaching to the faithful. A random thought prompts Francis to inquire,

"Mr. Hale. What of the elderly? How would they fare with such a climb?"

"Francis, the elderly were the originators of the space."

Francis nods his head; he is impressed.

The evening spent with Mr. Hale inspires Francis. He successfully convinces him to meet in the sacred space above the barn. The awkward climb once again sparks the interesting thought, *a difficult task for the more seasoned faithful.* Their conversation about Bunyan draws the young itinerant to Bunyan's commitment to the Gospel. Mr. Hale shares of Bunyan's two imprisonments and the resulting separation from his wife and children. The account of Bunyan's blind daughter who aches for her father's release saddens Francis. It reminds him of his older sister, Sarah, a sister who is largely the product of his mother's sharing of the girl. In light of Bunyan's productive second imprisonment, when he wrote *Pilgrim's Progress,* Francis desires *the same ability to persevere as Bunyan.* He vows to do so.

The next morning once again finds James and Francis moving out. Four miles northwest of the Dallow Farm resides Sundon Manor. Lord Sundon's affluent home is a large property in the English tradition of stately manors. Impeccably landscaped, its grounds are a complement to the surrounding forest that canopies the wilder portions of the estate. Umbrageous oaks and leafy hardwoods tower more than eighty feet in height and diameter as they shadow the acreage.

The early-eighteenth-century façade of the mansion with its castle-like crenellations delineates a royal architecture. Its original Lord and Lady, William Clayton and his wife, Charlotte, had set out to remodel the magnificent natural-stone structure. Charlotte, an attendant of Queen Caroline's bedchamber, and William, the manager of the Marlborough Estates for the Duke of Marlborough, handsomely accomplished their goal.

Currently a young couple, Mr. and Mrs. William and Elizabeth Cole, own the luxurious home. Elizabeth, the niece of the late Lord Sundon, and her husband, William, a magistrate and sheriff, inherited the estate upon Lord Sundon's death. More importantly, William is a close friend of John Wesley and a member of the Foundry Church in London. As a favor to Wesley, James has agreed to pay a visit to the Coles.

Approaching the home, Francis and James marvel at the magnificent three-story structure. James suggests,

"Perhaps we shall promote a preaching engagement for the evening."

"We shall?"

"We are itinerants, aren't we?"

Staring at the home, Francis doesn't answer. James comments,

"You seem hesitant, Francis."

"My apology. The home invokes a memory . . ."

The revelation surprises James. Sensing a young man in need of a listening ear, he waits for Francis to continue. Francis rides on in silence.

After a few minutes of quiet, James prompts,

"A memory?"

"Yes. One that fails to end well."

"I see."

"Mother and Father for a time placed me with a wealthy family. A wealthy and kind family."

"In Staffordshire?"

"Handsworth."

"The Wyrley Birch residence, Hamstead Hall?"

"Correct. The Birch family treated me to the theatre. And other items."

"Oh. Items of finery?"

"Fine items, clothing. 'Pure finery,' as Mother designates them."

"I see. According to your mother and father, shall finery necessitate despair?"

"Far from it. Finery on its own is simply finery. To my mother and father, finery is an opportunity to do well."

"Why the trouble?"

"Perhaps my attendance. At the theatre."

"I see. You enjoyed the performance?"

"Far from it. A burlesquing of dear Whitefield."

"Oh, the dilemma is quite clear now. Perhaps you shall share with the wealthy Cole family about your times in the theatre."

Francis frowns at the thought. James chuckles.

"Very well, this fine couple awaits our arrival. Come, Francis; Wesley depends upon our efforts."

Standing on the front porch of the home, William and Elizabeth Cole watch the arrival of the itinerants. James dismounts, secures his horse, and proceeds to the front door of the opulent residence. Turning around, he finds Francis still atop his horse.

"Come, Francis; we've work to do."

Francis reluctantly dismounts and joins the itinerant.

Elizabeth and William have lived at Sundon Manor since they inherited it nearly five years ago. After the unexpected death of her uncle eleven years before their acquisition, the ownership of the home passed through the hands of several family members. The first decade found little attention given to the property, the unwanted result prompting William and Elizabeth to take up residency in the home. Elizabeth's cousins were more than happy to allow her an attempt at managing the colossal estate. The perseverance of the young couple resulted in a complete restoration of the manor. They clearly do well at their task; the grounds and the structure continue to reflect their excellent care.

With his hand extended toward James, William gives greeting.

"Ah, yes; John Wesley is a man of his word. My wife, Elizabeth, and I, William Cole, humbly receive your visit."

"Thank you, William. It is an honor. Pastor James Glasbrook and my fellow laborer on the Bedfordshire circuit, Francis Asbury of Great Barr."

Francis nods his head. In her elegant white dress, Elizabeth curtsies. William extends his hand to shake his. Francis does so, admiring the cotton waistcoat that William is wearing; *beautiful material.* This prompts the thought, *perhaps the wealthy gentleman shall give me a coat to replace the tattered one I possess.* Francis forces his foolish thought from his mind.

Inside the home, their host departs to fetch some needed refreshment for the travelers. Left to themselves, Francis and James stare at the ceiling. The thirty-foot-high ceiling tops out with a three-foot-tall cornice, carved in stone. The detailed piece creates a heavenly scene of cherubic children linked by vining boughs that surround the entire ballroom. The fifty or so angelic carvings each grasp the decorative vine in a unique fashion. Some gently hold with an extended hand, others wrap their entire body, as if clinging to a cherished friend. Below, at the second-story level, a continuous gallery, complete with a cast-stone balustrade, delineates a walkway. The cantilevered balcony is supported by carved granite brackets and corbels, each four feet in length. On the top of the ceiling, a carved roundel thirty feet in diameter displays several styles of dentil and grapevine applied moldings, also carved in stone. From the center of the focal piece, a chained chandelier hangs twenty feet down from the three-story ceiling height. Francis snaps his neck to the side; his eye for detail has caused him to stare straight up for the last five minutes.

Moving his focus back toward the chandelier, he is impressed with the meticulous iron work. *If Foxall could view this—such craftsmanship!* The fixture is far beyond anything crafted in the West Bromwich mill. *One, two, three, four, five, six, seven, eight . . . and double . . . sixteen.* Francis counts the candles on the hanging piece that is eighteen feet in diameter.

Around the perimeter of the second story, several doorways—each with a carved pilaster and an ornate architrave banding surround, also of stone—mark several rooms immediately off the balcony. Again, Francis cracks his neck; *I must lower my focus.* He looks to the ground-floor level.

Around the main room measuring forty by sixty feet, several architectural pilaster features, also carved in stone, display sculptured busts of unknown men. *I must inquire as to these figures;* Francis logs a mental note.

William Cole returns to the main room. With him, Elizabeth carries a silver tray bearing four tea cups and a richly ornate ceramic container. *What of the household staff?* Francis finds it odd that no servants are carrying the refreshments into the room. *The Birch family required several hired servants.*

William offers,

> "Gentlemen, please have a seat. Elizabeth and I would delight to join you
> in a cup of tea."

James and Francis move toward the chairs. Strategically placed beneath the massive chandelier, each carved wooden chair is covered with a fine fabric, unfamiliar to James and Francis. Francis guesses, *much like a ribbed cotton.* The itinerants take a seat.

William begins,

> "I have informed Wesley of our intentions."

James and Francis remain quiet, unaware of these intentions. William continues,

> "For some time, Elizabeth and I have considered the better-world
> approach to our existence—the gift of this home affording many
> opportunities for such living."

I should say so. Francis keeps this thought to himself. He has his opinions of the wealthy. *Most are kind; somewhat self-focused, but kind. Perhaps they aim to use their wealth to win favor with Wesley.* William goes on,

> "Elizabeth and I are not people of the polite society; we fall far short of the lives of the lords and countesses. We strive to take that which has been given and invest it in the kingdom."

James clears his throat and asks,

> "Do you wish us to convey a gift to Wesley?"

> "I shall see Wesley in London; plan to arrive in the week following. Elizabeth and I aim for something of much more worth. We shall sell our home and offer some of the proceeds to build a chapel."

> "Incredible!"

Francis's audible expression of his thought is a surprise to the young itinerant and the rest in the room. William chuckles.

> "You believe so?"

Francis fidgets; noticeably uncomfortable, he places his hands under his thighs. He responds,

> "My apology, sir; your revelation is a unique surprise."

> "Apology accepted. Elizabeth and I will relocate to London. We shall plan our efforts from there."

Elizabeth offers,

> "William and I shall sell the residence to one Archibald Buchanan, a local merchant. The transaction shall allow us to remove the finery which can easily bind. Perhaps our gift will allow for a larger kingdom presence in London."

> "On behalf of John and Charles Wesley and their efforts to spread the Gospel of Christ, I offer a clear word of gratitude. I am confident that your generosity shall escort many into the glorious light of the kingdom."

Elizabeth and William are thankful for James's kind words.

The rest of the day and evening finds James and Francis enjoying the fine estate. That evening, the couple invites a few of their neighbors for an exhortation. James's preaching delights the couple and their friends.

In the morning, the Coles treat James and Francis to a splendid breakfast before their departing—again, with no servants assisting. By eight o'clock, the itinerants are once again on their way.

During their travel, the events of the preceding day and evening prompt James to comment to Francis,

> "Incredible happenings."

> "Indeed."

> "Would Mother and Father approve, Francis?"

"Most assuredly."

"Very well. Would Francis approve?"

Francis does not respond. James turns toward the young itinerant and inquires again,

"Have you not considered my question?"

"A rather unreasonable question."

"Unreasonable?"

"Somewhat; why would I disapprove of such an agreeable act like that of the Coles?"

"Your 'incredible' response to William's proclamation seemed to indicate your surprise."

"If I must be honest . . ."

"You must."

"I truly was surprised. I have seen the wealthy act kindly, but seldom with risk of discomfort."

"The Coles shall do well. My worry is for Francis, for your continuing punishment."

"Punishment?"

"Yes, punishment. Why would you disapprove of your attending the theatre when it clearly displayed the depravity of those around you?"

Francis and James ride on quietly as the young preacher considers James's insightful suggestion.

From Sundon, the pair travels ten miles northwest through central Bedfordshire. The yellow and orange carpeted path below the waning beech trees undulates slightly, periodically changing the scene for the itinerants from an above- to below-tree-line view of the lime-yellow leaves that refuse to acknowledge the end of autumn. The tiny town of Millbrook is the itinerants' destination.

Up ahead in the distance, James and Francis can see the bell tower of the Millbrook Anglican church building. The stone structure sits high above the Bedford Valley, the entire town in a gap between the hills west of Ampthill. James and Francis are in this valley, making their way toward the tiny village of eighty-five residents. Long before reaching the hillside that rises to the church, the travelers observe a large wooded forest on the valley floor, a portion of which appears to run right up to the holy structure. James prompts Francis, who has once again pulled out *Pilgrim's Progress,*

"Bunyan's Valley."

Francis slowly raises his eyes from the book and looks to James. The elder itinerant responds,

> "Bunyan's Valley of the Shadow of Death. It lies ahead."
>
> "It does?"
>
> "The approaching forest vale is the inspiration for Bunyan's dream. Are you prepared to walk through the Valley of the Shadow of Death?"
>
> "I shall proceed wherever the Lord calls."

James smiles at his young helper. He baits Francis,

> "Are we truly prepared?"
>
> "Yes, James. In fact, Churchy and I shall connect with you on the far side of the forest."
>
> "One word of caution: beware Apollyon."

James's caution of the devilish character from Bunyan's tale prompts Francis to prod his horse, and the pair gallops on ahead. James is surprised; his next comment is meant for his ears only.

> "Connect we shall."

Descending into the valley and entering the darkened wood, Francis pulls sharply on the reins, carefully slowing Churchfield to avoid running into the numerous tall, thin fir trees that tower above the forest floor. Arching his back, Francis peers skyward. The grey sky of the beginning of November is barely visible through the overgrown extensions of the thicketed forest. Remembering his recent reading of Bunyan's passage and the infamous valley, he experiences a slight sense of alarm; *shall Apollyon launch from behind that strand of trees just ahead?*

Francis regains a proper perspective. He takes a deep breath and seeks to refocus his thoughts. *From whence shall my help come? From the Lord, Maker of heaven and earth.* Despite his proper reasoning, he is a realist—the winter sun with its southerly route will soon bring a near darkness into this north-facing valley forest. He pushes on.

Francis and his faithful animal continue at a slow pace, the spaces between the trees gradually growing smaller. The tightening environment returns his thoughts to Bunyan's tale. *An awful eternity—Lord, shall You equip me to deliver many from this final destination? Souls in eternal torment, shrieking, screaming, moaning with constant discomfort; shall You fail to endow me?*

The scurrying sound of footsteps crunching freshly fallen autumn leaves catches Francis by surprise. He spins to his rear left side. Nothing.

Stopping Churchfield, Francis peers in several directions. Again he finds nothing, save the continuous settling of spent leaves heading for their final destinations. *The forest is strangely silent.* The gentle offerings of the wind as it weaves its way through the stalky timber fail to extinguish his frantic search.

Overhead, a piercing sound breaks the flowing silence. The noise nearly startles Francis out of his saddle. Grasping the reins tighter, he prods Churchfield to continue. The horse moves forward, slowly.

Shifting his focus from the sky to ground level, Francis attempts to lighten his emotions with the thought, *I have had my dealings with the harvest mouse before.* Thinking that he has acted foolishly, he yearns for James to catch up.

Again, the rustling of the leaves and the subsequent darting-away sound rivet Francis's attention. Spinning in his saddle, he darts his eyes in several directions behind him. Nothing again.

The approaching dusk with its visually dimming effects causes Francis's sense of hearing to sharpen. He is hearing more sounds now—again the scurrying, then another screech from above. The cracking of a tree limb off in the distance quickens his heart; he nearly jumps from Churchfield at the resulting thud of the branch crashing onto the forest floor. He continues his frantic search. Still nothing. *Oh, for the company of Faithful.*[126]

Ahead of Francis, a loud commotion erupts. Scurrying creatures race in several directions. From the corner of his right eye he catches a shadow, or some object, moving up a tree. He looks mid-height, then up high, then down low. Still, he finds nothing. The noises cause him to instinctively bring Churchfield to a complete stop.

He darts his eyes again near the suspect tree.

Then onto the tree right next to it.

Then another.

And another.

And another.

Sitting alone in this dense stand, Francis senses his heartbeat; the thick, methodical rhythm knocks on his chest. He ventures the thought, *I shall turn back and find James.*

Bunyan's Christian and his conversation upon meeting the two turning from the Valley of the Shadow of Death comes to mind: "We also saw there the hobgoblins, satyrs, and dragons of the pit: we heard also in that valley a continual howling and yelling, as of a people under unutterable misery, who there sat bound in affliction and irons: and over that valley hang the discouraging clouds of confusion: Death also doth always spread his wings over it. In a word, it is every whit dreadful, being utterly without order."

---

[126] The traveling companion of Christian in Bunyan's tale.

Perhaps I shan't. Francis takes a deep breath. *These ramblings border upon the absurd—there is no Apollyon; this is far from a pit of death. I shan't do battle with a creature from Bunyan's dream. I must continue.* He again prods the horse.

Churchfield will not move forward.

Looking about, Francis realizes that daylight is soon to end. He prompts Churchfield,

"Come, Churchy, it is all in the mind. Let us proceed."

The horse will not move.

Despite the cold weather, Francis can sense a bead of sweat, one tiny bead, inching its way toward his brow. He quickly brushes it away.

"Come, Churchy."

He prods his horse hard; Churchfield reluctantly moves forward.

The deliberate, slow pace of the animal causes Francis to continue his animated visual search. After several paces, the crisp, crunchy sound of the dead autumn leaves changes to a slushy, morbid squish of the valley floor. Several local dams, once used to force water toward a closed mill, impede the natural flow of several local springs. The redirected liquid huddles into several precariously located low-edged ponds, which occasionally overflow and threaten to drown the strand's fir-tree saplings.

The damp and marshy bottom level of the forest reminds Francis, *Bunyan's quagmire.*

Francis's thought spirals toward the prophet Jeremiah. *A wilderness, a land of deserts and pits, a land of drought and the shadow of death, a land that no one crossed and where no one dwelt.*[127]

In the distance, an unexpected movement catches his attention. He can make out a creature, a four-legged creature, moving from his left to his right. It turns toward Francis, spotting him and Churchfield. As quickly as it appeared, it darts away. Churchfield this time stops on his own. Francis urges him forward, but the horse does not respond.

Looking to his right, Francis notes that the darkness of nightfall is not too distant. In the same moment, the opening notes of the chirping crescendo of the cricket creation begin. Sitting still, Francis looks rearward for James. He is nowhere to be seen. By his estimate, Francis perceives that he is two-thirds of the way through the forest.

Looking to his left, he spots a dark object. The thickened forest makes it difficult, but roughly one hundred yards off, he can see it moving slowly. He decides to sit still and watch. The moving object continues until it is slightly in front of Francis's position, still nearly one hundred yards to his left side.

---

[127] From Jeremiah chapter 2, verse 6.

Another bead of sweat oozes onto Francis's forehead.

On his own, Churchfield resumes a slow pace forward.

"Oh, we've decided to lead, have we?"

The horse responds with a snort and a nicker.

"Welcome back, Churchy."

Francis continues his watch of the shadowy being in the distance. From behind, a tree creaks as it bends in the wind. The eerie sound once again galvanizes Francis's emotions; he darts his eyes in the new direction, toward the tree. Once again, he breaks into prayer: *Though I walk through the valley of the shadow of death, I will fear no evil; for You are with me.*[128]

Francis and Churchfield continue. In time, the crisp sound of four hooves stomping on dried leaves returns as the pair begins the ascent into the town of Millbrook. Through the few remaining rows of trees ahead, Francis can make out the large silhouette of the St. Michael's and All Angels Anglican church building. Its distinctive green sandstone is unmistakable, pitched atop the hill where its ideal location captures the last glimmers of daylight. Francis is relieved to complete this harrowing journey through the Bedfordshire valley. He welcomes the settling peace that signals the end of the forest and the beginning of the gentle slope to the small village. Above, he spots James on his horse, waiting for Francis to arrive.

Francis blurts toward the itinerant,

"James, however . . . ?"

James smiles and responds with lines from Bunyan's tale:

"Yea, snares, and pits, and traps, and nets did lie

My path about, that worthless, silly I

Might have been catch'd, entangled, and cast down;

But since I live, let Jesus wear the crown."

Francis's smile acknowledges both the source of his safety and the source of the quote. But James's silence on his ability to arrive without going through the forest fails to extinguish Francis's inquiry.

Ascending the sloping field, Francis welcomes a stop at the yard of the church. St. Michael's is a fourteenth-century building. Its main structural components are the local sandstone and clunch, a tough clay, also found locally. In spite of the intimidating valley forest that abuts the church, several open fields and farms producing wheat, barley, and oats surround Millbrook. One of these open fields was utilized by James to reach the church apart from Bunyan's valley. The view from the hilltop is without equal.

---

[128] From Psalm 23, verse 4.

James offers,

> "If you cherish this view, perhaps you should view it from the top of the church."

Francis's calculating smile cannot hide his sense of adventure. James replies,

> "Very well."

The men venture toward the entrance of the ancient church building. Pausing to admire the stone-wrapped arched doorway, they enter the thirteenth-century sanctuary. As Francis peers toward the ceiling in appreciation of another magnificent structure, James darts toward the opposite end of the building. Surprised by his partner's lack of wonder, Francis ends his admiration of the architecture and hurries a few steps to catch up.

> "Why all the hurry?"

> "Follow, Francis. We must not make ourselves known."

Francis once again sports a calculating smile, aware that James is up to something. The pair enters a small wooden doorway that leads to an adjacent room. In it is a small landing and a set of stairs.

> "Come, Francis. Quietly."

At the top of the stairs, James leads Francis through an opening to the top of the church, outside. The strong autumn winds cause the men to draw close the stiff collars of their jackets. Francis stands silent, admiring the Bedford Valley. The fading sunlight cascades upon the fall colors that permeate all he can see. Rolling carpets of orange, lime green, and red flow in all directions from the hilltop that lifts the church above the surrounding rural landscape. After several minutes of the enjoyable view, James advises,

> "Come, Francis; we've to meet the small gathering in Millbrook. We've no sunlight remaining and we mustn't get caught atop St. Michaels, either."

> "Are we not intended to climb here?"

> "Come, Francis."

James's reply advises Francis that they were not supposed to be on the rooftop.

On horseback, the pair travels outside the church grounds and through a series of small farms. While traversing one of the farms, Francis offers,

> "Perhaps the child James ventured upon the rooftop?"

> "Perhaps the child James ventured one too many times upon the rooftop. I was instructed never to return, on risk of eternal damnation."

> "Ah, I see."

Francis laughs at the look on James's face, a look of boyish mischief.

Approaching a small home in the field, James informs Francis,

> "The Bunker family. Perhaps they shall become the instrument used of the Lord to further His work here. Come and meet them; they are a large family."

Dismounting, the itinerants secure their horses and walk to the entrance door. The house that sits at the center of a wheat field is simple, a two-room, single-story structure with a thatched roof. The exterior walls boast of the local sandstone.

A fourteen-year-old boy answers the men's knock and invites them indoors. Thankful for the warmer temperature inside, James and Francis loosen their coat collars. The lad, a thin boy with arms appearing too lengthy for his frame, advises them,

> "Mother and Father shall arrive soon."
> "Thank you. My name is Pastor James Glasbrook. This is my co-laborer, Pastor Francis Asbury."
> "I remember you, Pastor Glasbrook. Mother and Father shall revel in your arrival."

The rear door of the home opens and in walks a young girl, the sister of the boy, wrapped in several layers of clothing to protect her from the cold. Without noticing the two men in the room, she instinctively begins to unravel the layers of cloth while she rambles on to her brother.

> "Now, Joseph, you know Mother and Father expect dinner ready; have you started the water?"

Before Joseph can answer, the young girl swings around and gains a view of the men sitting at the kitchen table.

> "Oy! My, oh my."

She abruptly stops her partial disrobing. The frantic waving of her arms desperately trying to gather the discarded items causes Joseph and the itinerant preachers to chuckle. James offers,

> "Ruth, is it? We apologize."
> "Not necessary. Please, I must . . ."

She retrieves her outer layers and runs for the adjacent room. Francis guesses, *she appears my age.* Francis is correct; the flustered young lady is exactly his age.

Bursting through the front door of the home, a robust man, along with two young men and a woman who appears to be the age of the younger men, are surprised to find the visitors.

> "Noticed the horses outside. James Glasbrook, once again you grace our family. Are you hungry? Mary is on her way from the barn. She and Ruth shall prepare the evening's meal. Where is Ruth? She left us some time ago . . ."

Mr. Bunker and his three children settle into the room. James responds to Mr. Bunker,

> "Blessed greetings from Wesley, Mr. Bunker. This is my helper on the circuit, Pastor Francis Asbury of Great Barr."
>
> "Great Barr. Umm? A solid trades town."
>
> "Spent my times in the trades."
>
> "Well then, perhaps as Pastor Glasbrook prepares for the class you may help me with a dilemma."
>
> "Very well, it would be my pleasure."

The young lady, the young and attractive Ruth, enters from the adjacent room. Slightly embarrassed, she curtsies toward Pastor Glasbrook. His gentle nod restoring her assurance, she rises and gives a slight turn in the direction of Francis. She is clearly pleased with what she sees.

Mr. Bunker, noticing his daughter's favorable view of the young itinerant, interrupts with,

> "Ruth, Mother shall have two guests for this evening's meal."
>
> "Yes, Father."
>
> "Francis, you must accompany me to the barn. I would like to share of my dilemma."
>
> "Very well."

Stepping into the dilapidated building reminds Francis of his father's barn. Several holes in the exterior boards allow the cold wind to easily sweep through the dirt-floor space, the smaller penetrations providing a constant high-pitched whistle. His initial glances affirm that Mr. Bunker is a farmer; the usual implements hang from and lean along the walls. There are several large wooden yokes and a variety of harnesses. Francis's attention is drawn to a work bench; he walks over to it for a closer look. On it is a smaller bench, made of wood. Francis surmises that the item has a unique function. He notices that it has four short iron legs . . . well, almost four; one of them is broken in half. Mr. Bunker asks,

> "Francis, are you aware of the item's purpose?"

Francis shakes his head. Mr. Bunker continues,

> "I am a cordwainer. When working correctly, this bench is utilized for repairing the boots and shoes of my customers."

Francis immediately calls to mind the shoe salesman who visited his home many years before. His thoughts drift back to the display of the various shoes and boots. He remembers the Baptist preacher sent out by the Countess of Huntingdon, Mr. David Taylor, as he laid out the footwear on the floor during his demonstration to Francis about solid foundations. He envisions the shoes placed next to each other on his parents' main-room floor, the delicate boot pumps, the . . .

Mr. Bunker's comment snaps Francis's thoughts back to the present.

"The horse stepped on the bench leg and it snapped."

"You've need of repair of the leg?"

"Precisely. Can you manage the repair?"

"Without a furnace and proper tools it would require some creative skills. I shall require time in the barn, to arrange the necessary items."

"Thank you, Francis. I shall leave you with my shop."

Francis walks around the dry and musty workspace. His first thought is, *without a makeshift furnace, no effort shall suffice.* He spots a pile of dried, cut wood; in fact, many random pieces of wood are scattered about the entire space. Locating a shovel, he digs a hole in the center of the barn floor. He then gathers a dozen pieces of the oak logs, several of which near eight inches in diameter and twenty inches in length. He places the logs in the bottom of the two-foot-deep hole.

"That shall not work."

He kneels down and pulls out the wood pieces. In frustration, he turns to a nearby pile of hay. He gathers the hay and places it on the bottom of the hole, then fixes the oak pieces on top of the thin layer of straw kindling.

"Much better."

"Father has informed . . ."

The delicate female voice spins Francis around. In complete surprise, he responds,

"Ruth?"

"Father asked that I assist you."

"Very well."

Francis is actually excited about the prospect. Ruth is a beautiful young lady. For a moment, Francis feels guilty; *Nancy* . . . His mission, as well as his new assistant, quickly change that thought.

Moving to the other end of the barn, Francis informs Ruth,

"I have need of a makeshift anvil and hammer. Does your father own a hammer?"

"Hammer? What is an anvil?"

"This shall prove most . . ."

Francis stifles his comment. His pace quickens, as Ruth follows closely behind him. On the floor, Francis spots an iron rod, two inches in diameter. He bends down to pick it up. Rising and turning, he hurries to place the item near the fire pit, and runs right into Ruth. She cannot control her laughter. Embarrassed, Francis blurts out,

"My deepest apology . . ."

"Quite all right, Francis. It was my fault."

The two stare at each other. Ruth's blue eyes draw Francis, deepening his attraction. She too finds a pull in his eyes. Each offers an uncomfortable smile.

Ending the moment, Francis darts for the far side of the barn.

"An anvil, or something thereof, is a solid surface upon which I can pound melted iron. Typically, I beat the heated metal on another metal surface."

"Father has a metal, beating item thing—in the loft."

Francis looks upward. A thin set of wooden rungs leads to the second level of the barn. He moves to begin climbing the ladder-like steps. Only because of the equal distance apart of the wooden crosspieces does the apparatus resemble a ladder. Ruth offers,

"Beware the second step; it moves a bit."

Moves a bit. Very well. Francis takes each step carefully. *The entire contraption moves a bit.* Francis keeps the thought to himself. Nearing the top, he is able to spot several planks of wood, a large wooden bowl, leather strapping, and other dust-covered items. In the corner of the loft is the reported *metal, beating item thing.* Francis smiles a humorous smile. Shaking his head, he asks,

"Shall the loft support me?"

"I believe so. Father has not ventured upstairs for a period. Harvest and all."

Francis proceeds with caution. The second-story floor is solid—a little creaky, but solid. Nearing the metal, beating item thing, he reaches down and lifts the steel object.

"Lord, You do supply our needs."

Moving to the ladder, he proudly displays the item for Ruth to see.

"This is an anvil."

"I see."

"Why would your father hide such an object of beauty?"

"Beauty? My, Francis, the trades are pouring out of you."

"It is true."

Francis sets the anvil down at the edge of the loft. Before he maneuvers his body around the top of the extended ladder, he reaches for a wide leather strip lying next to the edge of the loft and places it in his coat pocket. Setting his boot on the rung next to the loft, he begins his descent. After a few calculated steps, he pauses to grasp the anvil. Up to this point, Ruth has been enjoying the proceedings; now, with the anvil in Francis's hands, she is slightly more cautious.

"Please do take heed, Francis."

"Very well."

Forcing the anvil between him and the ladder rails, he guides the object. The process is slow, but transpires safely. At the floor, Francis turns and sets the anvil down. Ruth proclaims,

"Precarious effort, Francis!"

"Less precarious than the River Severn."

"You've been to the Severn?"

"Itinerated along its banks."

"All the way to Bristol?"

"Not quite; was turned around before Bristol."

With a wry smile, Francis adds,

"Smashing time."

"I see."

She doesn't catch the analogy. However, she ventures,

"Do you enjoy the itinerancy?"

"It is that which I seem called to. I enjoy the freedom of wandering about."

"I would love to wander about."

Francis's thoughts are pure; however, he is drawn to Ruth. *Attractive, easy to converse with, slightly older than Nancy* . . . these musings settle agreeably in his mind.

Returning his thoughts to the task at hand, Francis realizes that he needs to create a tool that would act like a monkey wrench. Outside of a consistent and strong furnace, the monkey wrench is the blacksmith's most important tool. At different times, the tool holds the hot iron, it aids in turning the hot iron, and it protects one's hands from the hot iron. This hot iron can also cause fire if carelessly dropped onto the random straw or fodder that lies around most barns. The dirt floor of Mr. Bunker's barn is strewn with straw in order to keep the dust down. Francis thinks aloud,

"If made of wood . . . perhaps a series of monkey wrenches; as one heats up to flames, another can take its place. Ruth, does your father possess a hatchet or axe?"

"Hatchet or axe? I believe so. Wait here."

As if I was to suddenly leave, Francis humors himself. Ruth departs and Francis continues his search. Uncovering several areas piled with wooden boxes, scrap wood, leather strips, and small tack nails, he stumbles upon a small box. Lifting the lid, Francis is excited by his discovery. In the box, several small cutting tools—cordwainer's tools, used for cutting leather—reside in the bottom of the wooden case. One tool, resembling a flat chisel, shows particular promise.

"Now if only . . . aha."

Also in the box is a hammer. The wood-handled object is smaller than the blacksmithing tool that Francis is accustomed to; *however,* he considers, *it shall work just as well.* Lifting the tool, he continues,

"Now to build the fire."

Ruth reenters the barn as Francis stokes the fire pit. He instructs her,

"Gather a cloth or object to act as a fan until the smoke settles."

Turning once again to depart, she tosses an axe toward Francis and runs. He calls after her,

"I shan't harm you!"

Francis busies himself with carving out several monkey wrenches from the scrap wood that lies around the entire barn. *Father would never accept such a system,* he thinks of his attempt to create a wooden monkey wrench. *However, he would appreciate the creative approach.*

Ruth returns and begins to fan the smoke through the barn door by waving a quilted blanket. Francis responds,

"Well done, Ruth; the Bedfordshire skies shall resemble Staffordshire in no time."

She laughs.

"Now, Francis, you are well aware that I shall ask of Staffordshire. Where do you reside?"

"My parents continue to reside in Great Barr, in the small hamlet of Newton Village."

"Been away long?"

"I have. Nearly eighteen months. Quite amazing that Mother has not given chase."

"Your mother loves you, Francis?"

"Very much so. Father as well."

" 'Tis sweet, Francis. I too enjoy the blessings of a loving family."

Ruth's enchanting smile would be hard for any man to ignore—and those eyes. Francis attempts to justify his attraction.

The strong fire turns into the prized embers that will heat the iron rod. Gathering the piece and the five monkey wrenches he has created, Francis places the iron piece into the smoldering grey and orange remains of the fire. He instructs,

"Shall not lie for long. Once the iron turns, it shall become pliable."

He drops to his knees in front of the pit. He leans back for the hammer and asks of Ruth,

"Can you lift your father's bench? If so, would you mind bringing it to me?"

"Not at all, Francis."

She acquires the bench and sets it next to Francis. As she leans over him, the two make eye contact again. Both faces beam. Rising to his feet, Francis busies himself with fetching the anvil.

She is most agreeable. Lifting the heavy object, he carries it to the pit, setting it down next to the shoe-repair bench. Again, he makes a request.

"Have you a block or chair to sit upon?"

"I shall . . ."

"No bother. I shall work on my knees."

Lifting the heated iron from the fire, Francis begins the manufacturing process. Placing the metal piece on top of the anvil, he advises,

"Wrap the quilt around you; ensure to protect your face. I shall have you hold down the iron rod with the monkey wrench as I remove a piece."

"Why the wrap?"

"Sparks. They shall travel as I slice with the chisel."

Afraid but willing, Ruth wraps herself in the quilt and extends her hand forward. Francis gently grasps her hand and places it onto the monkey wrench.

"Grip it tightly as you push down. I shall cover your arm with a piece of leather."

Removing from his coat pocket the piece of leather he took from the loft, he wraps her wrist and forearm.

"Must guard from the sparks."

Ruth appreciates Francis's concern; she is attracted by his attention to detail as he seeks to guarantee her safety. Upon completion of the wrapping, he gathers the chisel and hammer.

With one solid stroke, he cuts off a two-inch piece of the iron rod. The piercing clang causes Ruth to jump. Despite her fearful reaction, she continues to hold onto the wooden implement. The orange slug hisses as it hits the ground. Francis instructs,

"You've done well, Ruth. Release the monkey wrench as I retrieve the slug and place it into the fire."

Lifting the cut piece with a monkey wrench, Francis transfers the heated iron into the fire. It soon turns the desired orange color.

Over the next thirty minutes, Ruth watches and admires the skills of the young man. Francis's focused efforts eventually result in the fully repaired leg of Mr. Bunker's work bench.

Upon completion of the process, Ruth cannot withhold her excitement; she grasps Francis's forearm and exclaims,

"Impressive, Francis! Well done! Father shall be grateful."

She darts off for the house.

The evening in Millbrook is a simple one. In addition to Mr. and Mrs. Thomas and Mary Bunker and their two children, Ruth and Joseph, their additional children are present for an informal class meeting. The Bunkers have nine living children; two others passed years before, the loss creating an extremely tight bond in the family. Two boys are between the ages of Ruth, twenty-three, and Joseph, fourteen. The other children are older than Ruth, three boys and two older sisters. During the evening, the older brothers are especially watchful of Francis and the older sisters; their eyes hint at hopeful expectations for Ruth. James teaches from the Scriptures and Francis helps with questions from Ruth's older siblings and their spouses. Among the family, the women silently wish that Ruth would have an opportunity to marry a man like Francis. To Ruth and Francis, the evening is less about formal arrangements and more about simply enjoying each other's company.

For the next few months, James escorts Francis around the beginning portion of this circuit. Their regular visits to Luton, Dallow Farm, the mansion at Sundon, and Millbrook prepare Francis to undertake this area on his own.

Departing Millbrook for the last time in January, the pair continues northwest toward Northampton. Getting there will involve crossing the Bedfordshire county line into Northamptonshire.

Northampton is a historic town bounded on the south and west by the River Nene. Parliament met in its ancient castle until the late fourteenth century. The castle no longer stands; as Francis and James approach, the royal compound's former location is a cherry orchard.

James informs Francis,

"We shall make for the riding school."

"Riding?"

"Yes, the King's regiment, the Royal Horse Guard, stations here."

Nearing their destination, James and Francis bring their horses to a stop and dismount. The animals simultaneously snort through their nostrils as the cool air makes them a bit frisky. Eager to continue, Churchfield finds it hard to stand still. He turns slightly and pokes his nose at Francis's ribcage as his master secures the reins for a walk. Francis pushes back.

"Now, Churchy, 'tis an opportunity to walk your rider."

Churchfield tilts his head. Francis smiles and muses, *seems you understand all that I offer.*

Walking their horses through two stone columns that support an opened metal gate, Francis and James enter the open-air military grounds. The cold January wind sweeps through the large timber-roofed space used to train the Royal Horse Guard. The center of the structure opens to the grey sky. Around the perimeter of the regimental riding building are several stables, a riding yard, and coach houses, built right into the surrounding facility.

The Royal Guard, or the Royal Blues, originated in 1650 by the directive of Oliver Cromwell. Appointed as the official regiment attached to the monarchy—the Household Cavalry—these units train and dress superbly, and their equestrian abilities are unmatched.

Today, the Royal Guard joins the nearly three hundred soldiers and two hundred townspeople crowded into the Riding House on this afternoon. This is far from capacity; when John Wesley spoke here last year, nearly two thousand soldiers and civilians populated the space.

Standing at the head of the entire gathering, which has placed itself in a series of seats on the dirt-floor pit, a soldier dressed in glistening black jack boots has his hands raised for prayer.

The extra-tall leather footwear of the soldier rises to the knee, with an additional several inches on the outsides of each leg, rising to the lower thigh. The stark white gloves, set against the black long-sleeved cotton shirt, proceed to the mid-forearm and visually balance his white skin-tight riding breeches. The polished metal cuirsass[129] embellishes his already thick chest and radiates brightly, obviously the recipient of hours of painstaking buffing. Its brass shoulder straps and belt match the brass scabbard and handle of a long saber hanging at the soldier's side in its black metal sheath. On top of the makeshift pulpit, which resembles a wooden podium, rests a large and ornate helmet, also made of the same metal as the torso gear. It stands tall, complete with a thick brass chin strap and a bushy black plume resembling the tail of a Newfoundland dog, tall and curved. This grand soldier is Captain Jonathan Scott.

A hero against the French in the successful Battle of Minden in 1759, Captain Scott experienced his Christian conversion at the famous Ote Hall, a mansion converted by Selina, the Countess of Huntingdon. The remodeled estate, complete with apartments and bedrooms for Selina and her children, nieces, and guests, continues to serve the farmers and laborers of rural Sussex. It was within this sanctuary that the Captain gained his saving faith years before.

His happening upon the place of worship was quite by accident. Driven by a severe thunderstorm to seek shelter at a nearby farmstead, he was urged by the resident farmer—a faithful member of the Ote Hall class—to attend services. Captain Scott obliged the hospitable man, his wise decision escorting him into the presence of the venerable preacher William Romaine. Romaine's message from

---

[129] A sleeveless metal armor molded and shaped around the chest.

John 14:6 influenced the captain to be born anew. In time, Captain Scott's conversion led him to preach to his regiment, the Royal Blues.

John Fletcher—the noted Wesleyan preacher from Switzerland, educated at Geneva, and a personal aide to John Wesley—regularly admits that Captain Scott is a fine preacher, noting, "I believe this red coat will shame many a black one. I am sure he shames me."

Captain Scott lowers his arms as he draws to the end of his prayer.

"Amen."

The civilians in the crowd take their seats and watch, as the soldiers remain standing. Everyone, including the soldiers, direct their attention toward the captain. Slowly raising his eyes from prayer, Captain Scott nods his head and the soldiers take a seat. One of the equestrian soldiers shouts,

"Well, Scott, have you read your Psalms and lessons today?"

The Captain smiles, as do the locals. They have witnessed this endearing banter before. Scott's congregation is made up of rough military men, men who love their commander, most of whom also love the Savior. Francis and James watch the captain for his response. Scott fires back,

"It is the Psalms that you beg of. All right, then."

The guffaws of the gathering border on a friendly roar. Not wanting to disappoint, the captain's lesson from the Psalms lasts nearly one hour. The men graciously depart only after their leader dismisses them; they dare not register a complaint for the lengthy lesson. Francis and James remain, eager to greet Captain Scott.

With the riding center emptied, Francis, James, and the captain sit on three wooden chairs facing each other. The hot tea delivered by the captain's attendant inspires the talkative leader to answer James's concern of the regiment receiving a call out of town.

"As happened with the call to the Midlands, I could receive a call once again, leaving Northampton without proper preaching. Wesley must make provision."

"He already has, Captain. In fact, 'tis the very purpose of our visit this day. Young Asbury shall continue with the rest of the circuit; I shall remain here for the remainder of the season. If the King requires the Blues, I shall fill in."

"Perhaps you shall fill in regardless of the King's actions."

"Very well."

Pastor Glasbrook is pleased to gain such confidence, and such a privilege. The townspeople and the soldiers have for some time hoped Wesley's itinerants would visit Northampton regularly.

Silent up to this point, Francis asks the captain a question.

"Captain Scott, I am unaware of the serious incident which drew you away from Northampton."

"Quite simple, Francis. The Bread Riots of the Midlands nearly resulted in another civil war. Leicester barely stood, aflame, while several hundred farmers attacked the wagons, determined to gain the precious cargo which was becoming unaffordable. The inclement planting and harvesting seasons had forced prices to rise. The inflated prices influenced the local suppliers to ship their bread out of the area, where they could receive a much higher price than in the rural locales. The starving residents no longer would go without bread. The King ordered our regiment immediately. The townspeople were ill-set on our arrival; however, despite a few nicks and bruises, we managed the affair."

"I see."

"James, I shall inform Wesley. As long as our regiment remains in Northampton, we can contrive to let them have our Riding House for worship and gatherings. Perhaps young Asbury could deliver my correspondence."

"Very well."

Before week's end, not only does Glasbrook preach to more than two thousand people at the riding center, but Francis is on his way to Bedford, carrying the captain's letter for Wesley.

***

To the west of southern England, across the Bristol Channel, lies the mountainous country of Wales. Surrounded by water on three sides, this "wild west" of Great Britain's maritime climate causes Wales to experience almost continuous wet and windy weather. Despite the potential for blustery conditions, the North Atlantic Drift, a branch of the Gulf Stream ocean current, causes the temperatures of the nation to remain steady, even rising slightly higher than other countries at the same northerly latitude. The rugged coastal terrain with its magnificent cliffs boasts of several birds of prey: the merlin, Montagu's harrier, the goshawk, the golden eagle and the red kite. These mighty creatures are a reflection of the strong-willed residents who for several centuries have continued to resist English rule.

Wales also possesses its gentler side. The winged commanders hovering above share the breezy coastlines with the kinder gannets and puffins below. Softer still, amidst the rocky crags of the highland landscape appear the striking spotted rock-rose with its crimson-spotted yellow flowers. The slightly fuzzy green leaves highlighted with red-trimmed edges put forth new pansy-like blooms each morning during the warmer summer months.

Northern Wales, bordering England south of Liverpool, is home to the highest mountains of the region. Tucked within the higher-elevation rocks, the beautiful alpine whitlow-grass waves its tiny, showy clusters of tulip-like yellow blooms as the short, upright green stems rise from the elevated landscape in early spring.

One of Wales's ancient cities in the northeast is Flint. The fortified castle town bordering on the estuary of the River Dee was the first settlement chartered in Wales, in 1284. The English King, Edward I, successfully subjected Wales to English rule and built the castle in an effort to establish British dominion over the Welsh nation. This desired domination did not last long.

Despite the turmoil of the past, Wales is a country that embraces the English Methodist movement. Due to the influence of George Whitefield, the tradition is slightly Calvinistic in style. Despite this, the Welsh people graciously receive John Wesley. Since the revelation from Whitefield in 1739 that Wales was in the midst of a revival of Christianity—a great awakening led by men like Howell Harris, Anglican minister Griffith Jones, Daniel Roland, and Howell Davies—Wesley has put forth an effort to itinerate the nation with his faithful biblical cavalry.

One of these faithful traveling Wesleyan preachers, Richard Boardman, currently takes a break from his arduous circuit in the Dales. Planning to meet his dear friend Joseph Pilmoor somewhere in the northeastern portion of Wales, Richard departs the Welsh town of Mould, heading north for the town of Flint. If Joseph is no longer in Flint, then Richard will have to cross the tricky River Dee estuary to the Wirral Peninsula and the town of Parkgate.

The six-mile trek on horseback is through hilly country, the moderate grade affording several boggy patches along the way. Several neatly crafted sheep stiles dot the dirt road to Flint. The expertly crafted stone encasing nearly fifty acres forms a life-saving barrier for the sheep, keeping each flock in a designated field accessible only by the sheep herder. The walls are unique, constructed by members of the Guild of Hedgers. Built of local stone, the key characteristic of the sheep stile is the series of steps hanging on the side of the wall. Each step juts from the main body of the wall—too close to the wall for a sheep to traverse, but perfect for the herder and his dog to gain the higher ground toward another field.

Richard raises his eyes toward the thick grey sky. *Perhaps an early snow;* he'd rather it didn't.

Several fields full of sheep surround Richard as he travels toward Flint. *Bleating creatures*, he complains to the thousand four-legged animals bordering both sides of the ancient path. The constant babble of the timid animals eventually becomes an endless hum of background noise as Richard does his best to block out the droning effects. In sharp contrast to the continuing thrum are the sounds of a lamb attempting to scale the steps of the stile, ahead on his right. It's an impossible feat; however, the young sheep refuses to cease his efforts. Several loud yelps attend each failed attempt. In humiliating fashion, his head is eventually stuck under one of the stone projections. With a shrieking volume, he cries for his mother. After several laments, the animal frees himself, bouncing toward the safety of the ewe.

Pausing for a break, Richard brings his mare to a stop, dismounts, and stretches. The long ride from the Dales several days before continues to inspire a rest. Richard walks toward the stone barrier and leans his elbows onto the four-foot-high wall. Fifty yards away, several hundred sheep send forth their continuous bleats, as if checking to make sure their companions are still where they should be. The non-stop murmur lures Richard into stopping for a nap, but he chooses otherwise. As he moves to return to his horse, the sudden shout of an elderly man causes the itinerant to spin around toward the opposite field.

Nothing.

Richard searches the landscape. No one is in view, only several hundred more sheep crooning their confirmations of their fellow residents. He turns back around toward the original field.

Again, the sound of an old man yelling an informal greeting spins Richard around; again, no sign of the originator is found. Richard decides it is best to move on; *perhaps a child plays a prank*. Before mounting his horse, the traveling preacher ventures toward the opposite field. As he does, dozens of the sheep skittishly launch in several directions as if each is possessed by an internal guidance system gone askew. Richard laughs; *darting fellows*.

"Hoy, yo'!"

The voice comes from his left. Richard turns to find an elderly man crouched behind a rock. Realizing that Richard has spotted him, he motions for Richard to come near. Richard secures his horse, hops the stone boundary wall of the field, and walks over to the man.

"Yo' one of Wesley's?"

"I am."

"Very well. Can I bother yo' to hold for a moment? About to complete da' transfer."

"Transfer?"

The elderly man shakes his head in disbelief.

"Sit here, beside me. I shall explain."

Walking over, Richard crouches behind the rock with the man. The man begins,

"See that ewe over dere?"

"I do."

"She's lost her lamb."

"Can we find the lamb?"

"Said she's lost her lamb. Killed by a wolf, night before."

"Why is she not eating?"

"Sad for da' loss of her lamb. Now look over to da' right. What do yo' see?"

"I see a dog."

"My dog."

"And I see a lamb. The little fellow seems to wear a fleece."

"Correct. Dere is still hope for yo' Wesleyan itinerants. We've placed da' fleece from da' dead lamb onto a lamb recently orphaned by wolves."

"Why the fleece?"

"Ewes are especially fond of dere little ones. Much like yo' own mother. It is my hope to transfer da' orphan to da' ewe. Da' fleece adds a little coaxing, a little remembrance of her lost lamb."

"I see. What of the dog?"

"Da' dog creates suspense."

"Suspense?"

"What does Wesley teach yo' men dese days? Suspense. Da' threat of a dog on a lamb usually incites da' protective nature of da' ewe. In dis', da' ewe should adopt da' lamb for da' long term."

"I see."

Richard turns and watches the dog slowly inching its way toward the lamb. The dog is crafty; step by step, the furry intruder aims for the lamb. The young lamb tries to move, but it is nearly impossible with the fleece draped over his tiny shoulders.

Looking to the ewe, Richard notices that she seems unaffected by the dog's advancement.

The dog takes two steps forward and holds his stance. The abbreviated advance causes the frightened lamb to tremble. Under this added strain, his spindly legs can barely support their load.

The ewe still seems unconcerned.

Richard whispers to the herder,

"Does not look well."

"Oh, give 'er time. Dat' protective instinct will kick in."

"Very well."

The herder raises his hand in the air. The dog spots the familiar command and launches himself at the lamb. With a well-trained touch, the dog bumps the defenseless lamb with his nose, then begins to circle him.

At this, the ewe erupts into action.

Aiming for the dog, she bears down on the four-legged imposter. The dog doesn't move until the ewe actually makes physical contact. Upon impact from her wooly shoulder, the dog bounds away. In less than thirty seconds, he is at his owner's side.

The men and dog watch as the ewe gently nudges the tiny lamb. The lamb contentedly nestles into the ewe's belly.

The herder turns to Richard.

"The transfer completes."

Rising from his hidden position, the sheep herder bids Richard a good day. Left alone, standing at the rock, Richard replies,

"Very well."

Leaving the field and collecting his horse, Richard mounts and moves on. He surmises, *the chatty fellow knows his sheep.*

Approaching the riverside town of Flint, Richard glimpses the prominent structure on the edge of the estuary's embankment, Flint Castle. Built in the thirteenth century when King Edward gained a foothold against the Welsh citizens, the royal building on the borderland is in dilapidated condition. Only the four prominent stone turrets and remaining portions of the site's perimeter walls mark the ancient stronghold of the English King.

Searching the tiny town, Richard fails to locate Joseph. After several attempts at the local Methodist meeting house and the homes of its members, Richard realizes his only option is to cross the estuary. As he considers the expanse before him, the weather worsens as a light November snow begins to fall. The floating precipitation instinctively causes him to raise the collar of his jacket. He bundles himself more warmly and proceeds over the embankment at the edge of the estuary.

The River Dee estuary is a three-mile-wide mud flat, shaped much like an elongated basin. The numerous tiny shellfish that inhabit the nutrient-rich environment attract an abundant array of migrating birds escaping the arctic chill of the Northern European winter. The dried clumps of marsh grass that cover the sands provide natural cover for the migrating birds.

Richard hasn't paid much attention, but at the hilltop, he realizes the snowfall has thickened. Blanketing the landscape and the atmosphere, the falling flakes have reduced visibility to a couple of yards. Richard contemplates the situation. In his mind, he knows he will find Joseph in Parkgate; an individual at the Methodist meeting house in Flint advised him of this. He also realizes the truth that this same individual offered: "Unless you ride fast, you will be in danger of being enclosed by the tide." *Enclosed by the tide.* The words repeat, resounding like the bleating of the sheep in the Flintshire countryside. Richard prods his horse with his heels, hard.

The mare plods forward, down into the estuary, over and around numerous mounds of marsh grass. The low visibility increases the suspense as Richard begins to perspire with worry. Holding on with one hand, he raises the other to wipe the nervous sweat bead from his nose. Continuing downhill, Richard shades his eyes with his raised forearm. Squinting, he tries to look toward the west; in these conditions, this is an impossible task. He sighs in frustration, wishing he knew where the incoming tide is at this time. Richard suspects that in the distance, the waters are already emerging from the river. He pushes the horse to quicken the pace, the slow trot picking up to a moderate canter.

He leans back in the saddle as the decline to the estuary floor steepens. The falling snow is now wetting the entire length of his wool coat. The lumbering leaps of the mare as she negotiates the steep terrain bring a jarring pain to his back, but he does his best to aid the animal's balance as they descend the treacherous slope.

At the bottom, the undesirable sound of horse hooves splashing in water alarms the itinerant. Sitting up completely, he pushes the creature to a gallop. The incoming water is now fetlock-deep to the mare. Richard is quickly soaked from the methodical pounding of four hooves beating the rising river. He covers his eyes for protection.

The snowfall thickens and visibility drops to within a foot. Richard's gloved hands begin to chill from the splashing sea water. *My window shall close shortly;* Richard is aware of the obvious. The floor of the estuary rises chest-high in less than fifteen minutes. He must hurry to gain the opposite shoreline, or at least the rising portion of the estuary as it nears the town of Parkgate. The water is now nearing twelve inches in depth, the horse's stride becoming more deliberate and more wetting to the rider.

The mare stumbles; Richard is tossed from the animal's back. The water is up to his knees. Fearful of abandonment by his mount, he instinctively yells the horse's name.

"Abbey!"

The mare nickers from only a few yards away. *Marvelous creature!* Richard is grateful that Abbey ceased her travel when her rider was lost. In the water, which now approaches mid-thigh, Richard treads toward his horse. Grasping the reins, he hops up and prods her to continue.

Father, I trust You are with me, Richard prays.

The snowfall slows, and the visibility begins to increase. Richard can make out the opposite shoreline ahead, *nearly one thousand paces*. The remaining half-mile causes him to look toward the west; his discovery alarms him. *The water is well on its way. I doubt I shall arrive successfully.* The water is now up to his ankles in the stirrups.

The mare can no longer run. She slogs through the flowing water as the dangerous current pushes the pair inland, toward the east.

From the opposite shoreline ahead, Richard notices the faint sound of two men yelling, attempting to gain his attention. They have it. In relief, he raises his hands and waves them frantically. The men race up the hill and over the crest, away from him.

Richard's short-lived solace ends. *I commend my soul to You, Lord.* Richard embraces the possibility of the inevitable: death.

Back toward the west, the water continues it swirling onslaught. It is now just below Richard's knees as he sits astride the horse. Abbey struggles to maintain any forward progress.

Looking in the direction of where the men had been, Richard spots them again. This time they are dragging a small wooden boat. At the edge of the estuary, the water is now weaving its way into the marsh grass at the embankment. The men push the boat into the approaching water. They hop in and shove off in Richard's direction.

Richard eases his panic. The water occasionally rushes above the horse's back; Richard can sense an occasional hop by Abbey as she experiences a slight buoyancy. He shifts his focus toward the men in the boat. They are paddling fast, but are still a couple of minutes away. *Maintain balance, Abbey.* Richard worries for the horse; he has never had to ride her in a full swim. Within moments, he faces a decision of staying atop Abbey or jumping in the water with her. He looks to the men. They are closer. However, the cold air and water have begun their undesirous effects; Richard begins to shake with cold.

Within a few yards, one of the men calls out,

"Surely, sir, God is with you."

Richard nods an affirmative. The cold water is forcing his entire body to tighten. The men realize that the effects of the low temperatures are causing Richard to remain silent. They continue to paddle. The man with the grey hat offers again,

"Surely, sir, God is with you."

"I trust He is."

"I know He is. Here, hop into the boat. We shall swim the horse."

At this, the men slide alongside Abbey and ease Richard into the boat. Grasping the reins, the man with the grey hat clicks his tongue against his teeth; Abbey responds to his audible prompt and swims alongside the tiny boat. The man holding the reins continues,

"I know that God is with you; last night I dreamed that I must go to the top of the hill. When I awoke, the dream made such an impression on my mind that I could not rest. I therefore went and called upon this man to accompany me."

He points toward the man rowing the boat.

"When we came to the place of my dream, we saw nothing more than usual. However, I begged him to go with me to another hill at a small distance, and there we saw your distressed situation."

Richard nods his affirmation, the chill in his body continuing to render him silent.

At the shoreline, several women join the rescuers as they deliver Richard. The women escort the itinerant into a home at the top of the hill. The two men secure the boat and escort Abbey to the barn adjacent to the home. Inside the barn, they feed the wet animal and give her a brisk rubdown.

Inside the home, Richard is relieved to sit next to a lit fireplace. The welcoming warmth aids in his recovery; the shaking of his body begins to slow. The women wrap the itinerant in warm blankets and offer several cups of steaming tea. As the two men return from the barn, one of the women remarks,

"Just last month we saw a gentleman in your very situation."

Richard responds,

"I trust he was equally thankful for your aid."

"Before we could hasten to his relief, he plunged into the sea—supposing, as we all concluded, that his horse would swim to the shore. But they both sank, and were drowned together."

Richard's hands, cradling the warm cup of tea, begin to shake. He sets down the cup and wraps his arms in front of his chest. His entire body shakes in a slight panic. Wishing to abate his frightened emotions, he inquires,

"What of Pastor Pilmoor? Has he arrived?"

"Afraid you have just missed your associate. He has departed, returning to Wales."

"Very well."

Richard unravels the multiple layers of quilts that warm him and reaches inside to his coat pocket. Pulling out all he has, he offers the money to his rescuers. They respond,

"You needn't part with your money."

"It is yours, all eighteen pence. Please."

The men reluctantly accept the offer. Richard inquires,

"Where might I gain residence for the night?"

"You may tarry at the inn. It lies a block away."

"Thank you."

After several hours and several cups of tea, the rescuing men escort Richard to the inn. They inform him,

"You may collect your horse in the morning."

Richard is grateful for their willingness to house Abbey.

In the morning, Richard realizes that he gave all his money away to the two men who rescued him the day before. He hesitates to approach the innkeeper, but he must.

"I am slightly embarrassed. Seems I have nothing to give . . ."

"The Lord bless you, sir; I would not take a farthing from you for the world."

Richard departs the inn, collects Abbey, and leaves for home.

***

Although he would have liked James to join him, Francis will venture alone to Bedford. Francis is confident that he can handle the appointment. He understands that James and Captain Scott are working to develop several new societies in Northampton and the surrounding areas. He also understands the importance of the Northampton society to Wesley and the significance of the letter from Captain Scott, which he is to deliver through a messenger to Wesley.

The twenty-five-mile trek from Northampton to Bedford takes a peculiar route. First, Francis departs to the northwest and travels twelve miles to a hamlet one mile northwest of Rushden, the town of Highham Ferrers. The majority of this initial portion follows the River Nene to the northeast. At Highham, the four-way intersection of two ancient paths has Francis turning southeast. For the next thirteen miles, he will continue in this direction until reaching Bedford. Eight miles out from Bedford, Francis's journey follows the beautiful and winding River Ouse.

Passing through his last town before Bedford, Francis travels through Clapham. A thirteenth-century church dedicated to St. Thomas provides the majority of the town's scenery. Continuing, Francis moves on to Bedford. Entering from the northwest, he proceeds to the town's main thoroughfare, High Street. This north-south road will lead him to the heart of the tiny village. Before his turn south, he will pass the abandoned friary. The Greyfriars, aptly named because of the color of their clothing, no longer preach the Gospel in Bedfordshire. These thirteenth-century Franciscan friars, later victims of King Henry VIII's sixteenth-century expulsion of the Catholic monks and friars, differed from their monk cousins. In lieu of seclusion, the friars freely interacted with the culture through their daily routines. Interestingly, if the Franciscan friars had utilized horses and travel, their actions would have paralleled the itinerant efforts of Wesley's traveling preachers.

Bedford is a town in flux, no longer a strong member of the wool industry. The residents mostly utilize the River Ouse for transport navigation, as goods to and from Bedford travel along the waterway. There is also a small fishing industry that strives to produce fish for market in London. Heading south on High Street, Francis passes the city jail. The prison on the northern corner of Gaol Street and High Street revels in its reputation for torturous conditions. For months, prisoners who eventually find themselves declared innocent suffer numerous indecencies associated with the poorly run facility. The location emits a coldness, a darkened presence. Francis turns his gaze away from the building. He can sense the vice and depravity that haunt the structure's residents.

Continuing south, Francis spots the tall spire of St. Paul's Church. Originally, a group of Catholic clergy called canons ran the eleventh-century church. The building Francis views reflects four centuries of additions to the religious structure. John Bunyan preached here in 1656, and ten years ago John Wesley preached his famous Great Assize sermon in this historic setting.

The Great Assize sermon is one of John Wesley's signature offerings. The sermon is significant for two reasons. First, the assize courts are and have been the Supreme Court equivalent for England since the twelfth century. In these courts, presided over by the higher-court judges of London's King's Court and located in the capital towns of each county or shire, crimes of a capital nature are decided. These life-and-death issues such as murder, rape, forgery, burglary, and kidnapping are also the natural segue for the alternative meaning of the expression, the Great Assize. Since the fourteenth century, the Great Assize is the common phrase referring to the last judgment as expressed in the Bible's New

Testament book of Romans: "We shall all stand before the judgment seat of Christ."[130]

The High Sheriff from Luton—the esquire William Cole, who recently informed Francis that he and his wife, Elizabeth, would be selling their magnificent Sundon Estate—organized John Wesley's preaching at St. Paul's in Bedford on Friday, March 10, 1758. This event ten years prior was a visual spectacle on the level of the services held by Selina, the Countess of Huntingdon. The royal trumpeters and javelin men proclaimed the presence of the Royal Court Judges. The men of law, dressed in their scarlet and ermine[131] fur, graciously entered the holy building, their attendance—as well as their white furs—signifying their dependence on the ultimate Judge, God.

From the stone pulpit of the church with the beautiful tower and octagonal spire, Wesley pounded home the key points of his discourse. The large congregation focused on every nuanced detail offered by the wise preacher. His opening words were a sure reminder of the significance of the event.

> "How many circumstances concur to raise the awfulness of the present solemnity! The general concourse of people of every age, sex, rank, and condition of life, willingly or unwillingly gathered together, not only from the neighboring, but from distant, parts; criminals, speedily to be brought forth and having no way to escape; officers, waiting in their various posts, to execute the orders which shall be given; and the representative of our gracious Sovereign,[132] whom we so highly reverence and honor. The occasion likewise of this assembly adds not a little to the solemnity of it: to hear and determine causes of every kind, some of which are of the most important nature; on which depends no less than life or death, death that uncovers the fate of eternity! It was, doubtless, in order to increase the serious sense of these things, and not in the minds of the vulgar only that the wisdom of our forefathers did not disdain to appoint even several minute circumstances of this solemnity. For these also, by means of the eye or ear, may more deeply affect the heart; and when viewed in this light, trumpets, staves, apparel, are no longer trifling or insignificant, but subservient, in their kind and degree, to the most valuable ends of society."

---

[130] Romans chapter 14, verse 10.

[131] A white-coated weasel.

[132] King George II.

Advised by James to stop at the Methodist meeting house in Bedford, Francis turns west at the road before St. Paul's. At the next corner, Angell Street, Francis turns north. A few hundred feet on the right is the meeting house. Francis brings Churchfield to a halt, dismounts, and prepares to enter.

The house is similar to the meeting house in West Bromwich, a two-story wooden structure. Francis knocks on the front door. The sound of footsteps beyond the entrance prompts Francis to remove his hat. The oak door squeals as it opens halfway. The elderly man who peers around it inquires,

"Yes?"

"Pastor Asbury, journeying for Clifton."

"Pastor Asbury? You are one of the young ones. Please do come in."

The elderly man pushes the door completely open and turns. Watching him shuffling his way through the short hallway, Francis is somewhat amused by the old man's unorthodox method of walking. One leg, the right, drags the foot along the wooden floor. The left leg follows, then the same again with the right. Following slowly behind him, Francis remains silent.

Entering an open room that functions as a kitchen and a bedroom, the old man invites Francis to sit, then offers,

"Tea?"

"Yes, please."

"Itinerants ride hard. Hungry?"

Francis is grateful; he hasn't eaten since Northampton the day before. He measures his response,

"Very much so."

"Very well. Fresh out of steak and kidney;[133] shall sausage do?"

"Very well."

Francis once again is thankful. Fried sausages are one of his favorites.

The old man takes out a well-worn iron skillet and places it on an iron grid above the low fire in the kitchen fireplace. Francis's thoughts go straight to his mother; he vows to write her again very soon. As the old man retrieves several links of the mysterious meat and tosses it into the iron skillet, Francis asks of him,

"I have need to excuse myself. May I . . . ?"

"Facility toward the south end of the property."

Walking outdoors, Francis looks for the outhouse. He spots the wooden shack, roughly twenty yards in the direction mentioned by the old man. Francis notices the symmetrical vertical boards the same width as a barrel stave. They are moldy. Francis is glad to see no visible holes in the siding; he proceeds. Along the way he discovers a wood pile, loosely thrown about. Several dried leaves from cut

---

[133] Steak and kidney pie, a savory meat pudding.

branches thicken the lifeless heap. As he walks by, a strange sound of movement in the brush causes him to stop. Staring at the piled scrub, Francis considers the possible source of the interruption. Rubbing his chin with the thumb and forefinger of his right hand, he bends down to investigate. He pulls one branch.

Nothing. He pulls another. Once again, silence.

With the branch, Francis moves some of the leaves. His discovery brings a wide smile to his face, the kind of smile that a young man wears when he pets a friendly working dog. Under the leaves lie three small creatures. The midday sunlight causes one of them to come to life; snuffling about, the thin-snouted animal raises its tiny eyes toward Francis. He responds,

"The ruddle-tinged gang. The awakening approaches."

The biggest of the three—each is only slightly larger than a man's palm—puffs himself . . . or herself; Francis isn't sure yet. The audible warning, a delicate snorting sound, brings Francis to laughter. Again, he has a word for his newly discovered friend.

"You needn't get all hedgehoggy—just as pushy as James at the forge."

The other two balls of spikes awake from their hibernating slumber. They mill about, trying out their skinny pink legs, which have been resting for nearly five months. Francis reaches to pick up one of the latecomers; the hedgehog balls up. The sharply pointed sphere remains motionless on the ground. Disregarding this act of rebellion, Francis lifts the animal. Drawing it close to his face, he remarks,

"Whiffy as I remember."

The animal's earthy smell prompts a memory; Francis reminisces about his childhood playing with wild hedgehogs and encountering their unmistakable odor. He rubs the tiny creature.

"Shall I see your tummy button?"

The hedgehog remains balled up, its spikes as stiff as a forge nail.

"Perhaps not."

Francis sets the animal down, careful to place it within the pile of leaves. He gently nudges the walker back to the pile. Gathering the two sticks and some removed leaves, Francis re-covers the little family. He rises to his feet and departs to attend to nature's call.

Returning to the meeting house, Francis enters the home. The inviting smell brings another full smile, the kind a hungry man makes when he walks into a room smelling of roasting sausage.

"Pleasantly whiffy."

Francis's comment brings a slight smile to the face of the old man. Francis walks to the fire. He prompts his hospitable host,

"I failed to gain your name."

"Fuller, Claude Fuller."

"My deepest gratitude for your generous offer, Mr. Fuller."

Claude nods his head. With little ado, he gathers a cloth potholder. Placing it around the handle of the iron pan, he lifts the skillet. It makes one last banging pop. Claude responds,

"Dinner is prepared."

Shuffling toward the small kitchen table already set for two, Claude places the pan right onto the wooden top. Francis notices several scars where a hot pot rested directly on the tabletop; *slightly different from Mother's technique*. Francis keeps this thought to himself. Claude and Francis take their seats. The oak chairs with the reed-covered seats remind Francis of home. Claude bows his head and waits. Francis bows his head and waits. The silence is genuine; Francis welcomes the sacred moment. After several minutes, Claude raises his head.

"Pastor Asbury, at times, God desires that we only listen."

Francis wants to respond, but wisely, he merely nods his approval. Claude continues,

"Traveling to Clifton shall place you across the Greensand Ridge. Familiar with the region?"

"No."

"I see. The passage is simple enough; remain on the high road, as the land further south will approach swampy conditions. Upon the westerly woods, you shall be near the sheep ford, Shefford. This is the highest point to cross river. The river runs east to west north of Shefford. Travel east along the River Ivel and you shall approach Clifton, which lies shortly thereafter."

"I shall."

Francis devours his meal. Claude doesn't mind; he gains satisfaction in knowing he has helped one of Wesley's itinerants. He graciously offers Francis additional meat. Francis gratefully receives it, quickly forking the fried sausage. The young man can eat well when provision is available. Francis inquires,

"Met a family of hedgehogs on the property; are you aware?"

"I am. The little fellows continue to hibernate in the brush pile—protects them from the hungry season."

"Hungry season?"

"Quite unlike Wesley's itinerants."

Francis's sudden tilt of his head, that quizzical nod he has a habit of repeating, prompts Claude to explain.

"The hedgehogs are smartly crafted; when their food source is scarce, they sleep until it returns. Not like Wesley's men—food or not, you continue to preach."

"It is as you say."

"Hidden food."

Francis smiles; he understands the scriptural reference. He responds,

"Yes, a sustaining food that is not consumed."

"Just as Jesus spoke."

Francis shares another thought with Claude.

"The town jail . . . passing it brought a dark feeling."

"A dark place. Many have expired, some guilty, some not so guilty. Some set free. Wesley would do well to push his efforts in changing such institutions."

Francis nods in agreement. Claude continues,

"Man's inhumanity to man."

"I see."

"Not one hundred years ago, a good man spent considerable time within those walls. A man of God, like yourself. Preached to the sixty or so prisoners each day."

Claude's conversation has Francis's undivided attention. He inquires,

"A family member?"

"No. However, a brother in Christ."

"Very well. Who was this prison resident?"

"A Bedfordshire resident."

"All right, then; who?"

Francis's enthusiastic response brings a slight smile to Claude's face. He sets down his fork, leans back, and rests against his seatback. Francis taps the top of the table with his fork. Claude offers,

"There, I've found it."

"Found what?"

"Something that would cause you to pause from your meal."

Francis chuckles.

"Very well, Claude. I shall not return to the gracious meal until you share of this prisoner."

"All right, then. John Bunyan."

"Again, Bunyan! The man's efforts seem a constant companion."

"Perhaps a sign from above."

"I fail to decipher such a notice."

"All right, then; you must pray. Bunyan was a man on a journey, much like yourself. A very long journey."

"I understand he never left Bedfordshire."

"Ah, yes; however, his itinerating took him farther than he could have ever imagined. Perhaps your journey is longer than you perceive."

Impressed with the story and challenged by the thought of a long journey, Francis sets down his fork. After Claude's insistence, the itinerant resumes eating, but the action fails to silence Francis's wandering thoughts. *Long journey, farther than I could perceive.* Dinner completes with a time of prayer with Claude, and Francis is on his way.

The bridge over the River Ouse resides at the southern end of Bedford. Francis and Churchfield head for the ancient structure. As they approach the waterway, Francis notices the green algae of spring beginning to form a top layer, occasionally accented with several clumps of reed grass pushing through the pane of the slick, slow-moving surface. Francis halts Churchfield. The bridge over the waterway is suspect.

On the right side of the 250–foot-long bridge, the short stone wall, a barrier against falling into the water, is mostly missing. On the left side, the eighteen-inch-high wall is still present; however, portions of the gravel roadway are missing. Francis peers at several holes and discovers he can see clear through to the river. Scraping his top teeth on his bottom lip, Francis considers the medieval span.

"Come, Churchy; we shall venture eastward for an additional passage."

Turning the horse, Francis urges Churchfield along the waterway. Within a few yards, a young boy rushes forward from behind them.

"Yo' needn't worry. Right side can bear up the load."

Francis reins in his horse and looks the boy up and down. The twelve-year-old is tall and thin, much like Francis at that age, with hands on his hips and a look that is confident that the traveler will return to the bridge. Francis looks to the stone crossing, then back to the boy. He looks to the bridge again. Rubbing the back of his neck with his left hand, Francis responds,

"Very well. Shall give it a go."

Moving toward the span, Francis counts the arches: *one, two, three, four, five, and six. 'Tis a lengthy exchange.* At the lip of the bridge road, Francis pauses again. The boy urges,

"Go on. The bridge shall hold."

Francis guides Churchy to favor the right side of the structure. It is odd, moving closer to the edge with no barrier—clearly not the normal procedure. Francis continues slowly. His teeth resume their nervous scraping. The habitual act aids him with the uncomfortable view straight down to the water below. *This is the widest part of the river,* Francis worries to himself. At the middle of the bridge, the boy prompts Francis,

"Yo've got it. Continue on the right."

The boy is correct; the bridge is stable. Francis and Churchfield proceed. Nearing the opposite side, Francis turns toward the young boy.

"Thank you. The Lord's blessings to you."

"Yo' a preacher? Yo' must stay and preach to me mum and dad."

Uncomfortable that his departure disappoints the lad, Francis considers the request. Impulsively, he responds,

"Very well. You know Mr. Fuller, Claude Fuller?"

"I do."

"Go to him. Let him know that Pastor Asbury shall return in a week."

"See yo' in a week."

"Very well."

In complete happiness, the boy runs off. Francis relaxes as he approaches the end of the bridge. *Much better.* He convinces himself that he made the right choice, both in the crossing and the promise to return.

Departing Bedford, Francis passes the old St. John's Church. The twelfth-century church also functions as a hospital for the elderly who have found themselves in poverty, through either misfortune or the infirmities of age. The residents receive housing, food, and care in exchange for a commitment to holy living, much like the monks of centuries before. This religious community is a direct descendant of the medieval St. John's Hospital, which reached out to local lepers.

The town of Clifton lies ten miles to the southeast of Bedford. Nearly two-thirds of the way from Bedford, Francis will cross the beautiful greensand ridge. The wooded range of lofty black poplars soaking in the overflow of flooded rivers gives way to the conifer-rich hills rising from the clay valleys. The rugged panoply invites a traveler to gently receive the best that Creation has to offer. For centuries, the locally quarried sandstone has dressed cathedrals and churches with a unique sage-green tinge.

Nearing two hours out, Francis arrives at his destination in Clifton. Outside the home, he secures Churchfield; the horse is happy to munch on a pile of dried rye grass and fescue. The simple brick structure reminds Francis of Great Barr. A neighboring oak is mature enough to support a healthy community of warblers and swallows. Before Francis can reach the front door, a tall, thin, well-dressed man bursts from the home. With four large, quick steps, the gentleman offers,

"William Parker, local preacher and mayor."

Surprised by the sudden appearance of William, Francis replies,

"Asbury, Francis Asbury from . . ."

"Very well, Francis. Wesley is sending them younger each year. Please do come in."

Once again startled by William, Francis nods and follows him into the home. William darts toward the opening at the far end of the main room. Francis stands alone. *Most peculiar.* Peering about, Francis spots a familiar sight: a tiny fireplace with an iron spit. The sight brings memory of his mother and father; *I do miss their company.* Continuing his impromptu inspection, he spots a Bible on the small table in the corner of the main room. He suspects the table is the location of the home's dinners. *This truly inspires welcome memories of home.*

Once again bursting into Francis's presence, William strides into the main room.

"You must join me for town."

Without hesitation, William heads for the front door. He exits, and Francis again stands in the main room of William's house, alone. He hurries to follow.

Walking toward town, William shares,

"Town is shaping up nicely."

Very well, I assume; Francis ponders the revelation. Noticing an elderly man walking toward them, he prepares a polite greeting. He tosses several ideas about: *good day, sir; most beautiful day, sir.* But wait—*most odd; seems as if he turned upon spotting William and me.* Francis sets aside his effort as the pair continue their hurried pace. Francis is unsure, *why all the rushing about?* Along the walk, Francis spots a beautiful weeping willow tree hovering over a small pond. The almost haunting reflection of the billowing foliage creates a shady cover at the water's edge.

Francis's view of the tree is diverted as several oncoming individuals appear. Spotting Francis and William, they suddenly dart away. Before he can ask, William offers,

"Difficult task, reforming the locals."

What are we reforming? Francis keeps the question to himself.

Francis considers a pair who recently walked the other way. *Perhaps Clifton shall prove most difficult for the Gospel.* Inside, familiar emotions emerge. A slight fear wants to grip him; the familiar tightening of his stomach and the discomfort in his back returns. Despite the worry of preaching to those who resist, Francis is confident of one thought: *if danger were imminent, James would not have allowed me to venture into Clifton alone.*

Francis abandons the silent conversation and aims in a different direction.

"Mr. Parker, what are your opinions of the Clifton society?"

"The Methodists are well. It is the locals who require much of my attention."

These are words Francis does not want to hear. He reassures himself, *James would not have allowed.* Coming to a complete stop, William looks in the direction of two women walking on the other side of the street. One of the women announces,

"William Parker, you shan't rule this town."

The pair abruptly departs. Francis looks toward William. The town's mayor purses his lips. Francis notices that his large Adam's apple agitates the white collar of his shirt when he swallows. William remarks,

"Those two never accepted me."

Francis attempts to converse on a subject he knows little about.

"As mayor?"

"No. As a Moravian brother. Some time ago that pair made things difficult for me."

Are you so sure it was their doing? Francis keeps this thought to himself. He inquires,

"You were Moravian?"

"Benjamin Ingham's original society in Bedford, subsequently Clifton. Slight disagreement with them."

Are you so sure it was slight? Again, the thought remains private. William continues,

"Jealous of my daughter. Never accepted her."

"A women's quarrel?"

"No, the society's quarrel. Objected to her marrying without their consent."

"I see."

William is finally silent. He kicks the dirt and begins to move again. Francis follows close behind.

"Francis, you shall preach this evening in town."

Francis didn't expect this. Once again, his anxiety attempts to surface. Francis resists. He approaches the recent subject with William.

"The Moravian society expelled you on account of your daughter marrying without their permission?"

"It is as you have said."

"Shall this evening's townspeople hold the same opinion?"

"More than likely, worse. They've yet to accept my reforms."

"Reforms?"

"Yes, as mayor I have attempted to improve the behavior of our town. Not many have accepted the mandates."

Very well, this evening shall prove most entertaining.

Arriving at the preaching house that evening, Francis recalls Wesley's words of warning about the location. The structure resides on wooden stilts, over a pigsty. As they walk up the wooden steps, a creaking noise seems to squeal a warning. Francis grabs the oak handrail and continues to the front door.

Inside, William points to a small wooden platform at the end of the narrow room. It is a large room, nearly thirty feet long, but only twelve feet wide.

"This will allow for you to talk down to those most in need."

"Are you sure . . . ?"

"I am confident this is for their well-being."

Francis decides to keep silent.

The villagers arrive in small groups, a dozen people at a time. Many of the women carry small woven baskets. Francis ponders, *what will happen if the contents of these baskets are for nefarious purposes?* By the six o'clock hour, nearly fifty people have gathered. As Francis moves toward his preaching platform, he overhears several men of the group as they approach. *They do not seem to hold William in a favorable light. Very well, perseverance is my call.* In the makeshift pulpit, Francis raises his hands to pray, the gathering quiets, and the people bow their heads. Wesley's words from last summer's London conference come to mind: "Surely they love the Gospel, who come to hear it in such a place." Francis makes a mental note of the crowd: *several young men in their teens to the right, a large middle-aged man dead center. Thankfully, many women.* He begins,

"Let this be the mark for us, that Christ may be all . . ."

Below the wooden floor, several pigs begin to squeal. The cause is unknown to Francis; however, several of the young men look to each other, shaking their heads in disgust. Even the large gentleman at the front wraps his thick arms on top of his ledge-like belly and offers a frown. Francis is grateful for their reactions; *seems I'm to have a few advocates.* The big man clears his throat and announces,

"William Parker, might you control your nephews?"

William avoids eye contact with the man. Francis begins again,

"Let this be . . ."

"William Parker!"

The high-pitched shrill from the woman in the front row catches Francis by surprise. He jerks back his head and views the woman. She is a short, skinny creature, her mouth downturned from a lifetime of scowling. With both hands on her hips, she awaits William's response. There is none. Francis wonders if she is one of the people who avoided William on the street this day. She continues at William,

"Once more, your relations have decided on feeding the pigs during our time of service."

By now, the stench from the frenzied pigs chomping and rolling on rotten vegetables is ascending through the thin spaces in the plank flooring. Several women raise handkerchiefs to shield their noses. Men instinctively wave the offensive aroma from their faces. Along with the piercing perfume arising from the activities beneath the structure, the crescendo of squeals, snorts, and grunts makes it nearly impossible to hear. The big man in the front looks to the young men and offers,

"Seems the banquet below is going along quite well."

The room's inhabitants rise from their wooden seats. The young men, now standing, chuckle at the large fellow's comment. The entire group heads for the door. The last to leave, one of the young men, turns toward Francis and announces,

"Seems your sermon shall be cut short this beautiful evening in May."

Francis and William remain alone. The mayor advises Francis,

"Perhaps your next visit shall meet with more favorable results."

Francis turns and exits.

Outdoors, Francis finds himself tailing behind the rest of the townspeople. He descends the steps and heads for Churchfield, finding the horse prancing in excitement. Francis comments,

"Is it your desire to join the banquet?"

Francis unties his horse and climbs into the saddle. From the rear of the building, several muddy youths race toward Francis. The eight or nine boys immediately surround him. Francis stands his ground; *Almighty Father, shall such little weapons prosper?* The boys call to a young man at the perimeter of the gathering, a dodgy-looking character holding a wrapped blanket. The group pushes the lad toward the itinerant. They stand there, grinning and twitching with hidden excitement. Surprised they have not attacked, Francis taps Churchfield to move. The horse walks forward. Although the boys permit this action, they continue to surround his path.

Francis ignores the development, confident that he and his horse are in no danger. The boys sneer,

"Banish William or we shall banish Wesley."

"Banish William? Who might this William be?"

"Our uncle, William Parker. He is a despot."

Francis almost laughs at the preteen boy with the slight lisp. He decides to keep his amusement to himself.

Without reply, Francis taps Churchfield again and furthers his departure. The teen boys laugh as one of them unwraps the blanketed package. From the corner of his eye, Francis can sense him removing whatever it contains and propping it above his shoulder. He ignores the development and moves ahead at a steady pace.

The boy hurls the object at Francis. It hits him in the left shoulder and falls to the ground. Looking down, Francis spots the group's weapon of choice: a dead cat. He ventures a look at the sleeve of his left arm; it is stained with the cat's blood. *A fine accessory for a fine jacket,* Francis wryly mocks. As he once again prods Churchfield, the horse and rider almost run over two lads who wisely decide to get out of the way.

For the remainder of the spring and into the summer, Francis continues the route as James prescribes. From Clifton, he returns to his initial stop in the Bedfordshire circuit, Hertford. From Abraham Andrews's school in Hertford he travels to Luton, the Dallow Farm, and Sundon Manor exclusively. Departing the grounds of the estate, he ventures through the dreaded valley, Bunyan's Valley of the Shadow of Death, on up into Millbrook. In Millbrook, Francis visits with the Bunkers. His tasks completed in Millbrook, Francis stops at Mr. Fuller's in Bedford. He also visits the home of the young boy who helped him across the suspect bridge in Bedford. Once the visit is completed with the young man and his parents in Bedford, Francis returns to Clifton. The entire sixty-five-mile circuit allows the young itinerant to preach, teach, and check up on the local society in each location once per week.

The antics of the boys in Clifton continue every time Francis visits the town. Over the pigsty, Francis leads as the boys outside do their best to cause a commotion. Throwing rocks at the building, stirring up the pigs, tossing rotted vegetables through open windows—none of this shakes Francis's focus. At times, he finds the acts bordering on the comical, especially when one of the hoodlums slips and falls into the muck. Their last act against Francis ends badly for the lad who attempts to steal Churchfield. The horse allows the boy to untie him and lead him from the meeting house; however, once the journey reaches an advantageous spot—one with much early-spring grass—the horse summarily kicks the would-be pilferer and knocks him to the ground. Slightly dazed, the delinquent scurries home with a nasty bruise on his rear end, and Churchfield remains to enjoy a tasty snack.

The month of July, 1768, finds Francis in Millbrook once again. Outdoors, Ruth and her younger brother, Joseph, join him.

In the family garden, Francis teaches the young boy.

"The plant is coming along nicely."

"Pastor Asbury, you say this is tato plant?"

"Tomato plant, Joseph."

"Great smellin' leaves. Do we eat the leaves?"

"No, Joseph! Francis—I mean, Pastor Asbury—has informed us before. The round fruits shall follow the tiny blossoms. The pastor and his father are quite the gardeners."

Francis's humorous smile aims more at Ruth than her young brother. *Pastor Asbury; sounds so formal.* He begins to respond,

"Joseph . . ."

"Pastor Asbury!"

Before he can finish, one of two men approaching on horseback shouts once more,

"Pastor Asbury!"

Francis spins around. As he squints their way, the sight of the men prompts his memory. He's seen them before, at the London conference in '67. Despite the visual recollection, he cannot remember their names. He clears his throat and waits.

The men bring their horses to a halt several yards from the trio. Dismounting, they approach Francis.

"Pastor Asbury, Thomas Hanby of Durham. This is my fellow laborer on the circuit, John Duncan. Wesley sends word: Continue your small circuit until the first of August. Then proceed for London straight away. The August sixteenth Bristol conference will send word of your assignment."

"Very well."

The itinerants on horseback depart as quickly as they arrived. Francis considers the instructions; *I shall leave for London in five days.* Ruth inquires,

"Shall you return?"

Francis hesitates to answer. Turning away, he bends to inspect a delicate yellow blossom of the tomato plant.

"I shan't witness the fruit of this flower."

Unhappy with his response, Ruth turns and hurries back to the house. Francis rises, not happy that his actions have disappointed Ruth. He rubs Joseph's head.

"I aimed for softness and fell quite short. Very well, Joseph; I must depart. Fetch Churchfield; we've a ten-mile journey to complete before sunset."

As the day's light descends below the horizon, Francis arrives in Clifton. He is grateful for the warm reception, but he struggles with the thought which has occupied the majority of his day: his attraction to Ruth in Millbrook and his attraction to Nancy in Bromwich. Thinking of the two brings a subtle frustration; *perhaps I'm to have neither*.

The dealings in Clifton go as expected. The faithful of the town gather with enthusiasm. Before long, several of the local boys set out to disrupt, and they do a fine job. The evening ends with Francis once again facing confrontation from the pint-sized hoodlums.

The following day, Francis departs Clifton for Hertford. Since the town is adjacent to London, only twenty miles out, he decides to remain in Hertford until the first of August. He is confident, *Abraham shall have me teach the students at his new school*.

Francis is correct; Abraham Andrews has plenty of work for the itinerant. After several lessons with the boys and girls, Mr. Andrews invites Francis to spend the evening. The next morning finds the itinerant enjoying the loving farewells of the students and local townspeople as he heads south for the capital city on the River Thames.

The sights and smells of London are unmistakable. The gritty city's ever-present smoke and fog remove the possibility of a penetrating sunray. The foul and unkempt streets once again greet the itinerant. Francis instinctively reaches into his coat pocket for a handkerchief; he raises it to protect his nose from the rotting-flesh smells of the butcher shops that toss the refuse of their industry into the streets. Churchfield flinches away from the numerous chaises that race through the puddled streets, nearly bowling over the crowded gatherers busy about their day.

Ahead, a man pushes several bystanders in his effort to chase someone who has stolen his bag. As if providing background music to the pursuit, a fiddler twiddles on his strings. The pursuer races past Francis and the fiddler, oblivious to the oncoming traffic. A team of horses nearly knocks him to the ground.

Nearing on his left, Francis notices one who seems out of place. The young man in the burnished-brown silk jacket is impeccably dressed. His taupe waistcoat, also made of silk, is partially unbuttoned to reveal a hint of a starched white cotton shirt. A sheer-white linen necktie, handsomely tied to hang midway between his neck and chest, adds further elegance. The outfit causes Francis to question his own tattered jacket. Carrying several thick volumes, the well-proportioned blade is obviously a student. He makes his way on foot down Tottenham Court Road, the road on which Whitefield's chapel stands.

Nearing the flawlessly attired scholar, Francis surmises that the traveler is approximately his age, and more obviously, is not from the West Midlands. He draws Churchfield alongside to offer,

"Good day."

The well-dressed wanderer turns toward Francis, his thin lips offering an engaging smile. His dark, almost perfectly round eyes are enlivened by his dark, slender eyebrows. He responds,

"Indeed."

"Francis Asbury, Great Barr."

"And where would Great Barr reside?"

"Staffordshire. Sojourning in London?"

"Yes. By way of Edinburgh. My deepest apology; my name is Benjamin."

"Welcome to London, Benjamin. Great Barr lies northwest of Birmingham, slightly more than one hundred miles from London. Shall you remain in London for a time?"

"For a time, in studies. As for today, I'm to meet Whitefield at his chapel. You wouldn't by chance know the way?"

"The way—the Almighty has bestowed upon us the way."

"Indeed. Francis, you talk like a preacher."

"Indeed. Unfortunately, you fail to talk like a Scotsman. Where are you from?"

Francis's wry smile causes Benjamin to chuckle; sensing a friendly bond, he responds to Francis with a quip.

"I believe you are a preacher, and a not-too-polite traveling one at that!"

"Your perception is correct. I am far from polite; one of Wesley's itinerants. Perhaps you might share that which leads you to such a bold conclusion - -

And from where you originate."

"Quite simple, Francis. Your jack boots appear most worn, as does your Bible in your right hand. The style and make of your jacket are far from anything I've experienced."

Francis is drawn to Benjamin's witty smile. Also sensing the bond of a new friendship, Francis fires back,

"Ah yes, the Bible—a preacher's first necessity."

"At Princeton, I too pursued studies for the ministry."

"Princeton?"

"Yes, Princeton. In the colonies. The Jerseys."

"The colony of the Jerseys?"

"Well, in a way, yes; East and West Jersey. In America."

"I see. Have you faith in the Lord and Savior?"

"I do."

"Why abandon the Lord's call?"

"I didn't."

"Are the volumes ecclesiastical?"

"Far from it. The books aid me in my calling."

"Well, shall you reveal your calling?"

The welcoming banter adjoins kindred spirits.

"At Princeton, I studied theology, law, and medicine. I could have chosen to pursue any of the three, but a day of fasting and prayer directed me to choose medical pursuits. Here in London, I am to gain a mastery of military hygiene under the Royal Court Physician, Sir John Pringle. The volumes I hold are my medical studies from the University of Edinburgh. I recently completed two years of study. Edinburgh was the recommendation of my mentor, Dr. John Redman in Philadelphia, under whom I apprenticed for six years at the College of Philadelphia."

"Impressive. Perhaps you shall join me on my itinerant travels. As of late, your medical talents should have aided me in my recoveries."

"Recoveries? Your efforts are met with opposition?"

"At times. The Savior warned of such. Although He failed to mention the pains of the lower back."

"Ha! Well then, I am here to address this thorn, if need be."

"Very well, I shall no longer question your faith."

"A persistent and wise preacher is Francis Asbury of Great Barr."

The two proceed to Whitefield's chapel. Along the way, they discover they are the same age, Francis slightly older by a few months. Naturally, his competitive spirit will not allow the younger Benjamin an advantage.

"I too have traveled much. Though no ocean crossings were involved, I have had my dealings with turbulent waters."

"Do tell."

"No need; do tell of the colonies."

"Francis, the colonies are fantastic! Whatever a man dreams, whatever a man attempts, the sole hindrance to his accomplishments is his departure from truth. God blesses the continent in numerous ways. The lands are abundant with forest and river life. Even the aboriginal residents, the Indians, have displayed an acceptance of biblical truth."

"You make it sound as if Paradise has emerged on earth."

"Paradise on earth does possess its limits. No need to surface domestic issues; tell me of Great Barr."

"An industrious town. Community life revolves around the trades. Surrounding lands are blessed with the beauty of the animal and plant creation, along with a beautiful river. Father is gardener to two wealthy families; a third also seeks his efforts. Mother - -

Mother is a dear woman; slightly governing, but meaning well."

"Francis, our mothers appear as sisters. Widowed when I was six years old, Mother sought the welfare of myself and six other siblings. The loss of our father caused us to move from the farm to Philadelphia. In Penn's city, Mother's industrious efforts soon opened the door for me to attend my uncle's school in Nottingham, Maryland. My uncle, the Reverend Dr. Samuel Finley, recently finished as president at Princeton."

"What of his current efforts?"

"He passed two years ago, when I left for Edinburgh."

"My apologies, Benjamin."

Struggling with the response, Francis remains quiet. Benjamin continues,

"It is well, Francis; my uncle's efforts shall remain a lifetime with me. It is largely due to his influence that I graduated from Princeton at fourteen years of age."

"Have you arranged your stay in London?"

"I have. Shall spend my time with another from Philadelphia, Dr. Franklin. I believe we board on Craven Street. He and Whitefield encouraged me to school in London. In fact, it was Whitefield and his dear wife who brought me to London one week ago."

"Dr. Franklin I have had the privilege to meet, as well as Whitefield. An ingenious man—Franklin, that is, and Whitefield proves a most amazing man of God."

For the first time since meeting Benjamin, Francis is uncomfortable. He realizes that his new friend is not only extremely intelligent, he also walks with well-respected company, polite company. *He dresses well.* Francis silently vows to read more, *and to replace this awful jacket.* Benjamin inquires,

"What of your studies, Francis?"

"Consistent with the Midlands; basic education and an apprenticeship in the trades."

"Very well, you must teach me to work the iron."

"And you must teach me Latin; Wesley requires it of his itinerants."

"Not only Latin, Hebrew and Greek as well."

Francis nods his head in agreement. He senses a true friendship coming to life. Nearing Whitefield's chapel, Francis and Benjamin proceed to enter the grounds.

Before dismounting, Francis observes,

"The men are wearing weepers."[134]

"Weepers?"

" 'Tis a time of mourning."

"How so?"

"We shall inquire."

Inside the chapel, several men preoccupied with a discussion approach Francis and Benjamin. They rush right by the pair. Benjamin offers,

"I believe I heard reference to a woman."

"As did I."

As they walk into the center of the sanctuary, a familiar face greets Francis. The tall figure immediately envelopes the young itinerant with his long, large arms.

"Fr'dancis, our dear Whitefield is in deep mournin'."

Alexander Mather pauses to wipe away a tear. Seeing the big man weep draws a trickle from the eye of Benjamin; he removes a silk handkerchief and wipes the descending drop. Francis pulls back to ask,

"What of our dear Whitefield?"

"His wife. She passed this mornin'. Most unexpectedly. Whitefield is torn. Remarkably, he speaks of departin' the end of the week to speak at the Countess's school in South Wales."

The young men and Mather each wipe away a tear. The three take a seat in the sanctuary. The mood is somber. Each nervously looks about, unable to speak. Benjamin is the first to break the silence.

"It was just yesterday that Mrs. Whitefield mentioned a tiredness; she spoke of retiring early last evening."

"George mentioned an inflammatory fever that lasted through the night. She is said to have fought off the effects from the day prior."

Francis remains silent. He barely knows George; however, he cannot escape the overall gloom that hovers in the souls of each person arriving in the chapel. Without his noticing, the building has gained nearly thirty men and women who have come to mourn. Benjamin continues,

"She and Reverend Whitefield spent several days with me in Edinburgh— personally saw to it that each of my needs was amply supplied. They even joined me in my coach to London. The Almighty numbers each of our days."

"Indeed, Benjamin; indeed He does."

---

[134] Black armbands signifying a time of mourning.

Francis's response to Benjamin coincides with a man in a black clerical robe taking the pulpit at the front of the sanctuary. With hands raised for prayer, the elder minister begins the service, a solemn event.

Out of respect for Reverend Whitefield and his wife, many of the town's inhabitants arrive. With the gathering flowing out of the main sanctuary, the ending of the last hymn sends many home, grateful to have drawn comfort from the gathering and also thankful for the promises of God and eternal life.

The next morning finds Francis and Benjamin at the temporary home of Dr. Franklin on Craven Street. The young men vowed to meet early for prayer. Upon completion of their time in supplication, Francis makes a suggestion.

> "We must visit several friends of mine here in London. Perhaps we shall aid them in working the streets."

> "Working the streets?"

> "Sharing the Gospel. Are you willing?"

> "I am."

The pace of the young men as they walk to The Cedars in Leytonstone instinctively picks up when Francis mentions to Benjamin that they are meeting several women. Benjamin inquires,

> "And you tell me they are committed to aiding the less fortunate?"

> "Yes, Benjamin."

> "Quite attractive."

> "Attractive indeed. Respectfully, this is not a social call; it shall invoke the deepest desire of my calling."

> "Yes, Francis. Although, a little social life may aid your efforts."

> "Perhaps."

Francis displays that frivolous smile.

At the home of Mary Bosanquet and her companions, Sarah Ryan and Sarah Crosby, Francis and Benjamin stand at the front stoop. The young men unconsciously straighten out their jackets, one of which is much nicer than the other. Catching each other in the instinctive act, the two laugh aloud. Francis's knock on the door is answered by the voice of a young girl calling,

> "Do come in!"

The young men proceed indoors. The attractive woman at the end of the hallway immediately recognizes one of the guests.

> "Francis!"

> "Mary."

She hurries up to Francis and curtsies. Francis bows his head and responds to her charming smile,

> "With delight, I introduce my new friend, Benjamin . . ."

Stopping mid-sentence, Francis finally realizes that Benjamin has never shared his surname. He turns toward his companion.

"Benjamin, oddly, I fail to know of . . ."

"Rush, Francis, Benjamin Rush. Mary, it is with great pleasure that I obtain your fellowship."

The resonant male voices rolling down the hallway draw the other women of Leytonstone toward the entrance; included is the nine-year-old girl who invited the pair into the residence. The elder Sarah Crosby walks toward the new arrivals. She spots the proximity of Mary standing shoulder to shoulder with Francis and offers a serious look in the direction of the young woman. Without hesitation and unnoticed by Francis, Mary sidesteps a few inches away from the itinerant. Sarah's face lightens in response as she offers,

"Mr. Asbury! Excuse me, Pastor Asbury."

She curtsies, then continues,

"London, as well as the residents of Leytonstone, welcomes you once again. I see we have an assistant."

"A new friend. Moreover, a doctor to study under the Royal Physician. I introduce Dr. Benjamin Rush. Benjamin, Mrs. Sarah Crosby, a prophetess in Israel."

Once again, the saintly Sarah offers the courteous gesture. She and Mary are dressed in their purple cotton dresses, the outfit agreed upon as their customary attire for their operation in London. She inquires,

"Seems you are not a resident of England. American?"

"Yes, Mrs. Crosby. Philadelphia."

"Our dear Dr. Franklin sojourns from Philadelphia. Despite the growing tensions in the colonies, the citizens of London love the man. Do tell of the American commonwealth."

"Discomfort and anxiety are on the rise. Fortunately, none have risen to agitation. On an opposite front, the settlement of North Carolina has offered a reconciliatory gesture. They have named their key city after King George's queen of Portuguese descent, Queen Charlotte. They call it Charlotte Town. It appears a good-faith attempt to appease the King."

"Perhaps. In London, the residents have yet to accustom themselves to a teenage Queen who speaks the King's English with a strong German accent, having darkened skin and Negroid features. Sadly, they fail to recall the sacred words of Scripture: "And He has made from one blood every nation of men."[135]

Francis realizes an absence; *where is Sarah Ryan?* It prompts him to ask,

---

[135] From Acts chapter 17, verse 26.

"Is Sarah Ryan about?"

"She is not doing well. Please come. She awaits in an adjacent room."

Walking toward the bedroom at the rear of the home, Francis is uneasy. The last time he saw Sarah Ryan, she seemed to struggle with an ailment. In fact, on several occasions she excused herself from participating in the street evangelizations. Francis silently prays for God's best. Entering the darkened room, they find Sarah lying on her bed under several layers of handmade quilts. She is barely able to open her eyes when the outside light peeks into the room through the opened door. She mumbles,

"Mary?"

"Yes, Sarah, we have a visitor. A dear friend who wishes to see you. Pastor Asbury."

Sarah turns her head to view Francis. Spotting him, she broadens a smile that has been missing for some time. She nods her understanding when Francis raises his finger to his mouth, advising her to refrain from speaking. He kneels beside her.

"Sarah, the Sovereign Lord is your strength. He shall enable you to go upon the heights, and you shall not affright."

Her smile returns. Francis leans forward and kisses her forehead. Behind him, Mary and Sarah Crosby wipe away a steady flow of tears. Francis rises and turns for the doorway. The women follow him out of the room.

In the hallway, Francis speaks with Mrs. Crosby.

"Has Mrs. Ryan suffered long?"

"For several months she has been in decline. Sadly, the last two weeks have produced much strain. We fear she hasn't long."

Francis's eyes lower to the wooden floor. Unable to meet Sarah's gaze, he asks,

"What shall result from her loss?"

"Mary and I shall continue. Before she experienced her ailment, we planned to move north, to Yorkshire. Sarah's sickness has temporarily halted our plans."

Francis raises his eyes toward Sarah.

"And of her ailment?"

Sarah looks away. The biting of her lip precedes a quiet moment. After several uncomfortable seconds she offers,

"It is best if spoken apart from mixed company."

As she looks toward the itinerant, Sarah captures Francis's look of concern. He nods and asks,

"May I change the subject?"

"Yes, Francis."

"This evening would greatly bless if you and Mary would join Dr. Rush and myself at the Tabernacle."

"We have planned to be there ourselves."

"Very well. Till this evening."

Francis bows his head and turns toward Benjamin, and the two make their exit.

Francis and Benjamin spend the next two weeks aiding Mrs. Crosby and Miss Bosanquet in their efforts to reach the desperate souls of London. On the morning of August 18, Francis and Benjamin once again make their way to The Cedars. They plan to invite the women and several residents of their home to attend the service at Whitefield's chapel. Upon their arrival, Mary informs them that three young women will join them for the service.

At Whitefield's chapel, Francis, Benjamin, Mary, and Sarah enter the building, followed by the three young women. The three are veterans of living on the street, each once addicted to gin and a former employee of a local brothel. They all proceed to the few remaining empty seats partway up the right side of the aisle. Allowing the women to sit first, Dr. Rush and Francis stand adjacent to their pew. Before Francis can take a seat, two gentlemen approach him. They are dusty and unshaven, and each carries a Bible.

"Pastor Asbury?"

"Yes."

"Peter Jaco and John Murlin. Wesley advised we might find you here. We perceive that Mrs. Crosby is in your presence. May we have a word with her?"

Francis backs up a step as he swings his arm in the direction of Sarah Crosby. The men do not hesitate.

"Mrs. Crosby!"   "Mrs. Crosby."

Peter defers to John, who quickly advises,

"Mrs. Crosby, you must follow at once. Sarah Ryan is delusional."

The entire group, Francis and Benjamin included, launch for the exit.

At the Leytonstone residence, they find Mrs. Ryan lying in bed and screaming,

"No! You shan't take me! No!"

Her head collapses into the pillow. Dr. Rush kneels beside the bed. He turns to ask of Mrs. Crosby,

"What ails Mrs. Ryan?"

Hesitating to answer, Sarah Crosby requests that the resident women depart the room. Only Francis and Benjamin remain, along with Mary Bosanquet. Closing the bedroom door behind her, Mrs. Crosby draws a deep breath and offers,

"The most dreaded disease that one can gain from one's husband. Syphilis."

Francis looks toward the floor, but his headstrong personality will not allow him to remain silent.

"However should she come across this?"

"Her second husband set to sea; he visited many ports."

Francis is slightly embarrassed, as well as angry—a new mix of emotions for the young man. The ailing Sarah breaks the uncomfortable silence in the room. Looking at Benjamin, she barely gasps the words out,

"Lift me."

Benjamin is confused. He turns toward Mrs. Crosby and then back to the ailing Sarah.

"Lift you?"

"Yes."

Benjamin shuffles the coverings of the bed, gently wrapping her legs and then her upper torso. Lifting her, he turns toward Mrs. Crosby and Mary. Mary responds,

"Sarah, the doctor has lifted you."

Partially opening one eye, Sarah whispers,

"To Polly's bed. I long to die in her arms."

Benjamin inquires,

"Who is Polly?"

Mary responds,

"It is I. Follow me to my room."

In tears, Mary leads Francis, Sarah Crosby, and Dr. Rush, who carries the ailing Sarah Ryan, to her bedroom. Entering the room, Mary instructs,

"Place her on my bed."

Benjamin and Francis lay her down softly. Lying alongside Sarah and wrapping her arms around her, Mary talks gently to her.

"Sarah, your daughter in the Lord is here. You may rest."

The elderly Sarah Ryan draws comfort from the warm embrace of her protégé. For the last few months, the ailing Sarah has found peace from her painful ordeal in the arms of her Elisha. Forcing the words, Sarah speaks to Mary.

"My dear, I want to lay in your arms once more, for the last time."

"My dear, we shall be one forever."

All in the room are exhibiting tears, including Mary. The ailing Sarah responds,

"There is no doubt of that - -

No doubt of that."

With these words, Sarah Ryan passes into eternity.

For nearly a month, the loss of Sarah Ryan lingers among the emotions of the ladies of Leytonstone. The sadness of bereavement is interrupted only by anger toward the sailor husband who not only gave Sarah syphilis, but also physically abused her. The women promise each other to continue with their plans, "just as Sarah would have liked it." With the past addition of another helper, Ann Tripp, when Sarah first displayed signs of illness, Mary Bosanquet and Sarah Crosby are able to move forward with their previous plan: the generous women will move their operation to Crosshall in Yorkshire.

After several days spent giving aid to the women at The Cedars, Dr. Rush and Francis bid farewell to the group. Benjamin is off to his tutelage under the Royal Physician, and Francis has word that his assignment from the Bristol conference, ending its meetings today, shall arrive this evening. He anxiously awaits news of his post.

Later that evening, Francis decides to spend time near The Foundry. Once there, he notices two stocky middle-aged men of medium height walking toward Windmill Hill. Their steps are deliberate, almost cocky. These two, dressed in plain clothes, are clearly in search of something, or perhaps someone. They stop an elderly man on Finsbury Fields Road, a member of Wesley's Foundry Church. The old man's quick response, pointing in the direction of Francis, sends the two bruisers walking once again. Stepping over the open sewer drain on the edge of the road, the men approach the young itinerant.

"Pastor Asbury?"

Francis is not certain why, but the faces appear familiar. *Have I shared the Gospel with them before? No, perhaps faces from The Foundry, or Whitefield's chapel.* The stockier of the two boldly announces,

"Peter Jaco, and my fellow laborer on the London circuit, John Murlin. Wesley has given his assignment."

The two men are Wesleyan itinerants, the ones who summoned Francis and the others when Sarah Ryan became deathly ill. Although nearly twenty years older, the men share similar life experiences with Francis. Peter, the son of a pilchard[136] processor, and John, the son of a farmer, hail from the barbarous southwest coast of England, in the county of Cornwall. The peninsula-like geography creates three coastlines which seem to goad a nefarious smuggling trade. Along these waterways, plundering shipwrecked sailors is an honorable profession—not much different from the brutish West Midlands of Francis's childhood, where drunkenness, cockfighting, and pilfering of and by street children is commonplace. Even some of the Cornwall Anglican clergy participate

---

[136] Small fish in the herring family, also known as sardines.

in the illegal activity as they provide cover for the smugglers in their church cellars, where they also hide stolen items.

Peter's and John's Methodist roots reside in England's palm-tree-laden town of Penzance. Nestled into the protected and isolated harbor that faces southeast and tucks between the neighboring hamlets of Newlyn, Mousehole, and Longrock, the area is a smuggler's dream. In addition to the landscape complete with hidden caves, canals, and ports, the local Anglican minister is also the local magistrate and a barbarian, constantly obstructing the sole opposition to the illegal trade: the Methodist faithful. He constantly provides cover for the smuggling rings. His proclamation, "I wish the Bible was still in Latin only, that none of the vulgar might be able to read it" symbolizes the man's detestable opinion of the Wesleyans and non-conformists who are systematically changing the undesirable views and actions of the citizens. He consistently has the itinerants arrested on faked charges; the unflinching verbal proclamation and assurance of his sins forgiven prompts the arrest of one of the non-conformist preachers. The Anglican minister attempts to force several other Methodists into military service by the obscure sixty-five-year-old 1703 act of Queen Anne, which seeks to push idle men into the royal army and navy. Preachers like Peter and John are men who provide the necessary encouragement for the Wesleyan faithful to prosper in such discouraging conditions. This environment and background qualifies Peter and John to speak to Francis about his next assignment.

Peter continues,

> "Bristol is complete. A beautiful time—precious yearnings toward the Lord."

> "You've my assignment?"

> "Yes, Francis; however, first a word of announcement. Wesley has officially accepted you as a full-fledged itinerant. Congratulations."

Francis silently rejoices. Although he expected the appointment, it brings comfort to hear it verbally. Peter inquires,

> "Have you returned home since the last conference?"

> "No, nearing two years away."

Peter's look of concern, the pursed lips and the contemplative tilt of his head as he looks to Pastor Murlin, brings a silence to the group. Not a complete silence, for the London nightlife scurries about, oblivious to the three men who consider much holier pursuits. John offers,

> "Colchester is unattended."

> "My circuit is Colchester?"

> "It is, Francis."

Francis's emotions border on panic. Colchester is sixty-five miles east of his current circuit, 135 miles from home. Unlike his twenty-four months away from home, never more than two days' ride away, Francis has never ventured so far; Colchester is easily a week away on horseback. *Colchester . . . Mother . . . and Father . . . more, Mother. Neither shall welcome such a distant charge.*

John Murlin breaks the silence.

"Francis, Wesley insists we prepare you. The coastal towns possess their unique challenges."

The young itinerant's eyes lock onto a jagged rock jutting from the hard-packed ground. He may not have sight of the men; however, he is securing every word they offer. Peter continues,

"Smugglers, Francis. Have you experience with smugglers?"

"No, sir, I haven't."

"Well then, it is a trade to those who've no grasp of sin. Wesley aims to distribute his *Word to a Smuggler* in all the coastal circuits. Here, take a copy for yourself. Read it, learn it, and most of all, preach it."

Francis receives the pamphlet written on vellum. Peter offers,

"Francis, you needn't read Wesley's paper now; we shall sum up its key points. Wesley is clear—smuggling is wrong. A smuggler is no more honest than a highwayman. They are far worse than the common pickpocket. For they rob our father, far worse than stealing from a complete stranger. King George is a loving father to his citizens, yet the smuggler chooses to steal away his rightful taxes. Remember the commandment, Francis: 'Thou shalt not steal.'[137] The duties belong to the King. Failure to pay them is stealing from the King. Do you follow, Francis?"

"I do."

"Very well; in effect, smuggling is not only robbing the King, the heinous act also robs every honest man in the nation. The more the King's revenues diminish, the more taxes must increase. Therefore, every smuggler is a thief general, who picks the pockets of both the King and all his fellow subjects. He wrongs them all."

John also offers,

"But for all this, cannot men find excuses? Yes, many do. 'I would not do this, except out of necessity—for I shall not live without it.' When this excuse comes your way, Francis, answer them, 'May not the man on the street say much the same? "I would not take your possessions, but I am under much necessity to do so, for I shall not live without them." ' "

---

[137] Deuteronomy chapter 5, verse 19, King James Version.

Francis responds,

> "I grasp the teaching—evil shall not be done so that good may result."

> "Yes, Francis."   "Yes."

The simultaneous response of Peter and John brings a smile to all three of the men's faces. Placing an arm around Francis's shoulders, Peter seeks to change the subject.

> "You know, Francis, we've word for you from Mather. He requests us to share with 'Fr'dancis' on a sensitive subject."

> "How I do miss his thick accent—or as Alexander would express, 't'ick' accent."

> "Indeed! Mather sends word . . . on William Orpe."

Francis's quizzical tilt of his head signals that they have his undivided attention. Peter continues,

> "Mather warned to preface our information with the expression that you were correct on the young man."

> "Oh?"

> "Apparently, you perceived that William would not remain as preacher for long. Well, we must inform that he has left to pursue his father's lucrative farm in Prestwood, Staffordshire."

> "As well."

Francis shakes his head. The thought is clear: *finery*. With a proud flourish, he wipes the arms of his beaten jacket.

The fifty-mile trip from London to Colchester, the head of the circuit, once again places Francis upon an ancient Roman road. The track leaves London, heading to the northeast. The roadway, with its characteristic camber crafted for proper drainage, travels through the towns of Ilford, Chadwell, and Rumford, then continues northeast, passing through Burntwood and Shenfield. It then leads on through Ingerstone, Chelmsford, Boreham, Hatfield Poverel, Witham, and Keldon, then east of Feering, through Marks Tay, west of the Stanway heath, then finally, at the fifty-mile mark, into Colchester. From Colchester, a nine-mile ride will take Francis through Ardley and Lawford to his first stop in Manningtree. Francis will itinerate along the River Stour's southern coast, from Manningtree to Harwich. As beautiful as the scenery is, the area sours with rampant smuggling.

Beginning the two-day trip, Francis departs early Monday morning, the twenty-second of August. Once again, he welcomes the cooling temperatures as the leading edge of autumn flirts with the trailing edge of summer. Two miles out, the sight of the Bancroft's Almshouses sparks a gentle memory. He is thankful for the Christian kindness of those private individuals who reach out to the poor; he remembers fondly *the loving efforts of Mrs. Percy* in Worcester. He spots the Jewish and Mile End burial grounds. These are the locations of the massive communal graves from the killer plague of a century ago. Unexpectedly, his eyes moisten as the sight provokes a memory. He still struggles with the near-death experiences of Worcester and Gloucester. He vows to persevere despite the opposition.

Crossing the ancient stone bridge at the River Lea signifies that Francis has left the cradling confines of London. From here northward to Colchester, he will encounter mostly forested lands. The road will rise and fall, ultimately placing him into the heart of the southeastern seaboard, the south end of the Northern Sea.

Between the eight- and nine-mile mark, Francis once again crosses a small river, Kings Watering, located slightly before Chadwell at Great Ilford. The forested surroundings continue. Sporadically, a small farm accompanies an isolated home along the route. At the twelve-mile mark, the town of Rumford[138] and its 1,300 residents in half as many houses is the first sign of civilization since leaving London. The hamlet is a major stopping point along the busy road full of traveling coaches and men on horseback. The River Rom bisects the town. Francis crosses the waterway and decides to stop for a much-desired break.

Entering the town, Francis notices another familiar sight: an open field holding a crowd of people and a corral for livestock. Rumford is a market town. Looking at the hogs within the wood-fenced areas, Francis surmises, *hogs on Monday*. He is correct. Rumford enjoys three market days each week: Mondays are for the trading of hogs; Tuesday's farmers deal in calves, lambs, and sheep; and on Wednesdays, corn, cattle, and horses are added to the previous animals for sale. There is also provision for fresh poultry and butcher's meats sold on Wednesdays. Not wanting to find himself trapped within the growing crowd, Francis proceeds for the main street area. Nearing an inn, he decides to dismount.

The sixteenth-century Old Cock and Bell Inn is the central hub of activities in Rumford. Since Rumford is a designated post town, the post office connecting the citizens with London to the south and Colchester to the northeast receives letters and items for daily delivery. In by eight o'clock in the morning, a letter will be in London by ten o'clock the same evening. The reverse is true with the letter-sack from London arriving by ten in the evening and allowing Rumford residents to pick up their mail at eight in the morning. Climbing off Churchfield, Francis secures his horse and enters the establishment that serves not only as the local post office but also as an inn for tired travelers. As he removes his hat and walks in, two women standing behind a wooden desk offer greeting.

"Welcome to Cock and Bell. Might we oblige the traveler?"

"You may, with an ample meal for my horse and a substantial dinner for a weary itinerant."

"A dissenting minister? We shall provide."

The women summon several young boys. In seconds, a few are off to handle the feeding of Churchfield. Two of the lads escort Francis into an adjacent room with three small tables. They advise him to sit, promising a sound meal. Francis is grateful to sit on a chair. Resting his elbows on the table, Francis's mind wanders in prayerful conversation. *Thank you, Father, for safety, for rest, for my persevering animal.* Blanking his mind in order to listen, Francis's parents come to mind.

---

[138] Eighteenth-century spelling for the town of Romford.

Perhaps it's the smell of the stew beef boiling in the nearby kitchen, or perhaps it is the Almighty's prompting. Regardless, Francis decides to act.

One of the women from the front approaches Francis.

> "Pastor, my partner and I have acted improperly by failing to introduce ourselves. Ann Smith is the name."

> "Not to trouble. Pastor Francis Asbury, a Wesleyan itinerant."

> "On your way to Colchester?"

> "Yes, Manningtree and Harwich."

> "Stormy towns."

Francis's reluctant smile reveals his understanding that she isn't referring to the weather. He nods in agreement and replies,

> "So I've been apprised."

> "My partner, Martha Fryer, also welcomes you. She is indisposed at the moment; the post requires urgent attention."

Realizing that the inn is a post location, Francis inquires,

> "Might I send correspondence?"

> "You may. Late departure heads out shortly—in London by midnight or shortly thereafter."

> "Very well. Might I impose for parchment?"

> "I shall have Martha attend to it."

Ann departs and Francis gathers his thoughts. He intends to write to his parents. *Nearly a year and a half departed—and Nancy.* Ann's partner, Martha, arrives.

> "Pastor Asbury, your quill and parchment. The London bag is delayed for nearly one hour; I could dispatch it if completed by then."

> "Very well, I shall complete it promptly."

Various thoughts crowd Francis, stymying his effort to write. Pushing through the clouded considerations, he begins the writing process.

> *Dear Mother:*
>
> *Being gone nearly 16 months, I think it my duty to let you know that Wesley assigns me to the Colchester circuit. I enjoy good health and strength, much contented with emotions and much settled from past adverse incidents. My way is clear; the Roman roads are as a Scripture, marking my path. One day removed from my expected destination of Manningtree, I enjoy a warm meal and the hospitable comforts of two women who operate a coach inn. As has been my experience, despite the opposite, the loving, good-natured*

people of the circuits continue to supply my bread and water, generously offering bed and shelter.

Please attend my friends; do they continue to find comfort in Jesus? Do they stay their souls on Him? What of Edward Hand, Thomas and James, and the other Thomas and James? What of fair Nancy and her delicate companions; do they continue in the Lord Jesus? It is my prayer that all do so abundantly.

Give my duty to my father, and my love to all friends. I do find much of the goodness of God to my soul, so that He leads me on my way by His power, and enlarges my heart in His work. Blessed forever be His holy and dear Name! You may send me a letter when you can; I advise delivery to Colchester.

I have much work on my hands and am put to it for time to do what I want. My efforts on the Colchester circuit are alone; no other itinerant is assigned to this challenging land.

The bearer of this correspondence receive as myself. Provide for him and his horse. May you meet together often and in love, and labor to keep one another warm, to stir up one another from day to day, and to build each other up in the holy loving faith.

From your son, in a measure dutiful, through grace,

Francis

The substantial lunch prepares horse and rider for departure. Francis is grateful for the hospitality of Ann and Martha, especially their help in sending a letter to his parents. Walking toward the front of the inn, Francis prepares to pay for his meal. Reaching into his jacket, he removes the few pennies necessary to accomplish the task. At the front desk, Martha offers,

"Pastor Asbury, you needn't compensate. The privilege is ours."

Surprised that the women are giving him dinner free of charge, Francis presents a thankful reply.

"The Lord bless your generosity."

Francis leaves Rumford, petitioning the Almighty, *prosper Your Word among the inhabitants of this kind town.*

It is Francis's goal to make the town of Chelmsford by sunset. The town at the thirty-mile mark is the next sizable village after Rumford. In between, the small hamlets of Burntwood, Shenfield, and Ingerstone dot the forest road. However, before returning to this northeastern track, the Roman road dips to the south, transitioning through the small towns of Hornchurch and Upminster.

At the fifteen-mile mark, a unique structure captures Francis's attention. The tall building with four extended arms invites Francis to pause. After several key searches, the windmill with the brick base inspires him to dismount.

Entering the four-story wooden structure, Francis is drawn to the series of metal cogs and wooden wheels, all connected to the four lengthy arms outside through a wooden axle. All are designed to rein in and capitalize on the prevailing breezes that blow through the shallow valley and hillside. The entire setup reminds Francis of his younger days at the grinding mill on the Wyrley Birch estate. Watching the facility operate, Francis quickly gathers its workings. *Fascinating, the entire housing rotates on one single post.* The post in question is of large diameter and allows the entire housing connected to the blades of the windmill to spin into the wind. This small feature optimizes the operation of the mill. *The brake wheel and wallowers.* Francis notices the familiar sight, *millstones used to grind grain or corn.* Reluctant to leave but mindful that the long road awaits, he exits the structure.

On Churchfield's back once again, Francis bids farewell to the Upminster post mill and continues on his journey.

At the twenty-mile mark, he passes another familiar sight: round oast houses, like the ones he viewed in the low round near Worcester. The oddly bent roof cowlings once again bring a slight chuckle to the itinerant. Continuing onward, Francis turns to catch the setting sun; it is well on its way to the western horizon. He worries about making Chelmsford by dark.

As if on cue, the low-lying full moon arrives to light the way. Approaching the twenty-seven-mile mark, the ancient Widford Bridge awaits. The town of Widford is named for the wide ford that resides within the hamlet's boundaries. A century before, Francis would have had to cross this waterway through the flowing current. A little more than a century before, Francis might have been an associate of the town's most notable figure to date, John Eliot.

Baptized at Widford in 1604, John Eliot left England in 1631, heading for the American colonies to evangelize the Native Americans of New England. His successful efforts earned him a welcome place in the hearts of the American aborigines. In 1661, his loving ministry produced a version of the New Testament Bible in the Algonquin Indian language. He followed with the Old Testament two years later. This Indian Bible was the first printed in the American colonies. Several generations of American Indians have referred to John Eliot as the loving "Saint John."

Before embarking upon the bridge, Francis walks around to the water's edge and allows Churchfield to drink. The horse welcomes the refreshment. Once satisfied, the horse and his rider step onto the bridge to traverse the waterway, illuminated by the moon's beams reflecting off the flowing river. At the apex of the bridge, Francis looks to the full moon floating above. *And take heed, lest you lift your eyes to heaven, and when you see the sun, the moon, and the stars, all the host of heaven, you feel driven to worship them and serve them, which the Lord your God has given to all the peoples under the whole heaven as a heritage.*[139] Strangely, Francis's morning devotion from the Bible's book of Deuteronomy comes to mind. He moves on, eager to complete the last mile into Chelmsford.

Standing at the junction of two rivers, the Can and the Chelmer, the city of Chelmsford stands as the midpoint between London and Colchester. It is an ancient city, a Roman city, with a cathedral dedicated to St. Mary the Virgin. The Roman name, Caesaromagus, means "Caesar's Field," thought to be the location of Julius Caesar's successful defeat of the British army before taking their capital in Colchester. The eleventh-century church built of flint rubble, brick, and freestone is located east of the river crossing. Long before Francis crosses into Chelmsford he spots the flickering candlelight within, through the windows of the richly adorned structure. The aesthetics Francis enjoys as he and Churchfield approach date from several fifteenth- and sixteenth-century renovations. During the seventeenth century, the cathedral enjoyed the preaching of Thomas Hooker, a Puritan who fled England for the American colonies. His efforts in America formed the colony of Connecticut, specifically the city of Hartford—named after his associate the Reverend Samuel Stone's hometown of Hertford, England.

At the building, Francis dismounts. Approaching the nave, he marvels at an inscription carved in the base of the early-fifteenth-century portion of the building. The inscription reads, "Pray for the good estate of all the townsheps of Chelmysford that hath good willers and procorers of helpers to this werke and them that first began and longest shall continowe in the yere of our Lorde I thousand IIII hundredth IIII." *The year 1404—a mere 364 years ago.* Francis admires the history of the structure.

Finding a comfortable grassy spot for Churchfield, Francis ties his companion and removes his saddle and saddlebag, setting them on a nearby stump. With his horse cared for, Francis reaches into his saddlebag and removes the blanket that

---

[139] Deuteronomy chapter 4, verses 19–20.

resides within. He bundles the blanket and sets it on the ground. Lying down, he places his head on the makeshift pillow. Looking to the clear summer sky, he considers the vast array before him; *a magnificent inheritance*. In time, the celestial embrace caresses the itinerant to sleep.

Rising near four a.m. from long habit, Francis instinctively begins in prayer. His conversation with the Almighty alternates between praying silently and speaking aloud. The cool August air invites him to rise from his kneeling position; up on his feet, he continues his supplication. Stretching his legs and arms, Francis welcomes the adrenal rush as it chases away his drowsiness.

Completing his prayer time, Francis considers his day ahead. *Must accomplish the remaining twenty-two miles to Colchester, another nine to Manningtree.* In Manningtree, there is a small Wesleyan society willing to welcome the young itinerant; from there, he will reach out to the surrounding villages. In Colchester, Francis is unsure what will transpire. Despite the lack of preparations, the large Wesleyan society in the ancient city should be able to give Francis a meal if needed. Francis collects Churchfield; the horse nickers his welcome. Saddle girth fastened, saddlebag stowed, a quick rub of the horse's nose, and the rider moves up top. The pair sets out.

Less than three miles into the journey, Francis spots a long, tree-lined road to the north. In the distance stands a magnificent estate home. In addition, he is pleasantly surprised by the beautifully gardened grounds that lead all the way up to the edge of the road to Colchester. He is certain, *this large estate has a history*.

Francis is correct; the fine structure is New Hall, once the royal estate of King Henry VIII and his second wife, Anne Boleyn. King Henry named the property Beaulieu Palace (Beautiful Place). It was here that the abandonment of the Catholic faith by the English began, when King Henry failed to gain permission from the Catholic Pope to divorce his first wife, Queen Catherine. Wrongly assured by the Catholic Cardinal Wolsey that the Pope would grant permission allowing him to abandon his wife, permitting him to marry Anne Boleyn, King Henry began to cohabitate with Anne at New Hall. Inaccurately utilizing a Scripture from the Old Testament book of Leviticus, the King portrayed his marriage to Catherine as having been forced upon him, and thus he was living in sin. Unfortunately for the King, the Pope knew the Scripture. He stood his ground and refused an annulment of the King's marriage to Catherine. As self-proclaimed defender of the faith, King Henry VIII began the process that removed the Catholic Church from the numerous cathedrals dotting the English landscape.

Francis ponders the extensive grounds of New Hall; *so many oak trees*. One thousand oak trees, a gift to the Duke of Buckingham from King James I, and an additional five hundred oak trees, a gift from King Charles I, are arranged in splendid fashion, creating beautiful arbors and wide avenues. Beyond the trees, Francis spots a tiny river, a planned water feature that weaves through a fruit-tree orchard. Closer to the ancient road, a series of stables and coach houses adds prominence to the grounds. Francis once again hearkens to his childhood experiences; *oh, for Father to gaze upon such stately eloquence!* He wisely decides to move on, mindful of the effort ahead.

Twelve miles into the day's journey, Francis approaches the town of Keldon.[140] As the ancient road continues in a northeasterly direction, he is surprised to see that it takes a sharp turn to the right. An almost ninety-degree bend places him on a south-by-southeasterly path. After nearly a hundred yards the road turns sharply left, toward the north. In front of Francis are the River Blackwater and a wooden bridge. Francis is reluctant to cross the bridge. It's not that he doubts the stability of the structure; he's seen wooden bridges like this in West Bromwich. He's leery of the wide spaces between the boards; *seems the carpenters stretched a little with the building material.* Actually, they haven't. What Francis doesn't know is that some of the townspeople have borrowed portions of the planking for personal use.

Francis contemplates aloud,

"Well, Churchy, 'tis our sole device across the river."

The horse shakes his head and whinnies loudly.

"By the confidence in your reply, I gather you've prayed up. Very well."

The pair moves forward. Ahead of the wooden bridge, a small island and then another bridge, this one more substantially constructed of brick, await their arrival. Atop the wooden bridge, Churchfield pauses. Francis gently nudges his companion. The horse remains still.

"Come, Churchy. Nearly across."

The horse begins slowly—one step, another, and then another. The slow-moving water below shimmers a gentle reflection as a slight splash draws Francis's gaze. Below, several ducks are entering the waterway. The purple-breasted male with his iridescent green head and yellow bill escorts the orange-billed female and her little ones along the banks of the river. The wide spaces between the bridge planks allow the private viewing.

"Churchy, you've become an admirer of nature? Very well, as am I."

Once safely across the wooden bridge, Francis guides Churchfield across the small wooded island and onto the next bridge. This more secure bridge allows a small rivulet to travel under its brick arches. Easily crossing the structure, the pair continues forward.

---

[140] Eighteenth-century spelling for the town of Kelvedon.

On the narrow stretch of road to Colchester, Francis proceeds. About a half-mile out of Keldon, the ancient road returns alongside the River Blackwater. At the bank of the waterway, two men on horseback, military men, sit atop their impressive animals. The horses are large, tall at the shoulder and thick in the chest, clearly war horses. Water drips from the magnificent animals as they take their morning's drink at the river, the cold water invigorating their twitching lips and noses. Francis approaches slowly, careful not to excite the imposing animals. He offers,

"Extraordinary steeds."

The men remain true to military standards, keeping their silence long enough to evaluate. Confident that Francis poses no threat, they respond,

"Best in the King's army."

Francis nods his acknowledgement. Looking over the men, he realizes that they, too, are large. The one with the stouter arms reminds him of some of the elder nailers in Bromwich. Francis inquires,

"How far to Colchester?"

"Not much, less than ten miles. Road is clear."

"Thank you, sir."

Maneuvering Churchfield to drink from the river, Francis dismounts and walks his four-legged companion to the water's edge. Standing next to the military horses, Churchfield appears as a miniature pony. The large hindquarters of the King's horses stand nearly two feet higher than those of the stocky little Connemara. Churchfield doesn't seem to mind; he moves right to the much-needed water and begins to drink.

As Francis waits, one of the military men offers,

"We are proceeding for Colchester as well. Mind if we join you?"

Surprised by the offer, Francis spins to reply,

"Not at all. Please do; I would welcome the company."

The remaining ten miles of hilly fields to Colchester pass without incident—perhaps not surprisingly, as the military men and their horses appear as Francis's escorts. The conversation is good, mostly of military life, itinerant life, the trades, the colonies, and the beautiful August weather. However, what greets Francis as he and the men pull up to the end of the long road from London is both fascinating and daunting. The structure, unlike anything he has seen before, is clearly an ancient wall. He correctly guesses, *one that predates English rule*, also noting, *an ancient wall with one lone passage for admittance into the town of my destination.*

The oversized bricks that make up this wall are unique to their period. The unmistakable two-inch-high by seven-inch-wide by fourteen-inch-long red bricks form a narrow arch, a cutaway through the magnificent guarding wall. As Francis ponders the narrow entrance, a portion of a Scripture returns to his memory: *as through the eye of a needle*. The brickwork, which is unfamiliar to Francis, reflects construction techniques dating to the first century. The bricks are laid mostly in a standard pattern, except for the arched opening where a mason chiseled and laid the clay components in the striking herringbone pattern. The stunning display of craftsmanship boasts of a prosperous time—an ancient time, an ancient nation: the Empire of Rome.

The Roman wall and entrance gate Francis is viewing are nearly 1,800 years old. However, the city of Colchester predates even the Roman occupation of the first century AD. This military town, with its view of the River Colne from the ridge above, was first inhabited in the seventh century BC. By the first century BC, Colchester had become the capital city of the numerous realms that formed ancient British civilization—the British civilization taken over by the Roman Empire by the middle of the first century AD. Francis and his military companions dismount and proceed to walk their horses through the limited opening.

Cautiously migrating through the Roman-named Balkerne Gate and entering the town, Francis looks due east. His distant view reveals a castle, the Colchester Castle. Francis recalls the instructions of John Murlin and Peter Jaco, the itinerants who prepared him for the Colchester circuit: "Wesley's great round meeting house stands adjacent to the castle grounds on Maidenburgh Street, just to the west." He advises the military men,

"My destination is in view; I shall proceed to Wesley's room."

"We shall as well."

Surprised by their willingness to join him at his destination, Francis nods and turns toward the distant castle. He does not possess a map with street names, so he aims for the ancient fortification.

Nearing Maidenburgh Street, Francis easily discovers Wesley's round meeting house. The twelve-sided structure's double-door entry invites the itinerant into the building. After the men secure their horses, Francis leads the way toward the building that represents the center of Colchester Methodism. Opening the door, he finds a large and open sanctuary. With no one in view, he casually calls out,

"Hello . . ."

My, my—the acoustics are amazing! Francis sports a broad smile, the kind that conveys enough mischief to get a young preacher into trouble. Looking about, he finds that he and his companions are alone. Again, this time for fun, he lets out a sweeping rendition of his previous greeting.

"Hellooooooooo . . ."

Ah, yes . . . he smiles with satisfaction. The military men chuckle at Francis as he ponders the hall's resonating properties. He moves to a wooden bench near the rear of the room and sits, inviting the men to join him. Looking about and then to each other, they seem to share the same thought. One of them responds,

"We shall return this evening for the service. Seven o'clock is the usual time."

"Very well. Thank you for your company on the London Road. Shall see you both this evening."

Leaning back on the wooden bench affords Francis the opportunity to stretch. He does so, pushing his long legs forward. The welcomed relief as his ankles pop causes him to do the same with his neck, bending it left and right to a chorus of cracks and pops. Relaxing completely, he leans back his head and allows his eyes to close.

He isn't aware of when it began, but the sound of voices near the entrance door causes Francis to awake. Rubbing his face and knuckling his eyes, he hastily prepares to greet the new arrivals. Walking into the large space, two uniformed soldiers approach the itinerant as he grabs his hat and stands to his feet. At first glance he thought these were his traveling companions, but he now realizes that the two men who approach are unknown to him. One of them offers a greeting.

"Good evening; service tonight?"

"Believe so. Happen to have the time?"

"It is near six o'clock."

"Thank you."

Francis cannot fathom the thought that he dozed off for nearly three hours. Watching the soldiers as they make their way into the sanctuary, Francis once again takes a seat. For the next thirty minutes, he watches as nearly 160 people make their way in for a mid-week worship service. His observations bring one consistent thought to the young and wearied itinerant: *in this group, my jacket seems far from out of place.*

The Colchester faithful are a rough gathering of locals. Amidst this impoverished group, the oyster dredgers along the River Colne, the cloth and textile workers who make the well-known and sought-after Colchester "Bays and Says," and the various merchants who desire to sell their wares in London but are limited to selling locally, all arrive and patiently take their seats for tonight's service.

The Colchester "Bays and Says" are the product of the Dutch Huguenot immigrants of the sixteenth century who brought to England, specifically to the town of Colchester, the cloth-working technique of teasing woolen fabric. The process involves running matted wool fabric over a series of dried teasel flower heads. The prickly vegetation invigorates the fabric as the hooked bracts of the spent flower heads work their plushy magic and thicken the tiny fibers of the wool. The large rolls of Bay fabric are sold to cover tables and to line exquisite pistol boxes. In the wealthier homes of London, Bay fabric is used to cover doors designating the boundary beyond which no hired help shall venture. The Says are a much-sought-after white fabric, gently worked in a similar fashion to the Bays and used by the religious community, specifically the Quaker men and women, for shirts and aprons.

Nearing seven o'clock, a local man steps close to the pulpit. He too is dressed in the manner of his financially strapped neighbors. Francis assumes this is the local lay leader. He rises to greet the man, who is now surrounded by three other men, each of whom seeks an answer from the local leader. When Francis introduces himself, the man replies,

> "Been waiting to hear from London. Perhaps you shall preach this night? Would bring relief to these who continue to ask of our preacher."
>
> "Very well."

The man is grateful; giving a polite nod to Francis and the men, he vacates the pulpit.

Looking out to the people who gather, Francis spots the two soldiers who escorted him to Colchester and nods his hello. The King's military men return the same. Francis raises his hands for silence, and the gathering becomes quiet. He opens with prayer and a hymn. The large group clearly enjoys singing; Francis is pleased with the response. With great expectations for tonight's service, and inspired by the presence of the King's men, he begins his sermon.

> "What is smuggling? It is the importing, selling, or buying of run goods; that is, those which have not paid the duty appointed by law to be paid to the King . . ."

For nearly one hour, Francis continues with his sermon subject. He cites Wesley's *A Word to a Smuggler,* the Bible, and the experiences of his fellow itinerants, Peter Jaco and John Murlin. The locals are attentive, paying close attention, as they are fully aware of the nefarious industry that flourishes outside their city limits. The military men are grateful for Francis's loyalty to the King. Few distract from his competent delivery. At sermon's end, many of the locals come forward to acknowledge their agreement with Francis's views. In the midst of their encouraging words, the two military men who escorted Francis to town come forward.

Reaching his hand toward Francis, the larger of the two soldiers offers,

> "Far cry from previous services. I especially missed the birds and the donkey."

Several of the locals laugh at the comment. Francis raises an inquiring eyebrow. One of the locals explains,

> "Few years ago, several opposed to Wesley's meetings here would send in flocks of birds to put out the evening's candles."

The military man continues,

> "When this failed to bring the service to an end, they sent in a donkey. Wild animal tamed; seemed captivated by preacher Laurence Coughton's gentle voice."

Francis begins to understand; he offers a slight smile to convey his comprehension of the military man's jest. More important, Francis's smile conveys his thankfulness for his new friend in uniform.

The locals begin their departure for the evening, one older couple offering Francis room and board for the night. He graciously accepts. As the people clear, he overhears two men, dressed all in black, conversing in a serious tone. Francis pauses to eavesdrop. It's not that he means to pry; he is merely concerned. Pretending to busy himself with his saddlebag, he tilts his head to capture the subject of their conversation. One of the men in black is adamant that "goods need to be stored in the river." Francis experiences a nervous twinge originating in his stomach and traveling to his lower back, an uneasy combination of nerves and fear. He continues to listen. The other man responds that "the Pembroke has only been sunk for a week. In Manningtree we shall prosper." Manningtree—that is precisely where Francis is heading. His thought is clear: *Perhaps, Lord, You have meant for me to hear.*

The next day finds Francis with his host family. They are an elderly couple, thankful for the Wesleyan itinerants who serve the Colchester circuit. Their generous offer of a place to sleep and an ample supply of food was hard to resist. These are Wesleyan faithful with a gift for hospitality. They offer Francis a gracious invitation to return, which he gratefully accepts. At midday he departs for his next stop in Manningtree.

Arriving in the town of Manningtree at dusk, Francis heads for the home of the local family who host the Wesleyan class meetings. The membership is small—a handful of families, none of them especially motivated to grow the community of the Wesleyan faithful. As the light of day departs, Francis squints to make out the figure of a man, walking out of the nearby river.

The River Stour is a wide waterway, running mostly east to west and connecting directly to the southern tip of the North Sea where it meets the northern tip of the English Channel, one hundred miles due west of Belgium and the Netherlands. Along its route, the gently sloping shorelines run for several yards to the ledge above. Stopping atop that ledge, Francis reins in Churchfield and pauses to consider the man.

The drenched wanderer, appearing to be in his mid-thirties, slowly approaches the itinerant. Francis waits, considering the prospect of the individual. *A smuggler? A sailor?* A slight nervous pounding in his chest and stomach urge Francis to pray silently, *Lord, shall I confront smuggling on my arrival?* The silent reply is straightforward and reassuring: ***BE STILL AND KNOW . . .*** Francis releases a deepened breath. The man offers,

"Evenin'."

"Good evening, sir."

"Right fine horse. Connemara?"

"Yes. Gift from a friend."

"Right fine friend. You 'aven't an acorn, 'ave you?"

The man is serious. Catching himself, Francis almost chuckles aloud. In a cracked voice, he manages,

"An acorn?"

"Well enough; good evenin'."

The man departs, and Francis scratches his ear as he tilts his head, thankful that his bemused smile is hidden in the dark. Prodding Churchfield, he and the horse move on for the Gorbell residence.

Captain Gorbell is a retired man of the sea. The veteran of the Royal Navy settled in the port town of Manningtree mostly for its views across the gentle waterway. The captain is a short, stubby man, his white beard thicker and longer than when he commanded a three-hundred-ton vessel of the King. He and his wife live by themselves, hoping that someday their two sons will pay a visit. They haven't done so in a long time.

Arriving at the Gorbell residence, he finds it as Peter Jaco and John Murlin described: "the only house painted red." As Francis looks about the town, the little home clearly stands out from the rest. With Churchfield secured, he walks to the front door and knocks. Within a minute, the door slowly opens. Standing as wide as the door opening, the older man with the thick white beard greets the itinerant. Francis notices that the captain is as thick as he is wide. He inquires,

"Captain Gorbell?"

"The same."

"Pastor Asbury."

The captain turns about and calls,

"Martha, Wesley's itinerant has arrived."

As he turns back to Francis, the itinerant notices the man's thick, hairy neck, the white hair curling from the edge of his shirt collar. Gorbell clears his throat and offers,

> "Please do come in, Pastor. Martha and I have been expecting you. Surely you are in need of refreshment."

> "Most grateful."

Entering the home, Francis views a simple room with simple wood furnishings—oak chairs much like the ones his father crafts, and a square oak kitchen table with square legs. These are neatly placed in one corner of the main room. On the other end is a small open hearth made of stone with an iron spit for cooking. On the walls hang a painting of a harbor and a black-and-white drawing of a three-masted ship. One of the main room's windows overlooks the waterway. The captain's closing of the front door causes the river's salty breezes to waft through the shuttered opening. The captain invites Francis to sit.

Before long, the table boasts several bowls of soup and numerous plates of bread and fruit. Francis stares at the provisions, unaware that the captain is watching him closely. Gorbell remarks,

> "Our provisions are simple—enough for a hungry itinerant."

Francis nods to convey his approval, somewhat distracted by his pleasant anticipation of the meal. Martha arrives with three ceramic cups, each steaming with tea. She places the cups onto the tabletop and takes her seat. Looking to her husband and then to Francis, she bows her head. The captain bows also, and Francis too bows to pray. He begins,

> "Almighty . . ."

The captain interrupts him.

> "Almighty Father, Creator of the heavens, the One who orders the dawn and sunset to shout for joy, we thank Thee for Thy provision of healthy food and healthy preaching. Bless this young man in his efforts; shine Your face upon his work. We beseech Thee, protect him from harm, and intervene in his life in the form of protection. Surround him with songs of deliverance. Amen."

Francis and Martha respond likewise,

> "Amen."   "Amen."

Martha places the bowls of soup in front of the men. She also delivers two plates of fruit and bread in front of each man. The captain nods his approval, and the men begin their meal. Martha waits a few seconds, then pulls the remaining plates of fruit and bread in front of herself and begins to eat.

The captain informs Francis,

"Manningtree has changed."

"Has it?"

"Yes. Used to be a simple port town; inland merchants sent their beans and their wheat. Occasionally, barley and malt also. Some woolen goods. In return, coal from the north went inland. The town soon became a victim of its success."

"Victim?"

"Yes, victim. The Rigby era."

"Rigby?"

The captain places his torn piece of bread back onto his plate. Taking a sip of his tea, he sets the cup back down. He picks up a napkin and methodically dries his lips and the outer edges of his beard. He finally responds,

"The Rigby clan. Settled not far from here, in Mistley. What the father failed to see to the end, the son aims to complete. Richard, the father, amassed his fortunes through ownership in the South Sea Company. With perfect timing, he unloaded his shares prior to the collapse of the precariously financed venture. He was a good man, a smart man. Took his fortune and built the magnificent Mistley Hall. Upon his untimely death, his son aimed to transform the area into a spa town."

"Spa town?"

"For the well-being of the body and mind - -

And void of the soul. The younger Richard is well connected. Members of Parliament attend his social gatherings. Is he as pure as his father was? Only time shall reveal."

"Social gatherings, dear? My husband is too kind."

"Ah, well then, social mischief is more apt a term. The young Richard shall run out of money; his indulgent ways are sure to bring ruin. Aside from the goings-on, the town has benefited because of Richard's connections to the coffers of the Royal Navy. Residents are grateful as well as watchful. One luxurious party at Richard's Mistley Hall brought out several spectators to watch from afar. The audacious Richard and his eminent guests ensured that the wintry conditions were of no effect, sending servants to administer a warm drink to the gawking townspeople. He easily curries their favor."

Francis had not expected the informative conversation. He does his best to accept the situation and give his undivided attention to his gracious hosts. The captain continues, switching stories as often as he feels led. One story that captures Francis's attention is of a recent shipwreck to the west. The River Stour claimed the lives of a couple of men who were transporting goods to the Mistley port. Among the villages, rumors of lost goods excite the interest of those who seek to gain the items for themselves. The captain shares of men, and women, who aim to prosper from the loss of another.

"It brings a distasteful emotion."

With the authority of a past commander, he places judgment on them all.

"Thieves."

Before evening's end, the captain informs Francis that he will publish in town of a preaching engagement tomorrow evening. Francis acknowledges that it will be his pleasure. Dinner's end sends the captain to his bedchamber while Martha busies herself with cleaning up the meal. Her task completed, she offers Francis his bedding supplies and retires for the evening.

Eager to take in the moonlight that reflects off the waterway, Francis leaves the Gorbell residence and heads for the water's edge. With Churchfield settled in for the night, Francis ventures out on foot. Nearing the edge, he finds the gibbous moon lightly accenting the shimmering dark water. The windy conditions of the past few days have settled, odd for the late-summer season. The lacking breeze also calms the waterway, allowing the sounds of several large splashes to draw his attention. Ducking behind a clump of *Pennisetum*[141] launching its fluffy spires toward the silken sky, Francis is confident he is out of sight.

Nearly a hundred yards offshore, a wooden skiff bobs in the water. The nearly flat surface of the water allows the small, inconspicuous craft to navigate such a wide waterway. As Francis focuses on the skiff, another comes into view. The two skiffs set anchor within a few yards of each other. Another large splash, and Francis's imagination runs wild. *Smugglers! Whatever shall they dispose of in the waterway?* Within a few minutes the boats are moving again, heading east. Francis decides to take a risk. Taking great care to conceal his movement, he heads back to the Gorbell barn to fetch Churchfield; *shall lay bare the mischief.* Francis mildly startles the horse, already settled for a night's rest.

"Come, Churchy."

Atop his horse, Francis travels east, along the waterway on the inland side of High Street. His plan is simple: he will travel a short distance, and then turn around to the beach. He aims to wait to the east, convinced these are the men who conversed with the soldiers from the worship service in Colchester, the ones he overheard talking about "the water arrangement." It is his belief that the boats are hiding something in the waterway near the bend in the river at Mistley; *however, does one secure smuggled items in the midst of the Stour?*

---

[141] An ornamental grass.

One mile downriver, Francis heads for the shoreline. The moon overhead, now partially obscured by clouds, continues to provide enough light for limited night viewing. Francis stops Churchfield and dismounts. Tying the horse to a tree, Francis moves closer to the natural bend in the river and begins to wait. It isn't long before the two skiffs row into his view, directly off the point at Mistley.

The two boats stop in front of Francis, again a hundred yards offshore. Having difficulty deciphering their activities, Francis focuses on the boats. *Four men, two in each boat.* The unexpected splash causes Francis to squint hard. He is certain, *two men have dived into the water.* He fidgets, pacing back and forth, eager to gain complete understanding of this mystery.

After a minute, the two men on board retrieve objects from the men floating in the water. After ten minutes of this repeated motion, the men climb back into the boats. They have obviously extracted something from the water, have loaded the objects into the skiffs, and are paddling back toward Manningtree. *How long shall You allow, Lord?* Francis is furious. Collecting Churchfield, he follows the skiffs to the west.

At the original location to the west, the two boats once again anchor. The same two men who went overboard at the eastern location once again jump into the water. This time, the two men on board hand their objects to the men in the water. After several similar actions, the men load up and head back to the east location.

This back and forth effort continues for several hours. Like a special agent bent on discovery, Francis travels back and forth also. He is certain the men are taking objects from the river, then moving them nearly a half-mile and dropping their mysterious cargo into the river once again. *Strange dealings.* Francis watches the unusual operation until the men fail to stop their small boats at the eastern location and continue onward to a distant location. At this, Francis and Churchfield head back to Gorbell's barn.

The next morning, Captain Gorbell approaches Francis after prayer.

"Pastor Asbury, your preaching in town is posted."

"Thank you. I shall depart at four o'clock."

"You're welcome to join Mrs. Gorbell and myself for the day."

"Shall attend to personal items. But thank you."

Francis reads his Bible while the Gorbells prepare to depart. Actually, he does not want them to know his real intentions for the morning: he plans to return to the spot of the late-night activities that drew his attention. All night he thought of the two boats. *What could they be smuggling? Should I report this strange and deliberate activity? What would Father do?* Once the Gorbell family has left, Francis gathers himself and exits the home. Excited for this sleuthing adventure, he trips on the last of the brick steps outside the front door of the home. Landing on the patchy late-summer grass, he quickly pushes to his feet. Slightly embarrassed, he searches for someone, anyone, who may have watched his ungraceful departure. He's glad to find that only one has witnessed his fall: Churchfield. The horse says nothing, but he does tilt his head in a rather suspect manner.

Once aboard Churchfield, Francis heads for the approximate location of last night's concealed activities. In an effort to hide his secret purpose, he reads his Bible as he rides. Francis contemplates, *most assuredly, nothing shall display in broad daylight. What shall I find?* Francis lowers his Bible; he cannot focus on the Scriptures.

"Father, forgive my thoughts that fail to focus on You."

Reaching around, he places the Bible in his saddlebag, the pliant leather made stiffer from the coastal salt air. He brushes the white sodium powder from the bag. Looking toward the water, he notices that it is somewhat rougher than the night before. Again, his mind floods with thoughts of, *is this safe? Shall these mysterious men return? If so, shall they bring harm to Churchy and me? What shall Mother think to find me investigating potential smugglers, or worse, confronting them and experiencing harm? Would I survive an attack? Why should I deal with smugglers? Francis, you must return to your itinerancy.*

He hadn't noticed before, but ahead, roughly a hundred yards offshore, a strange object floats upon the water's surface. Then it disappears. *Lost it!* The object is clearly not there. *There!* The object returns into view. Francis reins in Churchfield. The horse stops and turns toward the water. *Lost it again!*

The gusty wind drives the sand of the shoreline against Francis. He instinctively grabs his hat. Several times he flinches in pain as the microscopic grains scour the skin of his face. He squints, in fear of injury to his eyes. Once again, he strains to find the floating spherical object. Its dirty translucent color glistening with the salty froth of the River Stour remains in his mind's eye. *I see it!*

Francis has once again located the strange globular object. With the steadfastness of a steel anvil, he will not release his visual hold of the bizarre body. *It must secure to an item below the surface. If only I had a boat! A boat? I shall endanger life and limb, for I cannot swim.* Francis shakes his head in disbelief that he would even ponder such a foolish thought. He dismounts, secures Churchfield, and walks to a clearing in the trees. From here, he can search for the mysterious float. Taking a step backward, he trips, bracing himself as he falls to the ground.

The small wooden barrel he fell over, made with the skill of a trained carpenter, has several broken slats. The remaining operable slats bend perfectly where they used to form a water-tight cask. Francis estimates the container can hold three to four gallons of liquid. Thick rope wraps around the top and bottom of the oak firkin.[142] In addition, a rope weaves its way around the item, as if to secure it for dragging. Francis ponders the container, tugging on the loose ropes. He envisions the two sections being placed over a beam, *or perhaps a man's shoulders.* Beginning to rise to his feet, he is startled by an unexpected voice.

"Pastor, the shoreline can be a rough place."

The deep male voice speeds Francis to his feet, flailing his arms and kicking sand in multiple directions. Thinking the worst, he gathers himself and begins to walk away. The tall, thin man dressed entirely in black grabs his arm and brings him to a complete stop. His veiny hands, aged and dry, hang several inches below the sleeve length of his jacket. The one holding Francis hostage grips strongly around his bicep; a slight pain warns Francis of possible bruising. The man's disheveled appearance completes the frightening experience as his scraggy grey hair hangs below a black-and-white-checkered cotton skullcap. Once again he warns,

"Shoreline can be a rough place."

The grip on Francis's arm tightens. Francis is barely able to give his response,

" 'Tis, I suppose."

"Suppose you move on back to Gorbell's."

"Very well."

With the release of his arm, Francis turns and departs. He hurries to retrieve his horse. With one motion, he hops atop Churchfield and the horse lunges forward at his urging. At full gallop, they head back to the Gorbell residence. His emotions shaken by the harsh man, Francis decides to remain at the home until the afternoon service.

The four o'clock service in the town marketplace is not a common occurrence. There aren't many Wesleyan faithful in Manningtree; in fact, there aren't many practicing Christians in the waterfront town. The residents gather, mostly curious as to Francis's intentions. Several men show up with their wives, some with wives and children. Other men, men who have the same rough and disheveled appearance as the man who confronted Francis at the waterfront, appear also.

Precisely at four, Francis raises his hands and begins a hymn. The piece, written by Charles Wesley, bellows across the gathering:

"A charge to keep I have,

A God to glorify.

A never-dying soul to save,

And fit it for the sky."

---

[142] A small wooden vessel, the British capacity of one quarter of a barrel.

The Gorbells are the only residents singing; the rest are polite, quietly watching Francis. *Perhaps they are ignorant of Wesley's hymn.* Francis ponders the thought and then continues,

> "To serve the present age,
> My calling to fulfill;
> O may it all my powers engage
> To do my Master's **will!**"

With a quick nodding of their heads indicating their approval, several of the husbands acknowledge Francis's spirited accent on the word "will." Francis sings on,

> "Arm me with jealous care,
> As in Thy sight to live,
> And oh, Thy servant, Lord,
> Prepare **a strict account to give!**"

The men chuckle at the emphasized lyric. Before Francis can continue, a tall, thin man at the back finishes the hymn,

> "Help me to watch and pray,
> And on Thyself rely,
> Assured if I my trust betray,
> I shall forever die!"[143]

Most of the men in the crowd cheer the roughly dressed nightingale. His black outfit and matching hat are threadbare and worn from his work on the sea. The women remain silent, seeming somewhat frightened by the man's appearance. Francis is silent also, the surprising revelation freezing his emotions: *my attacker.*

The man from the beach makes his way from the back of the gathering. As he walks toward the front, the people in the marketplace separate, forming a clear path to Francis. Francis is worried; he nervously moves his Bible from his right hand to his left as thoughts race through his mind. *Gloucester, Worcester, Stourbridge–the results are the same. Why must my efforts meet with resistance and persecution? Very well.* Francis raises his Bible to his chest. With both hands on the book, he gently taps the binder of the volume on his chin.

Nearly three feet away from the itinerant, the advancing man stops, spreads his arms, and bows his head to offer,

> "Pastor, I insist you continue."

From behind the crowd, several soldiers arrive. With them are four or five other men, clearly townsmen. They all place themselves directly behind the man in black and nod their approval toward Francis.

Francis continues.

---

[143] Charles Wesley hymn "A Charge to Keep I Have," 1762.

For the next thirty minutes, Francis preaches about the Savior. His words are clear: "Jesus offers eternal life to all. A life not only in the hereafter, but more importantly, life in the now. An intimate, loving, and vibrant father-child relationship for those who believe." The crowd is polite as it listens. The service closes with prayer and singing. Other than the hoodlum soloist, the afternoon has been uneventful.

That evening, Francis is restless and distracted. He rushes his dinner with the Gorbells, his hurried actions going unnoticed by the family. After dinner, the itinerant closes with prayer and dismisses himself outdoors. At the barn, he toys with several small tools in the workspace. With Churchfield foddered for the night, he bids farewell and sets out on his own.

On foot under cover of a sky darkened with passing clouds, Francis heads east. Seeking to avoid detection, he remains one hundred yards inland as he parallels the bending shoreline. Without the full light of the moon, the trek is hazardous. Francis wisely slows his pace, avoiding obstacles that would cause harm, thankful for the intermittent moonlight. Adjacent to Mistley Point, he searches for a comfortable spot to hide. Behind a clump of ornamental grasses holding hostage a pollarded[144] oak stump and branches, Francis tucks himself out of view.

It isn't long before two skiffs once again arrive. In the distance, Francis can make out the two boats as they float above the infamous spot from the night before. He watches intently, searching for clues of their activities. *Oh, for a ray of light.* Francis's request goes unanswered. Fearing he is not seeing clearly, he moves from his cover. One measured step at a time, he quietly makes his way toward the shoreline.

Closer, he can make out the boats more clearly. He also can see the men on board—four men, two on each boat—peering overboard, searching in the water. Francis finds this strange; *impossible to see in the water.* As one man holds a rope, another sitting in the bow of the craft reaches over and guides the rope through the water. Several times, he drags the line from the bow, along the side of the small boat to about the midpoint. Once the maneuver is complete, he scoots forward again and repeats the process. Each boat is doing the same strange activity.

Moving closer still, Francis ducks behind a large rock resting on the sandy edge of the river. From the watermarks on the stone, it is clear the boulder nearly submerges during high tides. Francis is confident that the men cannot see him. He takes a deep breath; he hadn't noticed before, but he is shaking slightly. The

---

[144] A tree cut back to the trunk in order to produce a dense mass of new branches.

nervousness causes him to sit. Turning his back to lean against the stony haven, Francis prays to relieve his anxiety. *Father, I raise my eyes toward You . . .*

All along, the evening's wind has been steadily growing. The blowing now stirs several trees nearby, whistling and swirling through their swaying boughs. The sound startles Francis. Peering into the darkness of the inland heath, he attempts to locate the source of the disruption. He looks to the right, certain the noise came from there. Nothing. To the left—again, nothing. *I am sure the noise is more than the swaying of a tree branch.* The disturbance repeats, this time in another location. On the other side of his barrier comes the sound of a man—no, two men—walking slowly along the bank. Francis's fear escalates. He slinks down for further cover.

The wind continues to blow, the waves of the Stour lap nearby, and the slurping sounds of footsteps in the wet sand continue to come closer. The footsteps stop. Francis takes a deep breath. He refuses to release it, fearful of detection. The steps once again continue. They are getting closer.

Looking to his right, Francis is startled by a sudden discovery: two pairs of boots stand within his view around the side of his temporary fortification. The feet are planted in the muddy soil. A closer look reveals that their footwear is military issue. Francis is relieved by the discovery. He rises to greet the men, who jump in surprise at his unexpected appearance. Peering at the itinerant in the shrouded moonlight, they respond,

"Deepest apologies, Pastor. Failed to realize, a preacher in prayer. We advise you move inland. The shoreline can be a hazardous location."

Francis's fears abate. He toys with revealing his intentions, but in the end says nothing. Looking over the shoulders of the men, he notes that the seafaring expedition continues. Francis watches for a reaction from the soldiers, but there is none. Willing to take the advice of the pair, Francis prepares to respond. One of the men interrupts,

"The goings-on behind us demand our attention."

Francis is once again relieved. He nods his approval as he decides, *the matter is in their hands. Perhaps they are luring the smugglers into their snare.* He responds,

"Very well, shall relocate."

"Might we recommend you collect that fine horse of yours and venture along the Roman road? Less than a King's mile, the forest on Furze Hill offers several locations for quiet contemplation. At one time, the Royal parklands."

The other soldier adds,

"The forest offers a six-hundred-year-old tree, Old Knobbley. The ancient tree provides a tidy clearing, total seclusion."

"Very well, I shall offer my petitions at the base of Old Knobbley, as you call it."

Francis departs on foot. He is grateful for the arrival of the military men. He surmises, *they must have watched the night before, as I did.* At the Gorbell barn, he readies Churchfield. The horse seems eager for adventure, the cool, moist air enlivening his short, sturdy legs.

On horseback, Francis heads for the small forest recommended by the military men. Nearing the Roman road, the pair heads back in the direction of Mistley. At the ancient pathway, Francis turns his horse southward toward the wood. The evening sky clears enough to allow the waning moon to shine its revealing beams into the oak-treed surroundings. Entering the woodland, Francis admires the dense forest as the evergreen scent provides a slight tingling in his nostrils. He and Churchfield continue inland.

Arriving at a small clearing, Francis marvels at the remnant of a thick, obviously ancient tree. Symmetrically reaching to the right and to the left, the base of the tree is nearly twelve feet wide. The two main branches that reach in opposite directions span more than thirty feet. The pollarded tree is dark and burly. Francis considers the history the tree has seen, *six hundred years. The Magna Carta signed, as well as the crowning of the Henrys and Edwards. The Black Plague. The Richards crowned. The Reformation and Shakespeare. King James and his Bible. King Charles, first and second. The first King George and the second. Our recent King George the third. The history you have experienced, and as conversational as James at Foxall's forge.*

Seating himself at the base of the massive tree, Francis discovers a cavity almost big enough to tuck himself into and hide. The hollow is perfect for leaning back against. Francis closes his eyes and begins his conversation, the continuous winds aloft providing a welcome setting for the itinerant. The swaying branches of the forest trees cause his thoughts to occasionally depart from prayer, mentally returning him to his childhood in the Bromwich heath. After an hour of prayer, Francis rises from Old Knobbley, mounts Churchfield, and departs for a night's rest.

The following day finds Francis bidding farewell to the Gorbell family. His plan is to head east to the coastal town of Harwich. He advises Captain Gorbell,

> "Shall meet in class on my return in three days."

Captain Gorbell is grateful, surprised that the itinerant would make time for such a small class. Mrs. Gorbell places several jarred fruits into Francis's saddlebag. She also includes one of his favorites, dried beef. He tips his hat and is on his way.

The town of Harwich nestles on a point sandwiched between the River Stour, the River Orwell, and the North Sea. The land jutting out from the mainland forms a protective harbor, a natural hook at the east end of the wide River Stour, forcing the merged waterways to turn due south into the great body of water, the North Sea. The village is located in the heart of that hook.

As a port town, Harwich is an international hub. From here, sailors travel to and from the Netherlands, Belgium, and France. Men on more substantial ships can reach Germany, Denmark, and Norway. Three fortifications constructed under the watch of King Henry VIII protect the harbor town, which busies itself in shipbuilding for the Royal Navy. From Harwich, as from Bristol, much of London's importing and exporting takes place.

Francis's arrival in Harwich concludes a wet and windy journey along the River Stour's shoreline, which at times found the young itinerant aching for shelter. The ten-mile journey on horseback easily inspires Francis and Churchfield to welcome the warm fire and hot meal offered by the vocal fisherman who greets them. Within minutes, the short, skinny operator of the fishing smack[145] shares many instructions with Francis and begs him to shelter Churchfield inside the barn. Francis doesn't want to inconvenience the man; the weather has not dipped to December and January extremes. However, the kind and talkative fisherman is serious about his offer.

"Da' horse goes to da' barn, Pastor."

"Very well."

The insistent man, Francis soon discovers, is Mr. Peter Firmin. Inviting Francis inside, the man holds open the front door to the simple one-story home. Immediately, the smells of a warm stew capture the itinerant's undivided attention. Francis's smile, the one that relishes the thought of a full stomach, beams from his chilled and reddened cheeks. Removing his wet hat, Peter insists,

"Place it abuv' da' fire."

Francis places his hat on an iron hook hanging above the fire.

Peter is dressed in typical fisherman clothing. As he removes his cotton skullcap and gloves, the salt particles practically drop from the worn threads. A regular of the Dogger Bank,[146] he works hard for his living. The area with the abundant plant plankton attracts many fishermen and their primary pursuit to the productive waters. Peter's recent abundant catches of cod and herring have drawn attention from the locals, who continue to harass him for becoming a fisherman. Peter is a brave man, regularly working more than sixty miles from the English shoreline; the North Sea is a treacherous body of water, especially for an open-deck craft like Peter's only thirty-five feet long.

---

[145] An eighteenth-century two-masted boat with a specific sail configuration that allowed for fast maneuvering.

[146] A productive fishing area sixty-two miles off the coast of England.

Mrs. Firmin darts into the room.

"Husband, please do introduce your friend."

"Yes, Wife. Pastor Asb'ry, ma' dear and lovin' Lydia."

"Pleasure to meet you, Lydia."

In her simple cotton dress, Lydia graciously curtsies. Francis returns a bow. Noticing Francis's thin build, Lydia offers,

"Wesley fails to feed his travelin' preachers properly."

"Ma' dear Lydia, we shall address dis' problem. Please sit."

Francis obeys Peter's request, thinking to himself, *I fail to appear as thin as Peter.* The two men sit as Lydia busies herself with the dinner preparations. Peter inquires,

"How fares Manningtree?"

"Well, I guess. The dreaded trade seems to permeate the entire lot."

"Know't well. Da' smugglin' trade was in ma' blood. Not even da' fury of da' North Sea could shake me from it."

"You participated?"

"Surely he did. Ma' husband was damn good at it, too."

Lydia's pause amidst her deep sigh reveals her disappointment with herself.

"I apologize, Husband. Moreover, to you, Pastor. Peter and I ar' new to dis' religious way of life. Oh, we love da' Savior; we jus' continue to struggle with unbefittin' behavior."

"Trust in da' Lord, Lydia; He shall deliva'."

"Spoken well, Peter. May I pose a question of the trade?"

"Ask away."

"When men drag a rope along the bottom of the waterway, whatever is their aim?"

"Draggin' a creeper. Da' men are hookin' a bag of shingles."

Francis's look of uncertainty prompts Peter to continue.

"Da' creeper is like a grapplin' hook. Drag it along da' river bottom to fetch ya' goods. Understand?"

"I think I understand. What are shingles?"

"Ya' goods, Francis! Shingles ar' ya' goods!"

Lydia delivers the meal to the table. Francis bows and all fall silent to pray.

"Dear Father, Heavenly Father, the blessing of a meal fails to escape our notice. Nor the blessing of a transformed heart. Two transformed hearts. Your mightiest blessings on Peter and Lydia, first for their kindness to a worn and hungry itinerant, and second for their birth anew. We thank Thee for Thy provision. Amen."

Francis is not shy; with wooden spoon firmly in hand, he heartily enjoys the meal. Lydia is pleased with the favorable results. Peter inquires,

> "Pastor Asb'ry, might ya' preach among da' townspeople tomorrow? I could publish notice in da' mornin'."

> "Very well. Publish for four o'clock tomorrow afternoon."

Peter looks to Lydia; their loving smiles for each other convey their hearts which seek to honor the Lord.

The next day's weather welcomes the preaching event. An unseasonably warm day with the clearest sky he's seen in months greets Francis as he enters the Harwich peninsula. Less than eight hundred yards wide in its narrowest location, the point experiences a constant wind from the ocean. Considering the favorable conditions, Francis is sure: *the Lord shines upon our efforts this day.*

Nearly sixty people arrive at the open field due west of Harwich's Anglican St. Nicholas Church. The magnificent structure pushes skyward as the highest landmark on the peninsula. Since the late twelfth century when the Earl of Norfolk gifted the church to an order of monks, St. Nicholas has ushered Christianity into the southeastern portion of England, welcoming many a traveler to and from these British shores. The arriving crusaders of the twelfth and thirteenth centuries worshiped at St. Nicholas. Christopher Jones, the master of the Pilgrim ship *Mayflower*, was on two occasions married in the church, his first marriage in 1593 and his second ten years later, in 1603. Standing across the street, Francis considers the rich history of the building. He steps forward, raises his hands, and once again begins his service with a hymn.

> "Forth in Thy name, O Lord, I go,
> My daily labor to pursue;
> Thee, only Thee, resolved to know,
> In all I think or speak or do."

The crowd seems to enjoy Francis's voice, but not much else. Francis boldly continues,

> "The task Thy wisdom hath assigned,
> O let me cheerfully fulfill;
> In all my works Thy presence find,
> And prove Thy good and perfect will."

Again, not many are responding. Francis considers, *these are nearly dead; shall continue.*

> "For Thee delightfully employ
> Whatever Thy bounteous grace hath given;
> And run my course with even joy,
> And closely walk with Thee to heaven."

Francis is surprised that none participate—well, almost none. Slightly off-key himself, Francis is thankful for the two who delightfully sing with him, Peter and Lydia. In truth, some of the lyrics they hum, but at least the smiles on their faces reveal faithful hearts. Drawing the singing to a close, Francis begins his message.

"For God so loved the world . . ."

Francis's sermon is a familiar one to him. For most of the itinerants, traveling to various locations allows for repeated sermons and lessons. Considering the lack of higher education among most of Wesley's preachers, this is advantageous. The repetition allows the traveling men to feel at ease in front of a group of people and is also a means of perfecting their approach and their deliveries.

At sermon's end, Francis raises his hands for a closing prayer. Before he can begin, the unaffected crowd disperses. He looks to the Firmins; their sorrowful nods convey their sadness for the spiritual state of their fellow residents. Peter comes forward.

"Pastor Asb'ry, our souls ache for them as well."

Francis purses his lips and nods in agreement. Reluctantly, he lowers his hands.

The following day finds Francis preparing for departure. His plan is to return to Manningtree. The Firmins wish him well, their kind words amplified by Lydia's loving gesture of dried and salted meats placed within his saddlebag. Departing the Firmin residence, Francis and Churchfield head west.

The route along the waterway is simple, the dirt-covered road almost perfectly paralleling the coastline from Harwich. Nearly twenty yards inland, the narrow path weaves through the heavily treed shoreline. The thinner trees allow a slightly obstructed view through the thick evergreens to the waterway. Francis makes a mental note, *today's winds churn the Stour.* A quarter mile out of town and nearing a clearing, Francis halts Churchfield. Up ahead, nearly twenty men stand blocking the pathway. Unsure, Francis decides not to push forward. He waits.

Several of the men realize that Francis has stopped. Among the group, they engage in discussion. Francis suddenly prods his horse, hard.

"Come, Churchy. Seems we've an audience."

At Francis's urging, the horse quickly picks up the pace. The loose gravel and dirt fly rearward.

Again Francis prods, and Churchfield is at a full gallop. Francis is not stopping; he pushes the animal again. Churchfield accelerates to his fullest speed. The men smile at the itinerant's audacity; several brace for the inevitable impact. Two men unravel a thick braided rope and pull it across the path. The group divides in half, each grasping one end of the rope on opposite sides of the path. One calls out,

"Raise as he approaches. We shall pit the preacha'."

The men brace themselves once more.

My bluff reveals their intent.

"Forward, Churchy!"

Hanging on with all his strength, Francis crouches as he prepares for impact. The men tighten. Churchfield thunders on. Francis's deep breaths grow faster.

Twenty yards away, Francis tightens his bent legs. The horse lowers his head as he senses Francis's bracing.

Fifteen yards away, Churchfield huffs the cold air from his bellowing lungs, the vapor trails channeling along his thick body.

Ten yards away, the men begin to yell.

Five yards away,

"Now, Churchy!"

The horse pushes off, his front legs rising six feet above the ground. The rear legs follow at the same height. Over the rope, Francis and Churchfield fly. With a startled and delayed reaction, the men raise their arms higher. Unfortunately for the aggressors, their lifting of the rope is not in unison; one side far precedes the other. Their attempt to trip the horse falls a split second behind and several inches short. The result of their efforts is to barely nip the edge of the horse's hind hoof, which does nothing to alter Churchfield's momentum.

Like Parliament rejecting a proposal rumored traitorous, the expletives from the men sail to and from many directions.

Landing front legs first and then the rear, Churchfield continues to discharge a barrage of stones, this time toward the men. The dust and debris incite the men to toss the rope to the ground. Several curse one another; others continue their invectives toward the rapidly departing itinerant.

Continuing forward, Francis relaxes after his triumphant escape. Convinced that he and Churchfield are far enough away from the troubling men, he slows their pace. The horse shakes his head as he resumes a slow walk. Through his shaken emotions, Francis pats the animal's neck with pride. *Churchy, you are an amazing creature.*

After a few minutes, Francis is not so hopeful. His doubts bring a slight fear as he mulls over the rejection from the townspeople in Harwich. He is thankful for the Firmins, but he realizes that for his efforts to gain a foothold in the peninsula town, he must return. *Surely I shall encounter the opposition once more.*

Five miles out, Francis turns to his left. He can barely make it out, but through the sparse tree limbs he spots a church at the top of a gently sloping hill. The building is small, and considering the grand cathedrals of his travels, for a moment he decides to push on. But the welcoming structure is too inviting to ignore. He gently directs Churchfield to turn off the path, and the horse eagerly directs his steps toward the structure. Crunching over several fallen and decaying limbs, the pair ventures beyond the edge of the forest. Francis can sense the slight rise in the landscape. Nearing the top, he turns in the saddle to look back toward the river. Over the tops of the diminutive trees, the expansive view toward the water is stunning. He slows the horse, turning him back around.

"Consider this view, Churchy."

The pair stare at the waterway. Beyond the protection of the trees, the chilling winds of the advancing autumn surge uphill, buffeting Francis's exposed cheeks. Coveting the warmth of his former course, he turns Churchfield toward the tiny church building. The wind is now favorably at his back.

The stone building with its Norman design is forty feet by eighteen feet, only one-fifth the size of the more massive monuments. Despite the limited dimensions, the one-story tile roof is steep. The walls of septarian rubble[147] and brick, dating from the early twelfth century, are beautiful in design. This is All Saints Church of Wrabness.

Wrabness is a small riverfront town, west of Harwich. The church overlooking the River Stour is the largest structure in the tiny hamlet. Practically a nature preserve, the riverfront grasslands, scrub, and woodland thrive adjacent to a flourishing marsh. At the hilltop, Francis's elevated viewpoint captures all of this.

At the church, Francis dismounts. Eager to view the architectural details, he walks up to the arched doorway. The stonework is impressive, as is the Norman archway. The sight of the ancient church stirs Francis's love for history. He remembers his mother's lessons of the Norman conquest of England, William the Conqueror, and King Edward. The thoughts remind him that he hasn't kept up his reading. *Must return to Bunyan's tale.*

Walking inside the church, Francis admires the impressive structure. Built in the twelfth century, the interior's simple wooden beams, made of hatchet-cut tree limbs, support the roof. Stepping back outdoors, Francis is drawn to a wooden cage, roughly ten feet square and eight feet tall, topped with a traditional roof. Peering between the vertical wooden slats, Francis spots the church bell. *Strange, the bell resides on the ground and in a cage.* Francis's thoughts cause him to rub the back of his head. With no explanation at hand, he decides to return to the trail. Walking from the bell cage, he collects Churchfield and the pair once again heads for the path along the shoreline.

---

[147] A mass of mineral substance having cracks filled with another mineral (usually calcite), resulting in unique inconsistencies that render it attractive.

Returning to Manningtree, Francis is informed by Captain Gorbell that several townspeople desire Francis to preach again. The itinerant is thankful; without hesitation, he urges the captain to publish for this evening. The retired sailor agrees to do so. Before Francis can depart to wash up for dinner, the captain mentions,

> "Almost forgot—correspondence from London arrived yesterday. Addressed to Pastor F. Asbury."

The thick hand of the sea captain hands the folded document to Francis. The lengthy piece appears to contain writing on three sides of two pieces of paper. On the outside fold, the remaining blank side of the two pages, "F. Asbury Colchester" occupies the center of the empty space. Francis opens the pages and begins to read.

> *Reproduced from April 1768 correspondence, Thomas Taylor, New York. Read publicly on any Sunday. You may then receive what the hearers are willing to give. And the Elisha-minded preachers who are willing to go.*

Reading the rest of the letter, Francis discovers that Thomas Taylor, a member of the John Street Wesleyan Church in New York, seeks financial help. In addition, Taylor pleads for competent preachers to settle in America, specifically to preach to the infant New York congregation. The letter goes on to detail the beginnings of the New York church. One Philip Embury, late of Limerick, Ireland, along with a retired British officer, Captain Thomas Webb, have raised a small but healthy society in New York City, specifically, on John Street. Francis receives the letter with gratitude, vowing to spread word to aid the new society. In light of this vow, one thing is clear to him: *New York shall never enter into my considerations; Colchester is far enough away from home.* Francis tucks the correspondence into his saddlebag and prepares for the upcoming worship service.

The evening's service occurs outdoors. The weather is crisp and moist, the lighted lamps reflecting their beams onto the wet paving stones of the marketplace. At the rear of the gathering of nearly fifty people, the wealthy Mr. Rigby stands with an entourage of key figures. The men are dressed in expensive silk clothing, their entire outfits of the same material and well embroidered. Their tricorn hats top their neatly powdered wigs, several of the hairpieces sporting a bow tie at the end of the tail. The women who attend with the Rigby group are equally extravagant in dress. The wealth of the burgeoning nation is well represented in the various oriental imports adorning the women. The women and a couple of the men are utilizing muffs to keep their hands warm.

In front of the wealthy group, several military men dressed in their regular attire converse with each other. Two of the soldiers are familiar to Francis—they are the two who accidentally discovered him hiding behind the rock at the river. At times, the soldiers peer in the direction of several suspicious-looking men dressed in threadbare, all-black clothing. Additional participants for the service are the Gorbell family and several local couples and their children.

At the front of the gathering, Francis raises his hands to begin the service. All fall silent, and Francis bows his head to pray.

> "Almighty Father, Creator of heaven and earth, of all that is seen and unseen. We thank Thee for those in attendance. Enter their lives with transformed hearts. Moreover, may You shine Your face upon their efforts. Bring to life their deeds, both good and bad, and allow for Your glorious provision of forgiveness to reign. Amen."

Upon completion of his prayer, Francis continues with raised arms and begins a Charles Wesley hymn.

> "God, the offended God most high,
> Ambassadors to rebels send;
> His messengers His place supply,
> And Jesus begs us to be friends."

Looking over those in attendance, Francis spots the Gorbells joining in song. To his right, the men in black sing also. Francis finds this strange. In the center, the military men and the men of wealth silently watch the proceedings. Francis continues,

> "Us, in the stead of Christ, they pray,
> Us, in the stead of God, entreat,
> To cast our arms, our sins, away,
> And find forgiveness at His feet."

Once again viewing his outdoor congregation, Francis's welcomed observance of the townspeople singing along is interrupted by a tall, thin man from across the street. He rushes forward toward Francis, loudly proclaiming,

> "Pastor, I beg of you."

The entire group turns to see the approaching man. Several of Rigby's friends are clearly intrigued by the disturbance; others are upset, their frowns mocking the intruder. Francis lowers his arms and inquires,

> "Yes?"
> "I beg of you, a couple in attendance are worthy of change."
> "Worthy of change, sir?"

"Their hearts are corrupt!"

Francis tilts his head and considers the comment, *couple worthy of change, their hearts corrupted.* He looks to the captain; Gorbell shrugs his shoulders. A few in the crowd verbally complain of the interruption, demanding the removal of the inconsiderate man. Francis silently rejoices at their disappointment. The man races into the group. Approaching the soldiers, he turns to the men dressed in black, who also begin making their way toward the soldiers. One of the men in black, a tall, thin man, prompts Francis's memory: *the man in black on the beach.* This is the individual who accosted Francis one week ago, the one who had tightly gripped Francis's arm. The man announces in the direction of the soldiers,

"You are under arrest."

The companions of the attacker and the man who interrupted Francis's singing grasp two of the soldiers—the soldiers who advised Francis to leave the beach. One of the soldiers' companions yells out,

"On what grounds do you arrest the King's men?"

With a stiff-armed hand to the chest of the disgruntled soldier, the tall man in black pushes back, replying,

"On the grounds that they have stolen barrels of brandy from the Pembroke. Stolen without tribute to the King."

The Pembroke is the ship that sank off the coast of Mistley, Francis recalls. The two accused soldiers lower their eyes toward the ground, offering no resistance. The man from across the street announces,

"If found guilty, there shall be a hanging in the morn."

With this proclamation, the removal of the soldiers disperses the crowd. Francis stands alone, looking to Captain Gorbell and his wife. They too are disappointed.

That evening, several of the soldiers approach Francis at the Gorbell residence. Their sincere efforts win Francis's approval; at their request, he agrees to pray for the accused. He also agrees to preach and pray at tomorrow's trial and, if required, the hanging of their fellow soldiers. Later that evening, Captain Gorbell advises Francis,

"With military men, things are not always as they seem. Despite the sacredness of the uniform, some men drift."

Francis receives the advice from the wise captain. He vows to pray for justice.

The makeshift gallows stands on its own in an open field outside of town. From its location, the beautifully scenic view of the river stands in sharp contrast to the stark wooden structure created for executions. Like a linen scarf around a sailor's neck, the gallows is out of place. To the local men and women, justice is expected to prevail. If the accused are innocent, free them; if guilty, hang them. Although the Pembroke was not a local ship, residents of Manningtree and nearby towns lost family members who worked onboard. Considering the loss of life, stealing from the sunken ship is tactless and socially unacceptable. The locals have no problem with the penalty for such crime: death.

The following morning, Francis arrives at a chaotic scene. Several soldiers stand shoulder to shoulder in a line, nearly face to face with several men dressed in black. These seafaring men and the soldiers are equally vocal. The soldiers demand proof of the accusations against the two men of their regiment; the rough-looking sailors bark back, "We'll have your proof!" Gathered around the soldiers and their opposition are nearly a hundred townspeople, while many more make their way up the slight hill to the middle of the field. At the gallows stands the magistrate of Manningtree. He is a small man, slightly balding, his simple black coat open to reveal a white cotton shirt and black waistcoat. At his side is a witness, an esquire of Manningtree. The two men spot Francis and wave him toward the gallows.

Turning Churchfield in their direction, Francis brings the horse to a halt. He dismounts and walks his companion up to the two men. Approaching the magistrate, he inquires,

"Where may I find the prisoners?"

"They shall arrive shortly. First, we must establish proof of their crime. Upon successful demonstration of their guilt, we shall summons them. You may spend a few minutes with them at the gallows before they climb."

"Shall I have the privilege to speak to the accused if found not guilty?"

The magistrate looks to the esquire, then turns back toward Francis with a devious smile.

"Itinerants! A man can stand at the precipice of death and you continue to push the Gospel. All right, then. It shall be arranged."

Francis nods his gratitude and walks to the side of the growing crowd. He secures his horse and waits for the proceedings.

The magistrate raises his arms to speak. When many in the crowd ignore the request, his esquire attempts to gain their attention verbally.

"Hear, hear! We shall proceed."

The people begin to quiet. The confrontation between the soldiers and sailors also quiets, but only after a gentle shove by one of the soldiers inspires a not-so-gentle reply from one of the sailors: he punches his fist into the sternum of the obnoxious soldier, leaving a nasty bruise. The town's magistrate orders several volunteers to police the antagonistic groups.

The first to present evidence are the local sailors. They produce a wooden cask, much like the one Francis tripped over at the shoreline. This one is slightly different: in lieu of one container, two similar wooden containers are connected together via a rope harness. The tall, thin man in black—Francis's confronter on the beach—demonstrates how the soldiers wore them when removing them from the water. He lifts the contraption, placing one of the casks in front of his chest and the other on his back. The ropes of the apparatus are slung over the shoulders, allowing for a comfortable balance when walking. He voices his discovery,

> "These dry-land smugglers clearly removed each of these half-ankers[148] from the Pembroke. The soldiers acted as tubmen, taking that which did not belong to them and, worse yet, seeking to import without duty."

The soldiers voice their disagreement. The sailors stand their ground. One of the sailors is a bruiser, standing nearly a foot taller and wider than the soldiers. Francis is thankful, *failed to make his acquaintance on the beach*. The lead sailor, who is making his case like a London lawyer, looks to the magistrate, whose approving nod indicates that he should continue. The lead sailor asks,

> "What of these?"

Next to the bruiser, another sailor walks forward with a length of rope and a grappling hook. The apparatus is the item Francis asked the ex-smuggler in Harwich to identify. He recalls Peter Firmin's reply, "Draggin' a creeper. Da' men are hookin' a bag of shingles." The prosecuting sailor proclaims,

> "We are clear; this creeper is the tool of smugglers. 'Twas found among the items of the accused."

The magistrate voices a question.

> "Have we any who will deny the item was among the personal effects of the accused?"

No one objects. The magistrate raises his hand toward the sailor to continue.

> "We are all aware that these half-ankers carry over-proof spirits. Not yet diluted, they can bring severe illness, even death. Explain the fact that two soldiers as of Wednesday last remain deathly ill. Two soldiers who not only lie nearly dead, but two soldiers who are also companions of the accused. Shall any rebut this?"

None in the crowd or among the soldiers will disagree. The sailor raises his right hand.

> "As the Almighty is my witness, my discourse is complete."

---

[148] The equivalent of half a barrel of liquid.

Stepping to the center of the crowd, the magistrate clears his throat and offers,

"Clearly, ample proof, proof without appeal, has been shown. I pronounce the accused guilty as charged. For the crimes of stealing and land smuggling, the accused soldiers shall hang."

The crowd cheers and the soldiers depart. Several of the military men brush by the sailors, bumping them with their chests as they maneuver past them to exit the gathering. Staring into the chest of the oversized sailor, one soldier decides otherwise and hastily steps around the bruiser.

Within moments, the guilty parties are escorted to the foot of the gallows. The magistrate motions for Francis to come forward. Leaning on Churchfield, Francis reaches into his saddlebag and removes his Bible, then walks toward the men about to die.

At the men, Francis removes his hat. The crowd falls silent. Opening to the New Testament, Francis invites the men to kneel, which they do. Francis kneels facing both of them. The people in the crowd also decide to kneel. Francis begins,

"Gentlemen, your guilty souls can be graciously justified through faith in the precious shed blood of the Savior. You should count it a privilege that before today neither of you has been struck dead by lightning or a bullet of war. This is your day, your time to choose eternal life. Do you choose eternal life, the Savior and Lord Jesus Christ?"

One of the soldiers stares at the ground; the other begins to weep. The weeping soldier exclaims,

"At one time in my life, I treated tenderly the blessings of the Savior. Sadly, I have neglected these longings. Despite my shortcomings, I choose to receive the gracious dealings of the Lord Jesus Christ."

"And you, do you too embrace the gracious arms of the One who seeks to bless you through eternal life?"

Lifting his head and his gaze toward Francis, his eyes swollen with tears, the second soldier nods an affirmative. Francis responds,

"Very well. Go to the Savior; He awaits your arrival this very day."

At this, Francis rises to his feet. He acknowledges to the magistrate that he is finished with the guilty. The crowd and the two soldiers rise to their feet also. The magistrate directs,

"Gentlemen, climb the gallows. Your days are complete."

The hanging is a standard affair. Bound and placed in the holds of the knotted nooses, the men await their sentence. The moist, sullen eyes of the men are the lasting view of their faces as they submit to the cloth hood of execution. At the command of the magistrate, the wooden floor opens and the men drop short of the ground below.

Upon the death of the guilty, several townsmen remove the bodies for burial. At the top of the hill, the men of the town dig two graves. They place the soldiers in the holes and the magistrate appeals to Francis for an impromptu funeral.

Francis is nervous; he has never performed a funeral. In fact, none of his Wesleyan mentors have had time enough to share a proper procedure with him. But he has an idea. Without hesitation, he clears his throat and walks forward.

> "Looking at these two men lifeless in the ground, their actions bringing on them the death warranted by justice, I am reminded of the words of a dear lady whom I sought to comfort. Instead of the comfort I sought to bring, as she lay dying, she brought comfort to me. Her last words to me were, "Follow the call, even in the face of a storm." If the two soldiers here before us had considered such sage advice, it is highly unlikely they would lie here staring lifelessly toward heaven. Following God's call for righteousness, even in the face of a storm-sunken ship, brings life."

> "Pastor, your words are a comfort to us all. Many here have lost loved ones on the Pembroke. In addition, we are certain these two soldiers possess family that shall grieve their departure. May we indulge in a local ceremony which continues as a reminder to us all for generations to come?"

Francis is surprised by this interruption from the magistrate; it temporarily produces in him a nervous trembling. After a deep breath, the anxiety subsides and he responds,

> "Very well."

The magistrate turns to the rear of the gathered group. He raises his arm and waves a man forward. From the back of the gathering, a man in his mid-thirties approaches the graves. Francis recognizes the man, but is unable to place the face. Dressed in the simple clothing of a laborer, the man moves with measured steps to the side of the first body.

Reaching into his pocket, he removes an item, small enough to conceal in the palm of his hand. His long, thick fingers shuffle the item to his fingertips. Clenched between the thumb, forefinger, and middle finger, the item appears between his curved and hairy knuckles as he kneels next to the deceased. Reaching down into the hole, he gently places the brown ovular sphere into the mouth of the deceased. *'Tis the drenched wanderer from the River Stour—'twas an acorn he requested.* This revelation of the first individual he met upon his arrival in the region some time ago, the man walking out of the river with wet clothing, brings a sense of uncertainty to Francis. Placing his hand on his hips, he contemplates why the man is placing an acorn into the mouth of a man about to be buried.

Rising from the first body, the man walks the ten feet to the second body. He drops to his knees and reaches into his pocket. Once again, he removes an acorn. He maneuvers it to his fingertips and lowers the seed into the mouth of the dead soldier. Upon completion, the man rises and looks to Francis. Noticing his bewilderment, he informs him,

> "You see, 'ere on da' river, our lives every day deal with all sorts. Good and bad, our shorelines receive dem' all. We welcome all, knowin' dey' aid us in providin' for our families. Occasionally, we must deal with dos' who fail to follow da' law—or as you so eloquently put it, 'fail to follow God's call even in da' midst of da' storm.' Dees' men who lie 'ere will be buried, dees' seeds will sprout, and da' resultin' trees will serve as reminder dat' crime fails to prosper."

Nodding his head toward the itinerant, the man turns and departs for the back of the gathering. Francis's only reaction is to watch as the man leaves the hill where the men will be buried—the hill that will gain two significant landmarks in the form of twin oak trees.

At the beginning of October, less than two months into the circuit, Francis receives word to head one-hundred and forty miles to the southwest, to Salisbury in Wiltshire. The correspondence from London contains a strange notation:

> Proceed south, to Wiltshire, Surrey, and Sussex, the Methodist Wilderness.

In addition to the correspondence, there is a private word from home. The young messenger delivers a personal message from Francis's parents, Joseph and Elizabeth. It is a worn piece of paper, folded once. Receiving the note from the dusty traveler, Francis opens it to find the following:

> She wishes you closer to home. Yearns for it.

Francis is used to this; his father's handwriting conveys no hurt within its subject. He understands his mother well enough to know that her current wishes do not coincide with the Lord's will for him. However, he wishes the same were true of the last announcement by the messenger.

> "Pastor Asbury, I am only the messenger. But apparently, there is a deep hurt and displeasure of your failing to visit a special young lady during your last visit. She accuses you of partiality."

Partiality? Francis is frustrated by the comment; he can feel the flush in his face displaying his embarrassment at the accusation. He considers Nancy's scornful comment. *Other than Nancy, I met with all—none did I refuse.* Upset by these developments, he prepares for his departure from the coastal town, his thoughts continuing to focus on Nancy.

The end of October is clearly a time of change in southern England. Autumn is departing and the stiff months of winter are beginning to emerge. The cold discourages Francis as he frets over his relationship with Nancy. He longs to talk to his father, or Pastor Mather or Pastor Glasbrook. *Each of these would offer sound advice.* These despondent yearnings occupy the majority of the first day of riding.

During the next day, Francis approaches London and decides to pass through the busy city. As he does, fond memories of Benjamin Rush, Sarah Crosby, Mary Bosanquet, and Sarah Ryan help to lift his mood for a time. But even these welcomed musings subside. When their encouragement falters, he flirts with the desire to abandon Wiltshire and head for West Bromwich; *shall my heart deceive?* His youthful eagerness to fix situations straight away, especially the situation with Nancy, urges the tempting distraction. Approaching Tottenham Court Road, he decides to continue on to Salisbury.

Moving southward on Tottenham, Francis spots a young man standing alongside a horse. The uniquely dressed man appears the same age as Francis. He is in a sizzling scarlet jacket, accented with a silver-grey waistcoat and white silk stockings. Atop his head is a laced hat. The red jacket is as eye-catching as a male cardinal landing on a black-iron fence post. The steel-grey waistcoat resembles the color of the London sky. Francis admires the fine clothing as he tips his hat to the stranger.

"Good day."

"Indeed."

The man nods his head with his response, the gentle tilting accompanied by a hand gesture. The right hand, palm up, welcomes Francis and Churchfield. The young man offers,

"Autumn in London has mostly departed."

"It has. As am I."

"Departing London, are we?"

"Passing through for Wiltshire."

"Fate seems to have brought relief, as I too head in your direction."

Francis is surprised by the revelation. He inquires,

"I'm to be in Salisbury by week's end. And you?"

"I shall terminate much closer: Basingstoke. Have you ever gone from London to Salisbury?"

"No—in fact, I am in need of sound directions."

"I see. After the first twenty miles along the Thames, the route is challenging—the first eight miles through a barren heath, the Black Desert, then fourteen miles on the coach road at Bagshot. Difficult territory, isolated and desolate. Perhaps we should travel together?"

"Very well."

"If it pleases, I shall meet you here in slightly less than one hour. I've to complete my business in London."

"Very well, Churchy and I shall look for you then."

Francis's smile reveals his happiness. Although he did not expect it, he is glad to gain a traveling companion—a well-to-do traveling companion who can offer welcome and challenging conversation. Before his departing, the young man offers,

"John is the name."

"Francis Asbury."

"Mr. Asbury, pleased to know you."

"As well."

Nearly one hour later, John returns. He's not alone; two young women have joined him. Francis is uneasy with the discovery; he didn't figure on traveling with women. John once again mentions that the upcoming journey is challenging. Francis wonders, *then why the women?*

For some odd reason, John repeats a description of the demanding route ahead of them.

"Twenty miles along the river, eight miles through the barren Black Desert, the Bagshot Heath, and another fourteen on the London Road to Basingstoke."

Even more baffling is the fact that John has changed clothing. He is no longer dressed as the dashing red cardinal with a grey waistcoat. The red jacket remains, but his steel-grey waistcoat has switched to one of blue satin trimmed with silver, even more striking than before. As Francis ponders this development, John offers,

"Mr. Asbury, the journey shall be long. My friends and I would like you to dine with us before our departure."

"Very well."

"Ahead, a most welcoming tavern awaits."

Francis turns Churchfield in the direction John points with his extended right hand, the opposite direction of where Francis was heading. John continues,

"We shall meet you there. Arrange for your horse as well; I shall pay for its provisions also."

Francis is impressed. He nods an affirmative and heads for the tavern.

Spotting the brick covered, two-story establishment, Francis secures his horse. A young man from the back of the building runs forward.

"Fodder your horse?"

"Yes, you may. Thank you."

Francis pauses to view the structure. It is large, as large as the manor house in Luton. The sign out front reads, "Adam and Eve Tavern." Francis facetiously notes, *all is well; a tavern for preachers.* Heading inside through the thick oak door, Francis once again pauses. Unable to see at first, he experiences an accumulation of noises. Several groups of people chatter. Male voices dominate; a woman cackles an awkward laugh. A large bird screeches; the wind whistles freely throughout the space. Widening his eyes, Francis attempts to focus.

It takes a few moments, but his eyes eventually adjust to the reduced light. As his vision sharpens, he notices a large, high-ceiling room with a dirt floor. The space is long and narrow and crowded with two dozen tables. At each table, several men and women sit talking or eating. Some drink. At the far end of the room, a miniature pipe organ and several wood-floor alleys line the wall. On his left, a wooden archway opens toward an attractive outdoor area planted in an orchard-like fashion. *Fruit trees?* are Francis's best guess. Around the perimeter of the exterior courtyard, a series of decorative wooden arbors are cloaked in last season's vines. Despite the biting temperature, the descending wind driving through the thinned foliage fails to inconvenience several more tables of people who reside under the oak pavilion. In the center of the open atrium, a pond gently ripples in the chilling winds. Francis shakes his head in amusement. He has never seen such a place.

Behind Francis, a strong beam of light enters the space as his new friend and his female companions enter the tavern. John rubs his eyes and offers,

"Francis, we shall sit over there."

Pointing to the rear of the room, John indicates a vacant table with four chairs, tucked on its own into a wooden niche. It appears set apart for a purpose. John and the girls escort Francis to the table. As they approach, a young lady dressed in serving attire comes forward from an adjacent room. With a thick forearm, she brushes a bead of sweat from her brow. She fumbles with her hair, neatly tucking it under a white cloth bandana that wraps around her head. She rushes toward the table.

"Hello, John. We've an additional guest today."

"My, Ran, you are a perceptive creature. The customary shall do."

" 'Tis my job, John."

Ran, short for Katherine, gives John a flirting nod as she turns to retrieve his usual fare.

Returning with a tray loaded with steaming tea, Ran places a cup of the hot drink in front of each individual at the table. Once all have been served, she moves the circular wooden tray to her left hip and informs the group,

> "The soup today is barley. As usual, the soup is a tad short on beef, but there are plenty of herbs."

> "Soup and bread for each of us, Ran."

John's instruction sends her off to fetch the day's meal. Raising his cup, John offers,

> "To Hogarth! Francis, does not Hogarth's artistry reveal the true Adam and Eve?"

The women raise their cups as well. Uncertain of the reference, Francis lifts his cup. When the tilt of his head reveals his confusion, John prompts,

> "Hogarth, William Hogarth. The painter?"

> "My apology. I am unfamiliar with his work."

> "Very well. He painted a scene of the street out front of this fine establishment. He presented it to the King. Unfortunately, King George was greatly offended."

> "Offended?"

> "Yes. Seems Hogarth's depiction of the soldiers fell short of Georgie's fair opinion of his men."

> "What of this depiction?"

> "Quite fond of the painting myself. I was especially drawn to the two women in the center of the work, ready to battle over the King's grenadier.[149] I believe the pregnant woman will win out over the wench dressed in the priestly robe; 'tis only right."

I shall agree with King George II. Francis finds the mere description of the artwork offensive. Before he can comment, John offers more.

> "The painting goes on to reveal the true identity of the British army. One soldier locks lips with a milkmaid, another playing the drum draws the undivided attention of a woman and a child. My favorite, though, is the soldier urinating on the tavern wall—the wall of the Adam and Eve—his face clearly pained with the effects of venereal infection."

Francis fumbles with his hands and almost drops his cup of tea. John's depiction of William Hogarth's piece has long lost his attention. He gives an awkward smile to one of John's companions. She returns a seductive gaze. John rambles on,

> "William completes the artistry with soldiers wielding a knife and robbing unsuspecting residents. The second-story prostitutes catch my attention too, as well as the soldiers in the painting. Francis, you seem to have lost interest?"

> "All is well. John, shall the ladies travel along with us?"

> "No, Francis; the heath is quite demanding. They shall remain in London, to take care of my affairs while I am gone."

---

[149] A soldier of the Royal Guard.

Francis is relieved. He had begun to dread the thought of traveling with the young women. Their general demeanor, as well as their occasional petting of John's arms and shoulders, prompts Francis to believe that these girls may have immoral connections with the enigmatic young man.

Soup and bread arrive. The women and John start in right away, scooping up several spoonfuls as Francis hesitates. He mentally considers praying aloud. Opting not to pray, he also begins his meal.

The rest of the meal is chaotic. Several patrons step forward to greet John; he is clearly a popular resident. Some of the visitors smell of gin, others attend with their mug of ale. As Francis watches the proceedings, he is somewhat ashamed. He thinks back to another young friend in London, Benjamin Rush. *O for a cup of tea with Benjamin.* Francis misses the edifying conversations with the young doctor. John breaks in,

"Come, Francis; you've finished your meal. Try a hand at the alleys."

Lifting Francis's hand, John pulls him up and away from the table. *Um, very well.* Francis is uncomfortable with the gesture, but he continues to follow.

Arriving at one of the wooden alleyways within the building, John points to the far end where nine wooden pins stand upright in a diamond pattern. At the end of the twenty-foot-long alley, each pin stands roughly fourteen inches high. The six-inch-diameter base and stubby roundness at the top give each pin the appearance of an oversized butternut squash. John hands Francis a round wooden disc.

"Here, Francis. Knock the pins by tossing the cheese without touching the floor."

"The cheese?"

"Yes, the cheese. The disc is called the cheese."

"The cheese is quite heavy."

"Well then, shall I have one of the girls show you?"

Not wanting to appear incapable, Francis grips the cheese, curling his strong fingers around the edge of the circular object. He directs the arm holding the cheese rearward in an arcing motion. John offers,

"Yes, Francis, you've grasped the idea. Swing it forward and launch without touching the ground. You've only to knock the pins down."

John delivers the last sentence with a manipulative smile. Francis rears back and tosses the cheese.

The wooden disc slams into the rear wall of the alley; he has missed the pins completely, the cheese sailing well over their tops. John lets out a guffaw.

"Ha! Not as easy as one would think. Try again, Francis."

By now, several of John's friends have gathered to watch. John's female companions also join the group, latching themselves onto John's arms. A young boy retrieves the cheese and returns it to Francis. He gratefully accepts the chance at another throw.

Massaging his palm on the disc, he maneuvers his muscular fingers into position. One of the girls comments to John,

> "Mighty hands on Francis."

> "Product of the trades."

Francis's reply is pure boasting. The girls giggle at his prideful revelation.

Francis swings his arm rearward, then forward, then rearward and forward again. He pauses. He draws his arm back and with a quick, sharp thrust launches the disc toward the end of the alley. John's friends and his girls audibly inhale as the disc sails through the air.

The cheese hits the head pin dead on, knocking down seven of the nine pins. The group gives a loud cheer. Francis exclaims,

> "I shall give it another go!"

> "Yes indeed!"

John is enjoying watching Francis have a good time.

For the rest of the afternoon, Francis perfects his approach to the game of London Skittles. Upon completion of the last game, John bids the girls and his entourage farewell. He tips the waitress with a gold coin and invites Francis to collect his horse. Francis departs for Churchfield, euphoric about his sporting success and an afternoon of enjoyment with a new friend.

Walking outdoors, Francis's spirits sink as he realizes there is only an hour of daylight remaining. The euphoric feeling of an afternoon of fun vanishes, leaving a self-condemning inner accusation of time wasted.

Departing London, Francis and John head for the surest route out of town in the direction of Wiltshire—which, John assures him, is the River Thames. According to John, the first stop, Chertsey, should take nearly five hours. They originally planned to arrive around six o'clock in the evening; this has changed. The afternoon at the tavern will place them in Chertsey around ten o'clock, forcing them to travel the majority of the trip in darkness—and worse yet, ensuring little rest for the challenging journey tomorrow.

Realizing that they will not reach the river until the sun sets, Francis is glad to have a traveling companion. He looks to the slate-colored sky; the moon is missing. He returns his gaze forward, into the darkened streets of London. John remarks,

> "Francis, you know, traditionally the game of Skittles is played for money."

> "Did not know this."

"As well. You could force a pleasant living with a strong arm like yours."

The thought finally surfaces for Francis. *I've failed to acknowledge my itinerancy.* He struggles with the revelation. In addition, he reflects negatively on his failure to pray before his dinner at the Adam and Eve Tavern. The shame-filled thoughts cause his emotions to plummet. Quietly, he and Churchfield plod along, viewing the candlelit windows of the approaching town of Westminster. *Such a poor, ignorant, foolish, unfaithful creature. How can I be called to such a work?*

Adjacent to the west of London proper is Westminster, its 140,000 residents making it the second largest city in England, only slightly smaller than London. Traveling southeast on Tottenham Court Road, Francis and John edge their way along the western boundary of London. The pair continue on Tottenham until the road runs into Broadstreet and then into St. Martin's Lane. At St. Martin's, John directs Francis onto the road heading due south; they now parallel the river. The large buildings associated with the monarchy crowd the street. There is plenty of traffic, mainly horses pulling tumbrils—the short, stubby, two-wheeled wooden carts used by farmers, which if not attached to the horses, could easily tip over backward. People freely wander in and out of the traffic. Sadly, the evening drives indoors the town's more welcomed Members of Parliament and the wealthier families. With the arrival of darkness, the road fills with many people in search of their next cup of gin or their next sexual pleasure.

The darkened sky removes the majority of visibility in the narrow corridors. Francis isn't comfortable with this. He complains to himself, *should not have participated in games.* With the thumb of his right hand, he rubs the knuckles of his left. He pauses to notice the dry skin of his hands, caused by the cold air. His fiddling resumes. After several minutes, he realizes he continues with the nervous habit and stops the rubbing, looking for a suitable place to rest his anxious hands. He fumbles with Churchfield's reins. Perceiving Francis's uneasiness, John offers,

> "You know, Francis, Westminster is a unique town. Not all is dark and hazardous. The gentry along with the aristocracy live alongside those who serve them. The tradesman, the craftsman, the butler, and the cook. All are welcomed."

Francis remains silent.

John continues,

> "The slums shall turn into the divine."

With an unsure nod, Francis silently considers the comment. Nearing the end of St. Martin's, the road veers into Whitehall and Parliament Street. On the left are houses of the Royal Guard, on the right the grander houses of Westminster. The wider street, accompanied by the sight of more substantial housing, lifts Francis's spirits. His thoughts move to his parents. He experiences a slight twinge of guilt; *Mother and Father have never had such opportunity.* His smile resurfaces. John welcomes the visible change with a generous smile and the tipping of his hat.

The larger buildings give way to the short and narrow St. Margaret's Street. Francis's smile turns to a pleasant stare, the kind of look one wears when unexpectedly making a happy discovery—in this case, the sight of the towering spires of Westminster Abbey. The thirteenth-century Gothic-style building is an architectural masterpiece, built on the site of a church started by the Benedictine monks in the tenth century. Since the year 1066, the abbey has been the church used for the coronation of the monarchy. The building in front of Francis and John was begun in the year 1245. The various towers and outbuildings were completed twenty-three years ago, in 1745.

Passing the abbey, the road turns into Abingdon Street and Millbank, the edge of the crime-ridden Westminster. The intersection of Millbank and Abingdon crosses perpendicular to Horseferry Road, the road onto the newly constructed Lambeth Bridge. The bridge crosses the River Thames to the east, to the residence of the Archbishop of Canterbury.

Continuing southward through the Horseferry Road intersection, Millbank abuts the river. It is along this portion of the journey that the river begins its slow turn to the west. As Millbank Row creeps away from its due-south direction, the crowded street turns into an open field. Halting his horse to stare into the blackness, John offers,

"Tothill Fields - -

If the dead of these four miles of barren soil could speak."

John's eerie smile brings a slight chill to Francis's spine. Peering into the darkness exaggerates the barrenness of the location and the uncanniness of the comment. John continues,

"It is from these unfertile grounds that magistrates deliver solemn public announcements. Here it is death for witches, criminals, and necromancers."

Francis remains silent.

For the next four miles, Francis and John will travel through an open field full of dark history. This they will attempt in almost complete darkness. The land along the bending river will rise eventually, making it the highest point in the flatland of Westminster. Until then, Francis and John will trudge their horses through marshy grounds.

Entering the field, Francis notices that his hands are trembling slightly. Adding to the suspense is the lack of sound. He ponders, *not even crickets.* Even the wind calms as Francis and his traveling companion enter the soggy glebe. The unholy past of the area and the slushing of their horses' hooves obscure Francis's ability to focus clearly. He mentally relives John's warnings, "unfertile grounds . . .

witches, criminals, and necromancers." *Why would someone worship the dead?* Francis's thought about necromancers furthers his anxious palpitations.

After a couple of miles, John reins in his horse. Francis is unsure, but he stops also.

"Francis, I've a confession to make."

Despite the darkness, Francis can detect an odd look on John's face. He thinks to himself, *we must be halfway through the field. The middle of the field, the furthest away from people.* John begins,

"I must ask you . . ."

A huge gust of wind swoops by the men, nearly knocking them from the saddles. The horses readjust their legs to gain a proper footing. As quickly as the interruption arrived, it departs. Francis looks to John.

"Did not expect such a startle . . ."

John doesn't reply, but continues to stare into the night. Francis pushes aside the lack of response and inquires,

"You were about to say?"

Gathering his reins, the visibly shaken John digs his heels into the sides of his horse and moves on. Francis shrugs his shoulders; *must not have been important.* He urges Churchfield to continue.

The end of the barren field brings the pair to a turn in the river. Over the next nine miles, the river twice makes a complete 180-degree turn from due south to due north. From here, the doubled u-shaped river adjusts to the west and then toward the south. It is the last leg, the southerly leg, which puts Francis and John at Twickenham. Here they depart the river, heading southwest through the Hounslow Heath. It is also here that Francis ponders John's earlier pause, the one interrupted by the gust of wind.

The four-thousand-acre Hounslow Heath begins as a slightly forested land, much like the Bromwich Heath, with its areas of wood and stretches of lowland grasses joining with limited marsh and reed-bed areas. Wild boars roam the grasslands and woodlands. Unfortunately for Francis, none of this is visible under a moonless sky; the light-borrowing orb remains tucked behind the clouds. He and John continue, slowly making progress through the gorse- and broom-covered grounds to the southwest. At this point, the men are halfway to their evening's destination of Chertsey.

Upon exiting the heath, the riders once again enter a thickly forested land dotted with several small lakes. They continue in this direction for four miles until reaching the town of Sunbury, where they rejoin the River Thames.

This part of the journey is much like following the river in West Bromwich. It brings to mind Francis's first horseback trip to visit Mrs. Hanson in Wolverhampton. Churchy is also pleased with this portion of the river; without notice, he pauses for a snack, bending down and biting at a clump of grass that is well beyond the growing season of life. The trip also brings to mind that all this traveling, all this time spent from home, is challenging. It is hard work, sometimes long and drawn-out, as is this night. The journey is at times exciting, and at other times, boring. Breaking the silence of the night, the horse's chomping of the dry reed grass brings a peace to Francis's emotions.

"Come, Churchy."

With a light prod, the horse once again moves forward. Simultaneously, a beam of light shoots to the ground. Above, through the thinning cloud cover, the full moon is revealed. Like a cotton ball floating above, the sight of the blurred illuminated orb brings a lightness to Francis's heart. *Surely, the heavens declare the glory of God.* This thought prompts him to speak.

"John."

From several yards ahead, John turns to see Francis. Facing forward again, he responds,

"Yes, Francis?"

"I've a confession to make."

"Oh?"

"I have failed to reveal my occupation. I am an itinerant for Wesley."

John and his horse come to a complete stop. John remains motionless. Looking to the reins in his hands, he says nothing, his gaze fixed in a blank stare. For a moment, he appears as a dead man, head slumped down and lifeless. Francis pulls alongside him and reins Churchfield to a stop.

"John, you seem dejected."

"Oh?"

"As if the revelation has brought a disappointment."

There is a long, silent pause. In the background, a frantic wind begins to push through the countryside, whistling its way through hundreds of dead ornamental grass clumps. Francis waits. John finally responds,

"All is well. Carry onward."

John and his horse move forward. Uncertain as to what has transpired, Francis prods Churchy and they travel ahead.

Across from the town of Chertsey, the men spot the Chertsey Bridge. The wood-timbered structure is a welcome sight for Francis. He looks to John and then to the bridge. Something seems wrong, but it's not about John this time—it is the bridge itself. The wooden structure has an odd look. It continues to rise from one side of the river to the other, giving it an off-balance appearance. In addition to the peculiar out-of-level construction, several of the support beams that reside in the water are floating about, evidently snapped off from the bottom and dangling from the underside of the bridge planking. The planking itself is suspect also, its varying widths revealing several large holes, big enough to catch a horse's hoof. The look on Francis's face causes John to laugh aloud.

"Francis, you appear to have seen a devil."

Francis doesn't respond. John continues,

"You mustn't allow the damaged appearance to hinder your effort to cross. So what if a barge or two has wildly smashed into several of the support beams, cracking them from their proper bases? Traversing the shaky, un-level assembly shall give you the courage to cross more properly built bridges."

Still no response from Francis. John tries again.

"The annoying slant is inconvenient, I will admit. Perhaps even dangerous. However, you have to admire a poem. Would you fancy a poem, Francis, or shall I say, Pastor? Well, here goes: 'Tumbling 'twixt Middlesex and Surrey land, we came where Chertsey's crooked bridge doth stand; which sure was made by all left-handed men; the like of it was never in my ken.' "

"The like of it we shall never see again."

"Ha! Francis, you are a wordy preacher."

Francis cannot hold back a laugh, his chuckling response matching John's own audible mirth. John offers,

"In you, Francis, I have found a friend."

Once across the bridge, John directs Francis to follow as he arranges accommodations in Chertsey. Francis finds it odd that several of the townspeople offer unlimited hospitality to John. *Perhaps they are friends also.* At least that is what Francis assumes. He is also challenging himself to allow more with John. *He is one who lacks the faith; perhaps my acceptance of him shall open the door for faith to prosper.*

A family of means amply supplies the night's accommodations. Their rough-edged hospitality is readily accepted by Francis. Uncivilized at first, their manners improve a little upon John's mention of Francis's ministry.

Rising early the next day, Francis commits to prayer. He opens with thankfulness for his new friend in John; *strangely, I've yet to gain his surname.* He reflects on the previous day's events. *Father, my deepest apologies. Failure to pray does not speak well of a pastor.* Francis pauses. He patiently spends time in silence, listening; *speak to my heart.* He struggles with thoughts of what transpired on the journey and continues to criticize himself. After several mental forays against himself, he questions his ability to remain quiet and hear from the Lord. Rising from prayer, he heads outdoors to fetch Churchfield.

His discovery of John in the barn with Churchfield is a pleasant surprise.

"Good morning, John."

"Good morning, Francis. About ready?"

"Believe so. I've yet to gain provision for the long day ahead."

"Already taken care of. I've made arrangements for both man and beast; the lad has loaded our bags."

Francis is thankful. He is well aware that the day's journey on horseback will occur in wind-blown, barren heaths. *Thank you, Lord;* Francis silently expresses his gratitude for the food supply.

The first leg of the trip takes place in the Black Desert, an open, dry heathland. The challenging landscape of the eight-mile trip requires nearly six hours to complete on horseback. The cutting winds greet the pair as they depart Chertsey in the early-morning light. Francis and John view the slight rise in the landscape; the first portion of the trip is toward high ground. Within a half mile, the pair nears the peak.

From the hilltop, an advantageous view of the entire landscape ahead of them draws the pair's attention toward several tree strands ahead. The isolated forests reveal the thick hardwoods spread from left to right in an elongated fashion. To the sides in either direction, several cousins of the tree strand, tree domes, spread in their circular pattern, displaying a mound-like appearance. Scattered among the groups of trees are many open areas of ornamental grass. The pair rein in their horses for a quick rest, knowing they have completed the easiest portion of the journey. Each looks to the other. Then, with a tip of his fancy hat, John kicks his horse and moves on down the hill.

Quickly prodding his own horse, Francis launches downhill also. The descending slope causes him to lean back for the short distance. Nearing the bottom of the decline, he sits up straight. Churchfield continues, the ground quickly changing to a marshy-soft loam, dotted with small clumps of dried ornamental grasses. This is wet going; the only dry locations in this swampy area of the heath are the tree strands and domes. The men navigate their horses through the scattered clumps of grass that resemble dried witches' brooms standing on their own, minus the center broomstick. The going is slow. When the ground is wet, the horses slow to a walk. When the ground is dry, the horses are able to accelerate to a slow trot. The ride is bumpy and, at times, slightly sloping from right to left. The vibrant purple colors of the summer heather attributed to the Bagshot Heath are gone. Apart from the sporadic groupings of trees, the nutmeg color of the waist-high grasses leads beyond the horizon in three directions.

Four hours into the journey, John slows his horse to a stop. Francis brings Churchfield to a halt beside him. John informs him,

> "Must relieve myself."

The brawly[150] man dismounts and heads for the tree dome twenty paces off to the right. Francis remarks to Churchfield,

> "Seems you haven't such problems."

After ten minutes of waiting for John, Francis decides to do the same. He dismounts and heads for a tree strand in the opposite direction of John.

When Francis returns to his horse, he finds John sitting atop his own animal, patiently waiting. Approaching Churchfield, Francis notices something unusual. His saddlebag is not as he normally places it, with the leather strap neatly tucked into the metal buckle. The strap lies loosely, unbuckled. He shrugs off the discovery, secures the strap, and climbs atop his horse. With a prodding of their mounts, the pair continues the journey toward the town at the end of the heath, Bagshot.

Neither man talks for the first five minutes. It is strange; there is an uncomfortable silence. Francis focuses his thought on the saddlebag. *Did I fail to secure it? Did I unlatch it before heading to relieve myself?* These questions continue to recur in his mind. Ten minutes into the ride, John offers,

> "We shall make good time to Bagshot. The coach road lies just west of
> town, less than one mile. Once upon the road, we shall make great time
> for Basingstoke."
>
> "Very well. Mind if I read?"
>
> "Not at all."

Francis pauses before reaching back to his saddlebag. His hands tremble slightly; he's anxious that he will discover something missing from the bag. He is certain that John can see his shaking hand as it reaches to undo the leather binding. He breathes deeply as he unwraps the strapping. Laying the leather flap over, he peers into the bag. The book he seeks is right there on top where he left it; however, he continues to look around the book's location. Not wanting to draw attention to his exaggerated search, he reaches in and removes the book, Bunyan's *Pilgrim's Progress*. He places it under his thigh and reaches back to the bag. Acting as if he requires something additional, he pokes inside the bag.

> "No. Well. All right, then."

---

[150] Finely dressed, a Scottish variant of bold.

His disguised and rambling sentence ends as he removes his hand from the bag, satisfied that all is present. He plunges the leather strap under the buckle and secures the saddlebag once more. Reaching under his thigh, he retrieves the book, opens it, and begins to read.

At the five-hour point of the journey, the landscape has changed little. Although the heath continues to deliver a worthy battle, Francis is largely unaware. He is enjoying his reading. John admires Churchfield's ability to tread onward, avoiding the nasty little clumps of dried grass. He advises,

"Less than one hour to go. Bagshot is just ahead."

"Uh-huh."

Francis is at the part where Christian is telling Hope the story of Little-Faith, a good man who lives in the town of Sincere, who has the harrowing experience of traveling into Dead Man's Lane, so called because of all the murders that take place there. Three thugs—Faint-Heart, Mistrust, and Guilt—spot Little-Faith and set upon him. When Little-Faith refuses to give them his money, they knock him in the head with a stick, the blow leaving Little-Faith unconscious. Francis pauses in his reading, his thoughts wandering in several directions. *Lord, do You speak to me? Shall I fear John as Faint-Heart, Mistrust, and Guilt? I've no riches, only books given from the itinerants. No money at all. I have You alone, Lord.*

Realizing that Francis is staring away from the book he's been reading for nearly two hours, John inquires,

"Has the story brought about strange musings?"

Francis continues his worried mulling. John tries again.

"Francis?"

"Huh? My deepest apology. Bunyan's tale captures my undivided attention."

"So I see."

Approaching Bagshot, the grassy heath turns to a well-forested land, though the surrounding areas are still part of the heath. The ground rises slightly, allowing traditional hardwoods to thrive. The horses welcome the dry ground, as do their riders. Noticing the change in landscape, Francis reaches behind and returns his book to the saddlebag. As he opens the leather pouch, he remembers, *in Chertsey, John loaded our food provisions. Very well, then.* Francis no longer doubts his companion; *he surely forgot to fasten the bag.*

The pace picks up slightly as the edge of town comes into view in the distance. Bagshot is a small country town located within the boundaries of a Royal Park. The main road through the village is the southwest artery, the coach road. Along its route, several small towns like Bagshot have sprung up to provide overnight stays for travelers enduring the jolting ride of the chaises heading toward Wiltshire.

John and Francis enter the town. Within minutes, they are on the coach road, heading southwest toward Basingstoke.

The next fourteen miles to Basingstoke will take less than three hours. The road is level and secure, although it continues to run through a forested heath. Not until Basingstoke are there signs of civilization along this route. The endless rows of trees and the overcast sky cast a gloomy mood upon the day. Urging their horses forward, the pair hang on as the animals accelerate to just under a full canter. If the horses maintained the fifteen-mile-per-hour pace, the trip from Bagshot to Basingstoke would take only an hour. However, the men realize that the previous journey through the heath has placed a strain upon the animals; moreover, the constant motion would cause its own burden on the men's bodies. They wisely choose to save their knees and alternate between a full canter and a walk every ten minutes or so. Halfway to Basingstoke, the men once again slow their horses to a walk. Francis again toys with the thought that he should return to West Bromwich. He worries that his relationship with Nancy no longer remains intact. *O for Father.* Francis longs to talk about this situation with Joseph. He nervously scrapes his teeth on his bottom lip.

Since the slower pace began, John has been watching the young man. He now comments,

     "Francis, you seem remote."

John waits for his reply.

Silence.

Sooner than expected, John prods his horse and takes off at full speed. Caught by surprise, Francis does the same. Trailing behind John, he pushes Churchy to catch up. *Seems more than a full canter.* Francis and Churchfield fail to catch up. He pushes Churchy again. John continues to drive his horse. The British Thoroughbred's longer and stronger strides pose a difficult challenge for the smaller Connemara. Francis continues to urge Churchfield. *The effort falls short.* Francis slows Churchy to a walking pace, while John and his mighty horse continue to speed on down the road. Within a few minutes, the horse and rider are out of sight. Francis is left alone with his horse and the several thousand similar-looking hardwood trees that swaddle the road.

The continuous offering of trees on either side of the road lends itself to tunnel vision. Francis catches himself staring without thought at the distant horizon. He ponders the recent development. *Why would John abandon me on the road? Hasn't he a worry for my safety? Highwaymen are notorious for seeking out a lone rider.* Without effort, Francis abandons the thought; he would rather sulk over Nancy then panic about potential harm by thieves. Besides, other than a few books and some food provisions, he has little to offer. He returns to the thought of Nancy's expression that she is unhappy with his failure to visit when he was last at home—implying that he was partial in his visits. He wrestles with this as Churchfield walks the lonely road toward Basingstoke.

Riding into Basingstoke by mid-afternoon, Francis pats Churchy on his thick neck.

"We have arrived, my friend."

Looking up, the itinerant is greeted by a familiar face.

"Hello, Francis! I see you've survived Colchester."

"I have, James."

Francis stops his horse, dismounts, and embraces his mentor, James Glasbrook. Francis's lengthy hug prompts James to inquire,

"Is all well, Francis?"

Not responding, Francis continues the embrace.

"Francis, look at me."

Francis releases and backs away. He looks to James, who again inquires,

"Is all well with the itinerancy?"

Francis looks at the ground. His emotions swell. Taking a deep breath, he manages,

"I am comfortable moving place to place . . ."

He pauses. After nearly a minute of silence, James inquires,

"Are you content?"

"Aside from one matter, very much so."

"Does the matter require advice?"

"It does; however, I shall address it when in Great Barr."

"It may be some time before you venture home."

"Very well. I am settled upon my duties."

"All right, then. I must inform you, we shall share the Wiltshire circuit. Our Sundays shall require one of us in either Portsmouth or Salisbury. In between, we shall venture into smaller towns like Whitchurch and Farnham."

Francis mentally notes the locations. As he does so, a well-dressed arrival interrupts the pair.

"Why, Francis! I was wondering when you would gather your thoughts."

Francis embraces the visitor—his riding companion, John. Upon release, John extends a hand toward Pastor Glasbrook.

"John is the name. Seems you're a friend of Pastor Asbury."

"Indeed. Pastor James Glasbrook, of Bedfordshire."

"Pleased to meet you, James. Young Francis and I traveled from London together. He is quite the rider and preacher."

"That he is."

"It would be an honor to buy dinner for my two favorite men of God."

Francis's grin towards James expresses both delight and gratitude. James replies,

> "All right, then. But first I must take care of quick business with Francis."

"It is well, James; John is a friend."

> "Very well. Wesley has sent allotment for temporal items. Specifically for clothing. You shall receive your salary for the year after the next conference."

Francis receives the money from James, counting out ten pounds. Thrilled, he immediately places it into his saddlebag. Turning toward James, he replies,

> "Thank you. My temporal needs are few. The good nature of people like John leaves me with little want. My bread and water are sure."

"Very well, Francis. Here is an additional item."

Reaching into his horse's saddlebag, James lifts a pamphlet and places it into Francis's hands. Francis opens the plain-covered publication. The opening page reads,

Extract of the Life of the late Rev. Mr. David Brainerd, Missionary to the Indians

James offers,

> "Wesley thinks highly of Brainerd's work. Suggest you make acquaintance with Wesley's writings on Brainerd's ministerial efforts in the American colonies."

"I shall."

Francis closes the pamphlet and places it too in his saddlebag. Once again, he thinks of the Indians in the colonies; *we seem to cross paths often.*

Finding an inn is not a problem in the travel town of Basingstoke, as the coach road daily ensures several new visitors. Francis, James, and John easily locate a place for the evening. As they enter the establishment, the smell of a warm stew entices the men to have dinner. First needing to wash up and take care of nature's call, the three men head in the direction of the appropriate rooms for both activities.

With all necessities taken care of, and having checked on their horses, the men make their way to the cozy dining room attached to the inn. Escorted to seats near an open fireplace, the three travelers relish the warming flames. The woman in charge of the inn has no trouble selling them an ample offering of the house specialty. Nearly an hour after their arrival in Basingstoke, three plates of steaming-hot stew are set before the hungry travelers. As only three men who have not eaten all day can do, they pray and set themselves to enjoying the meaty offering. For more than three hours the men exchange stories of their lives, families, and friends. As he did with his initial meal with Francis in London, John aims for a warm reception with James. By the time the men complete their devouring of several servings of the juicy stew, cups of hot tea, and loaves of freshly baked bread, the sky outside has darkened and the lamps of evening have been lit.

At dinner's end, John calls the waitress over to the table.

"I shall pay for each of the meals. In fact, I shall also arrange to stable our horses. By which direction can I care for such details?"

"Through the side door and on to the left, you shall find the barn."

"Thank you."

John places two coins into the waitress's hand. She is grateful for the generous offering. John turns back to the itinerants.

"Gentlemen, I shall go and take care of our beasts."

"Francis and I would like to thank you, John."

"It is the least one can do for godly men."

John departs, and James looks to Francis.

"How well do you know John?"

"Not very. We met in London. He expressed he was to travel in this direction and agreed to go with me."

"I see. Very well, our horses demand our attention before retiring for the evening."

The two men rise from the table and head outdoors. Outside the building, they locate their horses. John is there also, mounted atop his horse. Francis's unsure nod accompanies his inquiry.

"Going somewhere, John?"

John gives no reply. With one quick kick, he sends his horse racing down the coach road.

Francis looks to James. James responds,

"Such an odd gesture . . ."

Instinctively, Francis peers toward Churchfield. He immediately notices that his saddlebag is unbuckled and slightly open. He rushes to investigate.

As he pushes open the leather bag, Francis spots a few familiar items, including the book of John Cennick's sermons given to him by Lord Dartmouth when he first began to lead the class at West Bromwich. Unfortunately, several items are missing: his copy of Bunyan's *Pilgrim's Progress*, the pamphlet from Wesley on David Brainerd, and, worst of all, his clothing money. He shouts to James,

"John is a thief!"

The two men vault onto their horses and launch down the coach road. In the darkness, nothing is visible. Frantic, Francis kicks Churchy hard. The horse accelerates down the lonely road. After several seconds, James and his horse catch up.

Francis yells,

"He cannot be too far down the road!"

James looks to Francis, but doesn't respond. The men continue to push their horses.

After several minutes, James advises,

"Francis, we must stop. You shall not catch him. His horse is too swift."

Francis pulls hard on the reins. The sudden stop has both horses and men catching their breath. Francis stares into the blank darkness, his top teeth grinding against his bottom lip. He scoffs,

"Of all the thinly-guised schemes! I should have recognized the falsehood."

"It's all right, Francis. Money and books are replaceable."

Looking at James, Francis shakes his head in a dejected fashion. He stares at the ground.

After several seconds, Francis dismounts, walks a few steps from Churchfield, and kicks a stone on the ground. He fumes, *the money would have provided cushion. Food for Churchy and me.* Again, he kicks the ground in anger, then stands with his hands on his hips. He kicks the ground again, and again.

James offers,

"Francis, all is well."

He stops the kicking. With an exaggerated exhale expressing his frustration, he sits in the middle of the coach road.

"Father, I know not what I am. Am I preacher, or sinner preaching for money? Do they take me for one who requires no money?"

Francis places both hands on the sides of his bowed head, his elbows planted on his propped-up thighs. He mumbles to the ground,

"No, I am going to live to God, with or without money."

Francis raises his eyes to the bright moon as it begins to peek through the clouds; he speaks aloud to himself.

"John wouldn't stop. John ran."

Pastor Glasbrook finally dismounts and walks up to Francis. He gently places a hand on the shoulder of the itinerant and offers,

"I suspect he's well on his way to London. Be there in a few hours."

"Few hours?"

"Well before daylight."

"Through the heaths?"

"No, the London Road."

"London Road? There is a road that travels straight to London from Basingstoke?"

"You're sitting on it—the coach road."

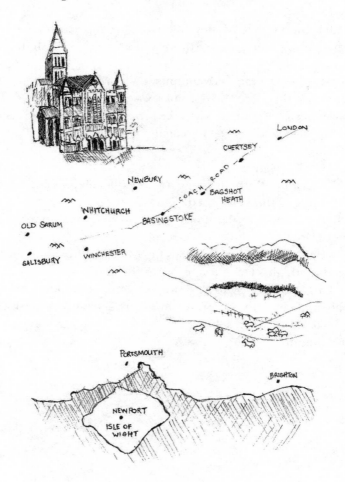

The next day, Francis and James are on the London Road, heading southwest toward Salisbury. The thirty-four-mile ride will take them under six hours. For the first few hours, Francis is silent and angry, feeling foolish and mentally berating himself for letting John take advantage of his kindness. *I border on a simpleton.* He feels dejected, even violated. The emotion is strong, like an iron rod thrust into his stomach. The effect temporarily cures his hunger for food. Instead, Francis longs for his book, *the one John stole.* And he longs for his pay; *John stole it as well.*

His anger rises dangerously close to spitting as he considers how John misled him through a barren wasteland. *He planned to rob me in the heath.* That thought prompts the memory of the sudden blast of wind; *perhaps at that precise point he planned his evil deed.* Through all of these anxious ruminations, Francis's riding companion, James, remains quiet.

Nearing Andover, James finally breaks the silence.

"Brother, you must speak of these things."

Francis says nothing.

James continues,

"Think it not strange. Yes, it is a fiery trial, but has not God seen you through? Could not the man have killed you in the midst of that barren heath?"

Still no response from Francis.

James offers,

"A fiery trial it is, which God in His goodness chooses to try you. At present, not all is well: anger, fear, confusion—they have their way. Joy seems distant, yet through His provision, the strain will birth peaceable fruits of righteousness. Was it not good for Daniel's companions to enter the furnace? Did not the fiery trial reveal One who is present at all times? Though you weary of the blaze, God will use it to purify and not consume. Allow your eyes to open; One holds you with everlasting arms."

Passing through Andover, the London Road continues toward Salisbury. Salisbury resides in a valley surrounded by several large, rolling hills. The hills are far from shallow, the change in height from one hill to the next approaching one hundred feet. The town nestles at the confluence of several rivers, including the Avon, the Nadder, and the Bourne. The road begins its undulation as it heads southwest; however, in the distance, the terrain is markedly different, as the rolling hills seem to deepen. The large expanse of undulating ridges seems to suggest that a rider will temporarily pass from view. Despite the attractive hills, James and Francis ride on in silence, but not for long. A strong rain begins to fall; the steady moisture, like columns of soldiers falling from the sky, advances with drenching results. The weather furthers Francis's grief as, for the next nineteen miles, he and James ride through the strengthening downpour.

Salisbury has a rich Wesleyan history. James and Francis will stay with a local family loyal to the works of John and Charles. In the winter of 1738, John Wesley first visited Salisbury to see his mother, who was staying with his sister Martha and her husband, Westley Hall. This visit occurred a few months before his evangelical conversion at Aldersgate Church in London. He returned in June of the same year to tell his mother and sister of this life-changing event.

The society in Salisbury owes much to John's brother-in-law, Westley Hall. At Oxford, Westley was originally a student of John, who said of him, "a student holy and unblamable in all manner of conversation." This was in the year 1730. In 1734, Westley secretly proposed marriage to John's older sister, Martha, and she quietly accepted. Oddly, a few months later, he openly proposed marriage to John's younger sister, Keziah. The family, unaware of his earlier proposal to Martha, accepted the offer to Keziah. Understandably, Martha did not remain silent. When the dual proposals become public, Mr. Hall wisely chose one spouse: the older sister, Martha. Mr. Hall's duplicitous actions rightly drew sharp criticism from the brothers John and Charles, but in time the wounds healed. Upon the death of the brothers' father, Samuel, their widowed mother agreed to move to the Salisbury home of the now-married Martha and Westley, taking with her the youngest daughter, Keziah. Despite his earlier breach, Mr. Hall became an important individual in the early days of Salisbury Methodism. Unfortunately, his true maxim eventually revealed itself; Mr. Hall believed in and actively sought out polygamy. In time, he abandoned the Wesleyan society and his wife in Salisbury, heading for the British West Indies with a mistress.

The incongruous actions of Westley Hall failed to harm the local Salisbury society. During the 1740s the little congregation continued to meet, and by the 1750s, their society had regained its earlier momentum. As is true in many Christian circles, the vacancy left by unprincipled leadership had allowed other leaders to surface—one of whom James and Francis will be staying with this evening.

The thatched roof and simple brick-chimney home of the couple who will house the itinerants is typical of the homes in the flatlands of the Salisbury Plain. This is sheep country. A simple structure, really no more than a one-room hut, appears as most houses in this area. Occasionally, as in the case with this location, a small add-on room is attached to the home. The house provides the desired protection from the numerous rains that enrich the surrounding landscape of flat, green, and fertile pasturelands.

After four hours of rain-soaked travel, James and Francis stop their horses in front of the simple home. The rain, too, finally stops. From the side of the building a shaggy-haired dog arrives, giving his barking greeting. James responds,

> "Here now; we've come to do well."
> "And to dry a bit."

James turns toward Francis and responds,

> "Well, well—he is alive! I've missed your voice, Francis. Come; considering the smoke which wrestles to escape the chimney, Barbara is sure to have a warm meal on the fire."

The thought of food brings a slight lift to Francis's emotions, evidenced by a hint of a smile.

The animated herding dog circles the pair as they dismount. The jubilant performance prompts Francis to bend down and pet the inquisitive animal. Two quick licks of Francis's boot leg, and the animal is off to an adjacent field dotted with sheep. Standing in the doorway, Barbara Hunt wipes her hands on the apron hanging in front of her dress. This is a working woman; when not toiling with the necessary tasks to support their farm, she is laboring to maintain and prepare her home. Despite the hard life, Barbara Hunt is a young, somewhat attractive woman. The thirty-two-year-old lives and works with her shepherd husband, Richard. The two met in Bradford, Wiltshire, when Barbara left home for a few years. Shortly after their marriage, they returned to Salisbury to raise sheep. They are both regular members of the Salisbury Wesleyan society that meets in the Methodist Chapel on St. Edmund's Church Street. But the neatly constructed chapel is not the original public meeting place for the Salisbury faithful.

During the 1750s, the Salisbury class met in a little meeting room the next street over, above a shop on Greencroft Street. Over the next ten years a small Wesleyan society developed. In 1759, the numerous Salisbury members erected a chapel on St. Edmund's Church Street, behind the shop on Greencroft Street. The church on St. Edmund's is where James and Francis will preach regularly in Salisbury.

As the itinerants enter the home, Barbara offers them a generous curtsey. The welcoming gesture appears out of place for the strong-looking woman. She rises with a flushed smile, less an indication of fatigue than a reflection of her light-colored skin. The men remove their hats and offer their customary bows. James inquires,

> "Shall we happen upon Richard? Failed to see him on our approach."
> "You shall. Busy in the barn he is. I suspect the smell of dinner will raise him."

The itinerants catch each other's look in the direction of the stew pot. Francis's slight improvement is a welcome sight to James; he is abandoning his woeful appearance.

Through the entrance door, a short, stocky man enters the home. His clothes are dirty, bearing the smell of livestock. Francis smiles at the sight of the man's trousers and coat sleeves, which bear numerous patches. Francis amuses himself as he considers his own materialistic leanings toward fine clothing; *perhaps I shall trade him for his jacket.* His thought turns to his mother and father arguing about Francis's time with the wealthy Birch family. This consideration lifts his emotions again; he is thankful for caring parents.

The man interrupts Francis's mental review.

" 'Allo, name's Richard. Richard Hunt. Believe you've met my wife, Barbara."

Extending a thick hand with its dirt-filled, roughly-cut fingernails, some of which appear chewed at right angles, Richard offers the kind gesture to Francis. Francis offers his own and the men shake hands.

"Francis Asbury, Pastor Francis Asbury."

"Pleased to meet you, Pastor Asbury."

Turning toward James, Richard offers,

"James, glad to see you once again. Barbara and I look forward to your stay. The room is always available to itinerants."

The room in question is a small addition onto the side of the house, which the Hunts built specifically to house the Wesleyan traveling preachers. In fact, Barbara worked alongside Richard, ensuring that the structure was built right— not due to any doubt about her husband's abilities, but merely a reflection of her innate personality.

A knock on the front door of the home draws Richard's attention, and he spins to answer the door. Attempting to lift the oak latch, he struggles with the release.

"Must attend to this . . ."

Richard successfully conquers the latch in need of repair and swings the door open.

" 'Allo, Jasper."

Jasper Winscomb is a friend of the Hunts. He is a short man like Richard, but thinner. His red hair, which is full and strewn about like the scattered hills of Hampshire, makes his reddened face look small. Overall, he has a fiery appearance, and this blazing look is a true reflection of his personality. His impassioned ways stand in stark contrast with those of the steady Richard. Richard's fascination with the lively Jasper is one of the key components of their friendship.

Jasper is also a local lay leader in the Wiltshire town of Winchester. For the past few years he has headed up the class and band meetings in the town twenty miles from Salisbury. In addition to his ministerial activities, Jasper runs a small shop in his hometown, an establishment dabbling in small notions and wares. He has recently added a modest line of men's clothing items: shirts, trousers, gloves, stockings, and hats. Recognizing Pastor Glasbrook, Jasper comments to the itinerants,

"As I've tried to sway Richard, his visit to my shop would greatly enhance his wardrobe."

Richard bursts forth with a loud laugh, as do the preachers, though not as loudly. They are drawn not only to Jasper's comment, but also to his fine gesture of delicately waving his hand toward Richard. Jasper continues,

"You see, even Wesley's preachers agree."

"I'm rather fond of my patches; at least they don't wear."

"At least, they don't wear well!"

Jasper's sharp reply brings Barbara into the conversation. Until now, she has been busying herself with setting a small kitchen table with bowls of the warm stew. She now offers,

"Jasper, you shall never improve on my fine stitching. Just ask Richard."

With a look that conveys years of wisdom in agreeing with his wife, Richard responds,

"Best stitches around."

By now Francis is enjoying the company, basking in both the meaty fragrances that fill the room and the friendly banter that feels like a day at the forge. Looking to Barbara, he awaits an invitation. Seeing many a hungry itinerant before, she recognizes the young man's look and nods for Francis to sit and eat. He doesn't hesitate, quickly taking a seat at the table. Richard responds,

"Gentleman, shall we follow the young man's lead? If not, I'm afraid there shall remain little for our consumption."

The men waste no time seating themselves. Richard is last to sit, gently nudging his wife closer to the table as she takes her seat. Richard looks to Francis.

"Pastor Asbury, your prayer."

Francis prays,

"Almighty Father, we pause to listen."

Francis's pause is unexpected; itinerants seldom wait to dive into a bowl of food, and certainly not a young man who has not eaten for almost eight hours. With head bowed, Francis's gentle breathing through his nostrils brings a quiet stillness to the famished men at the table.

After nearly a minute of silence, Francis continues,

"Father, forgive me, for I have failed to watch as well as pray. I have fallen short in my responsibilities. When You have provided, I have neglected. When You have been patient, I have pushed. When You have entrusted, I have gone forth irresponsibly.

"We thank Thee for this meal; bless our bodies and especially the loving hands which prepared. Amen."

The men do not hesitate to begin, Francis included. The eyes of Barbara watch keenly as the men enjoy the stew. She draws great comfort from their spontaneous efforts, which border on the unrestrained. But she is surprised as she watches Francis. His actions are in contrast with those of his companions; he eats slowly, his muscular hand steadily ensuring that his appetite is satisfied. After several spoonsful, she inquires,

"Francis, your prayer was quite reflective. Does the Lord prompt you to make amends?"

"It would prove near to impossible."

"How so?"

"My fault, actually."

"Oh?"

"I should not have trusted."

Signifying that she doesn't appreciate the indirect answers, Barbara clears her throat. Francis politely responds,

"My apology. Recently, a highwayman making himself out to be a friend deceived me out of my yearly allotment for clothing."

All but James stop eating. Barbara replies,

"I see. And you take it to be your fault?"

"I do."

The impetuous Jasper joins in.

"Well there, Francis, seems that the sinnin' is not with you, but with that deceptive highwayman."

Jasper slops an overfilled spoonful into his mouth, and onto the front of his shirt. Without looking, with an undignified stroke, he grasps his cloth napkin and wipes the front of his clothing. Undaunted, he continues, tiny bits of stew escorting his words.

"Now, Francis, we have all fallen victim to some. You need to accept the fact that you serve a God big enough to make things right. In His time, He will."

Francis nods his agreement as he lifts another mouthful. Barbara offers,

"A reflective man is a thinking man."

Richard and James look to Jasper, wondering if Barbara's comment was meant for him. Barbara continues,

> "Richard, it seems that you should expose Francis to the wisdom of the dim centuries."

Relieved that his wife was not taunting Jasper—unlike many in these parts, she is not afraid of the fiery man—Richard smiles his relief toward Jasper. James does the same. Jasper, it appears, remains unenlightened. Richard responds,

> "I could. Perhaps tomorrow we shall go."

> "We shall go?"

Richard hesitates to answer Jasper's question, aware of Jasper's prejudice towards the sect of Christianity to which Barbara refers. Francis inquires,

> "Take me to where?"

James sheds slightly more light.

> "Depths deeper than the Midland coal mines. The depths of civilized society."

The group has Francis's undivided attention. He sets down his spoon and asks,

> "Well?"

All at the table have that "we know something you don't know" smile on their faces. Francis can't help it; he smiles back.

> "Well, tell me."

All at the table pause in silence. Their eyes dart toward one another, their smiles conveying great patience in this teasing of the young itinerant.

> "All right, then."

Richard's reply accompanies his sliding of his chair. He rises, walks about the room, and begins,

> "Here in Salisbury we have an Anglican cathedral. I know what you're thinking, Francis: 'I've seen several cathedrals in my travels.' Well, young man, you have not experienced such a cathedral as the Salisbury Cathedral. Quite different—not for what is outside, but for what resides inside."

Richard returns to his seat.

This is too much for Francis.

> "Come now. Have I not patiently awaited? James, what is so special of this cathedral?"

Silence.

Francis tries again,

> "Richard, Jasper, what shall I expect from this Salisbury Cathedral?"

Barbara responds,

"Gentlemen—I almost refuse to use the term—you must inform Francis."

"Very well."

Richard once again rises.

"In the muniment room of the great cathedral resides a five-hundred-year-old document—a document that provides the foundation of liberty among the English-speaking portions of civilization. The Catholic Archbishop, Stephen Langton, penned it in the year 1215."

The mention of the year 1215 sends Francis's emotions soaring; *history!* He nervously taps the tips of his fingers on the wooden tabletop. The heel of his left foot taps also, raising his left knee several times before he leans forward to inquire,

"Well, what of this document?"

"All right, then, I shall continue. In 1215, drawing sharp criticism for his lifestyle—which exhibited an attitude reflecting a king who thought he could live above the law—the leadership of the Catholic Church asked King John of England to sign the Magna Carta. The Archbishop and the Catholic Church of the thirteenth century had long disliked the King's domestic actions, as well as his foreign policies. There were arrests and punishments by the King, punishing or imprisoning free men without lawful judgment. The Magna Carta dealt with these issues, providing lawful judgment by judges governed not by a king, but by the law of the land.

"But the everyday details of the document are far from the most important principles of the Magna Carta. Long before the establishment of the British Parliament, the thirteenth-century document affirmed that there is a supreme law, above civil governments and, ultimately, above the King, and that these laws of the land were inspired by this eternal fact."

Francis drinks in the significance of the document, first with his fascination for history and next, with the enthusiasm of the storyteller. Next to him, James lifts his spoon and plunges it into his stew. Balancing the lifted spoonful like an artist, he offers,

"Francis, you may ask, why such emphasis on the supremacy of Law? I shall tell you. For we are all subject to God's laws—the world around us, the laws of nature. And the world according to its Universal Sovereign, nature's God. Before any man is a citizen of civil society, he is a subject of the Great Governor of the entire universe. What Richard and I are conveying is that just as the Creator provides the contents of this spoon, so is English law. Our laws and our ability to make and judge laws come from the Creator. No civil law should ever violate the Law of the

Sovereign's revelation. No civil law should ever violate the Law of Scripture. These words are not mine; they are the words of those who were inspired by this amazing document, men like Locke and Montesquieu. This is the foundation of English-speaking governments, Francis. And this is the bedrock principle that emerges from the Magna Carta."

The room is silent. Francis quietly looks to the men around the table. His thought is clear: *despite their simple appearance, these are wise men.* His thought enriches the experience; he is thankful for living in an English-speaking country.

After a few quiet moments, the piercing eyes of Jasper meet those of Francis.

"Well, what have you to say, Francis?"

"We should go and see this fine document."

"Tomorrow we shall."

The following morning a thick fog lingers long, like an unmovable guest. The fuzzy view through the moist air reveals that the end-of-autumn cold has worked its artistic splendor once again. The ride to Salisbury Cathedral follows a scenic route, with the trees along the dirt road ablaze in color. The dimmed perspective slowly displays in the distance the seasonal transformation of the lush green plains into a soft caramel hue—and to the southwest, a tall, amazingly tall, thin spire.

Departing the Hunt residence on the north end of Greencroft Street, the four men on horseback ride alongside each other. If not for the traditional dress of a Wesleyan itinerant worn by Pastor Glasbrook, their appearance would be intimidating—at least, as intimidating as three large English thoroughbreds walking alongside a smaller mountain horse. Francis's little Connemara is nearly five hands shorter than the other horses. Churchfield, however, does not appear to notice. As the group walks southeast along the street, Churchy bobs his head to the right and to the left, obviously considering himself as formidable as his four-legged colleagues. He verbalizes this feeling with a proud snort.

Nearing the end of Greencroft, the road becomes Guild Street. Until recently, Guild Street went by the name of Bell Founder's Street, in association with a local mill on the street. The mill closed in 1730, bringing about the name change to Guild Street. Further on, Guild turns into Culver Street, which 150 years earlier was notorious for its prostitution; brothels once lined this section of the street. Thankfully, this is no longer the case. At the end of Culver is the intersection of St. Ann Street, running from the northeast to the southwest. The men pause at the end of Culver. In front of them, a beautiful meadow gently slopes downward. This low-lying land is the Bugmore Meadow, which in the summer is a fertile grass area; in the winter, the area is prone to flooding.

As the men enjoy the view of the open bog in its transitional state brought on by the change of seasons, Jasper inquires of James,

> "James, have you conveyed to Wesley the need for reinforcements?"

> "Not at this time, Jasper . . ."

Before he can finish his sentence, Jasper fires back,

> "The Isle of Wight, Portsmouth, Salisbury, and Winchester—these prove too much! You must make a case."

The outburst catches Francis by surprise; his quick glance at Jasper is abruptly halted by the stern look he receives in return. Jasper's reddened face and long, fiery-red sideburns appear almost devilish. He turns back toward James and demands,

> "Well?"

> "Jasper, as I've conveyed to you on previous occasions, the idea does not square with Wesley's ideals for the itinerancy. You've once talked of an itinerant solely stationed on the island; you've also talked of multiple preachers handling Wiltshire on the mainland. Wesley has made his aim clear: no circuit where a preacher travels less than four hundred miles in four weeks."

> "I've spoken more than itinerants. I've mentioned additional preaching houses. I shall have to write Wesley myself."

> "You do and you shall risk all that you strive for."

> "I don't take well to threats, James. I must be off. Pastor Asbury, Richard, good day."

Prodding his horse sharply, Jasper launches down into the meadow to make his abrupt and unexpected departure. The hooves of his horse stir up muddy clumps of dead grass as he pushes the animal from the group; clearly, he shall not spend the day with the men at Salisbury Cathedral.

The sudden departure brings a sigh of frustration from James; he bows his head towards the neck of his horse. Francis, not sure of the exchanges, treads cautiously. Of one thing he is certain: James and Jasper sharply disagree. Francis is also certain of something else: James is a wise man. He decides to postpone his questioning, confident that James knows what he is doing.

The three remaining men turn their horses onto St. Ann and head toward the southwest, in the direction of the cathedral. Already the towering spire of the church dominates the distant view. As the fog begins to thin, portions of the building's edifice also materialize. Francis tries to imagine what the entire building must look like.

This first portion of St. Ann Street is mostly residential; the stylish brick houses, with their cast-stone quoins delineating the corners of the buildings, signify the more upscale portion of Salisbury. Francis admires the two-story homes.

Although they are more noteworthy, the houses on St. Ann remind him of Great Barr. Not surprisingly, his mind drifts toward Nancy. Within moments, he determines to play the man and make amends as soon as possible. As the road turns due west, a clearing surrounding the cathedral property takes shape, and a beautiful field on the left and to the east of the cathedral reveals a methodically prepared landscape. Francis is quick to recognize the pattern: *a fruit-tree orchard.* He is correct; he has spotted the remaining property of the friary. The neatly produced space serves as a reminder of the cathedral's Catholic past, the convent with its communal approach to taking care of the poor. The square building tucked within the organized district is a remnant of the friary cottage; additional outbuildings are the friary hospital for the poor.

At the cathedral, the three men on horseback pause to admire the awe-inspiring sight. James looks to Francis, enjoying the young man's reaction. Francis's keen eye for detail is nearly overwhelmed as his thoughts race from *the tallest spire I've seen to date* to *the intricacies of the stone work are unbelievably magnificent.* His eyes drop to the roof lines; *each is superbly steep and covered with lead.* The details of the English Gothic architecture are impossible to grasp at first view. The groined-arch covered walkways, the quatrefoil windows with cast-stone surround, the more than 70,000 tons of Chilmark and Purebeck stone, the roof with its 28,000 tons of oak and 420 tons of lead—each of these deserves limitless time to consider. There is even a fourteenth-century clock. But however glorious these items are, it is something much more valuable that the men have come to see: the document that resides in the chapter house, the Magna Carta.

James urges his horse forward and Francis and Richard follow, guiding their mounts toward the north side of the cathedral. James directs them to dismount at the north aisle entrance.

Climbing down from his horse, Francis can sense his heart beating a little faster than normal. He loves history. Equally important is the concept of community, the eternal perspective that all of history is God's working, connecting all of human creation to each other. This concept never fails to inspire him to invite the subject of history with excitement.

From the side entrance of the cathedral, an Anglican priest arrives. The tall man in the black clerical robe inquires,

"Pastor Glasbrook?"

"Yes. We've returned. Our young companion is an admirer of history."

"He shall find plenty of history here. The muniment is free. Shall you take long? We've service within an hour."

"We shall depart before then. Thank you."

The men nod their thanks to the priest.

Once inside the north aisle entrance, Francis is amazed to discover an enormously large space. Running longitudinally from his right to left, the eighty-five-foot ceiling height gives the appearance that the nave is narrow, but the space is actually seventy-eight feet wide. Large stone columns line both sides of the interior, which is in the shape of the cross. The men make their way toward the left, toward the focal point of the cathedral, the Trinity Chapel. They continue down the ornate area reserved for worship. Passing through the quire area, they veer to the right, toward the vestry which leads to the sacristy and their upstairs destination, the muniment room.

The muniment or document room at the cathedral contains more than six centuries of statutes and ordinances of the governance of the cathedral, culminating in the year 1697. This copy of the Magna Carta was handed to the first Earl of Salisbury, William Longespée, when he was present with the author, Stephen Langton, and the monarch, King John, at the signing of the document. Entering the dimly lit room, Francis, James, and Richard are greeted by a musty smell. Looking toward the ceiling, they notice an oak-beamed roof supported by a single wood column in the center of the room. In addition, a large wooden cope chest, in the shape of a half-circle, sits along one of the eight walls of the octagonal room. The cope chest stands on several wooden legs fifteen inches above the floor. The case itself is twelve inches deep and has a large wooden lid operated by a rope lift. Above the chest, the rope is weaved through a windlass, the pulley easing the opening operation. Francis walks forward and touches the top of the chest. He inquires,

"Does it reside within?"

"No, Francis. Richard, direct him to the documents."

"Before we look at the charter, what is contained within the wooden chest?"

"Nothing now. It used to hold the ornate clerical robes of the Catholic clergy."

"I see."

To his left, Richard has already made his way to the documents bin and lifted its hinged wooden top. He immediately begins inspecting several piles of documents.

"Here it is, Francis."

Francis takes a deep breath as he stares at the lambskin document. The writing is familiar, but hard to read; Latin is the language of the document. Francis recognizes a few of the words, and the funny little abbreviations of the medieval period catch his attention. The archaic extra letters representing the "gh" and "th" sounds, the strong letter "s" which looks like the letter "f," and the strange symbols used to save valuable space—parchment in the medieval days was expensive. James comes alongside Francis and offers,

> "The foundations of the 'rule of law.' All from a riverside location in the Runnymede Meadow."

> "Runnymede, west of London?"

> "Precisely. It was along the River Thames, not too far from Chertsey that King John and the Archbishop made the agreement."

> "Chertsey. Fond memories of the highwayman."

> "Oh?"

> "I am careless. The infamous John took me through Chertsey. As you were saying, James?"

> "Very well. The Magna Carta owes its success to the wise Langton. His twenty-five years of study and lecture on the Bible afforded him quite the reputation with learned society. None in the Roman-influenced court were equal to his wisdom. His efforts caught the eye of the Pope. Pope Innocent and the King were in sharp disagreement over Langton's appointment."

> "King John clearly had someone else in mind."

Richard's interruption is accompanied by a sly smile. Through the beard stubble, Francis is quick to notice *one of his teeth is missing*. Francis nods a surprised acknowledgement, amazed that a sheep farmer possesses such wisdom. James continues,

> "The King feared Langton's reputation could sway many against the monarch. Included in that fear was Langton's longtime friendship with the Pope."

> "Did Langton side with the Pope? Were the King's fears to materialize?"

Francis's eager questions cause the men to chuckle. James is pleased with Francis's reaction to this fascinating history; Pastor Mather had indicated to him Francis's avid interest. James responds,

> "Interestingly, Langton honored neither the King nor the Pope. Instead, he moved the argument in favor of the common law and the English people. His work clearly held two items in great regard: the Bible and the English constitution. Two items which inescapably link. More precisely, Langton was urging King John to return to the principles of the Bible and the ancient rights of Englishmen, as expressed in the Charter of Liberties by the King who preceded King John, King Henry the First."

Richard adds,

> "Francis, without the book you and James carry and teach from, there are no concepts of human rights and liberty. The Bible births the wisdom found in Langton's great charter. Before it, widows and daughters of deceased barons were sold by the King for marriage and for monetary considerations. Are not the stars and planets applicable to everyone? Can anyone escape them? Neither can anyone escape the universality of the Bible."

Francis nods in agreement. He finds it difficult that women could experience such cruel treatment. His thoughts move to his mother, and to his sister Sarah.

Moving on from the painful memory of his sister, Francis contemplates the wisdom of the rule of law as expressed by James; *it inextricably links with the Bible.* Sensing Francis's mulling, James offers more.

> "Despite the wisdom of the ancient document, none of it stands without the influence of the Bible. To put it another way, though good laws do well, good men do better. As I am confident you know, all men shall be governed, either by a power within or by a power without."

> "James is correct; in my years as a sheep herder, I have found it safe to add that anything other than law which sources from the God of the Bible is a sophisticated form of idol worship, expecting saving by that which is created by man. Shall we bow down and worship a carved idol?"

> "Shall we take advice from a Hampshire sheep herder?"

James's quip has all three men laughing. He quickly adds,

> "We shall."

The exposure to the Magna Carta is an enlightening experience for Francis. His excitement not only broadens his mind, it touches something deeper. His strong yearnings for context, the why's of life, the blueprint and original intents of creation, are bringing a sense of fulfillment as he considers the information shared by James and Richard. He departs the musty room upstairs with a deep appreciation for the governing principles found in the Bible. Moving onward, the men head downstairs and back into the nave.

James directs them toward an adjacent space outdoors. Nearing the south transept, they turn left, heading toward the outdoor cloister garth, a covered walkway 190 feet long by eighteen feet wide, laid out in a square pattern. In the past, the outdoor portico was used for the clergy's daily processions. The large green space in the center of the rectangular hallway was at one time a prison, during the English Civil War a century ago.

Entering the exterior walkway with its decorative arched ceilings, the men walk a few yards and find themselves midway of the east side of the cloister. On their left is a wooden door. The round-topped entryway is open; it leads to the chapter house.

The chapter house at Salisbury Cathedral is a designated space built in the mid-thirteenth century. It resides on the south side of the cathedral, tucked between several full-bodied evergreen trees. The octagonal structure is traditionally the meeting place of the cathedral clergy and principal leaders of the church. The building gains its name from the tradition of the Benedictine monks and their ritual of reading a portion of the rule of St. Benedictine before their meetings. The name also links to the chapter divisions made in the Bible by the key author of the Magna Carta, the thirteenth-century Catholic Archbishop, Stephen Langton.

Entering the chapter house, Francis is speechless; he stands still, his gaze soaring upward. The fifty-eight-foot-diameter room is a large and dominating open space. There is so much detail to take in. The eight groined-arch ceiling sections vault from the stained-glass window arches to a center stone column fifty-two feet in the air. James watches as Francis's eyes wander about, then come to rest on a singular attribute of the architectural genius. One-third of the way up the wall, above the leafy quatrefoils delineating arches and doorways, a decorative frieze wraps all eight walls at the same level. Francis drops his eyes to meet James's gaze. His exaggerated exhale leading to a gentle smile, he returns to the ornate detail to study the encircling band.

The carved marble within the frieze depicts scenes from the Bible. On the north wall, the ornate strip begins with the fall from Paradise. Francis studies this opening scene, then moves to the next. The first labor, the killing of Abel by Cain, the punishment of Cain, Noah's commission and the Ark—each of these scenes draws Francis's undivided attention. The story line continues on the northeast, east, southeast, south, southwest, west, and northwest walls. From the Bible's opening book of Genesis to the ending book of Revelation, various scenes meticulously carved into the stone banding are displayed.

One vignette halts Francis's exploring. Even after taking in the entire eight walls of the strip, he returns to the scene on the south wall. On this wall, Joseph from the Old Testament is depicted as the ruler in Egypt. The picture of the eleven Jewish brothers and their parents, on their knees and bowing toward Joseph, inspires Francis. He considers the story of Joseph in Egypt. *The story has never failed to comfort, even excite. God's rich provisions available to all –to me. Nothing is impossible with God.* Francis relishes the inspirations.

Tapping Francis on the shoulder, James motions for the young man to follow. It is time to leave.

Back at the little room attached to the Hunt residence, the chapped lips of James and Francis welcome a cup of hot tea. As the men sip, they stretch forward from their reclined positions, inching their stocking-covered feet closer to the inglenook fireplace. The occasional spark and pop from a random piece of green hardwood keeps the men from dozing off. The warming flames not only aid the drying process of their shoes and socks, which never seem to stay dry, but also offer a pleasing aroma that masks the ubiquitous smell of horse and body odor.

Thinking deeply, Francis inquires,

"James, today when Jasper rode off . . . may I ask what transpired?"

James lowers his cup of tea. Staring into the leaping flames, he responds,

"We shall meet this crossing once again. We depart for Portsmouth on the morrow. The road will take us to Winchester, Jasper's hometown."

Francis drops his eyes, uncomfortable with the revelation. James continues,

"Additional preachers do not a circuit make."

Francis ponders the statement, puzzled. He too lowers his cup of tea. Setting it on the floor alongside his chair, Francis stretches his arms and legs. Retrieving the cup, he takes a sip, the steaming liquid satisfying his yearning for warmth on this cold October evening. Scraping his teeth over his bottom lip—not with anxiety as usual, but with an inquisitive look—he replies,

"An itinerant travels, as do preachers. Preachers are itinerants. You've lost me, James."

"An itinerant travels, period. Wesley is convinced that the success of Methodism is linked to itinerants, traveling preachers who seldom spend more than two nights in one place. Remember this well, Francis: when preachers locate, they open themselves to many a risk. And that risk usually takes the form of comfort."

"But if a circuit is large enough to require aid . . ."

Realizing that Francis is not understanding the implications, James elaborates.

"Francis, our circuit is large, as are most of Wesley's circuits. The size of the circuit ensures a busy itinerant. Wesley desires four hundred miles in four weeks, minimum. Jasper yearns to be a preacher on the Isle of Wight. With barely enough round for three days of preaching, what shall that preacher become after six months on a circuit that he can accomplish in three days? He shall become one who requires more and more comfort. Four hundred miles prevents us from becoming milksops."[151]

---

[151] A milksop is one who is ineffective.

The loud pop of the slightly wet piece of oak places an audible exclamation mark on James's point. Francis smiles at the impeccable timing of the wood. Even with the sudden and random interruptions coming from the fireplace, it is far from the reason that he hasn't fallen asleep for the evening. Francis's inspiring day of history keeps him from nodding off. Wanting to focus some of this jubilation, he decides to address something he has neglected. His excitement moves him to pen a letter to his parents.

Borrowing a quill from Richard and a cherished piece of handmade rag-paper from the table next to his bed, Francis pauses to write. The parchment is an off-white color, spotted occasionally with a darker color—more than likely from a piece of blue or black fabric that contributed to the parchment's manufacture. Francis begins:

My dearly beloved in the Lord and also Parents Dear:

Being moved from the place I was in, I think it my duty to let you know, and I hope you will not repine or be uneasy. I am now in health and strength and very well contented, settled upon my good behavior in Wiltshire. There are two preachers of us in the round. We have many places and in general a loving, good-natured people, so I see nothing to complain of; there is no want of anything, for our bread and water are sure, only there is a great want in me of wisdom and grace for the work; but I hope my God will supply all my wants. We shall spend our Sundays at Portsmouth and Salisbury; there we have two large congregations and very large and good preaching houses. I had no choice this year, and now I think I am as well settled as I could desire. As to temporals, that is the least of my cares. If my heart is upright, I shall not want them, I am sure.

Francis raises the quill. *Mother.* His thought prompts him to address his mother directly. He debates over the approach. He loves his mother; however, he senses an urgency. He writes:

I hope, my dear Mother, you are more easy. Why will you mourn in such a manner? If you have given me to the Lord let it be a free-will offering; don't grieve for me. I have cause to be thankful that such a poor, ignorant, foolish, unfaithful, unfruitful creature should be called to the work, chosen of man, and I hope and trust, of God; though I have done enough to both to cast me off forever.

Francis leans back in his chair. Setting the quill down, he considers the last section. *More?* He suspects more should be added. Tapping his fingers on the tabletop, he decides, *shall leave as is.* He is confident that his mother will accept his strong urging. Again tapping his hand on the small wooden table, he is distracted by several thoughts. The flurry of reflections easily subsides as he is drawn to one in particular—a dearly beloved one. He continues,

Nancy Brookes, your manner of speaking made me begin to think and wonder. I know very well that it becomes me to be without partiality and if you or any other will convince me of it, I would be ashamed of it, and shake it off as I would the mire of the streets. I don't say but I may be guilty of it, but I do not know wherein and in regard to what passed when I was over at Barr; I can't tell wherein, and it is a pity, but you had told me or would do it. My time was short; I was with all the people but you, I think, and also I was at your house but you were not at home. I could have been as glad of your company as anyone at Barr, and wanted it but could not have it; but my dear heart, I shall think no more of it if you don't, tho' it gave me some little pain. For who is offended, and I burn not? Dear child, I have travailed in birth for you and never sought any more, God is my witness, but His glory and your good. Tho' you have ten thousand instructors in Christ, you have not many fathers, for in Christ I have begotten you to a lively hope. My dear child, I am jealous over you with a godly jealousy, lest as the serpent beguiled Eve, you should be drawn from the simplicity of the Gospel.

Once again, Francis sets down his quill. He looks to James. James has fallen asleep, his feet instinctively drawn to the toasty fire. Francis looks to his own bed. He knows he should gain his rest; tomorrow the men will begin their almost fifty-mile journey to Portsmouth. Francis also realizes that according to James, the road to Portsmouth leads through Winchester—the thought of which brings a harsh realization: he is certain of another encounter with Jasper.

He decides to lay aside the letter; *it shall wait.*

Hark, how all the welkin rings,
Glory to the King of kings;
Peace on earth, and mercy mild,
God and sinners reconciled!

Charles Wesley[152]

The stiff October breeze continues to sway the entry door to the prophet's room attached to the Hunt residence. Inside this room, James and Francis sleep for the night. The gentle creak on the inward motion and the lulling hiss on the return motion, like a slow, soft lullaby, ensure that the men do not notice its ill effects. It's not that one of them has been forgetful; the latch of the door is set. The problem lies in the locking mechanism itself: it is broken at the door jamb, one of a long list of items which Mr. Hunt never seems to have time to complete.

The reason for the door's movement hinges on the movement of a strategically placed chair. Earlier, when James fell asleep in the chair, the piece of furniture kept the door from opening. Unfortunately, seeking the warmth of his bed, James moved from the chair in the middle of the night. As the winds grew stronger during the early morning hours, the chair inched further and further into the room, pushed by the invisible force. Now, two hours after midnight, the door swings more than twelve inches, rushing in the chilling effects of the oncoming winter. If not for the fact that the door jambs are out of plumb, the door would not swing closed again after a strong gust of wind. Regardless of this slight advantage, the temperature inside the cabin is near freezing, causing the sleeping men to instinctively raise their cotton quilt above their chins.

Reaching a hand to rub his nearly frozen exposed cheekbone, Francis shakes with a slight chill, the bodily reaction sparking a conscious thought: *'Tis freezing this morn.* He curls into the fetal position, tightening the quilted wrap around his thin body, but the maneuver fails to warm him. He opens his eyes and moves them in search of his jacket.

The slim offering of moonlight allows the discovery of the coat, but the revelation brings disappointment: the garment resides on the other side of the room. Not wanting to disturb James's sleep, Francis considers his options. There are only two: one, run for it in his night shirt—a somewhat painful option—or two, take the quilt with him on his journey. One problem: the quilt also covers James, as the two men are sharing one large bed. *Perhaps if I gently remove . . .*

---

[152] Charles Wesley hymn "Hark, How All the Welkin Rings," 1739.

Inching his way toward the edge of the bed, Francis is careful not to wake James. The position of the moon and the darkness outside cause him to guess it is near two o'clock; *shall rise in a couple of hours.* James's snoring is steady, *and loud . . .*

Arching his feet to the floor, Francis's legs are slightly exposed. The movement is a difficult one; the wooden edge of the bed is rough from the numerous strings that tie and support the floppy, feather-stuffed mattress; the ties form a tight checkerboard network, secured perpendicular to each other every six inches along the oak stringers. The movement is also a cold one; he shivers from the effects on his exposed legs and reaches to rub them briskly.

He then slowly raises his upper body, watchful that James remains in his deep, snoring sleep.

Turning toward the jacket, Francis once again considers running for it; *too cold.*

He begins his covert mission.

Dragging his arm rearward, he lifts the quilt above James's body and sighs in relief that the effort goes unnoticed. Francis bounces his fingertips under the warm cover, the movement nudging the edge of the quilt closer. Confident that he is at the end of the fabric, he pulls the covering toward himself.

Next, he eases the last portion of James's warm wrap off his legs, careful not to touch his feet. *He possesses the most sensitive feet.* Upon successful completion, he pulls the quilt around himself. With the entire covering wrapping him, Francis stands and turns toward James; with a squinting smile, he offers his best: *Sleep tight.*

The walk to the other side of the room is a comfortable one for Francis. Through the only window, he relishes the sight of the distant gibbous moon as it slowly floats toward the western horizon. The light casts a simple artist's stroke of dim shadows on the hardwood trees that surround . . . *the snoring has stopped.*

"Francis! What of the quilt?"

Francis doesn't flinch at James's exclamation. Focused on his task, he leaps for his jacket. With one hand drawn from the warm, comfortable wrapping, he snatches the coat and stuffs it under his left armpit. A cold draft works its way under the quilt, and Francis shivers, thankful for the warm covering. With one quick returning step, he turns toward his right and, with the skill of a Galilee fisherman, tosses the heavy quilt over the entire bed. The covering lands perfectly over the shivering frame of the elder itinerant.

Fumbling in the glacial air, Francis scrambles to put on his jacket. In less time that it takes James to finish an unexpected yawn, Francis completes his ensemble and climbs back into bed.

James offers,

"Francis, we shall speak of this in the morn . . ."

In the morning, Francis is careful not to apologize. It's not that he lacks care for his preaching companion and friend; it's that, in his mind, it is best to avoid the subject. The event doesn't enter into any of the men's early-morning conversation. Within two hours of rising, James and Francis move on from Salisbury and head northwest toward Old Sarum.

The fading remnant of a Roman road leads directly from the hills on the north side of Salisbury. The point of origin is actually the Salisbury of the last millennium, Old Sarum. The road heads east from there to Winchester. There is a slight bend to the south, as the twenty-nine-mile path rises and falls along the way. The sight of the numerous hills scattered along the route, intersecting in all directions, resembles a view from the helm of a rudderless ship in not-so-calm waters. The scenery is beautiful, affording several fantastic elevated glimpses of the surrounding countryside, including the never-ending supply of sheep farms scattered in many directions.

Sitting atop their horses on this cutting autumn morning, James and Francis estimate that the temperature is barely above freezing. Looking about and catching the strong-handed sway of several large trees on the Hunt property, they are sure of one thing: the gusting winds will not allow the wind-chilled temperatures to rise much. They wrap a protective layer around their necks and chins in hopes of lessening the effects of the slicing weather.

The first mile is a slight uphill ride. The dense forest of the High Wood cradles the ancient road, providing cover from the slashing winds above. The whistling swish of the wind draws Francis's gaze upward. Over the tops of the hardwood trees, the dimpled pewter sky hovers like a demanding parent. The tips of the evergreens sway toward the south; *dreaded northwest wind.* Despite the complaint, Francis is grateful for the non-deciduous sentries and their hearty protection.

As the riders exit the High Wood forest, the cleared hills of a sheep farm roll into view. Despite the accelerating wind that seems to revel in the open hills, it is a beautiful sight. Scattered among the fields, several small strands of trees appear as isolated islands. Within each of these timbered havens, a healthy dose of sprawling plants buffers the base of the tallest trees, which appear as bark-covered soldiers emerging from the thick underbrush. Francis glimpses the late-season fruit of a climbing bush prominent among the undergrowth. The branches, now void of their green leaves and scented white flowers, sport the end-of-season display of the white, clumpish mounds that proliferate along the grooved limbs. The long, thin, silky appendages burst from the branches, each bountifully arrayed with the curly white hairs that give the entire plant a bearded appearance. The sight of the clematis bush, also known as "Old Man's Beard," brings a welcoming smile to Francis's face; the plant is becoming a regular on his itinerant journeys. He ponders the appropriateness of the plant's other common name: *Traveler's Joy.*

The open view of sheep farms, ornamented with the occasional tree strand, helps to take Francis's mind away from the biting cold temperatures. His gaze drifts to a small town and a handful of cottages along the road in the distance. Perceiving Francis's discovery, James responds,

"Bossington Cottages."

Francis gives the obligatory nod.

As they near the miniature town, nine small cottages stand out in the open as they dot both sides of the ancient road. To the south side, a large farm with several outbuildings slopes in several directions, with the scene to the north side much the same.

Riding through the quiet town, Francis yearns to go inside where it is warm. He longs to stop at one of the houses, enjoy a hot cup of tea or a plate of leftovers from the night before. Looking at James, Francis realizes this is not an option. James stares into the distance ahead. The pair continues toward Winchester.

A little more than midway on the five-hour trip, the men on horseback approach a small stream on the north side of their path. Originally part of the Wallop Brook, the waterway slowly flows to the south and joins a larger body of water, the River Test. The men cross the Test over an old wooden bridge. Ahead lies another river crossing and then another, each a part of the forking River Test. At the crystal-clear waters of the chalk stream, James and Francis pause at Horsebridge Road. Nearly one hundred yards off to their left is the Houghton Mill. The three-story brick building with the slate roof stands adjacent to the mill wheel that turns in the waterway. The strong flow of the river matches the strong winds that continue to bully the traveling preachers. The winds leave their mark, chafing the faces of the itinerants. Francis inquires,

"Perhaps a corn mill?"

"Quite sure. The fertile hills grow more than grass for sheep."

Francis forces an amused smile, the short nod of his head upsetting the placement of his neck scarf. He adjusts the garment as the men continue on the ancient trail.

The next hour takes the itinerants through several thickly wooded areas. Francis notices that the trees appear unusually small. He inquires of James,

"Seems the trees have been cut for a purpose?"

"Copse woods—the periodic cutting provides smaller-growth limbs. Excellent for firewood."

"I see."

The beautiful scenery of the Hampshire countryside, its rolling hills, its gentle woods, accompanies the men for the entire trip.

Nearing the edge of the town of Winchester, James and Francis rein in their horses and pause to view the settlement. The city rises upon a hill. To the east, in the continued direction of the Roman road, the Winchester Cathedral rises above the wood and brick residences scattered within the ancient city's walls.

Located along the western bank of the River Itchen, the walled city of Winchester is the medieval capital of England. Within its ancient streets—which continue to match almost identically their original layout during the early Roman period—the ninth-century King Alfred the Great created a safe haven for his wife, Ealhswith, the daughter of the King of Mercia. At the time England was a divided nation, settled by Scandinavian immigrants. Over a period of almost seventy years these Danish Vikings had conquered most of the English coastline, and their success emboldened them to begin their conquest of the inland settlements. By the year 867, the strengthening Vikings had captured the majority of ninth-century England, consisting of Northumbria, East Anglia, and Mercia. The conquering invaders needed to capture only one remaining portion of the English mainland: the southern portion known as Wessex.

Leading the kingdom of Wessex was King Aethelred and his younger brother, the twenty-one-year-old Alfred. In the year 870, the Vikings attacked Wessex. The future of the Anglo-Saxon kingdom fought for its existence through the hands of the brothers. The fighting was fierce. Lives were lost, including that of Alfred's older brother. At the battle of Ashdown in the year 871, the Wessex army soundly defeated the Viking forces, with Alfred himself leading the charge in an uphill defense.

The fighting went on for the next seven years. For a time, Alfred and his mighty men took refuge in an area where he had hunted as a young man, the Somerset tidal marshes. From the counties of Wiltshire and Hampshire, Alfred led his men in raids on the Vikings. In May of 878, Alfred accomplished the ultimate task of defeating the Danish invaders at the famed battle of Edlington.

The reign of King Alfred the Great brought a much-sought-after peace to the island. In his efforts to protect the populace, he built stronghold settlements around the country. Centered from the city of Winchester, these military reinforcement cities, or burghs, ensured that no citizen was ever more than twenty miles from military assistance. King Alfred also established the first navy for the protection of England.

In addition to the protective villages, King Alfred built churches, aiming to reestablish the monasteries and convents at several towns including Winchester. The efforts of the religiously devout man focused on removing the paganism and ignorance—the unwelcomed companions of the Viking invaders—that had long permeated the English country. The religious places became centers where King Alfred encouraged scholars and teachers as well as artisans and craftsmen to bring change among the populace. The estate King Alfred constructed for his wife in Winchester eventually turned into Nunnaminster, a home for Catholic nuns from the tenth to sixteenth centuries.

King Alfred's ability to bring the Viking onslaught to a halt, along with his ecclesiastical and educational efforts toward the populace for the benefit of future generations, ushered in a new focus. The King's efforts opened the door for the eventual unification of Anglo-Saxon England, with his nation-building work originating from Wessex. Because of these accomplishments, King Alfred alone bears the title "the Great."

In the center of Winchester, High Street, the "*decumanus maximus*" or major east-west street, connects the east and west gates of Roman Winchester. The ancient road which runs from the direction of the sunrise to the direction of the sunset bisects the settlement into two portions, north and south. At the time of Francis's arrival, remnants of these stone gateways, though slightly deteriorated, continue to mark the ancient doorways to the city. There are four gates to the city, one at each major point on the compass. From these strategic doorways, the ancient Roman roads depart for the rest of England.

As the itinerants approach the center of town, the Winchester Cathedral dominates the view. Nestled in the midst of a large open field, the tenth-century structure rests on the south side of the Roman road. The church at this location actually dates back to the seventh century, and as with other cathedrals throughout England, it has a rich history. The cathedral started by King Alfred the Great and furthered by his son, Edward, boasts of limestone imported from the island off the southern coast of England, the Isle of Wight. Francis views the building consecrated in the year 1093. Several large additions since that date have enlarged the original structure, all built to the glory of God.

Before reaching the cathedral, the riders encounter a large religious-looking stone structure standing beside the Roman road. Francis estimates the height of the monument; *over forty feet tall.* James offers,

> "The High Cross. Some call it the Butter Cross on account of the trade that used to occur beneath its octagonal steps."

Francis considers the marker; *it clearly defines important figures. The Blessed Mother and some Catholic saints.* James interrupts Francis's thoughts.

> "Turn here."

Directing his horse to the left, James departs the ancient road for a smaller dirt road leading north. The road is Middle Brook Street and is lined with two-story brick and wood-frame houses, each with a tiled roof. The itinerants continue a few yards before turning to the east again. Their right turn puts them onto Silver Hill Road. The Methodist meeting house is ahead on the left.

The meeting house is also the home of Jasper Winscomb, the man who rode away upset from James's insistence that Jasper's request for additional itinerants in the Wiltshire circuit fails to fit with Wesley's plans. Jasper is also the local leader for the Wesleyan movement in Winchester.

Standing at the front door to Jasper's home, Francis is nervous. He doesn't visibly shake on the outside, but inside, his emotions cause him to think that he may. The face of the man who answers the door once again inspires a slight fear in Francis—the disheveled red, almost orange-colored hair that surrounds the small, reddened face; the bushy eyebrows that seem to smother the tiny round eyes—the look gives Jasper a fiery appearance. Francis knows well Jasper's ability to quickly lose his temper. Without any polite veneer, with a quick nod, Jasper offers his greeting.

"Preachers, please do come in."

James and Francis enter the dimly lit room on the bottom floor of the two-story building. The narrow hallway darkens as the front door closes. The methodical sound of Jasper's boots walking on the wood floor guide them forward to a small room at the end of the hallway, which serves as a kitchen. The inglenook fireplace to the left provides a place for cooking. The room also serves as a transition to the stairwell adjacent to the hallway the men passed through. The smattering of light from a window at the rear of the room shows Jasper grasping the handrail of the stairs at the end of the hallway. He makes his way upward and the itinerants follow.

The upper room is the local Wesleyan meeting room. The men arrive upstairs to find a young couple sitting in two of the twelve wooden chairs that line the perimeter walls, enjoying cups of hot tea. Without hesitation, Jasper offers the introductions.

"Pastors Glasbrook and Asbury, these are our guests, Edward and Hillary Ipsley."

Francis considers the man and wife, guessing them to be about five years older than he is. Their presence brings a pleasant thought of Nancy.

Jasper inquires of James,

"Has Wesley sent word?"

James's face reveals his disappointment with the pushy Jasper. He looks to Francis; *surely, this is a teachable moment.* He invites Jasper and Francis,

"Please, take a seat."

The three men sit across the room from the young couple. James offers,

> "Perhaps the young couple should be excused."

> "The young couple will do. James, what of Wesley?"

> "Jasper, at the risk of dissatisfying you, I shall not approach Wesley on the subject."

Across the room, the young man sitting next to his wife leans forward, scowling at the reply. He looks to his wife, Hillary, who gently pats his shoulder. The soothing action causes him to settle back again. Jasper speaks again.

> "James, young Edward would make a fine candidate for the Isle of Wight."

> "A precarious proposition, Jasper. You fail to work within the system. Edward is free to preach on the island if he chooses. But it is the decision of the conference to sanction his efforts under our cause - -
> Or not."

> "Our cause—you sound as the Anglican priests; they squelch the Gospel."

> "Jasper, it is precisely because of the Anglican leadership that Edward's efforts require approval of the conference. Wesley is adamant; the child shall honor the parent!"

James's forceful words at the end of his statement solidify Francis's thought, *Wesley knows best.* He also remembers the other key point of this argument: that Wesley's itinerants must be on the move; there should be no room for complacency. James's words from the last confrontation return: "no circuit where a preacher travels less than four hundred miles in four weeks." The reliving of these words recalls the precious thought Francis had when first he heard them: *Poor Churchy.* The words also recall another thought, though he is uncertain of its origins: "The Wesleyans shall submit to the authority of the Anglican Church structure."

Unexpectedly, Jasper jumps to his feet. He walks over to Edward and proclaims,

> "The Wesleys dictate otherwise."

Not happy with the mocking tone, Francis rises to his feet and blurts toward Jasper,

> "The Wesleys fall short of a dictatorship. You do well to heed their advice."

Spinning from the young couple, Jasper's face ignites with anger. He lunges for the young preacher. Within inches of Francis, Jasper's thick finger points upward toward Francis's reddening face.

> "You do well to respect your elders."

Jasper storms from the room, the solid beech-wood heels of his jack boots pounding the steps toward the first floor.

Francis's bowed head is a revealing gesture. James stands and walks toward his wounded companion.

> "Come, Francis. Our arrangements for the evening are with the man to
> whom you have just brought challenge."

James and Francis's stay in Winchester is a short one. Jasper allows them a simple dinner as well as the night's lodging, but it is clear that the itinerants should be on their way to Portsmouth. The pair leaves promptly at five o'clock, after morning prayers.

The twenty-seven-mile journey from Winchester to Portsmouth once again occurs on an old Roman road, which now also serves as the main coach road. The pathway delineates well, from Winchester southwest to Morested, through the Owlesbury Down to Bishop's Waltham, bending south to Wickham and Fareham. At Fareham, the road turns east as it crosses the Fareham Creek. It then moves further east to Portchester, next to Wymmering, and finally to the tiny settlement of Cosham. At Cosham, James and Francis will turn south to the Portsea Gate; once across the bridge over the Portsmouth Harbor waterway, the pair will find themselves on Portsea Island. From there the ancient road continues south to Portsmouth Common, the location of the Wesleyan meeting house.

Portsmouth is the reason the British navy is the most powerful navy in the world. It is the center of a large undertaking: the massive ships of Great Britain come to life on this island city as it gains from the American colonies the many raw materials needed for the manufacturing of these three-hundred-ton fighting machines. Key among its imports from New England are the white pine trees used for the masts of ships.

Harvesting the mature white pines that grow spectacularly straight in colonies such as Connecticut and Massachusetts requires colonial legislation forbidding the colonists from taking for themselves any trees that exceed twelve inches in diameter—a precarious subject, especially when clearing land for life's necessities like food and housing comes into question. The gathering of this much-needed timber also demands talented crews who can fell these beasts growing to more than one hundred feet in height. The challenge is to avoid splintering the trunks when they crash to the ground. If this extensive effort weren't enough, the final act of moving these large specimens to a river for transport usually requires sixty to seventy oxen to drag them to the waterside. From here, the trees are loaded in specially designed ships constructed to transport the heavy lumber from America to England. The shipments arrive in Portsmouth once a week.

James and Francis enter the island as they cross the Portsea Gate. Heading south, they eventually wind up at Portsmouth Common. From there, it is a short distance to Bishop Street, the home of the Portsmouth lay leader.

The large man who greets James and Francis is William Norman. Contrary to the disheveled look of Jasper Winscomb in Winchester, first impressions of William are the opposite: a large man, as large as the Portsmouth ship-building industry itself; neatly and modestly dressed—simple and clean clothing for a simple and clean lay leader who declined a call to preach when he decided to marry. Three months ago, William took over the lead spot for the Portsmouth Methodists on the heels of a scandalous incident forcing the removal of the previous leader. Several "under-the-table" money exchanges between two Portsmouth merchants uncovered the illegal activities of the previous class and band leader, more than likely connected with a smuggling ring. Though somewhat young in the faith, when approached, William eagerly accepted the elevated position in the large group.

The cordial greeting from William escorts the wearied itinerants into his simple two-story home on Bishop Street. Mrs. Norman invites the men to dinner. James inquires,

"William, may we wash before we sup?"

"You may. Outdoors are facilities. Running water in the shed behind the toilet hut."

Both itinerants make their way outdoors.

Dinner this evening meets every expectation of the tired and hungry preachers. Eager to begin settling themselves for the night, James inquires of the arrangements. William rises from the table and invites the men to follow. In the adjacent room, a stairwell leads to the second floor; the men proceed upstairs.

The men enter the room to the right of the second-level landing. It is a small room, roughly twelve feet square. In the middle is one large bed. Next to the sole window is a small table with chair; on it are a used taper, a quill, and paper. William offers,

"I've heard you are early risers. The table should suffice for morning prayers; there is a quill and paper for writing, if you desire. If privacy is required, please, utilize the kitchen table downstairs."

The itinerants graciously nod their understanding. William departs, and the men get ready for sleep.

The gracious reception of William Norman inspires Francis to finish his letter home. In fact, he's feeling confident that Portsmouth will prove a prosperous stop. The euphoric feelings not only have settled his injured emotions from his encounter with Jasper in Winchester, they also urge him to do some spiritual housecleaning back home.

After the kind invitation from William to utilize his personal writing desk, Francis obliges, taking a seat at the small writing space. Comfortable with the arrangements, James departs for conversation with William downstairs.

Francis sets his saddlebag onto the wood-planked floor. Looking at the desk, he guesses it to be carved by a local carpenter. The edge carvings of the oak top display a small rope-like detail; *beautiful*. Francis's gleeful thought moves him to retrieve the letter he began in Salisbury.

Aiming to check up on several whom he used to lead, he reaches out to many in the West Bromwich society. Although this is a letter to Nancy and his parents, he is confident that his mother will surely pass his thoughts and concerns to each one he yearns to direct toward the Lord. Besides, it's not as though his mother would be unaware of the town's goings-on. He begins,

Sister Smith, you have many trials, one upon the back of another, but you can't trust. Set up your Ebenezer and say hitherto the Lord has helped you, and He will if you look at Him in every trial, and help you to keep your garments always white . . .

Friend Thomas Smith, where are you? Yet out of Christ, host to Christ, shake yourself from the dust; arise and fly to Jesus, the City of Refuge. Make haste, my dear friend, make haste; the avenger of blood is at your heels. Oh, cry earnestly and instantly, "Jesus, thou Son of David, have mercy on me."

To my friend Sheldon: Oh my dear heart, where are you, tossed like a ship upon the ocean, here and there, but no rest. Return to Jesus, weeping aloud to Him, and give a divorce to your sins. He will receive you and comfort you with a sense of His love. See the harbor, make for it notwithstanding it is high. He may put forth His hand as He did to Peter and save you if you reflect on Jesus. You cannot help but love Him, but you may say, my heart is worldly, hard and unfeeling. He shall maybe this moment cast a

> *look, melt it into love, thy love; thy flinty heart shall turn and get it.*
> *To Mother Perkins, do you love Jesus? Do you increase with the increase of God? If so, watch and pray and go home and prosper.*

Francis continues his letter with several other inquiries. He ends, advising all to direct correspondence and communication for him at the chapel house in Salisbury. His closing to his mother is encouraging but firm.

> *I cannot by any means come over till the conference, so you must not desire it, but I hope to see you then. I think if I can go to the Leeds Conference, it will be in my way.*
> > *These from,*
> > *F. Asbury*

Comfortable with the letter, Francis sets down his quill pen and rises to walk outdoors.

Heading out of the Norman residence, Francis walks to the large stone in the front yard. Sitting on the stone brings a fond memory from his time in West Bromwich. The thought focuses on the rock in that town, the rock where he spent many a Saturday night talking with Nancy. Francis misses her company. He silently rejoices that he finished the letter home. *Shall mail in the morn.*

Francis's thought moves to the weather; the strengthening west wind delivers a vapor of moisture. In the midst of this activity, he notices a strange object, moved along as if dancing a few inches off the ground. It is flat, swirling in its motion, to the left and then to the right. Francis rises and jumps to catch the floating object. He misses. Having to try again, he thinks to himself, *this must look odd, as if I am jumping from one spot to another for no apparent reason.* He successfully pins the floating paper under his boot and leans down to retrieve the sullied parchment.

Looking it over, he fails to recognize the writing. The paper is strangely marked. Despite this fact, the unfamiliar symbols and slashes draw his attention. He turns to move inside; *James shall know of its origins.*

Inside the home, James continues to nurse his drink, his legs propped on an oak chair in front of him. His right elbow rests on the kitchen table. Sitting across from him is William. The two appear relaxed, almost jovial, as two merchants celebrating a business transaction. However, this deal is toasted not with ale, but with cups of hot tea.

Rushing into the kitchen fails to interrupt the men, until Francis extends the handwritten document toward James. This action gets his attention. Setting his tea aside on the table, James leans forward and arches his neck to view the paper. With a wide grin, he turns to William. William nods, as if he can read James's mind. James offers to Francis,

> "I suggest you approach Mr. Abraham Wolfe. You shall find him three doors down to the west, on White's Row."[153]
>
> "Mr. Wolfe?"
>
> "Yes, he is a short gentleman, nearly twenty years your senior. An accomplished silversmith and pawnbroker. His congregation meets there once each week."
>
> "Very well."

Francis pauses for a moment. It is clear by his distracted look that he is thinking of something. He raises his eyes toward James and asks,

> "What is a pawnbroker?"
>
> "The pawnbrokers purchase the wage tickets of the sailors required to stay aboard in port. With cash in hand, the sailors then return the cash as they purchase items from the pawnbrokers."
>
> "I see."

Francis immediately departs for White's Row.

White's Row is the next street to the west from Bishop's Street. The short walk is a cold one, the temperatures near freezing. Arriving at the street, Francis makes a left-hand turn to the south. *Three doors down, west side.*

At the front door of the brick residence, Francis removes the strange document from his pocket and takes a quick look. The markings fascinate him. With paper in hand, he knocks on the front door to the home.

The short man who answers the door looks kindly enough. His hair is a little grey on the sides, almost silver, and his easy smile precedes his inquiry,

> "Yes, may I help you?"
>
> "Well, yes. This document—I was instructed that you would know of its origins."
>
> "Let us take a look."

Reaching for the paper, the gentle-mannered man pulls it close. He holds it closer than most, his eyesight apparently failing with age. With a quick nod he offers,

> "The name is Abraham Wolfe. Please do come inside."

---

[153] Eighteenth-century name for Curzon Howe Road.

Francis is thankful for the invitation; the air is biting cold. Moving into the home, he offers,

> "Francis Asbury, Pastor Francis Asbury."
>
> "One of Wesley's, I assume."
>
> "Yes, traveling with Pastor Glasbrook."
>
> "You must tell James hello. He is a most welcome friend in this house."
>
> "I shall."

Abraham escorts Francis into an open space. The room not only serves as the kitchen and dining room of the home, but its oversized depth also allows for a dozen or so additional seats, which line the perimeter walls. Francis surmises, *his class meetings must meet within this room.*

Advising Francis to sit at the kitchen table, Abraham joins the itinerant. Francis eagerly awaits Abraham's interpretation. Sitting across the table from Francis and raising his gaze from the document, Abraham nods his head. He puts one hand to his chin, stroking it with his thumb and forefinger. Clearing his throat and lowering his hand, he begins,

> "The writing is Hebrew, written by myself. An announcement of an upcoming departure for a faraway land."

Francis's enthusiasm is elevated by the discovery that the symbols are Hebrew as well as by the gentleman storyteller's eyes, which swell with excitement at the proclamation of "an upcoming departure for a faraway land." Abraham continues,

> "Our synagogue meets here each Sabbath eve. At the last meeting, I gave this written notice of a ship which shall depart Portsmouth for the American Colonies. The paper gives the name of the ship, its departure date, and its port of arrival: Savannah, Georgia."
>
> "The colonies?"
>
> "Yes, many of our congregation, especially the young, seek greener pastures. I cannot blame them. The opportunities in the colonies are unmatched anywhere. Any young man unafraid of traveling about should consider the option."

Francis doesn't reply. His thoughts dart back and forth. Abraham is a Jew. *He leads not a class, but a synagogue.* Unexpectedly, Francis remembers the young doctor who aided his leg injury on the steps in the West Bromwich meeting house—his tales of the American aborigine. *I like to travel about.* With startling abruptness, his thought moves to the elderly Mrs. Hanson as she lay dying on her bed—the article about the colonies and the aboriginal tribes killing each other. Again a random thought, back to the time when he was laid up with the injured leg—his idea that he did not share with anyone, his thought of going to the colonies. *I did not share this even with dear Nancy.*

Realizing that the young itinerant is lost in thought, Abraham interrupts,

"Thinking of the colonies, are we, Francis?"

No reply, only a blank stare at the wooden floorboards.

Actually, he is. Abraham's words spark the memory of the deceased Mrs. Hanson in West Bromwich. Her words seem clearer now: "God has called you to preach the Gospel. His call will require you to leave the familiar. For some unknown reason, the unfamiliar will bring strife, perhaps pain."

Abraham nods.

"Many do. Correction, many young ones do. Despite the brewing storm in the colonies, you should consider the option if called to do so."

Abraham hands the paper to Francis. The young man receives it, still clearly preoccupied. His thoughts move to Mrs. Hanson's words again: "I urge you to follow that call, even if it were to lead you headfirst into a storm." Abraham continues,

"I could teach Francis Hebrew if he were interested."

Francis nods his acceptance and rises from the table.

"I must depart."

"Please give James my warmest regards."

"I shall."

Turning from the room, Francis fumbles his way to the front door and abruptly exits the residence.

The Jewish community in Portsmouth is an interesting group, clearly the result of the English Civil War one hundred years before and the proclamation by the victorious Oliver Cromwell lifting the four-hundred-year ban on Jewish residents in England. The new arrivals were mostly young men drawn to the busy seaport towns of Dover, Plymouth, Bristol, Liverpool, Hull, Chatham, and Portsmouth. In Portsmouth, the majority of the Jewish settlers reside in Portsea, also known as Portsmouth Common, the same area inhabited by the Methodists. The men are mostly traders and silversmiths, selling their wares to the lower ranks on board the numerous ships of the British Navy. The sailors who are desertion risks cannot go ashore in port, and these are the captive audience the local traders desire. The creative salesmen easily gain permission to board the ships, the result of which is a healthy trading industry. Yes, there are risks for men like Abraham—the occasional sailor who sells his wage ticket at an attractive discount, only to desert the navy and thus void the value of the ticket. However, these instances are rare. Abraham and several other members of the local Portsmouth Jewish synagogue prove honorable businessmen and most welcome onboard the King's ships.

As he walks back to the Norman home, Francis focuses on Abraham's last piece of advice. His words about a brewing storm inspire the memory once again of the deceased Mrs. Hanson. That evening, Francis's thoughts of going to the American colonies will not desist. He falls asleep thinking of the potential move.

The next morning finds Francis and James waking early. This is their day of separation from each other, James to Salisbury and Francis to remain here in Portsmouth. Rising from their time of prayer, James is the first to stand, brushing off his knees. As he takes his first few steps, the joints pop and crack. Francis's knees don't behave in the same manner; his youthful limbs spring to life. As James exits the Norman home, he turns toward Francis.

"I shall miss bunking with you."

The comment brings a tinge of red to Francis's face; he is slightly embarrassed. He responds,

"As well."

"Well, almost."

Climbing atop his horse, James laughs. As horse and rider set off for Salisbury, James offers his parting words,

"I hope you haven't assumed that I have forgotten the quilt incident. Good day, Francis."

Francis smiles sheepishly as he raises his hand and tips his hat toward James. *I felt he had laid it aside by now . . .*

That evening Francis is to attend his first Portsmouth class meeting. William informs him that he should expect the lively Portsmouth society to arrive by seven o'clock. Francis replies,

"Very well, I shall prepare a sermon."

"Very well . . ."

For most of the day, Francis gathers his thoughts. His efforts switch back and forth between Scripture research and prayer. A couple of times during the day, he is tempted to take a break—to visit Mr. Wolfe. Francis earnestly desires to learn Hebrew. He chooses otherwise, however; *must prepare my sermon*. At five o'clock, Mrs. Norman calls William and Francis for dinner.

After dinner, the two men settle in the main room to discuss plans for the class meeting. Francis's excitement to meet the group gives lift to his efforts. This is one of his favorite experiences on the circuit; he loves to meet new people for the first time. It ranks slightly beyond his second-favorite activity on his six-month round: getting to know each member as best he can before departing from his circuit.

With plans set, William escorts Francis two doors down to the Methodist meeting room, known as "The Long Room" by its owner, William Pike. Mr. Pike is the founder of Messrs. Pike, Spicer and Co., brewers in Portsmouth. The establishment is a descendent of several breweries set up by the reigning King Henry VII in the fifteenth century to service the sailors of his growing navy. Mr. Pike is a generous man, friendly to the Wesleyan Methodists. He rents the large building to the Portsmouth society so they can hold their class, band, and worship services. His fascination with individuals who profess that the Gospel has transformed their lives makes him a regular at the love feasts.

William departs for his home, vowing to return shortly. Francis takes a seat at the front of the room, daydreaming of how the Bromwich Heath society could utilize such a grand structure as this. Looking about him, Francis plans to deliver his prepared sermon from the front of the room.

Within minutes, several local families arrive. The familiar scene brings a slight feeling of homesickness to the young itinerant. These feelings slowly fade with each new introduction; he brushes off the saddened emotion, eager to jump into the evening's proceedings.

Introducing himself to a young couple, Francis stops mid-sentence as he catches sight of William entering the meeting. The big man has decided to change his clothing. In fact, his outfit rivals anything Francis has seen in the richer set. William is dressed in a brown silk banyan, the kimono-type garment reflecting the shimmering candlelight throughout the room. Astonished at the man's high style, Francis takes in the entire impeccably matched ensemble. A white linen shirt with black waistcoat and breeches complete the well-fitted outfit. Francis has nothing to say, or think. He stares with mouth agape.

Moving to the front of the room, William announces to all in attendance,

"Welcome. Please have a seat. We shall begin immediately. Francis, shall you open with prayer?"

"I shall."

Standing next to William, Francis raises his hands toward heaven and begins,

"Heavenly Father, Creator of the universe. Our hearts, as well as our lives, are Yours. Examine our thoughts and deeds and purify them with your cleansing waters. Amen."

William Norman steps forward and begins to speak. For the next twenty minutes, he offers a sermon. The gathering quietly listens as the well-dressed orator struts about the room. Several times he lowers his gaze toward a sitting listener. His voice is booming, at times bordering on an uncomfortable level. Never once does his pacing reach Francis, but conveniently turns in the other direction when approaching Francis's position in the room.

At sermon's end, William raises his hands and prays. His short, direct prayer ends and he dismisses all for the night. Francis stands in amazement, shocked, hurt, and somewhat angry at William's behavior. The people depart. Before Francis can confront him, William departs for his home. Francis remains alone, thinking to himself, *this is most odd*. Realizing that he will spend the entire next day alone with William, Francis doubts it shall remain an enjoyable experience.

It doesn't. By the end of the second day, Francis's feeling is as clear as Wesley's words: "A preacher shall not remain more than two days." Francis departs Portsmouth, shocked at his treatment at the hands of William Norman.

The next two months find Francis alternating between the towns of Portsmouth and Salisbury. In Salisbury, the society that meets at the Hunt residence is receptive to the young itinerant. They are a patient group, always encouraging Francis in his efforts. More satisfying for Francis are the meetings in the Salisbury chapel, the New Room on St. Edmund's Church Street. The crowds are large and friendly, clearly a reflection of Barbara and Richard Hunt.

In Portsmouth, the experience is the opposite. For the last three meetings, William has not allowed Francis to preach—in fact, he limits the young itinerant's work in the class meetings to opening and closing prayers. A few of the local members have slowly built a relationship with Francis, but the majority have held back in fear of the dominating William. Francis is patient, not wanting to incite William as he did Jasper in Winchester. However, his patience is flirting with the thought of a quick departure.

In Winchester, Francis makes the home of Jasper a regular stop in his transition between Portsmouth and Salisbury, but the stays there are awkward. Mrs. Winscomb is accommodating enough, but Jasper remains distant and cold. Whenever Francis arrives to find both his hosts present, Jasper conveniently finds something to do outside. Other than their small talk during dinner, the two men have said little of substance to each other for almost two months. Francis is determined for this to change, but is unable to discover a workable solution. In his room in the mornings and evenings, he resorts to prayer. Thankfully for Francis, Jasper seems to travel often. When Francis approaches Mrs. Winscomb regarding Jasper's strange disappearances, all she can offer is that he is "traveling about, spreading the Gospel."

Adding to the abandonment by Jasper, during one night's sermon when the fiery preacher is out of town, Francis finds himself surrounded by a noisy rabble. The crowd that shows up at the Winscomb residence is clearly unfriendly to the Methodist cause. As Francis begins to preach, one member of the crowd, a sinister-looking man, stands with pockets bulging. He stands next to several men of equally sinister appearance, about ten feet from Francis. Throughout the sermon, the mean-looking man continually points his finger at the young preacher.

Alarmed by this activity, Francis finally inquires as to the man's intentions.

"What have you to do with me?"

Without flinching, the man replies,

"I have filled my pockets with rotten eggs, to throw at you."

Before the man can reach into his pockets, a local boy about ten years of age runs up to the man and smashes every egg in his trousers. The sulfuric smell that smothers the room is far from sweet. Francis wisely dismisses the gathering, but only after quickly pressing the first three stanzas of a Charles Wesley hymn onto the handkerchief-waving congregation.

In Portsmouth, William's antics have become the least of Francis's troubles. The little society is growing. In fact, under the direction of William, the group is desirous of purchasing The Long Room on Bishop Street. What is surfacing is less the need for ownership and more the need of fulfilling William's prideful desire. William's delusions of grandeur bring emotional distress to the young itinerant as well as to the Portsmouth faithful.

Approaching The Long Room on horseback, Francis's thoughts are fixated upon a cyclonic array of emotions. He is not looking forward to an encounter with William. His journey from Winchester was long and cold. The egg incident in Jasper's home raises memories of Francis's persecutions in Staffordshire's low round: the knocking from a table in Worcester, the near drowning in the town's "baptism" outside Gloucester. In addition, while lying in bed the night after the crushing incident at Jasper's home, the nervous trembling of his body returned. This was unexpected. Not since the verbal and physical harassments of his schoolteacher—aside from that one time after the persecution at his friend Edward Hand's home—has he experienced these anxiety attacks. He presses on, silently asking God for help.

Inside the new location, Francis's emotions lessen as he admires the structure. The room is large enough to handle one hundred people. In addition, its high ceilings invite future improvements, such as a loft. Francis continues to marvel at the facility. The closing of the door at the rear of the space informs him that someone has arrived. The new arrival is William, who is accompanied by several townspeople, members of the Portsmouth Wesleyan society.

William notices Francis, but he chooses to ignore the young man. He begins directing several of his companions to set up chairs and tables for a love feast. Francis watches the proceedings. As the members labor to accomplish William's desires, William departs through the rear door. His departure prompts Francis to inquire with one of the locals, an elderly gentleman whom he recognizes.

"Shall William return?"

"He shall, but not until this evening."

Francis is thankful for the reprieve. He walks from the man and takes a seat in one of the two dozen chairs placed around the room. Before he can raise his leg to cross them, the elderly man, joined by two older women, approaches Francis.

"Pastor Asbury. You must confront William. You are the circuit's man—designated by Wesley. We long to hear you preach."

Francis is shocked. He never expected the Portsmouth members to want anything besides William's preaching. The older man continues,

"We long for leadership, but not at so high a cost. You must confront William. His actions border on despotism."

Again, Francis is shocked. He failed to recognize the deep feelings of the members. One of the women urges,

"Pastor Asbury, your flock is asking for help."

"Yes. I see."

That evening, nearly thirty-five people gather for a class meeting. The members inform Francis that afterwards a love feast for fifteen members will take place. Francis is thankful for the notification, but unfortunately, he doesn't see much chance to confront William.

As the evening's class meeting progresses, as usual, William is in complete control. His mannerisms begin to plague Francis. Especially troublesome is the way he completely ignores the young preacher, even when Francis asks simple questions. He comes across as too busy to pay attention to minor matters, let alone consider a conversation about the preaching issue. The only time William responds to Francis is when he needs the young man to do something—and with that comes several monotonous and controlling details of how it is to be accomplished. The man continuously, through both his words and his actions, belittles Francis's abilities. *Tonight it shall end.* Francis is surprised by his sudden thought.

The first woman to share during the class meeting rises from her seat. Francis knows her; she has shared at the past three class meetings he has attended in Portsmouth. She is a small woman, soft-spoken, always accompanied by her husband. Tonight he is not in attendance. Uncharacteristically, she rises and steps toward William. Standing in front of the man, she offers,

"William Norman, your actions are despotic."

With that, she returns to her seat. William says nothing. He remains seated, his chin firmly held high.

The next woman in line rises, walks to William, and repeats the line.

"William Norman, your actions are despotic."

Before she can return to her seat, William rises from his chair. With a proud and haughty stance, he peers at his congregation. Bringing his arrogant survey to a halt, he struts toward Francis. Standing in front of the seated itinerant, William inquires,

"How old are you?"

Francis fails to respond. He senses his nervous trembling. Catching himself mid-breath, he rises from the chair, noticing he is still shorter than the domineering William. William asks the question once again.

"How old are you?"

Francis remains silent. William turns toward the gathering and demands,

"Am I not due respect?"

One older woman in the group steps forward, her intentions clearly far from noble. Her husband pulls her back. From the other side of the room, another woman blurts out,

"You treat your flock as below you."

Several more women step forward and surround William. Francis finds it odd, not that the women are confronting their lay leader, but that their husbands remain quiet. Most of the men, even the two who accompany the women who have spoken aloud, continue to sit, arms folded, silent. Francis also realizes this is something the elder preachers have not prepared him to handle. He wants to confront William, but he also does not want to risk what happened with Jasper.

Francis walks toward William and offers,

"William, does not the Scripture offer those who fail to amend, to acquire a few in the church for help?"

One of the town's women restrains the older lady whose husband had earlier stopped her, catching the elder woman's arm as she swings it to strike the back of William's head. William turns away from Francis and the group. Another woman is quick to speak directly to his face,

"The Scripture instructs to know the condition of your flock, not condition your flock for your own."

Her husband rises and pulls her away from William.

Finally, Francis summons the ability to approach the subject. He calls out,

"William, what of these claims?"

The young man's voice is precisely what William needs to spin him back toward the group. Launching for Francis, clearly set on a verbal battle, his words aim for the young preacher.

"Abandoning your circuit—is it not what you are known for? More precisely, a wanderer, one who refuses to submit."

Francis's confidence diminishes, more than he expects. The nervous trembling in his body turns to a fearful self-deprecation. The heart-splitting persecutions of his past disobedience unsettle him much. He swallows the truth—or at least, the half-truth—hard. Again, William attacks.

"Nearly destroyed your animal—correction, someone else's animal, graciously loaned to you. Care you not for your horse?"

Again, the self-condemning feelings further his emotional bondage. Focusing on his innocent equine companion is too much for this moment. Francis dismisses his thought and remains silent. William again urges,

"Francis . . . ?"

Francis cuts short William's intentions.

"Sir, if you refuse . . ."

William is within inches of Francis.

"Young man, I am not in need of change!"

"Then you can no longer minister."

The gathering spontaneously erupts in cheers. Several offer their verbal and visible approval, shouting "No more William!" and raising their hands in the air. William knows he's beaten. Sneering at the young man before him, he turns for the front door as the verbal attacks of the townspeople continue.

At the front door, William turns and shouts his departing reply.

"Portsmouth shall not decide my fate!"

He storms off, slamming the wooden door behind him.

The departure of William brings a feeling of relief to Francis. He expected more trouble than a departing reply; *perhaps he shall return.* For the rest of the evening, the locals convey their thankfulness to Francis. He too is grateful, focusing on the thought that now the Portsmouth society will prosper even more. For now, Francis is happy to move on. He is to be in Winchester for Christmas. However, the dealings with William have his emotions nearing collapse.

The approaching Christmas celebration is a simple affair in eighteenth-century England. Francis longs to celebrate the occasion in the friendlier Salisbury, but with James on the opposite end of the circuit, the lot falls to the more advantageously located Winchester.

The night before Francis departs Portsmouth, the local society allows him to preach. They are well pleased. They are also thankful for his gentle approach in the class and band meetings, which stands in sharp contrast to their experience with William Norman. Added to this enjoyable experience is the evening spent with Mr. Wolfe, who took some time to give Francis preliminary instruction in Hebrew writing. Having heard of Francis's confrontation of Mr. Norman, Mr. Wolfe was the first to offer Francis a place to stay. Francis kindly refused, knowing that the Wesleyan society in Portsmouth would make other arrangements. The limited teaching of the Hebrew symbols was overwhelming, but Francis is confident, *I shall not remain ignorant of Hebrew forever.* He vows to spend time with Mr. Wolfe on his return trips after Christmas.

The cold December winds escort Francis out of town. In his mind, he is thankful for having dealt with the William Norman situation. At the same time, he is anxious about spending Christmas with the Winscomb family in Winchester. It is his prayer that he and Jasper can repair their relationship.

Arriving at the Winscomb home, Francis is surprised to find that Jasper is not present. His wife calmly offers Francis the usual accommodations. He is once again grateful for the place to stay. She informs Francis that there will be a small gathering for prayer this evening. He nods his head as he makes his way toward his room. He longs to set down his saddlebag and rest, but his rest will have to wait. Dinner is ready and he is hungry.

The evening's prayer service begins right after dinner. Nearly one dozen attend. The faces are familiar, absent of unseemly characters. Mrs. Winscomb takes a seat, surrounded by several of her closest friends. Taking turns around the room, both men and women offer supplications to the Lord. Each of these women is an encouragement to Francis. Over the last two months their numerous offerings of food and clothing have kept the itinerant well-fed and warm. Salted beef, canned fruit, and handmade scarves and socks make up the thoughtful gift list. The men, too, are always willing to give help.

With hands raised, Francis continues praying.

From the back of the room, a glass window shatters.

One of the three glass windows in the home lies shattered throughout the eating area of the room. From that window and from the front door, a mob pushes into the room. The prayerful women scream and their husbands leap to confront the rushing group. One of the intruders barks out,

> "Are you listening to this cast-iron preacher? The whole thing is going to steam."

Another offers his street wisdom,

> "These men are all play-actors, working you as an audience. Seize him!"

The newly arrived men of the mob launch for Francis. The men of the prayer group push back. Francis looks to Mrs. Winscomb; her eyes direct him to exit upstairs. He does so swiftly. As he does, a man with a lead pipe enters the room. He is a large man, nearing six feet tall. His thick hands and wrists seem capable of much damage. He raises the pipe and proclaims,

> "Tonight, I shall have the preacher's liver."

The disorderly group hails his announcement. The big man rambles through the crowd, in search of Francis. The others give notice,

"He's exited upstairs!"

The burly man races up the stairs.

On the second floor, Francis feels compelled to leave the room immediately; he is confident the random thought is God's prompting. Searching the room, he finds the only exit is a window. To the window Francis runs. Pulling away the wooden shutters, he eyes his only option. *Fifteen feet to the ground.* He steps to the sill and pauses, then turns back toward the bed and removes the quilt covering. Balling it up, he clutches the thick material under his arms, in front of his chest.

He leaps.

Landing on the hard ground forces a deep grunt from Francis. The wrapped quilt acts as a pillow to protect his chest, but it is barely an improvement. He rises to his feet, realizing that his lower-back pain from the Gloucester river baptism has returned. He rushes into the Winscomb barn and detaches Churchfield from the stall railings. Quickly collecting his saddle and bridle, he swiftly secures them on the horse. In less than a minute he is riding out of the barn, heading southwest for an adjacent field.

Nearly a mile from the Winscomb home and without other options, Francis brings Churchfield to a halt. He dismounts and listens. The quiet evening doesn't offer much beyond the occasional gusts of a steady northwest wind. The temperature is cold, below freezing. Francis searches for a place to secure his horse.

Tying Churchfield to a clematis bush, he takes the Winscomb quilt, still wrapped in front of his chest, and places it on the ground, securing himself for a cold night outside.

The first thing Francis notices is that the quilt is small. He doesn't understand. He grasped for the bed covering that was over the entire bed at the home. As he retraces his steps, it becomes clear: the piece he snatched was actually in the center of the bed. In reality, the fabric is a crib coverlet, though Francis doesn't realize it fully. He does his best to keep warm. He doesn't want to build a fire; the light of the flames could attract the rowdy townspeople. He decides to nestle up to the bush that secures Churchfield. Doing so reduces the wind's chill factor, which pushes the temperatures even lower.

As he lies on the ground, he remembers there is a quilt secured to the bottom of the horse's saddle. He leaps to his feet. Happy with his discovery, he loosens the saddle and removes the quilt. Leaning to the ground, he places himself on top of the crib coverlet. Once in place, he pulls the large bed quilt over himself. With more secure feelings, Francis falls asleep, watching several stars and planets shimmering above him on this clear, cold night.

The frosty air of Christmas morning coats the hillside where Francis is sleeping. He rises as usual, at four o'clock. As he gathers his thoughts, he looks around the snow-covered landscape. The chill in the air gives him a slight tremble. He locates several small wooden branches and twigs. Although the sun has yet to rise, it is safe; he can build a fire.

Francis crouches next to the small fire. Even Churchfield leans in for comfort. Francis begins his prayer ritual. In silent conversation with the Almighty, he thanks Him for the safe exit from the attacking mob at the Winscomb home. As he proceeds with the usual supplications of continued protection and provision, his thought wanders a little—he's thankful for the quilting that kept him warm through the night. His thoughts refocus and he finishes with reading a chapter from the book of Job.

As the sun rises, Francis raises his eyes from the pages of his Bible. In the distance, he notices an approaching rider. He instinctively reacts with worry, but soon changes his anxious thoughts to prayer. The completion of the prayer coincides with his visual discovery that the figure in the distance is Jasper on horseback. He rises to his feet, willing to greet his elusive friend.

Jasper draws near to Francis, his fiery appearance beaming in the snow-reflected sunlight. He offers,

"A mighty Christmas to you, Francis."

Francis smiles, amused at the irony. Jasper continues,

"Have you spent the night outdoors?"

Francis chuckles. He replies,

"Yes, I have, Jasper. Seems some of the Winchester residents thought it proper to storm your home in an effort to obtain my liver."

Jasper turns his eyes away from Francis. He is silent for a moment, contemplating Francis's predicament and another important issue. He finally offers,

"Come, Francis; we shall check on the wife."

At the Winscomb home, Jasper finds his wife. She is safe, though distraught over the loss of the prized kitchen window. In spite of the loss, she is grateful that Francis is safe. Looking at the home, it is difficult to detect any of the nefarious activities from the night before. Even at the kitchen window, Mrs. Winscomb has covered the opening with a small quilt tucked in between the broken frame and the closed wooden shutters. She turns toward the two men and exclaims,

"It is Christmas; let us rejoice!"

Christmas celebrations in eighteenth-century England continue until the day of Epiphany, January 6. In Anglican households, the celebrations reflect a holy reverence to honor the birth of Jesus, culminating with a festival on the last day. The celebrations occur both in the home and in the church, and much singing accompanies the small gatherings.

The twelve-day Christmas period is preceded by the season of Advent, four weeks of solemn reflection and expectation. The word Advent means "to come." The first day of Advent, November 30, coincides with the feast of St. Andrew, one of Jesus's Apostles. The day also represents the beginning of the Church calendar. During Advent, the faithful spend time fasting, in prayer and reflection, and reading the Bible. The Anglican faithful also include reading from the Book of Common Prayer.

Thankful to enter the warmth of the Winscomb home, Francis draws close to the open fireplace. Jasper advises,

> "Francis, pull up a chair. The wife has lit the Yule. It shall bring forth a glorious warmth."

Francis grasps one of the kitchen chairs and slides it up close to the oversized log aflame in the pit of the firebox. Mrs. Winscomb quickly drapes a quilt around Francis's shivering shoulders. As the covering begins to embrace his body warmth, Jasper offers,

> "Francis, dry clothes would benefit you."

Francis turns toward Jasper and nods in agreement. Jasper departs for the bedroom upstairs. Again Mrs. Winscomb approaches, this time with a steaming cup of tea. As the itinerant clutches the cup, the white-lined ridges of his hands, dried out by the cold, seem to rejoice. Francis draws the cup near his face to gather the rising thermals. He takes a deep breath and then a cautious but celebratory sip.

Jasper enters the room with a message for Francis.

> "Not to worry, Francis—none of the likes of Richard Hunt's trousers."

Francis's strained smile indicates that he is fighting back the urge to spit out his tea and laugh aloud. Jasper drapes several pieces of dry clothing over Francis's shoulder. Successfully getting the drink down, Francis offers,

> "Thank you, Jasper. Shall attend to it shortly. For now, the warming log is my dearest friend."

Jasper pulls up a chair next to Francis.

> "Ah yes, Francis, the glorious glow of the Yule log. The Saxons are truly our predecessors."

The Saxon word for mid-winter was Yule. When they accepted Christianity, they changed the meaning to reflect Jesus's birthday. In honor of this, and to honor Jesus bringing light into the world, the English Christmas tradition of Francis's day is to light a Yule log. There are other traditions, simple acts to honor Christmas; one of these acts known as Boxing Day takes place on the day after Christmas.

Boxing Day is an old Christian tradition. In its early days, the medieval Catholic Church would open up the alms boxes and distribute the monies donated to the local poor. The holy day also coincided with St. Stephen's Day, a solemn time set aside to remember the stoning death of one of Jesus's followers in Jerusalem, Stephen. The eighteenth-century tradition for Boxing Day continues to involve giving away an offering to someone in need.

Rising from his chair, Jasper departs once again for the bedroom upstairs. Francis considers rising to change his clothing, but finds the fire too warm to abandon.

Jasper returns. In his hands he grasps a clay sphere. On the top of the round object is a lid made of the same earthen material. Jasper approaches with the vessel, extends his arms, and offers it to Francis. Francis is reluctant at first to pull his arms from the toasty covering, until he suddenly realizes that Jasper is offering him a gift. As he maneuvers his arms and hands to receive it, Francis catches a rare sight—a beaming smile on the face of Jasper.

> "Go ahead, Francis. Although tomorrow is the traditional day, I wish for you to open it. I would like to offer you a gift."

A blend of several emotions rises in Francis. He is confused; *why a gift? Why a gift from the fiery Jasper? I fail to deserve a gift from Jasper.*

Jasper urges,

> "Come, Francis; we serve a God big enough to make things right. Open it!"

> "Very well."

Francis lifts the lid. Looking inside, he is surprised to find money. He looks to Jasper. He hopes that Jasper cannot see his eyes watering. He wants to rub them dry, but won't, too embarrassed by the emotion. He struggles with the shame of his past actions of confronting Jasper. *I failed to honor my elder.* Francis's extended silence is uncomfortable for Jasper as well. The tangled mass of orange hair bobs earnestly as Jasper offers,

> "When first it was known that you were a victim of the highwayman, the Lord placed it upon my heart to bring aid. Please accept this as that which was taken from you."

> "I shall, Jasper. And please accept my apology for failing to understand your position."

"Oh, Francis—James and Wesley are correct. How long I can live with
that . . . well, time shall bare that tale."

Jasper's hearty laugh brings a smile to Francis's face. He wipes the tear trickling
down his cheek, but only when Jasper rises to depart.

The knock on the door can mean only one thing: James has arrived from
Salisbury to celebrate the holiday with Jasper and Francis. Jasper launches for the
door. With a quick raise of the latch and a sudden swing of the door, the
emblazoned lay leader greets Pastor Glasbrook.

"Well, James, a mighty Christmas to ya'. Come in out of the cold. The
Yule awaits to bring comfort to a toiled master of the Roman roads."

James enters. Strangely, he fails to remove his hat, but gives a polite bow of his
head toward Jasper and his wife. Making his way toward the fire, James pulls up
a chair next to Francis, nodding his hello to the young itinerant.

"Good day, Francis. What have we?"

James points to the clay sphere in Francis's hands. Francis responds,

"The Lord's provision, enough to cover that which was lost."

"Jasper, you are a kind soul - -
When you long for it."

Jasper bursts into a full laugh. He walks up to James, puts his hand on his back,
and responds,

"And James, ye are a determined soul."

"Not as much as Jasper."

The men smile at each other, the kind of smile that acknowledges both their
friendship and their differences.

Reaching forward to draw the warmth of the blaze, James offers,

"Francis, I've word from Great Barr."

Francis quickly looks up.

"Oh?"

"Seems Mother and a special young lady have both expressed their
dissatisfaction with the lack of contact and correspondence of a certain
Staffordshire itinerant."

Looking to his boots, Francis regrets the news. He's thankful he has recently
penned a letter, but regretful that the writing has not occurred more frequently.
James continues,

"Francis, Elizabeth is far from happy. Perhaps Leeds will find you closer
to home. I shall put a word in with . . ."

James pauses, uncomfortable with the words that proceeded from his mouth. He looks to Jasper. Jasper tilts an ear; with eyes wide, bushy eyebrows spiked, and face cocked for a quick response, the lay leader locks his gaze on James. But Jasper cannot wait long; he responds,

"A word with Wesley? Now, is that so difficult, my friend?"

James and Francis look to each other, then to Jasper. The three burst into laughter. James declares,

"Why, you are a persistent fellow!"

Mrs. Winscomb interrupts,

" 'Tis Christmas, gentlemen."

Clearing his throat as he remembers that he is the senior figure on this circuit, James returns to serious conversation.

"On my last round through Winchester, I decided to pay visit to Farnham. Persecutions there run rampant as well."

Jasper interrupts,

"They don't call southern England the Methodist Wilderness for nothing."

James smiles, the weathered creases of his cheeks and forehead revealing one who spends much time outdoors. Looking straight at Jasper, he continues,

"A crazed man came running toward me through the crowd. Upon his arrival, he placed his gun in my face. With language improper to repeat, he vowed he would blow my brains out if I spoke another word. However, I continued, informing him that I was prepared to enter a pleasant eternity. He continued with the rude language, at times pushing the muzzle of the gun as if to place it in my mouth. Other times, he maneuvered the weapon to one of my ears. I pressed on."

Francis's eyes are riveted on James as he proceeds with his confident retelling. Jasper darts his eyes back and forth from James to Francis; he enjoys watching Francis hear of these distressing tales. James continues,

"At the closing hymn, he placed himself behind my stand and fired the rifle. Kablam!"

The exclamation sends Francis to his seat-back. James resumes,

"Shot singed the back of my hair. Here, have a look."

He removes his hat to reveal a bald spot, complete with tender blood blisters. Francis and Jasper shake their heads with disgust. James goes on,

"I quite enjoyed the end of the service. Several of the men worshipers set out to give him a sound beating. They did such a thorough job that reports acknowledge several days in bed for the obnoxious persecutor. I must say, he weathered quite a thumping."

James's wry smile brings laughter to Francis and Jasper.

Setting his hat on the table, James suggests,

"A hymn, shall we?"

The men nod their approval, and Mrs. Winscomb moves in to join the gathering. James begins and the men and Mrs. Winscomb join in,

"Hark, how all the welkin rings, Glory to the King of kings;

Peace on earth, and mercy mild, God and sinners reconciled!

Joyful, all ye nations rise, join the triumph of the skies;

Universal nature say, Christ the Lord is born today!

Christ, by highest Heaven adored, Christ, the everlasting Lord:

Late in time, behold Him come, offspring of a Virgin's womb!

Veiled in flesh the Godhead see, hail the incarnate Deity!

Pleased as man with men to appear, Jesus, our Emmanuel here!"

The men and Jasper's wife enjoy the day's singing. Later in the day, after a filling meal, all retire for the night. In their private room, James informs Francis,

"We really must get you back to Great Barr."

That evening, as Francis lays himself to sleep, the repeating of the Charles Wesley hymn focuses his thoughts on the Lord. Despite the persecutions that he and James have endured, of one thing he is sure: *my storms fail to reside in some distant land; they reside here, in England. Father, empower me to face them as You will.*

***

The man in the black frock coat sits in his saddle atop his horse. Protected from the harsh winds outdoors, he finds warmth and comfort inside a spacious wooden barn. The protecting structure resides in a Welsh village along the sometimes rocky western coastline of the east end of the Bristol Channel. The channel is an extension of the Atlantic Ocean; it continuously drops water into the local bay and eventually into the waterway that climbs to the northwest, into the heart of Wales: the River Taff. Cardiff is the town in South Wales where the itinerant preacher escapes the harsh winds and temperatures of the cold December morning.

The preacher is a good preacher, with a strong voice that many describe as honey-smooth. A successful preacher, he has received from Wesley the assistant's position for the growing circuit in South Wales. A charismatic preacher, his sturdy good looks are enriched by his exceptional height, compelling gestures, and erect frame. A well-accepted preacher, his tender compassion, pleasant demeanor, and earnest efforts draw many to his ministry. Despite the impressive attributes, the tears of the preacher fall on the pommel of his leather saddle. What is it that troubles this blessed man of God, this man who meets with little opposition?

The path this man rides never produces a faith-challenging obstacle. The throngs of people continue to accept and encourage his efforts. In each of the towns, families flock to his side, offering provision and shelter. Nevertheless, the successful preacher struggles with feelings of anxiety and confusion.

This circuit-riding preacher is Joseph Pilmoor. Unlike the life-threatening reactions to the preaching of James Glasbrook and Francis Asbury, Joseph's efforts meet with great acceptance. Joseph is aware of the trials and tribulations that continue to plague the Wesleyan itinerants. He is also aware of the nearly forty years of Methodist persecutions. Joseph's unchallenged ministry is driving him to consider the worst: that he is a stranger to the true spirit of the Gospel—ultimately, a stranger to his Savior.

Joseph is well educated, a graduate of John Wesley's acclaimed Kingswood School in Bristol. The young man skilled in Latin and Hebrew met with similar results during his year on trial and his first year as an itinerant in the smugglers' haven of Cornwall. The coastal town raised no resistance to Joseph. All this strikes the itinerant as odd, even disturbing.

His yearning for inclusion among his brethren drives his saddened emotion. His aim is to gain a strong sense of identity with his fellow preachers—not for personal boasting, but for healing the vacancy of growing up without a father. He longs to belong.

***

The winter of 1769 has been an especially cold season throughout England, but unlike last year, the River Thames has not frozen over. The Londoners express their disappointment at missing a return of the unusual occurrence. The rare occasion of the iced-over waterway has for centuries continued to spawn an impromptu celebration known as the Frost Fair. At the freezing, an entire street of wooden booths is dragged onto the chilled arena. In the festive open market, traders in metals and pottery, makers of toys, and bakers of breads and cakes all set up shop. On one side of the river, men can receive haircuts and a shave; on the other, a fresh-brewed cup of tea or a steaming bowl of potato stew. There are puppet shows, as well as vendors of gloves, scarves, and whalebone skates. Shoppers can purchase food items such as hot chestnuts, sticky gingerbread, baked apples, and pork sandwiches cooked on the open spits dragged onto the frigid platform. Those who arrive only to shop receive a custom-made souvenir memorializing the unique event. "This was bought at the faire kept upon the Midle of ye Thames against ye Temple in the great frost on the 29 of January 1768" was the inscription made on commemorative cards by printers who pulled their printing presses onto the icebound watercourse.

For Francis and Churchfield, the traveling between Salisbury and Portsmouth this winter silently ages them both. In addition to the inclement weather, tempestuous dealings with William Norman and Jasper Winscomb continue to plague the young itinerant. Even Churchfield agitates the situation, stepping on William's right foot in one unfortunate encounter. As for Jasper, despite his occasional kindness to Francis, the wild man's better efforts are clouded by intermittent bursts of anger and loud disagreement. Francis eventually feels comfortable with making a gentle rebuttal of the determined lay leader's opinions. But the overall effect keeps Francis awake most nights as the winter slowly gives way to spring.

As for William, the pompous man eagerly seeks to return to the Portsmouth society. Because of his continued efforts, several of the local members jump in to help Francis, adamantly quelling such attempts. With his direct-approach confrontations of Francis, William threatens his return regardless of the locals' and Francis's opinions to the contrary. Francis faces the issue as directly as William does. However, unlike the thoughtless William, Francis's conscience restrains him, as it does with Jasper.

Nearing the month of May, Francis's spirits are lifted by the sight of James arriving at Winchester, to the home of Jasper, at the same time Francis arrives. The two approach each other from opposite sides of Jasper's property. As they near the Winscomb home, Francis offers greeting.

"James! How delightful it is to see you."

"I'm sorry, Francis; what's that you say?"

James yells his reply. In Francis's eagerness, he is trying to converse with James while he's too far away to hear. Abandoning another attempt at communicating, Francis launches in the direction of his approaching friend. The sight of Francis suddenly dismounting and running with excitement towards James and his horse brings a smile to James's sunburned, wind-chafed face. He responds with a chuckle,

"Not even King George has received such reception."

"James, I have longed to speak with you. I thought you would have taken in Farnham or some distant hamlet as Guildford. So happy to catch you in Winchester."

"I see."

The approaching darkness signals the men to take care of their horses' needs right away. Completing their tasks, they head indoors to enjoy a meal with Jasper and his wife. Jasper inquires,

"James, how fares Salisbury?"

"It is well. The unseasonably warm weather this week has eased the effort. Wesley is delighted that Francis and I are able to supply both Salisbury and Portsmouth. Despite the occasional opposition in some of the surrounding towns, I am well pleased with the results."

Francis finishes a spoonful of dinner and asks,

"James, when shall we depart for the conference in Leeds?"

James halts his spoonful midway to his mouth. Setting the utensil back in his bowl, he grabs his cloth napkin and wipes his face. Clearing his throat and looking straight at Francis, James responds,

"Francis, it is the wish of Wesley that you remain until after the conference."

Francis sets his spoon onto the table. His gloomy expression broadcasts his thought, *I shall not make it home to see Mother - -*

Nor Nancy.

James purses his lips as he struggles with Francis's reaction. He offers,

"If up to me, Francis, I would offer you Great Barr. I yearn for it, as do you. However, Wesley knows best. I shall send word upon completion at Leeds."

"Very well. Can you allow one favor?"

"Anything, Francis."

"Please send Mother my fondest affections."

"I shall."

The spring and early summer months do bring a warmer season for Francis. As welcome as the stunning sight and sweet smell of the bluebell plants that carpet the forest floors as far as the eye can see, transforming the loamy ground into a solid-blue mat indicative of the month of May, the fair weather also escorts fairer treatment for Francis in Winchester and Portsmouth. Jasper, like the weather, softens his edges. And William, like the departing cold weather, discontinues his efforts to pester the Portsmouth faithful and simply vanishes from town.

On August 10, 1769, word from the Leeds conference arrives for Francis in Salisbury. In the chapel on St. Edmund's Church Street, several of the local families surround Francis. One gentleman standing next to his wife offers,

"Francis, we shall miss your preaching. The wife and I have grown fond of your teaching from the Scriptures, and your occasional use of a Hebrew word, as well."

His wife joins in,

"Hessed—the Hebrew word representing kindness and compassion. I shall hold to it because of your efforts, Francis."

Francis looks to the floor, struggling to choke back his emotions. As he raises his eyes to the man and his wife, tears slowly form on his lower eyelids. Another couple comes forward.

> "Francis, Bedfordshire will once again gain the thoughtful work of the young man from Great Barr. With a holy yearning, we wish it not so."

Francis again attempts to look away, but finds that he can't. Another set of tears builds.

From the back of the room, a soft-spoken woman in her seventh decade offers,

> "Dearest Franky, on many nights you have prayed away the fears of an old woman. Fears of going without, fears of death, and fears of change. With this, I am at peace. Your prayers have aided this peace. I thank you."

Francis walks to the elderly woman. She embraces the itinerant. Wanting to hide his emotions, he turns to look away from the others in the room. As he does so, he catches sight of several who stand at the perimeter wall. They, like Francis, shed tears.

At this, Wesley's messenger taps Francis on the shoulder. He urges the itinerant,

> "It is time. We must depart."

Releasing her embrace, the elderly woman grasps Francis's coat sleeve. With a gentle squeeze of his forearm, she winks and smiles. Francis's smile conveys an acknowledgment of a kindred spirit. Also conveyed is that Francis sees in the face of this elder lover of Jesus a glimpse of what someday could be his own mother. He wipes away the moisture running down his cheek and departs.

Outdoors, Wesley's courier advises Francis,

> "Your trip to Bedfordshire shall have a stopover."
>
> "Oh?"

The revelation is not what Francis expects. He voices his wish in his reply.

> "A visit home?"
>
> "Not quite. But a visit to one who cares for you. Wesley offers a stay in Oxfordshire."
>
> "Oxfordshire?"
>
> "Yes, one awaits your arrival."
>
> "Who awaits?"
>
> "Richard. Your friend Richard - -
>
> Whatcoat."

A most pleasant surprise.

Francis nods his head and readies his horse for departure. The messenger offers again,

> "Pastor Glasbrook has planned a route for you. Shall you have need of it?"

> "I shall. Suspect I could make a go of it on my own; however, the map shall bring a confident comfort."

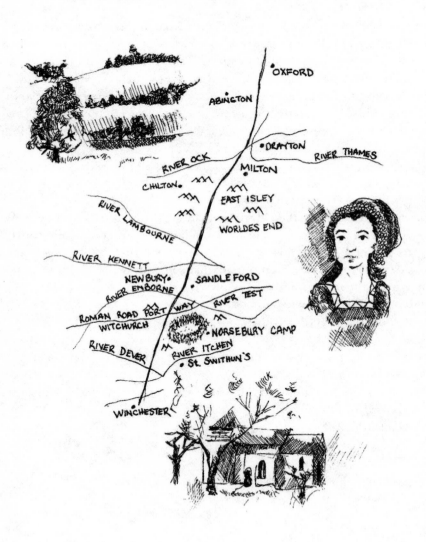

With map in hand, Francis looks over the hand-drawn document. He responds, "Appears clear enough. Peculiar route, yet clear. I shall make way for Oxford. Once I've said my hellos I shall make way for Bedford."

"Francis, in kindness, Wesley offers more than a friendly greeting to Richard; he longs for you to spend the autumn with him. Richard is currently stationed in Oxfordshire, preaching from St. Giles. Wesley wishes you to stay and enjoy the Christmas celebrations. At the first of the year you are to once again return to Bedfordshire."

"Very well. Oxfordshire until Christmas has passed. Please send a word of thanks to Wesley and company. Good day to you."

"Good day to you, Pastor Asbury."

Francis urges Churchfield onward, happy for the opportunity of seeing Richard once more.

Peering at the map, Francis realizes that for the first time in his itinerant career, he will travel mostly on small back roads through scattered towns and hamlets. James begins his map of tiny villages and farms with the town of Headbourn Worthy. James's map notes, "Ancient church dedicated to St. Swithun, Catholic Bishop who mentored King Alfred the Great when he was a child in 9th century." James includes a rough sketch of the building, depicting a simple stone structure. Francis chuckles at James's attempt to sketch the church building. *Very well, St. Swithun's shall mark our way.*

Nearly one mile out of Winchester, Francis views the approaching St. Swithun's. Despite the almost child-like rendering, it is quite as James drew it, a simple structure made of stone. The ancient church is hard to see, flitting in and out of view as it nestles among numerous trees and thicketed woodland. The building is set within a small waterway, the split of the river Itchen, which surrounds the church property on three sides.

Continuing northward, Francis views the tiny dirt road as it meanders ahead. From James's map, he determines that he will travel the next two miles through the civil parish of Barton Stacey and then an additional three miles to the town of Stoke Charity. James notes passing through Waller's Ash and Ash Farm. He has drawn a picture of a windmill on the right side of the pathway. Beyond the second town, he notes, "Cross river north side of Stoke Charity."

The current path undulates slightly, rolling five to fifteen feet in height difference as Francis proceeds to the north. The gentle days of summer have blessed the surrounding hillside; many bushes and trees spread forth their foliage to receive the life-giving beams of the sun. Not much is depicted on this section of map, only a juvenile drawing of a tree. *James, you must obtain better marking skills.*

Before arriving in Stoke Charity, Francis spots the field containing the early eighteenth-century windmill. He also finds a small village with several thatched-roof, one-story houses lining both sides of the rural dirt road. He points Churchfield forward. Passing through town, he arches his neck to gaze onward, looking for James's noted river. He soon spots the waterway ahead. Pulling the map from his coat pocket, he unfolds it to find that the river he is to cross is the River Dever, a tributary of the larger River Test. Only about eight to fifteen feet wide, the waterway supports abundant fish and plant life in spring and summer.

Beyond the little town, Francis approaches a narrow wooden bridge leading over the clear chalk stream. Looking into the waterway, he spots several fish hovering above the river bottom in front of a large bed of starwort plant, where the fish cherish the coolness of the shady location. Besides providing cover from the sun, the native plant of the English waterways acts as an oxygenator, replenishing oxygen to the river. The small, star-shaped masses of green leaves perch themselves atop the gentle flow of the river's surface. From there, several insects buzz and land upon the overlapping leaves that float atop the waterway like an emerald blanket. It is these unsuspecting insects that the river's trout are seeking for food. Francis watches as one fish gently sways its colorful tail, floating itself nearer to the surface. At the waterline, the trout raises his sturdy jaws and slurps down a bug. Francis notes, *quite efficient–like a highwayman.* He pushes back the unhappy thought attempting to steal his joyful appreciation of the fish's unique abilities and presses Churchfield over the bridge.

Francis continues northward, aiming for James's next town of note, Norsebury Camp. At Norsebury, he is to turn to the northwest for Cranbourn Farm. Francis's eyes focus on a strange marking on the map: two concentric circles mark the Norsebury Camp. Along with it, James writes, "Norse Ring. Pre-Roman fortification." From there, James has drawn several lines merging into one another. There is also a caution: "Choose wisely." Francis decides to worry about the convoluted arteries when he arrives at that section of the map. For now, he is intrigued by the Norsebury notation, "Pre-Roman fortification."

Nearing Norsebury Camp, Francis spots a hillside of trees. From a distance, it appears as one large hillside covered in thick woods. Drawing closer, he is surprised to find that the trees that should have filled the entire hump of the hill methodically thin out into two circles surrounding the entire hillside. Like two concentric rows of sentries, poised to stand guard against approaching intruders, the large hardwood trees provide the first line of defense against intruders set to take the hill.

Unknown to Francis, he is standing amidst ancient history. The Norsebury Camp is one of almost fifteen hundred hill forts scattered throughout England and Wales, the majority constructed eight hundred years before the birth of Christ. The natural predecessors of the castle, their use died out by the time of the Roman conquest of England in 200 BC. These hill forts provided a communal approach to civilization, trade, and safety. Within the confines of the fort, meetings of a settlement's leaders took place, as well as trade with surrounding communities. Naturally, the major reason for the fortification was protection against those who would bring harm to the fort's residents. The majority of the hill forts were nothing more than a high spot of land with minor additions of surrounding ditches and timbered fences. Some had walls of stone built around the hilltop. The Norsebury Camp that Francis is viewing utilized the thick forest of trees to create its safety barrier.

Digging into his saddlebag, Francis removes a piece of salted beef, a gift from Jasper's wife. He retrieves the blanket she gave him as well, tossing it on the ground. He dismounts and sits to enjoy his midday snack. As he eats, he thinks of the Norsebury Camp. *Pure genius.* He looks at the orderly layout, trying to envision a life that required such means of safety. *Blessed to be alive in this day.*

From Norsebury, Francis and Churchfield proceed to the northwest, toward Cranbourn. On the map, James details the route. It is a confusing reproduction; somehow, Francis must decipher the scribbled ramblings. From what he can determine, he should travel nearly two miles and turn to the north. The dirt road should eventually run into the town of Tufton, five miles north of where he is now. Slightly confused, he proceeds.

Within fifteen minutes, Francis is at the point on the map where three roads emerge from one. He turns to the right, heading north. The surrounding forest is thin, not overly dense. He can see a considerable distance through the numerous trees that filter the sunlight as it hits the ground. The scene is a familiar one, reminding him of the surrounding forested valley in West Bromwich. His childhood memories bring a smile to his face, a smile that conveys confidence. Several hundred yards up the north road, the path turns almost 140 degrees to the left. In fact, Francis is now heading in a southwesterly direction. *Strange . . .* Despite his silent questioning, he continues on this road.

Approximately four hundred yards in the southwestern direction, the road turns left again. Francis's confidence departs. Before long, he is at the intersection of the multiple roads which he left nearly forty-five minutes ago. Rubbing the back of his head, he removes the map from his coat pocket once again. Looking it over, he cannot determine why the road looped back. Analyzing James's drawing, he figures that the looped road is two of the three paths that James has drawn. He decides to take the remaining road.

The third option, the road Francis is now traveling, departs in a northwesterly direction. Francis is feeling slightly better about the choice. *James marked only three paths. This path must be correct.*

After thirty minutes of riding, the pathway stops. Francis and Churchfield stare into a thick forest. No road nor path, not even a walkway, exists from here. *This proves most difficult . . .*

Francis talks to his horse.

"Churchy, we shall turn around. Let us make way for our starting position."

Churchy nods and snorts as if he understands.

Retracing his last thirty minutes of riding, Francis grows frustrated with the development. He is not happy to waste time. By nature much like a John Wesley or a George Whitefield who strive to make every moment count, Francis focuses on the lost time. *James, you must learn to draw. I've traveled as you prescribe; why do you fail to depict accurately?* The ruminating thoughts deepen his impatience with the situation.

Francis pulls out the map once more. He is certain that he has now taken all three paths. At their original starting point, Francis turns Churchfield around. He places his horse at the exact spot he calculates to represent the infamous intersection on the hand-drawn map. He removes his hat to rub the top of his head. He scratches his head, trying to envision James's intentions. *All that remains is the path in the middle—the one I am sure that I returned upon.* Placing his hat on Churchfield's head, he offers to the horse,

"What do you think, Churchy? Perhaps you shall make a wiser choice?"

The horse taps his right hoof and moves forward. Francis laughs aloud.

"Very well! Proceed, my four-legged friend."

The horse chooses the path on which they originally returned. He continues to the point where the path turns back to the south, then stops, turning himself slightly to the northeast. He taps his right hoof once again. Francis responds,

"Well?"

The horse doesn't respond; he stares forward.

The parenthetical silence focuses Francis's attention.

He searches for a solution, looking in front of his horse, over his hat perched upon the perky ears of the animal.

For a moment Francis thinks to himself, *the itinerancy has driven me mad. I'm listening to a horse.* The completion of the thought arrives at the same time as Francis's discovery.

Nearly ten feet in front of Churchfield is a footpath, an overgrown walkway hiding within the leaves and branches of numerous bushes and trees. Francis missed the path on the first go-around. The clear demarcation indicates that it continues with a purpose. Francis nods his approval.

"Yes, Churchy, I believe you have discovered the missing path—a footpath."

Churchfield snorts and bobbles his head, as if to say, "I told you it was a footpath." Francis prompts the horse forward. The crunching sound of branches and leaves breaks the silence. After nearly ten minutes, the path opens up into a dirt road that continues in the northwesterly direction. Francis retrieves his hat from Churchfield's head and smiles, the kind of smile one gives when realizing his horse knew better than he did.

For the next five miles, Francis and Churchfield travel through the Cranbourn Wood, a beautiful chase of forested hills. The landscape eventually opens to broad, rolling hills, many of which serve as corn and wheat farmland. Francis considers the expansive view; *magnificent*. Before long, the welcoming sound of a flowing river and the pleasant sight of a small village greet the pair. Francis pauses at the river, happy to dismount and enjoy a drink with his companion. Before doing so, he pulls the map from his pocket and announces his discovery.

"The River Test. From here, we follow northeast to Whitchurch. Seems James has procured a place for us for the evening in Whitchurch."

Francis peers at the name written by James. It is hard to make out at first, but then Francis believes he has it.

"Elizabeth and Joseph Web. Elizabeth and Joseph?"

Francis lowers the map; without notice, he releases a short cry. The burst originates from deep inside. He pauses to take a deep breath. *This is most unexpected . . .*

After several silent moments, he gathers his thoughts about the incident. He dismounts and heads for the riverbank. Kneeling by the waterway, he reflects, *never expected such a reaction.* Yes, the couple have the same names as his parents. And yes, he hasn't seen his parents in more than two years. *Why the sudden sadness? I miss them; indeed I do. Perhaps in Great Barr something dreadful has occurred. Oh, that they are well . . .*

The riverside path from Tufton to Whitchurch is slightly less than one mile long. Francis is thankful that his day's journey is nearing its end. He longs to sit—in a chair. He longs to eat and he longs to rest for the evening. Climbing atop Churchfield, he and the horse set out for the Web residence.

At the home of Joseph and Elizabeth Web, Francis finds a couple who are nearly the same age as his parents. Like his mother and father, they are a family of simple means. No luxury items reside in their home. The Wesleyan faith is their style of worship. Joseph is willing to submit to the Anglican system, while Elizabeth has her doubts.

Joseph is a local baker. He adds to his income as a coal merchant, representing several miners who sell the raw material to jobbers. His efforts provide for a sturdy home and a small corn and vegetable farm for distribution to family members residing in Whitchurch. Joseph and Elizabeth are close friends with another Wesleyan family, William and Mary Butler. William is a local corn and flour merchant, and in the years that Joseph decides to grow more corn than is needed by his family, he sells Joseph's corn for him. Joseph has a brother, Caleb Web. Caleb resides in Whitchurch where he works as a grocer, tea dealer, and provision merchant.

The dinner table set for Francis holds a generous offering of neck of lamb and tarts. There is also a roasted rabbit stew. The simple family eats well. At the dinner table, Joseph engages Francis in conversation.

"Well, Francis, how long until you return to Great Barr? Seems a long time to be wandering about from family."

"Agreed. I long to see Mother and Father. And I long to see my companions. I shall spend the next year in Oxfordshire and Bedfordshire. Perhaps Wesley shall allow a circuit closer to my West Midland home. For now, I labor at the Lord's work, surprised that He would use one as lowly as I."

"You mustn't rate yourself too low. Wesley's itinerants, though simple in the beginning, do not remain that way for long. Are you reading well?"

"The few books I possess. Correction, used to possess."

Francis sets down his fork. His vacant look prompts Elizabeth to offer,

"Francis, Joseph and I possess many books. It would bring great pleasure to give you your choice of them."

Francis purses his lips. He can feel his cheeks cramping from the restraining of his emotions. He longs to complain over the loss. He longs to scream in anger at the thief. He longs to allow tears to well up at the kind gesture. Instead, he responds,

"A cherished gift of Bunyan's *Pilgrim's Progress* fell victim to the highwayman."

Elizabeth places her hand on top of Francis's, which lies flat on the tabletop.

"Very well, then. A copy of Bunyan's *Progress* shall depart with you on the morrow."

After dinner, Joseph proudly escorts Francis into a room adjacent to the kitchen. The descending light of the sun, yet to set nearing nine o'clock, sneaks through a window. Francis thinks of the many late summer nights he spent outdoors with his father, checking the garden, securing the tools for the night; he longs for home. His thoughts are soon distracted by the informal library in this room. On several oak shelves reside nearly two hundred books, leaning on each other and on several iron bookends. Francis draws closer to the iron bookends, remarking,

"Clever idea."

Joseph responds,

"Made them myself."

"You've a furnace?"

"A small one—nails, shoes for the horse. I enjoy the process."

"As do I."

Joseph turns his head in surprise. He responds,

"An ironworking preacher?"

"I suppose."

The two smile at their common experience. Looking at the books, Francis spots one he would love to own. He motions toward the work.

"May I?"

Joseph reaches for the volume and hands it to Francis.

"Consider it yours to keep."

Francis thumbs through the large pages. Measuring fifteen by twenty-two inches, the large book contains nearly five hundred pages. Francis responds to the kind gesture,

"I've only recently appreciated the writing. A gentle man in Portsmouth.
His efforts birthed my knowledge of Hebrew."

"Take it; it now belongs to you."

Francis is uncertain why Joseph and Elizabeth own a copy of a Hebrew Bible. The ambiguity doesn't matter; he is thankful to obtain the book. That night as he lies in bed, he arches his neck off his pillow as he reads, in search of Hebrew symbols and words he understands.

Early the next morning, as the sun rises above the horizon before five o'clock, Elizabeth approaches Francis as he sits atop Churchfield; she has gifts for the itinerant. She blesses Francis with additional blankets. She also gives him three colored handkerchiefs, a night cap (Francis almost laughs aloud on receiving this, but wisely holds back), three pairs of stockings, and a white flannel shirt. Francis's gratitude encourages the childless couple. After checking James's map one more time, he is on his way northward, bound for Oxfordshire.

From Whitchurch, Francis travels the dirt road leading due north toward Litchfield. The three-mile journey passes through the tiny village of Cold Henly, the Cold Henly Farm, and the Bradley Woods. Nearing the two-mile mark, Francis crosses over the Roman Way or Port Way, the ancient road from Salisbury to Silchester. He must continue north another mile to reach Litchfield.

The fields outside Litchfield are abundant with wheat, barley, and oats. The beautiful amber waves roll with the cresting hills. Other than a handful of houses, the main structure is a small twelfth-century church building. Francis pauses to admire the tile roof of the flint-and-stone church. The simple cornerstones accent the cobblestoned look of the main walls. The enduring one-story structure moves him to silent prayer. He prays for his parents, wondering if they are faring well.

Moving on, Francis continues toward the north. On the map, James notes a heavily wooded area and a four-way intersection, where Francis is to turn toward the northeast. Upon the discovery of the four roads that meet, Francis prays silently, *oh, that James's rendering is correct.*

At the intersection, Francis trusts in James's rendering and heads for the town of Burrowclere.[154] Less than one-half mile beyond the intersection, Francis finds the twelfth-century All Saints Church. At this monument, James notes to take a turn toward the north. Francis does so.

The next marker on James's map indicates that Francis will travel slightly more than three miles to Well Street. It is barely a town, with less than a dozen houses scattered in several directions. The remote area affords several opportunities to view deer as they wander through the sloping landscape. Francis pauses as a pair of the long-legged creatures dip to enjoy the dry, fertile moss growing on the sandy forest floor. Churchfield snorts and the animals raise their heads, turning their ears slightly to capture the origin of the sound. The horse repeats his snorting and the deer are off, running toward the northeast for cover. Pushing his horse forward, Francis resumes the journey. Within a few minutes, the pair arrives in Well Street. They take in the limited view and continue northward for Newton.

The hilly woodlands Francis travels are bursting with rich undergrowth. The coveted violet-blue flowers of the bluebell spires common in the month of May have long departed. However, the green ground cover of the cherished plant remains, continuing to cover every available inch of forest floor. Francis longs for the attractive flowers of the fairer season. The memory of the colorful blooms sparks a thought of Nancy. Francis longs to spend a day with her, strolling amongst the bluebells. *Lord willing, next spring.*

---

[154] Eighteenth-century spelling for the town of Burghclere.

Arriving in the small woodland town of Newtown Common, Francis finds the rise to the hillcrest ceasing as the road begins its descent to the north. As he peers down the narrow dirt-covered artery, the view through the silver birch trees reveals the southern bank of the River Enborne. The eastward-flowing waterway moves slowly as it crosses his path from left to right. He gently nudges Churchfield forward. They both welcome the sight of the clear stream; another water break awaits the weary pair.

Several handfuls of the chilly water splashed across his face invigorate the itinerant. He dips his cupped hands again, this time raising the life-giving liquid to his mouth. The sound of his swallow dominates the quiet setting. Churchfield lowers his head for a generous helping, his thick, pink tongue ladling more than a handful to his mouth.

Turning his eyes to the east, Francis looks along the grassy banks of the narrow river. Its twisting path is bordered by the tall, green wisps of ornamental grasses. Mixed among the reeds, which easily reach the height of his stomach, several layers of late-season flowers perch atop their tall, thin scaffolds. The brilliant pink color of the red campion plants has replaced the blue and purple haze of the bluebells. The attractive plants with the cosmos-like flowers sway gently about, easily appeasing the more persistent winds. Francis focuses more closely, catching sight of several butterflies and bees as they draw nectar from the flamingo-like blooms. Also spotted are the spent flowers of the wild garlic plant; no longer does the thick white blanket of scented blooms cover the river's banks. The late-summer sun encourages the silver birch trees to push up their dense foliage, eliminating the partial sunlight that brings forth the prolific displays of plants like the bluebells and wild garlic; the fruitful light no longer reaches the forest floor.

Looking up from the waterway, Francis finds a most attractive sight. In a nearby clearing, as the birch trees thin out, a large area of rambling heather proudly displays its bold purple-blue color. The tufted blooms billow about, completely covering the field toward the north. *Marvelous!* Francis's thought inspires him to collect Churchfield and continue across the river.

Francis swings into the saddle and urges Churchfield forward. Wading across the shallow portion of the river is an easy task, as the water barely reaches two feet in depth. Within moments the pair is on the northern bank of the Enborne, no longer in Hampshire, but now in Berkshire.

Proceeding north along the path into the arable woodland, Francis draws James's map from his pocket. The detail shows a small town, Sandleford.[155] It also depicts another of James's "renderings," a structure labeled, "house and chapel, call upon the Queen of the Bluestockings." *James, whatever do you reveal?* Francis is slightly confused. He has no problem with the house and chapel, but the queen reference is a complete mystery. Shaking his head, he neatly refolds the map and places it back in his pocket.

Scaling the northern slope of the Enborne Valley, Francis ponders James's odd notation. *Bluestockings? Perhaps an indication of blue worsted stockings, in lieu of black silk stockings?* Francis's thought is that black silk stockings are usually associated with formal attire, while the blue woolly stockings reflect a more subdued approach to clothing. The blue worsted stockings worn in public are associated with the less formal, everyday attire worn by everyday, hardworking people. He presses on, and the Sandleford building comes into view.

Gaining the subtle slope of the neighboring field, Francis halts Churchfield in front of the home. He hesitates. In addition to James's recommendation to stop, he too has a desire. James's map after Sandleford is somewhat unclear—it is as if the next town magically appears on the page. Francis wishes to obtain advice from the home's resident. Worried that he might lose the trail north to the next town, Newbury, he needs confirmation that he is heading in the correct direction.

Standing in front of the stone structure, Francis guesses the home to be built around the twelfth century. He dismounts near a large cedar tree and secures Churchfield to the massive trunk, fortuitously on a thickly grassy spot.

"Shall this do, Churchy?"

The horse snorts and nods his head. *Peculiar companion.*

Walking toward the home, Francis regards the simple structure. He estimates the main part of the building no longer than thirty feet, *perhaps twenty feet in depth.* Built clearly as a recent attachment, another section runs perpendicular to the focal point of the building. At the oak entry door, Francis knocks. He thinks to himself, *the structure also serves as chapel?* His mental question ends with the opening of the door.

The woman standing in front of Francis is middle-aged, her thin frame bending slightly at the shoulders. Despite her posture which sparks a doubt of good health, her eyes are strong. Through the grey hair hanging on either side of her face like spent blooms, the blue orbs penetrate Francis's own. He inquires,

"Sandleford?"

" 'Tis. May I inquire of your intention?"

---

[155] Eighteenth-century spelling is sometimes Sandhall Ford.

Francis removes his hat. Clearing his throat, he offers,

"A weary itinerant wishes advice on the road to Newbury."

"Itinerant? Please do come in. I shall provide sustenance to the weary traveler."

Francis is grateful for the invitation, even more so for the promise of food. He nods his acceptance. The woman turns and leads him into the main room of the home. Her walk is slow, almost methodical, her gentle steps barely audible as they precede the leathered tapping of Francis's jack boots. Francis gazes toward the skirts brushing the floor in front of him; *strange, no blue stockings.* The woman wears black silk stockings.

Pointing a long, thin finger to her right, she invites Francis to sit. He does so, moving the chair from the wooden table. Looking around, he takes in the building's simple layout. The rectangular room bears a fascinating ceiling. Built of local timbers, the beams arc upward to a center joist that runs perpendicular to the cross-framing. The magnificent work of the carpenters gives the entire room a cathedral appearance. Nearer to the ground level are three south-facing windows, set equidistant from one another along the length of the room. In addition, there is one window on each end of the long room. The interior is actually forty feet by twenty feet, with the peak of the cathedral ceiling at fifteen feet. In the middle of the room, a large table with chairs sits adjacent to several pieces of furniture, wooden tables, chairs, boxes, and trunks. Lying open, their two halves spread like oversized bolts of fabric waiting to be cut, are two large portmanteaus, their contents of numerous pieces of clothing exposed for anyone to see. Many quilted items also lie strewn about. From his quick inspection, Francis gathers that the woman is wealthy.

The woman walks forward with a tea tray and offers a cup to Francis.

"Name's Montagu, Elizabeth Montagu. Wife of Edward Montagu, MP of Huntingdon."

Francis receives the cup and nods.

"Asbury, Francis Asbury of Great Barr - -
West Midlands."

"West Midlands . . . as well. Fitting with your spiritual father; no corner of the earth shall inhibit his selection of preachers. You know, the Angli priests despise the thawing of their cold religion."

Francis barely manages a nod before the woman continues,

"Bunyan was a Midlands man."

Before he can respond, she is on to another subject.

"I'm unaware of a Wesleyan society in Newbury. Shan't be your final destination?"

"It shan't. Actually, Oxford. To meet with a friend."

"Oxford, well then. Not even Sandleford shall keep me from witty discussion. Francis—may I call you Francis?"

"Would be my pleasure."

"Well then, Francis. In London, I have a social group. More of an intellectual gathering. Along the lines of the French salons but without the political connection of the court and the sometimes-present immoral behavior. The group affords stimulating conversation in lieu of card playing and drinking. I suppose you and your fellow itinerants would greatly approve."

"I believe we would. Do many join your women's group?"

"Oh, Francis, you must allow the light of reason to open your view. These groups are not merely for women. The gatherings attract many of the noble citizens of London; both men and women participate freely."

"My deepest apology. Your husband approves?"

"Oh, I am not so perfectly the rib of Adam."

Francis smiles, the kind of smile that says he doesn't know what to think of this independent woman. She notices the indecision and responds,

"Apology accepted. As a woman, I can think for myself, even act for myself. As a wife, I am obedient because it is my duty. This is not so painful or irksome a task, for I am married to a man of sense and integrity. Edward is fond of the intellectual conversations. However, I fear they soon may have to end."

"Oh?"

"My husband struggles in health. I believe this summer shall be my last in Sandleford for quite some time. My duties shall involve taking care of him in his ailment."

The disheartened look on her face is not what Francis expected. Seeking to redirect the conversation, he inquires,

"Please, tell me more of the intellectual group."

"What started as literary breakfasts quickly became large evening gatherings. Not unlike Wesley's class meetings, people of varying backgrounds come together. Unlike the French, the dress is informal. Hence the name of my social soirées, the Bluestocking Gatherings. The evenings are open to many by invitation."

Francis thinks as she continues, *could I find myself participating with Nancy? Perhaps. Most definitely, with the men from West Bromwich.* Raising the cup of tea to his lips, he drinks in the warm liquid as Elizabeth continues.

"Well then, Francis, I propose a subject. Do you mind?"

Rushing his drink, he nods his head and responds,

"Please do."

"All right, then. Your philosophy, is it eternal?"

Francis lowers his cup. He hasn't an answer. For the first time in a long time, he feels inadequate. Not the humiliating pain of his school instructor—this is different. He has never considered his life's philosophy. The shrugging of his shoulders and the tilt of his head inspire her response.

"Your philosophy, Francis, is it eternal? In our Bluestocking Gatherings, the idea is tossed about that a philosophy which is not eternal is not philosophy at all. Do you grasp the concept?"

"I am afraid that I do not."

"Very well. The ability to reason, from whence does it come?"

"The Creator."

"All right. Can a philosophy exist outside of the Creator?"

"I suppose."

"Yes, it can; however, it fails to be true philosophy. A private philosophy is inconsistent with the Creator of the universe. A private philosophy can no more be obtained than a private moon or stars. Do you comprehend the concept now?"

"I believe I've sorted it—somewhat. The moon and stars are for all to see."

"Yes! True philosophy must apply to all! Is this not great fun?"

Francis reluctantly nods; *I suppose it is.* Elizabeth takes the concept one step further.

"Francis, there can be many philosophies that disguise themselves as true philosophy, but all they can offer is not a connection to the Giver of Truth, but a connection to the lesser concepts of newness or difference."

"All they are is new?"

"Yes, Francis! Or different."

Francis takes another sip of his tea. He is beginning to see the enjoyment in such discussion. He prompts Elizabeth,

> "The moon and stars existing for all is often overlooked. Well, I mean, true philosophy."

> "Yes, Francis. Hard to grasp a sound reason for this failing. The cosmos display the handiwork and glory of God. Your Charles Wesley has expressed it best: 'Hark, how all the welkin rings.' "

> "Indeed, Mrs. Montagu, indeed."

Elizabeth's joyful expression emboldens Francis; he decides to bring forth a question.

> "What of your faith, Mrs. Montagu? Do you possess the Savior?"

Elizabeth draws a focused breath. Her almost teal-colored eyes—which, depending on the light, alter from azure blue to emerald green—look to the glorious ceiling of the structure. After nearly a minute of silence, accented by an occasional pursing of her lips indicating her deep thought, she finally responds,

> "As a child, my family was not overly religious. We were Anglicans, members of the King's Church; however, rarely did we attend church or give heed to theological pursuits. Much of this followed into my marriage."

Her pause brings an uncomfortable moment for Francis; he worries that his question was too forward. He is relieved when Elizabeth continues.

> "After marriage, Edward and I enjoyed the privilege of childbirth. Our son, Punch, was born on the most beautiful day in May. My recovery delayed; however, Edward and I enjoyed Punch's endearing expressions - -
> We loved our little boy. With him, we joyfully traveled to the Berkshire estate. We also divided our time between here at Sandleford Priory, Yorkshire, and Allerton. It was at Yorkshire that our lives spiraled downward. Unexpectedly, our precious Punch departed this life, a few months after his first birthday."

Francis looks away, uncomfortable with the revelation. *How I regret my question! Could not I have waited to know more?* He rubs his top teeth on his bottom lip. Noticing the nervous gesture, Elizabeth assures him,

> "Francis, you needn't feel ashamed of your question. It is a valid question. You see, after the loss of my son, a dear friend wandered into my life. Into both our lives. Gilbert was a brilliant man, part poet, part man of faith. He allowed Edward and me a time for grief. Once the waters settled, his counsel brought much-desired comfort. Nevertheless, the loss did allow for a chasm between Edward and myself. Although we are fond

of each other, I am convinced there shall be no more children for us. It is well; the Bluestocking Gatherings bridge the gulf which divides."

"This Gilbert brought the comfort of the Gospel?"

"He did. Unfortunately, Gilbert West, as our dear Punch, departed this life prematurely."

"I see. Forgive me for asking a second time: what of your faith?"

"To be direct, Francis, I consider myself a Christian. I subscribe my heart to the Maker of the moon and stars. Does it arrive with fanfare? Rarely can I say so. My heart yearns for the joy that you and the Wesleyans enjoy. Perhaps my times in London should afford a visit to Wesley's Foundry. For now, I am content to rest assured in the eternal philosophy found in the historical pages of the Scriptures."

Francis's young face offers a gentle smile. Elizabeth responds,

"Your face seems to convey that you are pleased that you asked."

"You are a wise woman. However, there is more."

"Oh?"

"My smile reflects a fond memory. One of my sister."

"You have a sister?"

"I do. In eternity."

"I see that loss touches many lives, even those dedicated to God."

"As I have mentioned before, you are a wise woman."

Changing the subject as quickly as a chased rabbit changes directions, Elizabeth offers,

"And not the only wise woman to reside at Sandleford. What of the Inclusa?"

"Inclusa? I am afraid you speak beyond my knowledge."

"Like other religious individuals who resided at the Sandleford Priory, this twelfth-century woman, a nun of the Catholic order, devoted her life as an anchoress."

"Anchoress?"

"An anchorite—one who on account of her faith chooses to live in seclusion."

"Seclusion? Why refuse to spread the good news?"

"Not all have Wesley's joy - -

Nor energy."

Elizabeth's grin prompts Francis to chuckle.

For the remainder of the day and long into the evening, Elizabeth challenges Francis with intellectual conversation. Rarely does he have a proper response. If witnessed from the outside, the discussion might resemble a teaching session. Francis gladly accepts the instruction; he is also grateful for the chance to share of his mother's recovery from the loss of her dear Sarah. He also enjoys the richly adorned banquet Elizabeth places before him. The obvious luxuries of a well-positioned family such as Elizabeth and her MP husband include several cuts of roasted meats and a variety of seasonal vegetables.

Early the next morning, as the sun begins its climb above the gentle slopes of Berkshire, Francis sits atop his horse. At his side stands Elizabeth, finishing the last folds on a brown wrapper containing several layers of roasted meats. Handing it to Francis, she advises,

> "Continue as detailed and you shall arrive in Newbury in less than one hour; stay the course and Oxford by nightfall. I have traveled to Paris, the Rhineland, and Scotland, and I doubt I have met with as many fascinating experiences as you itinerants. I envy your freedom."
>
> "And I am grateful for your hospitality. And for your understanding in my sharing of my sister."
>
> "The loss of your sister and the subsequent triumph of your mother trumpet the eternal philosophy."
>
> "They do indeed. Good day, Mrs. Montagu."
>
> "Good day, Pastor Asbury."

Francis's departure places him once again on James's intended path for Newbury and eventually Oxford. The artist's rendering improves, as does the weather. The sunny, warm day welcomes the itinerant as he travels through the heart of Berkshire. Nearing Newbury, he crosses two rivers, the Lambourn and the Kennet. Continuing northward, he encounters rich, flat farmlands and pasturelands. This view remains the same for the majority of the trip. More than halfway on this journey he will encounter a town by the name of Worldes End—an unusual name for such pleasant, gentle scenery.

Before the town of East Ilsley, Francis decides to answer the call of his empty stomach and reaches into his saddlebag. The rich aroma of roasted meat greets the unwrapping of the brown paper that secures Elizabeth's gift. Even Churchfield catches the smell and promptly stops to eat some grass. Francis welcomes the interruption in the journey.

> "Very well, Churchy. We shall both enjoy a bit to eat."

After a short rest, the pair are once again on their way. At East Ilsley, they encounter fields of wildflowers called yellow rattle. The resulting waves of yellow from the late-summer blooms spread an irresistible canvas for the occasional purple bloom of clover. Every so often, the minority plant pops into view, a lone ship bobbing atop a lemon sea. The flowers prompt the memory of his visit with Elizabeth Montagu. The woman challenges Francis's view of women leaders. He thinks of the women preachers he encountered in Derby and the women in London as they reach out to the destitute and hungry of that city's dirty streets. Before long, he thinks of John and Charles Wesley, *they the true beneficiaries of a wise and discerning mother*. The thought of Susanna Wesley begins to ease his discomfort with women leaders and, to a degree, women preachers.

The ten-mile trip from East Ilsley to Abington occurs late in the day. Crossing the old Roman road, the Ickneild Way, at East Ilsley, Francis continues northward. Looking to the west and east, he estimates, *four hours until sunset*. He removes James's map to consider the amount of time left on his journey to Oxford. Unfolding the document, he looks to James's notes. The details reveal roughly seventeen miles to complete to Oxford. He is relieved; he should arrive at sunset.

Far off to the west, the Cuckhamsley Hills come into view. The gently sloping hills prompt Francis to look again at James's map. He surmises, *according to James, I am approaching the town of Chilton*. He soon discovers this to be true.

At Chilton, the path continues northward. Four miles north of Chilton, he crosses the Mill Brook. The waterway runs to the east, eventually emptying into the River Thames. The pathway now directs Francis through the towns of Milton and Drayton. After Drayton, there is another river crossing: the River Ock, which resides south of Abingdon.

Entering Abingdon from the southwest, the dirt road takes Francis into the heart of the town. Abingdon is one of the oldest towns in English history—according to many, the oldest. Advantageously located at the junction of the rivers Ock and Thames, the ancient town continues to benefit from the abundance of trade and food within its borders. The village dates back to a tenth-century settlement of Benedictine monks. Some reports place the religious camp in the seventh century. Its age makes Abingdon the clear county town of Berkshire. The town is also odd in the fact that eight years ago, it held an unusual event during the celebration to honor the coronation of King George III. Apparently, the ceremony dated back to an ancient tradition of the town's leaders gathering in the center of town to distribute baked buns to the poor. Abingdon decided to turn the benevolent tradition into a ceremony marking significant national events. The unusual aspect of the ceremony is that the town's leading citizens toss the baked items to the waiting citizens from a rooftop. The bun toss borders on the comical as bunches of the baked items fly in all directions. In addition to the distribution of the bread, in celebration of the royal honor, a generous supply of locally brewed ale usually makes it into the hands of the adult residents. Despite this new way of celebrating, there isn't any bread being distributed on this day that Francis passes through. He continues northward. The instructions from James read simply, "Upon Oxford, proceed straight away, St. Giles Church." Francis plans to do so within the hour.

Some fifty minutes north of Abingdon, Francis finds himself south of the waterway that fingers its way around the west side of Oxford. Here the river seems to gently cup the ancient city, proclaiming to the rest of the island nation that this is the geographical and educational center of Great Britain. Francis halts Churchfield to take in the view. His explorer-like peering along the wide horizon causes him to silently rejoice at the numerous steeples and towers ascending within the boundaries of the university town. Nudging the horse forward, he moves onto Folly Bridge.

Atop the span, he stops once again to view the River Isis, the waterway that runs to his left toward the northwest, into the heart of Oxfordshire, and to his right southeast, where the river receives a new name: the River Thames. From the bridge, more well-built structures come into view. Nestled within the city limits, a neatly packaged offering of colleges, churches, and homes stirs the young itinerant's emotions, each stone structure appearing as a study in proper historical architecture. *Most pleasant and compact.* Urged by this thought, Francis again nudges Churchfield forward.

Proceeding northward, Francis's eyes are drawn to several locations competing for his attention. The beautiful meadow on the north side of the bridge, east of the roadway—this is the lush green grass of Christ Church Meadow, dotted by the occasional weeping willow with its gentle, sage-colored boughs arching toward the emerald-carpeted ground. *Each demands a deeper consideration.* His insightful thought prods him further northward.

Pulling out James's map, Francis orients his location. *James's depiction is clear; the first of the Oxford roads is St. Aldate's. Upon High Street intersection, the road becomes Cornmarket Street. Upon the north end of Cornmarket, it becomes St. Giles, eventually forking into two, St. Giles Church to reside on the east road and on the west side of the street.* Francis raises his eyes from the map, but something of James's work recalls his attention back to the drawing. *Now, wherever . . . ?* Francis finally finds the object of his search and reads aloud the notation which carries a strange remark.

"Broad Street, location of the Oxford Martyrs."

The Oxford Martyrs? James, you must be more specific.

Francis looks for the infamous lane. According to the map, as St. Aldate's takes a slight bend to the northeast, the roadway widens and continues toward Cornmarket Street. Lifting his eyes, Francis can see the wide road ahead, adorned with its luxurious attachments. Francis cannot fathom such beauty. *The city proudly displays its monumental buildings.* This is indeed a wondrous place. Francis strangely remembers a quote from a visiting preacher who stayed with him and his parents in Great Barr: "God Himself would choose to make His abode in Oxford." After his first glimpse of the city, Francis agrees. The welcomed traveler to the Asbury home many years before also related the fact that Oxford continues to attract England's most famous citizens. The kind gentleman related the story of "one William Shakespeare staying at the Crown Tavern in Cornmarket Street" a century ago. This long-forgotten memory inspires Francis to daydream of other key people who may have graced the extraordinary streets of Oxford.

At the junction of St. Aldate's and Cornmarket Street, Francis proceeds northward. Again, he looks for Broad Street, James's map showing that it lies ahead. Before the searched-for lane appears, he notices a stone tower on his right. The tall, vertical, perfectly square structure is the entrance to the oldest church in Oxford, St. Michael at the North Gate. Francis admires the stonework. Alternating-length cut-stone quoins make up the attractive corners highlighting the random-patterned fieldstones. In the center of the side facing the street, several arched openings appear from the lowest level to the top of the magnificent narthex. Francis returns his attention to street level and continues north along Cornmarket.

Francis once again refers to James's map. It is clear that Broad Street should appear shortly. Looking up from the drawing, he notes his approach to a street intersection and halts his horse at the junction. Looking down the street to his right, Francis catches sight of a university building. The richly adorned stone structure resides on the north side of the street. To Francis, *the college seems to coincide with James's demarcation of the Oxford Martyrs.* Francis takes a deep breath, looks to the east, and directs Churchfield to the north. *Shall have a talk with Richard about this.* Francis's eventual talk with Richard will reveal the story of the burning at the stake of Hugh Latimer and Nicholas Ridley 220 years before.

Moving onward, the beautiful buildings continue. Francis has already passed St. Mary Magdalen Church and the St. John's College buildings. As the road begins to widen, each new structure invites the itinerant along to his final destination, St. Giles Church. Scattered about the spacious avenue which is now St. Giles Street, a small herd of sheep waddle along the route, on their way northward, out of town. On both sides of the street, many oversized canopies of hardwood trees line the perimeter of the causeway. Under these shady locations, several small groups of university men, in their traditional gowns and caps, gather for conversation. On his left, at building number 49, Francis passes an inn, The Eagle and Child. The sign above the doorway acknowledges that the establishment has been in Oxford since the year 1684. Francis continues on his path along St. Giles Street, following the puffy sheep toward the outskirts of Oxford, the location of the church.

Outside the city's boundaries when constructed, St. Giles is an eleventh-century church dedicated to the patron saint of lepers, beggars, and outcasts. The Catholic Church placed this honor on Saint Giles because of his monastic characteristics and the injury he suffered by an arrow shot by a hunter aiming for his lone companion, a red deer. The injury resulted in a permanent limp.

The historical account is that Giles was a wealthy aristocrat from Greece. After the death of his parents, he depleted his huge fortune helping the poor and destitute. After much public attention for his acts of kindness, as well as his piety and learning, he sought seclusion in the dense forests of France, near the mouth of the River Rhone. The injurious shot by a hunter aiming his arrow to kill the red deer occurred while Giles was a hermit and living with the gentle animal. Upon news of Giles's discovery in seclusion, and having learned of his injury, the French King arranged for his care. Giles's refusals of care inspired the King to accompany the numerous doctors he sent for help. In addition to the King and his physicians, many local residents were drawn to the cave by the miracles Giles continued to perform. The desperate seekers came to the cave in search of divine deliverance from physical, emotional, and spiritual ailments.

In Francis's day, the once-Catholic church dedicated to this saint is the center of Anglican and Wesleyan activity in Oxford. Ironically for Francis, Saint Giles is not only the patron saint of beggars, cripples, the disabled, outcasts, and lepers; he is also the patron saint of blacksmiths.

St. Giles Church is a structure built in the Norman style, situated north of the end of St. Giles Street, where it forks into two different roads. The church aligns east and west between Banbury and Woodstock Roads. Despite civil-war-era damage to the south aisle of the structure, the building is in relatively good condition. The beautifully crafted architectural windows continue to draw the viewer's attention. Keeping with the custom of churches dedicated to St. Giles, the location of the church in Oxford is outside and away from town, north of the city wall.

Approaching the church from the south, Francis pauses in front of the adjacent graveyard. The nearly three-quarters of an acre begins at the veering of the two roads and continues right up to the south side of the church. Numerous above-ground tombstones do their best to stand plumb. Over the years, several of the granite monuments have not fared so well; they tilt at a slight angle. Francis dismounts, gathering Churchfield's reins, and walks forward toward the church building.

Securing the horse to a tree, Francis can hear the voices of a choir. The singing members are no doubt students from a local university. The melodic voices draw Francis to the entrance door of the church. Pausing, he imagines the scene inside. He pushes open the thick wooden door and enters.

The central nave is bordered with a series of stone columns leading to the front of the building on each side. At the end of the long, narrow space, the altar resides below three Norman arched-top windows. The occasional clear panels of the stained-glass window beam natural light into the space. Above the area with the holy gleam, a white plaster vaulted ceiling comes to a peak, becoming the uniform backdrop to dark-brown wood beams spaced four feet apart from front to back. The ridgeline of the space is nearly thirty feet in height.

The all-boys choir stands to the right of the altar, tucked under a stone-wrapped archway, their harmonious singing resonating amidst the sanctuary's walls. Nearly two dozen people stand in wooden pews nestled between the columns, singing along with the choir. In the front row, one young man stands nearly eight inches taller than his companions. The back of his head is a familiar sight to Francis. The young man, as well as those who stand next to him, is dressed in a black clerical robe. Francis approaches the gathering, taking a seat in the last row.

The singing comes to a close and the tall young man steps to the left side of the altar space. There, a wooden pulpit awaits. As he steps into the space, his gentle, pleasing face raises toward the congregation. The sight of his face brings a sense of kinship to Francis; *my friend Richard.*

Richard Whatcoat begins his prepared sermon.

"As Sodom and Gomorrah, and the cities around them in a similar manner to these, having given themselves over to sexual immorality and gone after strange flesh, are set forth as an example, suffering the vengeance of eternal fire. Likewise also these dreamers defile the flesh, reject authority, and speak evil of dignitaries. Yet Michael the archangel, in contending with the devil, when he disputed about the body of Moses, dared not bring against him a reviling accusation, but said, 'The Lord rebuke you!'

"But these speak evil of whatever they do not know; and whatever they know naturally, like brute beasts, in these things they corrupt themselves. Woe to them! For they have gone in the way of Cain, have run greedily in the error of Balaam for profit, and perished in the rebellion of Korah. These are spots in your love feasts, while they feast with you without fear, serving only themselves. They are clouds without water, carried about by the winds; late autumn trees without fruit, twice dead, pulled up by the roots; raging waves of the sea, foaming up their own shame; wandering stars for whom is reserved the blackness of darkness forever."[156]

Richard has everyone's undivided attention. Raising his eyes from the pulpit, Richard peers about the room. His face is far from capricious, but the staid look brightens upon the discovery of Francis. Francis returns the warm response, happy that his friend has recognized him. Richard continues; with a raised right hand he pronounces,

"The quoted writings from the book of Jude inspire that which I am prepared to deliver."

He lowers his hand and continues,

"In verse seven, these are cities which gave themselves over to fornication. The word clearly means unnatural lusts. These cities are set forth as an example, suffering the vengeance of eternal fire. That is, the vengeance which they suffered is an example or a type of eternal fire. In like manner, these dreamers, sleeping and dreaming all their lives, despise authority. They despise those whom Christ invested with authority and were made by Him the overseers of His flock. In simple words, the dreamers despise the overseers of God's flock. They rail at dignitaries—though not at worldly dignitaries; for these they had an admiration for the sake of gain. But those holy men, who for the purity of their lives, the soundness of their doctrine, and the greatness of their labors in the work of the ministry, were truly honorable before God and all good men; and who were grossly vilified by those who turned the grace of God into lasciviousness . . ."[157]

Richard's words continue to challenge the minds of those who sit listening attentively, revealing their power to discern and judge properly. One lad in particular, his rigid posture identifying him as a student of the university, has fixed his eyes unflinchingly on the preacher. Several of the local students are not as bold; the amplified words of the tall, sinewy preacher impose upon them an apparent desire to avoid recognition. Richard's last details of wandering stars—planets which shine for a time, but have no light in themselves and will soon be cast into utter darkness—is the final point in his sermon, and a final point that several young men will accept. As Richard raises his hands for a closing prayer, these are the first to rise from their pew and leave.

The completion of the prayer invites Francis forward. As the congregation departs, Richard's rubbing of his arms with his hands catches Francis by surprise. *Richard, you appear as an anxious puppy.* Francis quickens his pace. He has never

---

[156] Book of Jude, verses 7–13.

[157] From John Wesley's commentaries on Jude.

seen such awkward movements from Richard; *unlikely for such a solid figure. Are we a bit nervous?* Francis spreads his arms and Richard drops his hands to his sides. With shoulders drooped, he stands as a small child facing imminent danger. Francis embraces his friend. The welcoming emotion brings a sense of calm to both men; these are kindred spirits.

Pushing back from their prolonged hug, Francis offers,

"Richard, are we well?"

" 'Tis the adrenaline, or the nerves. Francis, your arrival is as grand as the Second Coming."

"But are we well?"

"I am well—somewhat hungry; however, I am well. You must be in need of a good meal. Come, we shall dine."

Without hesitation, Richard escorts Francis to the door, eager to enjoy a meal with his friend.

The white-painted, low wooden ceiling of the establishment contrasts nicely with the interior brick wall painted in a dark brown color. Only a handful of seats line the table along the wall. Opposite the table, a long bar occupies nearly the entire length of the space. At the end of the narrow room, a separate area juts toward the rear of the building. Inside this adjacent space, Richard and Francis walk past three men in lively conversation, their audacious laughter drawing the trio together like an English sheepdog. Francis and Richard take their seats at a small, round wooden table beyond the men.

A man with a white apron arrives at their table.

"Hello, Richard; shall your guest eat as well?"

"He shall."

"Shall he require coach and stabling?"

"No. He shall reside with me, as will his horse."

The man departs and Richard begins,

"How long since you have seen your mother and father - - And Nancy?"

"Too long. Currently well past the two-year mark. How is Great Barr?"

"Oh, the Wednesbury class was mine until the Leeds conference. Your pals have asked often of you. I failed to have an answer."

"What of a fairer friend? Has she made request of my whereabouts?"

Richard darts his eyes; the tight-lipped look of his face causes Francis to sense this as an unfavorable reaction. Looking back at Francis, Richard responds,

"She has."

"Has she indeed, Richard?"

Once again, like a hummingbird flitting to a more favorable bloom, Richard darts his eyes to an adjacent window, and then to another window. Returning to his friend, Richard says quietly,

"She has not."

Francis's crestfallen expression reveals his deepest disappointment. Richard is quick to offer a change of subject.

"So much has transpired, Francis! The conference in Leeds was desirous of those who would consider the American colonies."

Still pushing through the turmoil of the blow, Francis inquires,

"The colonies?"

"Yes, seems another letter from John Street Church in New York arrived to Wesley. In it, the author begged for preachers. Oh, there was a small request for money, but the larger issue lay in the need of competent preachers. Wesley put forth the appeal in the morning. His appeal met with the deepest silence. Later that evening, Wesley once again offered his desire. This too met with a strange and uncomfortable stillness."

"Silence to Wesley? Have we gone mad?"

"Ha, Francis, you amuse me. Yes, the reaction seems extraordinary. However, so does preaching in the colonies."

"For some."

"Oh?"

"Never mind. I'm familiar with the correspondence. Continue."

Francis's fumbling with the table edge coincides with his snappish reply. At first Richard is slightly offended, but he ignores the comment, conscious of what is happening with Nancy in Great Barr. He kindly responds,

"Very well. Wesley's reaction to the lack of response was telling. We all sat quiet, surprised that none would offer their service."

"What was it like?"

"A dreadful silence. One would rather have turned loose a wild bird in a sanctuary . . ."

Francis's fumbling stops. His brilliant eyes lock onto Richard's, whose gentle smile conveys the recalling of the fond memory. Francis replies,

"What was it like for you?"

"As I said, dreadful. A most uncomfortable feeling of inappropriate inadequacy. I actually ached for qualification to go myself—yet I knew better. My response would surely have met with resounding confrontation. In Wesley's urgent plea, he was looking for a seasoned itinerant. However, none responded. At least, not until Richard Boardman and Joseph Pilmoor stepped forward to offer their service."

"Boardman and Pilmoor, far from seasoned itinerants."

"I know. However, far from our rank. Francis, could you have done so? For me, the colonies seem so distant a field."

"Could I have done so? At one time I thought I could. Several indicators: rich stories of the land, a prophetic woman who shared a prophetic word. I believed then it was a possibility. Even the gentle healing of a doctor familiar with the aboriginal remedies of the continent led me to believe so. However, today I am convinced these were only a distraction. My heart knows His call, and His call for me is here."

"As is mine. To England we shall proclaim the Gospel Truth."

"To England, we shall."

The young itinerants find Oxford the perfect location for them. Not only is there a chance for an old friendship to revive, but the university town also affords them many opportunities to share the Good News with young men their age, young men who seek a proper education, young men not afraid to air their opinions on almost anything. The Sunday evening preaching at St. Giles is fruitful, but Richard and Francis have other streams to fish.

Drawn to the cheerful atmosphere of the pubs and inns, Richard and Francis regularly attend the establishments—not for drink or revelry, but for food and fellowship. In reality, this is the closest they will come to attending university. Some nights prove more successful than others, and tonight is one of those nights. Richard and Francis sit at a table in the center of The Lamb and Flag, an inn that lies across the street from The Eagle and Child pub. Several young men sit with several courses of food. A roasted shoulder of mutton and a plum pudding join veal cutlets, frilled potatoes, cold tongue, ham, cold roast beef, and eggs in their shells. To drink there are three open bottles of wine and a bowl of puncheon.[158] Although Richard and Francis decline to imbibe, they are the center of this dynamic environment—and the center of the students' challenges.

One young student consistently badgers Francis. He is a strong-willed individual, self-confident, boastful, determined to come across as the life of the party. He is also studying for the Anglican priesthood. His harassment of the itinerant usually settles on his dusty appearance, his shabby jacket, his lack of drinking strong drink, or the fact that the Anglican Church considers his leader, Wesley, a rebel. Consistent with previous outings, the young man now stands and delivers, directing his barb directly at Francis:

"You may talk of brisk claret; sing praises of sherry; speak well of old hock, mum, cider, and perry; but you must drink punch to be merry."

The student raises his glass, and his companions join him in a drink.

---

[158] An eighteenth-century rum punch.

Francis has no response. He quietly taps his fingers on the wooden tabletop.

The drunken rabble, all seminary students, seem to have once again triumphed over the simple West Midland preacher. But not for long, as Francis now stands and counters the wag.

> "As you imply, punch does tend to make one merry. However, I would venture a more substantial consideration. Your philosophy—is it an eternal philosophy? More clearly, does it possess truth?"

Already sitting and leaning on the shoulder of one of his friends due to too many dips in the punch, the student of St. John's College once again stands, looks to his mates, and replies,

> "These Wesleyan itinerants possess considerably too much time to read . . ."

The gathering's boisterous response echoes off the plaster walls of the inn. The laughter continues long enough to invite the attention of the establishment's manager, who arrives and shares his reservations concerning the group's inappropriate noise level. The young men at the table acknowledge his concerns and the manager departs. The boisterous student who confronted Francis gives in to the stunning reply and sits. Richard's look toward his friend says it well: "I believe you have silenced this dandy; checkmate!" Wishing to continue his theme, Francis offers,

> "Very well, if you . . ."

The inebriated lad holds out his hand to interrupt Francis; with a wobbly push off the table, he stands again. His friends, as well as Francis and Richard, watch as he begins to remove his stunning blue coat, a cotton garment. Obvious to all, this is a costly accessory. His efforts are temporarily halted as he considers why the jacket will not open. A revelation brings a slight wobble to his tall frame; a raised finger points upward as if to say, "I failed to remember one last button." He methodically places the fingers over the oaken knob and successfully maneuvers past the last hurdle to his jacket removal. He then folds the fine garment in half lengthwise and offers it to Francis.

> "Cost me four pounds, ten shillings. A true-blue coat for a man with a true-blue philosophy."

Francis stares at the coat in disbelief as he realizes the garment cost nearly half his yearly allotment for clothing. *One piece of clothing equal to half . . . ?* He quickly responds,

> "I cannot receive such a lavish gift."

> "You must."   "You must!"   "Oh, you must."

The lad's friends respond for him, all agreeing that Francis must receive the garment. One of them offers,

> "You have earned it!"

The leaner tosses the coat to Francis and struggles to retrieve his seat. While all at the table silently pray that he makes it safely back to his chair, Richard proclaims,

"Francis, you must receive the jacket. Wear it well."

That is precisely what Francis does. Excited to put on the coat, he removes his own, grateful for its replacement. He carefully dons the stunning blue jacket, delighted to find it's a perfect fit. He happily buttons the wooden buttons and pokes his hands into the front pockets.

"Oh!"

His face conveying his surprise, Francis raises his right hand from the jacket pocket. In it is a beautiful gold watch. Richard exclaims,

"Oh my! Splendid timepiece, Francis."

Francis turns to the giver.

"Here is your watch . . ."

"Oh no, the watch and the jacket are one and the same. You must have them both."

"I shan't! This is more than I earn in a year."

"All right, then . . ."

The wag slowly rises to his feet again; it is a difficult maneuver. With hand raised, he offers,

"Might I suggest you ask Wesley for an increase?"

The entire group at the table bursts into laughter. Francis shrugs his shoulders and looks to Richard, the kind of look that conveys uncertainty. Richard responds,

"He said to keep it, Francis; I suggest you accommodate his wish."

The giver once again urges,

"As Elisha, receiver of a double blessing."

Francis returns the watch to his pocket, and the students rejoice in the "holy traveler's" victory over their colleague. The rest of the evening brings one recurring thought to Francis: *Truly, Lord, You are my provider.*

Later that evening, when the itinerants are alone in their lodgings, Richard raises the obvious question, the question he has been aching to ask.

"Francis, wherever did you gain 'eternal' philosophy?"

"From the Queen."

"The Queen?"

"Queen of the Bluestockings."

"Francis, you make little sense. Just as well; goodnight, my friend. Some day you must inform me of this Queen . . ."

"I shall. Goodnight, Richard."

For the next few weeks both Richard and Francis are a regular sight in the pubs and inns, Richard quietly standing alongside the preacher in the dashing blue jacket. Francis wears it regularly, except when he preaches at St. Giles Church. It is good that he wears it, for the story of his outwitting one of their fellow students is widespread; nearly the entire Oxford student body knows of the event.

The third week of October brings the expected decline in weather. Since late August and early September, the temperatures, like a preoccupied kitten playing with a ball of yarn on a set of stairs, have bobbed and weaved, gradually descending to their pre-winter level. The changes are once again the stimulus for a grand autumn display of the native foliage. Despite the magnificent show of color on this late afternoon, Francis can't help reflecting that, as with the declining weather and temperatures, his relationship with Nancy is on a downward spiral. He prompts his friend,

> "Richard, you must speak frankly. If she has decided for another, I must know."

Richard's quiet manner is normal, for he is a gentle man. However, when one of his closest friends is asking about a girl who may desire to end their relationship, the silence conveys something much more severe. Richard will not reply. Francis seeks to construct a sound dialogue.

"Richard, Nancy is a loyal friend . . ."

"Perhaps only your mother would consider her so."

Richard's eyes squint. Francis perceives Richard's accompanying smile as conveying a slight chance for hope. But is there any? Francis trusts there is. He decides to put the topic aside. Almost.

> "You are aware, Richard, she has always been at my side. As long as I can remember. Was present my first night of preaching, and the dreadful night in Sutton. She braved a stoning, clutching my hand as tight as any smithy from the forge. Oh, how I desire to clutch that hand at this very moment . . ."

"I know, Francis, I know."

On Tuesday, October 24, 1769, as the evening arrives, Richard and Francis once again take dinner at an inn, the Angel Inn. The coaching inn is busy and heavily populated. From three o'clock in the morning until midnight, a coach departs the inn for all parts of England every couple of hours.

The usual stragglers from the university are present, some from New College, some from Magdalen College, one from Christ Church, and yet another from Exeter College. The table is set richly, compliments of the wealthy students. This evening's fare is skate fish, a neck of roasted pork in applesauce, three boiled chickens, knuckle of veal, and tongue. There are also tarts and tartlets neatly placed on one end of the wooden table, as well as several bowls of boiled late-season vegetables. As always with these students, the wine and ale flow like the Thames. Tonight's beverage of choice is the strongest form of ale, a barley wine known as Hadley's. The young men, excluding Richard and Francis, drink the intoxicating English ale for nearly two hours straight.

Nearing eight o'clock in the evening, several people from the streets run into the establishment and begin urging everyone outdoors. Their excitement renders their words incomprehensible. Richard stands and invites all at the table to rise and exit.

"Perhaps there is grave danger."

The group, along with several patrons from another dining room and many more from the rooms of the inn, force their way forward to the exit. Rising from his seat, Francis aims for the front door. Richard grabs Francis by the arm, slowing his departure. Turning toward his friend, Francis captures a look on Richard's face that conveys a noble gesture. Francis understands; *allow others to exit to safety first*. Peering forward as the group struggles to pass through the narrow doorway, Francis's eyes are drawn to the window next to the front door. It is ablaze in red. He quickly motions to Richard.

"Fire?"

"I see; push them forward."

The itinerants corral and nudge the stragglers closer to the departing group as they force their way through the only exit. Francis's brow begins to sweat, not unlike when he stood inside the forge at West Bromwich. He worries for his own safety. The task is difficult, as several travelers wrestle with their luggage bags, accidently bumping others with the large leather cases. The chaotic scene quickly elevates the adrenaline of all inside the structure.

Outdoors, nearly one hundred people gather in the middle of High Street as the bright illumination casts an instant daylight onto the entire city, brighter than any full moon. Francis and Richard are the last to exit the inn. Looking to the north, they discover the flashes of light beaming a returned twilight onto the beautiful streets of Oxford. Richard exclaims,

"Not fire after all, but an awe-inspiring wonder!"

Francis cannot speak. He stands still, removing his hat he had recently replaced on his head, and watches the sky. A young man in a clerical robe proclaims to the crowd,

"The welkin from east to west declares the glories of God."

Richard and Francis catch the words of a nearby student: "That is Mr. Parsons; standing next to him is Reverend Whitchurch. Both of Christ Church College." The gatherers nearest to Richard and Francis nod in approval, their awed expressions conveying that Parsons and Whitchurch are important figures in Oxford.

Another student exclaims,

> "From Ursa Major to the northern horizon, the royal arc and drapery do
> hang."

The young people in the crowd react with shouts of joy, as do Richard and Francis. For the next hour, the residents of Oxford enjoy the celestial phenomenon that hangs above the northern hemisphere. The colors are strong and beautiful. This is the rare aurora borealis.

The quick and numerous ascensions of the white, blue, yellow, and scarlet colors are visible for most of Europe. This is an unusual occurrence for these locations. The sky-show is actually visible as far south as Gibraltar. Several reasons allow for this. Unknown to the crowd, the first reason for this phenomenon is that the solar activity of 1769 is one of great turbulence. This year, the sun hurls its energetic particles more than in other years. The second reason is that the Earth's magnetic north pole is farther south than in previous decades, pulling the charged atmospheric collisions into visual range over more of the northern hemisphere.

Glancing away from the sky, Richard spots several people at the road's edge. They're no longer looking upward. Nudging Francis, he gently pulls on his coat sleeve.

> "Come, Francis."

Turning toward Richard, Francis understands. He follows close behind.

On the other side of the road, Richard and Francis approach about fifteen people who kneel in tears. Their sobbing is unable to penetrate the sporadic roars and cheers of the Oxford revelers. Nevertheless, these penitent residents obviously ache with sorrow. Richard advises Francis,

> "These are aware of their sinfulness. Let us convey the rescue of the
> Savior."

Until midnight, three hours past the display of the brilliant night sky, the two itinerants minister to those who see the celestial array as a sign that they are not the center of their world. Their feelings conveyed to the itinerants reflect individuals who feel unholy and unworthy of knowing a Creator who could construct such beauty as seen in the sky this autumn evening. Their hearts lie open, yearning for a healing salve that might clean away the festering chaff of their wound. Richard and Francis lovingly share the generous and bountiful offerings of God to those who believe.

As their efforts draw to a close, Francis and Richard look around. Other than the two itinerants and the sobbing worshipers, the streets are empty; none of the Oxford students or clerical leaders have lent a hand.

Richard and Francis's walk home finds them reviving a familiar discussion. The pair has talked often of the topic. At times their observations are slightly different, but actually, their opinions are the same. Turning up his collar against the early-morning temperatures that tinge the broad leaves of Oxford's deciduous trees, Richard rekindles the dialogue.

"Unfortunately, Wesley is correct of our brethren."

"I have conveyed my opinions before, Richard."

"As have I. However, we do well to work through these matters."

"It is clear, Richard; this evening's events once again give a resounding confirmation to our and Wesley's conclusion: they come very near to becoming useless."

"Useless? Is that not a harsh term? Is it not also somewhat inaccurate, Francis?"

"It may very well be harsh and inaccurate, but it reflects the deep frustration of Wesley and myself. And your own, as well. I vow to submit, however; it is a decision of which I must remind myself daily in this substantial town."

"As do I, as do I . . ."

The two continue their walk in silence. Every now and then they look to the northern sky, in hope that the beautiful aurora borealis will return. Nearing their lodgings, Richard offers,

"You know, at Leeds, the entire conference was shocked when Wesley announced that he has given up writing them. His words were sharp and direct: "I've written them off as a rope of sand." Yes, Francis, at times I feel the same as Wesley. Even the handiwork of God, written across the heavens, shall fail to wake the Anglican leadership."

The cooler temperatures of autumn soon turn to the colder conditions of winter. January of 1770 finds Richard and Francis both being stationed on the Bedfordshire circuit. The surprise news arrives as a Christmas present to the pair. Francis was expecting to go it alone, so the note from Glasbrook stating that the pair should minister together is a double blessing for Francis. And it is a welcomed opportunity for Richard, as well.

On the evening before their departure, Francis pens a letter to his mother and Nancy. Again he urges his mother to accept his traveling. And with Nancy, he urges her patience, expressing his desire to once again sit with her upon the tree stump in West Bromwich. At the completion of the letter-writing, Richard proposes that they sing a hymn. Francis's sense of humor causes him to suggest a particular one written by Charles Wesley.

> "In honor of the beautiful Oxford skies this past autumn, I suggest Charles's *Lo, He Comes with Clouds Descending.* "

"Very well."

The two begin the hymn,

> "Every eye shall now behold Him
> Robed in dreadful majesty;
> Those who set at naught and sold Him
> Pierced and nailed Him to the tree,
> Deeply wailing, deeply wailing, deeply wailing,
> Shall the true Messiah see."

Continuing with the lead voice, Francis goes on,

> "Every island, sea, and mountain,
> Heaven and earth, shall flee away;
> All who hate Him must, confounded,
> Hear the trump, proclaim the day:
> Come to judgment! Come to judgment!
> Come to judgment! Come away!"

At the finish of the hymn, Richard looks to Francis with one eye slightly squinted. The chewing of the inside of his cheek conveys his perception that Francis may have been a little sarcastic in choosing this song. Richard prods,

> " 'Come away,' Francis? Now, is that what Wesley is suggesting with the Anglican leadership?"

"Perhaps the leadership - -
Perhaps others."

Francis smiles that wry smile from his youth—the one that conveys he is up to something. Richard responds,

> "Very well. Good night, Francis."

Behold the prophet in his tow'ring flight!
He leaves the earth for heav'n's unmeasur'd height,
And worlds unknown receive him from our sight.
There Whitefield wings with rapid course his way,
And sails to Zion through vast seas of day.

Phyllis Wheatley[159]

The thirty-five mile trip northward from Oxford to Northampton will place Francis within fifty miles of his home county, Staffordshire. This revelation brings a satisfying feeling to the weary itinerant. Thoughts of his home in Great Barr, his friends in West Bromwich, the forge, and Nancy inspire him to give thanks. Nearing three years away from home, he aches to return to the West Midlands. Despite the occasional correspondence to and from his parents, the random letters fall short of his personal need to connect with those he loves, especially Nancy.

As he and Richard push their horses forward, the thought of home also lessens the effect of the winter weather as it slows the pair's travel. They expect to cover barely ten to fifteen miles in a day; what normally would take two days to accomplish will now stretch to include a small portion of the third day. This extra half-day is a welcomed opportunity for the young men, for they love to converse. Nearly twenty minutes into the first leg of the journey, Richard furthers the dialogue.

"Word spreads that Wesley is to address a serious issue in London this summer."

"The conference?"

"Yes. Many will question Wesley. Perhaps persecutions again, from the unbelieving crowd and, sadly, from the Wesleyan faithful."

"The faithful question Wesley? Seems a bit steep."

"Steep it is when the issue is women preaching."

"And how have you come about this?"

"A friend of a friend."

"Whose friend?"

"Your friend, Francis."

"Oh?"

---

[159] Phyllis Wheatley, an African poet in the Massachusetts colony.

The comment causes Francis to consider which friend it might be. Richard offers,

> "One Sarah Crosby. When in London last, I had privilege to speak with her."
>
> "London, was it? I had heard she has departed Yorkshire."
>
> "She has. For some reason, she intended a short stay in London."
>
> "Well, Richard, you have brought forward a profound subject. Care to offer your views?"

Francis's almost mocking hand gesture indicates that Richard seldom does otherwise. Richard replies,

> "My views on the matter focus on Wesley himself. I am confident that you see him as I do, well-versed in the Scriptures. Nothing that I have witnessed in his life, his writings, or my own perusals of the Holy Word renders his opinion suspect. I do believe he shall experience a progression."
>
> "Progression? How so?"
>
> "Lay preachers, like you and me. Has Wesley ever struggled with laity preaching? For that matter, has the Anglican Church struggled with lay preaching?"
>
> "Most certainly the Anglican Church has struggled with this, Richard. From what Pastor Mather has shared, Wesley was convinced to allow lay preaching on account of changed lives—what he termed 'validation of the Holy Spirit,' as seen in those changed lives."
>
> "Correct, Francis. Despite those who termed this transition the first serious deviation of Anglican discipline, Wesley said yes to lay preaching. What are Wesley's words? Are they not, 'These lay preachers are God's extraordinary messengers, raised up to provoke the ordinary ones to jealousy'? The natural question presents itself: Do the sharing in the class meetings and love feasts by women like Sarah Crosby and the eloquent Mary Bosanquet bring about changed lives?"
>
> "I suppose . . ."
>
> "You seem almost opposed, Francis."
>
> "Well, on occasion their preaching, or teaching, has brought forth the work of the Holy Spirit. In Derby, I witnessed it myself."
>
> "It is only natural that Wesley shall arrive at the same for women who exhibit this extraordinary gift. I ask you again, Francis: How long before Wesley's opinion transitions to the validation account? What shall he say upon the validation of the Holy Spirit in the changed lives brought about by the exhortation of these women? Methodism currently possesses nearly forty women able to deliver life-changing messages."

"Forty? Richard, you sound as if the deal is complete."

"Yes. I've heard several itinerants speak of these women whose words seem anointed by the Holy Ghost. Most are limited to speaking in class meetings and love feasts. How long shall these limitations last when several long to preach in the open air?"

"I see where this may lead, Richard, but are you not risking the pushing aside of St. Paul's admonition that women should not preach in the church?"

"Where has Wesley's opinion fallen in this? Has he not studied the ancient texts? Has he not arrived at the opinion that Paul's words were local and limited for a season? And has he not determined that in these instances the women in question were interfering with church discipline and government, nullifying the application of the prohibition to the gift of preaching?"

"Richard, you speak beyond my understanding. Perhaps I may attain your knowledge if I shall remain in Oxford and you take Bedfordshire for your own?"

"Francis, you amuse me. Perhaps you seek an additional fine garment. May I continue?"

At this Churchfield snorts and shakes his head as if to convey, "Do we have a choice?" Francis thinks to himself, *where has my gentle and encouraging friend gone? Seems someone else has taken residence in the body of my dear Richard.* His friend continues,

"Very well. What of the wise woman who handed over the reckless Sheba after he lifted his hand against King David?"

"Second Samuel twenty?"

"Yes, the handmaid. With her as well as with Deborah, did not each have a public declaration from God?"

"It is as you say, Richard. Deborah is truly a prophet and not a priest. As is the handmaid."

"It is as you say, Francis!"

"Perhaps Wesley shall eventually accept this change. But it shall invite the scorn of many."

"Sadly, it shall, Francis."

"And you are confident this matter shall be dealt with in London?"

"Seems so."

The end of the first day has the two men staying at an inn at Bicester, a town conveniently located on the ancient Roman road that Francis and Richard are traveling. The inn on Stratton Road is a center of activity; coaches leave from here for Oxford and London four times each day. The inn's host, out of conviction that he hasn't been to church in a while, offers a room for the itinerants.

"My only request, remove the boots before sleeping in the bed."

Up at four a.m. and on the road by half past five, the itinerants find that their second day's travel soon brings another discussion—this one also involving the fairer sex.

"I must be honest with you, Richard; there is a young girl other than Nancy."

"Oh?"

"She resides in Clifton. It is my hope we shall pay visit to her and her family."

Richard is surprised, especially in light of his own friendship with Nancy. Not that he would encourage Francis in either direction, but he has seen the relationship of Francis and Nancy from early on. He also, like many others in the West Bromwich society, is accustomed to seeing the two together, and has never thought of them apart. He inquires,

"What of this girl?"

"She is a gentle and caring girl, and from a pleasing family. Unfortunately, she expects more."

"More than what?"

"More than a visiting itinerant."

"How did this come about, Francis?"

"Clifton became a regular stop in east Bedfordshire. Clifton, Millbrook, Sundon, Luton."

"Bunyan's country."

"Yes, our dear Bunyan. Before long, I became accustomed to seeing her on my visits to Clifton. Never intended more than an innocent friendship. Perhaps my distance from home caused me to lead further than I should have."

"Do you intend Clifton after Northampton?"

Francis stares at his gloved fingers loosely grasping Churchfield's reins; the pause indicates an uncertainty, or worse, an ulterior motive. He responds,

"Almost seems improper."

"Improper in what way?"

"Not in form, but in person—to her."

"To her? To whom do you mean, Francis?"

Silence.

The unanswered question goes unanswered for the rest of the day. Out of respect for his dear friend, Richard does not push. He brings up other, unimportant topics: the weather, the unusual height of the trees, and the possibility of snowfall. None of these delves any deeper than seed that falls on thorny ground, or even less so, on exposed slate. Nevertheless, the truth is that Richard deeply wishes that the seed had fallen in good soil, multiplying fruit many times over.

The second night finds the itinerants at the home of a woman in Towcester who is friendly to the Wesleyan movement. From here, the young men should arrive in Northampton around noon the next day. The woman and two others of this small village find their little Wesleyan society a challenge—so much so that the society is not truly a society, but resembles merely a social gathering of three women. The other women are not religious, nor are the townspeople. They do respect the woman who is devoted to the Bible, but to most of this little town, God is far from the central focus of their lives.

Mrs. Spencer is a gracious host. Her roundish, motherly looks return nostalgic childhood memories to the itinerants. For Francis, even before he entered the simple thatched-roof home and met the dear lady in Towcester, the approaching village with its many trees scattered about, their spindly bunches of branches iced over in the artistic grey of January, inspired happy thoughts of the West Bromwich countryside. Inside the Spencer home, the smell of a bubbling dinner evokes favorable reminiscences of his mother preparing a warm meal. Another distant memory of his mother emerges: the way she demanded that he dress warmly before heading out to school. The bunching of his sock in his boot spurs the memory of her mending his socks, which he occasionally tore each spring when defiantly walking outdoors in them without shoes on—an act clearly against his mother's demands. How he wishes for his mother's mending abilities, here and now.

Mrs. Spencer's gentle voice interrupts Francis's distraction.

"If you could share anything with your mother, what would it be?"

The question astonishes Francis. He fumbles in his chair, nervously picking at an exposed edge of the wooden seat. He wants to reply, yet strangely, he hesitates. Sensing his reservation, his hostess sets down the kitchen plates she has been wiping clean, then walks over to the table and seats herself in the chair at its head. After setting aside the dishrag she holds in her smooth-skinned, stubby fingers, she asks again,

"If your mother were here, what would you say to her?"

Clearing his throat while glancing across the table toward his traveling companion, Francis politely returns his eyes to the kind woman and responds,

"However did you realize that she occupies my mind?"

"A mother can tell these things. Besides, not many of my visiting preachers watch as I prepare dinner. She must be a wonderful woman."

"She is. Father is exceptional as well."

Once again, Francis pauses. His empty look toward the tabletop lasts only for a few seconds; he then raises his eyes toward the woman and responds,

"Perhaps I would express my sorrow for troubling her on my account. I would set her heart at ease, sharing that I am in health and continue strong in the Lord's work. I would share that I daily pray for her peace and assurance, assurance that her work for the Lord is good and prosperous to her soul. I would also offer my duty to my father. Share of how I miss our times together, managing the plants in the gardens. I would ask that they would share my love to all my friends at home. And, I would close with the fact that I do find much of the goodness of God to my soul, so that He leads me on my way by His power, and enlarges my heart in His work. These things are my deepest desire to share with my dear mother and father."

Looking to Richard, Mrs. Spencer inquires,

"And for you, Pastor Whatcoat?"

Richard sits upright in his chair, methodically adjusting the sleeves of his jacket. He folds his hands on the table in front of him and responds,

"My past is not as friendly as Francis's. My four siblings and I lost our father when I was nine years old. The shock to Mother and me failed to depart for quite some time. Oh, there were years where I felt over it all, but the sense of abandonment would on occasion return. The loss sent my brothers and me in several directions, gaining apprenticeships where we could. My mother is well, though now and then she struggles with a foreign ailment."

Richard stops. His nervous fidgeting inspires Mrs. Spencer to interrupt his pause.

"What would you say to her?"

"What would I say to her? I would assure her that I continue well in the work she so happily embraced for me. Like Francis, I would share that I pray for her daily."

Richard unfolds his hands and places them below the table.

Francis is familiar with Richard's background. At times he is amazed that one who has dealt with so much is so capable of generosity and grace. Francis offers,

"If Richard were a papist, he surely would have received canonization."

Richard shakes his head at the quip. Mrs. Spencer's leaning back in the chair is void of indication. Richard jumps in,

"You must make provision for his view of life—he really is a close friend."

The itinerants' laughter is cut short by a look from their hostess. Rising from her chair, Mrs. Spencer responds,

"I see. You two possess a sense of humor as deep as your hunger. Come, let us eat."

The stay at the Spencer home is a warm and fulfilling one. The open prayer and conversations with the dear lady continue well past midnight. Mostly the prayers touch on God providing for His Word to prosper in the town of Towcester. The sense that this will indeed happen visits Mrs. Spencer several times by evening's end.

Setting out early the next morning, the men gain the snow-covered road that leads them to Northampton. The trees lining the ancient road offer a stark welcome as the first rays of morning wrestle with the thickened sky and work their way through the iced trunks to the east. Against the backdrop of the fallen powder, the only color in the entire landscape is the brilliant red glow of rose hips scattered among the never-ending white of the snow and the Old Man's Beard tucked amidst dormant hedgerows. The chilling effects of the wind and below-freezing temperatures cause the men to tighten their outer coverings.

On this day, it isn't long before Francis opens up the conversation.

"Mrs. Spencer seemed as though she could read my thoughts. 'Twas an uncomfortable experience. Thankfully, the Lord gave assurance to share. The sweet woman desires the Gospel for Towcester, and I believe she may have as she wishes."

"She may. Francis, may I share a deep-seated feeling with you?"

Surprised, Francis peers in the direction of his companion. Reaching up to once again cover his neck with his jacket collar, he responds,

"You may."

"I envy your childhood."

"Oh?"

"I do. I love Mother and vaguely remember Father, but as a child, I longed for that which you share each time someone asks you about your mother. Without fail, you include your father. I envy this experience. Not with an unholy envy, but one that considers deeply the rich blessing of having such a perspective. You truly know and love your father."

"Do you desire I cease such activity?"

"Of course not. I look forward to what may come out of your mouth next. You truly love the man."

"I do. Many fond memories he has built into my life. I am sorry you were not privileged to the same."

"It is well with me, Francis. I shall draw from your experiences—I shall make them mine."

"Ha! Well then, perhaps if Wesley shall ever permit us back to Great Barr, I shall volunteer you to work Father's vegetable garden. The hard work will do you some good. As will cleaning and sharpening the tools before replacing them in the barn—mind you, each has its proper place. Afterwards, you may undertake one of my favorite tasks: cleaning out the horse stall. Yes, I can see Richard excelling at that specific labor—almost a divine appointment."

"Oh, Francis, all your traveling has corrupted you. Perhaps you shall aid me in the horse stalls. Yes, I believe a good shoveling shall cure your deepest discomforts . . ."

The fourth hour of the journey places them on the southern bank of the River Nene. Crossing the river, the itinerants enter the town of Northampton. Francis advises Richard,

"Straight away for the riding school."

Within one mile, the pair nears the fine structure. Francis is surprised to find little activity. He directs Richard through the two stone columns and the opened metal gate. Inside the timbered arena, Francis advises Richard,

"We shall dismount and walk from here."

On foot, the itinerants search the huge structure as the cold wind zips through the open-air setting. The strange silence is interrupted occasionally by the fretful wind as it slashes through gates and fences specifically designed for the equestrian ring. All this and the dark sky above prompt Francis's greatest fear. He voices it to his friend.

"Perhaps the Royal Guard has departed."

Richard and his horse follow as Francis leads Churchfield in the direction of the perimeter stables and coach houses. Approaching the door to one of the coach houses, Francis knocks on the wooden slab. The door slowly moves open under his hand. He peeks inside the dark, cold room, but there's nothing to see. He moves on to the next door.

A small window next to the door glows with flickering candlelight. Francis urges Richard,

"Hold Churchy; I expect someone is here."

Handing Richard the reins, Francis knocks on the door. Quickly, a man answers.

He is a short man, in regular civilian clothing—the kind a smithy would wear, minus the leather apron. Francis inquires,

"Looking for Captain Scott, Captain Jonathan Scott?"

Scratching the back of his head, the elder man replies,

"Cromwell's Blues have departed for some time. Nearly one year ago."

"I see. Perhaps you can direct us to the local Wesleyan meeting house?"

"I can. Not many make up their gathering. Pressure from the Anglican priests. They meet on Bridge Street. One-oh-nine Bridge Street. Next to the slaughterhouse, south quarter."

"Very well. Thank you."

Francis looks to Richard and exclaims,

"This is most disappointing!"

The south quarter of Northampton is north of the river, between the old south-wall boundary of the city and the waterway. The walls defining the city are long gone, destroyed by the order of King Charles II. The slaughterhouse and the meeting house are tucked inside the abandoned wall limits, less than two blocks from the riding school. The trip takes only a few minutes; the men are thankful for the short distance as the snow begins its delicate descent.

Nearing the tall, narrow building, Francis and Richard secure their horses to the two-story structure and approach the entry to the meeting house. After several attempts to rouse the house's resident, the door is opened from inside.

The woman standing in the low opening is an older woman, perhaps around sixty years old. Upon the completion of their introductions, she invites the itinerants indoors. Grateful for the gesture, the men step inside, shake the effects of the snowfall off their shoulders, and walk into the dark, cramped living space. The dank smell of the hallway reminds Francis of an underground cellar. The men make way for an adjacent room at the back of the building. Pointing to the wooden table in the corner, the woman offers the travelers a place to sit.

Francis inquires,

"Captain Scott and the Methodist soldiers—where have they gone?"

With a slow turn toward the men, the frail woman braces herself as she sits at the table with them. She draws a deep breath, the action of sitting having demanded much of the aged lady. She responds,

"London, I assume. Many of the King's soldiers are departing for the colonies, a place called Boston in newer England. The King had need of the Royal Blues in London."

"I see."

Francis's response is short, giving an air of uncertainty. His curiosity will not hold back for long.

"Boston. What of Boston?"

"I have heard that the citizens have rebelled against the King. Our mad English brethren."

Richard inquires,

"The local Wesleyans—Francis has expressed that there were nearly two thousand when last he heard Captain Scott preach. Where do so many meet? The meeting house seems inadequate."

The woman wraps her arms in front of her. Slowly, she raises her right hand and with her wrinkled thumb and forefinger gently grasps her nose. The extra skin of her right elbow cascades over her left palm as it firmly plants into the midsection of her thick frame. Lowering her hand to speak, she responds,

"Inadequate; the meeting house is adequate. We've barely fifty members at this time."

Both men sit back in their seats. The news is unexpected. Francis tries to understand how this could happen. Richard, too, silently searches for reasons. The itinerants have no words. The woman continues,

"When Captain Scott departed the military for the ministry with Whitefield and the Countess, the society experienced its initial decline. When the soldiers left shortly thereafter, the society suffered the fatal blow. Oh, several of us shall remain faithful to the end; however, this result delivers the fact: our town and our society were highly dependent upon the military."

"I see. Perhaps Richard and I could offer prayer for your society?"

"It would be most appreciated."

Richard and Francis's prayer for the Northampton society brings comfort to the old woman. *Why should such a healthy community dwindle?* The question is almost verbalized during Francis's prayer, but he keeps the thought to himself, knowing that he and Richard will have ample time to discuss the dilemma.

Another interesting result of the prayer is the old woman's suggestion that the men head back in the direction they came, to Whittlebury, a tiny town residing on the Roman road. She is adamant in her request.

"You must pay visit to my dear Betsy in Whittlebury. Miss Padbury, along with others, leads a prosperous work in the little town."

The next morning, the men agree to return in two days for the class meeting at the Bridge Street meeting house. The elderly lady is grateful, offering food and lodging to the men once again on their return.

Outdoors and atop their horses, Richard asks the obvious question.

"Are we heading to Clifton?"

Francis's pause is revealing, indicating that his struggle to decide is unexpected. In time, he responds,

"We shall head back, to Whittlebury, as instructed by the dear woman."

The all-day ride back to Whittlebury puts the men in town around four p.m. Along the route, the pair spot several red deer anxiously looking for food. Several of these magnificent creatures wander freely into the tiny village. In town, at the cut-stone house at 34 High Street, Richard knocks on the door. A middle-aged woman answers, and Richard offers,

"Miss Padbury?"

"No, I'm Mrs. Padbury."

After the usual introductions she graciously receives the itinerants, then hurries off to begin spreading word of the preaching this evening.

One by one, Mrs. Padbury's guests arrive and greet the itinerants. Included in the arrivals are Mr. Padbury, Thomas, and their daughter, Elizabeth. Elizabeth, or Betsy, as they call her, is an attractive young woman. She is the woman referred to by the lady in Northampton, and is also single and of the right dating age for Francis. This revelation fails to escape Richard and Francis.

As the members of this farming community arrive, they are far from empty-handed. The women present Richard and Francis with food items of various kinds. Salted beef, jarred fruits, and a loaf of freshly baked bread are among these precious offerings. One woman offers each of the men a neck scarf, saying,

"This shall aid in protecting you from the harsh elements."

Several men offer their services for foddering and shoeing the horses. With each adult arrival, several children spill into the happy home. Within an hour the house is crammed with fifty people waiting in eager anticipation for a sermon from the traveling preachers.

Standing at the front of the room, Richard prepares to deliver a short sermon. When he raises his hands for prayer, the room falls silent, and he pauses before offering his thanks to God. Looking toward Francis, he catches his itinerant partner deep in reflection—not of prayer, but of Betsy. He continues anyway.

At the completion of the prayer, Richard begins a Charles Wesley hymn.

> "Praise the Lord Who reigns above
> And keeps His court below;
> Praise the holy God of love
> And all His greatness show;
> Praise Him for His noble deeds,
> Praise Him for His matchless power;
> Him from Whom all good proceeds
> Let earth and heaven adore . . ."

The gathering joyously sings along until the completion of the hymn. Richard raises his hands and begins,

> "When God wants to convert the heathen, He will do it without consulting either you or me."

For the next twenty minutes, Richard preaches on the unbounded work of the Holy Spirit. The residents of Whittlebury rejoice in the teachings.

The completion of the sermon and subsequent closing prayer coincide with the arrival of an unexpected guest. The room's inhabitants fall silent as a man in his thirties dressed in a long grey coat walks into the room. Immediately, several young boys and a young girl, all preteens, rush to greet him. With arms wide open, he embraces the youngsters. The oldest, a tall, thin young boy who could be mistaken for one of the Brummies in Francis's past, drops from the loving huddle and bursts forth with an indignant anger,

> "Father, you are a sinner who is destined to hell."

Richard and Francis gasp at the brazen disrespect shown by the lad. Looking around the room, the view is even more upsetting. Several of the adults nod their mistaken approval of the young boy who confronted his unbelieving parent. Each of the boy's siblings stands away from their father and turns to their mother for advice. She nods approvingly toward the older sibling who scolded their dad. Again, Richard and Francis gasp with dismay at this act of disrespect.

Raising his Bible in his right hand, Francis interrupts the group.

> "Children, a word with you and your neighbors."

The children do not understand, nor do the adults in the room. Pushing further, Francis offers,

> "Do not the Scriptures call for each of us to honor our parents?"

Again, the room's visitors are speechless. Clearing his throat and stepping to the middle of the gathering, Richard lends his effort.

> "Despite your focus on truth, and regardless of their behavior, you must on all accounts honor your parents. Seek to reprove the man you call father, the man you love, with honor."

The young boy who verbally attacked his father droops his shoulders and weeps. His brothers and sister do the same. Without hesitation, the father and mother come together and embrace their children. Several of the remaining gatherers also embrace the family.

As the evening progresses in a more subdued fashion, Richard and Francis pull aside Mr. and Mrs. Padbury and the Whittlebury class leader, advising them to earnestly teach this evening's valuable lesson. The pair vows to do so.

The next morning, Richard and Francis head north again. They will need to be in Northampton the following day. For tonight, their plan is to stop once more in the town of Towcester. Despite the snow, which does not seem to slow, the four-mile trip will take them a couple of hours.

The motherly Mrs. Spencer welcomes the arrival of the itinerants in Towcester at eleven a.m. Despite the cordial greeting, the woman does not appear well. Immediately upon their entrance to her home, she begs the men to accompany her to an adjacent bedroom. The itinerants drop their saddlebags to the floor and follow.

In the room, a woman lies silent on the bed. The men look to the motherly figure of Mrs. Spencer, but she isn't saying a word. She stands at the doorway to the room, clutching a handkerchief to her nose and mouth, tears running down her stout cheeks.

The woman in the bed sits up and begins to sing,

> "When I shall leave this house of clay,
> Some glorious angels shall convey,
> And on their golden wings shall I
> Be wasted far above the sky."

At the completion of her singing, she turns toward Richard and proclaims,

> "Lend, lend your wings! I mount! I fly! Oh grave, where is thy victory? Oh death, where is thy sting?"

Turning toward Francis, she offers,

> "Good day, Pastor; what are these which are arrayed in white robes, and whence came they? These, they came out of great tribulation, and have washed their robes, and made them white in the blood of the Lamb. He is the life of my life, and the soul of my soul; He is the altogether lovely. These owe their revelation to His blessing."

Lying back down, the woman screams in agony, gripping the right side of her abdomen. Hastening to the woman's side, Mrs. Spencer kneels and prays,

> "Almighty Father, sweetly catch her parting breath, and make her gently glide to Your bosom. Take her carefully to her eternal home."

As quickly as the screams began, they come to a halt. Opening her eyes, the ailing woman turns her head toward Mrs. Spencer, who gently inquires,

> "How about some wine for your stomach?"

The ailing lady nods in agreement.

After drinking from the small cup, she leans toward the itinerants and the caring Mrs. Spencer. She whispers,

> "The next shall be in my Father's kingdom."

At this, she lays her head back on the pillow and closes her eyes.

Several hours pass as the men patiently wait with Mrs. Spencer. They watch as the ailing woman weaves in and out of consciousness for most of these hours. Nearing dinner time, a strange sound draws the men outdoors. Standing outside the front door of Mrs. Spencer's home, Richard points toward the northeast.

"I heard it coming from that direction."

Francis and Richard begin walking in that direction. A scream from the house sends them running back indoors.

At the bedside, the ailing lady stops her wails. She sits up and speaks to the itinerants.

"I see the glorious convoy prepared to conduct me to the mansions of bliss. I see them, harps in hands, dressed in white linen, palms of victory, and the never-fading crown."

Francis kneels beside the woman. He bows his head and offers a silent prayer. As he does so, the sickly woman lifts her hand and places it upon Francis's head.

"These that come out of the great tribulation require your telling."

Raising his head, he looks to the woman; her eyes are wide open, very wide open. They almost gleam. Francis's first reaction is, *I can see a glorious eternity in her eyes.* She continues,

"Jesus said to me, 'Did I not say to you that if you would believe, you would see the glory of God?' I have seen the glory of God. I will praise Him while I have breath, and I will praise Him again when I pass over the Jordan."

From over Francis's shoulder, Richard proclaims,

"Then shall we sing."

Immediately, Richard, Francis, and Mrs. Spencer break into a Wesleyan hymn. The ailing woman joins in, but only for the first line of the opening stanza. By the end of this first verse, she is singing the hymn in eternity.

For the next three months, Richard and Francis decide to alternate their efforts between the small groups in Northampton, Whittlebury, and Towcester. Although in Towcester the gatherings are small, the time with Mrs. Spencer helps Francis to bridge his homesickness. His evening prayers silently ask for a time to return home.

***

On Sunday, March 18, 1770, the blowing snow will not relent. The slashing waves of tight powder billow like a furled blanket suddenly unrolled and snapped in every direction. With each thrust of whirling snow, one expects the lashing effect to end in a loud pop. However, the thrashing wind doesn't offer an explosive snap; instead, it bellows a low, hollow cry of anguish. *This cannot be good* is the thought of John Wesley as he makes his way on horseback from Birmingham. The four-mile trip to Bromwich Heath, the home society of Francis Asbury, is made arduous by the hostile weather.

On this day, John Wesley is scheduled to preach in the West Bromwich meeting house, the two-story brick building on Paradise Street across from Dagger Hall and the heath. Francis and his young friends renovated this structure many years before. The residents of the local area buzz with the news that Wesley is stopping in to preach to the Bromwich society. Word has it he even plans to stop at nearby Wednesbury, the site of many persecutions more than a decade ago.

Everyone from the Bromwich society will be there. All of Francis's friends are expected to attend: the two Thomases, Thomas Ault and Thomas Russell; the two Jameses, James Mayo and James Bayley; William Emery; Edward Hand from Sutton Coldfield; Jabez, the younger brother of Thomas Ault; several young ladies traditionally associated with Nancy Brookes; and Nancy. Francis's parents, along with several groups of his friends' parents, will also participate in this special occasion. There is also the Foxall forge clan, many of the young and older men who worked with Francis and James Mayo. These and their families are among those eager to hear the famed Wesley.

At 1:30 in the afternoon, Wesley finally arrives at the Methodist meeting house on the heath. He ties his horse among the several already attached to the downwind side of the building, where a small roof overhang provides limited shelter for the animals. Walking back to the front of the building, Wesley pushes the front door open and makes his way to the stairs. Upstairs, he can hear the voices of a multitude. He silently whispers a prayer for divine assistance in his preaching. Ascending the steps, he finds the stairwell dark and fusty. The moist smell occupies his thoughts until an errant cobweb decides to lower into his path. Brushing away the dangling silk, he proceeds to the second-floor meeting room.

At the top of the stairs, he moves to push open the door to the room. It won't budge. He knocks on the oaken slab, and several gentlemen pull open the door. To their surprise, Wesley stands there with Bible in hand.

"May I enter?"

"You may if there was room. Seems the space is far from adequate for the likes of you, Mr. Wesley."

"Very well. Is there a place . . . ?"

"Mr. Wesley, those who are here represent only half who wish to attend. As strongly as we disagree with the solution, the only viable option seems outdoors, near the heath."

"Very well. Please, if someone would kindly accompany me to the intended place, I shall begin."

The men scramble about, each volunteering his service. Wesley and his three escorts descend the stairs as the word is shared with the rest of the room's inhabitants.

"Wesley shall preach outdoors."

The entire group of fifty people heads for the doorway to the stairs.

Outdoors, nearly two hundred people already stand in an area of the heath that is somewhat protected from the driving snow and wind. Wesley thinks to himself, *the conditions are too cruel*. However, it is clear that this group is determined to hear Wesley regardless of the challenges.

Led to a large boulder that stands on a slight rise in the landscape, Wesley thanks his escorts as he asks one for help to climb the stony pulpit. With his assistance complete, Wesley's aid moves to the front of the gathering. The entire group huddles together for warmth.

Wesley raises the Bible in his hand, and all in attendance fall silent for his opening prayer.

> "Brothers and sisters of Bromwich, let us pray. 'Carry them back! Carry them back!' This was the cry of the heathenish husband, who after his wife joined the Methodists and laid off swearing, urged the magistrate of this town to send me away. 'My wife used to possess quite the tongue! Now she is quiet as a lamb.' With a grateful heart, Almighty Father, we thank Thee that this region has embraced the Savior. Amen.
>
> "I have chosen an applicable hymn, penned by my brother Charles: 'Depth of Mercy.' Shall we begin?"

Raising his hands, Wesley counts the time and begins,

> "Depth of mercy! Can there be
> Mercy still reserved for me?
> Can my God His wrath forbear?
> Me, the chief of sinners, spare?"

The entire gathering sings joyously above the swirling winds of snow,

> "I have long withstood His grace,
> Long provoked Him to His face,
> Would not hearken to His calls,
> Grieved Him by a thousand falls . . ."[160]

At the completion of the fifth and final stanza, all settle into silence for Wesley's sermon. He begins,

> "As for me and my house, we will serve the Lord. Joshua, now grown old, gathered the tribes of Israel to Shechem, and called for the elders of Israel, for their heads, for their judges and officers, and they presented

---

[160] First two stanzas of the Charles Wesley hymn "Depth of Mercy," 1740.

themselves before the Lord. And Joshua rehearsed to them the great things which God had done for their fathers, concluding with that strong exhortation: 'Now therefore fear the Lord, and serve Him in sincerity and truth, and put away the gods which your fathers served on the other side of the flood.' Can anything be more astonishing than this that even in Egypt, yea, and in the wilderness, where they were daily fed, and both day and night guided by miracle, the Israelites, in general, should worship idols, in flat defiance of the Lord their God!"

Everyone in the crowd focuses on each word that comes from Wesley's mouth. He continues,

"He proceeds: 'If it seemeth evil to you to serve the Lord, choose ye this day whom ye will serve, whether the gods your fathers served on the other side of the flood, or the gods of the Amorites in whose land ye dwell. But as for me and my house, we will serve the Lord.' A resolution this worthy of a hoary-headed saint, who had had large experience, from his youth up, of the goodness of the Master to whom he had devoted himself, and the advantages of His service. How much is it to be wished that all who have tasted that the Lord is gracious, all whom He has brought out of the land of Egypt, out of the bondage of sin, those especially who are united together in Christian fellowship, would adopt this wise resolution! Then would the work of the Lord prosper in our land, then would His Word run and be glorified. Then would multitudes of sinners in every place stretch out their hands unto God, until the glory of the Lord covered the land, as the waters cover the sea . . .'"

The sermon goes along smoothly; some rejoice verbally, others fall to their knees in tears. Some in the front proclaim the glories of God, accenting Wesley's key points in his sermon. Nearly halfway through the sermon, a woman in the back of the gathering screeches. Her husband, who stands next to her, catches her as she faints. Several women around her huddle in closer.

"Elizabeth, are you well?"   "Let us remove her indoors."
She fights back.
"No, no! You mustn't. I scream not because of conviction. I scream for my son has arrived!"

The men and women attending Elizabeth look around. Her son is nowhere in sight. She pushes herself upright.

"Look, near the front and to the right—there he is!"

Those standing close by immediately spot the young man. Elizabeth's husband hands her to two friends and launches himself around the perimeter to greet his son. A couple of those helping Elizabeth also dart to the outside. Nearing the front, her husband finally reaches the young man.

"Francis!"

Joseph extends his arms and embraces Francis.

For a moment, Wesley continues his sermon. However, the crowd's polite yet excited reaction to the welcoming home of Francis soon causes him to pause. With his hands tightly grasping his Bible, and his eyes fighting back tears, Wesley smiles at the sweet event.

Racing around the outside of the gathering, Elizabeth runs to greet her son. Several attendees whisper the arrival of Francis. Before long, several of Francis's friends discover the pleasing revelation. Elizabeth embraces Joseph and Francis as the entire gathering, Wesley included, applauds the loving embrace.

Wesley offers,

"Many have commended my sermons, but never only partway through."

Wesley's sermon on grace and mercy completes to a receptive crowd who are grateful for his visit.

At sermon's end, the crowd surrounds Wesley and it surrounds Francis. In time, Francis and his family move indoors to rejoice upstairs in the Methodist meeting room, surrounded by all of Francis's childhood friends. The atmosphere is one of jubilant celebration. James Mayo, the quiet James Mayo, pronounces,

"Francis is home; let us celebrate his return!"

As the group applauds and shouts, John Wesley strolls into the room. Francis immediately releases from his mother's embrace and walks to his leader. Spotting Wesley and noting Francis's approach, Richard also makes his way toward the father of Methodism. Francis offers,

"Mr. Wesley, I am most grateful for the opportunity to return home."

"I believed it so. I assume Pastor Glasbrook has also given you and Pastor Whatcoat your assignments for the remainder of the year?"

"He has. Although it will pain me to depart from my dear friend Richard, I welcome this two-week break from my circuit. I shall return to Bedfordshire promptly upon its completion."

Wesley replies,

"As well. In spite of the harsh weather, I must depart for nearby Wednesbury. The funeral of a dear woman, Elizabeth Longmore, awaits. This long-time member of the Wednesbury society recently passed, and I promised my sendoff."

"Very well. Again, Richard and I give much thanks for this privilege to return home."

Wesley nods his approval of the young man's polite expression. He tips his head toward Richard also, then turns and heads for the doorway to the stairs. The townspeople of West Bromwich are sad to see Wesley leave, but they are happy for the return of their long-time resident and local preacher, Francis Asbury.

From the other side of the room, Thomas Ault calls out,

"Does anyone recall Francis's preaching at the front of this stuffy room? What of that rickety three-legged pulpit with the three narrow wood spindles and the thin, flat oak top?"

James Bayley offers,

"A thin table for a thin sermon . . ."

The informal group erupts with laughter. All look to Francis for his response.

"Some in the assembly failed to handle a worthy sermon."

The boys respond in kind, their mocking gestures broadening the smile on Francis's face.

Glued to Francis's side are his mother and father. Elizabeth continues to wipe away tears.

"This is most unbelievable."

Joseph's thick arm is secured around his son's broad shoulders.

Peering about the room, Francis looks for the gentle and pleasing face, the one that has for so long warmed his heart. It is absent. Francis finds it odd that Nancy is not present, but decides to hold off further inquiry until he can separate from his mother. Until then, he enjoys the impromptu celebration.

The first evening home lasts well past midnight for Francis and his family and friends. The townspeople do not want to depart. Not until Francis agrees to visit many of them, as well as to conduct the next two weeks of class meetings and Sabbath worship services, do they depart for the night. Heading home with his mother attached to one side and his dad to the other, Elizabeth makes a comment.

"I would not fault you if you were to venture to find Nancy on the morrow."

Francis's sudden stop brings the trio to a halt. His welcomed feelings surprise him. He has never felt that his mother completely approved of the relationship. *She may not;* the thought causes him to hesitate in replying. However, it fails to hold Francis back for long.

"I may proceed to find her now."

"Very well, Francis; your mother and I shall await your arrival. Your room is ready and waiting for your return."

"Thank you, Father. Thank you, Mother. My heart aches to . . ."

Francis decides not to share that his heart aches to discover if Nancy and he still have a relationship. Instead, he offers,

"My heart aches. I shall return shortly."

Making his way toward Nancy's home, Francis's body trembles with nervousness. The feelings originate in his abdomen, a swirling morass of emotions that seem destined to pilfer a pleasing outcome. He continues to the front of her property. The heavy night air flows from his uneasy breaths. The light snow has finally stopped, for which Francis is grateful. The day's storm and the subsequent lighter snowfall have covered the heath in white. Pausing to gaze at the glistening surroundings, he wipes away a tear; *so long have I been gone.*

It takes several minutes, but he eventually gathers his emotions and looks to the sky. The clearing in the clouds allows a partial view of a distant constellation and a closer, friendlier, half-moon smile. Francis considers his current situation, standing in front of Nancy's home after midnight; *this is an odd occasion. Late in the evening, the distance in time is great. I don't know if I should stay or run. I cannot run home, but I cannot stand here any longer, either. I must move forward.* His sporadic thoughts move him at last to the front door.

The light tapping on the wooden slab is repeated twice before the door finally opens. Nancy's father wipes away his obvious grogginess and inquires,

"Yes, may I be of assistance?"

"Mr. Brookes, 'tis Francis, Francis Asbury."

" 'Allo, Francis. Nancy has retired for the evening."

"I understand, Mr. Brookes. It was my hope that I could see her."

From behind Mr. Brookes, a gentle hand is placed upon his shoulder, the delicate skin sinking into the thick cotton coverings that protect him from the harsh weather. Francis's methodical breathing pauses for a second. He lifts his gaze to the pleasing face that accompanies the long, thin arm.

Realizing that his efforts to postpone this meeting have fallen short, Mr. Brookes excuses himself.

"Nancy, invite Francis in; the night is cold. I shall retire."

Mid-departure, Mr. Brookes turns back toward the pair, who are silently staring at one another.

"Francis, no more than fifteen minutes. You can resume on the morrow."

"Thank you, Mr. Brookes."

For nearly two minutes, the couple sit in complete silence. The flickering candlelight shadows the vertical edge of a nearby china cabinet onto two hands that tightly grasp each other. The gentle sniffles trickling from Nancy are hard to decipher. Francis cannot determine if the tears are for a joyful reunion or for bad news she may be harboring. Fighting the urge to embrace her, Francis wipes the tears from her soft cheeks and chin, then reaches up to place his hand on her shoulder.

> "Failed to see you at Wesley's service."

With her free hand, Nancy grasps Francis's shoulder. She replies,

> "Didn't plan on attending."

> "Oh?"

> "Oh, Francis, I beg to talk of this tomorrow. Allow me to just sit and enjoy your quiet company."

> "Very well."

The two sit in silence. There is the occasional stroking away of a tear by Francis on Nancy's smooth skin, followed by his gentle touch on the back of her hand. Francis shares,

> "Almost feels alien to sit with you."

> "As well with me. As if we shall have to start again."

> "A pleasant task."

Nancy does not respond. She reaches up and wipes one of her tears away. Grasping Francis's right hand with both of hers, she offers,

> "Perhaps we should take this up tomorrow. It is rather late, and my parents shall remain until you leave."

> "Very well. I shall visit in the afternoon, tomorrow."

Leaning forward, Francis kisses her on the forehead. Again, she wipes away one of her tears, this time refusing to look Francis in the eyes.

Walking out the front door, Francis toys with several emotions. He is glad to be home. He is also glad that Nancy invited him in. He struggles with her not attending the visit by John Wesley, and is troubled by her push for silence. *Why did she refuse to converse?* Trudging through the cold and windy conditions, Francis eventually drops the self-doubting questions and focuses his thoughts on Nancy. *My, how I have missed that pleasurable face.*

The next day finds Francis up at four a.m. He spends an hour in prayer at the table in the main room of his parent's home. A montage of sweet memories thwarts his efforts, and his focus lingers on the flickering taper lighting these quiet moments of his first morning home. He remembers the many hours spent reading at this window, his mother warning that he would ruin his vision by reading in such a low-light setting. He remembers the many times he sat at this table, praying that he wouldn't have to return to school. *That churl,* he thinks of his cruel instructor, *I should have walked out on him long before I did.*

Heading outdoors, Francis catches the first morning rays. Despite the unbearable cold, he needs to use the toilet hut. He reminisces about his many trips to . . . chuckling, he decides to let the fond remembrances stop there.

On his way to the facilities, his foot knocks against an oak board submerged beneath the light snowfall. The impact startles him to the point of anger. He rears back his leg, ready to launch the unwelcomed intruder. Bearing down for impact, he abruptly brings his leg to a stop. Next to the wood, he has noticed a familiar sight: a curled ball of spines, a tiny creature lying motionless in the cold, white powder. Abandoning his morning visit, as well as his not-so-admirable outburst, he lifts the tightly wound creature and attempts to warm him against his clothing.

"Come, hedgie, 'tis far too cold to lie about."

Racing into his father's barn, Francis locates a small wooden crate. He uses a wheeled barrow to fetch hay, which he places into the crate. He then buries the tiny hedgehog snugly under the hay.

"This shall warm you to life."

Francis searches the barn, looking for a suitable lid to keep out the cold. Locating an old piece of his father's clothing, he places the fabric over the rough-sawn edges of the crate. Lifting the makeshift box, he quickly sets off for the inside of the Asbury home.

Next to the fireplace, Francis sets down the box with the tiny animal in it.

"The warmth of the fire shall lend aid."

Watching her son, Elizabeth knows what he's doing. She doesn't stop him; Francis's effort to save the hedgehog from freezing to death is a welcome return of Elizabeth's memories of her son's childhood. He's done this so many times before. The occurrence is normal in the Midland winters. These tiny animals usually abandon their hibernation spots prematurely, placing them in grave danger. Francis calls to his mother,

"He shall keep until I return."

"From circuit? I don't think so, Francis."

"No, Mother, from Bromwich. I shall visit a friend today."

"Oh? I had hoped you would spend the day with Father and me."

"I shall return soon. Need to talk with James at the forge."

"Very well. Shall you at least eat dinner with your parents?"

"I shall. And on second thought, I shall take the box with me."

Elizabeth departs for her bedroom upstairs. One thought occupies her departure: *I hope he is visiting James and not that young girl.*

Entering Bromwich, Francis detours his journey to the forge and heads straight for Nancy's. Standing at the front door, with the box in hand, Francis knocks. Nancy opens the door, expecting to see Francis, but not expecting to see the box. She inquires,

"Now, Francis, what is in the box?"

"I shall show you. May I come in?"

"I suppose so; it is rather cold outside. And you brought me a gift . . ."

"And I brought you a gift, now Nancy."

Nancy's eyes and smile beckon him into the warm house.

Standing at the kitchen table, Francis slowly lifts the cover off the box. At this, Nancy's mother enters the room.

"Good day, Pastor Asbury. Whatever resides in such a large box?"

"Mother, a gift can never be too large."

Slightly shocked by Nancy's comment, Francis decides to interrupt.

"Well, Nancy, it is less a gift and more a discovery."

"Discovery?"

Now Nancy's mother is intrigued. She joins them at the table as Francis continues,

"This morning's discovery."

Digging through the hay, Francis lifts out the balled-up animal. He still has not uncurled his tiny, chubby body. Perhaps fearing danger, the hedgehog will not open to expose anything. In fact, Francis wonders if the little fellow is indeed alive.

"Ah!"

Nancy's gentle exclamation is exactly what Francis was hoping to hear. His face beams with an appreciation of her compassionate heart. Nancy's mother, on the other hand, expresses a different sentiment.

"Blasted hedgie. By spring we shall be inundated with the nosy nuisances."

Ignoring her mother, Nancy reaches forward and urges,

"Hand her over, Francis."

He does so, as he informs her,

"We shall have to nurse him back to health."

"Let's give her a name."

"I have thought of his name already."

"Well, give me time and I shall gain her a name."

Nancy's mother shakes her head, the kind of shake that conveys that these two aren't hearing each other. *Rather like marriage . . .* She keeps that thought to herself. She offers as she departs the room,

"Advise me later of the outcome."

Francis confronts,

"Her? I have thought of a boy's name. We should name him a boy."

"I say girl. We shall give her a girl's name. I like Victoria."

"Victoria? Why Victoria, not William, James, or Henry? If it must begin with the letter V, then why not Victory?"

"Francis, it shall be a girl. It is final—Anne shall be her name."

"Anne? Wherever did you get Anne?"

"She is a royal, like the Queen."

"A royal hedgehog. Borders on anarchy."

"Far from anarchy; she is monarchy."

Francis doesn't fight it. He is happy that Nancy is drawn to the tiny animal. Even more so, he is happy that the two of them are together. Reaching to the creature in Nancy's arms, Francis strokes its spiny back. The hedgehog still isn't moving. Francis advises,

"He is breathing, barely. He really should remain in the warmth of the box."

"Very well, I shall place Anne back into her castle."

Their battle over the sex of the animal wages for the rest of the day. Nearing dinnertime, Francis departs, leaving the box with Nancy. He plans a visit to the forge and then home for one of his mother's fine meals.

Nearing Foxall's forge, the chamois-colored reed grass lies thickly along the free-form borders of Forge Mill Lake. The snow-topped reeds appear as if they've been dipped in powdered sugar. Darting in and out of the clumpy ornamental grasses, tiny sand martins chase various edible winged insects. The birds blend into their natural surroundings, at least until they expose their soft white underbellies, seen easily from below. Their slightly notched tails are distinctive, as is the tiny dark band around each of their breasts. Francis stops to watch and listen. Listening is easy, as their loud, harsh, staccato twitters echo across the water. In a month, when thousands more are present at the lake, the sight and sound of the large flocks darting over the water and land will dominate the valley region and continue into the summer.

Entering the front entrance to the forge, Francis stops. He peers into the heated space. Steam rises from the furnaces, as does smoke from the chimneys outdoors. Above all this is the piercing clanging from the hammers beating out steel on the anvils. As several of the employees notice the preacher standing and watching the operation, the sparks cease to fly from their work stations. As the unexpected silencing of these locations catches on with the other workers, they also bring their pounding to a halt. After a few seconds of quiet, one of the workers yells out,

"Mayo, seems you've company today!"

Looking up from his station, James replies,

" 'Tis only a preacher. Thought it was an old nailer."

Francis laughs as he removes his hat and walks toward James. On his way, several men step forward to join him at Mayo's station. After a dozen or so steps, the two friends are face to face. James extends his hammer toward Francis.

"Know what this is for?"

Francis peers silently at his pal, then looks toward the men who are now gathered around the pair. The younger workers who never knew Francis have no idea what is transpiring. They look at the tall, thin preacher, wondering what he is going to do. He surely doesn't appear capable of holding a hammer, let alone knowing what it is for. They look at James, whom they do know. To them, James is a tough nailer, not to be trifled with. Is James going to punch the preacher? Is the preacher here to confront James? A couple of the boys whisper to each other their worry for Francis: "James will surely take him." Francis removes the hammer from James's hand. He walks over to the anvil and readies the head of the hammer on top of the steel bench. Slowly lifting the hammer, Francis looks to one of the young boys. The lad's wide-eyed stare reveals his anxiety for the man of God. He blurts out to James,

"Don't 'urt the preacha'. He's good man."

James replies,

"How do ya' know he's good? Seems rather full of himself to think he can work the forge. All he's good for is spreading the Holy Word."

The young boy's friend joins in to help.

"Ya' know the Word is good, so he has to be good. My momma loves the Holy Word."

James shakes his head.

"Now two of you like this preacher. I will deal with the both of you later. As for now, this preacher better know what to do with the hammer."

Slamming the hammer onto the anvil, Francis causes the two young boys to jump. The men in the group laugh aloud. So does Francis, and so does James. Before Francis can set the hammer down, James hugs him. The boys are confused.

Releasing his hug, James darts for the boys, who disappear in a flash. James returns to Francis.

"The boys probably have need of an outfit change."

"Ha! We don't scare that badly, James."

The men of the forge who knew Francis approach to congratulate him on the itinerancy. Their questions are many, several at once. Francis does his best to weather the onslaught. One by one, he answers everyone. With James's arm over his shoulder, Francis offers to the men,

"Can you spare James for a little?"

A tall, thin man, taller than Francis, walks over and offers a gap-toothed smile.

"Don't make much difference if he's here or not."

The surrounding men burst into laughter. Francis nods his approval, and James protests,

"You didn't have to agree with them as easily as that, Francis!"

"I know."

The two men head for the forge's chapel.

Inside the tiny space, Francis and James take a seat. Looking around the simple room, Francis remarks,

"Such a special place. I have missed its regular occurrences very much."

James responds,

" 'Tis indeed a special place. Here for long, Francis?"

"Two weeks."

"Two weeks, well then. I assume you will conduct the class meetings next week also."

"I shall. James, may I ask a question?"

Pulling his chair closer to Francis, James responds,

"What is bothering you, Francis?"

"Does it show?"

"It does. I noticed it the other night. You appeared to be searching - - For someone special."

Moving his eyes from James to the dirty wooden floor, Francis pauses. His silence is interrupted by James's question.

" 'Tis about Nancy?"

"Yes, it is. Nancy seems . . ."

Again he pauses. James urges,

"Go on."

"She seems different."

"Francis, you've been away for three years. We all are different. Even Thomas Ault is different . . . well, not that different."

They both laugh. James continues,

"The only constant is our dear Foxall—he still drives us hard."

"James, this is far from trivial. Something has changed."

"Have you approached her?"

"She seems guarded, almost careful."

"In what way?"

"I cannot say."

"Give it time, Francis; three years is a long time. At our age, three years is almost unbearable."

Although James's encouragement eases Francis's worry a little, he continues to sense a barrier with Nancy. Walking home, Francis calms his fears with thoughts of his mother's awaiting home-cooked meal.

Eating dinner with his mother and father, Francis experiences a most welcome sense of peace. This is his home, his childhood home. And it feels good and secure to return. Leaning forward for another piece of bread, Francis inquires of his parents,

"How are the Bromwich class meetings?"

"They are well attended. Your mother and I especially enjoyed when Richard led the meetings. We encouraged his entry into the itinerancy. We are looking forward to your efforts for the next two weeks. Many will attend because of your return. I would not expect much empty space in the meeting room."

"What of Nancy and her family? Have they attended regularly?"

Joseph and Elizabeth look to each other, the kind of look that communicates they haven't noticed. Their visual exchange goes unnoticed by Francis. Joseph offers,

"Do you think Edward Hand shall attend? On the night of your return, he seemed to indicate so."

"I could not say. I assume he will, along with many of the young people from Sutton. What of Nancy, has she attended regularly?"

"Believe so. Elizabeth, do we have more bread?"

"Joseph, must I? I'd planned to save for the morn. Very well, then; hold steady."

Elizabeth departs for the bread. Francis thinks to himself, *perhaps I shall ask Richard about Nancy.*

The next day once again finds Francis at the home of Nancy. The two of them occupy their time with the hedgehog. The little animal is alive and quite appealing. His tiny legs somehow manage to support his chubby frame. During the night he began to walk around the box, and the nocturnal activity woke Nancy from her sleep. She instinctively secured the cloth lid, knowing from experience that the animal is a climber, capable of getting out of the box and causing mischief.

Cuddling the hedgehog, Nancy offers,

"Francis, do you want to hold her?"

"She seems at home with you. Perhaps later."

Surprised by Francis's compliance with her opinion that the hedgehog is female, Nancy replies,

"She is a lovely companion."

Sitting next to Nancy, Francis asks,

"How large are the class meetings these days in Bromwich?"

"Oh, I don't know. I would guess about the same."

Her reply strikes Francis as uncharacteristic. He presses for more.

"Have you not attended?"

Failing to look directly at Francis, Nancy occupies herself with the hedgehog and replies,

"It has been some time since I have."

"How much time?"

"Francis, must we talk of this now? Are you hungry? I am sure Mother has bread and some meat in the kitchen."

"I'm not interested in food, Nancy."

"Very well."

"Nancy, how long since you have attended class meetings?"

"Francis, must we talk of this now?"

"Nancy, am I to expect you at the meeting tomorrow night?"

"I will try to make it. Unless Mother requires me here."

Francis's thoughts run away for a moment. *What is transpiring here? Is this the doubt which troubles me? Is she attending at all?* Nevertheless, despite her refusal to answer, Francis is both happy and upset. He is thankful he has narrowed the topic of his anxiety with Nancy, but upset by the result—she seems distant to the faith. *This is who I am. How do we maintain our relationship when we are of such differing opinions?*

The night of the class meeting finds Francis at the helm. Richard Whatcoat is happy to sit and watch his friend in action. Leading this group generates a sweet emotion in Francis. These are his people, the ones who first believed in his ability to teach, preach, and lead a community of believers. Throughout the night, Francis lovingly approaches each member about his or her faith. He encourages and he confronts where needed. Standing tall at the front of the room, he appears as a delegate of the King and an ambassador of a distant land.

Francis's efforts encourage even himself, despite the fact that Nancy fails to show. Completing his class meeting duties, he walks over to Richard and asks,

"Richard, did you ever expect such a fine evening?"

"Now, Francis, with you leading your old group—how could it turn out otherwise?"

"You are too kind, my friend. It has not all gone well."

"Oh?"

"Nancy neglected to attend."

"Does this trouble you, Francis?"

Silence.

Richard draws a deep breath. He expected this revelation to eventually reach Francis. He puts an arm on Francis's shoulder and responds,

> "I expected this. In your mind, she seems to have walked away from the faith."
>
> "Did she attend when you led?"
>
> "She did. Didn't notice when, but at some point, she just stopped attending."

Francis's face conveys his pain. Richard notices and offers,

> "Francis, not all is lost."
>
> "It isn't? Seems very much so. This is my life. God is my life. Does she not see that I have left home for Him, left family for Him? How do I yoke myself with one who does not value God as I do?"
>
> "Is this really the issue, Francis? Perhaps you should give her time? After all, she has shared much."
>
> "Shared much? How so?"
>
> "She has shared you with God. Perhaps she never considered the effects."
>
> "I don't know, Richard. It pains me."
>
> "Effects, Francis. Focus on how the itinerancy affects her. I know this pains you. I wish it were not so. But you need to observe. In time, she will feel confident enough to communicate."
>
> "I hope so."

The following week busies Francis with society activities, a Friday night love feast, and a Sabbath sermon, followed by another class meeting. As the second week home nears an end, Francis has one more opportunity to work through this troubling issue with Nancy. Approaching her home on an unseasonably warmer afternoon, Francis once again pauses to view the front of her house. He realizes this is his last evening before he returns to the circuit. *This relationship is in Your hands, Lord. Help Nancy and me to accomplish Your will for us.*

With temperatures seeming less like winter and more like spring, Francis and Nancy decide to walk to their favorite spot, the large rock on the edge of the Bromwich Heath. Sitting next to each other, the pair look out into the shrubland, where the warmer weather is melting the snow from the week before. The low-growing vegetation yearns for the approaching spring weather. And Francis yearns to leave for the circuit with this relationship intact. He inquires,

> "Have I wronged you, Nancy?"

She fails to reply. He continues,

> "For the last two weeks of class activities, you failed to attend any save one. Are you not in love with the Savior?"

Silence.

"Have you lost your affections for me, Nance?"

"Francis, I don't know why I failed to attend the class activities. I enjoyed the Sunday night service. I would have attended the love feast and class meetings; however . . ."

She doesn't complete her comment. Francis closes his eyes to keep a tear from falling down his cheek. He is uncertain; *is this a test of my commitment to God, and is it the end of our relationship? Does she require . . . ?* Nancy cuts off the completion of his thought.

"Francis, since a child, I have always considered you and me as one. But I am torn."

"Torn?"

"Francis, this is difficult. I don't want to bring hurt."

"But I am hurting, Nance. It is as if I am standing, alone, in a swampy mire. There is no real footing for my feelings. What type of hurt do you intend?"

She doesn't reply. After a minute of silence, she raises her right hand to wipe away her own tear. With both hands, she nervously pats her dress against her legs. She glances at Francis, then to the ground.

Francis once again asks,

"Hurt, Nancy—what hurt are you referring to?"

Again, silence is her reply. Pointing toward the low land in front of them, Nancy offers,

"Perhaps we should return to my home and retrieve the hedgehog."

"Retrieve the hedgehog? Nancy, you are not making any sense."

Jumping down from the rock, Francis walks with his back to Nancy. He stares out into the still landscape—there are no signs of life, no birds nor animals. He places both his hands on his hips and silently begs God, *help me.*

Returning to Nancy, he places his right boot onto the boulder and sets his chin on his clasped hands resting upon his raised knee. Saying nothing, he looks into Nancy's moistened eyes. Realizing he will not relent, Nancy persists,

"This would be an excellent place to release Anne."

The evening's walk back to the Brookes home is without conversation. Francis escorts Nancy to the front door and departs. Not wanting to indicate his sadness, he walks home without raising his hands to wipe away the tears that stream down his face.

Finding Richard, Francis draws comfort from his friend's embrace. His uncontrollable sobbing worries Richard.

"I am sorry, Francis."

Pushing back from his friend, Francis retrieves a handkerchief from his coat pocket. He wipes his cheeks and chin, which are covered with the signs of his lamenting. Richard inquires,

"Care to talk?"

"I do. She has said nothing in word. But she implies much."

"How so?"

"Seems she wishes I would release her."

"I see. Will you?"

"Hadn't planned on it. Perhaps I haven't a choice."

"Perhaps. Has she indicated why?"

"No."

Richard invites his friend to sit. Taking the chair next to him, he offers,

"What are you called to, Francis? Is it marriage or the itinerancy?"

"I've always thought the itinerancy. But it pains me so to think that she shall no longer stand as an option."

"An option? Francis, marriage is more than an option."

"I did not intend it as you say it, Richard."

"I understand. However, you must make a decision. Look at Jesus; did He not accomplish His ultimate task? How would humanity have fared if all He did was teach the truths of the Bible? Would not mankind remain in its sinful despair?"

"What are you indicating?"

"What I am trying to get you to consider is that Jesus came not only to spread truth; His ultimate goal was to die. What is the ultimate goal of God's call on your life? Is it as a married and located preacher, or is it as an itinerant? Only you and the Lord can know this. Either is commendable. Perhaps Nancy refuses to keep you from that which she is confident of? You must ask her."

Francis lowers his head as he nods his agreement.

The next morning finds Francis and Richard at the Asbury cottage. There, Elizabeth and Joseph pack their saddlebags with delicious food. Elizabeth also offers a blanket to each. Despite Elizabeth's verbal reluctance, the goodbyes are short and to the point. By six a.m. the men are on the trail, Richard returning to Oxfordshire and Francis to Bedfordshire.

Wesley's instruction to Francis via Glasbrook's letter is to attend to the western portion of the circuit. The Wesleyan societies in the eastern Bedfordshire towns of Northampton, Clifton, Hertford, Luton, and Millbrook are sadly on the decline. Wesley made it a point to provide these with more seasoned preachers, planning to preach himself at Northampton before the summer's conference in

London. Before his visit home, Francis was upset that he could not visit Clifton, the town where Ruth resided. After his unsettling dealings with Nancy, this obstacle no longer threatens any damaging effects.

From Staffordshire, Francis travels Watling Street to the southeast. The ancient Roman road that lies east of Sutton Coldfield runs directly into Francis's desired destination of Towcester. Entering Towcester, he spots the thatched-roof house of Mrs. Spencer. No longer do the groupings of trees marking the edges of this tiny town expose themselves within the artistic grey of January. The deciduous trees sprout their first signs of life as tiny shoots emerge from the spindling branches.

Dismounting from Churchfield, Francis secures the animal at the side of the home, where a small farm bin of straw has been placed against the stone structure. The fodder is intended specifically for the itinerants who visit the Spencer home. Walking around to the front, Francis is greeted by Mrs. Spencer.

> "Oh, that look on your face tells me you have seen your mother."

> "How do you accomplish such feats?"

> "Oh, that little farm bin does come in handy."

Francis's chuckle reveals his understanding that one of his fellow itinerants must have shared that he was heading home for a time. Tipping his hat, he follows her into her home.

Once again, the smells of a warm meal embrace Francis. Mrs. Spencer bustles about, setting an additional plate for dinner. She advises,

> "You've plenty of time to wash up before dinner. You know where the basin is, in the back room. You'll need to draw water from the spring out back."

> "I shall."

Making his way to the back room, Francis admires the creamware bowl; *most definitely the fine work of the Staffordshire artisans.* He carefully lifts it and heads for the spring.

Outdoors, the crisp air dances its annual waltz, gliding slowly between winter and the beginning of spring. Francis bends down and places the bowl under the natural spring and collects his water. The clear liquid is cold to his hands, even colder as he splashes it upon his face. The end-of-the-day beard stubble rasps against his calloused hands. As he leans forward on his knees, a slight burning sensation rises in his lower back; he realizes this strain is from the countless hours on horseback, aggravated by his dousing in the River Severn, near Gloucester. He straightens up, pressing a balled fist into his lower back. The stretch brings a quick relief.

Back on his feet, Francis retrieves the basin and heads indoors. The welcoming smell of dinner is one of his favorite sensations. He gently replaces the bowl onto the table in the adjacent room and makes his way to the dinner table.

For the next four months, Francis alternates between the little towns in the western portion of the circuit. The main location is Whittlebury, and in time, Towcester emerges as a tiny society. During that time, he does his best to meet the needs of the struggling societies. A letter from home brings a slight relief, but the work is hard. Several of the local societies are dwindling, and Francis cannot understand why.

A little way up the Roman road to the northwest, the little town of Weedon is also a regular stop for Francis. In fact, the ancient road, now known as Watling Street, was for a time called Weedon Street. Despite the locals who do not welcome the Methodists, the small start can be credited to Francis's consistent return in the face of opposition. While in Weedon, Francis pauses to write his parents.

> *Dear Parents:*
> *I send these few lines to let you know that I am well, and that I had your last, though I have put off writing through the hurry of business. At present I find myself a little at rest to write to you, though in past life various have been the exercises of my afflicted mind, and still I cry out, Woe is me! For I am a man of unclean lips. A want of holiness bows me down before God and man. I know that I am not what I ought to be, in thought, word, and deed. And O how hard to be borne is this, when well considered. Thou tellest another he should not speak evil. Dost thou? Thou that sayest another should have no unholy desires, hast thou such in thy heart? When I meet with fightings without and fears within, my heart trembles, my courage fails, my hands hang down, and I am ready to give up all for lost. I despair almost of holding out to the end, when I think of the difficulties I have to wade through. I can say with Job, I would not live always. Or, Oh! that Thou wouldst hide me in*

the grave! Or with Jonah, 'Tis better for me to die than to live. Oh! The peaceable dead are set free. The bliss that I covet, they have.

At this time, I am in trying circumstances about the people and places; but sometimes I please myself that I shall go hence and leave these parts. But then I shall take my nature with me that starts at suffering, and the devil will be hard at my heels to tempt me; and if my trials are different, still they will and must come.

I do not expect to stay here another year. Where I shall go I cannot tell. Most that know you ask after you, and give their love to you— Miss Tyers, in particular, and her mother, and Mrs. Spencer. I read those lines to Betty Gent and her husband, and both of them seemed much affected. I have been most of my time in Bedfordshire since you left me. Mr. England's people are well. They have had the things you sent; not one broken. I hope both of you will keep on in the good way of God, and will seek to Him, that you may increase with the increase of God. In so doing you will do well.

If you write, let it be quickly. Direct to Towcester. I believe I shall go to the Conference, and when that is over I will come home, unless something very pressing falls out. And if so, I will watch for an opportunity, and will take the first to come home. If I do come, it will be about the first Wednesday after the Conference. If I do not come, I will send a letter by some preacher. Give my love to all friends. I am glad to hear of your prosperity. May the Lord increase it a hundredfold in every soul and among the people in general.

So prays your unworthy son, yet in dutiful respect,

Francis Asbury

In Whittlebury, the vibrant class with fifty members and friends seeking the faith begins to dwindle. Francis astutely avoids any misconceptions of interest in Mrs. Padbury's daughter Betsy, but locals who throw rocks through the windows of the houses in which he is preaching continuously harass him and the members. Some even seek to harm the preacher for "wantin' to date the Padbury girl." Many of the members no longer wish to put themselves in harm's way. Francis's unmistakable focus on the ministry informs Betsy that he is not interested, but it fails to convince the violent locals. The aggression soon taxes Francis's self-confidence.

In Towcester, Mrs. Spencer is grateful for Francis's efforts. By the time of his departure for the 1770 conference, her class of three has swelled to a society of seven. The additions are clearly an improvement, but in Francis's mind, *not much of an improvement.* The new members are new to the faith; they are also leery of the Methodist movement, victims of slanderous accusations made by unbelievers and the Anglican faithful who object to John Wesley. Francis struggles; *I am in trying circumstances about the people and places.* These thoughts plague him constantly, so much so that another thought resurfaces, the thought he wrote about to his parents: *Sometimes I please myself that I shall go hence and leave these parts.* Go hence and leave these parts? *Where am I planning to go?* For now, Francis's thoughts of his deepest yearnings for change must move to the upcoming conference in London. He makes plans for his departure from Bedfordshire.

The members in Towcester, all women, bestow many food items for Francis's day-and-a-half journey back to London. Departing the home of Mrs. Spencer on Monday, August 6, he heads straight away for London.

On August 7, 1770, the London conference opens in its usual fashion. The Foundry Chapel is decorated with evergreen boughs, hand-selected and cut by many of the local men. Their wives and daughters have lovingly placed the greenery around the sanctuary, with many of the boughs hanging from the second-level balconies that border both sides of the main room. From outside, the joyous melodies of unaccompanied singing flow through the open entry doors. Inside, the singing by the locals is joined by the robust voices of the traveling preachers. The weary itinerants endlessly pour in from Ireland, Scotland, and England. Twelve women who unofficially preach in the Wesleyan movement are here also, obviously present because of the rumor that Wesley will address the issue of women preaching. With them is their vocal leader, Sarah Crosby. She approaches several of the arriving itinerants, eagerly inquiring if they have any word on Wesley's plans. None have an answer.

Another young woman present is Mrs. Mary Bright. The talented teacher, currently out of work as a schoolmistress, resides with her husband at John Wesley's residence in London. Wesley himself introduces his friend's wife to the arriving itinerants, making clear that she is in need of a job. Several of the men vow to send word of any developments.

Standing at the front of the gathering, Wesley raises his hands. The entire assembly falls silent as he begins the opening prayer of the conference.

"Lord of immortality, before whom angels bow and archangels veil their faces. Enable me to serve You with reverence and godly fear. You, who are spirit and require truth in the inward parts, help me to worship You in spirit and in truth. You who are righteous, let me not harbor sin in my heart, or indulge a worldly temper, or seek satisfaction in things that perish."

Following his prayer, John's brother Charles comes forward to lead the large group in singing hymns. Nearly two hundred locals and half as many itinerants eagerly wait to join in the joyous choruses. Also present is the Countess of Huntingdon, Selina. Dressed modestly for a member of the nobility, but still impeccably outfitted, the elegant Countess is accompanied by several of her women friends. Each of these ladies of faith regularly gives aid to Selina in her ministry outreaches throughout England, Ireland, Wales, and Scotland.

Charles opens with *Jesus, Thine All Victories Love.* Many in the group, including several of the itinerants, drop to their knees for the closing stanza:

"Refining fire, go through my heart,
Illuminate my soul;
Scatter Thy life through every part
And sanctify the whole."

For the next hymn, Charles chooses *Ye Servants of God.* The last few lines unite the followers in a crescendo of praise:

"Then let us adore and give Him His right,
All glory and power, all wisdom and might;
All honor and blessing with angels above,
And thanks never ceasing and infinite love."

For the third hymn, Charles naturally transitions from the last, without announcing the title. The gathering bursts forth in joyous praise, familiar with this favorite:

"O for a thousand tongues to sing
My Great Redeemer's praise,
The glories of my God and King,

The triumphs of His grace!"

O for a Thousand Tongues to Sing is one of Charles's most popular hymns. Many of the locals who with unbridled joy lift up their voices at this conference learned to read by memorizing these verses. Reading the written words after memorizing the hymn brought a sweet revelation of language.

For his closing hymn, Charles chooses *Thou Hidden Source of Calm Repose*. In this, the third stanza resonates with Francis in such a way that he senses God gently encouraging his melancholy heart.

> "Jesus, my all in all Thou art,
> My rest in toil, my ease in pain,
> The healing of my broken heart,
> In war my peace, in loss my gain,
> My smile beneath the tyrant's frown,
> In shame, my glory, and my crown."

Charles leads the group through all four hymns before his brother John steps back to the pulpit. Taking the pulpit, John delivers a closing announcement,

> "This evening I shall give an opening-day sermon. This shall conclude the public portion of the conference. Starting tomorrow morning at five o'clock, the private conference shall begin and I shall preach."

The evening's sermon by John Wesley pleases the local residents, who are thankful to hear the inspired teachings of Methodism's leader.

Early the next morning, Wesley's sermon focuses the sleepy thoughts of the itinerants. Per conference rules, no locals are present for the first official day of the conference, when business matters will take place. After his opening prayer, John begins,

> "Everything I meet with seems to carry this voice with it: 'Go thou and preach the Gospel—be a pilgrim on earth; have no parties, or certain dwelling place.' My heart echoes back, 'Lord Jesus, help me to do or suffer Thy will. When Thou seest me in danger of nesting, in pity, in tender pity, put a thorn in my nest to prevent me from it . . . And He said unto them, 'Go into all the world and preach the Gospel to every creature.' "

Wesley's sermon could not be more on target for Francis. His recent troubles at home and abroad cause him to crave encouragement. In particular, he finds encouragement in Wesley's talk of his American mission to Georgia decades before. The thought returns to Francis: *I am in trying circumstances about the people and places.* This thought, coupled with Wesley's opening lines, *"Go Thou and preach the Gospel—be a pilgrim on earth; have no parties, or certain dwelling place,"* gives credence to Francis's other utterance, *but sometimes I please myself that I shall go hence and leave these parts.*

After completion of his sermon to the preachers, John Wesley opens the business portion of the conference.

"What preachers are admitted this year?"

A tall preacher at the side of the room steps forward.

"William Whitaker, Samuel Wells, James Hudson, Francis Wrigley, Samuel Smith, Robert Wilkinson, Thomas Dixon, Richard Whatcoat, Thomas Wride, John Peacock, John Duncan, Joseph Thompson, Jonathan Crowle, Jonathan Hern, and William Ashman."

Wesley nods his approval. Each of the men steps to the front and Wesley blesses them for the work. Francis is happy for Richard's appointment. He watches as his tall friend returns to his seat next to him. Richard beams as he leans into Francis, whispering,

"Congratulate me, Brother."

"Congratulations, Richard. Now go and preach the Gospel."

"I shall."

Moving right along, Wesley continues with the next items of business, the usual questions of "who shall remain on trial, who is admitted on trial, who desists from traveling (either from death or marriage), and who act as assistants this year?" The next concern is the reading and noting of the long list of itinerants' names, one hundred and twenty this year. A subsequent issue deals with objections to any of the preachers in the list—there are none this year. The following item of business is the key reason for the conference: the assignment of the circuits.

At the front of the room, Wesley raises his right hand for silence. The soft murmuring of those bored with items of business quickly fades away. Upon this silence, Wesley begins the offers that no one ought to refuse.

"London: John Pawson, John Murlin, Thomas Rankin, John Allen, John Helton.

Sussex: Edward Slater, Francis Wolf.

Kent: Benjamin Rhodes, John McEvoy.

Essex: George Shadford.

Norfolk: John Murray.

Bedfordshire: John Easton, Richard Whatcoat, James Perfect.

Oxfordshire: John Furz, John Duncan.

Wiltshire south: John Catermole, Francis Asbury.

Wiltshire north: James Cotty, Barnabas Thomas, John Magor . . ."

Wesley continues until all fifty circuits are assigned. The fiftieth circuit is simply titled "America." The preachers assigned to America since the last conference are Joseph Pilmoor and Richard Boardman. Two additional preachers will join Pilmoor and Boardman unofficially; these men volunteer on their own. Wesley only makes note that they had chosen the previous year to leave

Ireland and England for the American colonies. These two men are Robert Williams and John King.

For Francis, the return to the southern portion of the Wiltshire circuit brings a slight measure of relief, as he had worried that another "Colchester" would become his assignment. Returning to Salisbury will put him among a friendlier crowd. And his return to Portsmouth will once again allow him to converse with his Jewish friend, Abraham Wolfe. In between these two familiar cities will be visits to Winchester and Jasper Winscomb.

Question sixteen of the conference asks, "What shall we do to prevent scandal, when any of our members becomes a bankrupt?" The answer: "In this case, let two of the principal members of the society be deputed to examine his accounts; and, if he has not kept fair accounts, or has been concerned in that base practice of raising money by coining notes"—known as the bill trade; it refers to bills of exchange or promissory notes to raise money on credit, a practice regularly sending many to debtor's prison—"let him be immediately expelled from the society."

Continuing at the helm, Wesley offers the date and location of the next conference.

"Our next shall convene in Bristol, first Tuesday in August."

After several smaller matters and an important issue of supporting forty-three of the stationed preachers' wives, Wesley raises one final concern.

"Take heed to your doctrine. We said in 1744, we have leaned too much toward the careless attitude of Calvinism—the doctrine of imputed righteousness of Christ allowing for the neglecting of God's holy laws."

These words keep everyone's focus. Wesley continues,

"Unchanged lives which afford no evidence of new birth. Wherein have we done so? With regard to man's faithfulness, our Lord taught us to use the expression. And we ought never to be ashamed of it. We ought steadily to assert, on His authority, that if a man is not faithful in the unrighteous mammon, God will not give him the true riches. With regard to working for life, this also our Lord has expressly commanded us. 'Labor' in the Greek literally means to work for the meat that endureth to everlasting life. And in fact, every believer, till he comes to glory, works for his life as well as from life."

In the back of the room, a low murmur begins to roll through the crowd.

"Works for his life . . . ?"   "Does he propose works salvation?"

Ignorant of the disruption, Wesley continues,

"We have received it as a maxim that a man is to do nothing in order to obtain justification. Nothing can be more false."

The murmurs grow louder. Wesley, unawares, continues,

> "Whoever desire to find favor with God should cease from evil and learn to do well. Whoever repents should do works which are meet[161] for repentance. And if this is not in order to find favor, what does he do them for?"

Many of the itinerants are uncomfortable with the statement. Several silently question Wesley's proclamations, nervously shifting in their seats. *Have we not progressed since Luther? Have not the Calvinist leaders substantially dealt with such failings of the past?* They keep their unsettling thoughts to themselves.

Near the back of the room, Francis finds himself surrounded by several itinerants who, while ensuring that Wesley cannot hear them, border on rudeness as they emphatically voice their disagreement. Francis remains silent, somewhat confused, but confident that Wesley knows what he is doing and saying. Above the growing din, Wesley continues,

> "Who of us is now accepted of God? He that now believes in Christ with a loving, obedient heart. But who among those that never heard of Christ? He that feareth God and worketh righteousness, according to the light he has. Is this the same as 'he that is sincere?' Nearly, if not quite. Is not this salvation by works?"

This last sentence causes several to rise to their feet. Wesley goes on,

> "Not by the merit of works, but by works as a condition. What have we then been disputing about for these thirty years?"

> "We are not Calvinists, nor papists!"

The voice issuing loudly from the back is a new arrival, an itinerant on trial. When several around him ask his name, his reply is simple.

> "Farewell, Wesley; I am to have no part of this works salvation."

The man walks out of the meeting. Wesley ignores the interruption and continues,

> "I am afraid about words. As to merit itself, of which we have been so dreadfully afraid: according to our works is our reward, yea, because of our works. How does this differ from 'for the sake of our work'? And how differs this from *secundum merita operum*, 'according to the merits of our works'—as our works deserve? Can you split this hair? I doubt it. I know I cannot. The grand objection to one of the preceding propositions draws from matter of fact. God does in fact justify those who, by their own confession, neither feared God nor wrought righteousness. Is this an exception to the general rule? It is a doubt God makes any exception at all. But how are we sure that the person in question never did fear God

[161] Suitable, proper.

and work righteousness? His own saying so is not proof, for we know how all that are convinced of sin undervalue themselves in every respect."

Wesley pauses to peer at the group. They are restless; several more have stood to their feet. One has even gone outside and escorted the Countess of Huntingdon into the assembly. She sits as Wesley resumes,

"In closing, does not talking of a justified or a sanctified state tend to mislead men? Almost naturally, leading them to trust in an act completed in one moment? Whereas we are every hour and every moment pleasing or displeasing to God, according to our works—according to the whole of our inward tempers, and our outward behavior."

As defined as the shoreline of a mighty ocean, a marked division makes the parting of this conference not as loving and united as others have been. The works issue ignites many of the itinerants to question their leader. The failure of Wesley to address the women preachers issue also dispirits the women who expected him to do so. As the itinerants surround Wesley to confront him, Sarah Crosby and several of her fellow female preachers push to the front. Sarah verbalizes her disappointment with the proceedings.

"We failed to address the preaching issue."

Holding her hand in his, John Wesley responds,

"Sarah, indeed it has long passed for a maxim with many, that women are only to be seen, not heard. Accordingly, many of them are raised in such a manner as agreeable playthings! But is this doing honor to the sex? Or is it a real kindness to them? No; it is the deepest unkindness; horrid cruelty. And I know not how any woman of sense and spirit can submit to it. Let all you that have it in your power assert the right which the God of nature has given you. Yield not to that vile bondage any longer! You, as well as men, are rational creatures. You, like them, were made in the image of God; you are equally candidates for immortality; you too are called of God, as you have time, to 'do good unto all men.' Be not disobedient to the heavenly calling. Whenever you have opportunity, do all the good you can, particularly to your poor, sick neighbor. Will this make provision for preaching? In private, yes, in the bands and in a few rare instances the class meetings, with the sick and with the imprisoned. Especially when no male is mature enough to lead. My very own mother was a shining example of this. For several years, she led a small class and prayer meeting nearing three hundred persons. Will this accommodate the speaking of women in the public arena of the congregation? What do the Scriptures say? I believe they are clear; provision for women speaking to the congregation is not present."

Several itinerants pull Wesley away. Sarah soon finds herself standing alone. She is not happy with John's closing sentence. *He has spoken otherwise before; why would he change?* This thought plagues her as she walks away, dejected.

Standing next to Francis, Richard Whatcoat is disappointed with Wesley's statement of faith. He also overheard Wesley's reply to the women preachers. Francis looks to Richard and asks,

>"Where is the progression?"

>"I do not know, Francis. Surely, Wesley has indicated otherwise not so long ago."

From the other side of the sanctuary, a tall, thin man makes his way toward Francis and Richard. His is a slow and deliberate walk, with shoulders rounded in a downward slant. The arch of his upper back pushes his head a little forward of his frame. Walking up to the pair, he silently nods his head, his focus moving from their eyes to the ground and back up again. Clearing his throat and adjusting his shirt collar, he introduces himself to Francis.

>"John Catermole."

With a tip of his hat, the spindly man who will act as Wesley's assistant on the Wiltshire low round, supervising Francis, offers his hand. Francis shakes the man's hand, noting that the preacher's grip is soft, almost limp. This is much different from Francis's handshake; in fact, Francis worries that he may have injured the appendage of the frail man. The two begin making their plans for departing this conference which has ignited such raging controversy.

Wesley's comments bring rejections from his itinerants, his brother, and many of the Methodist faithful. John's longtime friend, the Countess of Huntingdon, immediately withdraws her invitation for John to speak at the second anniversary of her Trevecca University in Wales, an institution started and supported by her for the purpose of training preachers. Her comments to John are strong: she warns that his words at the conference border on Roman Catholicism. To her, the comments indicate that he has abandoned the faith and that until he recants his statements, he can no longer preach in any of her chapels.

Under this billowing cloud which threatens a deluge on the movement, Francis and John Catermole depart the conference. On horseback on their way to Portsmouth, the two have nearly an hour to discuss the matter.

>"Works is madness. Do you not agree, Francis?"

>"Agreed. Perhaps what Wesley is conveying is other than that. He is obviously not a papist."

>"I know, but at such cost these words! He must pull us together. As we stand now, the movement's health is in jeopardy."

This time, the seventy-mile trip from London to the Wiltshire circuit will take place on a more agreeable road, and most definitely with a more agreeable companion. Francis directs John onto the coach road. The direct route, in lieu of the heaths and barren wastelands of the robber's directives, offers several safe stops along the well-populated and well-established path. Francis grimaces at the memory of the highwayman; he is thankful for preacher John.

The beginning of the transition to autumn richly adorns the approach to Portsmouth. Nearing the seaport town, the abundant gardens of the residents' homes draw Francis's attention. He comments,

"This town boasts of some of the best broccoli - -

And cauliflower. Have personally enjoyed them on many occasions in Portsmouth. None I have found elsewhere, not even in my father's garden, can match the rich color and flavor. Plants seem to grow bigger here. Remarkable size. Look forward to partaking of the vegetables this very night."

"I see. And where shall we enjoy such blessings?"

"Follow me."

It's not long before the itinerants are at the home of Abraham Wolfe, where Mrs. Wolfe promptly invites the itinerants to sit for dinner. The preachers are grateful for the offer; without hesitation, they take their seats at the table. Mr. Wolfe helps his wife to sit and then offers a prayer of thanks. Bowing his head, he begins,

"Barukh ata, Adonai Eloheinu, melekh ha'olam hamotzi lehem min ha'aretz." [162]

Peeking with one eye, Francis watches for John's reaction. The lanky itinerant interrupts his arching lean over the table, involuntarily straightening in his chair. For the first time since Francis met him, John's eyes open wide as he turns his head toward Francis. The look on his face says it all: "This man is Jewish!" Francis nods in return, the kind of nod that indicates all is well.

The dinner table is stacked with many delights. Francis is especially glad for the broccoli florets which complement the meal. Mr. Wolfe passes a plate of meat to the weary travelers, and they enthusiastically help themselves. Abraham inquires of Francis,

"Shall your circuit remain as before?"

"It shall. John and I shall alternate between Salisbury and Portsmouth. I am to depart for Salisbury in the morn."

"John, have you traveled to Portsmouth before?"

---

[162] Blessed are You, Lord our God, ruler of the universe, who brings forth bread from the earth.

"I have not. But I am familiar with a seaside setting. I am a native of Cornwall. Traveled to many of the towns of the southeastern coastlines. Plymouth Dock for a time."

"Cornwall? Francis, have you traveled to Cornwall?"

"No, I have not. Was in Colchester for a time."

John offers a turn in the conversation.

"I have spent time at Kingswood in Bath. Wesley's fine school."

Francis finds this encouraging; *perhaps this fine man can teach me*. He offers,

"Abraham has taught me a little of the Hebrew alphabet."

"Has he? Wesley would commend your thirst for the language. Tell me, Abraham, is Francis a good student?"

"He is. A little impatient, but thorough in his approach. We met nearly every week he preached in Portsmouth. I missed our regular appointments when he departed for another circuit."

"Well then, Francis, perhaps Wesley shall have you assist in the Hebrew lessons at Kingswood."

"I doubt that very much. I fail to tell the difference between the letters *dalet* and *khaf*."

"Oh, Francis, you do not let on to your abilities. John, the young man does well. Someday I expect a letter from a far-off place, written in Hebrew and with Francis's name attached."

"You think too highly of me. Especially on the far-off place. Perhaps London or Derby is as far as my Hebrew will take me."

The men laugh at Francis's self-deprecating comment.

The next morning finds the men departing Abraham's home, where he and his wife graciously offered hospitality for the night. Heading out for Winchester and then Salisbury, Francis tips his hat to John.

"Shall meet you at the home of Jasper Winscomb in Winchester, one week from today."

"Shall see you then, Francis."

Mounting Churchfield, Francis departs for Winchester.

Several hours into the ride, the thought occurs to him, *today is the anniversary of my birth*. August 20, 1770. *Twenty-five years of age.*

Entering the town of Winchester, Francis aims for the home of Jasper. In the distance, a large gathering of people populates High Street. The group borders on the raucous, with several men shouting protests as they raise wooden clubs in the air. Francis strains to hear, but he cannot make out the angry words which fly from all directions. Despite his inability to learn of the dispute, Francis can see at whom the objections are being aimed. One man, an elderly and chubby man, stands on the top step of the Butter Cross monument. With no sign of relenting, the people scream and point at the individual.

Francis reins in Churchfield, not willing to come any closer to the mob. *Are they in protest of something like Wesley or the Methodists?* He quickly recognizes the inconsistency of this thought. The city of Winchester, although not a large society for Wesley's followers, is somewhat friendly to the efforts of Jasper and his helpers. In fact, the last time Francis was here, the townspeople had recently heard Jasper speak outdoors in the middle of town. Jasper described the event as a rewarding experience. *This protest is for something completely different.* Francis decides to watch the proceedings from a safe distance.

One man holding a wooden club points his weapon at the chubby man.

"Mr. Dummer, the cross stays here!"

Mr. Dummer doesn't respond. He stands with arms crossed, nervously rolling his fingers on the tops of his forearms. Obviously uncomfortable, he finally offers a reply.

"I've paid good money for the cross. Winchester hasn't need of it."

"Yes, Winchester has need of it!"   "We have need of our history!"

The shouts are unanimous in their sentiment: "The cross is staying in Winchester!"

The Butter Cross is a fifteenth-century monument built on High Street. The tall structure, comprised of several spires acting as architectural brackets for carved statues of key people from English and biblical history, is the town's focal point for commerce. Indeed, this is how the former High Street Cross gained its current name. But apparently the Paving Commissioners of Winchester decided that if they sold the cross, much-needed revenues would result. Their plan appears to be failing, however, as the townspeople will not allow the sale and subsequent move of the monument. Mr. Dummer, the purchaser, is at a point of decision.

Mr. Dummer waves his thick arm above his head, motioning to several large men on the perimeter of the gathering. The half-dozen men begin pushing toward the center of the group, aiming to stand alongside Mr. Dummer. This proves an unwise decision, for the crowd decides to attack the approaching men. Several of the town's men raise their wooden clubs and strike. The first of Dummer's bodyguards goes down hard. Unconscious, the large man is subsequently trampled by several of the townspeople.

From behind Mr. Dummer, several young teenage boys grab the elder man. He doesn't resist. They sense his peaceful response and escort him out of the riotous group. At the edge of the mob, they advise him,

"Leave; the rest of the group will not deal with you as kindly."

Mr. Dummer departs. Behind him he leaves a raucous crowd set on pummeling his bodyguards. As they begin the abusive process, Francis wisely moves to circumnavigate the town's riot. The event evokes the unpleasant memory of his persecutions in the low round of the Staffordshire circuit.

At the home of Jasper, Francis is grateful to have arrived safely. Jasper invites the itinerant inside.

"Come, Francis; there's to be a small uprising sometime today."

"Already seen it. Several men bloodied and beaten unconscious by a riotous crowd."

"Already? Seems the town's leaders sold the High Cross. Crazy fools—the people shall not allow it. I suspect the men beaten were sent by the purchaser to remove the cross."

"I wouldn't know, Jasper. I remained far away, unable to gather the details of the dispute."

Back in Portsmouth, John Catermole prepares for the evening's class meeting. He sits alone inside The Long Room on Bishop Street. The inside of Mr. Pike's building dimly flickers with the light of several tapers hanging in iron holders on the walls. The written words of his Bible prompt John to silent prayer: *Let the words of my mouth and the meditation of my heart be acceptable in Your sight, O Lord, my strength and my Redeemer.*[163]

The members of the Portsmouth society arrive. Each goes out of his or her way to graciously receive the itinerant. Several men step forward to introduce themselves.

"Pleased to meet you, Pastor Catermole. We've word Pastor Asbury will once again grace our class."

"He and I shall work the circuit, 'tis true."

"Francis rescued our little class from the hands of that tyrant Norman."

"Norman?"

"William Norman, our deported steward. His strong hold on our worshipful society frustrated many. We are thankful for the efforts of Pastor Asbury."

"And what might those efforts have been?"

"He forced Norman out!"

The forceful response of the local startles the preacher. His thought brings a slight fear; *this Norman must have been a frightful fellow.*

Of the Portsmouth faithful, one seems especially drawn to John. A woman of about thirty years of age manages to work her way near the group of men who converse with him. In the midst of their discussions, John catches the eye of this

---

[163] Psalm 19, verse 14.

woman. She quickly diverts her focus from the preacher, looking to the underside of the roof structure, to a window near the entrance—but only briefly; within moments, she nervously returns her gaze to the itinerant. John is flattered by her warm consideration. This is a new experience for him—he is not overly attractive; tall, but with a plain and folksy look to his appearance, especially his face. *That woman is attracted to me.* He enjoys the revelation, repeating the thought to himself often.

Pastor Catermole takes his place at the front of the room. Each of the two dozen members takes a seat on the oak benches set out before him. On his left the women gather, his admirer conveniently placing herself in the front-row aisle location. John admires her gracefulness as she sits upright in almost perfect posture.

To his right, the men of the gathering have also taken their seats. John begins,
> "Almighty Father . . ."

The slamming of the wooden entry door echoes through the building, its startling crash interrupting John's opening prayer. Through the doorway, the large figure of William Norman struts into the room.
> "I've returned to take charge of my class."

The gasps of the women rouse the men to rise and turn toward William. They immediately move to approach the obnoxious intruder. Norman barks,
> "Who is this preacher? You will be gone, if you know what keeps you from harm."

One of the men rebukes him.
> "William, you are not welcome here. You know that. Why do you challenge the authority of the itinerants?"

> "The authority . . . I shall show this itinerant what authority is all about!"

Rushing the informal pulpit, William storms toward John. John reacts by darting in the opposite direction. Unable to see the wooden box in his path, the itinerant trips and falls to the dirt floor. Within seconds, Norman is towering over John.
> "Preacher, you'd best move on to the next town. Portsmouth belongs to William Norman. Anything otherwise shall meet with stern opposition."

From behind William, a shove causes the big man to temporarily lose balance. The woman who pushed the brute bends down to comfort John. It is his admirer. William gathers himself and retorts,
> "Don't tell me you have feelings for the fellow."

> "Perhaps I do. You should leave, William; no one desires your efforts."

> "I will show you who should leave."

William pushes the woman aside. Her dismayed grunt coincides with her impact with the floor. William reaches down and grabs John by the collar. With one sharp tug, he raises the preacher to a sitting position. With no small amount of spittle escorting his words, Norman advises,

> "You depart on your own. Now! Or I will see to it that you depart with my help."

John rushes to push himself to his feet. With Bible in hand, he runs for the doorway and exits the room. His admirer, along with several men and women, follow him outdoors, seeking his attention.

> "John, this shall pass. We will not sit for William. He shall preach to an empty room."

The words of the wise man escorting the female admirer bring comfort to John. He nods a hesitating approval, unable to determine the correct decision in this incident. His admirer grabs his hand and offers,

> "Come, my mother and I shall dress your wounds."

Realizing that he hasn't any physical wounds, John once again is attracted to the woman's interest in him. He responds,

> "As well."

The following Sabbath finds John still in Portsmouth. However, he advises the class members to attend the Anglican service in the newly constructed church, St. George's. The residents erected the church in Portsea to honor King George. The members listen to John's advice to visit St. George's and wisely submit to his recommendation.

That same Sabbath finds Francis in Salisbury. For him, the scene is completely different from his visit here almost two years prior. Approaching the location of the chapel on St. Edmund's Church Street, he notices that the men and women are outdoors—not in their usual dress for service, but dressed for working in their gardens. In fact, many of the familiar faces from the Salisbury class are not only working their gardens, but some are out in the fields digging and raking weeds and potatoes. Near the meeting house, Francis finds men sawing wood and building. Their helpers haul several timbers around a structure currently under construction. *On the Sabbath?* The thought shocks Francis. *Such a vibrant society, now resorting to abandoning the Sabbath!* This revelation brings emotional pain to the itinerant.

Nearing a woman who tarries in her garden, Francis asks,

> "Woman, are you not worried for your soul? I surely am."
> " 'Tis none's business but my own. Never has the clergyman asked me of my whereabouts on the Sabbath. Be gone with ya'!"

Bowing his head with dejection, Francis pauses. *We build, and another tears down.* His thought furthers the pain. Lifting his head, he notices a young boy and several of his friends walking toward him and Churchfield. With them is a woman who appears to be their mother. In her hand is a Bible. Recognizing Francis, she offers,

"Pastor Asbury, we have need of your efforts. The efforts of Barbara and myself fall short."

Francis realizes that this woman is a friend of Barbara and Richard Hunt. He responds,

"What of all this activity on the Sabbath? Has not the class met regularly?"

"Sadly, no. Several tried to maintain, but their attempts were smothered by strong opposition."

From an adjacent building, a man storms toward the woman and her children. He shouts,

"Lydia, have I not spoken of this?"

Stopping next to the woman, the man snatches her Bible from her hand and scolds,

"Home, Wife! As for you, Preacher, Salisbury no longer requires your unholy work. We have a church—the King's church."

Fortunately for Francis, a small remnant in Salisbury remains. From this tiny base of three families, Francis sets out to reestablish the Salisbury society. He struggles with the task ahead. *Lord, You seem to show me something that I am unaware of. The work to reestablish seems overwhelming; at least, the opposition seems overwhelming. Shall I depart? Shall I remain? Shall I leave England altogether? Surely Wesley's work would achieve more success with one whose efforts are better than mine.*

Mid-week finds Francis and John meeting in Winchester. At the home of Jasper, the two itinerants share their experiences. Noticeably shaken and disappointed from their respective events, John and Francis offer and receive advice from each other and from Jasper. Jasper's concern is a welcomed encouragement for Francis; long gone are the negative emotions and slight fear he used to experience with the fiery man. By day's end, the pair vow to do their best in the alternate towns.

The following weekend, John's Salisbury Sabbath is slightly better than Francis's experience. Two local families, the Lacy family and the Marsh family, along with Barbara and Richard Hunt, manage to raise several other families for a class worship service after the local Anglican service.

Especially drawn to John's sermon is sixteen-year-old Jeremiah Lacy. The oldest of his parents' thirteen children (they talk of having more), Jeremiah recently completed an apprenticeship for cabinetmaking in Borough Walls, Bath. He had gone there three years earlier, after his father sold some property to raise funds for his son's training. The Lacy family and the Marsh and Hunt families welcome Pastor Catermole and a return of the Wesleyan preachers.

In Portsmouth, Francis's arrival inspires many of the local worshipers to attend the class meeting. His arrival, coupled with the fact of his past confrontations with Norman, also incites many locals antagonistic to the Wesleyan movement to show up at The Long Room on Bishop Street, in hopes of seeing a confrontation between Norman and Francis.

Outdoors, Francis can barely get through the gathering of nearly two hundred people. Among this loud and rough-looking crowd, several crews from ships docked in the harbor have gathered, eager for a brawl. Their appearance is as sharp as their odor. Several bob and weave, inebriated from an afternoon of drinking. Their breath and their clothing smell of gin.

Francis tips his hat as he maneuvers through the mob. A couple of men who work the shipyards also seek to antagonize the preacher. One pushes Francis from behind. Francis ignores the tactic and continues to the door.

Three men from the Portsmouth society quickly open the door for Francis, and he darts inside. The men immediately push back several of the group outside, who voice their right to gain entrance. The men know it is foolish to acknowledge the request.

Making his way to the front of the room, Francis receives warnings from several of the members.

"William has raised a mob!"   "He shall return this evening."

Francis scratches the back of his head and nervously scrapes his teeth over his bottom lip. His emotions rise and fall as fear and disappointment plague his thoughts. He struggles for a solution. At the front of the room, he raises his hands for prayer. The leader of the three men guarding the door admonishes his partners,

"Eyes open for this prayer."

The men nod in agreement. The rest of the worshipers bow their heads.

In the silence, the noise of the rabble outdoors swells and sways like a growing sea. The sound of a rock hitting the side of the wooden structure occasionally breaks the flowing mumbles. At one point, as Francis is ready to utter his first words, the unmistakable voice of William Norman emerges from the disorderly group.

"Let me in, Pastor!"

Raising his eyes, Francis looks to the three men at the door. They have secured the wooden slab; its locking bar is in place. Francis is relieved. He remembers the words of an ancient Puritan prayer and offers them aloud to the Creator.

"Expel from my mind all sinful fear and shame, so that with firmness and courage I may confess the Redeemer before men, go forth with Him hearing His reproach, be zealous with His knowledge, be filled with His wisdom, walk with His circumspection, ask counsel of Him in all things, repair to the Scriptures for His orders, stay my mind on His peace, knowing that nothing can befall me without His permission, appointment, and administration."

With this, the noise outside subsides.

Inside, the class meeting proceeds as planned. Several hymns join the prayers from the members. Francis begins his process of sharing the condition of his faith and seeking the condition of the members' faith. Although this is not his regular duty as a traveling preacher, Francis correctly assumes that tonight the members need their faith encouraged not with a sermon, but with a personal reassurance from a Wesleyan itinerant. By meeting's end the mob is absent, as is Norman. Francis welcomes the uneventful evening. However, later that night, while lying in bed, the nervous fear from his youth returns. His thoughts are clear: *Almighty Father, why do You allow this fear and shame to remain? I am uncomfortable with these trembling emotions.*

The mid-week meeting in Winchester is a welcomed break for Francis. He is eager to communicate with John about his experience. Seeing him at the home of Jasper, Francis shares the surprising results of the class meeting.

"You know, John, seems we've convinced Norman to move on. He showed this past meeting."

"He showed?"

"He did. A mob with him also."

"Mob?"

John's demeanor changes, the look on his face conveying that he isn't happy to hear about a mob. Francis continues,

"William, as well as the mob, seemed restrained by a higher power. For they departed without incident. We continued our meeting in prayer and song without a return from William Norman or the group."

John doesn't reply. His vacant stare at the main room's firebox is inconsistent with the results of the event. Francis inquires,

"John, did you not hear my account? Are you well?"

John doesn't answer. Francis inquires again,

"John?"

John stands to his feet. His eyes dart about the room, first to Jasper, then to Francis, but lingering only briefly on Francis. He moves toward the window and stares outdoors. Turning around, he offers,

"Francis, I am departing."

"Why not spend the evening? Portsmouth can wait."

"Francis, you are not hearing me correctly. I am departing - -

The circuit. I am leaving the ministry."

With this, John places his hat on his head and exits through the front door of the home. Francis and Jasper are left sitting in uncomfortable silence.

The next morning does little to ease the shock of John's exit. Both Francis and Jasper avoid bringing up the subject. In Jasper's mind, the conversation will only lead to his deeply-held opinion that the circuit demands several more preachers. For Francis, the avoidance of the subject stems from a completely different cause. Not only does he lack the wisdom to deal with John's quitting, but also, more significantly, a deep truth has surfaced in his mind: he wishes he had departed the Wiltshire circuit himself. Where would he go? He has no idea. His thoughts focus on the immediate. *Can I handle so heavy a cross? The isolation in this Methodist wilderness . . . am I able to stand alone?* Aside from these worries, he also wrestles with a part of him, deep in his core—his heart, mind, and soul—that continues to indicate the need to move on. With great pain of heart, he moves on to Salisbury, mindful that he will now handle the low round of the Wiltshire circuit on his own.

Francis has been ministering in Portsmouth and Salisbury for several weeks when word arrives that John Wesley is on his way to visit the low round and will preach next Sabbath in Salisbury. At Jasper's home in Winchester when the news arrives, Francis drops his plans for returning to Portsmouth and immediately heads back to Salisbury.

On October 9, 1770, John Wesley arrives in Salisbury. The twenty-mile trip from Shaftesbury takes him nearly three hours. The late-afternoon sun parches the cathedral city and its magnificent focal structure, which took a century and a half to build. The cathedral spire glistens, as do the town's residents as they welcome the unseasonable warmth. The rays offer a rare occurrence: the potholes of the dirt streets are dry, and no longer do they hold the nefarious liquid that mysteriously attaches to every person and object venturing into the Salisbury streets. Heading for the chapel on St. Edmund's Church Street, Wesley marvels at the cathedral completed in the fourteenth century. He travels eastward with the cathedral on his right side, the setting sun casting an elongated natural arrow pointing in a slight northeasterly direction.

The Salisbury faithful arrive, jubilant for this rare occasion. In addition to the main families of the local Wesleyan society, many of the locals, eager to see the famed preacher, also attend.

At seven o'clock in the evening, Wesley takes the pulpit. The Hunt, Lacy, and Marsh families surround Francis as they await the opening words from Francis's distinguished leader. Wesley stands on the wooden platform, participating in small talk with several key men of the city. Amidst the large gathering, standing near Francis and the core of the Salisbury Methodists, several groups of local musicians patiently wait for Wesley. The cathedral town boasts a large music community, the majestic structure offering a beautiful venue for singing and instrumental groups. Standing in the crowd among the young artists, James Harris, the MP for Christchurch and the unquestioned leader of the Salisbury music community, talks with his talented companions. The enthusiastic musicians gravitate toward this gifted player of the harp, a friend of the late George Frideric Handel. The musicians and Harris quietly discuss Handel and his magnificent work, *Messiah,* and the recent musical event of the year: the St. Cecilia's Day musical festival, a three-day event that originated nearly thirty-five years ago. Performances here in the Salisbury Cathedral take place in the mornings and evenings. During the day, several impromptu gatherings of musicians occur in the local business establishments that welcome live music.

Raising his hands to begin, Wesley silences the expectant crowd.

" 'King of Kings and Lord of Lords'—is this not the glorious proclamation of Handel's 'Hallelujah Chorus'?"

Pausing for the reaction, Wesley looks to James Harris and the young men. The musicians fidget with grateful delight that Wesley would tailor the message to them. Wesley smiles, confident that he has gained their undivided attention. He continues in rhythm and on key,

" 'Forever and ever, Hallelujah! Hallelujah! Forever and ever, Hallelujah! Hallelujah!' Oh for the day on which we may proclaim it continuously . . ."

For nearly one hour Wesley delivers a powerful sermon, during which several fall to their knees in repentance. Among the musicians, one of the sons of the Marsh family bows his head to weep during the sermon. Young John Marsh toys with making entrance into the music community. His parents desire a life of ministry for the young man, but he has a love for music.

At sermon's end Wesley prays and closes with one of his brother's hymns, his smile conveying his clear thought, *not in any other town does the melody blend so sweetly.* Wesley then descends the outdoor pulpit, where James Harris and the youthful entourage greet him. Wesley revels in the opportunity to chat with the young men. Harris graciously allows the exuberant group to engage with the world's itinerant. Back and forth, the elder clergyman holds his own. His numerous quips and encouragement, given with marcato-like[164] strokes, strike the young men with inspiration to continue toward the faith.

After nearly twenty minutes of this exchange, Wesley forces himself to separate from the young men and find the local Wesleyan leaders. Successfully doing so, he approaches Francis standing with the Marsh, Hunt, and Lacy families. As he nods his greeting to them, the families extend their kind hospitality.

"May we offer a place for the night?"

"The prophet's chamber at Hunts' is always a welcome stay. I shall also enjoy the opportunity to converse with young Pastor Asbury in private."

Francis is grateful for the invitation to stay with Wesley, although a little nervous about sleeping in the same room with the great man. *Perhaps it shall remain warm through the evening.* Francis chuckles as he considers the cold nights with Pastor Glasbrook. The families arrange for the evening's stay and breakfast the next morning.

Surrounded by the families while walking to their horses, Wesley advises Francis,

"Only two retained their mirth. Pray for them, Francis. Their outer beauty reduces their level of understanding to a six-year-old."

"I shall."

The two young, attractive women who mocked Wesley during his sermon are not members of the local society, nor are they part of the local music community. Despite their inappropriate behavior during the service, Francis considers their presence a welcome occurrence—not for their beauty, but for the fact that they are a natural draw for young men to the service. He wisely keeps this consideration to himself.

The next morning, Wesley and Francis depart for Winchester. Francis is happy to escort his mentor to the home of Jasper. Along the way, Wesley surprises Francis by commenting,

"Francis, as you know, this evening we shall stay at the home of Jasper Winscomb. I request your aid. I shall agree to send an itinerant to the Isle of Wight. Jasper has requested this for some time. After our stop in Portsmouth, I would like you to depart the port city for the Isle of Wight. I have arranged for your travel to Wooten Bridge on the island. From there you shall walk to Newport."

"Newport, very well."

"Newport is in its infancy; perhaps Jasper is correct. May He whose seed you sow give it increase."

---

[164] A violin technique of short, sharp strokes of the bow.

Francis finds the temporary assignment exciting. He's never departed the mainland for an island. From what he has heard, the Isle is a beautiful place, with sloping hills like Hampshire's and stunning shorelines like Dover's. *Oh, for Mother and Father to enjoy such liberty!* His thought inspires him forward. Amidst the silent jubilation, another thought occurs: *What shall I do with Churchy?* Francis considers his options. A sense of peace arrives as he realizes that he can leave his horse with the kindly Abraham Wolfe.

Realizing that Wesley has opened the conversation, Francis prompts himself to ask,

"Reverend Wesley?"

"Yes."

"The commotion at the conference in London - -

Over the works comment. What did you imply? I assured your assistant, John Catermole, that you are not a papist. Why do some tend to see otherwise?"

The two men ride along on horseback. In his characteristic way, the leader of Methodism tilts his head in thought. Taking his time with choosing his words, Wesley turns toward Francis and smiles, the kind of smile that conveys his thankfulness for Francis's vote of confidence. He asks,

"How doth a man gain salvation?"

"Plainly, through the finished work of the Savior."

"I abhor the doctrine of justification by works. Have I not made this clear?"

"You have."

"Works is a most perilous and abominable doctrine. In the sight of God, I declare that there is no trust or confidence but in the alone merits of our Lord and Savior Jesus Christ. Only He provides our justification. Is this clear enough, Pastor Asbury?"

"It is. But respectfully, sir, what were you implying with works?"

"Simply, no one is a real Christian believer, consequently cannot be saved, who doth not good work where there is time and opportunity. Works not of saving, but of meriting the truth of the believer's conviction."

"I see."

"Our freedom of religion is our freedom in Christ. It demands our conviction, demands evidence of the birth anew. You cannot have freedom of religion without freedom of conviction—the freedom to believe and the freedom to act upon that belief. Remove the ability to act upon your beliefs, and you remove the freedom."

The gatherers in Winchester, like those in Salisbury, lovingly receive their spiritual leader. The crowd, as in Salisbury, is large. Many from the neighboring towns of this cathedral city travel great distances to see Wesley. With the preaching in Winchester complete, a night's stay at Jasper's becomes the sendoff for Portsmouth.

Along the way to Portsmouth, Wesley offers,

> "Francis, I am aware that you have no assistant for this circuit. I shall send help. I am confident my new leader for Wiltshire's low round will lend proper aid."

> "Thank you."

The full day's journey to Portsmouth tires the itinerants, and they welcome the hospitable reception at the meeting house on Bishop Street. Inside the overcrowded building, Wesley decides to move everyone outdoors. In the crisp autumn air of the evening, Wesley once again delivers a resonating message. The locals as well as the Portsmouth faithful are grateful for the privilege of Wesley's visit. Wesley himself is well pleased with the reception; *indeed, the people in general here are nobler than most in the south of England. They receive the Word of God with all readiness of mind and show civility, at least, to all who preach it.* These favorable thoughts, as well as the strains of the thirty-mile ride earlier in the day, lead the itinerants to an early evening at the home of one of the Portsmouth families. With Churchfield's accommodations taken care of with Abraham Wolfe, Francis and Wesley head indoors. Nearing nine o'clock, the pair find comfortable seats in which to rest. It isn't long before Francis is asleep.

Sleep is precisely what Francis requires; the strain of the day's travel is bearing its full weight on the young itinerant. Even Wesley closes his eyes for a much-needed rest.

At midnight, Wesley wakes Francis.

> "Francis, we've to arrive at the dock before two."

Groggy, Francis rises to head outdoors. Wesley is out the door before he can gather his things; Francis rushes to follow.

Departing the friendly home, Francis and John walk toward the harbor. Arriving at the waterfront, the pair decide to tour the area where a fire broke out in late August. The account of the blaze continues to occupy the front page of several national newspapers. The event destroyed much of the dock area. Nearing the charred remains, the two men carefully traverse the large facility, *much larger than any other in England.* Wesley's thoughts prompt him to ask a dockworker,

> "The recent fire—why here? This location seems remote."

> "It is as you say. The fire was in the middle of the night, at low water."

Wesley raises his hand to his lips. Rubbing them with his right forefinger knuckle, he thinks to himself, *a place where no one comes, at low water, and at a time when all are fast asleep. This can only be design.* Wesley keeps these thoughts to himself. Peering at Francis, he nods his head and grimaces, his expression conveying his doubt of the accidental nature of the event. The dockworker catches the look; out of conviction, he offers,

> "The violent flame advanced quickly, increasing among the tow and cordage. The dry wood of the dock escalated the flames. No one could come close without risk of life. Nothing was expected but that the entire dock would fall victim to the raging fire."

Wesley comes to a stop. His condemning stare compels the man to continue,

> "Nothing but the utmost danger. The dock, if not the whole town, lay at risk!"

> "What caused this tumultuous disturbance to cease?"

Wesley's methodically paced question once again puts the man on the spot; he nervously fumbles with the collar of his coat. Under a holy conviction, the dockworker launches his finger toward heaven and hastily replies,

> "God! God would not permit it. Just as it was set to seize the town, the wind changed direction and drove it out."

> "I see. Come, Francis; you've a **wherry** to catch."

Oddly, Wesley mispronounces the object of his last sentence. Francis fights back the urge to laugh aloud. The scruffy-looking dockworker scurries off, and Wesley grabs Francis's coat sleeve. He offers to Francis,

> "I was growing **weary** of his tale."

The dock fire is an odd occurrence. It clearly indicates foul play, but no one has been implicated yet. Despite the dockworker who improvised the story of God's involvement, there is divine intervention of sorts. The flames the dockworker describes as suddenly turning were certain to destroy the commissioner's house at dockside. In light of this favorable turning, the fire fails to consume the important building. However, the rampant blaze does consume much of the dock, forcing several nearby buildings to undergo a forced pull-down lest they too succumb to the flames. It is the only way to salvage the wood and furnishings of these buildings. Not until nearly five weeks later is the fire fully extinguished.

At two o'clock in the morning, Wesley departs the dock in a chaise, bound for London. Watching the covered vehicle until it disappears in the darkness, Francis turns and boards the wherry to the Isle of Wight.

A wherry is a mid-sized sailing vessel used to navigate small channels and straits, carrying cargo, passengers, or both. These thirty-ton ships are unmistakable in their key characteristics: a gaff-rigged sail with a single high peak, its mast set forward in the boat; and a long, overhanging bow which aids in keeping the arriving passengers dry when going ashore. Clinker-built[165] ships of this size make the ten-mile trip from Portsmouth across Stokes Bay daily and, as with the one Francis will ride, through all hours of the night. Francis is not sure of crossing this much water in a boat that sits only twenty inches above the surface. He silently prays as he steps down into the boat, which he estimates to be around sixty feet in length.

The Isle of Wight is located to the southeast of Portsmouth. Getting to the twenty-two-mile-long, diamond-shaped island will take roughly three hours. Francis sits on a long wooden bench in the middle of the ship. In front of him is a covered area for protection from the weather. In front of the dry area resembling a wooden tunnel, the pilot and two other men of the ship adjust several lines, setting them for departure. Turning around toward Francis, the captain advises,

"Departing Portsmouth."

With the release of a dock line, the ship inches away from the shoreline. With a long wooden pole retrieved from inside the protected area between the men and Francis, one of the shipmates moves behind Francis to the stern of the vessel, where he pushes off the river floor to further the launch. Within minutes, the pole is secured in its original place and Francis awaits the unmistakable sound of the main sail catching a favorable wind. The wind engages, the ship tilts a bit, and Francis begins his wrestling match. After several sudden shocks of dozing off while sitting up, Francis leans forward, tucks his head, and crawls toward the dry protected area. Finding a wooden bench that runs the length of it from front to back, he lays his tired body upon it.

The captain turns to offer,

"Francis . . ."

He doesn't complete his sentence. Spotting the itinerant asleep with a Bible as his pillow, the captain wisely leaves the tired young man alone.

A little over three hours into the trip, the captain advises one of the shipmates to awaken Francis. After several moments of regaining his whereabouts, Francis crawls to the seat at the rear of the boat. Within minutes, the wherry enters Wooten Creek. The captain advises,

"Shall dock in less than half an hour."

---

[165] Ships with a long overhanging bow.

Twenty minutes later, Francis carefully walks the extended bow and goes ashore.

Stepping from the ship, he notes the woody smells of hardwood trees—many hardwood trees— sailing through the chilly autumn air. Although the sun's rising has not yet occurred, the first lightening of the sky reveals a thick woodland. Francis instinctively takes a deep breath, and memories of the Bromwich forest waken the sleepy itinerant. The welcomed sensation of the earthy smells also has its negative effects: they awaken his hunger. With his stomach reminding him that it too is on this journey, Francis desires to find breakfast.

The town of Wooten nestles on the water's edge of Wooten Creek. The wide body of water originating from Stokes Bay travels inland nearly two miles, all along the winding path hidden amidst the dense forest that gives the town of Wooten Creek its name. Formerly known as Woodytown because of the thick forest that resides on both sides of the waterway, the name eventually was transformed into Wooten. Although Francis will not follow the creek inland, he will not depart from the thick forest. His four-mile journey toward the southwest will continue amidst the hardwoods, placing him in the island's largest town of Newport in two hours.

Walking is the ideal manner to experience the beautiful island. As daylight arrives, Francis finds himself walking amidst trees harboring hidden caves and ancient burial mounds. The caves belong to animals now, but had sheltered aboriginal inhabitants centuries before. The mounds are also a sign of previous peoples. In addition to the sacred raised areas, monuments to the departed dot the island. These standing-stone megaliths vary in size and shape. Large stones are predominately used, placed upright in a circular pattern, or as a tripod support of one large, flat stone. Each structure is unique. Even the virgin ground draws his attention as Francis occasionally finds himself walking on the soft, velvety sward of moss. This food is a favorite of the animals native to the island. Stopping to admire the thick ground cover, he reaches down and pushes on the spongy surface, releasing the cool moisture trapped within. Rising again, Francis continues his pleasant journey toward the town of Newport.

The Wesleyan society in Newport is very small, with only two families enjoying regular weekly class visits. The gatherings have a lay leader, but his fishing business occasionally forces him to miss the meetings. Approaching the home where the families expect the traveling preacher from the mainland, Francis once again struggles with a deep hunger for food. He pushes the thought aside, trusting that the families will offer some form of sustenance.

After he enters the simple home, the middle-aged couple who welcome him invite Francis to breakfast. He gratefully accepts. At meal's end, his hosts advise him that they shall move to the empty building next door for the meeting, where they will meet the other family in the society.

Stepping outdoors just before the noon hour, the three suddenly find themselves facing nearly two dozen townspeople. The gathering swells as additional people rush to the scene. Soon, a mob nearing one hundred men and women confronts Francis as he prepares to enter the building next door.

"Yo', play-actor!"

The comment catches Francis by surprise. Unwisely, he turns toward the accuser. Immediately, two dozen swarm him at the large rock where he stands and drag him into the middle of the street.

"Yo' a cast-iron preacha'!"

"Dat's right, a cast-iron preacha'. Da' entire work is goin' by steam. Wesley 'as done it now—papists!"

The verbal abuse continues as they call Francis a papist, a charlatan, a purveyor of lies. No doubt the turmoil over Wesley's comments this past summer brings this opposition. Francis worries for his life. Looking toward the outer edge of the gathering, he sees a group of twenty men approaching, wooden clubs in hand. He inches his retreat toward the nearby door. The crowd is not allowing such an escape, however; they push him back into the middle of the street. With his return there, rotted fruits and vegetables begin to fly. The thrown objects impact and splatter on Francis's chest, back, and shoulders. Several pieces barely miss his face. In addition to the throwing of the decayed items, several in the crowd spit on the itinerant.

From his far left, a group of men from Newport run toward the men with clubs. Confronting the mob, the Newport leader pleads,

"Come now, gentlemen—wouldn't you rather hear a good sermon?"

"Good sermon?"

The burly man's reply is deep and dark, his voice resonating in the outdoor air. Francis watches the proceedings, unable to make out the communication. The burly intruder raises his hand without the club, and the murmuring and throwing of objects ceases. Francis is now able to hear the exchange. The friendly Newport leader continues,

"Yes, a good sermon. Pastor Asbury is not a papist, nor is he an unworthy preacher. Come now and give him a chance. If by sermon's end you do not agree that he is a worthy preacher, you can deal with him. My friends and I will not interfere."

Hmm? Francis's thought has him whirling to look in several directions, to his right, then left, in front, and spinning behind. He finds himself surrounded by unfriendliness.

The rugged man with the club, a hard-looking man, considers the offer. Curling his lip down and to the side, he asks,

> "Dis' preacha' is dat' good? Good enough to risk a beatin'?"

> "He is. Come now."

> "All right."

Francis still cannot fathom the thought, *my safety depends on my sermon?* The club-wielding men push their way toward him. Before they reach the itinerant, the local leader who is favorable toward Francis makes one more request of the dreadful men.

> "Would it not serve well if you left those clubs behind?"

The mob's leader considers the suggestion. He doesn't reply. Francis's advocate once again offers,

> "Perhaps some of the women will affright?"

The mob's leader nods his head and shouts to his men,

> "Toss the clubs!"

At this, the men throw their weapons into a pile. Francis, the local leader, and several of the friendly men are much relieved by this act. They hurry to open the door to the room designated for the gathering and escort the men inside. As the people and the mob make their way into the building, the local leader waves his hand to summon two teenage boys. They respond to his request and he quietly instructs,

> "Gather the clubs and burn them."

With eyes wide, the excited youths grin, the kind of grin that conveys astonishment that someone would actually ask them to burn something. With impassioned gasps as the realization sets in, they turn and run off to raise a flame.

Inside, at the front of the gathering, with dripping fruit and spittle adorning his expensive blue jacket, Francis delivers his sermon on Elisha. It's a lengthy message, Francis fearing an unhappy response at sermon's end. After nearly two hours of preaching, the local mob, as well as the society members, continues to listen well. To the surprise of both Francis and the Newport faithful, no one causes an interruption.

Continuing into the late afternoon, the event ends with a hymn, a prayer, and a solemn dismissal of the group. The two Newport families and the friendly locals stay throughout the departure of the opposing group. Everyone holds their breath as the mob exits the building and leaves the grounds.

With the danger past, the leader of the Newport group walks over to Francis and comments,

> "Today you inherited a double blessing—much like that of the subject of your sermon. Not only did you save a life, you also saved your own."
>
> "Thank you."

Francis's gratitude reflects not only his relief for the favorable results of the meeting, but also a confirmation of the stirring that occurred while he preached to the precarious grouping on his subject: Elisha receiving a double blessing upon the death of his mentor, Elijah. The stirring in Francis's heart this afternoon is that he too is to receive a blessing. What this blessing is he doesn't know, but the communication on his heart while he preached was overwhelming. It stood in sharp contrast to the predicament he found himself in, preaching for the safety of his life. Despite the fearful occasion, he is certain: *This double blessing came about upon the death of a mentor. Am I to lose a mentor? Mather? Wesley? Glasbrook?*

The next morning Francis departs for Wooten Bridge and eventually Portsmouth. The overland journey and the seagoing trek place him in Portsmouth around eight o'clock. This October evening finds Francis tired, hungry, wet, and chilly from the cold rains that plagued the ride across the bay. Expecting the port city to have already settled down for the night, he is surprised to find the town abuzz. Crowds of people walk the streets. Several of these informal groupings utter words that don't make sense.

> "Would rather wear out than rust out! That is what he said."
>
> "Wear out he did. I heard tell he ignored the asthmatic symptoms; against all recommendations to stop he kept going, in a field, atop a barrel!"
>
> "Word is, on ship before his arrival, one of the shipmates ran to him in tears."
>
> "Wasn't a shipmate, it was the pilot, smothered in tears, saying, 'May the great and never-failing pilot, the Almighty Jesus, renew us and take us all into His holy protection, and then all must necessarily end in our safe arrival in the haven of eternal rest.' "

The last words are clear enough to draw Francis in for a closer review. Next to the sailors, many are kneeling and crying. Francis considers the discovery; *something is amiss.* Next to him, a woman companion of one of the sailors lets out a startling wail.

Francis leans in to catch what has transpired. What he hears from the sailor who recited the lines about the "never-failing pilot" brings great emotional pain.

> "Whitefield is dead."

Francis bows his head and weeps.

The sobbing is strong; he didn't expect this. He wipes his eyes, which burn from the mixture of the tears and the dried sweat from the day's journey. He reaches into his coat pocket to retrieve a handkerchief, but his fumbling ends in failure; the cloth is soaking wet like his jacket. Again he sobs, his neck arched, his head hanging down, his face buried in his hands.

A gentle touch on his forearm causes Francis to raise his head. Standing next to him is a sailor, a tiny sort. The European man holds in his hand a handkerchief. The silk cloth appears too fancy for a man of the sea. A woman walks up while Francis is contemplating the incongruous item. She too reaches for Francis's forearm.

> "Take it, please. It is evident you are one of his companions. Whitefield and the Methodists have done much for England."

The tall, thin woman retrieves her handkerchief from the sailor, then reaches the fancy cloth to Francis's cheek and wipes away a tear. Francis gratefully grasps the expensive fabric and quickly buries his face in it.

From the group of sailors, one of the men approaches Francis and tugs on the weeping preacher's jacket sleeve.

> "We must get word to London straight away. Have you an itinerant heading north?"

Francis manages,

> "Wesley does not know of this?"

> "John Wesley?"

> "Yes, John Wesley. And what of the Countess?"

> "The Countess?"

> "Selina, Countess of Huntingdon—since the death of his wife, Whitefield's closest friend."

> "Pastor, the word of Whitefield's death has just arrived with me and my fellow sailors. Thomas, the short man who stands over there, he actually worked the ship which delivered Whitefield to the colonies nearly one year ago. He witnessed the Portsmouth pilot's tears in front of Whitefield before departure from this very port. A little shaken are we who ride the sea. You should know, Pastor, not all who ride are pagans."

Following the long, thin finger that points to the man's shipmate, Francis spots the sailor who was present on Whitefield's last trip to the colonies. In the distance, the older man raises his thick hands to wipe away tears. Somewhat embarrassed by the sailor's sharp words, Francis responds,

> "Did not imply the contrary; the revelation catches me by surprise also."

The slight clearing of Francis's grief affords a simple thought: *Is the loss of Whitefield the gateway to my inheritance? What am I to inherit?* Francis once again wipes his tearing eyes, looking toward the tall woman accompanying the sailor. His questioning gaze prompts her to offer,

"Portsmouth truly is the gateway to the American colonies."

Francis's face conveys his confusion. The sailor senses this and responds,

"At times, sir, it truly is."

George Whitefield passed away in his sleep on the morning of September 30. Against the recommendations of a doctor and several friends, the fifty-five-year-old with the portly build preached his last sermon the night before, in a field, atop a wooden barrel. His words were sharp, thundering against the inefficiency of works to merit salvation. "Works! Works! A man gets to heaven by works? I would as soon think of climbing to the moon on a rope of sand." Clearly, word of Wesley's August conference troubles had already reached the shores of America and, more precisely, the ears of George Whitefield. On word of his death, the African poet in the nearby town of Boston, Phyllis Wheatley, wrote a poem in honor of the passing of the Methodist preacher.

> "Hail, happy saint, on thine immortal throne,
> Possest of glory, life, and bliss unknown;
> We hear no more the music of thy tongue,
> Thy wonted auditories cease to throng.
> Thy sermons in unequall'd accents flow'd,
> And ev'ry bosom with devotion glow'd;
> Thou didst in strains of eloquence refin'd
> Inflame the heart, and captivate the mind.
> Unhappy we the setting sun deplore,
> So glorious once, but ah! It shines no more.
> "Behold the prophet in his tow'ring flight!
> He leaves the earth for heav'n's unmeasur'd height,
> And worlds unknown receive him from our sight.
> There Whitefield wings with rapid course his way,
> And sails to Zion through vast seas of day.
> Thy pray'rs, great saint, and thine incessant cries
> Have pierc'd the bosom of thy native skies.
> Thou moon hast seen, and all the stars of light,
> How he has wrestled with his God by night.
> He pray'd that grace in ev'ry heart might dwell,
> He long'd to see America excel;
> He charg'd its youth that ev'ry grace divine
> Should with full lustre in their conduct shine;

That Saviour, which his soul did first receive,
The greatest gift that ev'n a God can give,
He freely offer'd to the num'rous throng,
That on his lips with list'ning pleasure hung.

"Take him, ye wretched, for your only good,
Take him, ye starving sinners, for your food;
Ye thirsty, come to this life-giving stream,
Ye preachers, take him for your joyful theme;
Take him, my dear Americans, he said,
Be your complaints on his kind bosom laid:
Take him, ye Africans, he longs for you,
Impartial Saviour is his title due:
Wash'd in the fountain of redeeming blood,
You shall be sons, and kings, and priests to God.

"Great Countess, we Americans revere
Thy name, and mingle in thy grief sincere;
New England deeply feels,
The Orphans mourn,
Their more than father will not more return.

"But, though arrested by the hand of death,
Whitefield no more exerts his lab'ring breath,
Yet let us view him in th' eternal skies,
Let ev'ry heart to this bright vision rise;
While the tomb safe retains its sacred trust,
Till life divine re-animates his dust."[166]

As Francis gathers his distraught emotions, he catches sight of a familiar face. A young man neatly dressed in a black robe, obviously a Wesleyan itinerant, approaches on horseback. Thomas Rankin, Wesley's stern disciplinarian, has arrived in Portsmouth.

Francis is not happy to see Rankin; he has heard the rumors of his uncompromising manner of aiding Wesley. As a gesture of reconciliation, Francis offers Rankin the news of Whitefield's death. All business, Rankin wastes no time in taking responsibility for getting word back to London.

---

[166] Phyllis Wheatley, "On the Death of the Rev. George Whitefield," 1770.

Unknown to Francis, Wesley arranged for Rankin to venture south of London to address the rumors spreading about the low round of the Wiltshire circuit: the declining membership and the possible departure from the ministry of an itinerant. Rankin hasn't had time to confirm Catermole's departure; he only knows of the dwindling membership. The impromptu meeting between Francis and Rankin in Portsmouth gives Francis the opportunity to raise the issue about Catermole. The news causes Rankin's left cheek to twitch as he taps the molars on that side of his face. He is not happy with the news of the itinerant's departure.

Sharing with Rankin about Catermole slightly eases Francis's worries. Although Francis is grateful to see another itinerant, he fears that working with Rankin will not prove an easy task. At Rankin's recommendation, the two take a late meal at the Butcher's Arms pub at 26 Bishop Street, just down the road from the Wesleyan meeting house. Rankin's suggestion causes Francis to look away from him and mumble,

"Fitting name."

"You were saying, Francis?"

Francis wisely diverts,

"Oh, just giving thanks for a warm meal."

The two seat themselves inside the establishment. Francis quickly inquires,

"When shall you see Wesley?"

"Lord willing, tomorrow evening. I shall depart this eve. I am hoping to find him at The Foundry."

"Had you received word of Catermole's departure?"

"Word arrived in Newbury that Pastor Catermole had abandoned his post. I was there to gain analysis of the circuit. The news caused me to venture to Winchester. There, I had no news of Whitefield's death, only the rumor of the itinerant's departure. Now you have confirmed both."

Francis fumbles with the edge of the tabletop. Rankin's cold approach furthers his concern. He consciously confirms his worst fears: he's afraid that his answers will appear as a mark on himself, or worse, that *Rankin may take to the circuit himself and send me to some smuggler-infested coastland.*

Rankin continues to say nothing, but the look on his face conveys that the information is worthy of note. Finally, the emotionally distant martinet breaks his silence and offers,

"On account of Whitefield's passing, you shall attend the circuit alone. I had planned to engage as assistant, but the death of Wesley's dear friend demands my immediate departure for London."

Francis nods his affirmative, the kind of nod that does its best to hide both relief and the fear of a different outcome. At dinner's end, Rankin bids Francis well and departs.

It will be almost two weeks before Wesley learns of Whitefield's death. He receives the news ten days later, in London. The revelation coincides with his return from Norwich. Wesley's words are telling: "Oh, what has the church suffered in the setting of that bright star which shone so gloriously in our hemisphere. We have none left to succeed him; none of his gifts; none anything like him in usefulness." Wesley's yearning for one with a Whitefield-like blessing, an Elisha-like double blessing, is strong.

At the home of Abraham Wolfe, Francis embraces his horse. Churchfield gives his enthusiastic greeting. Looking over the animal, Francis admits,

"Seems you have not missed many meals."

The horse shakes his head and snorts as a friendly voice speaks from behind Francis.

"Pastor Asbury, please come inside. The wife shall prepare some hot tea. We've a warm, comfortable bed for you to reside in this evening. Might I offer you some food?"

Francis's reaction is strong; his love for this kindly man allows him to relax. He bows his forehead onto the arched neck of his horse. Abraham places his hand on the young man's shoulder. Francis is drawn to the elder man's fatherly compassion as it brings him relief.

Inside, sitting by the warming fire, the two men talk of Francis's travels and the recent news of the passing of George Whitefield. Not sharing too much, Francis stares at the brick hearth in front of the flames. Abraham offers,

"The world shall miss Whitefield. The colonies have long experienced his uniting spirit."

" 'Tis so?"

"What your religion has termed a 'great awakening,' a shaking of the spirit, if you will, unites the various peoples of the American colonies. Despite their differences, many are united in the spirit of your religion."

"God's religion."

The awkward silence causes Francis to respond to his own comment.

"My apology."

"You need not apologize. I too am a man of strong conviction. Francis, you seem distracted. Are you well? Do your efforts bring strain? Do they meet with opposition?"

"At times, it seems God's will. Even my personal life—a dear woman whom I have known since childhood is near to breaking under the strain of our separation. Perhaps I am to leave the ministry."

"Ah, the thorns of the flesh do not sink only into the Hebrew."

Francis raises his bowed head at this intriguing comment. He asks,

"You talk of Paul's thorns?"

"No. I speak of that which Paul spoke of: the thorns originating in the Torah. These are those who persecute the godly."

Francis is confused, and Abraham senses it. He offers,

" 'When you have come into the land of Canaan, which I give you as a possession, and I put the leprous plague in a house in the land of your possession . . .' "

Now Francis is even more confused. He lets out a tiny laugh and looks to the wise man. Abraham asks,

"Do you know that which I refer to?"

"I assume it is of the Old—correction, of the Torah, perhaps the book of Deuteronomy."

"Close. Leviticus. The Lord commanded that the houses which the Israelites inherited in the Promised Land were to remain free of mold."

"Mold?"

"Yes, a special type of mold. The presence of this mold warranted the destruction of the wall in which it showed, or in some cases, the entire house."

"So, the new settler would lose their home?"

"In a way."

"How can this come to pass? Did not God wish for them to reside in a home?"

"God wishes for their blessings. However, God's blessings are dependent upon obedience. The Promised Land once belonged to pagans. Their practices were contrary to the holiness of God. When the mold showed up in the newly adopted homes of the Israelites, the entire area containing mold would require destruction. This at great inconvenience and expense to the new resident."

Leaning forward to stare toward the floor between his feet, Francis shakes his head, conveying his doubt of the rule on mold. Abraham continues,

"God was communicating that this presence of the mold is much more than physical; it is actually a spiritual indication of a physical problem. In many instances, these innocent Israelites, those who had done nothing contrary to God's laws, would find the mold on their walls."

Raising his head, Francis responds,

"Why would those who are living according to God's will have to suffer?"

"I will tell you why. The Canaanite pagans were like most men of the day. When they gained income or riches from their labors, they would store the wealth in the hidden cavities of the walls. When the Israelites lived according to God's laws, they would tear down the infected walls, only to find hidden treasures which were left behind."

Francis's smile indicates a revelation. Abraham continues,

"The Hebrew word is *tzaraat*. The *tzaraat* affliction. Francis, look at me."

Abraham reaches his arm forward to gain the young man's attention. Placing his hand on Francis's knee, he offers,

"Sometimes, what appears as a series of unfortunate circumstances is a blessing in disguise. What appears as unmerited harm from God is more often an opportunity of great blessing."

These words allow Francis to enjoy a restful night's sleep in the Wolfe home.

The month of January in 1771 is quickly upon Francis. He continues in the low round of the Wiltshire circuit, but it is rumored that in a few weeks he will be moved to the upper round of the circuit. Until word arrives, however, he is to remain in the low round. The faithful in the towns of Portsmouth and Salisbury grow weary of receiving visits from Francis only every second week. The lay leaders do their best, but their efforts fall short of the polished ministry of the experienced itinerant. Unfortunately for the Portsmouth and Salisbury societies, their complaints are heard by the locals who hold the meetings suspect.

The Roman road from Winchester once again places Francis in an abandoned city to the north of Salisbury. Francis is drawn to the remaining relics of the old cathedral and castle. On his right, the stem-footing walls, stone blocks laid out in the exact pattern of the exterior walls and barely reaching a man's height above the ground, are covered with overgrown, frozen vegetation and a light snowfall. To his left, the same type of surviving memorial reveals the floor plan of the castle torn down by decree of King Henry VIII, when he generously gave the stones away to his close friend and Groom of the Stool,[167] William Compton. Francis guides Churchfield through the remaining weather-worn boulders. Descending from the raised mound, the highest point in the deserted town of Old Sarum, he resumes his journey to Salisbury.

Arriving in Salisbury, Francis enters the meeting chapel on St. Edmund's Church Street. Looking into the dark space, Francis finds no one. *Most unusual.* His thought almost echoes in the damp room lit only by the sunlight pouring in from the entry door. Returning outdoors, he searches for something to prop open the door while he lights the wall-mounted tapers in the room.

Spotting a rock slightly larger than his closed fist, he bends down to retrieve the impromptu doorstop. Rising again, Francis finds himself staring into the faces of several local men.

---

[167] The King's personal-hygiene assistant.

Beyond these men, Francis views three additional men who have Churchfield by the reins. The biggest man in the group in front of Francis offers,

"Please, gain your horse and depart."

Please? Why would one seemingly set on cruelty ask politely? Francis responds,

"Might I ask why you have untied my horse?"

"Gain your horse and depart."

The man refuses to answer. By now, nearly two dozen men have arrived, each rougher-looking than a Colchester smuggler. Francis nods in agreement and moves toward his horse. Cautiously walking through the men, he finds himself surrounded.

At the horse, several of the men raise objections.

"Let us deal with 'im!"   "What shall we say, we let da' preacha' go? Let us deal!"

The large man who originally confronted Francis raises his hands in the air. The hecklers cease, and Francis takes this as a sign to mount his horse. As he pulls himself up into the saddle, the men of the group ignore their leader and yank him to the ground. The impact with the January-hardened soil explodes a sharp pain in Francis's shoulder. As he struggles to gain his feet, the men aid him in the process, pushing him into Churchfield. The horse stands his ground; however, he begins to twitch.

Pushing Francis up onto the horse, the men who hold the reins begin to drag the pair forward. The movement makes it difficult for Francis to gain a secure footing. *If only I could catch one of the stirrups.* The men hold Francis, stomach down, across the saddle. The bumpy walk of the horse jolts his stomach and paining shoulder.

Nearing a small pond, the men bring their march to a halt.

The leader pipes up with,

"Well, what are we to do with horse and rider?"

"Send 'em in!"   "Make 'em walk!"

Raising his head, Francis sees before him a frozen lake. At first glance, he cannot determine if the ice is thick enough for their passage. A slap to the back of his head causes him to duck; he raises his hands and protects his head. The men crowd in and, unexpectedly, the pushing and shoving raises the preacher into the saddle. He secures himself in the leather seat. *Now to gain the stirrups.* But the frantic movement of his boots does little to secure his desire; from both sides, the rough treatment of the mob crushes his legs against Churchfield. The horse begins to nervously stomp his hooves, aiming to rid himself of this obnoxious group. After several well-placed impacts, the men oblige and part to create an exit.

Churchfield leaps forward, straight for the iced-over lake.

The first few steps onto the pond confirm Francis's greatest fear: the ice is too thin. Frozen chunks of ice and mud scatter as the horse and rider crash into the chilling waters. In less than a hurried breath, the pair is submerged.

Churning his thick legs, the horse raises his head above water and attempts to swim, the surface-level ice chunks cutting into his broad chest. Francis reaches for the reins; he secures one and tugs hard. The horse turns. The turning to the left allows Churchfield to regain the cleared, shallow waters from his entry. It is a struggle, but the animal slowly inches his way back to the rising shoreline.

The men raise a cheer as the horse and rider gain dry ground.

With hands and body trembling from the cold, Francis urges Churchfield to run. The horse doesn't hesitate; he launches. Through the men, the pair flees for the meeting house.

At the chapel, Francis guides Churchfield straight into the darkened structure. Jumping from the horse, he quickly secures and locks the entry door.

Inside, in total darkness, Francis and Churchfield struggle with the cold that causes their bodies to shake uncontrollably. Francis wraps his arms around himself and stumbles toward Churchfield. At the horse, he leans on the large chest of his companion. He draws warmth from the deep exhalations of the wet animal.

Despite the natural warmth of the horse, Francis needs the warmth of a fire, and so does Churchfield. Francis desires to open the front door to let in light, but he knows better; *the men surely await such happenings.* Huddling close to the front of the horse, Francis offers,

"Come now, Churchy; we shall find warmth, with the Lord's help."

Rubbing the cold, wet nose of the animal, Francis silently prays for help. In time, the pair find themselves standing and leaning on each other, silent and in total darkness. After nearly an hour, a light knock on the entry door startles Francis. He says nothing.

Walking Churchfield toward the oak entry, Francis awaits.

The gentle knock recurs. Francis still says nothing.

Another knock, this time accompanied by a woman's voice, causes Francis to respond,

"Are you alone?"

"Yes. I witnessed their dealings with you. Only recently have they departed, having hoped you would surface again. May I come in? I can light a fire. My father has sent warm clothing."

"How can I be assured?"

"I am of the Lacy family."

"Which Lacy?"

"Elizabeth."

Francis remembers Elizabeth Lacy. He opens the door.

Within moments, several other women join Elizabeth. Their husbands have also come, but they remain outdoors to secure Francis's safety. A large fire in the fire pit, a change of clothing, and a thick quilt wrapped around his shoulders provide instant comfort for Francis. He continues to shiver, but the generous offerings promise an end to the struggle. Churchfield stands near the fire as several of the women brush his wet coat.

The contents of Francis's saddlebag, along with the saddlebag itself, lie across the brick hearth near the fire, placed with much care by the concerned women. In a relaxed moment, Francis emerges from his warm covering and reaches for these items that constitute his sole possessions. He lifts one of the books, the Hebrew Bible, and fans the pages, acknowledging to himself that they will dry. He does the same for each book.

In another pile, letters from his mother and father are spread out to dry. He picks up one of the letters and enjoys a rereading. Setting down the slowly drying pages, he notices one obscure letter, one he hasn't seen since the circuit in Colchester. The correspondence is a reproduction of an original, painstakingly copied by hand. Thumbing through several of the pages brings forth a thought: *Shall departure reveal a hidden blessing?*

The letter is Thomas Taylor's letter from New York, written to John Wesley, urging Wesley to send competent preachers to America. Francis's attention is drawn to several key words written at the top of the facsimile:

Read publicly on any Sunday. You may then receive what the hearers are willing to give. And the Elisha-minded preachers who are willing to go.

Elisha-minded preachers . . . There it is again—Francis's sensing of a calling linked to the story of Elisha.

For the remainder of the afternoon, the Salisbury families provide for the weary itinerant and his horse.

After Francis spends the night with the Lacy family, they ask him to talk with a young couple planning to marry. The Lacy's daughter, Elizabeth, the girl who first arrived to aid Francis after the icy-lake ordeal, and her fiancé, Richard, seek a preacher's blessing for their engagement. After dinner, over a cup of hot tea, the family leaves Francis alone with Richard and Elizabeth. Francis opens with prayer. His thoughtful considerations for the couple are apparent.

"Elizabeth, your faith is well exemplified in your works. You have stood alongside your family, in the face of opposition, without fail. Richard, what of your soul? Do you fear an awful eternity?"

"I long for a pleasant eternity."

"How so?"

"I too am of a faithful family. For several generations, we have loved the Savior."

"I see. But Richard, do you love the Savior?"

"I do."

"Enough to exhibit this faith through the works which go with salvation?"

"I do."

"The caution of the Apostle Paul is clear: 'Be ye not unequally yoked with unbelievers.' "

The counsel ends with the young couple praying aloud with Francis. Francis closes with the admonition,

"Marriage is a gift from the Creator, never to be entered into without sound, biblical advice. Let all be advised to take no step in such a weighty matter without first gaining advice from the most serious of brethren."

The next day brings an unexpected visitor, Thomas Rankin. Wesley's man of discipline is thankful to find Francis in Salisbury. He hands a letter to Francis, saying,

"For you—correspondence from home. In addition, I shall assist you on this circuit. You are to remain; I have made other arrangements for the high round."

Francis is not happy to hear this. The last thing he needs now is a lover of strict discipline assisting in a difficult circuit of which he himself has grown weary. However, Francis nods his head and acknowledges,

"Very well, Thomas. I shall depart for Winchester at once. Portsmouth the following Sabbath."

"You shall remain here, Francis. I shall make for Winchester and Portsmouth on the morrow."

"Very well."

Francis doesn't want to, but he accepts the assignment. He ponders his new boss. *Thomas Rankin will not run from responsibility. But how will he hold in the face of violent opposition? Only the experience itself will bring light to the subject. Shall he face opposition at all? His clerical robe gives an appearance of the Anglican clergy.*

The letter from home brings a slight encouragement. Francis is thankful to hear from his parents. The words of his mother and father become the few kind exhortations he experiences for the next few months of winter. By late spring, the Wiltshire circuit's low round is taxing Francis. He struggles with his preaching, his prayer time, his time of reading the Bible and quiet meditation on the holy words. His yearning is for something different, something more significant. *I struggle with the insignificance of opposition; all that I do seems to prove unprofitable.*

The beginning of summer, June, finds Francis arriving once again in Winchester. To his surprise, he is greeted by the thickened accent of a dear friend, reviving a slight hope in the heart of the weary traveler.

"Pastor'd Asbur'dy, Jasper informed me ya' were to arrive."

"Pastor Mather!"

Francis's embrace of the large man almost knocks the Scottish itinerant off his feet. He responds,

"Fr'dancis, ya' are about to put me in the gr'dound."

Francis will not release his hold. Recognizing the strain and anxiety in the young man, the seasoned preacher allows Francis to hang on as long as needed.

Over dinner at the home of Jasper Winscomb, Francis and Alex enjoy a private conversation. Jasper is off on a merchant's duty, while his wife sits quietly in an adjoining room, having recognized Francis's need for a quiet conversation with his mentor and friend. With a slow and deliberate motion, the kind that implies hesitancy, Mather reaches into his coat pocket and hands Francis a letter.

"Fr'dom ya' friend Thomas Ault."

Francis unfolds the single page. Writing appears on only one side of the linen page. In fact, only one paragraph conveys the full content of the correspondence. Francis reads the short note written by Thomas. Setting down the page, he bows his head. Raising his right hand to his face, he rubs his eyes with his thumb and forefinger. Tears slip past the muscular appendages. Alex sits quietly, not wanting to interrupt Francis's emotional struggle.

Moving his hand to the tabletop, Francis offers,

"Seems Nancy is no longer a worry. She courts with another."

Rising from the table, Francis departs for the itinerants' room next door. After nearly an hour, Alex departs the room and walks to the door that leads to the prophet's chamber. From outside, he can hear Francis in deep audible prayer, crying out to God,

"I know that You are for me; I know that You are for me . . ."

The lament brings tears to Alex's eyes. He returns to the main room of the Winscomb home. The itinerants do not speak to each other for the remainder of the evening.

The next day finds Alex and Francis walking in a field adjacent to Jasper's home. The gentle summer breeze does little to lighten Francis's lament. Alex stops, then turns toward his fellow preacher and offers,

"There is another correspondence. Ah' suspect much more encouragin'. 'Tis fr'dom Abraham Andrews, the carpenter in Hertford. He mentioned that ya' may br'ding relief to a current problem."

"As well. I will look at the letter."

Receiving the paper from Alex, Francis opens the two pages neatly folded in thirds. Nodding his head as he reads, he responds,

"I can help. I shall write this evening. Perhaps on your return to London you can see to the reply."

"Ah' shall, Fr'dancis."

The men continue their walk among the rolling hills of Hampshire. The numerous sheep and the herding dogs that work the fleecy animals bring an occasional smile to Francis. Looking at the dogs, he comments,

"These never seem to give up."

"They don't, Fr'dancis."

"Alex, may I share something with you? Something that I have failed to share with another?"

"Ya' have my complete confidence."

Fumbling with his hat, Francis hesitates. Alex notices, but continues the walk. Francis stops and offers,

"America is looking better now."

Stunned, Alex brings his long strides to a halt. Turning to his protégé, he inquires,

"America? What of the colonies? Better yet, what do ya' know of the colonies?"

"The Lord's tug. A slight push in that direction. An Elisha pursuing the double blessing of an Elijah."

"Elisha? Elijah? Tell me, what do ya' know of America, Fr'dancis? 'Tis a barren, unforgivin' wilderness."

"I know very little. However, the leading is strong."

"Ah' see, Fr'dancis. How strong?"

"Very."

"Very well. There has been a work of God in America, some of it movin' among the Friends,[168] and then among the Presbyterians. Unfortunately, wit' both, the work declines."

---

[168] Quakers.

"Why do you mention this?"

"Fr'dancis, in America, many have come to the faith. The works of Whitefield have accomplished much of this. Unfortunately, as wit' any large movement, there are many followers, but few to disciple the new converts."

"I think I see."

"The people God owns in England are the Methodists. The Lord has greatly blessed the doctrines we preach and the disciplines we enforce. These are the purest of any people in the three kingdoms; they must therefore please Him."

"Precisely, Alex; if God fails to acknowledge me in America, I will return to England."

"Whitefield's death strangely unites the colonists of differin' faiths; there is a need for someone to br'ding depth, to provide order'd. The Anglican priests and the rumors of war cause them to shudder wit' the thought of departure for England."

"I see."

Despite Alex's warnings, Francis's thoughts of America continue. Raising his eyes, he takes in a remarkable sight. The first signs of summer further the encouragement brought by the arrival of the letter from his old friend in Hertford and the honest discussion of America with Alex. In a nearby stand of trees, the purple forest floor of gently waving bluebells offers a flowing invitation. Francis declines the woodsy proposition and departs Alex and the fields for the Winscomb home.

"I shall write Andrews."

"Very well."

In the correspondence from Mr. Abraham Andrews of Hertford, he expresses his wish that Francis once again pay a visit to his little schoolroom. Francis would love to return. Abraham advises that his school has doubled its number of students; Francis is glad to hear this. Andrews adds that he is in need of a schoolmistress for the girl students. This comment causes Francis to yearn to help his friend. The strong desire sparks his memory: *In London, at the conference, had not Wesley a young woman in search of a position as schoolmistress?* The thought moves Francis indoors.

In the kitchen, he retrieves a writing implement, then sets about writing to Mrs. Mary Bright at The Foundry near Upper Moorfields in London.

My dear Sister:

Grace and peace be multiplied to you, so that you may be kept in the evil day and be upheld, by the everlasting arm, thro' all trials, inward and outward. I had a letter from a friend of mine, Mr. Andrews, in Hertford; in it he gave me an account of a person he had had in his house for a schoolmistress, but he had turned her away, and I judge he must want another. I think it would do for you. Observe that he is a person who has a school under his own roof, at his own expense, for boys and girls. He has a man to teach the boys and I suppose wants a woman for the girls. They are very spiritual people; they are well known at The Foundry. It is but 20 miles from London. You may write to him to know his mind and to know on what terms he will take you, and what your work must be, what the children must be taught, and then you will know whether you can do it. I have thought of it some time as I have been looking out for you, but I did not think you would have gone to London so soon, but I take the first opportunity to write. You may make use of my name and tell him I directed you. The direction to him must be thus: To Mr. Abraham Andrews, a Carpenter in Castle Street, Hertford. From one that wishes you well and is your friend and brother,

F. Asbury

Handing Alex his letter to Mrs. Bright, Francis prepares for Portsmouth and Mather departs for London. On his departure, Mather proposes,

"Perhaps ya' should return to the topic at the conference in Bristol."

"Which topic?"

"America."

I shall. Francis's thought solidifies his decision.

A few days later, Francis once again finds himself in the port town of Portsmouth. At the home of Abraham Wolfe, the elderly man reads aloud from the Old Testament book of Isaiah, chapter 54, verse 2:

"Enlarge the place of your tent, and let them stretch out the curtains of your dwellings; do not spare; lengthen your cords, and strengthen your stakes."

From the opposite side of the table, Francis replies to Abraham,

"Precisely."

The older man nods his head, the kind of nod that conveys full confidence that God's Word is speaking to Francis. He reaches forward, shuts the Bible, and offers,

"Does God wish to stir you from your current troubles? Perhaps so. Does He bless when it seems like all is utter failure? He does. Perhaps God is asking you to strengthen your tent poles, to enlarge them for a bigger canvas."

"It seems as you say."

"Then if God says 'Go!' you needn't hesitate; you must go!"

By Virtue and Industry[169]

Happy we as those above,
We who keep the feast of love,
Urge each other on to press
Toward the crown of righteousness!
Call'd to different climes away
We in Christ together stay,
One in spirit, mind, and heart,
Parting, we can never part!
Charles Wesley[170]

Tuesday, August 6, 1771. The fifty-mile journey from Salisbury to Bristol is wearing on Francis. Aside from the overnight stay in a bed filled with additional "guests"—bedbugs—in Westbury, the nearly two days in the saddle brings a strange ache to his legs. With the balls of his feet, Francis pushes on the stirrups to ease the pain. He continues on his journey, Wesley's New Room looming into view in the distance.

For the last few hours, Francis and Churchfield have held the winding River Avon in view over their left shoulders. Approaching the center of Bristol and its Castle Green, Francis ponders the route in front of him. Pausing to enter Merchant Street, he looks to his left down Newgate Street and beyond to the corn market on Corn Street. To his immediate left is the infamous Newgate Prison. The smell of death that emanates from this facility, known for its overcrowding and unhealthy conditions, bears down on all who pass near its gates. Francis instinctively covers his nose. Of the prison's twenty thousand inmates, five thousand die each year of various maladies. Beyond the prison, Francis views Bristol Castle and its church, St. Peter's. Beyond those are St. Mary le Port Church and All Saints Church. The castle was constructed in the eleventh century and the churches in the twelfth century. Along Corn Street, he spots several brass tables at the road's edge on the approach to the Corn Exchange. The "nails," as these are called, are the impromptu battlegrounds for farmers and merchants as they

---

[169] The motto for the English seaport town of Bristol. In Latin: *Virtute et Industria.*

[170] Charles Wesley's poem about the biblical account in Acts chapter 20, verse 11. Also a Wesleyan reference to the love feasts before a departure of one of the society's significant individuals.

haggle for a coveted price. Several men occupy the first few tables, their animated gestures indicating their impassioned pleas.

Before him along Merchant Street, across a tiny river, Francis can see Wesley's New Room. He can also see what appear to be an inn and an almshouse on opposite sides of Merchant. The greatest sight, even more spectacular than the large conifer trees of the Avon Gorge to the distant west, is the sight of nearly one hundred Wesleyan preachers on horseback as they ride single file down Merchant Street toward Mr. Wesley's room. The outfits are typical, with one common characteristic: the men's clothing is covered in dust. Ignoring the impoverished appearance of the itinerants, several hopeful local vendors rush the holy cavalry, attempting to sell their wares.

Continuing northwest along Merchant, Francis joins the Wesleyan parade across the River Froom. Beyond the north bank of the narrow river, on his right, are the Quaker meeting houses. Several of their male members gather outside to enjoy the Methodist arrivals, the silhouettes of the riders set against the summer sun as it sinks beyond the magnificent gorge. On Francis's left is the Taylors' Almshouse, and ahead, on the corner at which he plans to turn toward Wesley's place of worship, is the Bachelors and Maids' Almshouse. This charitable house owes its beginning and continuation to Sarah Ridley, a maiden lady herself, and her bachelor brother, Thomas. Thomas and Sarah Ridley intended for their donated funds to help "five poor and decayed bachelors" and "five poor and decayed maids," and since 1726 the facility has been doing so. At the corner, Francis follows the train of horses and men as they turn left onto Horsefair. The New Room stands on his left side, not far from the corner.

The New Room at Bristol, the first Methodist building ever constructed, is the result of an invitation from George Whitefield when John Wesley visited the seaport town. In the open air, Wesley preached his first "scandalous" sermon in St. Philip's Marsh at The Brickfields—scandalous because the preaching wasn't taking place inside an Anglican church building. Subsequent preaching in Hanham Mount and additional local spots brought the formation of a Wesleyan society, which eventually increased enough to warrant the purchase of the plot of land on Horsefair. The original purpose of the "New Room in the Horsefair" was the teaching of the Scriptures to the Wesleyan faithful by the Wesleyan leadership no longer allowed to preach in the Anglican churches. Further growth of the Bristol Wesleyans inspired the first society to utilize the class meeting with lay leaders. By 1748 the chapel had grown crowded and so expanded again, adding worship services timed to not interfere with the local Anglican services.

Entering the courtyard, Francis dismounts. Despite the painful jolt as he lands on his feet, Francis welcomes his arrival in Bristol. Standing alongside many other preachers and their horses, he peers again to the far west, where the Avon Gorge lies in the distance. The magnificent display of the parallel slopes cradling the River Avon, covered with towering conifer trees, inspires him to comment,

"The Lord's handiwork."

One of the nearby preachers responds,

"Indeed."

With Churchfield secured and feeding on the generous offerings of several local families who have put their children to work blessing the itinerants' animals, Francis approaches the double doors to the chapel. The elliptical-top doors are propped open, and many of the preachers work their way into the chapel. Inside, Francis pauses to enjoy the view of the beautiful structure. The center of the room is filled with eight or nine rows of wooden benches, each row capable of holding ten to twelve adults. At the right and left ends of these oak pews are tapered columns supporting the two-story ceiling. In the center of the ceiling, an octagonal parapet floods natural light into the sanctuary. Around the perimeter of a second-level gallery, fine wood wainscoting, painted white, is topped by an oak ledge. Francis comments to himself, *splendid carpentry.*

At the head of the room, a two-tiered pulpit becomes the focal point of the staircases descending from each side of the upper-level galleries. Behind the top portion of the pulpit is a large paned-glass window, which also fills the room with natural light. Francis considers the reasons for the double pulpit; *perhaps the upper is solely for the preaching of sermons. At least that is what I have heard.* Francis is correct; the top pulpit is for preaching while the lower portion, where John Wesley currently stands with his brother Charles, is for the rest of the church service.

A familiar voice interrupts his studied view of the interior of the building.

"Francis!"

Looking to his left, Francis spots his dear friend.

"Richard!"

Francis moves to his friend, and Richard Whatcoat graciously receives him. Amidst their embrace, Richard inquires,

"Are you well, Francis?"

Richard's look conveys that he knows something of a deeper matter. Sensing this, Francis responds,

"The Lord provides. Yes, life has taken a turn; however, I believe the new path shall do me well."

Richard assumes Francis is talking about Nancy; Francis assumes something else.

Richard offers,

"Come, let us take a seat."

The pair walk three rows into the sanctuary. Recognizing two who are already seated, Francis nods his hello to the familiar faces as he and Richard move to join them. The young men have decided to sit next to the itinerants who taught Francis about the smugglers of Colchester. Francis offers a cordial greeting.

"Hello, Peter. Hello, John."

Peter Jaco and John Murlin rise to greet Francis. Each offers the young man a sturdy embrace, the stocky Jaco almost collapsing one of Francis's lungs. He offers to Francis,

"Please, sit between John and me."

Francis looks to Richard, whose expression urges him to accept the invitation. John Murlin informs them,

"Word is, Wesley's critics shall arrive in numbers, continuing with their agitation over the works comment. I hope you boys are ready for a fracas."

Francis swallows hard; *not here also.* His worry prompts a nervous folding of his arms. With a laugh, Richard remarks,

"John, you needn't pull out the clubs just yet. I am confident that the Countess leads a non-violent protest."

"She does, Richard, she does."

Francis unfolds his arms, glad to hear that civility will be the rule of this conference.

Looking about the room, Francis notices that the itinerants have filled the center pews. To the right and left of the support columns, several rows of first- and second-level side galleries running perpendicular to the pews have begun to fill with locals from the Bristol society. Here, young and old, rich and poor, nestle together. Many enjoy light conversation and laughter. Some sit still with eyes closed, appearing in silent prayer—or perhaps sleeping. Others, especially the young boys, have their eyes fixed on the itinerants. These itinerants, especially the young men like Francis and Richard, inspire many a young boy to consider a future in the ministry—their dusty appearance, their broad-brimmed hats, their trustworthy beasts tied up outside, all add to the attraction for an adolescent boy set on adventure.

From the front of the room John Wesley raises his hands, and the audience falls silent. His opening words are simple and few.

"Welcome. My brother Charles shall open with prayer and a hymn."

Charles maneuvers his pudgy frame around his slender brother. John remains in the pulpit, clasping his hands in front of his chest. All in the chapel rise as Charles begins,

> "Ye Servants of God, your Master proclaim
> And publish abroad His wonderful name:
> The name all-victorious **of Jesus extol,**
> **His kingdom is glorious and rules over all."**

What begins as spoken prayer naturally transforms into song. This is a time of peace for Francis. It is in this setting that he reminisces of his first exposure to the Methodists back home, amidst the joyful singing and the friendly congregants of Wednesbury and West Bromwich. This is home to Francis. Charles's powerful, melodic voice continues the hymn in 3/4 time:

> "God ruleth on high, Almighty to save,
> And still He is nigh, His presence we have;
> The great congregation His triumph shall sing,
> Ascribing salvation to Jesus, our King."

Peter places his arm around Francis's shoulders. To his right, John Murlin also places his arm around Francis. Amidst this holy setting, Francis is emboldened with a youthful confidence: *I can face anything with the support which surrounds me.* From the front, Charles continues,

> "Salvation to God, who sits on the throne!
> Let all cry aloud and honor the Son;
> The praises of Jesus the angels proclaim,
> Fall down on their faces and worship the lamb."

He leads the congregation into the final verse,

> "Then let us adore and give Him His right,
> All glory and power, all wisdom and might;
> All honor and blessing with angels above,
> And thanks never ceasing and infinite love."

The completion of the prayer-turned-song brings John to the front. Standing alongside his brother, he proposes,

> "Shall we continue in prayer? Almighty Father, the all-victorious Savior. We beseech Thee, govern our proceedings in these coming days. Allow for the fellowship of the brethren today and the proper care of business in the days that follow. In the mighty name of Jesus, our Lord and King, we pray. Amen."

Charles descends from the pulpit and the itinerants relax in their seats. John opens,

> "Our missionary efforts are ridiculed by the press."

This stark and unexpected comment causes the gathering to fall silent once again. They keenly consider John's comment. Reaching onto the wooden pulpit, John raises three recent copies of the local newspapers, *The Bristol Journal, The Bristol Mercury,* and *The Bristol Chronicle.* Ironically, family members who disagree on religious issues own all three newspapers, plus a fourth. A Methodist, Felix Farley, owns the fourth local paper, which he publishes under the name *Felix Farley's Bristol Journal.* The three papers Wesley holds up are not friendly toward the Wesleyans and seek to rouse locals to oppose the movement.

The itinerants slide forward in their seats, straining to make out the headlines John is referring to. John repeats,

"The press ridicules our efforts - -
In America."

The men relax back into their seats. John continues,

"Seems I've been elected Bishop of Pennsylvania."

The men let loose with laughter. The back-slapping by the dusty preachers floats airborne evidence of thousands of miles traveled on horseback. Looking to the pulpit, they notice that John appears serious—very serious. As the men gather their composure, they catch John's stern face as it lets slip a wry smile. The laughter of the men rises again with this gesture. As the gathering begins to recover, John suggests,

"And Charles, the Bishop of Nova Scotia."

The men erupt in uncontrollable laughter. The locals in the gallery don't know how to react. They are not used to seeing these holy men participating in such frivolity.

Near the front of the room, itinerant John Pawson rises to his feet and proclaims,

"Praise ye the Lord, for the press recognizes the priorities."

The preachers burst into laughter yet again, instinctively looking to Charles— but he is not impressed. He shakes his head and looks to John, his expression clearly conveying, "You started this foolishness." Undeterred, John laughs at his brother.

Tossing the papers aside as worthless scrap, John offers,

"I've word that Thursday I am to meet with the Calvinist Methodists on the issue of my works controversy. I invite you men to attend. Then and there I shall lay this controversy to rest."

The demeanor of the group changes; the men sit up straight, the women tap their children to mind, and Charles Wesley once again stands at the front.

The rest of the first day goes as with conferences before: a day of hymns, prayer, and fellowship among the local community. The evening ends with John in the upper pulpit, preaching a sermon and conducting a love feast.

The morning of Wednesday, August 7, finds the itinerants present for a five a.m. service. No locals are allowed now; this is a day of business. John preaches and Charles leads in song. At the completion of the opening, John begins,

"What preachers are admitted this year?"

Standing to his feet, John Pawson offers,

"John Bredin, Joseph Garnet, James Perfect, William Linnell, Richard Wright, William Winbey, John Floyd, John Undrell, George Wadsworth, Robert Swan, James Watson, George Mowat, Charles Boone, Michael McDonald, and William Horner."

John offers the customary hand wave and the men come forward.

After the confirmation ceremony, John continues with other matters of business: Who remain on trial, who act as assistants, are there any objections to any of our preachers, and the all-important question, how are they stationed this year? John handles the assignments for the fifty circuits, and Francis is once again assigned to attend the Wiltshire circuit. *More confirmation;* Francis keeps this thought to himself.

The seventh question of the conference is a weighty one. Not as weighty as the works issue which will be handled tomorrow, but this issue is important to the ones it affects. Wesley offers the question,

"Our brethren in America call aloud for help. Who are willing to go over and help them?"

The resulting silence reveals several itinerants who have a slight cough. Their polite hacking, unnoticed before, now stands out in the stillness. An itinerant clears his throat. Others look about the room. The inner thought is unanimous: "Who shall volunteer for such a demanding assignment?"

At his pew, John McEvoy rises to his feet. Alongside him, Joseph Garnett and James Perfect also stand. The gathering remains silent. This time the inner thought is a different one, but still unanimous: "These are infants, barely one year on the circuit. Is there not one with more experience?"

At the back of the room, Richard Wright stands to volunteer—again, another itinerant young in the work. McEvoy was admitted to the itinerancy the year before, Wright and Garnett this year, after only one year of preaching. James Perfect has preached one year longer than the rest, but only because he didn't qualify for admittance last year. His preaching skills and faith walk both lack fervency.

At the pulpit, John Wesley looks to the wooden desktop of his pulpit. He nervously taps his fingers on the oak slab. He twitches his bony nose. He appeals again,

"New York asks for experienced, competent preachers."

The volunteers bow their heads, feeling slighted by Wesley's indication that they have little experience. Then each offers a nod to their leader, the kind of nod that acknowledges his wise insight. One by one, they return to their seats.

In the middle of the chapel, Francis sits with Richard. Several times during the proceedings, the pair have shifted their gazes between the volunteers and each other. For Richard, he didn't expect so many willing to leave England. He also didn't expect the free exchange of harsh criticism toward the young, bold itinerants. For Francis, he didn't expect to be sitting so long. Rising to his feet as Richard looks on in astonishment, Francis offers,

> "I believe I have a call to America."

Near the front, an itinerant dressed in a formal black robe turns and comments,

> "The incompetence continues."

Francis peers at the antagonistic preacher. He didn't expect opposition, especially concerning an almost afterthought circuit like America. He also didn't expect his personal reaction to the harsh statement; Thomas Rankin's comment incites anger in Francis. He takes a deep breath and wisely remains silent as Rankin continues,

> "Pastor Asbury's circuits dwindle under his influence. Bedfordshire, Colchester, Wiltshire—all suffer. Check the numbers as I have and you shall arrive at the same conclusion."

> "All the more reason to send him; he is expendable. Based on the lot before us, he is the most experienced to lead such an inexperienced group."

John Pawson's rebuttal of Rankin is loud and sure. His words hurt Francis's feelings only slightly; he chooses to focus on the fact that Pawson sees him as a leader, at least somewhat. John Wesley interjects,

> "I shall not send five. I believe two shall suffice. Boardman and Pilmoor are on the circuit already; they shall provide sufficient supervision."

The itinerants nod their approval. All but Rankin. He barks back,

> "What of the Staffordshire low round? Asbury abandoned his post."

> "The young man is a wanderer!"   "He shall weaken the effort!"

The additional criticisms from other itinerants ignite a sense of guilt in Francis. Unexpectedly, he recalls his personal assault of William Orpe. Despite Orpe's scathing letter, Francis now realizes that his criticism, although soundly proved later, should never have focused solely on Orpe's inexperience. Before these seasoned preachers, many of whom have been preaching longer than he has been alive, Francis too is feeling young and inexperienced.

Despite these feelings he wrestles with, his attention is drawn to the front once again. There, a stocky Scottish itinerant stands. Clearing his throat, he booms,

> "R'dankin, take a seat. And those who oppose Fr'dancis can take a seat as well. Ya' criticism is unfounded. Ah' sent the young man to the low r'dound. And that on account that he was only revealin' what time itself brought forth: that the assistant in charge of Pastor'd Asbur'dy was lackin'. Ah' too believe Pastor'd Asbur'dy has a call. He has my support to go."

A dozen preachers stand to offer their support of Pastor Mather. In addition, Peter Jaco and John Murlin rise from their seats. Standing on either side of Francis, they place their arms around his shoulders. Peter offers,

> "I too support sending Pastor Asbury. His were not the refined members of Wesley's Foundry or Whitefield's tabernacle. His were the sheep herders, farmers, and sailors of Portsmouth and Colchester. A smuggler's preacher. The American wilderness awaits a man with such advantageous qualifications."

> "I support him as well. His ways may seem unorthodox to some, **but this fails to disqualify**."

The recommendation of Jaco and Murlin prompts more itinerants to stand, especially after Murlin's smug look at Rankin as he emphasizes, "but this fails to disqualify." Nearly the entire room stands in support of Francis's call. Francis purses his lips, touched by the kind gestures of his fellow preachers. He nervously fumbles with his coat sleeves and crosses his arms.

At the pulpit, John Wesley raises his arms and offers,

> "I too sense a call to America for Pastor Asbury. I move that he go forth."

> "As do I."

With Pastor James Glasbrook's agreement, Wesley announces,

> "Pastor Asbury, you are reassigned to America. Now, who shall join Asbury?"

The itinerants who stood in support of Francis take their seats. The four initial volunteers, some of whom ironically opposed sending Francis, stand again. At the front of the room, Thomas Rankin peers at the group like a stalking wolf. He finally makes a selection, declaring,

> "I nominate Richard Wright; his walk is steady."

The itinerants who stand in his support bolster the decision for Wright. By day's end, Richard Wright has joined Francis in the group bound for America.

At the end of the evening's closing prayer, John Wesley approaches Francis. The young itinerant can barely meet Wesley's gaze; the steely look of the wise leader causes him to look away. Sensing his own discomfort, Francis forces himself to look Wesley in the eye, or at least at the bridge of his nose. Francis does not feel worthy of the call. He doesn't doubt the call, but fears he is one who is prone to mistakes. Wesley stands within arm's length of Francis and offers,

"Following God's call may not come easy, but it surely rewards."

Francis nods his agreement. John continues,

"The Lord provides for those who step in faith."

Francis bows his head. John gently lifts the chin of the dejected preacher.

"Give me one hundred preachers who fear nothing but sin, and desire nothing but God, and I care not a straw whether they be clergy or laymen, such alone will shake the gates of hell and set up the Kingdom of Heaven upon earth."

On Thursday, August 8, the five a.m. sermon is attended by eight new guests: seven Calvinist Methodist preachers and one Countess of Huntingdon. After the sermon, John Wesley steps down from the upper pulpit to the lower pulpit and offers,

"Before we begin, I am pleased to announce that our society in Birmingham, the one that took over the Moor Street Theatre seven years ago, is making plans to expand. We are in search of property to build a chapel."

Francis silently rejoices over the Birmingham society's need for more space. He is familiar with the Moor Street Theatre, recalling the time the Wyrley Birch family took him to see the mocking theatrical portrayal of Whitefield. This play caused his parents to argue and cut short his apprenticeship on the Wyrley Birch estate. He rejoices for the development of a future chapel in Birmingham, but more for the fact that the theatre has thrived as a Wesleyan place of worship. Looking to Richard, he comments,

"Mother shall receive this with much joy."

"I am sure."

Francis cracks an early-morning smile at the wry reply.

At the front of the room, Wesley offers a welcoming wave and announces,

"Kind Selina, you may begin your proceedings."

At this, almost all of Wesley's itinerants rise from their seats and leave the room. The gesture is almost rude, but the brothers Wesley do not rebuke the silent protest. Selina politely waits for Wesley's preachers to depart. All that remain are Francis, Richard, and a couple more. The Countess's seven escorts are not pleased with the departure; however, they intend to confront John Wesley and not his preachers.

Selina's chaplain, Walter Shirley, begins by pronouncing Wesley's statement from last year's conference as "popery unmasked." He delivers an opening statement which is followed by Wesley's reply,

> "It is my hope by meeting's end that you shall no longer consider me a dreadful heretic."

For nearly two hours, a debate rages back and forth. The proceedings are for the most part cordial. Each side delivers a sarcastic barb now and then, but overall, much good is accomplished. Wesley makes his case well, that "the works are on account of salvation, not unto salvation." Selina and her preachers are satisfied; they draw up an agreement for Wesley and his preachers to sign. Wesley advises,

> "Upon my approval, I shall encourage my preachers to sign."

The clarifying statement is simple enough, and Wesley writes it out in his own hand.

> *Whereas the Doctrinal points in the Minutes of a Conference held in London, August the 7th, 1770, have been understood to favour justification by works: Now the Rev. John Wesley and others assembled in Conference do declare, that we had no such meaning; and that we abhor the doctrine of justification by works, as a most perilous and abominable doctrine. And as the said Minutes are not sufficiently guarded in the way they are expressed, we hereby solemnly declare, in the sight of God, that we have no trust or confidence but in the alone merits of our Lord and Saviour Jesus Christ for justification or salvation, either in life, death, or the day of judgment. And that no one is a real Christian believer (and consequently cannot be saved) who doth not good works where there is time and opportunity, yet our works have no part in meriting or purchasing our justification, from first to last, either in whole or in part.*

Fifty-three of Wesley's preachers sign the document the next day, day four of the conference. The signatures of Richard Whatcoat and Francis Asbury are missing, as is the signature of Richard Wright. Francis and Wright not signing is understandable, as they must proceed home to prepare for their departure to America, scheduled to board ship in Bristol in less than a month. For Whatcoat, the situation is slightly different. His circuit assigned by Wesley is in Ireland, the town of Enniskillen along the River Erne. Making matters more unsettling, Richard's mother is ill, near to dying. This news causes Richard to race home to her side, only to receive a word of blessing from her. Despite the grave situation, she begs her son to go to Ireland, saying, "We shall meet again in eternity." Sadly, the sudden departure to his mother's deathbed does not allow Richard to say goodbye to Francis.

Collecting Churchfield and departing from the conference, Francis heads straight for home. The eighty-mile trip takes a direct line through the towns of Gloucester, Tewkesbury, Worcester, West Bromwich, and finally Great Barr. The route is the Staffordshire low and high rounds combined. After the first ten minutes of the trek, Francis suddenly brings Churchfield to a halt, dismounts, and kneels in an open field. With hands cupped over his eyes, he speaks aloud,

> "Father, I fail to know what makes a preacher. I am willing to go. May I find peace in Your provision."

Rising from his knees, Francis walks to his horse. He pauses. Reaching to rub the side of the animal's neck, he breaks into tears. Wrapping his arms around Churchfield, Francis weeps.

The trip home is an arduous journey, once again nearly two days in the saddle. Entering his home, Francis announces his return.

> "Mother, Father . . . ?"

> "Francis, oh, Francis!"

Elizabeth's joy launches her into the main room, where she embraces her son.

> "Oh, how I have missed you! Must tell Father. Joseph!"

Elizabeth's attempt to call her husband almost deafens her son. He responds,

> "Mother, you shall injure my hearing at this range. Hold on, Mother; I shall fetch Father."

Releasing his mother, Francis walks to the back of the house. There is Joseph, tending his garden. Joseph catches sight of Francis and exclaims,

> "Franky, so glad to see you! Has Mother . . . ?"

> "Yes, the first, as always."

> "Come, we've much to talk about."

> "Yes, Father, we have much to talk about."

Inside, Francis asks,

"Father, Mother, may I ask you to sit at the table? I have need to share a development with you."

"Come, Eliza; sit. Francis wishes to talk."

"Oh, that can wait; let me prepare a lovely dinner, for our son has returned!"

"Mother, I really need to speak with you and Father."

"Come, Eliza."

"Oh, very well."

At the kitchen table, Francis nervously taps the tabletop as he waits for his parents to sit. As they settle into their chairs, Joseph inquires,

"Francis, you wish to share something of importance?"

"I do."

Francis takes a deep breath, the kind of breath that indicates the seriousness of his next words and the fact that he is overwhelmed by the enormity of the task. Joseph reaches and gently takes his wife's hand as it lies on her lap. Squeezing it, he offers her a comforting smile. Less than comforted, she inquires,

"Francis, what is it? Are you to marry?"

"No, Mother. Not marriage. Father, Mother . . ."

Francis cannot get the words out. Joseph urges,

"Go on, Francis."

"Father, Mother, I have accepted assignment as an itinerant in America."

"What! Francis, are you mad?!"

Launching from her chair, Elizabeth stomps her feet. The scene in the Asbury cottage borders on the hysterical. Elizabeth races around the main room, mumbling and arguing, her words slowly crescendoing to the level of an angry outburst. Joseph vainly attempts to hold and comfort her.

"Leave me alone, Husband!"

Francis sits quietly. He struggles with the pain he has brought, watching as his mother's tirade moves her from one side of the room to the other. Joseph lovingly follows, aiming to comfort her. However, she is having no part of it. Her actions do one thing for Francis: they calm his struggle and solidify his decision. He loves his mother, but at almost twenty-six years of age, her attempts to manipulate his decision appear almost comical.

Out of love and respect for his mother, Francis looks to his dad and offers a nod, the kind of nod that says she must come to accept this. Rising to his feet, he calls to his mother,

> "If it does not work in America, I shall return. Even so, I plan to return for my thirtieth birthday."

> "Four years! What shall I do with four years? What shall you do for four years? The colonies are a desolate wasteland. Animals, mountain ranges, aborigines, all these set for harm."

> "Now, Mother, I have faced as much here in England."

> "Aborigines, you've faced aborigines in England? Why have you held this from your mother?"

> "No, Mother, I haven't, but some do border on the savage. You know this. Have I not shared of these dealings? Mother, I plan to return. Please, accept my decision not as your son, but as a man. In the hopes you shall eventually accept it as God's will."

This brings Elizabeth's plotting march to a halt. She raises her hands to her face and weeps. The always-strong Joseph motions to Francis, and they rush to embrace the dearest woman in their lives. For the next five minutes, Joseph and Francis calm Elizabeth. She eventually agrees to sit in a chair at the kitchen table and talk.

Joseph opens,

> "Eliza, America is a distant land, I will not argue. Franky's decision brings worry to myself as well. However, let us give him a hearing. I am confident this decision did not arrive without notice."

Wiping the tears, Elizabeth snatches her hand away when Joseph attempts to hold it. Returning his attention to Francis, Joseph asks,

> "Tell us, Son, how did you arrive at this decision?"

> "For nearly a year, or perhaps six months—I am uncertain of the time, but I am certain of the indication. Several times, through preaching as well as through several individuals God placed in my life, has it been so indicated."

> "Eliza, see? This decision is not the result of youthful exuberance. The Lord is calling our son. We must allow this. Correction—despite our feelings, it shall happen. Francis is a man."

Elizabeth nods her approval. It isn't a strong approval, but one that comes with hesitation. She looks to Joseph and continues to weep. Joseph places his arms around Elizabeth and looks to Francis.

> "She shall come to accept it. Now, you must need to make provision. When and where shall you depart?"

> "I am to arrive in Bristol in three weeks."

"Well then, this leaves just two weeks for Mother and I to help you prepare."

Due to Elizabeth's controlling nature, demanding every minute that Francis can spare, his preparations for the trip actually amount to little. His parents spend much of the time traveling with him to neighboring towns as he offers his farewell sermons. The people are grateful for his preaching, but little appreciation appears by way of donated support. This doesn't disturb Francis; he is content to move on. But Elizabeth gives a curt nod each time this happens, the kind of nod that indicates Francis should seriously reconsider.

His final night in Great Barr brings many to the Asbury home. With the cottage filling beyond capacity, the family agrees to move the evening's event outdoors. Part class meeting, part last sermon at home, and part love feast, this time marks Francis's final night in the company of those who know him best. In the morning, he shall depart for Bristol.

In a corner of the main room downstairs, a table is set out to gather items for Francis to take with him to America. At the beginning of the night's proceedings there is little on the table; a bag of salted beef is the lone item. Elizabeth and Joseph hope for more, maybe even money. Joseph struggles with the fact that he and Elizabeth have little in the way of worldly wealth to give their son.

In attendance are the usual members and friends from Bromwich, Wednesbury, and Great Barr. In addition, Pastor Mather joins Lord Dartmouth and several of the Dartmouth family. Henry Foxall and his family, along with many employees from the forge, also attend. Nearly three hundred people congregate outdoors on this beautiful August evening.

Also in attendance are Francis's close friends from childhood: the Ault brothers, Thomas and Jabez; the two Jameses, Mayo and Bayley; Thomas Russell; William Emery; Edward Hand; and, escorted by Edward, Nancy Brookes and several of her friends. Francis is confident that Nancy is here as a friend; he is also confident that she is not being courted by Edward Hand, for the letter he received clearly indicated another young man as her intended. Francis has checked; that young man is not present this evening.

Francis approaches Edward and Nancy. As he reaches the pair, Edward lifts away Nancy's hand, which is wrapped around his forearm, and remarks,

"I would guess you two have to talk."

Edward and the group depart, leaving Francis and Nancy alone, yet still among the crowd. The two move beyond the gathering for privacy. As they walk, Nancy opens the conversation.

"Nice jacket."

"Won it in a wager with a student at Oxford."

"A wager?"

"Not really. The young man, somehow impressed with my side of a debate, gave it as a gift. Strangely, after I discovered his watch in one of the pockets, he advised me to keep it. So I did as he wished."

"Impressive. You can wear it to the theatre."

"Oh, Nance."

Nancy's jesting smile causes Francis to focus; once again, his emotions are drawn to her. He comments,

"Your face. It has always started with your lovely, smiling face. The sight of which never fails to quicken my emotions."

Nancy bows her head, slightly embarrassed by the comment. She gently pulls on his arm to stop. Facing him, she raises herself to gaze into his eyes. Surprised to find them slightly moist, she reaches to take his hand. He forces a smile, the kind of smile that conveys an understanding sorrow. Nancy responds,

"I, too, am drawn to you."

"But it cannot be so."

"I know, Francis. However, you must hear me. For some time, it has wearied my heart that you do not know what I have ached to share. Please allow me to do so."

"Of course, Nancy."

"If I have learned anything of Francis, it is that you are most sure of what you want. As desirable as this is for a young lady, I do not wish to stand in your way."

"You never have."

"True; however, the indication would have done so."

"Oh?"

"What does Wesley have for a married itinerant? Is it not a life of placement? Francis, where shall placement fit into your life? Placement is far from you. You are a traveler; if you had a ship, you would fancy yourself an explorer. If it were possible, no doubt you would soar to the moon."

Francis nods his agreement. With his other hand, he grasps the hand that holds his.

"Go on."

"Francis, it is my wish for you to go. Go forth to the ends of the earth. Go, Francis, for the Creator has designed you for such."

Raising her hand to his lips, he gently kisses her soft skin. Not wanting to lift his eyes lest they reveal the tears, he responds,

> "Thank you, Nancy. Thank you for your understanding and friendship. I shall always hold you dear."

> "As you with me. Now go. Your friends and family eagerly await your presence on this important evening."

Patting her hand, he releases his hold of Nancy. As he turns, Nancy holds to one thought that pains her: *The Lord has such different plans for you and me, Francis; if only it were not so.*

Nancy moves toward her parents, who stand on the other side of the gathering. Reaching them, she sinks into her father's embrace.

With the departure of Nancy, several of Francis's childhood friends rush toward him. Nancy feels a gentle relief at the sight of the young men surrounding Francis.

> "Franky, you've a word for us this evening?"

Thomas Ault's mocking tone invites a gentle slap to the head by Francis. Thomas continues,

> "Perhaps a word to help poor James Mayo—his life is in disarray."

Pushing Francis toward the outdoor pulpit, the young men continue their banter. Nearing the front of the gathering, his comrades pause. James Mayo, the usually quiet one, begins,

> "You know, Francis, we shall pray for you each day. We are proud of your willingness to go to the barren wilderness of the colonies. Hopefully, the four years shall pass quickly."

Francis is grateful for the kind words. Thomas Russell inquires,

> "Four years?"

> "Yes, Thomas. This is my plan—after four, I shall return home."

> "Well then, I shall withhold my words until your return."

> "Come now, Thomas!"   "Thomas, tell Francis your thoughts."

The two Jameses goad Thomas until he responds,

> "Well, all right. Francis, this town owes much to your efforts. The preaching and teaching affects all of us in a good way."

> "Thank you, Thomas."

Spinning Francis around, James Bayley adds,

> "And this town shall surely miss its Wesleyan itinerant, the only one ever to spoil the clothing of Lord Dartmouth."

James pulls Francis into a husky embrace. The rest of the group join in the show of affection.

Barging into the huddle, Pastor Mather commands,

> "All right, enough already! He's yet to preach this evenin'; don't know if he'll get to keep that fancy blue jacket."

The group erupts into laughter. Pulling Francis slightly aside, Mather informs him,

> "Asbur'dy, word from the conference: Wesley is not a heretic."
>
> "As I thought. I assume the others returned to sign the clarification."
>
> "They did. Come now, preach to ya' class. They eagerly await."

The evening's sermon is a powerful one, based upon Psalm 61, verse 2: "From the end of the earth I will cry to You." Many in the crowd marvel at Francis's booming voice, which one man later comments, "was like the roaring of a lion." Francis's childhood friends also stand in amazement; in the six years he's been commissioned as an itinerant, a handful of them have heard him only once. By the end of the evening the locals, Francis's dear friends included, have experienced the efforts of an impressive preacher—a seasoned preacher who has no problem sharing his inner emotions through the selection of a sermon topic that was more for himself than for his hearers.

Following the sermon, a bountiful feast feeds the entire group. From several surrounding towns, the visitors contribute food and drink. By evening's end, Francis is ready to spend his last night at home with his parents. Pulling Joseph and Elizabeth toward the front door, Francis waves a farewell to the gathering. As they enter the home, Francis suddenly leaves his parents to pull aside his friend Edward Hand.

> "Edward, might you pray with me this evening?"
>
> "Yes, of course."
>
> "Wait here; I shall inform Mother and Father."

Edward waits outdoors as Francis heads indoors to talk with his parents. Within a few moments Francis emerges from the home, slightly amused by his mother's anxiety. Apparently the evening's offerings for Francis's trip to America were minimal—food supplies for his trip to Bristol, nothing more. His parents were hoping for a blanket or two, or additional clothes for America. Despite the limited offering, Francis is happy for the townspeople's eager participation in the night's events. He comments to Edward,

> "We shall pray for provision in Bristol."

Edward nods his agreement as he and Francis head for their prayer closet, his father's dilapidated tool barn.

In the barn, Francis walks around, regarding the various tools of his father's trade.

> "I shall miss the sight of this barn. Each item has its proper place."

"Indeed? Look at the walls—the siding barely hangs on, Francis."

"Provides for a welcomed summer's night breeze."

"And a most unwelcomed winter's night blizzard."

"Ha!"

"Come, Francis, let us pray for your provision. I am sure your parents desire your undivided attention this evening."

"They do."

Kneeling on the dirt floor, both men grow quiet. Edward begins,

"Heavenly Father, Almighty Father, our loving and caring Father. We kneel before Thee, fully aware that each good gift comes from above. Fully aware that apart from You, we can accomplish nothing. This evening, this most glorious evening which You allowed, we lift up our request for provision. For safety and provision for my dear friend as he proceeds to follow Your call upon his life . . ."

Edward's prayer continues. He covers all necessary items: provision for the trip, the itinerancy in America, safety in crossing the Atlantic, safety in lodging in the colonies, provision and safety for Francis's parents. At the end of Edward's supplication, Francis bursts into tears. He didn't expect this reaction, but it happens upon him. Edward leans into him; placing his arm around Francis's shoulders, he silently comforts his friend.

After taking a few minutes to gather himself, Francis reveals,

"As strange as it sounds, I shall miss my parents. Haven't been home for several years, but I shall miss them dearly. And Edward, even stranger, I weep for my animal, my dear Churchy. He has . . ."

Francis cannot finish the sentence. The tears flow, his breaths deep and measured. In the quiet moment, Edward patiently waits.

After nearly a minute, Edward offers,

"Your horse. Francis, he is more than a horse. I'm sure he has been your constant companion and friend. Tell me of Churchy. I would value the sharing."

"Not much to share. He's just always there. Braved crazy opposition, raging rivers, and unforgiving Roman roads. Almost drowned by an ignorant group of heathens. Always a welcome greeting, even on the most frigid of mornings or after plunging through the ice of a winter lake. I wish I could take him to America. Nevertheless, I can't."

"I see."

"Will you take him, Edward? It would honor me to give him to you. Lord Dartmouth refuses his return. Please, take him from me."

"I shall be honored, Francis."

"I shall leave at daybreak. Would you make arrangements?"

"I will. My father and I shall accompany you and Richard Wright to Birmingham. From there I shall receive Churchy."

"Edward, I wish for you to take him this evening. I cannot bear to weep over my horse and my parents at the same time."

Edward pauses, then, tossing good judgment aside, offers,

"Mother would react sorely."

Francis forces a smile, the traces of tears highlighting its perimeter creases.

"I believe she would. Come, I must say my goodbye to him alone."

Leaving the barn, Edward walks toward the house to wait for Francis. Francis moves toward Churchfield. The horse responds with his usual snort, except this time it is less effusive, almost in knowledge that this is a solemn moment. Francis leans into the animal; he hugs the thick neck and weeps again.

Gathering himself, he says to Churchfield,

"The righteous man shall take care of the needs of his animal. Isn't that what the Book proclaims? Churchy, at this moment, I do not feel righteous. I feel I am abandoning one who unconditionally accepts me in all seasons. I shall always remember your tireless efforts. Farewell, my friend."

Francis rubs the neck of the animal. Churchy twitches, seeming to return thanks for the loving neck rub. A swish of his tail brushes a light breeze by the pair. Backing away from the horse, Francis walks outdoors to find Edward. Approaching his friend, Francis advises,

"Please, remove him. It bears heavy on me to untie him. I would like to think that I shall untie him once again in the future."

"As you wish, Francis."

Within moments, Edward exits the barn with Churchfield. As they turn in the direction of his home, away from Francis, the horse stops. Edward gently pulls on the reins to continue, but the horse will not budge. Turning his head toward Francis, Churchfield lets out a loud, snorting whinny. The neigh brings tears to Francis yet again. Raising his hand to wipe his eyes, he struggles to reply,

"I shall return, Churchy. I shall return."

The next morning finds Elizabeth and Joseph eating breakfast with their son. The mood is quiet. With breakfast complete, the family moves outdoors, where they begin final preparations for Francis's departure. The walk to Birmingham will occur in ideal summer conditions. Francis's coach doesn't leave until two o'clock in the afternoon. The four-mile walk will take them nearly two hours to complete.

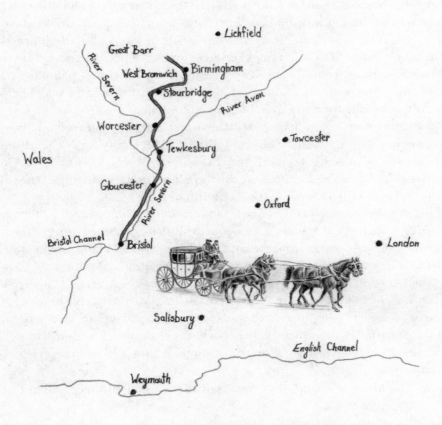

Busying herself with last-minute preparations for Francis's trip to Bristol, Elizabeth's saddened emotions silence any chance of conversation. Joseph does his best to comfort his wife; he is her rock in these times. With the last items tucked into the linen travel bag, Joseph hugs Elizabeth from behind. Saying nothing, he draws her close. Without resistance, the couple accepts the situation, drawing strength from each other. Francis and his parents depart for Birmingham.

In Birmingham, the Asbury family awaits the arrival of the coach that will deliver Francis and Richard to Bristol, which is due to arrive at noon. Richard has already arrived, he too with limited provisions—a small bag, not unlike the one Francis has, filled with little more than enough dried food for the journey to Bristol. Their entire life's belongings reside in their coat pockets and saddlebags: for Francis, a Bible, some books, a watch, and some Wesleyan pamphlets; for Richard, the same, with the addition of a writing quill and a jar of ink. The two seem far from ready for a trip to Bristol, let alone America.

The Birmingham Flying Stage Coach departs each day from Birmingham with a direct delivery to the seaport town of Bristol. The eighty-mile trip will take thirty-two hours, placing Richard and Francis in Bristol around ten o'clock tomorrow evening. Several stops along the way allow for the changing of the four-horse team before final arrival at the Lamb Inn in Bristol.

In the distance, Francis and Richard spot the approaching vehicle. The coach from Bristol arrives on schedule at noon. The two coachmen jump down to release the four passengers from the covered chaise. Several young boys from the coach inn leap onto the chaise and quickly unleash the leather straps that hold the travel boxes of the passengers. One by one, each piece of luggage is lowered to the ground. The boys then carry the leather satchels into the establishment.

The lead driver, a big man with a peculiar smell, retrieves a stocky firearm from the side of his driver's seat. It is obviously a means of self-defense. The driver, sensing the questioning stares of Francis and Richard, offers to the itinerants,

> "The blunderbuss, a nasty muzzle-loader. A convincing greeting to the highwayman."

The driver's smile reveals a missing tooth, maybe two. The preachers say nothing. Elizabeth raises her hand to her mouth to cover her astonishment. Joseph nods, the kind of nod meant to convince his wife that the boys will be safe. Unfortunately, she isn't convinced.

The driving team as well as the horses are changed out; a new set of horses and drivers will deliver the coach back to Bristol. The new horses are stocky and edgy, the drivers as surly-looking as the previous team. They too make use of the blunderbuss; in fact, each of them carries one.

Looking to Elizabeth, one of the drivers comments,

> "Night passage tends a bit more adventuresome."

Elizabeth says nothing.

At precisely 1:45 p.m., the inn's director announces,

> "Coach is departing."

At this, Richard and Francis prepare to leave. Richard shakes Joseph's hand and tips his hat toward Elizabeth, then turns and climbs aboard the chaise. Francis, fighting back tears, embraces his mother. She shakes with sadness, her uncontrollable trembling prohibiting her from speaking. She begins to weep, as does Francis. Turning to his father, he hugs his dad. His father, too, shakes with uncertainty. Releasing his grip on Joseph, Francis reaches into his coat pocket. Removing his watch, he places it into his mother's hands. The act seems to bring a peace over her; she no longer trembles.

"Please, take care of this until my return. I love you, Mother . . ."

Francis fails to complete his sentence as his tears cause a similar trembling. Elizabeth replies,

"I shall, my son. Your father and I shall pray daily."

Seeing his son in tears, Joseph also begins to weep. His words are quick and forced through uncontrollable sadness, the last words Francis hears from his parents.

"I shall never see him again."

At this, the driver roars,

"Departing for Bristol!"

Francis turns and climbs on board the chaise. With one last look at his parents, he nods his head and closes his eyes, seeking to secure their faces in his memory.

It is several miles out before Francis can speak; the dryness of his throat and the swelling of his eyes inhibit him. Richard leaves Francis to himself, silently praying for their safe passage to America. When he can, Francis offers,

"I have never seen Father cry . . ."

The revelation is interrupted by a sudden jolt of the chaise. The impact from the large hole in the road indicates that they have traveled beyond the well-funded Birmingham portion of the road. For the next thirty-plus hours, the travelers will experience the lesser-funded sections of the narrow, dirty road.

Six hours into the ride, the chaise stops at Stourbridge to change out the horses. Francis and Richard exit the car. Stretching and walking off the first segment of the trip, Francis notes,

"My body already aches. The road is far from adequate."

" 'Tis that, Francis."

"Far less painful on horseback."

"I wouldn't know. I've never crossed the country as you have."

"And now we shall cross an ocean."

The thought is not an easy one for the men. Francis advises,

"Best we make use of the inn's facilities."

The men head indoors. Having enough food for the trip, the men refuse the generous offerings of the inn for dinner. This is an obvious choice, considering that neither of them has any money. After a thirty-minute break, the chaise once again travels the road west to Bristol.

The late-summer setting of the sun allows daylight to linger late into the evening. The men decide to read their Bibles and pray, but this is a difficult task because of the unforgiving road. As the sun finally sets, bringing a cool darkness to the chaise, the men stretch their legs, put their heads back, and fall into sleep.

After midnight, the men awake to a stopped chaise. This is standard procedure; once again, the team of horses is switched for a fresh set. The thirty-minute break offers another rest stop, and the men take advantage of it. They are returned and asleep before the chaise departs again.

At five o'clock the next morning, the chaise continues to wrestle with the rutted passage, as do the men's bodies. Despite their linen bags which they have improvised into pillows, several times each hour their heads collide with the side of the car. The chaise will not stop for another ninety minutes. As the men yawn themselves awake, Francis leans to retrieve his bag. Reaching into his supply of food, he announces,

"Fresh fruit."

The jar of sliced peaches, nestled within a tightly wrapped dish towel, is a welcome sight. Francis removes the jar and opens the wax-sealed lid. With his fingers, he removes a large peach slice. Down it goes, deliciously soothing his parched throat. He comments,

"Mother – has – sent – only – enough – for – one – person."

"Well – then, – now – that – you – have – had – a – sample, – you'd – best – hand – over."

The sudden jolts in the road continue to make conversation difficult. Francis laughs at Richard's quip, but more so that the last bump almost sent both of them to the floor. He hands over the jar, making sure Richard understands he is welcome to one slice. Francis isn't a stingy individual, but he rarely shares his food.

At 6:30 a.m. the coach pulls off the road in Tewkesbury to change teams. Francis and Richard race out of the coach to attend to the necessary business.

With necessities complete, the men exit the inn. Francis advises Richard,

"That bridge there is King John's Bridge. Look over there . . ."

"Oh my, it is . . ."

"Beautiful, I know. And Tewkesbury Abbey. Was there one time before."

"You preached in the abbey?"

"No, visited. Viewed Milton's organ and spoke with the man in charge of tuning the instrument."

"Milton, the poet?"

"Yes, John Milton."

Spotting the drivers leaping on top of the chaise, Francis and Richard hurry back toward their confining compartment. A passerby calls out,

"Preachers!"

Francis and Richard turn in time to view a short, well-dressed man offering his paper.

"*Felix Farley's Journal.* Enjoy."

Francis receives the newspaper, tips his hat, and jumps back to join Richard in the coach. From outside, the resonating voice of the driver announces,

"Departing Bristol."

Promptly at seven a.m., the coach once again begins bouncing its way toward Bristol. Francis voices his opinion,

"One of the first objects upon my arrival in Philadelphia is to obtain a horse."

Francis does not wish to spend much of his life traveling in coaches. Richard nods his agreement, the kind of nod that indicates he is doing his best to accept the current conditions.

Francis reaches over and picks up the Bristol journal. The front page of national news from London, Portsmouth, and Liverpool fails to gain his interest; neither does the international news from Prague, Madrid, and Paris. He opens the pages and browses the various ads for vendors and departing ships. One ship advertises passage to the colonies; another promotes the recent arrival of American-produced goods, providing a long list of lumber and other items: "5,500 feet of inch oak boards, 15,000 feet of 1-1 qtr. inch ditto planks, 1,300 feet 1-1 half inch ditto, 1,200 feet of 1-1 qtr. and 1-1 half inch pine plank, 23 logs of cedar, 5 poplar planks, 2,050 spokes for wheels, 30 barrel staves, 13 barrels annotto,[171] 1 barrel cow tails." The ship's contents are advertised as "Just Arrived on the ship Warwick."

Another advertisement catches Francis's attention:

For Sale, a Negro man, near 20 years of age, well limb'd, fit to serve a gentleman or be instructed in a trade.

Francis sets down the paper.

---

[171] An herbal plant.

He has heard of the enslavement of Africans; Wesley has spoken against the infamous trade. However, Francis has never faced it in real life, never even seen a slave auctioning block. Noticing that Francis has set down the paper, Richard inquires,

"Finished with the journal?"

For the next six hours, the men shift their bodies, their posteriors, and their perspectives, withstanding the worst of too many hours on the heartless road to Bristol. Too awake to nap, the men alternate their focus from the outdoors, to the inside of the coach, to each other's clothing, to the Bristol journal, only to repeat the process. This portion of the trip is the hardest for a wanderer like Francis.

At one p.m. the coach stops again to change out the horses and drivers. The drivers are as rugged as the previous teams; they too carry their blunderbusses as they board the coach. At precisely 1:30, the coach is off. The men encourage each other, voicing the fact that the trip has one more stop and then a short three-hour leg into Bristol.

Roughly thirty minutes into the trip, one of the drivers offers a strange comment:

"Can't stand preachers."

The comment is clear enough for both itinerants to hear, and it stands out amidst the constant chatter of the men up top. Francis and Richard fall silent, listening.

"The worst of the bunch—Methodists."

"I hear ya'."

The ride for Francis and Richard is now bumpier. If permitted to escape as steam, the anger of the young itinerants would rise immediately from the coach cabin. Francis shifts restlessly in his seat, leaning from one side to the other. He fidgets, not knowing where to let himself settle. The driver continues,

"What of this Wesley clan? Have they the keys to the kingdom?"

"What kingdom?"

"Precisely. They have forgotten their King."

These words do not sit well with Francis. When he suddenly grips the coach's door handle, Richard urges,

"You're mad, Francis—let it be. These are an ignorant group. Let us not leave a damaging impression."

Francis doesn't want to, but he acknowledges that Richard is correct. He settles back into his seat, releasing his breath in an explosive sigh.

"Friends of prostitutes . . ."

This last comment from topside, however, is more than he can take.

"Bladdered buffoons!"

"Francis, you stoke a fire which shall eventually burn."

Richard's reaction to Francis's rebuke of the drivers is quick and sharp. Francis slumps back into his seat.

For the next three hours, the comments of the drivers further Francis's aching to retaliate. He keeps silent, or nearly so—in his unique manner, he privately offers more retaliatory comments, many of his father's favorites toward the drunks from The Malt Shovel. In time, Richard waves his hand and ignores Francis, despairing of any further efforts to silence the West Midlands preacher. However, Francis soon finds that his comments are not helping him with his overall feeling toward the drivers; he is about to erupt with anger.

Nearing the five o'clock hour, the coach driver lets out a loud call to his team. The horses immediately come to a stop. Francis and Richard find this odd. Peering out the side windows, the men spot the driver and his assistant climbing down from the drivers' seat. Francis warns Richard,

"These are set to harm us."

"Now, Francis, calm down. Let us see."

The burly men grumble incomprehensible words as they cautiously carry their blunderbusses. The sight of the guns causes the itinerants to sit back and consider their options. Francis concludes,

"We haven't any."

Leaning his head out of the coach window, Francis inquires,

"Your side?"

Looking out his window, Richard responds,

"Nothing. Just a horse standing in the middle of the road."

Richard reaches and unlatches the coach door. With a deep breath, the pair step out.

The driver and his assistant walk slowly toward a few bushes at the side of the road. The Old Man's Beard plant once again sparks a memory for Francis, as he notices the last stage of its blooms abounding within the bushes. However, the unexpected events quickly supplant that happy thought. Francis cautiously pulls Richard to the far side of the bushes, convinced that the driver is looking at something within their branches. Richard acknowledges to Francis,

"Whatever the driver and his assistant are looking at, it resides in the thick brush."

From the other side of the road, Francis and Richard can hear a strange groaning in the thicketed area. The driver takes his blunderbuss and pokes it into the bush. The groaning intensifies. The driver offers to his assistant,

"Obviously too much drink."

The comment eases the itinerants' anxiety; they immediately walk over to the driver and his assistant.

In the bush, half asleep, disheveled and drooling, lies a mail carrier. The driver scratches his head with the underside of his weapon. Pointing to the horse, he advises his assistant,

"Move the animal; tie him to the bush. We've a schedule to keep."

Lying beside the postman, a dog patiently waits for his master to awake. The assistant moves to the horse, ties him as the driver instructed, and turns toward the preachers.

"London post carrier—too much of the bitters."

Looking at scene, it is obvious the inebriated man fell from his horse into the bushes. The driver summons Francis and Richard to board. They do so and the coach is once again on its way.

A few minutes after the departure, Richard continues to think about the drunken postman. He aches for the man, *well employed, but sadly mistaken.* Wishing to engage Francis in a discussion of the ill effects of intoxicating drink, he asks,

"What do you think of the recent event?"

Francis pauses. He raises his right hand to grasp his chin. Looking to the ceiling of the coach, he responds,

"It is my deepest conviction that the London mail for Bristol shall arrive later than expected."

Before eight o'clock, the coach arrives for its last stop before the final leg of the journey. The men step out, eager to relieve themselves and to eat dinner. The last of their provisions from home are inadequate for grown men; the portions are more appropriate for a child. A few minutes later, the coach driver emerges from the inn in Falfield with two wooden cups in his hands. He approaches Francis and Richard, commenting,

"Best soup around."

He hands the cups to the men. Reaching into his coat pocket, he removes a half loaf of bread.

"You'll require the assistance of this. Enjoy."

Stepping to the coach, the driver announces,

"Departing for Bristol."

The itinerants hurry into the coach. They do not know how to respond. Their stomachs ache for the food, their heads ache from three hours of anti-Methodist ranting. The pair look to each other. Outside, the drivers are no longer cursing Wesley and his preachers; they seem focused on the arrival in Bristol. The drivers push the coach forward as the itinerants inside use great skill to devour the generous offering.

Three hours pass with no additional rude comments from the drivers, and at twenty minutes past ten, the coach arrives in Bristol. The men quickly gather themselves and their belongings and depart for the New Room.

From the Lamb Inn, the men walk through Lawford's Gate, one of the remaining medieval gates into the town of Bristol. The darkness of the moonless night adds to the eerie appearance of the ancient portal. Proceeding west through Old Market, the men pass through to the castle path. Other than a few intoxicated Newgate prisoners who have earned a night out, Francis and Richard walk alone. Nearing Merchant Street, the nefarious odor of the prison greets the men. Holding his hand to his nose, Francis responds,

"Wesley's New Room is just ahead."

Onto Merchant Street, the route from here requires a short walk by the almshouses. These too are quiet, settled down for the night. At Horsefair, the men turn left and walk to the west. At Wesley's New Room, they pause to catch their breath. Francis offers,

"Shall sleep well tonight."

"Indeed."

Entering the grounds, the young men proceed for the entry door. Once inside, the quiet space flickering with the light of several lit candles brings a feeling of relief to the weary travelers. They head for the stairs and their rooms on the second level.

The New Room sleeping accommodations for the itinerants are simple. A common meeting room acts as the central hub of the upstairs space. The room is complete with tables and chairs for study and eating. Here, fellowship among the preachers takes place. One of Wesley's extensive libraries stocked with books for the itinerants is also located in the common room. Off this room, several doorways lead to the tiny yet private bedrooms where the traveling preachers sleep.

With the candlelight dancing on the whitewashed walls of the common room, Francis and Richard bid each other a good night's rest and depart for their beds.

The next morning finds the men up by five, washed, and in quiet prayer in the common room. Nearly an hour into their supplications, the sound of boots climbing the wooden steps to the second-level room breaks their concentration. The two look at each other, their expressions identical: "Wesley?" Their guess is correct. Francis stands and offers,

"Good morning, John."

"Good morning, gentlemen. Quick passage from Birmingham?"

"As quick as can be."

"Sleep well?"

"I am confident I speak for both Richard and myself, the best of the last two days."

"Very well. Several people downstairs would like to meet with you."

With an almost skipping motion, Wesley turns and departs downstairs. Francis and Richard once again find themselves looking at each other, the kind of look that conveys their surprise that someone would venture to see them at this early hour—and that Wesley could be so joyous at this early hour. Francis urges,

"Come, Richard; several request our presence."

Francis sets aside his desire to go through the numerous shelves of books; *there shall be time enough to browse Wesley's library.* The pair race toward the steps.

Downstairs, the atmosphere is almost festive. Nearly a dozen people, men and women, nod their greetings as the itinerants step into the sanctuary. Francis and Richard chuckle as John Wesley rushes across the room to pick up a young girl of about six years of age, her shoulder-length ringlets framing her adorable face. With one quick scoop, Wesley raises the child in his arms, gives her a kiss on her head, and gently sets her on her feet again. Seeing her little brother admiring the activity, Wesley drops to one knee, places his hand on the young boy's head, and offers a prayerful blessing. With the blessing complete, the lad is all smiles as he darts back to his mother's side.

Looking to the pews, Francis and Richard view several piles of clothing—trousers, shirts, and socks—alongside two leather pouches. The tallest man in the group summons the young men, saying,

"The locals have put together some things."

Pointing to the piles of clothing, the man gestures for Francis and Richard to receive them. The itinerants nod their acceptance, the kind of nod that hesitates to let on that they are pleasantly surprised with the gifts. Moving to the piles, they find each item neatly folded, then bound into bundles with hemp rope. The leather pouches are small, the size of a big man's fist. Picking one up, Francis inquires,

"For Richard and me?"

The tall man replies,

"Yes. The Bristol society raised ten pounds for each of you. I suspect this should hold you for a few months in the colonies."

Francis once again feels hesitant to express his gratitude. Richard offers,

"Thank you all. The Lord's grace abounds."

Turning to Francis, Richard points out,

"Seems all our needs are accounted for."

Francis smiles as his doubts of God's provision fade away.

The group slowly move forward to make introductions. Some offer their prayers, others whatever they know of Philadelphia and America.

From outside the group, two young boys, preteens, suddenly rush the itinerants. Their mother, slightly embarrassed, scolds them to back away. Acknowledging her concern, Francis and Richard respectfully nod to the mother as they wave the boys closer to pray. As each lad expresses his excitement at the chance to kneel, the itinerants kneel alongside the enthusiastic youths. The prayer is short in length, but lasting in memory for the rambunctious fellows. Within seconds, the boys are off, headed outdoors.

The talk with the Bristol society continues.

Glancing up from one of the light conversations, Francis catches Wesley's eye; he appears to be summoning Francis. He politely excuses himself and walks over to Wesley. Pulling Francis toward one of the first-level side galleries, Wesley offers,

> "I wish to speak with you."

Uncertain of his leader's expectations, Francis experiences a nervous surge that prompts a light sweating of his hands. Rubbing them together, he follows Wesley to a secluded area. John begins,

> "I wish to speak to you of the colonies. As in England, itinerancy is the key. Location prompts complacency. The success of Methodism owes much to traveling. Yours is to travel, to open new doors, and to find those who shall become leaders. Promote the small group versus the large gatherings. This is the truest route of success. Location shall sound the beginning of the end of this movement."

Nodding his agreement, Francis is relieved that Wesley would encourage him with such information. Wesley offers again,

> "I've made arrangements with a pilot in the Back.[172] You're to meet at the White Lion Inn. From there he shall escort you to his wherry and eventually to your ship, the Warwick. Your passage for the wherry and the ship has been taken care of by the Bristol society. They have also raised fifty pounds for you to deliver to the New York congregation. I entrust the money to you. Please deliver at your first opportunity."

> "I shall."

> "You're to meet the pilot today at noon. I trust you and Richard are ready for departure."

> "We are. Might I ask one favor?"

> "Go ahead."

> "May I look through your library?"

> "Francis, you may look and take from my library. It is expressly set up for the itinerants."

> "Thank you, sir."

---

[172] Present-day Welsh Back, north of King Street.

Richard is surprised to view Francis racing up the stairs. Considering this, he detaches himself from the group, offers his gratitude for their provisions, and makes his way toward the stairs.

Upstairs in the common room, Francis peruses the extensive library. With great expectation, he looks to add to his small collection of books. As Richard joins him, he advises,

"Only that which can fit in our saddlebags."

The two begin their search. It's a difficult task; Wesley is highly considerate of his itinerants. Francis already has a Hebrew Bible, thanks to Abraham Wolfe in Portsmouth, who has helped him with learning some Hebrew. He has a copy of Bunyan's *Pilgrim's Progress*. He struggles with what to add. He loves history, and would love to regain the account of David Brainerd's work among the Native Americans. He continues to look.

A sound from the steps signals the return of John Wesley. The short, thin leader walks over to Francis, where he stands perusing the bookshelves.

"Francis, may I make a few suggestions?"

"Of course."

"Let us see."

With a decisive prod of his pointed index finger, Wesley directs Francis,

"Over here, Pastor Asbury. Yes, this shall serve you well. First, the Appeals: *An Earnest Appeal to Men of Reason and Religion* and *A Farther Appeal to Men of Reason and Religion*—both written by a most wise man."

Francis laughs at the inference, well aware that Wesley wrote both books. Tapping his chin with that decisive index finger, Wesley continues,

"The abridgment of de Renty's life. Yes, a fine rework."

Again, Francis laughs. Wesley abridged the voluminous work of the French ascetic's biography; de Renty was a counselor to King Louis XIII in the seventeenth century. Looking straight at Francis, the wiry Wesley ponders the next selection. Francis clears his throat and stands up straight, somewhat intimidated by the little man's confidence. Wesley exclaims,

"Norris! Yes, John Norris. Let me see . . . ah yes, here where I spotted it last. You must take the works of this Platonist."[173]

Francis considers the suggestion. *The philosophies of Plato? I shall attempt.* Now the indefatigable Wesley launches himself to the other side of the room, and Francis does his best to follow. Perusing the extensive display on the shelves, Wesley's searching finger comes to a stop.

"Yes, you must take the works of Edwards."

"Jonathan Edwards?"

---

[173] One who follows the teachings of the philosopher Plato.

"Yes, Francis."

He pulls out two abridged works of Edwards's writings—these abridgments also done by Wesley—and hands them to Francis: *A Narrative of the Late Work of God, At and Near Northampton* and *Some Thoughts Concerning the Present Revival of Religion in New England.* The growing stack in the itinerant's hands is getting heavy, and is far from what can fit in the travelers' saddlebags. Francis begins,

"May I set . . . ?"

"Ah yes, sermons! You've need of my published sermons. Come, Francis."

Abandoning the setting down of the books, Francis lumbers over to the corner of the room. Keeping up with Wesley is nearly impossible. The weight of the books brings an ache to Francis's forearms; he wryly reminisces, *not since the forge* . . . But his thought is soon lost in the bustle. Wesley reaches for the book of his sermons and places them onto the pile, noting,

"Quite a stack of books; you should set them down."

Francis withholds his reply. Before he can set the books on the table, Wesley stands at the top of the steps and offers,

"Shall make arrangements for the books. Would you desire an additional saddlebag? I am in possession of a few extra."

"That would be fine. Thank . . . you."

Wesley is heading down the stairs before Francis finishes his reply.

With books, clothing, and monies packed for safekeeping, Francis and Richard depart the New Room and head for the White Lion Inn.

Nearing the well-populated establishment, Francis and Richard discover an effigy, tarred and feathered, hanging outside the inn's doorway. The figure, made of hemp bags and string, waves about in the riverside wind. Pausing to consider the object, Francis and Richard are confused, unsure as to its meaning. A passerby offers,

"Ol' John Adams, ungrateful colonist—how many more acts shall he protest?"

Francis and Richard remain mystified. Shrugging off the comment, they continue their search for the pilot who will escort them to their ship, having been instructed to meet him at the American Coffee Shop attached to the White Lion Inn.

It's not long before the pilot arrives. He is a short man, thin, with tiny hands. With him is his companion, a long-haired dog similar to the one that greeted Francis at the abbey in Tewkesbury years before. The wheat-colored hair, in matted strands, thickened by the salt air (and the fact that he hasn't been bathed in a few years), blows in the wind. Occasionally when the dog shakes, the resulting spread of the strand-like fur gives the appearance of an oversized porcupine or hedgehog.

The pilot offers his greeting, extending his wiry hand with a smile.

"Departing for Pill?"

"Yes. We're to catch the Warwick for Philadelphia."

"Philadelphia; a little further than I plan to go."

The jest causes the dog to bark. The pilot offers,

"Ol' Pilot, now, now. These boys don't want no extra companion for the colonies."

With an odd look—Francis is sure one of the man's eyes is slightly askew—the pilot asks,

"But would you be interested in one of his pups? Seems he's had a few intimate nights with a lady Wheaten in Pill. The owner dumped the whole lot on the missus and me. Happy to give you one."

"Gracious offer, but no, thank you."

"Ah well. You let me know if things change."

"We shall."

The dog sighs deeply as it leans against Richard's leg. Richard reaches down to stroke the matted hair, mentally describing the feel of it as *rather gritty*. Pilot is grateful for the petting.

Within a few minutes, the men and the canine Pilot board the Pill pilot's wherry and set off down the River Avon. On board are two other passengers, apparently men of commerce. Francis surmises that they are merchants, their cotton clothing indicating they are probably dealers in colonial items.

The beginning of the journey involves strategic maneuvering around several large one-hundred-ton ships anchored in the Avon. The task involves floating near the north bank of the river—a tricky undertaking, as the water is dangerously shallow at the river's edge. Only a skilled and experienced pilot would attempt such a route. For the Pill pilot, this is just another day spent doing what he does best.

Traveling near the north bank affords an opportunity to view the various shops and people who inhabit the docks. Butchers, weavers, sellers of various imported items—all these populate the busy port town. The people scurry about like those in London, except these are less concerned about appearance and more concerned with accomplishing the day's tasks. So perceives Francis, until he spots one particular individual, obviously a man of the sea. Dressed in a gaudy coat trimmed with lace and sporting a cocked hat, the seaman struts along the docks. The jacket is adorned with large alternating silver and gold buttons on the elongated lapels and oversized sleeves; even his shoes flash a pair of metallic buckle-type ornaments. At his side walks a black adolescent boy, obviously his servant, ready to address his master's needs.

The sight causes Francis to inquire about this individual. The pilot's response is short and to the point.

"The post of captain for a slaving ship is not without its financial benefits."

Francis has for the second time faced the issue of slavery. He acknowledges to himself, *I am to encounter a world far different from my expectations.*

The wherry pilots of Bristol are in high demand. Unlike the captains of the large one-hundred- or three-hundred-ton ships that cross the Atlantic with passengers and cargo, the pilot is a specialized worker, capable of braving the peculiar channel. The Bristol Channel possesses a unique tidal phenomenon: at low tide, a majority of the waterway becomes a mud flat. This is advantageous to the waders,[174] but a major inconvenience to boats. The Avon dries up twice each day, leaving boats grounded near the banks and in the shallower portions of the river. The stress on the cargo-filled hulls is a cause for concern, as is the possibility of fire as dangerous chemicals shift in the leaning boats.

Continuing due south, the pilot points out a large park-like setting on the west bank.

"Queen Anne's Square."

The open area is a favorite gathering spot in the milder months for ceremonies, punishment of criminals, and communal assemblies. The green space dedicated in honor of Queen Anne resides in the middle of the most fashionable addresses outside of Bristol town proper. The pilot points to a bronze equestrian statue in the center of the square.

"William the Third."

Francis responds,

"William and Mary."

"Correct. Perhaps an equestrian statue of yourself will someday mark your life."

Odd comment. Francis keeps this thought to himself.

As the waterway turns to the west, the pilot instructs the young men to look due north.

"Hotwel,[175] the playground of the well-to-do. The Prince of Orange ate here once, as did the Duchess of Marlborough and the Duchess of Kent— with their husbands, of course."

---

[174] Wading birds that feed on the exposed sea life stuck in mud.

[175] Eighteenth-century spelling for the town of Hotwells.

The dog barks his acknowledgement of the pilot's announcement, then shuffles over to Francis and leans his hairy body against his leg. Looking up, the disheveled tilt of the animal's head causes Francis to smile. He comments to himself, *you are an ill-smelling companion.* Nevertheless, he bends down and pets the friendly animal.

The Avon takes a slow turn toward the northwest and then due north. Looking east, Francis spots a beautiful sight: a sloping hill, mostly covered in blooming foliage. It is an aromatic delight, as steady winds distribute the scents of heath, eyebright, wild thyme, marjoram, maidenhair, wild sage, and geraniums. Competing with the favorable scents, fields of pasturing horses, cows, sheep, and donkeys offer their own unique fragrance. The combination of smells becomes close to unbearable, but the occasional waft of the herbs alone is still pleasant.

Looking forward past the bow of the wherry, Francis spots the magnificent Avon Gorge. For more than a mile, the widest part of the Avon displays jutting stone cliffs rising more than three hundred feet above the waterway, mostly on the eastern bank, clothed in dark-grey limestone with occasional veins of brown sandstone. On both slopes, towering conifer trees blanket all that isn't stone, giving the western slope a solid-green appearance. Francis eagerly awaits this passage.

Before entering the gorge, Francis's glance up the sloping land to the east brings into view the tiny town on the top of the hill, Clifton. A few minutes elapse in which to appreciate the view, and then the ship tucks itself into the gorge.

Within the secure bounds of the gorge, Francis fixes his gaze on the plants that attach to the rocky slopes. He silently wishes his father could see this. His enchantment with the natural landscape is interrupted by a comment from one of the merchants on board.

> "Only a bastard kind of popery, Methodism, has troubled Bristol for some time."

The pilot smirks, the kind of smirk that is set on mischief, confident that the merchants are unaware that Francis and Richard are Methodist preachers. He prompts,

> "Gentlemen, as you were saying?"

The short, stocky merchant scowls.

> "The Methodists—ungodly rabble. Theirs is a beastly sect. Their women fail to keep house; the men, worse yet, fail to provide for their women. The women flock to Wesley and Whitefield. Not so sure they aren't running brothels."

For a moment, Francis is set to pounce upon the ignorant dandy. He has reached his limits. The nearly three hours of mocking by the coach driver the day before has diminished his ability to resist an angry outburst. It is a difficult veto, therefore, but he chooses otherwise. He clears his throat. Gripping hard the wooden edge of the cover that provides minimal protection from the rain, he steps forward to comment. Wanting to intervene, Richard grabs Francis's arm. Turning about, Francis stares at his companion, the kind of stare that brings an immediate release of his arm. Francis continues his approach to the merchant.

"Methodist? Seems you know very little of the sect."

"Oh, might we have a Methodist on board? Pilot, you allow Methodists on board your ship?"

The pilot smiles that crafty, mischievous smile again. Ignoring both the smile and the comment, Francis responds,

"You speak of corruption; from whence does it really derive?"

"Religion is corruption."

"Precisely. The corruption of the Anglican Church is the seed that brings forth Methodism."

"Precisely, preacher."

"No, you fail to grasp what I'm saying. Methodism is far from corrupt; it is the cure for a cold, dead religion deceased with corruption."

"Preacher, you seek to tangle me in a web."

"Far from it—I seek to set you free."

"The church seeks to return us to the Dark Ages."

"Dark Ages? Christianity is the only thing that ever brought mankind out of the Dark Ages."

"Preacher, you speak of the church as if it is Parliament."

"Precisely; the Anglican leadership is Parliament."

"Parliament is corrupt."

"Correct. Unchecked, government corrupts all that it touches, churches included. Right and wrong are written on every man's heart, put there by the Creator. Corrupt religion shall never keep people from the truth written upon them. Neither shall the miter and the crown encircle the same brow."

Taken aback by the itinerant's verbal flurry, the merchant pauses. He looks to his partner, but he has nothing to offer, nor does he want any part of this conversation. Francis stands silent, his hands upon his hips, panting from his last words. He appears as a man set on getting the facts out into the light.

The merchant returns his questioning gaze to Francis and responds,

"The miter and the crown—you speak of religious things of which I know not."

"Not religious—truth, eternal truth. The miter is religious, the headgear worn by the Jewish High Priest, and the Roman priests. It symbolizes the church. The crown is simple enough: the monarchy. When the miter and the crown are worn by the same person, corruption follows."

"That I understand. But what of Methodism?"

Francis relaxes his stance. He lowers his hands, then raises them in front of him and rubs them together. He continues,

"Methodism, like the reformers and dissenters before, seeks to put things aright. Church and commonwealth remaining separate. History is unmistaken in this."

"Remove the church and anarchy shall follow."

"Now you are on my side? Wise insight. The miter and the crown must separate; however, separation of church and state does not imply the complete cutting off of the state from God, or the nation from Christianity. It does not imply the exclusion of God, righteousness, and morality from the state, only that the state is in no way equipped to designate what is righteous and moral. These designations derive from the church, or more precisely, from the Bible and its revealed evidence in the Son of God."

The merchant looks to his partner. This time, instead of turning away, the partner shrugs his shoulders and comments,

"Must say, I see it as he has presented it."

"I see."

Francis offers,

"Civil leaders face dire consequences when attempting to lead the church also. The Scriptures are clear enough; an Old Testament king became leprous for attempting the same![176] This is the cry of the Protestant reformers like Hooker.[177] Do you hear this same cry from Parliament today? I think not. Parliament, the Church of England, and the monarchy are all one and the same. What has this brought upon them? A corrupt populace, illiterate and addicted to gin. Methodism, like the Puritans, the Separatists, the Moravians, the Dissenters, and others of a like mind are the remedy for a corrupt populace. Strangely, we have returned to that which we fought to leave."

---

[176] King Uzziah, found in 2 Chronicles chapter 26.

[177] Reverend Richard Hooker.

The merchant turns away. Francis is comfortable with what he has said, but uncomfortable about the way he went about it. *Was I too harsh in my reply?* With this thought, he backs away also. Looking to Richard, Francis catches his friend's eye. Richard's look conveys much, and he decides to verbalize it.

"Such depth from a Black Country naila'."

Appreciative of Richard's attempt at a West Midlands accent on the word "nailer," Francis nods his agreement. After thoughtful consideration, he offers to his traveling companion,

"Less a Black Country naila' and more a Hampshire sheep herder."

As the waterway bends, making several turns to the west, the port of Pill comes into view. Looking toward the shoreline, Francis spots a familiar sight: a peregrine falcon. The bird of prey with the almost limitless top speed gracefully perches itself on a wooden pier post. Francis thinks back to the falcons he and his father regularly spotted in Bromwich; the thought is a pleasant one.

Nearing the port, Francis and Richard step to the front of the long, narrow boat. Within minutes, they will walk the elongated bow of the wherry to depart. As they gather their possessions, the pilot offers,

"For the Warwick, see William Hiorn or Thomas Flowers, Goodman's wharf. Or the Captain, Samuel Davison."

The itinerants nod their thanks and leave for land.

Walking toward Goodman's wharf, Francis and Richard look for the master of the Warwick. The port of Pill is a famous port. In 1497, famed explorer John Cabot sailed from Pill, intending to reach Asia for trade. Instead of Asia, he landed on the coast of Newfoundland, North America. It is common Bristol knowledge that Bristol citizen, sheriff, and businessman, Richard Ameryck, financed the Cabot expedition. It is also common knowledge among the Bristol citizens that Cabot named America after the financier who provided his ship, the Matthew.

Along the dock, Francis notices a strange sight: seven old women are chained together, their hands behind their backs, as they cower in the scorching sunlight. The unusual and disturbing sight of the elderly procession causes the itinerants to stop their search for Captain Davison. Leading the procession is a jailer; his rough treatment of the women prompts Francis to intervene.

"Sir, might I . . . ?"

"Tend to your own business, sir."

Francis is silenced, but he continues to look. Uncomfortable with Francis's staring, the jailer responds,

> "These women are too old to serve their sentences; enterprising captain
> has decided to take them to America, to sell."

"Into slavery."

> "Well, if you want to call it that. The women are convicts, too old to serve
> their sentence of transportation to the Indies. The captain is doing them
> a favor, keeping them from rottin' in a cell, or worse, dying in a field."

Again, slavery. This time it is different for Francis—the women are white.

The approaching sound of the solid heels of jack boots knocking upon the weathered wooden dock captures the attention of the jailer and the itinerants. The stout man who stops a few feet from the women prisoners tips his hat toward the preachers. The itinerants return the gesture. The arrival of this stub of a man, standing as tall as he is wide, prompts the jailer to offer,

> "Beautiful day, Captain Davison."

The captain remains silent, peering at the inglorious group of women prisoners on the wharf.

As the jailer awaits the captain's response, another group of white emigrants, male and female, approach the ship's captain. These are not bound by chains, only an obligation to work off their ocean passage. The usual indenture is seven years. The captain's pause once again moves the jailer to offer,

> "We've got weavers, tailors, blacksmiths, spinners, and masons. All
> prepared for seven years' indenture."

The well-dressed captain nods his approval and responds,

> "They have been informed of the terms?"

> "They have. Any turn up sick or dead in the voyage and their children
> will serve as collateral, with servitude until their twenty-first year. All
> agreed upon, sir."

> "Very well. Any in the coach-making business? I've a request for one in
> the colonies."

> "None, sir."

> "Well, if we happen upon one, consider his passage free of charge."

The jailer's recital of the terms shocks Francis. He ponders the situation: *all white, and risking their children to enslavement. A blacksmith . . .* Francis considers the loving community of believers who have paid his passage; he is grateful he chose to preach.

In addition to the chained women, another jailer brings along three white convicts, chained at the feet and wrists. These are also purchased by the captain—purchased from their sentence of death, they will be sold for the captain's profit as slaves in America.

Francis has no comment.

Within one hour, the ship's mate asks the men to board a skiff for the Warwick. They do so, riding the small craft along with the women prisoners and several white emigrants indentured for the colonies. The tiny craft floats to the side of the three-hundred-ton Warwick. The three-masted ship towers over the men. Pointing to the rope ladders that hang over the side of the ship, the pilot of the landing craft advises,

"Your passage aboard. Mind your step."

Francis is shocked. Not only do they have to climb a nearly fifteen-foot rope ladder in order to board, the old women in chains must do the same. Immediately, to Francis's relief, the pilot begins to remove the bindings of the women prisoners.

Within moments, Francis and Richard find themselves climbing the side of the enormous ship, which, not surprisingly, remains unmoved by their activity. Stepping onto the deck of the Warwick, the itinerants bow to one knee and give thanks. As they pray, one of the ship's crew cries,

"We've preachers on board—away with the bitters!"

The mocking comment from the seagoing wag fails to interrupt the men. With their prayer complete, Francis and Richard rise and walk to the far side of the ship. Ignoring the various noises of the crew, the indentured passengers, and several other obnoxious shipmates, the itinerants lean onto the ship's bulwark and stare into the waterway. They remain silent. For Richard, the struggle is limited to leaving the familiar. For Francis, it is the memories of the violent opposition to his preaching, the departing from his close friends, the criticisms of the itinerants who objected to his going to the colonies, the abrupt and awkward ending of his relationship with Nancy, leaving his loving parents—especially his mother—and the uncertainty of what lies ahead in the colonies. At the wooden rail, with their few belongings lying on the deck beside them, Richard holds on to what might be, while Francis holds the exposed end of the white ribbon in his Bible—the same white ribbon given to him by Nancy Brookes when she bandaged his arm cut by his cruel schoolteacher, thirteen years before. Francis droops his head and closes his eyes; he thinks to himself, *shall return before my thirtieth.*

About the Author

Al DeFilippo is a Writer's Digest award-winning writer with a passion for writing the history of America's founding generation, told through stories of individuals who exhibit a "fish-out-of-water" characteristic.

Al's involvement with the story of Francis Asbury started in 1996, when he was approached by an associate pastor at the Methodist church he attended with his wife and children. The Reverend David Broadbent asked Al if he knew what a circuit-riding preacher was. Growing up Catholic, Al had no idea what David was talking about. What was a circuit rider and what did he do? When Reverend Broadbent told Al he reminded him of a circuit rider, it naturally piqued his interest.

Drawn to the friendship of Francis Asbury and Harry Hosier, Al knew he had to write a story of this unique pair—a young, inexperienced British pastor away from his homeland and an ex-slave—traveling the thirteen colonies during the Revolutionary War between the American colonies and the British Empire.

Al's first attempt to write this "fish-out-of-water" story was in the form of thirty four-minute radio episodes. Eventually, Al wrote several versions of a two-hour film screenplay, one of which received an award from Writer's Digest. Al has also created a treatment of the story of Francis Asbury and Harry Hosier in the form of a twelve-hour television miniseries. In 1998, a national sports figure was interested in producing Al's take on Francis Asbury and Harry Hosier as a weekly one-hour television drama. For more on the sports figure and the television series, see the author's bio page on *The Asbury Triptych Series* website at www.francisasburytriptych.com.

Al and his lovely wife of thirty years, Kim, live in southern Florida with their two daughters and a Wheaten Terrier named Riley Flynn. He enjoys watching the British television show, *Top Gear*. He also enjoys playing the drums and African percussion, when time permits.